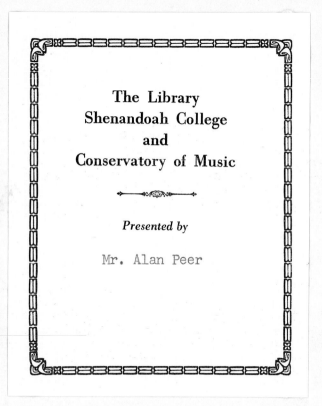

the voices

of Glory

*the voices
of Glory*

by DAVIS GRUBB

CHARLES SCRIBNER'S SONS *NEW YORK*

for my friend
Saul Isaac Heller

and for Eleanor—

whose whispers came to me

*"When I get to the other side
I shall tell God Almighty about West Virginia."*

—Mother Jones

table of contents

Millard Filmore Rogerson

So you think it undemocratic that I—Apple County's wealthiest man—should be first chosen to speak about the woman, Marcy Cresap. My God, the snobbery of the people against the Rich! Or do the civil liberties of this Republic stand for the rights of free-speech only of the average, the unambitious, the ungifted, the mediocre and the illiterate? Whereas, the fact of the matter is that I was not chosen at all. I simply am the first one of all those yonder waiting multitudes who knows exactly what he wants to say and how to say it. If you trouble to look back at four decades of Apple County history you'll find the name of M. F. Rogerson was first in a lot of things. But you'll not take the trouble and it doesn't matter what you think of me. It's this woman, this Marcy Cresap—it matters what you think of her. Yes, your opinion of her—that matters a great deal. God only knows how you shall judge her. God only knows there are those whose voices shall rise tonight,

1

striving to be heard above the wind, who would like to see this woman Marcy Cresap dead and buried in her eternal grave. Everyone here tonight thinks he knows Marcy Cresap and all the secrets of her strange mind and even stranger life in all its bright, queer beauty. There is not one citizen, dead or alive, whose voice shall praise or damn her or pass her off as worthy of neither praise nor damnation—not one, I say, who doesn't think he knows Marcy Cresap best of all his neighbors. And I think that they're all wrong. I think they're wrong for the simple reason that I think all opinions of people in mobs are wrong. And I believe that any group of people is a mob and that the motives of mobs are either savagely cruel or hideously sentimental. And if you doubt me—and I have a feeling of certainty that you do—just listen a spell to what these others have to say about Marcy Cresap—all of these odd, selfish, madly opinionated men, women—even children—in this small West Virginia town which some misguided and probably drunken pioneer once gave the name of Glory. Just listen.

Each of them is fighting, fairly stepping on the faces of his neighbors to be first to have his say. There are some whose eyes glisten with hatred at this moment at the thought that I—wealthiest man in the town of Glory—should be first to have spoken at all. Hold still, have patience, my worthy neighbors, and you shall have your turn. The voices of Glory, indeed! The clamor of Babel is more like it! The shuffling, sweating crowds who gather now to speak out for or against the woman Marcy Cresap and no matter which way the scales tip she'll be the loser in the end: damned by the shameless contumely of her enemies, smothered beneath the funereal flowers of her advocates. As for myself—as usual—I stand apart and alone from all the others. I am on the side of Marcy Cresap and yet I have nothing to do with the motley and mismatched creatures of that unwashed and sanctimonious brotherhood which is on her side. I am for Marcy Cresap because I love a lonely, stubborn fighter in a hopeless cause. As for the trash of humanity whose cause she is said to champion they fill me with nothing but disgust and nausea.

There are some who will tell you that some of this garbage of the human race has been murdered here in the town of Glory—murdered by the hands of Marcy Cresap's foes. That charge touches neither outrage nor pity in my thinking. There are some who improve the mortal breed by leaving it. Diseased and feeble-minded infants growing up to be sick, half-wit adults—can you honestly defend that process? Really? Well, your unrealistic sentimentality doesn't surprise me! Because *you're* a mob yourself and therefore don't need nor want the elegant condition of thoughtfulness! That is why I so seldom mix with the people of Glory or, for that matter, people of Apple County—people of anywhere! I play with my little son David—I dream of the greatness which it is his choice to make and shape someday—*alone!* We two— my boy and I—we stay indoors and I tell him stories of how to win the world round to his ways. He is three years old now and I am a man of sixty-two and it may seem hard for some to believe how much we share in common. His small eyes light on a toy he wants—his small, rosy hand reaches out and seizes it—*alone!* Oh, I know it—he will be a captain of men when he is grown!—he will be greater than I in all my grandest dreams—and he will fight his way to that estate *alone!* Sometimes I think this woman Marcy Cresap understands me better than any living person. That is why she is the only person—aside from my two housekeepers—who is welcome to set foot across the threshold of my big home on the high ground above Tomlinson Avenue here in this town of Glory. There's scarcely a week goes by that she doesn't come and sit a spell with me and the boy and share a cup of tea and talk of my plans for my son and her part in helping him to find his way into the world on the day, sooner or later, when I shall leave him to it to find his way. *Alone.*

It's really queer about that woman, Marcy Cresap—sometimes I catch a glimpse of her that tells me that underneath it all that we are spiritual kinsmen. Sometimes I think she hates the dirty, greedy masses of men every bit as much as I. Maybe beneath all the twisted, cranky beauty of her stubborn, losing fight for them—it's all a game she plays against her soul: beating back something she can't admit dwells there! When I think sometimes of all that wasted strength she has!—Lord, what a world she could have conquered if she'd seen men as I see them. The crawling, verminous mobs of mankind! They've never fooled me. Never! When the five hundred miners walked out and struck against my company at Glory Number Twelve in nineteen and twenty-four I did not hesitate a moment. It was the mob versus me and the only way to fight mobs is with mobs so within twenty minutes I had personally contacted my friend Governor Jackson and by noon of that morning I was personally leading a detachment of convicts from our excellent state penitentiary here in Glory—I led them up Parr's Run and every man of them armed with government issue Springfield rifles and we smashed the strike by sundown of that day. Though I limp still—yes, my right leg still is stiff from some hunkie miner's bullet through my knee.

The woman Marcy—she would not speak to me for a year after that. Maybe she would have kept that angry dumb-show with me forever but there came a time when she was trying desperately to raise money among the businessmen of Glory for the Apple County Sanatorium. She walked up boldly that bitter, February morning and rang the doorbell till I answered it.

So you have forgiven me at last for shooting down the murderous riffraff of Parr's Run Mine shantytown, eh, Marcy? I asked quietly, determined to ask her in or shut the door in her face on the strength of how she answered.

No, Millard, she said. I'll hate and loathe you for that until my dying day—or yours. But I just can't afford the pride of angry silence any more. I need some of your money.

Come in, Marcy, come in, I said, delighted with her as always. And she came and sat in the big library and sat leafing through some of my first editions and looking at the Durer Christs glistening in their frames among the shining shadows between the bookcases, and my housekeeper fetched us tea and toast with damson-jam and Marcy told me again that she had come to me for money.

For what purpose? I said, smiling patiently and yet with profoundest admiration.

For the tuberculosis sanatorium, she said. I want five thousand dollars from you, Millard.

But why, Marcy? I asked, teasing her out to make her give the answer that would let me drive her away in disgust—and disappointment. Why, Marcy? I haven't got tuberculosis. Neither has my boy, Davey. Why should I give you five thousand dollars to fight a disease that neither I nor those I love have got?

And I waited—half-praying that she wouldn't—for her to start the sickening, usual stuff about the suffering masses of Glory folk who *did* have the disease and how it was my duty to help fight it for their sake as well as for my own because, Heaven knows, it might attack me or my Davey after all. But that wasn't what she said at all. And I was glad; I was proud to know a lonely, stubborn fighter like that woman, Marcy

Cresap. But she was still awhile, considering her answer before she spoke, studying me levelly with those brown eyes of hers that hold the beauty of both chill and warmth and borrow beauty from both.

Why, Marcy? I asked her again, with my hand already inside my coat pocket, the tips of my fingers resting on my checkbook and my fountain pen, something in my hoping and praying, like a man at poker, that she would play the right hand and beat me after all.

With me, she said, her eyes wandering from my face to the frosted windows beyond which palely shone the winter wastes. With me, Millard, it's revenge. That's a thing you can understand, I suppose. Revenge. I'll not stop, Millard, till I've won or worn it out or worn myself out trying.

Revenge on who, Marcy? I said, already feeling the glow of damned admiration she somehow always gave me.

Revenge on it, she said. Revenge on the death that took my husband and my child, Millard. Revenge on sickness, Millard, that stole two good years of my youth and kept me flat in a bed when I could have been out in Glory and in Apple County fighting. You're a man that appreciates revenge, Millard. I saw that in your face that day your prison strikebreakers shot to death Sophie Sochek's husband Paul. Everybody needs revenge against something in this world, Millard. Now help me get mine. I'll be everlastingly grateful if you do. But if you don't, by God, it won't matter for I'll get it anyway!

Well, I laughed shamelessly, I laughed till my eyes filled with such tears that I could hardly see to make out the seventy-five hundred dollar check. And then I laughed some more and hugged Marcy Cresap and lifted her lightly off her heels and squeezed her a minute, laughing still, and smelling that queer, unfeminine perfume she always wore: the smell of some disinfectant or medicine or other. And after a spell she thanked me with that cold light burning in her eyes and went off somewhere to some preposterous, unsanitary and stinking pesthole of a shack in Angel's Swamp, most likely, and left me with the faint scent of her drifting in the wake behind her and suddenly seeming to me the most elegantly female perfume I had ever smelled since Molly died. And I sat a great while alone in my library, listening to Miss Gaunt playing games upstairs in the nursery with Davey and I fingered the stub of the check and thought about the thing that had not been mentioned there between us, Marcy and me, that day: the strange and solemn promise which she had made me once. I suppose now I must permit you to spy and pry a little more into my private life—enough to know that the only, single gracious act of love my wife Molly Jane Bender ever accorded me was to present me with a son—our only child —late in the summer of eighteen ninety-nine. And I loved that son as I could never love her. Never. Because he was more of me than ever he was of her. More—eternally more.

And when the Great War came and he let the ragging, bullying, teasing trash of Glory boys goad him into joining up and he needn't have gone at all because his poor vision would have spared him in the draft. And the evening he came to me with his young eyes all shining with pride in his new uniform and the town band down under the courthouse trees was playing "Over There" and "Keep the Home Fires Burning" and he stood there before me in the library with the noise and clamor of fools thumping and blasting all around him and he waited for my blessing. And it was my curse I gave him. It was my curse and I would give it to him again if he rose from the grass of the Meuse-Argonne tonight and came to me in death. It was my curse that he had joined the mobs—the damned, blind, sickening mobs! And I knew when he went away from me to his mother that night with his face hot with anger at me that I would never speak to my boy again. And I was right. He went off with the mob. And the other mob murdered him. And that has been nine years ago and I have forgiven neither the mobs he followed nor the mobs that killed him nor the mother who gave her blessing and the kiss of death that sent him proudly out to die for the folly of a handful of kings and a Princeton University professor.

My wife and I lived the six years until her death without speaking. And I find a queer and bitter comfort in the thought sometimes that the place where she lies on Glory Hill and the place where Jim's buried in the meadows of France have oceans and five thousand miles between! I think, with comfort, what a bitterness that must be to her who sent a son out to die for a myth. And in the years after Molly passed on and I was left alone in this big house in Glory with a fortune in beautiful, rare books and Boschs and Blakes and Botticellis and all the joys of the spirit and the mind with no one to share them with except the mob who imagined, I suppose, that I would leave all these to Glory's poky, fusty little city library. And I looked round me at the rich trash of my contemporaries who had made their fortunes in Wheeling steel or the glass factories or the mines I didn't own (and they are few) and the ones who had gotten rich off the clothing factory in the penitentiary and stacked up hundreds of thousands out of prison labor and then spent half their fortunes on Packards and uncut sets of leather books they never opened and trips to Paris and all the rest of the nauseous, nouveau-riche mindlessness and waste and tastelessness. And I knew that I had to have a son. I knew that I might not die for ten or perhaps twenty years and I knew that without a son I would go mad. And I knew that I hadn't worked and battled my way up from the meanness and poverty of an Apple County childhood spent in shacks and shantyboats to see my life go crumbling and my fortunes dwindle as my mind went mad for the longing, like a sickness, for a son.

Sometimes I think that in the weeks of that April four years ago Marcy Cresap read from my eyes what lay in the heart of me: that yearning and that need. And I know her well enough to know she understood. Because when I got my young housekeeper Jenny Maxwell pregnant with child and kept her living in my house all through her pregnancy with Glory's best medical hands attending her—Marcy Cresap was the only one in all of Glory who did not sit back high and proud in sneering, sniggering judgment. And when my son Davey was born and I knew that Jenny would love neither me nor the child ever, was in fact incapable of loving anything but her own pleasure in the fun and frenzy and frolic of mobs and mobs of her kind, I called her to me in the library as soon as the child was weaned, presented her with a one-way railway ticket down river to Cairo, Illinois, and a check for ten thousand dollars for services rendered. For the service of giving me a son.

And that was something else which, strangely, Marcy Cresap understood with swift and sure instinct. For it isn't only swarms of the lazy and whining sick folk that Marcy deals with in Glory; it is homeless children, too. And when my son looks for the last time upon my dead face he will not be looking over my shoulder at some heaped brilliance of inherited millions. Marcy understands. And though you sit there shaking your head at me in puzzled or angry judgment, I do not care. On the day I die Marcy will take young Davey away to the home of strong, independent country folk: a couple just beginning on a farm somewhere. A lonely place, I hope. A place from which, with what I have left to him of my spirit and my hatred of conformity, Davey will strive and struggle forth like the butterfly from the cocoon. He will flutter and be banged by this world's winds; he will learn still more from what, if anything, he will have learned from me. He will learn to fight. He will learn to stand alone. Or he will perish. And that's as life is and should be.

You stare at me, strange faces. Why? Is single, lonely strength— once the proudest virtue of our Republic—is this so cheap and mean a coin to own these days? Well, think what you will. Marcy understands. And I understand Marcy: that lonely, strong-faced woman with the dark and fighting eyes who stands up there in Apple County Courthouse these aching-cold mornings and yellow, chill-lit afternoons in the first week of January in this year of gracelessness nineteen hundred twenty-eight. The doctors, the big dairy-men, the real-estate men, the lawyers, the bankers—their mob's mostly out in the fight to destroy Marcy Cresap. The littler mob—the socially less respectable one—it's out to make her into some sort of plaster saint in Glory. My curses on them both! I could bring down two or three of my own smart lawyers from Pittsburgh that would smash Marcy's enemies in one single afternoon of legal argument. But I'll not do that. I wouldn't cripple Marcy with lawyers she doesn't want any more than I will cripple my boy Davey with a fortune he didn't earn. The butterfly fights and struggles loose and flutters free—or dies. No, Marcy will have to go her fight alone. When Marcy stands alone there's a splendor to her that no little mob of tricky lawyers need embellish. Marcy's like me—she stands and fights or falls alone. Marcy needs God just now—not mobs of men or lawyers. And so there has not been a single night in the whole, cold month in this, Marcy's winter of her discontent, that I have not had my boy Davey kneel by me on the draughty carpet by his bed and pray to the Lord God Almighty for Marcy Cresap and against this town of Glory, Apple County, West Virginia, the whole Earth! And you sit there yonder and wonder to yourselves that a man like Millard Filmore Rogerson believes in God? Well, that's about the best I would expect from the likes of you and your rabble kind: the mob. Of course I believe in God, you eternal fools! For Who in Hell makes coal and sons and creatures like Marcy Cresap if it isn't Him?

Juney Hankins

Marcy Cresap was right about me. Well, I know that now. Even if it's too late now for me to tell her so. Lordy, I sure wisht it wasn't too late to tell her; just to walk up to her and take off my cap and come right out with it like a man: Miz Cresap, you was right about me and you was right when you tried to get me fired from my job waiting on tables at Brother's Lunch. And I'm sorry, Miz Cresap, and I only wisht to God I could take back those mean things I said about you. And I'm sorry you're in such bad trouble now. I only wish I could come back to Glory long enough to tell them all the truth which now I see so plain.

Maybe one of you out there. Maybe you'll get close to Marcy Cresap tonight. Can you hear me out there? Well, if one of you can hear me, you go tell Marcy how sorry I am and tell all those men and women for God's sake to let her be. No, it's too late for that, I know. Well, it's been too late for me since the day I was born. Everything I've touched just seemed to turn to dust or death or misery. Even when I was little,

9

on Grandma Swisher's farm, I never could keep a pet dog or cat alive. Grandma gave me a baby lamb once and showed me how to feed it milk from a bottle with a baby nipple on the end but it died that spring before the redbud blossoms was even gone from the hilltops. I cried all that afternoon and when sundown came I taken Grandpap's spade and wrapped the dead lamb up in my good red flannel shirt and I buried it up yonder on the ridge under the little trees where the redbud blossoms had bloomed bright as the pieces of broken dishes against the old, tired gray of dying winter's sky. Nobody—not even me—could find that little lamb's grave today. And nobody—except maybe Marcy Cresap—could find the grave of Juney Hankins. I don't care. The Lord knows where I'm at. And maybe some day His voice will call me to rise and come to Him.

When the last sleep taken me in her arms that April morning last year, Grandma and Aunt Love Jackson quarreled the livelong day about where I was to be buried. My ma and pa was long dead in the flu epidemic and buried somewheres out near Chillicothe, Ohio, and there just wasn't any more grave room on the Jackson plot so they buried me clean out to the edge of Glory Hill where the lots is cheap and there was a tombstone salesman came through town that spring with a big line of flashy, snow-white markers and Aunt Love Jackson bought one because it was such a bargain and put it at the head of the little mound I made. It had my full name Floyd Jackson Hankins and the years of my time: nineteen ten to nineteen twenty-seven and I was real proud of it with it shining so pure and white above me there in the moonlight stillness of that first spring on Glory Hill. But it was just like everything else; the same in death as it had always been in life: everything about me, even the final shape of my name and the years of my time upon that stone among the violets gone to forgetfulness and dust in the end. For, the reason them tombstones come so cheap was they was cast in plaster instead of chiseled out of stone and it wasn't more than five or six rains before the gorgeous plaster letters and the numbers started crumbling and running down the stone like tears and disappearing at last into the earth which is my poor eternity's last home.

Don't pity me though. I don't want that. It's the last thing a body needs over here on Glory Hill. Pity the ones I left behind. Pity Grandma and Aunt Love Jackson for the pure mean blindness of their eyes and the blacker blindness of their souls for fighting Miz Cresap that time

she tried to get me fired. Pity the ones that will die themselves and come
to lie on Glory Hill or Potter's Field because of me. Pity Miz Marcy
Cresap if you want with all them big powers fighting to cut her down
like a great strong tree before the axe of the woodman. Pity or not—
maybe it won't matter in the end; maybe what's to be is to be and
there's no sense in wanting or praying or fighting at all. Do trees commence to praying when they see the faraway flash of the axe on the
woodman's shoulder? Well, I reckon not. And it's like the Book says,
we're all like trees and grass cut down in the end and our time on earth
is of a little space. Still I wish there was a way of coming back just long
enough to unsay some things said long before.

When Ma died in the great flu epidemic in nineteen and nineteen it
was just a matter of weeks till Daddy taken down sick and followed her.
So they taken me and sent me to live with Grandma and Aunt Love
Jackson on the farm in Apple County down river a piece from the town
of Glory. I was only nine but God knows I was full of mischief and sin
even then and one day in the pantry while I was crawling around under
the big stove where Aunt Love Jackson was making apple butter I just
suddenly got gripped by the notion that I had to lift up Aunt Love Jackson's dress and take a look up her legs to see what was there. Well, I
done it and Aunt Love screamed and called Grandma and she got the
old man down the meadow from the hay harvest and he read me three
long chapters from Bible and then he taken me out to the barn and
thrashed me with a buggy whip till even my hair ached with the pain of
it and sent me off to bed, too sore even to cry, and without any supper.
Well, don't you know it wasn't a week until I got the same wild need to
look up Aunt Love Jackson's skirt and this time they threw me in the
back seat of Grandpa's buggy and taken me in for a lecture and a threat
from Mister Arbogast, the probation officer. He got me confused because I knowed he was threatening me with terrible things and yet all
the while he smiled at me with his eyes all pursed up thin and said that
boys like me who got out of hand got sent to the Apple County Orphan
Asylum up beyond the town dump at the head of Misery Creek. I think
I knowed even then, even that very day with Mister Arbogast's eyes
grinning at me like catfish gills that I'd end up at the Asylum anyway,
no matter what I did, and no matter how hard I tried not to do it.

I was sure full of black sin back then, even when I was ten years old,
and by the time I was eleven it taken a turn for the worst. It was spring

again and there was a carnival went in business down on the flats below
the smelter and I run into some boys my own age down there one night
when I should have been home at Grandma's and long ago prayed over
and in bed. But there was just something sinful come over me that night
and the carnival lights was all a blur of beautiful colored lights like the
kind of moving, rainbow stars-and-moon a child would order up if he
was in charge of such heavenly matters. I never could see anything plain
in those days and I used to get a whipping once or twicet weekly down
at the old school at Hannibal Junction because when it come my turn
to stand up and read I couldn't make out half the words. Most of the
time when I'd get to one I couldn't see I'd always make up the word
"stovelid" and say it instead, whether it made good sense or not, and
Miz Jewell, the teacher, said I was a willful, impudent smart aleck and
off I'd go by the ear to the cloak-room for a good strapping. That was
the thing I liked about those lights at the carnival that night, I guess,
because it didn't matter if I couldn't see them plain: I could see the
beauteous rainbow of their colors moving up yonder in the dark and the
first thing you know them kids I was running with taken the notion into
their heads to bust into Mister Ganz's Novelty Store and steal some toys
and candy and stuff. So I went.

God, I was so full of sin in them days it's a wonder He never struck
me down in my tracks. And back we all run through the dark to Glory
and up through the river fog beneath the trees on Purdy Avenue till we
come to Mister Ganz's place. I was scared so I just followed along
behind and let someone else break the glass in the little doorway out
back in the alley and followed the others inside when the door was open.
Jake Likens and Stanley Thorpe and them other kids had their mouths
so full of taffy directly that you couldn't make out a word they was saying and some derned fool turned on the lights so we could see what we
wanted to steal. It's a funny thing but nobody but me knowed exactly
what it was they wanted when we first busted in. Everybody but me had
the general idea of swiping candy and toys and peashooters and such
but not me. I minded once I had bent down close enough to the case by
the window in Mister Ganz's store to see exactly what I wanted more
than anything in the world. Never in all my life can I mind ever wanting
anything so much as that and sometimes when I look back through all
the years to that spring night I'm not sure it wasn't me that first brung
up the notion of busting into Mister Ganz's store in the first place. I

groped my way around in that blinding light and heard the other kids winding up dollar watches and stuffing their cheeks with jaw-breakers and I just fumbled my way through the blur of them till I come to that counter and what was in it. It was glasses. Ain't that the damndest fool thing in the world now? A pair of glasses!

It just come over me that night that if I just had a pair of them glasses nothing in the world could ever hurt me again and I wouldn't ever have to say "stovelid" again and Grandma wouldn't switch my legs for stepping on fresh laid eggs among the hay in the morning. I got a pair, too, and I swear to God it was like someone rubbed the magic lamp because when I lifted my face it was the world all come into shape and that's something that's hard to explain to someone who's never been half-blind and then suddenly had the whole world jump plain right there on the bridge of their nose. It was queer. The first thing I ever saw real plain in my life was Chief of Police Smithers coming through the front door of the little store there with his big hands outstretched for me. I was the only one he found there, too, because the other kids had spied him through the front window and run out the back and left me there to take the punishment for them all. Well, it was just the kind of joke I deserved having played on me. Maybe them other kids yelled a warning to me before they run, I don't know. I wouldn't have heard them anyhow I was so fascinated trying them spectacles out that I'd found in the little glass case. You take your first look at the world and try listening to someone talking to you at the same time! Well, they taken me to the Apple County Jail and called Grandpap on the line and he come in the buggy two hours later, taken one look at me, heard Chief Smithers telling what I had done, and Grandpap told him to keep me locked up in the jail over night. He said in a real loud voice that he didn't much care what they done with me after that and he said maybe he'd come to fetch me in the morning and maybe he wouldn't, it all hung on what Grandma and Aunt Love Jackson had to say.

So they locked me in the cell and there was some poor lady over yonder in the corner on the floor beside the toilet screaming and thrashing around like the Devil was trying to climb inside her gaping, squawling mouth and directly some old constable with a big gun on his hip come round and warned her if she didn't shut up her hollering he'd fetch her out in the hall and turn a fire hose on her and she just screamed and throwed herself around all the more but he never done it. And directly here come Chief Smithers with a tall, soft-faced lady with brown hair and glasses and an old squashed-up pocketbook and the Chief taken out his big key and unlocked the door and she come in. And I was hid in the shadows so's the crazy woman wouldn't see me and wondered what this lady was being locked up for because she didn't look like she was drunk, nor colored, nor nothing illegal like that and directly she went over to the crazy woman and got down beside her and lifted the crazy woman's head and held it in her arms so's she would stop banging it on the stone floor and she taken a handkerchief out of her pocketbook and wiped the sickness and slobber off the crazy woman's chin and directly she lifted her up and carried her to the old iron bunk and laid her down and stretched herself out beside her, still holding her like she was a baby and whispering something to make the poor soul stop her shaking and her screaming and directly the woman give a big sob and a big sigh and fell sound asleep. Then I seen this other woman—yes, you guessed it: she was Marcy Cresap—she taken a little bottle that she'd given the woman something out of and put it back in her purse and then her eyes lit on me. I crouched back in the shadows as far as I could because I had the notion she was one of them women that fetches children off to Orphan Asylums and I prayed she wouldn't see me. Well, she seen me all right because directly she called two or three times for the Chief of Police and when he come directly she demanded to know what right the Law had locking up a little child. And the Chief beat around the bush awhile until directly Marcy Cresap got mad and said if he didn't surrender me into her custody that she'd have the Law on him. Well, that was the first I ever heard of having the Law on the Law because when you're poor there's just nothing higher than the Law, not even God Hisself, and it's usually not till you come over here to rest in Glory Hill that you learn any different. Well, the Chief he raised hell.

Miz Cresap, he said. This here's a Law matter. It's got nothing to do with you.

No, she said. But it'll have something to do with you, Mister Smithers, gainst I get on the phone and call the Governor in Charleston.

So I spent that night in the little attic bed in Marcy Cresap's own big house down by the end of the river road where the willows bow down grieving to the shore and the little stars lay with catfish in the bottom of that black and talking stream. And Marcy got me a boarding home with Mister and Missus Jamieson who had a little farm down Proctor way and they was good to me and I stayed with them till I was sixteen and got this queer, deep longing for the faces of my own kin again. It got so I couldn't sleep of a night in the hay of the tick in my own good bed: this longing for the faces of Grandma and Grandpap and Aunt Love Jackson, so strong it was like an ache in the bones and it didn't matter if they wanted to see me or not, I wanted to see them and ask their forgiveness for my sins and beg them to take me in a while.

Yes, I said a while because even that far back I seemed to know deep inside that I hadn't long to be there among them and it grew and grew in me that spring and so did the bad cough I had—that longing for their faces and that racking, nagging cough they all seemed part of the knowing that I'd sure better hurry if I wanted to see them ever again this side of Judgment. Well, I was seventeen before long and even though I loved the Jamiesons for all their loving kindness through all them years I knew I had to get to Glory then and there and make that try to see my own again. That was the week I got the job waiting tables at Brother's Lunch and they give me a little money, two meals a day and my bed and soon as I'd saved up three dollars for a good pair of pants I went to see Aunt Love Jackson. She cried and pawed all over me and Grandma hugged me and said they were glad to see me again and I told them about my job at Brother's Lunch and my nice bed. They never once asked me to come and live with them, although I had made up my mind ahead of time I was going to say No if they did. Being on my own that way made me feel proud for the first time I could remember. Still it would have pleasured my heart if they had at least asked me. So I worked on and on into the summer and winter and my cough got worse and worse and twice in the kitchen I grabbed up a towel just in time and coughed up blood bright as a brakeman's flag. I kept it hid from everyone but Mister Brother's wife Jessie—she knew—and I hoped and prayed it wouldn't get me fired because having that job even with no more pay than a dollar a week, two meals and my bed meant more to me than anything had ever meant to me except maybe that pair of glasses that night. It was like them glasses, in a way: a look at the world at last, a way to keep proud and a way maybe to make Grandma and Grandpap and Aunt Love Jackson love me enough to ask me home with them.

That was the winter I saw Marcy Cresap again and she bundled me out of work one day and into the back seat of that old Model-T touring car of hers and drove me down to Apple County Courthouse and scratched my arm and listened to my chest and taken pictures of it and two days later she sent a letter to Mister Brother's saying he would have to fire me that afternoon or she would have to take it up with the Apple County Health Nurse. Mister Brother called her on the phone and told her to mind her own business so I reckon Marcy must have gone to Miz Challoner, the County Health Nurse and demanded her to order me fired because she said I was as dangerous as a murderer up there among the tables at Brother's Place. So Miz Challoner called up Aunt Love Jackson who is a Democratic Committeewoman here in Apple County and asked her what she wanted done with me. And Aunt Love said how much good the hard work was doing me and she said how healthy I looked to her and she told Miz Challoner it would make her mighty angry if the Health Department was to get me fired from my job. But that was far from the end of the matter. Marcy Cresap fought day and night to get me fired and she wrote me long letters and tried to explain something I couldn't even see to read, let alone understand, and I just got madder and madder by the minute. That old bitch, Marcy Cresap! I thought, while I waited tables there at Brother's and run back in the kitchen every now and then to cough up phlegm into my apron and look anxiously for little specks of blood like red flowers there.

And Marcy Cresap even come in person to see me in my little room one winter's night and tried to plead and reason and talk to me. But I was like a stone. Oh, Marcy Cresap, My God, can you ever forgive me? Someday, Marcy, when I have come to learn the ways of speaking over here maybe I can come to you in a still room and kneel and speak and make you hear the words! Forgive me, Marcy Cresap! Maybe someday, too, I can beg the forgiveness of all the rest, the quick and the dead, who suffered and will suffer more by all my blind and wicked willfulness. Lordy, if only I hadn't been so puffed up with pride over that little job. Lordy, if only I'd known! Because in a few weeks I had to quit the little job anyway and it was Marcy Cresap who took me away to the white, narrow bed in Apple County Sanatorium and by then it had grown upwards like a fatal and pale flower blossoming within my breast, filling my throat with its petals till I could no longer speak. And it was Marcy Cresap who came every day toward my end and everytime my throat would make that queer, thin sound, trying to speak, trying to shape words to ask forgiveness. But it was no use. And even that last night in the week before Christmas I tried the hardest I had ever tried to tell her, to beg her, to get it out if it killed me. And it did. Because I tried too hard and something broke like a warm, thick bubble in my chest and I fell asleep suddenly.

May you never know the sorrow of having cursed someone in life and then to have them hold you dying in their arms while your aching, wild, full throat strains to plead for pardon and cannot make a sound! And if you see Marcy Cresap tonight, will you tell her I was here? No. I know. I understand. It is all too far away somehow—as distant as the sound of the death of a star in the summer sky. Still someday I will speak and they will hear me. I swear it! First it's got to be Marcy Cresap I talk to. And then the others: Mister Flynn, Bessie Moon, Mister South, the little children who came for ice cream in the hot nights of that summer, the young girls with their beaus who came for sodas after the show was out. I remember. When the folks were finished eating I would write it down so carefully in my thick, slow hand and then Mr. Brother's missus would add up the sum for me. Then I would hand them the little check with everything listed and what it cost: the apple pie, the milk, the dish of fresh peaches and cream. Everything there on the paper except the hard, slow death that came free with the meal. Forgive me for the deaths my fingers gave! O, forgive!

The Reverend D. Webster Toombes

My father always used to say a man should know which side of his bread is buttered. I never forgot that and in my thirty years' faithful service of the Lord I've discovered that goes for communion bread just as much as the table variety. There are certain principles and pillars of this great land we live in that a man of the cloth cannot oppose and still hope to prosper. And if he doesn't prosper then how can he preach the Word? It's that simple. Now I've been pastor here at the Glory First Presbyterian Church for going on twenty years and I've been Protestant Chaplain up yonder at the State Penitentiary for more than ten. Besides that I'm a member of the Rotary, the Kiwanis and the Lions Club and I was a chaplain in France for a year with the rest of the Apple County boys. I'm just mentioning all these things so you'll be able to understand it when I say that there are few men in Glory that know as much about the way human nature goes on than I do. I've watched men come and go. I've stood beside them when they

18

fell through the gallows trap, I kneeled beside them and brought comfort to them as they died in Belleau wood, and I've held their hands when they died in bed. I could tell you a few stories about the way men face death's many faces but I might have to use language unbecoming to a preacher. I know a few things about women, too. I know the kind of saint on earth my mother was and the kind of Christian and devoted mate my late wife India was. And I know a thing or two about the other kind of woman, too—the kind this Marcy Cresap is always coddling and caring after. Now you may rest assured I know all about Mary Magdalene and all her fallen sisterhood since then. Maybe a few of them can be helped to better ways. Frankly, I doubt it. The biggest percentage of them don't want help at all—they're more than content, they're even willing to keep going right on down the primrose path. And it seems to me that it's this big majority of the unrepentant ones that Marcy Cresap seems to favor.

Some of you will probably remember that big scandal here back in nineteen twenty-two when Marcy Cresap openly took that girl Bessie Sochek into her own home to live with her that whole summer. Mind you now, here was a girl fresh out of a Benwood whorehouse and Marcy Cresap welcomed her in like she was a long lost sister. Well, I've always suspicioned that there is a lot more to Marcy Cresap's own life than meets the eye. The Sochek girl was born, raised and grew up right here in Apple County. Her father was one of the Hunkies who got killed during the big Parr's Run Strike here a few years ago and from all I could gather he was not only a foreigner, he'd been one of the top radical organizers for the Wobblies out West somewhere before the Great War. Anyhow the girl Bessie is said to have told Marcy Cresap that, since her father got killed, her mother Sophie had gone crazy and couldn't take in washings any more and that she had tried getting housework to support her mother and eight brothers and sisters but that nobody in the whole town of Glory would give her a job.

Well now, in the first place, we've got the Associated Charities for people like that. In the second place, feeling around Apple County is still running pretty high about that Parr's Mine Strike—they made up a troop of convicts from the State Pen—as a matter of fact, as chaplain I was one of the men who handpicked the trustworthy ones—and in the fighting that followed an Apple County Deputy was killed and a member of the Glory Police Department got a bullet in his spine and is paralyzed for life. So you can appreciate that the daughter of one of those Bolsheviks wouldn't exactly be welcomed through the front door of any Glory homes. Besides that, work has been so hard to find since the War that the people of Apple County have all they can do finding work for Americans. Anyhow, this Bessie Sochek claimed the only way she could support her insane mother and the rest of the family was to hire out her body in a Benwood brothel. And that might have been an end to the matter then and there as far as we were concerned here in Glory. But then one night the girl showed up on the streetcar with a cardboard suitcase and tried to get a room in a Water Street rooming house. Well, she was crying and carrying on that men were coming in cars to kill her or worse and the old woman who rented her the room got on the phone and called up Marcy Cresap. And then she called six or eight other women on the party line to tell them that Marcy Cresap had come in her old touring car and driven away with the girl.

Next thing any of us knew Amelia Post the wife of Marcy Cresap's mailman said the girl was hiding out in the attic bedroom of the Cresap house. And the girl Bessie Sochek was crying and yelling so loud that all Marcy's neighbors could hear the preposterous things she was claiming—that she gave a Social Disease to Wheeling's highest public servant and that he had sent out two or three carloads of thugs to have her taken care of. Well, there were no cars showed up in Glory so we all knew that part was nonsense. And I'll speak for the Wheeling gentleman and tell you that I know him as a fellow Kiwanian and a man whose morals are above reproach. Anyhow, a week went by and the girl stayed on at Marcy Cresap's. And at the end of the month I personally headed a delegation of six men and women from my little flock and on the front porch of Marcy Cresap's house I read aloud to her a short letter of protest. I think it is to my credit that I kept an even tone of voice during the reading and that, furthermore, I made no mention of Marcy Cresap's having been a member of Glory First Presbyterian Church since she was born and had not set foot inside that house of God in nearly thirty years. She stared at me a minute and she looked at the others behind me and then she said:

This girl is sick and I am giving her treatments.

Doctor Ed Follansbee nudged me twice with his elbow and I took the hint.

Miss Cresap, I said. You're not a doctor. What right have you got giving anybody treatments for anything?

Do any of the three doctors in your church care to take this girl in their homes and give her treatments, Preacher? she said.

Miss Cresap, that is a shameful insult to the decent wives of Doctor Follansbee here and to the good Christian women who are married to Doctor Blick and Doctor Stone.

Just the same this girl is sick, said Marcy Cresap. So I am keeping her here. She is my guest. She is my friend. And I am going to see that she gets treatments until she is well.

Without the supervision of a certified doctor? I said. What gives you the right? Who do you think you are, Miss Cresap?

I am an employee of the U. S. Public Health Service, she said. And they pay my salary. Not a penny of it comes from Glory or from Apple County. As for a doctor's prescription for Bessie's treatments I have them. Doctor Cecil who has time for such duties is taking care of that.

Well, we knew what a joke that was. Old Doctor Will Cecil is a senile fool who carries on with his young housekeeper and who harbors the most radical notions about doctoring. But there the matter lay. And the Sochek girl stayed on shamelessly at Marcy Cresap's for the rest of that summer and in the fall Marcy Cresap had the nerve to come right down to the Mercantile Bank and Trust Company and draw out a check for a hundred dollars made to the name of Bessie Sochek. Then she drove her up to the Biddy-Bye Ladies Furnishings on Jefferson Avenue and had her outfitted in a new dress, hat, shoes, and a winter coat and put it all on her own bill—or tried to. Lem Carmichael told her that the whole affair of having to outfit the girl at all was a slur on his own wife Nevada and he sent Marcy Cresap right back to the bank and made her come back and pay for the girl's outfit in cash. Well, after Marcy Cresap put the girl on the evening train south the affair was ended. Or nearly so.

A year later J. W. Tinkle told me in utmost confidence that he had seen the Sochek girl on the porch of the biggest whorehouse on the Parkersburgh waterfront as he chanced to drive past one evening on his way to prayer meeting. Well, we were thankful enough down at the Church that, at least, Glory was rid of the Sochek girl. Though the bad taste it left in everyone's mouth made us wish we had seen the last of Marcy Cresap as well. But Life is never that Simple, my friends. A woman like Marcy Cresap seems born into the world to go against the grain of things that be and were meant to be. There are lots of her kind on the earth. The do-gooders, the troublemakers, the nay-sayers—the folks with two left feet who go through life sneering at things that are established and settled and beneficial to the community. And that brings me to the business up at the Penitentiary last year and the big stink Marcy raised which all but ruined the spring celebration of the Ohio Valley Electrical Booster's Club. Well, the whole drive meant a lot to the business recovery of Apple County and the town of Glory. Since the Great War industry hereabouts has made great strides in the direction of enormous electrical expansion. It looks like we put it over— despite Marcy Cresap—and the business folks around here are looking forward to nineteen twenty-nine with a lot of zip and ginger. Still it was Marcy Cresap who did her best to throw cold water on the biggest attractions of the Booster Association's program for nineteen twenty-seven. I mean, as you probably know, the big change up at the West Virginia State Prison from the gallows to the electric chair.

On the whole it was agreed by everyone that the publicity of the change was strong enough in itself without the risk of criticism involved by talking about the thing in too much detail or even by slogans such as "Everything in Glory Goes Electric." It seems that just a simple news announcement works best in things like this—folks get the idea without pounding away at it too much. As chaplain at the Penitentiary naturally I had great interest in the change and I even spent some extremely pleasant evenings talking with the men from the big Pittsburgh electrical supply house who had the contract to build the chair. Of course, before that we had got it through the State Legislature and got the Governor's signature and, fortunately for Apple County, the lawmakers all seemed to feel that it dovetailed pretty nicely into the whole, big electrical expansion theme of the Valley. It was in the last week in September that the chair was installed. As it turned out they didn't take the gallows out until late in November because there were two prisoners from down state waiting in death row to be hanged. I find it not impossible to imagine that these men probably felt some emotions of disappointment that they were not going to be able to enjoy the swifter and more humane form of execution. Naturally, everyone in the Booster's Club, and quite a few Apple County businessmen who weren't, were extremely interested in seeing how the new chair worked and one afternoon that month after the Kiwanis luncheon we all went up to the Prison on Jefferson Avenue and were treated to a mild demonstration.

I say "mild" because, of course, there was no one in the chair and so the boys just asked a lot of natural questions and two or three took turns switching the current off and on. That night the *Glory Argus* came out with one of the most unfair and vicious editorials against capital punishment that it has ever been my misfortune to read. No one was much surprised, I guess, for it's hard to tell how Editor Tadd Cockayne is going to react to anything. He's a staunch Democrat and that puts him, often enough, on the other side of the table from business and every now and then he comes out with some strange and unpopular attitude which no one can predict. Such as this thing he wrote about the death penalty. At the time none of us had any inkling that Marcy Cresap was mixed up in it in any way, shape, or form. And so far as Tadd Cockayne's attitude about the death penalty goes, that was all his own and I'll not abuse his name by suggesting that Marcy Cresap put any ideas in his head. Nonetheless there had been a good deal in his paper throughout the fall and late summer about the coming change and he had had plenty of chance to attack it at the beginning which he did not. Doctor A. A. Blick is the prison doctor and has seen almost as many men hang as babies born and he and seven other prominent Glory doctors all came out with a statement the night after the *Argus* editorial, saying that they had definite medical proof that electrocution was less painful than hanging. That was the evening that Marcy Cresap walked over to Doctor Blick who was eating supper alone in the dining room of the Baldwin House and, in the presence of a whole group of the doctor's good, Christian friends and neighbors told him that the statement which he and the other doctors had made was a "shame and a disgrace to the profession of medicine whose purpose is healing and not death."

Madam, said Doctor Blick, a short, fat man who likes to enjoy his meals in peace. The purpose of medicine, for your information, is not healing alone—it is also the alleviation of pain and suffering.

And you say that electrocution is the alleviation of pain and suffering, Doctor? said Marcy Cresap, standing there beside his table with that incredible impudence of hers.

I say it is, Madam, said Doctor Blick, ready to get at his pie and coffee.

And I challenge you, said Marcy Cresap, far from content to let the matter be; having already embarrassed Doctor Blick and spoiled his dessert she must now go on with her haranguing.

You challenge me, Marcy Cresap? said Alf Blick. Are you a doctor, perhaps? Have you been hiding secrets from us all these years, Miss Cresap? Tell the truth now—*Are* you a doctor?

No, Doctor Blick, she said. And have you ever been electrocuted?

Well, that incident in the Baldwin House dining room was only the beginning of this woman's impertinence and meddling. Three days later she got Tadd Cockayne to publish a report of hers proving that there were almost two hundred active cases of tuberculosis among the inmates at the prison. Well, by that time half the respectable people in Glory were mad enough to ride Marcy Cresap out of Glory on a rail. All the doctors in the county wrote angry letters to Tadd Cockayne which, in all fairness. I must say he published dutifully in the *Argus* and Doctor Blick himself came out and denied the report of two hundred TB cases in the prison and said he would have his own figures on how many there were any day now. As a matter of fact, the very next spring he did that very thing and said in his report that there were only sixty or seventy really hopeless cases and they were managing to get at least two hours of sunlight every day in the prison yard and all the rest that Marcy Cresap had counted were nothing but mild cases which would just naturally clear up by themselves what with all the rest and good, nourishing food the convicts had.

Well, in November they sent us a man from Gilmer County under sentence of death by electrocution and things seemed fairly peaceful and quiet for a while. Thanksgiving was over and what with business picking up and only a few weeks till Christmas every man, woman and child in Apple County seemed filled with natural happiness. The storm over capital punishment in the *Argus* had all but died down and it wasn't till the morning the man from Gilmer came in under guard on the ten o'clock eastbound that Marcy Cresap started up her malicious crusade again. The condemned was scheduled to go down the first week in December and naturally all of us concerned in the actual execution and quite a few interested members of the business community were all a little uneasy and naturally anxious anyway that the prison's first electrocution come off without a hitch. Once, before that winter, Marcy Cresap had shown the people of Apple County her true colors: That was back in the spring of nineteen nineteen when our State Penitentiary was unfortunately chosen as a place of two or three months temporary confinement for the nation's arch-radical and Bolshevik Eugene V. Debs. There wasn't a week while that damned dynamiter lounged up yonder in comfort in our prison that Marcy Cresap didn't bring him a box of home-baked cookies or a caramel-fudge layer cake from her own oven. The memory of the Apple County boys who had laid down their lives among the blood and poppies of Flanders Fields— that memory didn't seem to trouble the sentiments of a woman like Marcy Cresap who brought cakes baked by her own hand to the national criminal who had dared to call the country's railroads out on strike while the boys and men of West Virginia and all the glorious other forty-seven states were giving their lives to fight the Kaiser to his knees. Well, the years hadn't changed Marcy Cresap any. Not a bit. It was a bitter cold night and just commencing to snow when I met Marcy coming in the prison as I was on my way out from an errand of mercy. I thought I would be as Christian and courteous as my position demands that I be.

I thought to myself: Web. Let's turn the other cheek to Marcy Cresap. Let's see how large this woman's soul is after all.

And so I bowed genteelly to her, took off my hat and I said: Evening, Miss Cresap.

And then I thought to myself that this might be a good chance to get in a little hint about her coming to church for a change.

Miss Cresap, I said. We don't seem to see much of each other these days and nights in Apple County.

She looked at me a minute and I swear to you I thought to myself then as I think now: The woman is mad. She had the queer, wild light in her eyes and she seemed to look clear through my face and out the back of my head and seemed staring at nothing but the stench and sin and depravity of the prison behind me.

No, Preacher, she said in that odd, far-off voice, almost like a deranged child. We don't. And perhaps the simple reason is that in the strange and miserable places that I search for God I never seem to find you there. And what is more I never find the slightest traces that our paths have ever crossed.

And she pushed on past me through the wheel-gate and it was then that I saw what she had kept half-hidden, keeping it warm no doubt, under the folds of her red wool shawl. It was a box with a cake in it. And I seemed to know by instinct that the cake was destined for the man from Gilmer. And I was right. Because I met Marcy coming out a week later as I was coming in. I looked at her and now her eyes were twinkling with an almost satanic mischief in their queer, unstable depths. And again I thought to myself that I would try—that I would reach out my hand again in loving kindness and mercy. Let no one ever say that any soul has been lost to hell because of the flaw of pride within my soul! And so I spoke again to Marcy Cresap. I knew very well that she had been to see the murderer in death row. The warden himself had told me that he saw no harm in it and that he had even let Marcy in the cell for a while and that she and the murderer shared coffee and some of her cake together. I thought this highly improper but beyond the rights of my Christian position to criticize. At any rate, I bowed again to Marcy Cresap and took off my hat.

Good evening, Marcy, I said, and my heart was truly filled with fellowship and forgiveness.

Good evening, Reverend, she said, already smiling rather impudently.

Marcy Cresap, I said, determined to go all out to save her. Marcy, why don't you ever attend religious services?

Why, Reverend Toombes! she cried out with a disrespectfulness with which I have rarely in my life been faced. Why, Reverend! she cried again, licking chocolate icing from her finger tips. Can't you tell? I've just come from communion!

From that night on I knew that the woman Marcy Cresap was beyond salvation, beyond prayer even. From that night on I knew her to be the implacable enemy of everything that I and every decent Glory Christian stands for. Our paths have crossed since then and now in her life's great battle up yonder in Apple County Courthouse I am proud to say that I stand on the side of the decent people of Glory. And I stand rock-firm against the woman Marcy Cresap.

The man from Gilmer went to his death a week later. And I could see that night what Marcy Cresap had done to twist his mind and spirit around her finger. For don't you know he turned down the last reading from the New Testament before we led him away? Don't you know he swore that he'd already done his Bible reading—with Marcy Cresap?

Do you see now how a woman like this can tunnel and burrow, digging and undermining the very pillars and posts of public decency itself? As for the man, he went to his death without repentance. He told me at the last—just as they strapped him in—that Marcy had told him not to worry about Heaven—that whatever it was over there, it would be all right for him. I glanced at the faces of the witnesses, hoping none of them had heard the man's shameless and unrepentant last words. I saw the faces of J. T. Langin and Roy Huggins and some of the other boys from the Booster's Club. Fortunately, I don't think they heard. As for that murderer I pray to God that there is a hell for him. And I think for a man who would spit words like that in the face of a Man of God will find his hell. Later I learned that nine years before he had been personally decorated by General Pershing with the Medal of Honor for killing eighteen Germans under heavy and direct machine-gun fire. Think of it!—a man so honored by his commander—by his country! —the grateful nation!—to go then and disgrace himself and that medal by an act of drunken murder! I tell you I can envision no mercy for that man from Gilmer. And that night as I watched them pull the switch I found myself thinking: Two distinctions. First, the Medal of Honor. Second, the first man to be electrocuted in the state. Two distinctions. And I don't think the son of a bitch appreciated one a bit more than he did the other!

Thomas Jackson Sorrell

There were three times in my life when I could have been Governor of
West Virginia. And that was the second thing I wanted most in the
world. The trouble was that the first thing I wanted was to be honest.
Born into an impoverished family in east Virginia, I began life with
no riches but those of a good name. My father and five of his brothers
fought under Stonewall Jackson in the War Between the States. A sixth
brother rode with Jeb Stuart and received all the highest decorations
attainable in the Confederate cavalry. The extraordinary aspect of
this achievement rests in the fact that Asa Sorrell was born into the
world without legs. When the War began he hired a master saddle-
maker to design and fashion for him a saddle much larger than ordinary
at the top and with two bucket-shaped hollows. Each morning two of
Captain Sorrell's orderlies would lift him into this saddle. Thus with one
fist clutching the reins and the other brandishing a big Navy Colt, Asa
Sorrell, his gigantic shoulders thrust forward over the horse's neck rode

forth like a raging centaur into most of the greatest cavalry engagements of the War.

When I was still a young man I crossed the mountains to West Virginia. I found work with the B & O in a railroad town in the eastern panhandle of the state. Born and reared with that lovely word Virginia always in my ears I was troubled and saddened by the name of West Virginia. It seemed to me one of the cruelest results of that terrible conflict—the sundering of the great and old dominion. Nights in the lonely mountain depot I would sit listening by the telegraph key and through the dusty window I could see the dark and woolly mountains of the great Appalachian Front rising to mingle treetops with the stars. And I would say to myself: It is still Virginia. It will always be Virginia. Nothing ever can really make it be West Virginia. But I was mistaken. Years later I came farther west. I settled clear across the state in the town of Glory. Within a few years I discovered that people here had traditions and a history peculiarly their own. They were West Virginians. Perhaps they had always been West Virginians, even back in the days when Washington and his rich neighbors lived elegantly in east Virginia while the mountaineers hewed out a tough life of a far more austere and lonely sort in the western counties. Soon I grew to love West Virginia almost as much as I had been raised to love Virginia. I found men and women here of rich character and honesty; people of integrity who could not be bought and sold with the easy bribes of privilege and politics. I met some of the other sort, too. And my upbringing enabled me to distinguish quickly one from the other.

My first friend in Glory was a banker by the name of William Davis Cresap. He was a retired steamboat captain full of memories of the days when the river was rich and great with glory. He had also been a farmer and a storekeeper. And then several years before the Great War he and several other prominent Glory citizens decided to gather together some capital and organize a new bank. The two other Glory banks, it seemed to them, were business organizations whose primary interest was not in the savings accounts of small, unimportant people, often foreign-born, with meager education, little future, and even less money. These two other banks, it seemed to Davis Cresap and the others, were little more than local offices for the speculations, wealth and further investment of Glory's most influential men: the mine owners, the steel and railroad men, the men with large and growing factories in Apple

County. Oftentimes these men had the biggest part of their vast fortunes invested far from Glory, some in Wheeling, some clear out of the state in Pittsburgh. And so the new bank was organized—amid loud, private laughter—announcing in its prospectus that it was for the investment of Apple County money for Apple County prosperity. And even a dime was enough money for a poor Polish coal miner to open an account. This seemed particularly laughable to most of Glory's most important men. And behind Davis Cresap's back they would make fun of his deep concern for the old age of miners and millworkers who spoke little or no English, with large families to support, and a working life which often did not last past the age of fifty.

It was A. K. Pyle who said after Kiwanis one day that the new Mercantile Bank and Trust Company was "a goddamned lot more trust than bank" and Harper J. Follansbee added that with the Hunkies and Spiks and Polacks saving their money the bank would end up with a capital of nothing but kopecks and pfennigs. No, added Bob Wolff, it would be shekels because he had it on good authority that a good percentage of the bank's initial capital was smart Jew money from Pittsburgh and New York. Nobody said any of these things, of course, within hearing distance of Davis Cresap. Perhaps it was his lean and lonely boyhood which gave his face that austere and Calvinist dignity which few men dared recklessly offend. Perhaps it was the long nights in the pilothouse watching the great river's channel and guiding his boat by starlight and guess which gave his keen blue eyes that icy coolness with which they answered offense. He was a man who joked seldom; he was a man upon whom no one made jokes. At least, not to his face.

At the age of nine his mother had called him and his six brothers and sisters to her bed. She told them she was going away to Heaven presently. She told them that it was up to their brother Davis to support and look after them now. She said nothing about their father. She made no mention of what they all knew: that he was a drunkard and that they probably would never see him again after she was gone. And so William Davis Cresap went to work cleaning brass spittoons in the cabins of the great Ohio Valley packets. There was nothing in his childhood lighthearted enough to let him learn to laugh. There was nothing but work and God and duty. And these were the things he brought unchanged into his later years of age. They had carved his face as rains and wind leave their traces upon stone. There was hardly room for even an occasional smile. And for the furtive smirk of compromise or dishonesty there was no room at all. Even his family were rarely able to reach him. I remember well the fair May morning his seventeen year old daughter Marcy, fresh home for spring vacation from Washington Seminary, ran up to him in his office in the bank and threw both arms around neck and kissed him impulsively on the cheek. Removing her hands from his shoulders he pushed her back to what he considered a proper and respectful distance.

Daughter, he said sternly, you forget yourself.

Sometimes I have imagined him as a lonely boy in those joyless river nights. I can picture him stifling sobs with a fist jammed into his teeth, his eyes clenched angrily to deny the tears that burned behind the lids. I can imagine him in those days learning to smother grief and self-pity and the longing for his dead mother. I can imagine that because he had to stifle these emotions he had to stifle the others as well: laughter and tomfoolery and the carefree shrugs of youth. Not that he was without emotion. Thrift, duty, honesty, concern for the prosperity of the helpless and those too old to work—these were the emotions that fired his life.

In those first days in Glory this man was to become, even more than my father, the guiding inspiration of my life. Without his example my life might have been far different. And without his example I might have become Governor of West Virginia. I had no profession and little education when I came to Glory. I worked in the B & O office as I had over in the eastern panhandle. I think it was during Debs' big railroad strike back in the nineties that I became interested in politics. My father and all my people had been Democrats in Virginia. It never occurred to me to be anything else. Soon I was beginning to learn the rudiments of politics. When Woodrow Wilson's campaign train stopped at our small depot in the fall of nineteen and twelve the Glory mayor and Apple County Democratic chairman each made a speech of welcome. I wrote both those speeches. I campaigned in eight counties of the Ohio Valley during that hot election campaign. And I can remember the zest and excitement of that November night when Tadd Cockayne had a lantern-slide machine in the window of the *Glory Argus* and kept the thrilled crowds posted on the triumphant returns with gigantic figures projected across the street against the wall of Ike Mobley's Clothing Store.

In those days politics seemed uplifting to me; to campaign for a man in those times seemed to be championing the greatest dreams of the Republic against the selfishness and greed of special privilege. I was as certain as I was certain of heaven that there were no thieves and bigots in the party of Andrew Jackson just as I was certain that every Republican was black as sin. With the nineteen twelve Democratic victory I rode into politics on the crest of the wave of Wilson. To be sure it was for me a little wave, hardly more than a ripple, but I was in. Soon I began attending political meetings all over the state and my name became fairly well known among the good Democrats in Charleston. Once when the great Mother Jones and the mine organizers met together in Pittsburgh I was sent along with four other West Virginians to represent the Democratic Party as a friend of labor. That night there was a beautiful dance at the old Schenley Hotel. I had no right being there. The dance was being given by one of the great coal magnates of the Ohio Valley. It was Marcy Cresap who got us both the invitation and she came down all the way from Washington Seminary to keep our date. The orchestra leader was Victor Herbert. Marcy looked more beautiful than I thought it humanly possible to look. Even now I can remember the scent and the feel of the elbow length kid gloves she wore that April night. And I can remember the enormous table of food in the center of the hotel dining room: the ice cream molded in the shapes of animals, the gigantic, carved palace of ice in the middle of the table with the crystal bucket of caviar sunk into the middle and glowing like a goblet of rubies. And Marcy was the prettiest girl by far among them all and she seemed to me so ritzy and smart because she had been to New York City that winter and she had been to see the latest Victor Herbert extravaganza *Princess Pat* and he was playing the tunes from that show tonight and Marcy, as we danced, sang the words in my ear to "There's a Message of Love in Your Eyes."

I never drank much, but that night I had a little champagne with Marcy who was being terribly daring that night and even smoked an Egyptian Deity cigarette. And after a while the glitter and the swirl of beautiful dresses and the music and champagne did its work on my feelings and I knew I would always be in love with Marcy, though I didn't even hint at such a thing that night. Because I had no right to be in love with her. For what would I have to offer her? And then I began to wonder if maybe I might not be on the wrong side of Things and I thought about that afternoon with the miners and that shrill, radical old lady from the coal fields and all the lusterless talk of safety and wages and rights. What did they have to do with me? And I looked at Marcy and she looked at me with her laughing eyes and she asked, A penny for your thoughts. And I made some answer, I don't know what. I made some kind of stupid answer because I realized suddenly that I was ashamed of my thoughts. It came over me suddenly that I had bumped up against a choice that would haunt me the rest of my life. Because it seemed to me that unless I were rich beyond dreams I could never hope to court a girl like Marcy. And I suddenly realized that I was nearly forty anyway and had achieved nothing at all in my life— not even a career. So you can bet your life I felt pretty blue all the rest of that evening and Marcy kept trying to show me a new dance by the Castles and stopping every now and then to ask what was wrong.

What could I tell her?—that I was in love with her and wished I was on the side of the millionaires instead of a bunch of dumb coal miners who didn't have enough sense to look after their own political interests? No, I couldn't say that. Because I knew the mind of Marcy Cresap's father. And more than likely Marcy's mind was like his when it came to matters of loyalty and integrity. And I was right. For even if I had been the richest coal baron at the Schenley that night it wouldn't have mattered. I didn't know it then but Marcy Cresap was already engaged and a few weeks later in the Glory and the Wheeling papers her forthcoming wedding was announced. He was a Wheeling boy—a young doctor—I'd never heard his name. It hurt at first but I drove it from my thoughts. I plunged into political work harder than ever and because I was close to the Democratic state government I had become a close friend of Governor James Gassaway Slade. I've never known for certain but I always thought it was Marcy's father who suggested my name to Jim Slade when the opening came for a new warden at the State Penitentiary. It wasn't a great enough job financially to be considered much of a plum but it carried considerable administrative prestige with it. I knew how Davis Cresap felt about the terrible conditions up at the prison and his opposition to capital punishment and I had expressed my sympathies and feelings on these views to him many times.

At any rate, I became warden at the West Virginia State Prison the same week that Marcy and Lou Delaplaine came back from their honeymoon in New York City. It was spring again. It seemed as if it was always spring when Marcy appeared anywhere. And even if it was winter she always seemed to carry a spring of her own around everywhere. She came to see me at the prison that April. She was dressed in the smartest nineteen-nineteen fashions and I was sure from the merry smile on her lips that she was going to burst out singing for me the latest Broadway hit. But instead of that she began to talk about the terrible health conditions inside the penitentiary and the awful exploitation of prison labor for the private fortune of John Wickerman and a few other Glory businessmen who ran the prison clothing shop. Marcy asked me what I intended to do about these things. I smiled a little, I guess, and got a little red around the ears and asked her what I could do. Her temper flared up then.

You can do your bit to fight it, Tom! she cried, pacing up and down my office in her narrow-toed, high-topped kid shoes. You can't let a job like yours just roll by without doing something against these rotten things.

I wonder if you've heard any of the talk around Glory, Marcy, I said, looking out into the prison yard where the band was rehearsing. The talk that maybe they might run me as Democrat candidate for State Senate next year.

What does that have to do with *this?* she fairly yelled at me.

I have ambitions, Marcy, I said. If I do a good job here at the pen there's no reason I couldn't go on to the Senate in 1920. And if I keep on growing maybe in 1924 I might be hot enough for the governorship.

Even before I had finished I knew I was ashamed of myself. And I didn't even have to look around at Marcy's face to know what she thought of me. I guess I knew that very day, the very moment I had finished saying that sentence to Marcy Cresap that I was never going to be governor nor state senator either one. That's the trouble with loving women like Marcy Cresap and being around men like William Davis Cresap. Some of them rubs off on you and—one way or the other —you're never quite the same.

I hope in years to come, Tom, Marcy said, that neither you nor I will ever let on to one another that we remember your saying that.

I covered my face with my hands, I couldn't look at her. I couldn't think why I had said it. I remembered that dance at the Schenley Hotel and Marcy in my arms and the gilt and smell of wealth all round us and the white hair of Victor Herbert bowing to the dancers after they'd finished "Three O'clock in the Morning." Maybe it all began that night—the temptation to wealth and glory. Or maybe it was because that night I knew I would always love Marcy. So that at last, this morning, a year later, in the warden's chair, I had said something that I knew would hurt her and make her sorry she had ever known me. But it wouldn't work. And I think she knew I didn't mean a word I'd said. Because she reached up and lifted my fingers away from my face and took my hand and kissed the back of it.

No, dear Tom, she said. I know you too well.

And she ran off into the morning up Jefferson Avenue and left me there with the heaviness of my damned principles weighting me down like a man being crushed to death by stones. I began to fight then, in little ways, against the outside powers that were making their fortunes in Glory out of the prison shops. I went so far as to make public statements of my feelings and I said things privately which I allowed Tadd Cockayne to print in the *Glory Argus* and it wasn't long before the fat was in the fire. John Grimm and a few other businessmen pointedly snubbed me at Kiwanis and finally, after I had sent a letter to Tadd Cockayne the night of an execution declaring my opposition to capital punishment, several of the big-timers in business and local politics came to me in a body. John Grimm was their chief spokesman and he let me know the Democratic Party had plans for me. And I began to realize that ironically in my attempt to turn these men against me, I had provoked them into offering me the temptation of a promotion which would take me out of the prison entirely and place me where I couldn't afford to go against them without committing political suicide completely. Nobody said anything specifically about the senate nomination but it was there unspoken in the air all right and I could sense it. I thanked them and made no commitment at all and the next day Marcy asked permission to finish arrangements which had been made for her as a nurse and her husband as a doctor to make a survey of health conditions inside the pen. And I agreed. If I had not agreed she would have had the right under her Federal job to make the investigation anyway but to the big men of Glory the thorn in their hide was that I did agree. Again that next week came promises of gifts. This time John Grimm came alone and this time he said that if I made things hard enough for Marcy and her husband the facts they gathered would be so sketchy that the report would have little meaning.

Do you think there's much sickness behind these walls, John? I said. I don't know, he said. And what's more I don't give a good goddam. Probably there's a fair share of the men in here are sick. Well, what do you expect, Tom? They are born diseased. They come into this world diseased. Want me to have Doc Blick come up here and give you the facts of life, Tom? Besides—what's your gain in all this? Everybody knows this whole stink is Marcy Cresap's fish-fry. What have you got in this, Tom? Is Marcy still letting you have a little now and then?

Not since my boyhood in Virginia, not for more than thirty years had I struck a man. But I hit John Grimm and I hit him so hard he staggered backward ten feet across my office and put his elbow through my glass bookcase. Then I took him by the collar and the seat of his pants and threw him out in the prison hallway. Which should have finished me forever. But suddenly that week a strange thing happened. The governor himself, Jim Slade, made a public statement about prison health conditions and followed it up shortly after with a strong statement expressing his disfavor of capital punishment. And the next time John Grimm came around he had forgotten everything, all the unpleasantness, the blow—he was all honey and oil and smiles. Some others came with him, too, and they said they were going to have a special Lion's Club dinner next month in my honor for the swell job I was doing as warden and for the fearless principles which I shared with Governor James Gassaway Slade. Twice they had come up and twice they had vaguely, barely hinted that, if they decided it, they might put me on the long, slick road that somehow would plop me down in the governor's chair. And there was a third and last time they would come.

Scarcely a week later a telegram arrived from Washington announcing that Eugene V. Debs, the Socialist, was being brought under heavy guard to the West Virginia State Penitentiary where he would be imprisoned until room had been made for him in the Federal Penitentiary in Atlanta. I tried unsuccessfully to get Attorney General Palmer on the phone. It seemed to me that the burden of trying to get along with the businessmen and politicians who held my political future in their hands was strained to the breaking point already. All I needed now was this world-famous radical under my authority and the slightest misstep would finish my career eternally. It all seemed too much. God of my fathers, I prayed in those nights, Why have you burdened my life with the yoke of caring so much about human beings? Nobody ever answered the question of that prayer. In a week Debs came, I escorted him to his cell, spoke briefly with the guard and went away. Within a few days the gifts began pouring in—cigars, candy, cakes, hand-knitted socks—presents from famous men and the unknown men all over the world. That night of the first wagon-load of gifts the guards brought them all to my office. I asked them why.

Mister Debs asked us to, said Harry Marlin, the guard captain. He says he doesn't want anything for himself. He says he wants you to pick out the things you might enjoy yourself and then distribute the rest of the gifts to the other cons.

Take them all the hell out of here! I shouted.

But it was no use. The next day, and the next they came. Rooms were filled with them. And always the prisoner would accept nothing. No, he would say, damn him, nothing for myself. And that frightened me. It was like an insurrection inside my prison: a revolt of love. I thought of the green and still strength of roots splitting stones. It seemed as if all this earth-wide love for this man had come to threaten and to split the walls of my penitentiary. I thought of burning them. I dreamed in the queer, lights-out quiet of the prison nights of an ocean of cigars and candies smothering me. And I would wake up listening to the slow, hard pace of the quiet guards and cursing the name of Eugene Victor Debs. And in the end that love did split the stones. No, it did not sunder the walls of the prison—though perhaps in its way it did. Surely, however, it split some stone in me; some hard and ruthless hold-out in my mind; some unbeauteous want to compromise myself. In the end I gave in to the love. I had Debs up as guest to my quarters, we dined together. The gifts were distributed among the prisoners. The broken, old and dying agitator became a kind of god among the men. John Grimm, Doctor Blick and seven of my fellow Kiwanians came to see me one night soon after.

Tom, you know, of course, what you're doing to yourself politically, asked John Grimm, by coddling this ruthless Bolshevik.

But he's not ruthless, I said. He accepts nothing for himself. Gifts come for him from plain people all over this earth. And he wants nothing himself. He gives it all away.

Tom, do you consider yourself a mightier humanitarian than Woodrow Wilson? asked Doc Blick.

Not a bit, I said. But wait—

It was Wilson that had the damned old traitor tried and convicted, Blick said.

I can't help that! I shouted. He is a gentleman. And a man. And so long as I am warden of this penitentiary I will treat him as a gentleman and as a man.

And as a Christian? asked Reverend Toombes of the First Methodist Episcopal Church.

He is a finer Christian than I am! I said. In fact, I cannot remember ever having met a truer Christian than Gene Debs!

Was it that last remark that finished me? Probably. I'll never know. Maybe I never would have won the governor's chair in the end. A year later Davis Cresap told me that the decisions I had made had cost me the candidacy. But he could be wrong. I hope to God he was wrong. Sometimes at night in the moment before sleep I feel this huge doubt like a great rock pressing on my breast—this wondering if I might not have done more good for my brothers of this life if I had made the compromises and gone to sit in the state capitol. And that's the hell of it: I'll never know. But I do remember a queer thing. Debs and I became good friends during the three months he was there in Glory in the pen. I told him of the old days in the eastern panhandle and how I had said he should be hanged during the great railroad strike in the nineties. Well, we both laughed over that.

I saw him to the wheel-gate on the morning the guards came to whisk him away secretly to Atlanta. I watched his tired, unbeaten shoulders in the cheap overcoat slumping away down the sidewalk through the morning mists. The two guards seemed almost holding him up. And for a moment in the odd way those river fogs in Glory have of changing things I saw quite vividly a man in a gray Rebel jacket and a battered old cavalry hat. On either side of him I saw Confederate soldiers about to lift this man into his saddle. Because, you see, he was without legs. And he was riding out to fight a battle he would lose.

A Child of Small Consequence

I will speak for the child. Since she was not given any name in her four years of life you will simply have to take my word that—in whatever world—names are neither here nor there. You understand, of course, that each of us in Glory has but one voice, one chance to speak. And so, in giving my voice to the child, I am forfeiting the right to speak for myself. Not that this matters to me in the slightest. It is not with the wish to impress you with my great goodness or generosity that I give this child's voice an importance greater than my own. It happened that this child of small consequence died before she could learn and so she cannot speak for herself. And even had she lived a few years more it would have made little difference—the words she learned would have been few and she would have said them poorly and understood them even less. For, you see, this child of such very small consequence came into the world imperfect of mind. She was what the doctors and most other nice people in Glory called a half-wit. She was what some even kinder—and surely wiser ones—give the name of *simple-minded.*

Why is it that most men can find love and praise for all of earth's great simple things except a simple mind? How is it that this most solemn and innocent of human creatures must often inspire horror and cruelty from those around it? So many of the world's unfinished and imperfect things do find their place at last and someone who will surely love and treasure them. On the dusty counters in the cheap bargain stores of the poor you will find beautiful and bright-tinted glass vases. And if you look at these creations in the sunlight of the even more dusty store window you will notice that each has some absurd imperfection. A bubble maybe—a wrinkle in the glass—perhaps a comic bulge. Who knows?—the glass blower may have had the hiccups. And not being perfect, these objects naturally sell for less—but still being beautiful they naturally are valued more. Certainly the grimy hands which lift so carefully these lovely bargains of broken delight—surely those frugal poor whose pennies choose these sweet, damaged things will not shrink with disgust nor grin with mocking at that bubble, this wrinkle, that comic bulge. Can it perhaps be that in the shape and blowing of the wonder that is man there is sometimes a hiccup in the breath of God?

Surely you can appreciate why I feel it so urgent, so absolutely essential that someone sacrifice the voice of his own time's telling to give some sort of tongue to this unfinished yet beautiful thing—this child of such small consequence. For do not imagine for a moment that because she cannot speak that she has nothing to say. It is true that behind the blue vacancy of this child's eyes there quaintly hoped and strove a mind less quick than yours and senses less exquisitely focussed. Yet that little which the eyes and stunted wits of this child did see and grasp and taste and smell was such a miracle of earth-staggering beauty and God-waking splendor as would make an angel blink. Perhaps for the very reason that the child's eyes made out a blurred and wordless infinity from the mystery of a flower—perhaps that swarming, nameless ecstasy of color was for her more wonderfully flower than ever it could be for you.

As for myself—Yes, I remember—I told you I was giving up my chance to tell you of myself. Still I must tell you a little. You must learn enough about me to realize how perfectly I am the one to do this thing

for the child and for you. For, in a sense, I am nameless, too. In my way
I have as little identity as the child. For I was a suicide. You would
know the name of my people if I said it. They are prominent in Glory.
So were the people of the girl I loved. Prominent and proud. And their
pride was such a sickness in them that when I got my girl with child she
became scared and went to the wrong man. I didn't know where she
was that summer night. And all night long I searched the starlit streets.
At last I came home. My father is a doctor. I saw my girl's mother and
father and my own parents standing around the small bed in my father's
office. They were looking down at my girl who had just finished bleeding to death.

I waited awhile outside that window in the warm night. I knew im-
mediately that if I went on living I would take the lives of four people.
And so I thought it better to take my own instead. My father had me
buried here on Glory Hill without a stone to say my name and time.
He does not want to remember that I lived. And so you see I am really
nameless, too. O, what sweet and grassy anonymity is mine!—I wouldn't
trade it for the earth. The awful hurt, the awful beauty—the senseless
striving, the moment's heaven—they're all over and beyond me here.
And I am, at last, no one. Which brings me again to this useless little
child—the one no one ever wanted, the one no one ever even named. A
child of such small consequence, indeed. And yet somehow she seems
to me at this hour, in this place, a creature of deathless and almost
incandescent holiness!

Some of you who lived in Glory may remember her. Her father was
the Apple County garbage man. I know, it's hard to remember which
child she was—the family numbered scores. And nobody in the garbage
man's family ever bothered getting wedded in the sight of God because
they were never out of it, what with all the cracks and tears and star-
bright peepholes in their shack's tarpaper roof. As for the inconsequen-
tial and uncompleted child no one in the family ever called it anything
but "Her."

Get *her* in here outa that road, Flory! the garbage man's wife would
shout from the porch.

Fetch *her* in for supper now and wash *her* good! she would howl
later.

Whar has her got to! one of them would cry at dusk when the broken
child had gone wandering off through stars-of-Bethlehem and staggered

now across the Glory garbage dump, her fingers chasing fireflies down the dark. And presently an older of the garbage man's daughters would fetch her cooing home and another would stuff her mouth with food and still another sit with her on the rickety porch for a while to watch the burnished aftermath of gone-down sun and all the sky it left behind now fired and stoked against the west. And had they been people of another land, another faith, another time perhaps they would have crossed themselves each time they looked into the hapless, sweet vacuity of the face of the broken child and said a magic word to keep away from themselves the demon that had cursed her dim and dumb. For a child of four she was large in a lopsided way and when the other children came to lift her good-humored unwieldiness they usually gripped one hand under an arm and with the other seized hold of her fair hair and so lugged her cumbersomely to and from the porch as if she were a fat laundry hamper with one broken strap. To these pains and indignities the child never complained, rarely wept, and seemed at all times to hoard beneath the Mongolian simplicity of her face the untranslatable secret of all human content. And so it seemed to all that the child had no real feelings and was indeed a creature of absolutely no human consequence. All that is except her mother, the garbage man's wife. The breasts of this poor woman hung flat, within the tattered and styleless folds of her hand-me-down dress, like the skins of dried and sucked-out oranges. Yet those breasts had been the fruit which fed first-food to more than twenty children. And beneath them even now there thumped a merciful and giving heart.

Tired as she always was this mother was never too tired to guard her broken child against the teasings and the meanness of the others. It was as if some organ deep within this woman's body comprehended with anguish the error it had made. As for the garbage man himself he was always angry enough at any new mouth to feed and at the sight of the child which, even his not-too-keen wits could tell, was absolutely of no consequence, he would often fly into rages and menace the child with his fists or a stick and curse it through the shack till its mother fetched it off to the shadows somewhere and safety. The other children teased it when they could find no dogs to tease. If the child had had a tail—and to many it was surprising it did not—they would have tied on tin cans and chased it clanking into town. And the garbage man's neighbors— some of them, at least—viewed the unperfect child as God's curse upon all the families and children of Angel Swamp. This belief was strengthened after the lemony bleakness of the winter's day when four or five of Glory's doctors accompanied some state inspectors on a tour through the frost-rutted alleys between the reeking open privies, poisonous wells, and tottering shacks of the shantytown.

You folks don't know it, said Doctor Blick to a group of children huddled together in the wind that day. But the best thing that could ever happen to Angel Swamp would be a good diphtheria epidemic.

And for those to whom that dreadful opinion was understandable it seemed certain that it was the broken child from the womb of the garbage man's wife that had made the men so mad. And then that Christmas came and with it the baskets from the ladies of the Glory Associated Charities. And there were old toys and dolls painted with new house paint and some of them were hardly broken at all. There were cans of food, too, and because there were no labels on them it was a jolly Christmas game—guessing whether it was peaches or string beans you were having for supper and some of the cans must have had extra amounts of food in them because they were swelled almost to bursting. Someone had taken particular pains with the three baskets for the garbage man's family because there was a present for every one of them and a red, merry tag with the name of each attached with a bright string. There was, of course, no Christmas gift for the child of small consequence. How could there be, with no name to write with crayon on the bright tag? With presents hard to come by anyways it would have been plain waste, thought Glory's ladies, to put one in the basket marked for "her." Besides, being broken, the child wouldn't know. Being simple it would not know what to do with a toy anyways, reasoned the wise women of Glory. Perhaps they were right. And so the child wandered off by herself that night and found a dead rat beneath the kitchen stove and cradled it and crooned to it like a child might croon to a doll and loved the dread thing with all the power within the shining fragment of her mind. Perhaps that one wild Christmas eve night in Apple County a dead rat was a sort of sacred thing. You can never really tell what will be sacred next these days.

In the hope that some of you out there may be Glory born—may I speak for the child of small consequence and chide you not unkindly by saying that you might have done better for her? In the winter of that year when she was so sick—her first and last sickness, by the way, so she didn't cost the county very much—in the last week of that illness it was only Marcy Cresap that night who would come. No other Glory woman came to stand beside the grieving womanhood of the garbage man's wife. No man among you came to comfort the shame of the man himself who now, in clumsy and bewildered unreason, fancied that Death had come to lay her dark wings round his roof and shadow his broken windows to punish him for something he had done. When Marcy Cresap came and saw the child, she turned and drove back desperate to Glory. Great and good, Old Doctor Will Cecil would have come but he was off in the cold, snowy, county on his own tireless rounds. And so Mary Cresap cranked the phone in the Mound Hotel for hours—pleading and cajoling, bullying and bribing, threatening and praying, promising and humbling herself to each of Glory's pajamad, warm, and long-retired doctors and none would come. But wait. Does it matter? Does it really matter? Weren't they being humane—those men of healing—when by not coming they could let nature painlessly erase a clumsy phrase of poetry she had scribbled: the broken child? Painlessly, you understand, because Doctor Blick and Doctor Stribbler both assured Marcy that half-wits don't feel pain. Mercifully, you realize, they both told Marcy, because disease was good sometimes: it helped clear out the weeds and trash from the human garden.

I tell you the broken child with the dead Christmas rat in her arms throws a long, long shadow across the grass where I am laid. For she is with us now over here. She will be a shame to her father no more, a game for her neighbors, disgust to the ladies, nor for the doctors a bothersome phone call in the night. She is with us now on Glory Hill. And that took a little doing. The garbage man's wife—she and Marcy the only ones who grieved—the mother of the child of small consequence, could not bear the thought that her child be dumped in a Potter's Field hole. And so one cold winter's night two women borrowed the garbage man's horse and wagon for a ride to Glory Hill. One of the women knew a place at the far north corner of the cemetery where there were a few scattered lots and the rest of it unbought ground. And with a pick and shovel the women, taking turns, hewed a hole in the hard, frozen earth and laid a small and shawled-wrapped shape inside. Then carefully they filled the hole again—both of them softly weeping—replaced the sod so the place would not show and went away.

My darling little one. In a place as unmarked and nameless as my own. O small unfinished thing. I will not let you be forgotten!

It's spring now and many of us who lie here busy with nothing but the industry of grass and our memories of life—we like the distraction of a running little child above our rest. In the deep gold green of spring twilights you can hear the broken child laughing at a rabbit which nibbles at our flowers in their tin vases. When the wild and vainglorious April moon lifts pendulous from the river willows in the west she croons a sound of loveliest delight and reaches up her hands to take it down. Lights like foxfire shine round her like a nimbus as she moves around this silent and stone-studded place. She casts out from her a light as if she were the old ghost of a toy. And here, at last, she has found a mind more simple than her own—someone to play with who will not tease or taunt or make mean faces and say mean words. At last, the useless child has found a comrade of even less consequence. And together the light of them moves, like twin haloes through the boughs and star shadows from the pines; beneath the moon and the hurtling, fateful galaxies.

Perhaps by now you will understand more clearly why there was no choice for me. My life's story is meaningless—it is a kind of rough joke. My voice would have told you only a story that you have heard too often before. I had to speak for the child. Though her story, too, is not perhaps so rare—God save us all. Every Christmas since that year the two women come back to Glory Hill in a big old touring car. Together they bring a small, bright bouquet of winter violets—blossoms like those the fingers of the broken child used to pick among the tin cans of the Glory dump. Together the women place the posy on the unmarked earth. And last Christmas Eve Marcy Cresap came back afterward, alone, stood awhile, prayed awhile, cursed a little, prayed some more and cried some, and then laid something else beside the tiny frozen bouquet. A broken doll the Christmas ladies had fixed as good as new.

If you are on the side of this world's reasonable ones you will dismiss forever from your thoughts all sentiments about this lowly and unfinished creature. Yet over here on Glory Hill things aren't so simply put aside. Over here we have a reasonableness, too, but it's free of all such facts as money and time and life or death. On Glory Hill these things don't mean much. With all the time we've got to spare it's hard to understand a man unwilling to give up a few hours of his sleep to go and fetch a child—even a child of such little meaning—back from the mouth of old, black death.

But I have almost forgotten to tell you what I began to say a moment or two ago—how, at last, the child of small consequence has found a child of even less! This is a comfort to us all—especially the very old ones here on Glory Hill. How they love it in the sweet hour after dusk to listen to these two laughing at rabbits and chasing meadow mice and shooting stars and fireflies up yonder among the cool pine trees in the vast and spangled night. There's no one can hurt them here on Glory Hill. There's no one can ever neglect or murder them again. They play together. And each—with that glowing, tiny fragment of the human spirit which endures eternally—each loves the other dearly in her way. Perhaps they will stay out here forever. Or perhaps, at last, they may grow weary of their little games and be drawn back again into the gigantic matrix of God's everlasting fire that's waiting to be blown anew in children yet unborn. We here on Glory Hill will miss them when they go. Forever will we love these two—the sacred idiot, child of the garbage man's wife, child of small consequence. And her small friend of even less— the litle girl unborn at all—the child my father killed that night within my darling's womb.

Doctor Edward Everett Follansbee

Since the spring night my only son Everett killed himself nothing has been the same. I have sent his mother Hattie to Europe every year since the tragedy but she is inconsolable and blames me for the boy's death. What did I have to do with it? What did I ever have to do with Everett —headstrong and incorrigible likeness of his mother's brother Jed. Whatever went wrong in Everett I know it was nothing he got from the Follansbee side of the family. It's something cursed in his mother's blood, I'll swear to that! All through school he was a shame and a hindrance to me. At the State University in Morgantown he was suspended twice. The first time was for forcing his way to the speaker's stand during a campus Armistice Day service and insulting America's war dead by reading aloud from the works of the native-born Bolshevist traitor John Reed. The second time was for organizing demonstrators outside the University Law School as a slur upon the teachers who had taken a brave and loyal stand against the anarchist-murderers Sacco and Vanzetti.

It came as no surprise to me that my son's life ended in suicide. But nothing has been the same for me in Glory since that shameful night. And when my brother Harper's boy Jack died violently the next autumn things got even worse. You have no comprehension of what even the faintest breath of scandals like this can do to a man. Since my boy's death my practice has fallen off more than a third. My brother Harper had a good Florida real-estate business going when his son Jack got killed that night and within six months he was selling cheap farm properties here in Apple County. I wonder if these two upstart youngsters knew what they were doing to the fathers who suffered and sacrificed to raise and educate them as decent Christian Americans. When I look at the rich practices of general practitioners like Alf Blick and Ira Stribbler and see the big new homes that they have built in the last two years it makes me sick. When I look at the prosperity of men like that I could fairly curse my son's memory. Because I was on my way up in Apple County till the scandal of that night hit Glory. And my brother who was on his way to becoming a millionaire outsmarting rich New York Jews in the Florida boom until his own boy died the following August.

Sometimes I wonder what it all means—this thankless sham we call Life. You fight and struggle to get through medical school, you fight ten years more to build up a decent practice, and then watch the whole thing go bang in a twinkling because of the moment's impulse of a thankless, spoiled son. I could never figure out why Alf Blick's practice didn't suffer, too. After all, it was his daughter Jane who played up to poor, weak Everett like the commonest Benwood whore and then when she got knocked up came whimpering to me. Why didn't she go to her own father? I was a fool. Not that I didn't know the odds with a girl in her seventh month. I don't know what got into me that night to make me even chance it. I knew my boy had been seeing the girl all that winter. I knew that a boy like Everett and a girl like Jane would be bad for each other. Both of them full of rebellious and dangerous philosophies—the kind of treacherous ideas Judge Ben Lindsay and atheist radicals like Bob Ingersoll and that lawyer Darrow preach and rant and write—polluting the minds and spirits of American youth.

When my boy came to me with questions about sex I thought about his questions as I lay awake all one summer night listening to Hattie snoring in the twin bed across from me. I knew I could give him the hard, cold, natural facts of life as a doctor knows them. But I didn't want him starting out on the Great Adventure that way. I knew with a boy like my son the truth might be dangerous to him. So I sent him and his questions to a man of God—Doctor Dan Tombes. Tombes put him straight on most of his questions. He told him if he played with himself he would break out in pimples and if he kept it up through manhood it would drive him insane. I know that's a lie but it seemed to me that a lie like that might be a good check on the high spirits of a boy like Everett. Well, it wasn't enough. Because the winter he got kicked out of the University for the self-promoted Sacco Vanzetti scandal he started going with Alf Blick's girl Jane. Don't think Alf hadn't told me plenty about that girl of his. I knew she was a hellion and a girl of loose morals from the mouth of her own father! That's why it came as no surprise to me to find her sitting in my waiting room that April night a few years back.

She was a pretty enough little thing—I had flirted with her myself in a kidding way one time when she had come to me for a vaccination. Well, I'll admit the place I asked her to show me wasn't the place I was going to vaccinate and when I put my hand on her she slapped me. I didn't want her running home hysterical with some exaggerated story to Alf so I apologized. But I had her number all right. That's why I wasn't surprised to see her in my waiting room that night. And that's why I wasn't surprised when she told me that she was seven months gone. Well, I knew my boy was the father all right. And I could just picture the disaster that was facing me if the news ever got around Glory that my boy had gotten Jane Blick pregnant. Alf would understand but what about the rest of Glory? Do you have any notion how much of a doctor's reputation rests on the pure and unadulterated b.s. of respectability? The thing I thanked God for that night was that Jane Blick was seven months pregnant but almost as slim as ever. She was one of those little, size five girls who never show until the eight or ninth month and then they swell up big as a balloon. I knew something had to be done before that happened. I told you what kind of mentality this girl had. Well, do you know she had the gall to sit there that night and tell me she wanted to have that baby somewhere up in western Pennsylvania and never let on a thing to Everett? That's a fact. She said Everett was still trying to "find himself" since his "misfortune" at college and she didn't want this to stand in his way. She said she thought

Everett was going to grow up to be something great such as a poet or perhaps a great labor organizer and she didn't want a thing like a wife or a baby to stand in his way.

I told her in no uncertain terms that I'd just as soon see my son dead as watch him become either one of those things. Well, I could see the defiance blazing behind those enticing brown eyes of hers but she didn't reply to that. Instead she went on to tell me that she couldn't go to her father with a problem like this because of his bad heart and besides she felt it was a problem of her own and wanted to work it out herself. Her plan was the sheerest case of bare-faced nerve and bad upbringing I've ever encountered. She asked if I could take care of her somewhere outside of Glory during her two months left and then deliver the baby. She began to cry then and promised me over and over that she would not bring the baby back to Glory but that maybe sometime she thought Everett was back on his feet and on his way in the world she might write him a letter. She said it would be up to Everett then whether he wanted to marry her or if he even wanted to see her and the baby. Because she said they were both "free souls" and neither of them was the kind who'd want to make the other do anything against his will or just because law or religion said they should.

Young woman, I said, do you have the slightest respect for law or religion either one?

She said: I believe in the law of God and the religion of humanity.

Well, if you had a little more of the religion of church, I said, you might not have such a faulty comprehension of what God's laws really mean.

I want to have Everett's child, she sobbed.

How can you be so sure it's his? I said. If you're such a "free soul" as you claim to be, young woman?

Because there's never been anyone but him, she said. Not before nor since.

And her voice had begun to become a little shrill and I didn't want Hattie to overhear any of this so I decided withour further hesitation what had to be done. I knew that if Jane Blick had a baby the news of it would eventually get back to Glory. And everybody would know my boy Everett was the father. And I could picture pretty clearly what would happen to my reputation and practice in Glory after that. Meanwhile the girl kept blathering on about her plans and she kept saying that it wasn't

a matter of money or anything. She said she had enough in her savings
account in the Mercantile Bank to see her through all the expenses for
a year or two. She said she wanted to live in Pittsburgh with the baby
until she felt it was time to let Everett know. I asked her why in the
name of God she had picked me of all the doctors in Glory to come to.

Because, she said, I felt that no other doctor in the world would have
deeper concern about a child of Everett's.

I knew that if I handled it wrong she might become hysterical and
run to her father. I decided it was time I took over. Now all of you can
sit there piously condemning me for what I did. Well, that's easy for
you. But try to put yourself in my place. The sanity of my wife at stake,
perhaps. What little reputation my son had left—that at stake, as well.
And last but not least a reputation of my own and a good practice that
I'd spent fifteen years and fought hard in the Great War to build up
and establish. By God, I was not about to watch these things go up in
smoke just because Dan Tombes failed to tell my boy there was something more to sex than playing with himself. I told the girl to stop crying and make herself comfortable and everything was going to be all
right. I went back to the parlor, to the old roll-top desk from my father's
country office, and I typed out a statement on his old Oliver. The statement said that the girl, Jane Blick, had come to my office in a state of
shock and hemmorrhaging severely from an illegal operation by Persons
Unknown. The statement said that the girl had no notion as to who the
father of the child might have been. It concluded by saying that she had
of her own free will and choice come to me for emergency treatment for
the aforesaid shock and severe bleeding. I took the paper in to the girl
in my waiting room. I had no other choice—can't you understand that?
I told her the paper was just a simple agreement that she would not
bring a bastardy charge against my son. Can't you appreciate the
alternatives that faced me? She was still crying too hard to be able to
make out what the words on the paper really said. I placed the pen in
her hand and told her to sign. When she had finished signing I told her
I was going back to my medicine cabinet and fix her up with something
for her nerves. When she was unconscious I did what I had to do. Would
most of you have done any different? As long as there was that one
chance in ten that she would have come through it that keeps it from
being cold-blooded murder, doesn't it. But why should I ask you? What
do you know of what it means to be born the only son of a dirty,

ignorant old back-country pill-pusher! An unambitious, illiterate old fool who would set a broken leg and then demand no more payment than a few pounds of rancid butter or a seven pound hen!

It was nearly morning before Alf Blick and his wife went home together. Alf looked at me once after he had examined his girl's dead body. That look was a look that only medical men can understand. Alf knew enough about his girl's brand of morals. He wouldn't have been surprised if she had come to him with the news that she was pregnant. There were tears in his eyes that night. And for a split second there he had the look of a man about to commit murder. Well, Alf is only human. I can't blame him for feeling that flash of hatred toward me. But it passed. We were both fathers. But we were both doctors, too. And when doctors are in danger they stand together. I don't think there is any more lofty nor ennobling fellowship in the world than that of one physician toward another. I think Alf knew that Jane's passing was the kind of end she would have come to anyway sooner or later. Or perhaps she would have lived to break her mother's heart. Who can say? God moves in a mysterious way. And it would have all been forgotten if it hadn't been for that Woman.

There was a nice little obituary in the *Glory Argus* two nights later. Alf Blick and his wife took a month's vacation up in New York State at Lake Chautauqua. For three days my boy Everett was missing. Well, at least we kept that out of the papers. And then four nights after the Blick girl died Marcy Cresap drove up in front of my office in her touring car. I hated her on sight, as usual, and politely asked her what her business with me might be.

It's about Jane Blick, she said.

Yes, I said. What stark tragedy.

You should know, said Marcy Cresap.

What kind of remark is that supposed to be? I said. State your business with me briefly, Miss Cresap.

I will, she said. I know about Jane Blick, Doctor.

You know what about her? I said, playing it cagey with this dangerous and notorious trouble-maker. You know that she died? Perhaps you didn't know that she died because some Wheeling quack performed a careless abortion on her. Maybe you didn't know that she came to me dying and I did everything in my power to save her life.

I had to tell her that much to throw her, if possible, off the scent of what could only mean mischief and real trouble for myself and perhaps for Alf Blick as well.

I don't know about that, Doctor, said Marcy Cresap. I just know it's all very interesting. I went down to Marple's Funeral Parlor this afternoon and made Jessie Marple show me the girl's body. There was nothing careless about what was done to her, Doctor. So I come to you. I thought perhaps you might throw a little light on things.

Why me? I said. Because the girl died in my office?

That, said Marcy Cresap. Plus the fact that your boy Everett got her pregnant.

That's a lie, I said.

It's no lie, said the Woman. And I have proof it's no lie.

What proof? I shouted.

The word of your boy Everett, she said. He told me he was in love with that girl. He asked me to help her. He said he wanted to marry her. He asked me to find her a place to have their child—a home where she could stay and take care of the baby until he could live with her honorably and support them both.

Live with her, I laughed. Well, that sounds like Everett all right. That would be about his idea of what the word "honorable" means.

Oh, he would have married her, too, said Marcy Cresap. And I had begun making plans for the three of them. I had even found the home down river a ways where Jane could have had her baby. And waited.

Waited forever, I added.

Yes, forever, said the Woman. And forever it will be now, won't it, Doctor Follansbee?

What does that mean? I cried at her.

It means your son is on his way home at this very minute, Doctor, she said. He's lying in the bottom of an old country buckboard with a piece of canvas thrown over him. The canvas is to keep the flies off. Because you see, Doctor, last night your son took his old ROTC rifle, stuck the muzzle in his mouth and blew the top of his head off.

By God! I shouted. He wouldn't have dared!

Can't you see what this meant to me? Can you just sit there and shake your pious heads at me in judgment without even trying to see my point of view a little? All of it now—the seamiest and meanest story in the world—just enough out in the open now for all the Glory gossips to go to work on it. And all the care that Alf Blick and I had taken together—both of us suffering and bereaved fathers—to keep all the sordidness away from the young people's mothers—away from the ears of Apple County.

Well, it's county history now. The Woman Marcy Cresap tried her best to get the West Virginia State Board of the AMA stirred up into a full-fledged investigation of the thing. Thank God, I had gotten the girl to sign that paper. Because nothing ever came of it. I told you how medical men know how to stand firm together. Women like Marcy Cresap never seem to understand a power like that till they come up against it.

For months my wife spent half her time and hundreds of dollars on a fake Wheeling spiritualist who claims he has put her in touch with Everett's soul. And she'd come home crying and tell me how Everett's ghost kept saying I was to blame. What did I ever have to do with it, really? What did I ever have to do with my own son? My wife said this spiritualist let her talk to Everett. I asked her what he ever said to her and she wouldn't tell me. And I asked her what she said to him and all she could say was: Forgive me. Forgive me!

Forgive what?—is what I'd like to know. Forgive her for marrying me?—a father who has worked himself nearly to death trying to make an easy life for his wife and son? Forgive his mother for suffering to bring him into this world only to watch him grow up to be disrespectful to his country, a disgrace to his father, and a rejection of all his mother's early religious teachings? Is that what she asks Everett to forgive? I don't know. I just don't know.

On top of all of that, last summer my brother Harper's boy John Wesley Follansbee died violently in an accident during that disgraceful riot in the minstrel show at the Opera House. And that was another smirch on our good family name. And don't think it didn't hurt Harper's real-estate business just as much as it did my practice!

You have got to believe me! My voice will keep on speaking to you until you believe me. I searched my soul long and hard that night before I took into my hands the life of Alf Blick's daughter. I thought of her life. I weighed it with the others. I weighed it against the lives and happiness of so many, many other lives. Then I acted as my conscience dictated. A murderer!—that's what the woman Marcy Cresap called me and several other respectable Glory doctors in County Court today. Imagine it—a murderer. If I were even guilty of malpractice, let alone

murder, don't you imagine the girl's own father—a man of the caliber
of Doctor Alfred Aikens Blick—would have been the first to accuse me?

Hattie is better these days. She never goes to the Wheeling spiritualist
any more. I have been giving her certain injections to help her sleep
better at night. I can't stand any more of her dreams! I give her
enough to make her sleep a little too deep for dreams. And sometimes
when she starts crying for no reason during the day I give her an extra
injection. True, she is becoming somewhat dependent on the medica-
tion. But what would you have me do?—sit by and watch her suffer?—
stand by and listen to those horrible, insane accusations from her lips?
—see her suffering those awful hallucinations about Everett? As a
physician I can't stand by like that and let her suffer. And now she
has these delusions no more. Now she sits quietly in the sun parlor
beside a frame picture of Everett taken in a sailor suit when he was ten.
From time to time she smiles quietly to herself and touches the picture
with the tips of her fingers. It is all quite moving. She was a nervous
wreck a few weeks ago; now she is at rest. Since I began her with these
mild morphine injections the voices do not seem to afflict her imagination any more. So if she imagines the voices still, she says nothing to
anyone about them. Thank God, I am a man of science and know these
things aren't real. I came right out and told Hattie if she didn't stop
seeing this spiritualist and talking about hearing voices and seeing
Everett's face that I would have her put away. I told her if she didn't
cut out all this nonsense and let me give her these injections I would
have her committed. And I would.

As it is we lost a wonderful little maid all because one afternoon
Hattie woke up from a nap and frightened the girl half to death with a
story of a vision she said she'd had. Maybe this will give you an idea of
how unbalanced poor Hattie really was. She said she saw Everett's face
smiling and she said there were these two little shining babies on each
side of him—infants who couldn't speak but only smiled, infants laughing with stars in their hands and fireflies gleaming in their hair.

Poor Hattie. For these were dreams, my friends, dreams!—not visions
from beyond. Surely now, sensible folks like you and I—don't we know
the difference?

Tadd Cockayne

The night after Jane Blick's sudden death and Everett Follansbee's suicide the *Glory Argus* carried nothing more than two decent, simple obituaries side by side. And when Harper Follansbee's boy John died violently that autumn we wrote the same kind of notice. There's a million light-years' distance between all the news that's fit to print and all that's fit to read. When my father founded this newspaper in 1893 he decided that's what we'd always try to print: what's fit to be read. A lot of other newspapers print a lot of stories that are fit to print—which is to say that nobody gets sued for libel. But when we've got a sordid, ugly, mean story that's going to hurt someone—living or dead—we trim it down to the kindest, plainest facts and print that. Don't worry—the gossips fill in the rest. So rest assured that nothing ever gets censored around Apple County. But that doesn't mean we print a tame or timid paper that's afraid to stand up on its hind legs and fight for something it believes in. My father fought for Bryant and Free Silver. Back in

56

ninety-four the *Argus* came out for Altgeld and the workers in the Pullman Strike and when Debs went to prison he wrote an editorial defending him. And this winter when some of the Great Powers in Glory decided to go all-out to destroy the Woman Marcy Cresap the *Argus* began to fight for her all the way. And being for the Woman is not a popular position either. We've already lost some mighty good advertisers and a lot of folks have canceled their subscriptions.

I don't know what all they've told you about the Woman so far. I know a lot of important men in Glory will tell you they'd like to see her dead; I know some others who'll tell you things about her life and character that will make you hate her like they do—if you believe them. Yes, there'll be many who'll tell you barefaced, naked lies to smear her name. As for me, I'll stick to the policy of the *Glory Argus* and give you what, to the best of my knowledge, are true facts. I won't give you all of them. Because I think in the long run you're bound to have to make your own mind up about the Woman. I want the others here in Glory to have full chance to have their say. You'll have to hear their side of it, too. I want it to be fair. So I'm not even going to tell you all I might.

I've known the Woman since the day she came into this world. I watched her grow and start school and I printed it when she had chicken pox and whooping cough. I printed her engagement notice, too, and carried the story of her marriage to a fine Wheeling man, Doctor Lou Delaplaine. And when he died and their child died, all in the same winter, the *Argus* printed that. And when the Woman herself was felled by that terrible sickness folks read about it right here in the pages of the *Glory Argus*. I guess I am a little prejudiced. Because the Woman has always seemed, in a very particular way, one of ours. I knew her father W. D. Cresap and I know the kind of things he stood for. I don't know whether his voice is one that's going to speak among all these voices of Glory. But I'll bet if he has anything to say about the Woman it will be something full of pride.

This fight against her—it's been gathering for a long time. And then this winter, like a storm, it broke. You'd see her proud, straight bold figure standing up there in the County Court if you were in Glory this week. And you'd see the faces of some mighty powerful men, twisted and knotted with passion in their hatred of the Woman. You'd recognize men among them, too, whose lives are supposed to be dedicated to the very things that the Woman herself has fought for. And you'd hear these men saying things against these very principles; you'd hear them saying things that someday they'll be mighty ashamed remembering. That show that's going on up at the Apple County Courthouse this January in the year 1928—it's not a very pretty thing to watch and hear.

But shows are nothing new for the Woman. She's put on a few pretty good ones all by herself through the years. When her husband and child died that cruel winter it seemed to a lot of us here in Glory that the Woman might be licked. And then when she came down with TB the next year a lot of people were sure of it. But something seemed to come over her. When she came back from the sanatorium, rosy-cheeked and well, there was a something queer and burning in her eyes. It seemed as if she had whipped the fever in her flesh and now she was left with another fever in her spirit. And those of us who knew the Woman best knew that there were things about her that would never be the same. Her eyes shone as if they were lighted by a feud fire. It put me in mind of the look I saw once in the eyes of a country boy from back up Silver Hill. A deputy had shot his old father in the back during a raid on a still. The boy came into Glory looking for that man who'd killed his father. And I remember the look in the boy's eyes. And when I saw the look on the Woman's face when she came back from the edge of death there was something in her look that rang a bell. And suddenly I knew where I'd seen it before. Except that the look in the Woman's eyes was a feud fire of another sort. It was tempered and sweetened with something. The feud-fire in the eyes of the country boy was pure. It was hate and nothing more. But the Woman's eyes had something that wasn't hate. It sounds odd, I know, but it was almost as if she was out to get even for love. And right away she started to do something about it.

From the beginning there were enemies. From the very start there were mighty important Apple County people who got sore. And there were a lot of middling-important and pure no-accounts who got sore, too. It seemed to many that the Lord had spared the Woman's life and sent her home well, expecting her to spend the rest of her days quietly giving thanks that she hadn't died like her husband and little boy. And to these people it seemed almost sacrilegious that the Woman did no such thing. It seemed to them pure ungratefulness to God that, instead of that, she just seemed to set herself on a course of trouble-making. She made the real-estate people mad and she made the dairy men mad. She made the doctors mad, too—most of them—and doctors swing a lot of power in a town like Glory. She made the bankers mad and the café proprietors and the chairmen of the Apple County Water Board. She even made Mister Parker, the garbage man, mad because she tried like the devil to get his little simple-minded baby sent to the Home at St. Mary's. You could throw a stone almost anywhere in Apple County and you'd be pretty sure of hitting someone who had a gripe of some kind or another against the Woman. But that just seemed to spur her on.

The thing sort of came to a head in the autumn and early winter of last year. Harper Follansbee, the real-estate man and County tax-assessor owns most of the land out beyond Misery Hollow behind the smelter. That's the part of Apple County that nobody's too proud of around here, the section known as Angel Swamp. Nothing grows there but polk-weed and poverty. One day late last summer the Woman went out to investigate a case of typhoid fever. She found a shack there a little worse than the others which were bad enough, God knows. But this one was right at the creek mouth of Misery Hollow, below the Prison Farm, and there three not one cases of typhoid. Harper Follansbee couldn't see any sense in the Woman's opinion that fifteen feet wasn't far enough distance from a privy for a well to be dug. Harper said his brother was a doctor and he had told him that the sandy ground in Angel Swamp was a natural filter and that, besides, most of the people who drank out of the well were so used to filth that they had built up more resistance than other people had. The Woman wouldn't accept Harper Follansbee's point of view. She also took issue with him over the particular shack in question. Harper couldn't seem to see anything unreasonable in the fact of a one-room shanty about the size of a large chicken-house which he was renting to twenty-three people. Harper, who is quite a wag, commented to some friends that twenty-three people wasn't too many for a shack that size just so long as one of them didn't get pregnant.

Well, the Woman spent two weeks at it but she finally found places for all the twenty-three to move to. And the evening of that day, about sundown, she went out to Angel Swamp with a five-gallon can of coal oil and burned the building to the ground. Harper Follansbee got his attorney, J. K. Foss, on the phone and tried to have the Woman arrested for arson. J. K. told Harper that he had seen the shack himself and he advised Harper to forget about the whole thing while he was well off. Nor was that the end of the matter. The following Friday was Armistice Day and naturally everybody in Glory was looking forward to the parade.

Harper hadn't been to France but he had made quite a name for himself contracting for the barracks for a big army camp in Georgia. And so, of course, Harper put on his uniform and led the Apple County veterans in the parade. Being at the head of the parade he did not know, of course, what was at the rear. It was a float, of sorts, designed and built by the Woman herself with the aid of a group of Angel Swamp children. Actually, it was no great shakes as a float, being nothing more than an old hay-wagon pulled by a windbroke mine mule. It was what stood on top of the wagon that caught everyone's attention and, in its way, it was the hit of the day. On top of the wagon the Woman had put the huge old privy those twenty-three people used and on each side of it she had nailed a sign that read: TYPHOID FACTORY. CLOSED FOREVER.

Harper felt the insult doubly—having everyone make fun of a build-ing—even one so plain and humble—from one of his lots. And he was sore, too, because the Woman had been the main attraction of the entire Armistice Day parade. And the Woman hadn't helped things any after-wards. Harper Follansbee had taken great pains to memorize his speech. And then right in the middle of it the people all spied a column of smoke rising above the elms and willows at the edge of town. The Woman had hauled Harper's privy out to the foot of Misery Hollow. Then she had set fire to it the same way she had the shack. It takes a pretty good speech any day to outdraw a fire in a town like Glory, and within a few moments the street in front of the bunting-draped speaker's stand was entirely deserted.

It was a good joke for a while. A lot of Glory people chuckled over it till well into Thanksgiving Week. That was the week Harper's boy John was to die so tragically. That was the week the Woman set in motion a plan which, through no fault of her own, was to end in death and shame and heartbreak. I've looked into Harper Follansbee's face on the street in Glory since that night. And I don't know whether I feel more pity for him or for the son for whose death he was to blame.

To begin with the Woman arranged with Denver Busby for the use of his theater for that one night to raise money for the Apple County Sanatorium. Denver agreed and everything looked as if it would run off smooth as silk. The Woman planned the show. At nine sharp the curtain rose. Seventeen scared, smiling boys and girls and one old man faced the audience. Each of them stood behind a white-painted box made up to look like a tombstone. Each of them said a little speech about how glad he was to be well again and back home again and back at school or his job again. For each of the seventeen were ones that the Woman had found out in time, had sent to the sanatorium, had gotten cured. There were a lot of people there in the Glory Opera House that night who hated the Woman. But there were a few others, too, with lumps in their throats as they listened to those queer, choky little speeches and watched as each one turned his tombstone around and showed what was on the other side: the scarlet, double-barred cross of the Apple County TB Association. There were a few of us there that night who looked at the eight other tombstones with no one behind them standing there waiting to make his little speech of thanks. They were out somewhere—those eight—sleeping that night in Potter's Field or in the autumn peace of Glory Hill. As for the seventeen, they went home and slept in beds that night, and slept safe and slept well. Because of the Woman.

And that was supposed to be all. At least, it was all any of us knew about. Denver had cancelled the movie that night which was Bebe Daniels in *Swim, Girl, Swim,* with Trudie Ederle. When the curtain rang down on the Woman's part of the show everybody got ready to get up and go out and start looking for their Fords. But then Harper Follansbee appeared from behind the curtains and held up his hands for silence. A lot of people wondered what right Harper Follansbee had up there. But a few of us remembered all too well that Harper owned some other real estate in Glory beside the stinking shacks of Angel Swamp. Harper owned Denver Busby's theater, too. And Harper had decided to ask for equal time, as it were. Harper had planned and organized a show that was sure to make everybody forget that puny little TB pageant the minute the curtain rose again. Harper had arranged to put on a small-sized minstrel show. Not so small a one, either, because he had hired Peabody's Band to play in the pit and he'd borrowed the minstrel costumes from the Elks. A fine, old-time minstrel show, it seemed to everyone, and yet, to those of us who sensed the storm now gathering between these men of Glory and the Woman there was a smell like scorching in the air, a smell of tragedy to come.

Folks, cheer up! cried Harper Follansbee, waving his bamboo cane. After all this *funeral* we've been watching!—all this business of tombstones and sickness I felt you good people deserved a little honest fun and merriment! How about that, folks!

And most of them shouted and clapped and stamped their feet and a lot of people went out front to Denver's little peanut stand for fresh sacks of buttered popcorn.

So let's get the gray taste out of our minds, folks! shouted Harper Follansbee. Let's enjoy ourselves with a good old-fashioned combination minstrel show and amateur night. No, wait. Hold your applause a minute, thank you—thank you—let me explain. Tonight behind that curtain—ahem, on the stage from which, I trust, the tombstones have been removed and the dead sent back to Marple's Funeral Home—. Behind that curtain sit sixteen talented—well, maybe only *eight* real talented—young people who are going to strut their stuff and do their turns! Yes, folks, when that curtain goes up you're going to be staring into the black faces and googley eyes of the boys in Harper Follansbee's Amateur Minstrel Show. Cheer up, lady! That's a bad cough your little boy's got down there in the third row center but if it's the galloping consumption, I'll buy him a sack of popcorn and he'll forget all about it.

And a lot of them laughed. Yes, God knows, a lot of them laughed. And some of them coughed. God knows, some of them coughed.

But wait a minute, folks. Behind that curtain sit eight healthy and talented young lads from Apple County's very best homes—most of which I rent! And they're all blacked up till you wouldn't know 'em from Little Black Sambo himself. Yassuh yassuh! I mean to say now they really look like the genuine, native-born, American-raised and watermelon-fed Homo Africanus. Do you follow me? Wait. Wait. No applause yet. Wait. Thank you. Now, the *other* eight—. Well, now what do you reckon they are, Mister Bones?

Real niggers! shouted somebody from the balcony.

Harper Follansbee smiled reproachfully and leaned a little forward over the footlights and his voice was a whisper of mock respect.

Cuh-luhd folks, my young friend up there in the balcony, he said in that cozening, murmurous tone. That's not a proper, nice word to use about our African neighbors. Not even if you *are* sitting up there in nigger-heaven.

And that got the biggest laugh of all.

The point I'm coming to, folks, friends and neighbors, shouted Harper Follansbee, is that we're gonna get the taste of this gloomy, tombstone, TB show out of our minds tonight with a *real* show, No, wait. Hold the applause till I finish. Thank you, Rastus, you up there in the fifteenth row of the balcony.

And they laughed again. God knows they laughed again. And some of us went slowly toward the door to the good clean autumn wind that blew that night in Glory's streets.

The eight African gentlemen! shouted Harper Follansbee, his voice cracking a little now to a strangely sinister scream of hoarseness. The eight Africans are dressed up just like the black-faced white-folks boys, my friends. And presently the curtain's going up, Mister Peabody's fine little orchestra will strike up "Swanee River" and the show will commence. Now! Now, let me tell you some mighty nice news! There'll be prizes tonight! Yes sirreebob! Oh, by the way—the colored gentlemen were kindly *loaned* to me tonight by Warden Bill Jackstraw who claims they're the stars of the West Virginia Penitentiary Frolic. There was originally nine but one of them did a dance at rehearsal called the Strut Away and one of the guards had to lock him in solitary!

And they laughed again. God knows they laughed and laughed again until he held his hand high for silence. And even the silence seemed a shameful thing.

Lemme get to the prizes now! cried Harper Follansbee. For the coon that does the best dance tonight he gets ten years off his sentence! No, that's just one of yours truly's little jokes. And, by God, anything sounds funny after that tombstone show we had, eh?

I could see Denver Busby in the wings and there was a look on his face that a man doesn't like to have another man see.

A free pass to every movie and traveling show at the Glory Opera House for a full year! cried Harper. And there's eight of them passes waiting for the very first eight of you bright-eyed folks out there tonight who can watch these sixteen performers and tell me—*and tell me—which one is the gen-uine colored man!*

I had gotten as far as the door now and I felt as if I was going to be sick. It was more than just the disgust and the shame of it. There was something gathering in the air: something that was part of the hatred for the Woman and part of it something that was just Hate itself, set free upon the air, Hate for whatever was frightened and helpless and shackled on the earth. I had felt it once before during the Great War when I was on a story in the coal fields down on Big Sandy and there was a riot because champion Jack Johnson had lost the world's title in Cuba to the white man Jess Willard. Even now I hardly remember when the curtain went up and Peabody's Band struck up "Swanee River" in five or six different keys and the sixteen figures on the stage went into

their little minstrel business with their canes. My eyes seemed glazed—
at first I thought it might be tears and angrily rubbed them with
my knuckles—and then I knew it was an unnamed and seemingly senseless fear. All of Harper Follansbee's hate for the Woman was there reeking in the close air of the Opera House; his hatred and that of the others
in Glory who were gathering themselves that cold autumn week to leap
upon her in destruction. And there was that other hatred, too; perhaps
only Hatred itself, incarnate, or perhaps the atmosphere of the sweating
audience was all it was, or perhaps the air was haunted with the ghosts
of the anger of those twenty-three who had lived in the shack that the
Woman and burned and for all I know, God help them, hating her for
that holy anger, for that torch of healing.

Dance, boy, dance! roared Harper Follansbee to a figure doing a fast,
inept clog in the center of the stage. Dance, black boy! Watch him, folks.
Which ones, now? Pick out the real nigras, folks! Some of these boys
are white except for a little burnt cork and a few imitation watermelon
seeds on their shirt fronts!

It was a farce and a sham. An idiot who was blind could have picked
out the Negroes from the white men in that hideous spotlit glare. I ob-
served that the third figure from the end was John Follansbee, Harper's
son, and the dark lie upon his face was streaked with tears of resentment
or shame, we'll never know. Because then it happened. Somewhere
in the balcony someone threw an empty popcorn box—it seems such a
curiously comic and somehow unangered gesture when I remember now
the way it sailed out into the glimmering air above the audience and
descended almost as lightly as a kite and struck someone harmlessly on
the shoulder. And then someone shouted something and it seemed that
everyone in the audience began standing up in their seats and straining
toward the aisles and the air began to ring with their curses. Harper
Follansbee shouted something and the orchestra idiotically continued
playing until Quill Peabody struck his music stand with his baton and
shouted something at them and snatched madly at sheafs of sheet music.
Apparently, Quill, in quaint and misled desperation, had thought that a
musically imposed mood of patriotism might quiet the fracas because his
little orchestra struck up "Over There." The performers meanwhile stood
gaping and thunderstruck at the massed hate clenching itself, as it were,
into a fist of resolution before their incomprehension until presently they
began straggling, in almost drunken bewilderment, toward the safety of

the wings. At that moment Denver Busby ran across the stage making wild gestures which none could interpret, followed by two prison guards armed with automatic shotguns. And these latter seemed unreal: it was as if the pathetic minstrel figures had been the horror of reality and these stone-faced armed men were part of some farce which would presently set the theater echoing with the boom of blank cartridges. In the midst of everything Harper Follansbee stood with a look both of god-like and idiot indecision. And he stood thus until his stare fell upon the gun in the hands of the first of the guards.

The niggers is escaping! screamed Harper Follansbee and with such authority as was, apparently, both believable and irresistible, seized the shotgun from the astonished man's hands and raced off into the wings with a look on his face of such deranged and implacable hatred that it seemed to me for an instant that it was the Woman, herself, who was his quarry. At that moment, indeed, it did appear as if the convicts as well as the other eight black-faced boys were escaping or were, at least, flee-ing to some kind of shelter. I stood for a moment back from the shouldering mob that thrust past me in a river through the exit and I thought to myself bitterly: This is news. And yet by the God of my father it is something so rotten and so evil that I cannot, could not and will not ever set a stick of type to tell of it.

Though much of it was left to tell. Long after Chief Smithers and Sheriff Holt and sixteen deputies with tear gas from the arsenal belong-ing to the Parr's Run Mine Company—hours, it seemed, later when the worst I thought that my eyes could witness had been witnessed—still there was sorrier, worse, more eternally, agelessly and fundamentally tragic than all the rest of it would ever seem. I rounded the corner behind the theatre and started down the alley among the choking, tear-faced men—moving now not as a newspaper editor but as a human being who is drawn by—by what? By his want to help the suffering? By his need to lend a hand to help mend things so savagely undone? Or was I moving at the impulse of something as atavistic and brutal as all that had nudged that mob that night and sent them hating outwards like a knuckled fist of flesh. What drew me down that alley behind the Opera House that night? Was it the horror itself? Was that what pulled me there so shamelessly wide-eyed?

The first thing I saw was Harper Follansbee, his face the tallow color of day-old buckwheat batter; a face bloodless, drained and dreadful. He saw me, our eyes met, for an instant he seemed to recognize me and then the lights in his eyes blinked out and he stumbled sideways toward some other human signal, like a baited blind man answering catcalls.

Harper! I said, moving after him, my mind white-hot and seething with a torrent of words, a fury of insult and rebuke which I had held too long inside. Harper Follansbee!

Don't bother him now, brother, I heard a voice say at my side and turned and saw that it was one of the prison guards. He was looking at me and shaking his hard face with a smile of curious apology and abashment, as if he were momentarily unnerved and dismayed by some recently woken sense of man's awful fallibility.

I wouldn't bother him now if'n I was you, brother, he said again firmly and yet with deference for fear I might be someone important. That poor soul yonder has made a tur'ble mistake, brother, he said, and spat into the fog as if to be rid of the taste of all pity.

What has happened? I cried, seeing the figure on the foggy pavement with the coat of a guard thrown over its face and shoulders.

Something just tur'ble, the guard said, looking toward the autumn sky as though, for the moment, it was necessary to avoid the encounter with a human glance. That po'r soul mistaken his own boy for one of them prison niggers that run out. And he let loose with both barrels of that pump-gun and like to blowed him clean in half!

I went back to the office of the *Glory Argus* that night. I was up till sunrise, at the old roll-top desk, writing the story as I tell it to you now. And when I had finished I looked at the sheaf of papers, and I read them through. And then I took them one by one and burned them in the old iron stove where my father used to warm his long, quick hands on cold election nights, with the red torchlights in the street touching his white beard with fire. So many years ago! After that I went back and sat down and wrote a brief, decent but somehow wildly strange obituary:

John Wesley Follansbee

1911 - 1928

"The Minstrel Boy to the wars has gone

In the ranks of Death you will find him."

Well?—Isn't it that?—a war! For any of us!—for the boy, for Harper, for the Woman? For me, for you? Is it anything if it isn't that for each of us—from birth to the grave on Glory Hill—a war? And then God calls us, in strange and fearful ways, to our reward! And is it blasphemy, is it too horrible for the soul of men to ponder on, for me to ask: Is it not that for Him, as well?—a War?

Louis McCoy Delaplaine

What could I say about her that wouldn't be prejudiced out of all sense or reason? When I look back at life from the clear, unclouded view of things over here on Glory Hill I know how lucky I was in the life I had. When I look at Marcy's face these evenings when she comes home, aching and worn by what the men are trying to do to her in the Court—when I catch a glimpse of her face when the light of sundown blesses it softly through the parlor curtains, I know how lucky I was. Forty-three is young to die and I know I didn't live as long as most men but somehow I know my seven years of marriage to Marcy was a time more precious and beautiful than some whole lifetimes are. And it was luck, I think—I don't believe much in Fate. It was luck when I saw Marcy that first time in the dining room of the Stratford Springs Hotel in Wheeling. How easy it would have been for me to have married one of the giddy butterflies I used to take to dances and parties at the McClure House; the season's musical comedies at the Virginia Theater. For her sake I like to believe that the seven years we had together were the happiest years of her life. With all the death and sorrow and fight that faced her in the years after those seven I like to think she looks back sometimes and tells herself: Well, at least I had that much. I had those years, that love, that man. Vanity is a funny thing—it takes us years to get rid of it, even over here. I know how popular Marcy was, how many beaux she had before she met me. But I have the quaint, old-fashioned satisfaction in knowing that no matter what a heartless flirt she was, Marcy never gave herself to anyone but me.

Some of you smile—does that sound unforgivably romantic? Of course. I know it does. And the only ones among you who don't chuckle at this shameless sentimentality are those old enough to remember that a world ended in 1914 and is still ending and no new world is anywhere in sight. Oh, believe me 1914 was so much more than just the year the Great War began. Even today school children who do not even remember their history lessons are living in the strange vacuum which fills the world since then. Whether they know it or not they move and breathe and go to bed within the long, fumed shadow of that year. I remember the small, half-hidden news story on the front page of the *Wheeling Intelligencer* that spring—the Archduke and his wife with names nobody knew or cared to know were dead somewhere in a town called Sarajevo which meant even less. Yet in the house of all of us the central rafter snapped, the shingles of the roof opened an inch, rains came in. And the waiters crept round and snuffed the candles one by one and the dancers departed. The year before, I was in Vienna and Paris finishing my medical studies. And I remember the feverish haste of people in the quest of pleasure; I remember the movement of lovers in the streets and theatres and restaurants by night, the couples moving faster and faster in the circling gestures of the waltz as if something infinitely small yet imperatively clarion cried: Haste! Haste! For the last sands of a thousand carefree years are swiftly running out! Even the cheeks of the women, the eyes of the officers, seemed feverish with that instinct. Faster, faster! cried the plaintive hour. For soon the waiters will be putting up the chairs, the last cab rattle home, and bitter shall come morning with the drums of fate and soldiers!

There was only one close shave for me and it's one I must confess . . . Marcy would laugh but you may think it shocking. I fell three-quarters in love with a young French dancer in Paris who was madly enchanted with the veil-dances of Loïe Fuller. Her name was Solange and she had not the slightest interest in me except that she worried obsessively about her legs and believed that she must, at any cost, marry a doctor to look after them. Poor little May-fly Solange! She was in England when the war began and was caught in the collapse of a music hall during one of the first zeppelin raids. No, her legs came through unscathed. It was both arms they had to amputate.

Those queer times. And the faces of those years: sometimes I glimpse them briefly over here. How plaintive are their eyes; they seem struggling desperately to remember a lost night, they clutch after fragments, love notes, souvenirs, and the pressed and long-dried roses of some evening whose kisses and gay waltzes are drowned and buried in the long guns of Verdun. The young Baron von Richtofen, Serge Lifar, and the aging agelessness of Réjane; Nijinski and my brief love Betty of the Brighton music halls and the Japanese lanterns, like impossible, pastel moons, at the midnight garden parties of a preposterous, improbable, pretentious and entirely charming English lady by the name of Eugene Pouter-Dickie. A lost time then, which from the timeless perspectives of my eternal-here seems buried beneath layers of a century's fall of autumn verdure. And then I came home and within a month came down sick and that meant rest and milk and sunlight and what seemed to me then the disappointment of a discharge before I'd even known a wound and the misery of not being where, certainly, doctors were needed more than ever in history. But I didn't know it then; that there were battle-fields of sickness for which there was never and will never be an armistice: the rank and pestilent slums of West Virginia. And a war there to be fought forever, so long as breath and strength hold up, and the enemy not always the invisible microbe but quite as often the virulent and visible enemy Man. And if I hadn't come home sick from that Europe which was burning down like flaming Troy I would not have cared to specialize in respiratory disease. And, of course—and by no means least in importance—I would not have seen the face of Marcy Cresap over the shoulder of her escort at the dance that night.

It's odd how nothing or no one could ever fool that girl of mine. I think she knew from our first gravely delirious encounter that nothing would ever stop the swift, sweet smoulder of our love. And I think she knew, within her deepest, if unspoken, instincts that just as surely nothing would ever stop the slow and silent murder in my lungs. What can one think of a girl who marries a man she knows must shortly die? No one in Wheeling could ever whisper round that it was money, for the last solid dollars of the Delaplaine fortune which my mother Elizabeth had not charmingly squandered in Europe, went for my education at medical school at Cornell and abroad. I do not like to think it was this; that Marcy was pulled to me somehow by an instinct which has always drawn her to those sick and in need of her. Perhaps it was a little that. But what I like best believing is that Marcy saw in me a chance for love with gaiety and carefreeness, a little year or two of that before she would have to face the fight and harshness of the years which, again through instinct, I think she knew would come. The years of war with little men with little, mean and covetous spirits: men who owned land and dairies and rotting, sleazy mine-town shacks; even men of medicine, in whom that lovely obstinacy of warriors against Death had died, blinded by the dazzling burn of gold. All these things, I think she knew would come. But meanwhile may we dance, may we not laugh and love a little spell?

I was well enough for our marriage and our honeymoon in New York City and it was still 1914 and enough left of the dying tune of that forgotten world for a song and a sip of wine. We stayed in a suite at the Ritz and that was the winter Marcy, like everyone else, was humming the songs from the *Girl from Utah* and raving over the beauty of Julia Sanderson, laughing at Joe Cawthorn and dancing at Reisenweber's and Delmonico's to the strains of "They Didn't Believe Me" and "The Land of Let's Pretend." As for me, nothing seemed more certain than that I would live forever and sometimes since I've thought of the nights in that old, lost winter in the gaiety of New York when I would find Marcy watching me, searching my face with that shine in her eyes which I thought was love and only love and never guessing that it was her anguish at the doomed destiny of an end which, with all the total medical wisdom and healing miracles in both our hands, she was powerless to stem. Sometimes here on Glory Hill, since then, I have wished with all my heart that we had never met. And though half my wish is that she had met a stronger man who would have lived and not grieved her with his death, the other half of my wish is selfish: that I did not have to hold within my hands such loveliness and wisdom of spirit for such a little while. But I have learned better about some things over here on Glory Hill. Marcy and I had seven years of magnificence together—though seven years is a span of pitiful, dismaying brevity. But Time comes into fresh and wise and unfamiliar focus over here: and I have learned that the time shared by the very old couple who lie ten feet from me beneath the locust tree was just as piteous and shocking in its shortness. And they were married and loved one another for more than sixty years.

Sometimes, at first, I pitied, too, my little son, Marcy's first and only born child William, named for her great father and dead in the sixth year of his life: ruler of all his backyard to the boundary marked by hedge and Chinaberry tree, captain of toy gun and wooden sword, king of the rope swing, high priest of the ant and master of the firefly, Merlin of the chemistry set, and emperor of toads and tiddleywinks. And why, why, why? I used to cry here in the stillness with the sad sod in my mouth. Why a child? I'd weep and strain against the prison of the grass. Why a creature with all the wit and wonder, all the zest and peril and the glory of a child? And then the queer, consoling focus filled my eyes. And I knew, strangely, that the death of a child, this scrap of sacred paper with nothing on it but the first, discovering crayon scribbles of infant astonishment—it came to my eyes so clear and terrible and true that this young death was, by that one harsh, inarguable measure not so wasteful as the death of that old judge who lies among the elm roots at my shoulder: a man who died at eighty, with such a legacy of piled wisdom and oaklike mercy written with neat script upon the heaped and hodge-podge pages of his days, that his loss to men in need of mercy at the dock of justice was as terrible as a piece gone from the sun itself. My child, my son. I wish you had lived! And yet you are only this, my sweet, my fairest fruit of love, no more than a perfect and spotless sheet of paper with some few and staggering wonders scrawled with colored pencils on its whiteness. For when that old judge went, a great tree left the sky and set the forest racketing with its fall: a man filled and wise, with all his sheets inscribed with the trove and motherwit of centuries, a creature who fought for justice with such a fervor that often the fight would find him fighting self and questioning the very grain of his own soul and taking his mind apart and painfully assembling it again into the cleanness of fresh concept.

Mind you, I do not believe (and I speak with total honesty), that I would have come to this opinion in any place but here on Glory Hill. For here's the place where Time's not calendered from then to now;

here is the place where Time may swerve and, like a bird, swoop sideways in its flight and contradict the very tick of watches and the sequence of man's days. When someone dies and goes to earth like that old judge, who found mercy and love for blackest murderers in the prayer and agony of his secret chambers, when such a man as this vast compendium of mortal charity passes, it is the Past that he takes with him into earth. But with a dead child there is only the future, and everything is future over here! That is the reason for which I would weep more sorrowfully at the death of old, kind women, their dried wombs forever wise with child, their gnarled and rooty hands cunning with safety pins and Bibles, their uncondemning eyes just in their witnessing of folly and mistake, their spirits quick as the tang of homemade quince jelly with wit and love and grace. It seems to me their down-going to death is a pity and a loss more to be mourned than ever is the dying of a child. And make no mistake—I loved my child. But over here his future still is his. And his interment in the earth is just the planting of a seed. For time will let his spirit rove and soar and find its place in space and let it shape an influence in the spirits of the living. I remember when I was small and Grandmother Delaplaine read me the death of Little Nell and how I cried until they had to fetch the nurse and give me chocolates and show me lantern slides. And now I smile at this. I love my child—more here on Glory Hill, perhaps, than ever I could back there in the happy ignorance of life. And yet I see him, and his death which came so soon, as the stopping of a tale whose telling had scarcely passed the story-teller's first preliminary clearing of the throat. Yet I see the death of that old judge whose wit and cunning mercy all lie prisoners in the white joke of his bones as the massacre and stifling of a saga, and a shameful smothering of a huge and sweet judicial kindness which men like him may not, unfortunately, leave behind them in their wills.

Mister Delaplaine! my grandmother used to cry to her husband in the steep and stacked cathedral of his books. Mister Delaplaine, why in mercy's name do you waste time and lamp-oil reading those old books in Greek and Latin and such outlandish dead tongues!

Because, Madam, my grandfather Delaplaine would say gently, these are the languages I shall expect to be required to speak in Heaven!

I wish Marcy could see life from the height of this low place. For well I know how she has grieved for me and our child. And sometimes I think, perhaps, that all that grief, compounded with her anger at the sickness which struck her too, has driven her almost to frenzy in her war against disease in Apple County. After we married we settled in the old, cream-colored house on Seventh Street; the home and land her father gave us as a wedding gift. We were happy there. But then I told you that before. And yet I never tire of saying it: We were happy there. It's a way that, by remembering as I speak, almost permits the miracle of return. Together we struggled for funds to build on Waynesburg Ridge the first TB sanatorium Apple County ever knew. In those days my fellow doctors were on the side of Marcy and her dream. They worked hard and well and uncomplaining to shape and raise that place. And it was almost a miracle because the people in the town of Glory, almost with the solitary exception of Millard Rogerson, gave us neither funds nor faith nor even the comfort of a half-wish for success upon a venture in which, for the most part, they could see no sense.

What good'll it do? old Mrs. Charmichael, the baker's wife, said at the first town meeting we held to raise some funds. When ever'body with a grain of sense and memory knows from plain fact and experience that the TB is something folks has in the family and passes on from generation to generation through some weakness in the seed. What's all this talk of germs and microbes and such? My grandpap had the TB and so did his daughter Belle and so did her last-born boy Albert. Now what earthly good is a costly sanatorium going to do for something that passed from pap to child just like freckles or red hair?

Marcy sat alone in the parlor that night so angry and so thwarted that when she came to bed I could see the row of teeth marks in the fist that she had bitten to keep back oaths.

My brother's boy Creedmore had the TB's, said a man at next week's gathering. And they taken him to Terre Alta to the hospital there. And them X-rays they give him didn't stop his TB no more than if somebody's snapped his chest with a kodak. You folks claim them X-ray pictures stops the TB's but I'll stand right here and testify that it's not true! My granny cured my pap up yonder in Shades of Death Holler more than forty year ago. And she didn't do it with nothin more than hot onion poultices on his chest ever' night!

Still we won. That much we won, at least. A sanatorium shining white and proud upon the sharp thin ridge against the western sky. But, as for me and our child William, all was lost. I wish so much that he'd gone first. Marcy was so alone when his death came. Sometimes I'd leave this place on Glory Hill and soar down to the town, all milky in the early mist of fall, and find my Marcy weeping in the yard, wandering like something lost beneath the Rose of Sharon and the little elm that we both so loved that spring; the elm she herself planted years before. Time is so queer and tricky over here. There is no Time, once you have learned to not count. Still, even now I find myself remembering, and even now my years with Marcy seem so far, so long removed.

We worked night and day that last year I was with her. I lied to her a thousand times about my cough. For many's the night I'd go without my rest, and go without it the night after that. Nights when Marcy had driven thirty miles and urged and cursed that old Ford up the ruts of muck and mud of unpaved mountain roads, and sometimes driving through four feet of snow as far as she could drive to some deserted mouth of some dead creek. And there someone would meet her in a sledge, pulled by the single, winded, sway-backed horse that was the family's only fence between themselves and unplowed hillside and the winters with no dried corn stored up sweet and sniffy with parched fragrance in its muslin sacks. And Marcy'd go five more miles in the sledge and when the creek banks leaned and shouldered close and no room for a sledge and little enough for even the width of a horse, she'd ride on bareback onwards eight miles more, and walk the other seven miles on foot, through cold and snowdrifts that would freeze a soldier's feet. And when she got there find that she had come that awful distance for no other cause than to wet gauze and wipe the spittle away from some child's dying mouth, gawping for air, like a poor landed sunfish drying in the sun. And stand by steady there to stanch the blood that gushed up like a hot red spring at last and hold the dwindled hand and say a prayer and stay another hour so two or three or five or six kinsmen could weep into the wool of her thick, tattered sweater and sometimes, in their anguish, sink their teeth in tongueless outrage through the wool, into her skin, and sob and gasp and curse God and the mystery of the deaths and microbes which He, in the queerness of His mercy, created with the same sweet majesty as He created man.

When she'd come home, days later sometimes, she would fall and sleep so deep that I would think she'd died, from driving, walking, struggling up those hills and find that, after all, she could do no more than tell them what they knew—that Life is strange. And Death a secret kept by stranger things—things infinite in their smallness like stars, or tears, or microbes in a cough. A cough—something man sometimes does so lightly—sometimes in shyness or apology—and slays his child with that cough, or his wife, or strangers in the streetcar going to a picnic: murder without the decorum of wrath. I smoked a lot that year. I smoked so that when I coughed, as I did almost constantly all winter, that I could tell Marcy it was smoking that made me cough. Smoking and not dying, I could say. And make it easier if ever dying can be made easier. Because she knew. And I hid the red tea towels when I'd hemorrhaged and kept them hidden so she would not see. And then I'd take them somewhere far from her. And burn them and stand and watch the smoke, my burning blood curling white among the branches of her elm and finding a purity among the antiseptic splendor of the sky. Yet I was bitter then. Bitter to die—yes, that, I won't deny. But bitter most that once more I'd been made to languish in the presence of a war. And so I'd pray to God that I could stay with her and fight on until we'd made a dent—a little scratch in the vast, scarred, gray wall of sickness. Some small chipped scratch in that most costly of human real estate: the house of ignorance and greed and I-don't-care. But I knew soon she would have to go alone. And I knew, too, that even our child would leave her, too. And that, I think, was agony worst of all. And for a while I blasphemed against God and saw Him answer blasphemy with love, and a beckoning away, and then with peace.

Most bitterness has left me now, I think. A man's got loads of time to think on Glory Hill. You lie here like a gardener upside down and witness the green harvest eternity which is grass. Grass and the roots of trees and burrowing things: moles and mice and children with their spades, making small, shallow comments in the earth: portends of graves their sweet minds never guess. You're that: a gardener watching growing upside down; and glad to feed that growing with the chemistry of hand and lips and eyes that never knew that the Almighty Lord above us all ever meant hands and lips and eyes for any task but touching, kissing, seeing the hair and lips and faces of those we'll leave. Sooner or later in some dark harvest year. Yes, immutably, in one harvest year.

But some bitterness is still mine. When I must lie and watch the men I stood beside with pride some years ago, men of healing, men of grave dedications: oath of Hippocrates; watching them strike and slash and slander, sparing themselves not even the sick humiliation which must surely follow on their pawky harangue. They'll fight her to the end—that girl of mine. They'll fight her to the end of them—or her.

Yet, sometimes I comfort and quench the seething of my wrath, remembering the last hours she was mine. It was a winter's night and it was cold with that cold that clutches at breath like fingers round your throat. And neither of us had coats on and it was the first time she hadn't scolded me for being out on such a night without one. Because, I think, she knew it couldn't matter. And we looked at the still and sleeping winter yard, the young frozen elm, the rosebush and the leaf-stripped branches of the Rose-of-Sharon by the cistern old, wise dousing hands had pondered-out and dug a century gone. And nothing lived, it seemed, and nothing grew. And yet we looked and knew and sensed the spring: the surging, coiled green leap clenched in the bud; the sap beneath the bark, where the roses' sweet and drifting scarlet sleeps like memory in the vine. And Marcy squeezed my hand and spoke to me more eloquently than ever in our lives, by opening her mouth, beginning, and then closing it upon the very breath of a word. Stopping because the word between us, the wisdom and the ecstasy of understanding, had always been that: a breath too keen for speech. And because there was nothing for her to say, nor me to say, that we had not whispered through all our years, wordlessly with the eloquent tongue of deeds, of labor for the sick, and love for our child. And the moments when we were too tired from our work, which was so common to us that it seemed sometimes as if she were the right hand and I all the left. And love the mind that lifted us and bade the fingers spread and close and do their work, or simply touch a child who wept alone, in that unspeakable orphanage which sickness is to little things alone in the camphor dark, beneath the hot chest poultice and the fire seen brightly ten times over with hot eyes and all the world of one room made so keen and brilliant and each shadow tinted more brightly with fever than a painter ever saw his chair and cat.

We said all this in silence and squeezed hands. And I went up to bed and she stayed there alone outside a while, doing perhaps the strongest thing of her life, knowing my pride and what I had to do, knowing that neither hand nor love nor wisdom could now help, knowing that staying there was honoring me. And waited there. Watching the glittering galaxies of winter. And waited there. Seeing the sleeping green blood of the rose. And waited there, hearing me go to bed. And waited there, in respect for this poor shred of vanity of mine: wanting to be alone to get it done. Not wanting pity, not wanting sympathy, not sobbed out words of parting nor questioning of the Lord in that justice of Him which often seems caprice. She knew me to be proud and wanted that to be, at last, untouched; unrotted by the germ. She stood there in the frozen night alone, willed by a stonelike willing, yet soft as summer flowers with love. She waited there and knew I wanted her to save all tears, touch, pity for the rest: the sorry multitudes of ones to come—those who would die in Glory and need prayers. We knew each other's hearts so well: my Marcy and me. And nothing I could ever tell you here could speak more strongly of the love we had, than what she did, staying down there that night. Nothing she ever did for me in life was bigger than what she gave me in my death. She waited. And she waited. And never came upstairs till I was gone; and lay as still as starlight in my bed, and froze at last to peace. And waited like the winter elm for spring.

Clackey Barker

I was born poor but we had our pride. Poor as we was we never asked for charity. The little piece of ground my Pap spent twenty years trying to farm was too poor to pick a fuss on. Nothing ever grew there and nothing ever will. But we got by somehow. Don't ask me how. Little food as we had I somehow learned to cook. That's why I got this job in the kitchen at the Mound Hotel when I got fired from teaching school. The school job paid good but somehow I just never had a particular hankering for it. There was hardly a boy in that whole class of first-graders who was under seventeen years old, though the girls was mostly younger. The school was a little one-room shack south of Glory and about seven miles east of Riggs Knob. Aside from the nearby privy there wasn't another building in fifteen miles. That school had six different teachers between 1925 and 1928. The reason there was such a fast turn-over was because of them boys. You never saw such a pack of rascals. Every one of them was mean as gar-broth. The cause for them being in first grade and most of them sixteen and seventeen year old was for the reason that most of them had to spend half their time working their Pap's fields. Whatever little time they had left they come to school. So it wasn't because they was dumb that they was so old and still in first grade. They just had to get their learning a little bit at a time.

So here I was teaching abc's to a room full of devils that was strong enough to whip a grown man. That's why Riggs Knob school had so many teachers. All the teachers was men and every time one of them taken a strap to one of the boys he generally found he'd tackled more than he could handle. Four teachers got chased clean out of Clay District, one got ducked in Hog Run and half-drowned and another got run clean across the Ohio River and out of the state. I was number seven and they never give me no trouble because I'm a woman. But they tell me the old man they hired when I quit has really got his hands full. But I reckon he'll make it. They tell me the first day of school he reached in one pocket of his coat and pulled out a five-foot blacksnake whip and laid it on the desk. Then he reached in the other pocket and pulled out a nickel-plated thirty-two pistol. He put that on the desk, too.

Now, boys, says he. I aim to teach school here for a while.

Last I heard he was still teaching. But they tell me he just can't wait till recess to get one of them girls up in the back seat of the old, broken-down Whippet he drives. They say that old Whippet just shakes like a shimmy-dancer when him and one of them girls is doing you-know-what. If ever he gets fired it'll be for that. They tell me he's got three first-grade girls knocked-up already and one is swelling but the cause is doubtful. Them Clay District girls hasn't hardly started hairing and titting till that old man has his eye on her. 'Deed, I think a carrying-on such as that is uncalled for. That Knob Hill School isn't nothing better than a bawdy-house the way I see it. The reason I quit was because the oldest of the Sigafoose boys tried to rape me. If it wasn't for me wearing three pairs of flannel drawers I reckon he'd have done it, too. And me going on sixty-two years of age, too! Ain't that a caution? I run nigh two miles up Hog Run that morning and taken the noon streetcar into Glory. And that very same afternoon I got me the job running the kitchen in the Mound Hotel. You'll not find any of us Barkers letting the grass grow under our feet.

I had done cooking before over in Webster County for a bunch of loggers in a little wide place in the road called Erbacon. It come to get that name back in the days when the county had a big stand of timber. There was this old Irish cook they had then and of a morning she'd come out and hammer on a skillet to fetch the boys in for breakfast.

And she used to yell: What'll you have with your eggs, boys?—ham er bacon.

That's how the town got named that and it's the God's honest truth. I got on just swell cooking at the Mound Hotel. There was two niggers to help me—one of them was a trusty from the pen—and this little gal by the name of Miranda Moon. They hired her there as a dishwasher though I'd sooner had a one-armed blind man for all the good she was. If it had been any of my say-so I'd have fired her first thing off the bat but Mister Lemley he was the hotel owner and he done all the hiring and firing. Mirey they called her and she was thirteen year old and I just wisht I had a nickel for every dish she broke. Uppity she was, too, and all the time having visions and going off into trances. Or so she claimed. She was a nervous little thing and if it wasn't for the way she was always bustling around I'd have swore it was laziness. Her Pap he got killed in 1924 in the mine blast up at Benwood and she claimed she knowed ahead of time he was going to die because the snowball bush come out in bloom that winter. She swore that whenever a snowball bush put out blossoms in the winter it meant there was somebody in the family doomed to go. Things like that. She was just full of superstitions and spells and premonitions and things like that. She used to give me the willies just hearing her talk. Half the time when we was the busiest like during the weekly Lions or Rotary luncheons she'd be standing there by the window looking out at fairies playing on the brick sidewalk acrost from the post office. I went once and looked but there wasn't a blessed thing in sight but fall leaves and sun shadows. One time she told me early in the morning I'd best watch myself for she seen it in a dream that I was going to burn my left hand with hot grease from the fried potatoes that day. It give me a sick headache all that morning and I got so nervous that afternoon that I did spill grease on my left hand and had to work all during the busy supper hour with my fingers wrapped in a wet dish-rag full of baking soda. That little fool.

Jason, the nigger trusty, was superstitious anyway and he fell for everything that girl said. Jason was a lifer for killing his wife over in the eastern panhandle. He taken a straight razor, a guard told me who is married to my sister Starr, and cut her throat so far that her head would have fell off if it hadn't been for the neck bone. Jason was slicing apples for a pie one morning and Mirey told him she seen his wife out under the willow tree and her neck was all healed-over and she was smiling and picking dandelions and singing nigger hymns. Mirey said she looked up when she saw Mirey watching and told her to tell Jase that she forgave him and her neck was good as new and she was just waiting till Jase come over to join her so she could give him a big hug and a long-time-no-see kiss. Jase put his pan of apples on the big wood table and asked Mirey to find out from his woman when that would be. But Mirey said she was gone by then. But Jase wouldn't let go of the idea. He had that shiftless girl running out back under the willow tree all afternoon to see if there was any more news from his wife and it ended up with me having to cook supper for a lot of big men and wash the dishes as well. That derned Miranda Moon. I declare I just wish it was up to me to do the hiring and firing around that hotel. That young missy would find herself out on Jefferson Avenue before she could say persimmons.

I don't hold with superstitions. It's just pure, stubborn ignorance. When I was a girl down on the Big Sandy there was an old granny-woman they claimed was a witch. I taken sick with the quinsy once and she come and claimed she had some powder made out of the ground-up skull of a hanged man and she and my Aunt Clory made me drink some of it in a glass of sheep-nanny tea and the old woman spoke in tongues over me for an hour. And it never done my quinsy no good and give me the horrors to boot. All that mumbo-jumbo is good for is half-wits and niggers and I want no part of it. That no-account child Miranda she was a scrawny, puny little thing to begin with and even when she was working I had to do half the dishes over again because she was too lazy to scrape them. I always suspicioned there was some finagaling going on betwixt her and Mister Lemley but, of course, I had no proof.

The evening before the day of the night she come down sick she claimed she had a vision of death. One thing about that nigger Jase he's a liar anyways and one that would beat Ananias in the scriptures. You ask that nigger if he's guilty and he'll tell you and swear on the name of his mother that he's spotless as a newborn babe. You ask him about that woman of his whose throat he cut from ear to ear and he'll swear there wasn't no knife nor razor neither one and all he done was give her a little push and she fell over dead. So naturally when that Mirey come out that night and said she seen Death in the hotel lobby Jase quit stringing beans and I couldn't get a speck of work out of him all that evening. Mirey claimed she was on her way to the cellar with a peck-basket full of pint mason jars when she caught sight of Death out in the lobby checking in for a room. I scolded her and even smacked her with a tea-towel and she just stood there with her big eyes staring at nothing and repeated it again. This time the nigger fetched out a little tattered Bible from his hip pocket and commenced to singing "I Know That My Redeemer Liveth." He's got a sweet voice and every time the prison puts on a show they get him to sing but this night I wasn't in no mood for hymn singing. It was the night before the weekly Lions Club Lunch and I had my hands full getting a cake baked and turkeys roasted for the next day. Mirey went on talking about Death signing the hotel register for a room and I just decided I'd try to nail her with the lie. I asked her what he looked like. And she had a good story made up, I'll say that for her; that girl had an imagination to beat the Dutch. She said he wore a straw hat with a band as black as a funeral wreath. She said he wore a crepe-black alpaca suit and had a black traveling case like a drummer. When I asked her what she reckoned he was peddling in that make-believe black suitcase of his she said it was deaths.

Deaths, says I. Do tell. Now kindly explain what that means, young lady, and don't give me any more of your impudent lies neither.

Deaths, she said, with them sick shadows under her big eyes darker than ever and Jason hunched on the kitchen stool shaking like an aspen. Hard deaths, slow deaths, easy deaths, she said. All kinds, Miz Barker, sudden ones and long, long expected ones. He's come to Glory a-peddlin his new spring line. And one of them—

Shame! I said. Shame on you, you young, brazen thing! Scaring that poor, ignorant nigger yonder by making up such tales as that! Now hush.

But one of them, she said, her voice hushed to a whisper for fear of my tone. One of them is for me, Miz Barker.

At that the nigger commenced in to singing even louder till I told him to hush up, too.

Now you get yonder and dry them dishes, missy, I said. For by the time I get done telling Mister Lemley about tonight's lies and mischief you'll wish you *was* dead.

Well, don't you know about sundown of the next day that girl commenced complaining of a pain in her side and hadn't hardly started for the back door till she fell down bent double and laid there on the floor beside the stove crying and gasping like she was dying. I expected the nigger Jason to turn white or throw a conniption or something but he was just cool as ice. The first thing to enter my mind was that she was putting the whole show on so's we'd all think what she'd said the night before had come true. But the nigger Jason said there wasn't any doubt about it: Mirey had the appendicitis and the onliest person to get hold of was Marcy Cresap. Directly, Mr. Lemley he heard the commotion out in the kitchen and the waitresses come back complaining they wasn't getting their orders. By now the girl's thin face had turned green and she was biting her lip and moaning and digging her skinny fingers into her stomach. It just made me boil—the idea of a nigger telling Mr. Lemley what to do but anyways Mr. Lemley said Marcy Cresap was about the only person in Glory he could think of to call so he done it. And directly we all see Marcy's old Ford touring car pull up under the willow tree across Lafayette Avenue by the post office. Marcy come in and taken one look at Miranda Moon and poked around awhile in her stomach and directly she said she had the appendicitis. I know all they're saying about that Cresap woman up at the Court House these days but, by jiminey, I'll have to give her credit. Because she'd just had a death in the family—her little boy—and the funeral was scheduled for next morning. But she went about looking after that fool Mirey Moon like there wasn't a thing on her mind. I reckon she knew better than to ask Chuck Lemley for money for a doctor to come tend the girl for she knew good and well she'd never get a plug dime out of that old tightwad. And there wasn't nobody to ask but me and the two niggers and we couldn't have got up the price of a mustard-plaster with payday three days away.

Well, Marcy went out and got on the phone and we all come along and stood beside her and listened while she called Doc Follansbee and wheedled and pled with him to come because the girl had a busted appendix, she said, and we could all hear old Doc's voice hollering in the phone that he was just sitting down to dinner and wasn't about to come out and look after some little scullery girl particularly when there wasn't a penny of money for his time and trouble.

Is it the money, Doctor? said Marcy Cresap. Does it really mean that much to you?

And we could all hear old Doc's voice squawking as plain as if he was there in the lobby.

I've worked like a dog all day, Miss Cresap, he said. And I think I'm entitled to a little peace and quiet while I sit down with my family to a good hot evening meal.

Well, that Marcy Cresap is mulish, I'll say that for her. Because she called Blick and Stone and Stribbler and Hallcraft and every other doctor in Apple County, it seemed like, and it was a funny thing: they all said the same. And you didn't have to have it written down in black and white that their reason for not coming was all the same. Money. Well, maybe I'd look at it the same way if I was them. Money. It sure don't grow on trees. And the good Lord will bear witness that every cent I've ever gotten I had to fight for it. Besides you look at all that time and school a man puts in before he can even come out for doctor you can't much blame them. Well, Marcy Cresap still wasn't whipped. I declare to see that woman that night you'd have swore she didn't have a thing on her mind except that useless little dishwasher. To stand there and watch her crank that phone and argue you wouldn't never guess her own little boy was stretched out cooling on a slab at Marple's Funeral Home. By granny, you'll have to give her credit for nerve if nothing else. She got somebody finally. And I had to laugh at that. Because I'd used to get mad as the dickens at that little Mirey Moon and call her a cat and a bitch and a sneaking mouse and a jabbering parrot and a few other flavors of animal, including a mule. And be derned if it wasn't old Doctor Dalrymple, the veterinarian, that was the only one Marcy Cresap could get to come.

He lived way down the river at Raven Rock and what with nothing but a dirt road up the river and thigh-deep in mud, at that, he was a good long time in coming. Meanwhile, they had Miranda Moon stretched out naked on the big meat-cutting table in the middle of the kitchen, with a good tablecloth throwed over her, and Marcy was whispering things to her and mopping her red face with a wet dish towel. An hour must have passed and directly Marcy had the nigger Jason fetch the cake of ice out of the big box and chip off a pound or two and wrap it in a rag and then she pressed it on the girl's belly but I swear I never seen what good that done. It fretted me something fierce: the idea of the girl laying there sick on that big table where we prepare the food: that big meat-table, and God knows what appendix-germs she must have been spreading all over the wood for decent, unsuspecting Glory folks to eat in their dinners. But I thought twice about making an issue out of anything with Marcy Cresap and I kept my mouth shut. Besides, it wasn't my hotel, nor my kitchen, nor good, nor liability neither. The nigger Jason had his Bible out by now—you might know it! And he was singing "He Shall Feed His Flock" and praying by turns and the gal was whimpering and Marcy was whispering and the ice sounded like blood dripping off the wood table onto the floor. And directly outside a whippoorwill commenced to whoop-whistling in the willow tree and the nigger's eyes rolled all the more and, deed, the whole thing commenced giving me the willies. Lemley was out front in the lobby reading the evening *Argus*—he'd washed his hands of the whole thing, and directly here come old Dalrymple up Jefferson Avenue in a rockaway buggy and the nigger Jason caught sight of him through the willow and went over by the stove and got down on his hands and went to praying. About time he stopped that derned hymn-singing, I thought: that sure gets on a body's nerves if it's anywhere but church. Dalrymple was a lanky, lantern-jawed man with dirty fingernails and I reckon the reason he looked so much like a horse was doctoring so many of them and he taken one look at the girl Mirey and shaken his head.

Can't cut without ether! he squawks in that scratchy old blackbird voice of his.

We haven't got any, Doctor, says Marcy Cresap.

Then get some, says Dalrymple, washing his hands off in cold water though I'm blamed if the water didn't just smear the dirt and make them look all the worse.

The only place to get ether, says Marcy Cresap, is from the office of one of the Glory doctors or the Glendale Hospital.

Well, where are the doctors? hollers Doc Dalrymple, pulling the tablecloth back from Mirey Moon's face. Are they all on cases?

Yes, said Marcy Cresap, with a pinched-up, queer-like smile on her face. They're all busy operating on beefsteaks.

I reckon she meant, by that, they was eating. Sarcasm.

Well, says Dalrymple, the gal 'pears to me like if her gut hasn't busted it's about to. What's the sense, Marcy? She'll die, like as not, whatever I do.

She'll a hell of a lot surer die if you do nothing, said Marcy Cresap.

I might as well say here and now that I don't hold with profanity from a woman. And it purely shocked me to hear a lady like Marcy Cresap cursing, no matter what the occasion.

Then she'll die from shock from the pain, said Dalrymple, shrugging his bony, old shoulders and cracking his dirty knuckles. Then he looked sidelong at Marcy Cresap with a shamed and sheepish grin.

Marcy, you know well and good, he said, that I never cut nothing open but sick dogs and mine mules since I went into practice in the Spanish-American War. Now if this poor child here was a mare with the glanders it'd be simple. I'd say shoot her.

Well, whether it was the word or the tone I'll never know but that nigger Jason stopped praying and dropped his Bible and ran across the kitchen to the meat table. He leaned across easy but it was clear what he was gesturing to do—he was covering that girl with his body. Marcy Cresap laid her hand gently on his back and I cringed to see a white woman make so gentle a move toward a nigger.

Stand away, Jason, she said. Nobody's going to hurt this child. Doctor Dalrymple here is going to try to save her life. Go back to your praying. Maybe we all need a little of it tonight.

If'n she was unconscious, said Dalrymple, I'd start right in and figure out how as I go. For it's not hard to see what shape she's in now. Another half hour and she'll be dead.

That was when Marcy Cresap called the nigger Jason back from his knees by the stove. The nigger looked scared, like he thought maybe Marcy Cresap had called him forth to tackle the figure of Death itself and rassle him and fight his shoulders to the floor. He looked at Marcy Cresap and he looked down at the twisting body and groaning mouth of the girl on the meat block. Deed, for a moment I almost felt half-sorry for that poor coon.

Jason, said Marcy Cresap, you're strong.

Yes'm, Miz Cresap, he said, twisting his big hands in terror.

And you're gentle, too, she said, and the nigger's eyes filled up with tears at that and he bowed his head.

I warn't gentle once, he murmured to himself. Else I wouldn't be up yonder in de pen.

You're gentle enough, said Marcy Cresap. And you're strong enough, too, for this.

She reached out and laid her fingers on his big, cut-scarred fist.

Jason, she said quietly, and I never knowed what a soft person that hard, hurt face of her hid. Jason, put the child to sleep.

It's queer: dumb as that nigger was, as we all know niggers are, he knew right away what she meant and he shut his right hand so tight hard that I could hear the knuckles creak and he shut the other hand close round his ragged Bible.

Yes'm, Miz Cresap, he mumbled.

And he bent close over the writhing figure under the tablecloth and he moved his big, sweating shoulders out over the face of that no-account Mirey. Slow as a snake his right arm coiled and rose, the big fist curved from the wrist in an arc and he moved it close till it was inches from her weaving chin.

Hold still, little lady, he whispered, and you could tell it was only for her he spoke. O, little lady, this nigger would take that ham-knife yonder and carve off this fist if it would help. But it wouldn't. Hold still, little lady. God Jesus, forgive me. God Jesus knows I hate this worser than ifn he was to bid them strap me up yonder in the chair and burn me alive for a year! Hold still, little lady. O, sweet Jesus, make this fist of mine go quick and slow and both at once. Hold still, little lady. Miz Marcy, sweet Jesus be my judge, I can't! I can't! But I will! Sweet Jesus be my judge, you knew I would. You know I will. Hold still, little angel! Now!

And I declare it was a marvel. Her head just barely rocked. I declare that nigger must have trained that fist all his life, like a pet dog. Never in all my born days did I ever see such a queer kind of hit. It went so fast no one could see it and yet there was something in it holding back. I declare I never seen a man hit someone hard and gentle all at once. And when it was over he looked at Mirey's sleeping face and he looked at Marcy Cresap's face and he looked at old Dalrymple and he turned and went back to the floor by the stove and commenced in to singing that scared hymn again and muttering prayers to the willow leaves beyond the window.

Dalrymple cut. Marcy fetched a bottle of vanilla extract from the cupboard and he smeared that all over the gal's stomach, though, I de-clare, I couldn't see the cause for that. Then he commenced cutting, sweet and easy as the nigger's fist had hit, and I just couldn't stand to watch—I've always been delicate and swoon easy at the sight of blood— and I went over and stood beside the black praying figure of the nigger and, I swear, the way I felt right then I was downright glad to listen to him praying down there on the floor, even if he was only a black murdering heathen, and I could smell his sweat and his fear from the little night wind that made the kitchen curtains blow like loose bandages in the darkening air.

Well, I heard tell later that they used the rest of the vanilla: they poured it into the place they cut open and they said it was to kill the infection though I can't fancy how that could be. Anyways, Miranda Moon come to after they was done and she looked down at the big place where old Dalrymple had laced her up like a shoe with a banjo string from Ike Water's Music Store and a darning needle from Marcy Cresap's bag. And she pulled through. And I was ashamed because I found myself crying despite myself because I hate vulgar displays and besides I always did hate that gal so much. But I cried. I reckon I even felt glad. Yes, I did—I felt glad. Ain't I the worst? But then do you know what? I hadn't hardly started feeling sorry for that Mirey Moon till she done something to make me mad all over again. She looked up at Marcy Cresap and she looked at old, ugly Dalrymple and then she turned her head and looked through the half-open kitchen door at Chuck Lemley leaning over the hotel register at the counter. Her voice was so faint nobody could hardly hear it and I, for one, wisht I hadn't.

He just checked out, she whispered.

Who, darlin? said Marcy Cresap, leaning over the thin shape under the bloody tablecloth.

He just left, said Mirey Moon. Just this very minute. And yonder he goes down Lafayette with his straw hat with the black, black band and his black suit and his black sample-case.

Who, Miranda? said Marcy Cresap, crinkling up her eyebrows and sticking her face even closer so's she would hear. Who was it just left?

And old Dalrymple stared out into the empty lobby and pursed his mouth and harrumphed softly. Nigger Jason's voice rose a little louder with his singing of that derned, nagging hymn.

He did, Miz Cresap, said Mirey Moon with a wan, little grin on her puny face. *You* know!

Well, maybe, said Marcy Cresap, smiling far-off a little, her eyes sad though, and thinking, I reckon, of that little thing of hers laying up there gone and cold at Marples. Yes, maybe, Marcy said.

Sure, said Mirey Moon, faintly but a little more pert by now. You know him, Marcy. He's gone now. Didn't you see him go? Well, no matter. He's gone now. But he'll be back, Marcy. Oh, yes, he will be back.

Maybe, said Marcy Cresap again, and there were small tears in her eyes now. I guess I know who it was, Miranda.

Sure you do, Miz Cresap, said Mirey Moon. You sure better know him. 'Cause he'll be coming back to Glory—time and time again.

Miss Nan Dandershott

Fifty years of children seems to me sometimes like all the children who ever lived. They walk into my dreams and their numbers stretch out till I can't see where they end. But I know each face, every one of all those thousands. Even now that they've grown up and aren't children any more; even now when some of their faces have softened and some grown harder, some dead and some moved away, I still know them all. A few have become pretty important people here in Glory and yet the most are just people and still others have gone to seed and sorrow, ended up in jail and become drunkards. The ones that got married and had children, I taught the children and when they had children I taught them, too. Some nights, behind my closed and sleeping face I see all of them: a flower garden of faces lit by the school-day suns of fifty autumns: and some of the blossoms are laughing, vivid, while others are flowers with broken stems. And there are the weeds. But I guess I even love the weeds when I think about them awhile and remember.

Half a century of teaching first grade at Glory Central; fifty years, fifty fresh starts. That may seem like a long time to you but to me it doesn't feel like much more than fifty days. Not that there haven't been the heartaches and disappointments. Maybe that's because I cared too much about each one. It's not easy to see a face whose nose you used to wipe grow up and go to the gallows. But then, too, one of my boys became a governor of the state, I've had a half a dozen senators, and another wrote a book of poems that got a good write-up in all the Charleston papers. And I don't know how many of my boys are now lawyers and doctors. The girls are mostly wives and mothers, and I think that's about as far up on the scale of things as a governor. And most of them seem pretty happy being that and the ones who never married became nurses or else went to State Normal like me and taught school. Though there were some of my girls went wrong and some settled down to be queer and cranky old maids. It's a fact that most of them that never married just seemed to drift through life with puzzled looks on their faces, like they were trying their best to remember something important, or else they were looking for something mislaid around the house and couldn't rest till they found it. And never found it.

I was born different, I guess. Because I never wanted that. Not for a minute. Most girls want a husband first and then children but I just seemed to skip the first part and only wanted children. And Lord knows I've had my share. Fifty years of them. As I say, I was different. Maybe it's because Papa was sick so long and there just wasn't a soul in the world to look after him but me. I don't think there were many Americans hurt in the Spanish-American war but Papa was one of them. He came home from the shouting and the glory with a Spanish bullet in his stomach and a framed, colored picture of Admiral Dewey. And then he settled down to twenty years of dying. Not that I ever once complained and I'm not whining now: Papa was a saint on earth. He was a cabinet-maker by trade and I guess being shot in the stomach was the only really important thing that ever happened to him. It was an event that meant so much to him that he never tired of talking of that day. And it had a glory for him that seemed to take away the fear of death. He was so patient and he suffered so and got so toward the end he could eat nothing but junket and clabber and soft-boiled eggs. And for me it was a pride, taking care of him. Mama died of the brain fever in 1889 and I was an only child, so who was left for Papa but me. Folks in Glory used to speak of Papa as the Cross I had to bear but I never felt that way about it. He was so patient and kind and he asked for so little. And that was just as well because it was little enough he had until I got my teaching certificate: a little pension from Washington and a few hundred dollars Captain Cresap made him put away in the Mercantile Bank when he had his little carpenter's shop. Still and all, we never wanted for anything.

Well, Papa's gone to his Reward now and I'm alone. Alone, that is, save for those thousands of faces that come to me in dreams.

I never taught anything but first grade. And I taught it for fifty years. That's a lot of chalk and crayons used up, when I think about it sometimes. It's a lot of readers passed from hand to hand till they wore out; a lot of measles and a lot of bean-shooters I used to have to take away and hide in my desk till after school.

There's a good deal of talk about new education methods these days and I think they're just fine. I always did. In fifty years I never struck a child. And when I found one who was retarded I never shamed him before the others. When a child seemed extra bright I used to recommend that the Principal let him skip a grade. But the School Board always called that too radical. Thumb-suckers were a problem every now and then. I remember the time I had with young Eddie Follansbee—he's the famous doctor now—but I soon broke him of it. I'll never forget that snow-white thumb on that grimy little hand of his. He always used to hold his reader up and suck his thumb behind it so's no one could see. One day I sent him into the cloak room where he could have plenty of privacy to enjoy his habit and not have to hide it.

Now, darling, I said, you just go in there by yourself and take that thumb of yours and suck real good. Meanwhile, the rest of us out here will take our scissors and colored paper and make pictures. Thumb-sucking is lots more fun than making pictures, isn't it!

And so he went while I hushed up the titters and giggles from the girls. And soon enough a shaggy little head poked itself round the corner of the cloak-room door. Eddie Follansbee had wiped his thumb dry and jammed it in his pocket. And it was plain to see he was longing to be in there with us, cutting out paper animals with the rest.

I'm not criticising Elsie Moore who taught third grade in the room next to mine. But I must say in all truthfulness that she kept a dunce-stool in the corner of her room and she used to strike her children's hands with a straight ruler when it seemed to her that they weren't paying attention. She punished little Stanley Sochek so often one semester that his hands developed blisters and his sister Bessie came to the school one morning and made a terrible scene; threatening to kill Elsie if she ever struck Stanley again. That was the day they found out what was wrong with Stanley all along. He was almost completely deaf.

Christmas was always the best time of the year. I used to take poster-paint and paint the window in our room: a picture of that midnight sky and the star and the wise men. Then I'd get the children to make a little paper stable in the sandbox and cut out the holy family with their scissors. The children of the better families never seemed to understand it how a king like Him could ever be born in a stable. But the ragged ones from Angel Swamp, the miners' children from Parr's Run and Benwood, and the children of the Polish and Slovak smelter workers— to them it seemed the most natural thing in the world. I remember one little girl from the alleys of Mingo Junction. I had just finished telling the children that the stable of the Holy Family was in Jerusalem. But no. She stood up and bravely contradicted me. She said it was old Dick Gallagher's Livery Stable out on the road to the Prison Farm. She said she'd seen the Christ Child there and all the animals and the star in the sky above it was shining over Misery Hollow.

Well, perhaps it is, I said. Yes, dear. Perhaps it is.

And—well, who am I to say? I used to go home beneath the naked winter trees those Christmas Eves alone. But the faces of the children— they never left my mind. And the house was empty: Papa and Mama both gone. And not a sign of Christmas in the parlor or the hall, nor any room. And not a gift in sight, waiting to be given. And I'd turn on the old Atwater-Kent to hear the Christmas carols from KDKA. And I don't think there was a house in the whole town of Glory that had more Christmas spirit than did mine. Because all I had to do was stand there beside Papa's old rocker and shut my eyes. And there they were: all the faces.

Marcy Cresap was one of the smartest pupils I ever had. But she was frail and poorly as a child and after I had her in First she spent most of the other grades being tutored by her mother. She was a strange little thing. I swear, sometimes she'd come out with sad, grown-up remarks that used to stump me for an answer. Sometimes I think children see the world in all its wonder, understand it, and then spend the rest of their lives forgetting all that precious wisdom. Surprise, that's it! They see things for the first time and then never see them again. A tree, grass, sun, the wild, red moon of autumn. That first look is such a miracle. "The wine of astonishment"—Isn't that what the prophet called that wonder in the Book?

Well the Board retired me just three years ago. They said I was too old. It's funny but I didn't feel old. I felt young!—I felt as if all the youngness of those faces and minds of all those fifty years had rubbed off on my heart. All those thousands that came to me like harvest every autumn—it was as if their youth and wonder was all piled up in my mind. Still, maybe the Board was right. I'd gotten forgetful. I used to write the prettiest hand you ever saw and that had failed and faltered and gone crooked. And they said I was too easy on the slackers and the failures. Lord, I don't know! It seemed that every year I taught I grew to love the children more and more. Like they were each my own. As if each child was child of my childless womb. So, maybe, the Board was right. Someone younger was what was needed now: someone who wouldn't care too much, who'd make them toe the line—someone who knew the latest ways. Grant was president when I started teaching. I'll be the first to admit that school has changed since then. Methods are new, teaching is all progressive now. There's just one thing that hasn't changed since then and never will. Children. Noses still run, ears still ache, pencils still break.

It's been four years now. My neighbors in Glory say I've gotten queer. Well, I expect I have. There's nothing to do any more; there's no autumn to look forward to, no flock of bright September faces. I've gotten so I talk to myself, too, these days. Or so they say. But they don't know—how could I ever explain it's them I'm talking to: those faces of fifty years. I keep as busy as I can. I have a little garden in my yard, and my persimmon tree: there's always children coming to my fence for pocketfuls. And I read the *Glory Argus* and the Literary Digest and the book that stood for half a century on my desk: the one the children loved best when I read to them aloud—*Hurlburt's Stories From the Bible*. It always seemed to me a so much better book than Scriptures for a child. It was gentler; not so full of doom and grief and killing and God's vengeance.

Yes, I expect they're right—my neighbors. I talk to myself sometimes and I am queer. But they don't have those fifty years of little
ghosts like me. There's none of them who looks into the face of Glory's
mighty men and sees a face that's smeared with licorice strap. There's
not a thing about my life I'd change. And nary a memory that's not
dear to me save one. And that's the day so dreadful that I dream about
it still. I look back at it now and wonder how I stuck there at my job.
That day still aches in me like some old wound. It was that kind of day
that hurts like holding your breath too long. And it was only four years
ago—the last year that I taught.

I never understood why Marcy Cresap picked Taddy Polk to be the
Clown that day. Taddy has worked for twenty years for the Apple
County Cemetery Association and if I were going to pick out someone
to be a Clown I'd hardly pick the grave digger out on Glory Hill.
Though the idea of the Clown was a good one. This was in 1924 before
the doctors here in Glory were up in such a steam about Marcy Cresap's
health work. In those days all of them were on her side. And they
helped her in her work all they could. I declare, I wish I understood
what all this County Court fuss is over and why the Glory doctors all
hate Marcy so. I've listened to the talk around town and I've read Tadd
Cockayne's editorials in the *Argus* and I still don't understand it. Why,
some of the most respectable businessmen in Glory swear she's the
worst thing to hit town since the flood of '84. To hear them talk you'd
think diseases like diphtheria and scarlet fever were something they
had shares of stock in.

At any rate, on the morning of that queer and dreadful day, Marcy
and Doctor Blick came to my room to give the children their toxin-
antitoxin shots against diphtheria. Every child in class was scheduled
for his shot except one. Little Adam Greever's father Garvey said if
anyone gave his boy a shot it would be him. He said he wasn't going
to have any fool doctor punching his child's arm full of poison when
he could just as well do it himself. The Greevers lived in the most
dreadful poverty in an abandoned streetcar six or seven miles back up
Hog Run. Garvey Greever was mentally unbalanced, poor soul, and
small wonder what with the hunger and misery that had been his lifelong lot. When the dirigible Shenendoah passed over Glory on her last
voyage Garvey, seeing the huge, silver shape of it in the sky, decided
it was the Angel of Death come to warn him and had not been the
same since that day. But that's getting away from my tale. The morning

that Marcy and Doctor Blick were due to come the children were half of them in tears from fear of the needle. Nothing I could say or do would help so I just kept them singing songs and hoped the inoculation wouldn't take long.

Well, leave it to Marcy Cresap to think of a way to make things easy. She'd taken her own money and hired a clown suit from a Wheeling costume house and asked Taddy Polk to wear it. And the first one to come through the door of my room that morning was Taddy Polk in his gay white and red silks, bouncing a ball on the end of a magic wand. The children stared an instant, gave a gasp, and then burst out in a gale of cheers. And behind Taddy came Marcy Cresap and Doctor Blick with his cotton and needles and ampules and all. I felt as if a ton of worry had been lifted from my shoulders and Doctor Blick had just rubbed alcohol on the little arm of the first child when it happened. It's queer. I mean that such a dreadful thing should make so little stir. Off somewhere south in the crisp morning air came a sound as if the hills had gently coughed. And the room stirred, the whole schoolhouse shuddered and gave a little shrug. I'll never forget it: a piece of chalk jumped from the blackboard trough and tinkled on the floor. And a little mason jar of autumn wild flowers one of the children had brought that morning sang like chattering teeth against the windowpane. And that was all. Except the silence after. And the looks. Doctor Blick looked at Marcy and Marcy looked at me and, I swear, in their silent, fearful glances all was told. They knew. And with their eyes told me. And the children froze and lowered their eyes to the desk tops and waited. And I knew for the first time that morning how valiant children are in waiting. In the waiting of children, I thought that day, there is something holy. Well, none of us waited long. It was a little while before we knew. Yet it was almost something you could feel those moments in the Glory air: a stunned and slow recovering hush upon the town. Then we heard footsteps running up the hall and Wilbur Fish, the school janitor, stuck his wild face through the door. I could have struck him, for he seemed to bear the news with the zest and pleasure of someone whose life of tedium and broom and disinfectants is so drab that to bring the tidings of disaster is a treat. And for the children he made it even worse by shouting.

There's been a blast in Benwood mine! he blurted, his voice untempered by either shock or mercy. And when he had made this dread announcement he smiled despite himself and looked from one face to the other of us all to relish more deeply the novelty of this break in his sour and humdrum rounds. No one spoke nor moved nor even breathed for a moment. And then one of the children began to cry and in a second others joined in, while those fortunates whose fathers were not miners turned and stared agape. Well, I must say I had a new and fresh respect that morning for Taddy Polk, the grave digger turned clown. He was the first to wake, the first to break that awful sound of wailing, against which all of us—Marcy, Doctor Blick, and I, the least of all— were helpless to comfort or still. And it was—or so it seems now—the simplest thing in the world.

Taddy turned a somersault and then he stood on his hands in the incongruous gaiety of his harlequin silks and began to sing in a voice that would have honored the finest traveling stage show in the land. Marcy meanwhile moved quickly among the most hysterical of the children and stooped by their desks to whisper and hold them close against her in her arms. And the miracle was this—and I shall never know if it was what she said to them or that awful, panic giggling of dread—most of them began to laugh. Though soon after she had moved away they fell solemn-faced again, with the brave gravity of children used to death, and stared hard into the wood of their desk tops. While Taddy never stopped. I heard later that he was so shocked and sick and worn by that day's feat, he slept a day and a night, still dressed, and never moved a muscle. It seems incongruous if you think of it on the surface: this digger of graves bringing laughter to the lips of children who so soon would stand by graves; this kinsman of death who so deftly, that morning, brought life back to us all. And yet I've thought of it—I have long hours to think these days—I've remembered and weighed and judged that day, and it seems to come queerly to my mind how close those two have always been in this small span of waking we call life— those two: death and his strange brother mirth. And since, I've read in old books how it once was so: obvious and clear to even the simplest mind of medieval times.

And soon they began to come: the foremen or whatever from the Benwood Mine. And each time they would take a child away, tuck him into the black van and drive him home to be with his mother and his brothers so they could slice the bread of grief and chew its bitterness together at the very table where, that sunless morning before dawn, their father had taken his last breakfast and said good-by. And I could tell that Blick saw nothing in the children's faces—he was not shaped that way—while Marcy's eyes and mine searched in anguished helplessness the faces of the children: each who was a miner's child flinching and tensed and praying the plain and shapeless prayers of children to be spared.

It seemed the morning was a year. Somehow it seems to me in years since then that morning never stopped. And the men came back, entering the schoolroom with their faces showing the shamed and hangdog air of those who have been made abashed at life itself, and presently they would stand, miserably searching the childen's ghastly faces for the one for whom they'd come. And they would beckon, feeling like Death himself, I would suppose, and lead some small and grieving figure stunned away. Yet Taddy never stopped. He sang songs, he told jokes, he pranced and leaped and vaulted, somersaulting like the finest circus clown and stood on his hands while the tears dripped downward, upside down, across the grease-paint of his forehead. And yet the children seemed not to see the tears. Or if they saw them knew that they were fitting, somehow, to the show. In the streets of Glory the sirens of the black mine-vans and ambulances choired like awful heralds. And still Taddy Polk danced and I have thought since how he must have surely known that there would be many graves to dig and it would be Taddy Polk to dig them.

Marcy Cresap was at her finest that day. Whatever they're saying about her up there at the County Court these days I know it's lies and I know it from her splendor on that day. Blick left. It is true that there was nothing to keep him there, the schedule of toxin-antitoxin was clearly out of reason on that day. Still, I think he might have stayed. It could have helped a child be brave in that dreadful moment to have heard the voice of a man who was neither clown nor courier of death. But Blick went home. Or should I say he fled. It's strange: a man inured to agony and death in almost every form, flinched and took to his heels like a thin-skinned woman at the sight of children's grief.

The toll of dead at Benwood Mine was twenty-four. Twelve children in my room that day were orphaned. And though they wept when first the news came hurtling like a dark bird toward them, they were straight and stoic when they, one by one, were led away. It awed and frightened me a little and I think Marcy Cresap shared with me that mute and wounded wonder at the braveness of little children. For in each of us was the fresh memory of a loss. Papa had died two years before. Marcy had lost both child and husband in the winter before that. And I think that both of us knew that we were not so brave; that we could not have walked with such a staunch and steady step out of that room that day, as each of those twelve children had marched into the pitiless and poverty-sickened future which awaited them. And till the very last had been beckoned to and led away, Taddy danced on. Songs and dances, jokes and funny faces, and tricks and sleight-of-hand: balls of scarlet that multiplied between his fingers, silks that vanished in the dread-filled air, while from his loose and gaudy sleeves, Taddy pulled wondrously everything but fathers.

I look back on that day. I remember it as one of the proudest and most dreadful days in all those fifty years.

And it's all over now—fifty years of glory, fifty years of what, for me, in all my barren fruitfulness, seems a kind of everlasting motherhood. What better can a woman say that in the goldenrod of fifty autumns she has found herself the mother of a glowing room of children? They say I'm queer. The neighbors whisper; they say I talk to myself. But it's not to myself I talk—it's to my many tawny sons, my golden daughters. I've been failing lately. And I've reached the age where Death lays before me as welcome as the summer holiday between semesters. My mind's not what it was. Yes, I've been here nearly long enough, I judge. There's no sense hoarding things: particularly life. One night last spring the rain beat like silver whips against my bedroom window. The wind cried and it was a cry of voices: child voices which seemed in the plaintive needfulness of their thin rise and fall to be the chorus of all those thousands: the little, learning, yearning voices of my fifty years. Well, what could I do but what I did? I rose from bed, threw some old thing around my worn old back, and made my way out into the night. The rain fell in torrents and the wetness of it was cool with spring. Still I wasn't cold. I walked for what seemed hours. For all I knew I might have walked for fifty years.

Someone found me later, nearly morning. The rain had stopped. I was standing stock-still and quite alone, knee-deep in the swampy marshes of the pastures beyond Misery Hollow. For a moment I had no idea who had come, who knew I had gone there, who had missed me, who in all of Glory would even care enough about a crazy, useless schoolteacher whose children had grown up and gone away. It was Marcy Cresap. I suppose she had come to visit me that night, to see if I was well, perhaps to talk of all our common, myriad memories. She led me to that ugly, preposterous, wonderful old touring car of hers and drove me back to town. We didn't speak. But we talked. All the schoolday mornings were the words we talked. Yes, we talked. Though neither of us made a sound. We thought and our thoughts were every bit as good as words between us: words about the thing we had not known back then, and didn't know till long days after the morning of the Benwood Blast; each of us remembering all the years of Taddy Polk's stark labors: like a dark gardener digging holes to plant the seeds of Apple County's dead: his quiet, thankless zeal and the grim and uncomplaining industry: a savage, morbid devotion to his job, working as if he had something brilliant and wonderful to work there for. And never knew back then that what it was was this: a son. I guess we found it somehow inconceivable that someone as sparkless and wooden as Taddy Polk could ever have won the heart of any girl and got from her a child. And, least of all that day, guessed that John Polk, son of Taddy, was foreman in the Benwood Mine and working on the morning shift that day. And now, on this spring night so long, long after, thinking back to the morning when Taddy Polk had laid aside the tool of his macabre trade and danced for children there in the silly, tinted silk of clowns, stoppering their tears, even making them smile and laugh, saving them, for all of that perhaps, from raving infant madness. While all the time the singing, weeping harlequin that day was wildly wondering where his son could be, and if he was safe, and even if he were living still. And Taddy Polk did not find out until that awful night that while he pranced and sang for children that his own lay burning to a cinder at the bottom of Benwood Number Two.

Marcy got me home, took off my cold and sodden clothes, gave me a rub with spirits, a hot lemonade and put me to bed. Then she stood at the foot of Papa's old oak bed, looked down at me awhile and suddenly began to sing a little song I'd taught her in first grade full thirty years before. Well, it was just too much: the years came flying back. I cried a little, and laughed some, then fell asleep and Marcy Cresap closed the door and left. The rain had stopped; the wind had fallen. And yet there in my dream it seemed that something tapped with soft insistence on my windowpane. Was it the rain again?—the wind come back? And in my dream I turned my head to see. It was not rain, not wind. I might have known!—it was my sons, my daughters, born of the love and patience of those fifty years. It was the thousands of my little ones, and each was waving his hand, his grimy fingers brushing on the glass, tapping devotion there against the pane. And each was crying out brightly in the sweetness of that spring night after rain: Good-by, Miss Nan! Good-by! School's out! So long, Miss Nan, till autumn comes again!

Reverend Scott Riggs Whitaker

The ministry was a calling wrong for me. I should have been a sailor,
or a poet or the landlord of a river bawdy house. Does that shock you?
Then ask yourself how far's a preacher's business from the trade of
human flesh. Look at the Sunday philistines in my church who say the
Apostle's Creed with piety—and then go whore their fellow men in
business all week long. Or search the story of our Lord—was he not
kind and close to one of them: the Mary Magdalene? And wasn't he
close to women all his life, even to the last dark day on Calvary? And
who stayed by him till the very end? It was Paul who smeared with
filth the female form and taught men shame of the secret and holiest
workings of their flesh.

It was my father's life that made me choose the Cloth. No—he was no
preacher, no man of God. He was the town drunk of Hannibal and he
beat his wife and sons each Saturday—beat them until his arm ached
with the effort and then he went and sought brawls in the square. And

if no man would waste the time to raise his fists to him, he'd find some thin, stray dog and beat it till it died. My mother was what the Hannibal women called a Saint. By God how I hate Saints! She stood my father's vicious deliriums every week and never raised her hand or voice once. And even as a boy I understood—I saw plain in her eyes the martyr's ecstasy. And grew up hating it with all my soul! And yet—life's strange. I married a girl who could have been her twin. I married Emma Glim, knowing she had my mother's zest and joy in suffering and sacrifice. God help the man who marries one who's proud to bear Her Cross. If ever I had the chance to live my life again, I'd marry a girl who'd nag me night and day, who'd sulk and rage at traits she couldn't bear, who'd have the spunk to tell me: Go to hell!

Now you know me: the pastor of the Glory Methodist Church. A man of God who is a man of men. A man who hates his collar and the lectern, the pulpit at which I stand four times a month and teach a creed that Jesus never meant. I made my early choice and I have paid: I have a wife who thinks the love of man for woman filth, a woman who for thirty married years has proudly denied me every human right of the marriage bed, except the time she chose to bear a son. So that, I reckon, she could raise him up and try to bind the instincts of his flesh, like mandarins used to bind their women's feet: making a crooked and deformed shape out of the splendor of a boy's loins. I fought her in this crusade but she won. Until my son was thirty years of age, hunchbacked and lonely in his sealed-up room, ashamed when he undressed to look down and see the shape of hell dangling down there, sterile as any eunuch in the East where he grew up, and never knew the sting of fleshly love except for those rare times, against which he fights like some hermit wrestling Satan in the parched desolation of some breathless desert, until at last Life's spirit takes his hand and makes it be for him a lonely wife.

Sometimes I wished for his own sake he could die. And yet even a life of madness is better than none at all. Not that I don't believe in some life after death. But I would never dare to preach to Glory Methodists what I believe it is: they'd stone me out of Apple County if I did—my firm faith that in Heaven abide sickly saints whose Life is nothing but Life's bleakest denial. That's Hell, in my belief, as it should be. And Heaven a place of peace for those who've learned that Life is half flesh and the other half Mind; Heaven a refuge for the brave, bold spirits who have conquered the toughest challenge facing men. And that's no more nor less than naturalness, and being yourself, and giving your neighbor the right to be his. Each Sunday morning for me is a lie; and nearly all the week that follows it I spend in asking God to pardon me. I stand there pious and solemn at my altar and preach the twisted sickness of that strange genius Paul. And know that if I told them what Christ really meant, they'd drag me out and hang me up like Him.

All week long Emma's busy with God's Work. Or what she calls God's Work. I'm not to judge. She spends long hours with the prisoners, telling them they wouldn't be there if they'd lived as the mild man of Galilee once lived. Forgetting, it seems to me, how he was wild and went around his people making trouble, and came to trial, was judged, and hanged between two men much like themselves. I wonder if they ever think of that. Especially the ones who are serving time for being wild and trouble-making, too. Down in the coal fields by the River Tug. Or up in Wheeling in the mills of steel. She plays the organ for them in the chapel, and makes them join in singing the old hymns. Murderers, robbers, rapists and the like. She says God guards her when she walks among them. Though I should judge the armed guards are some help: men with clubs and whips and high-powered guns, shoving the men to Jesus with a stick, mixing Salvation with the taste of steel, standing over the praying men with shotguns, with bullets as an answer to a Doubt. What a long distance that place is from the mountain where He spoke few, simple words or the still seaside of His fishes and warm loaves. And when she went one night to the brothel of Cleo Parez by the freight yards in Benwood and smashed the piano and broke the chandelier and drove Cleo and Bessie Sochek and Jewel Clem out into the streets and thrashed them with a leather whip one of the convicts had woven, I said nothing. But I had my thoughts. Careful, proud lady, careful! Remember that among those crouched and weeping by the cross there was one weary, grieving whore.

In 1900 Emma got the Call. It took a little doing and some letters and some influence but at last we got the notice from the chief in Baltimore and in the fall of that year we sailed for India. Hubert was only one year old and far too frail for the journey and we had hardly docked in Calcutta till he came down with dysentery. Emma said Hubert's suffering was only the Lord testing our strength. But when I stood at night looking at the twisting, sweaty body of the child beneath the mosquito netting I couldn't think how to explain that to him.

It was during that first year in India that Emma nearly finished my career in the service of the Lord. There's something in the air in those hot lands and it's a something more than heat itself. It's as though there was a lustfulness about the very sky. Or maybe it's the gaudy brilliance of the cloth these people wear, the fieriness of all the curried foods, the tantalizing monotony of their songs. It's in the air, I think—maybe the spirits of Asia's millenniums of heathen, honest folks whose ghosts glory in the memory of flesh.

It was a sultry night, I know, with no air moving and what little there was heavy and clinging, it seemed, with the weight and warmth of tropic water. Emma had put the child to bed. Something—some memory, perhaps, long shamed and quenched and smothered deep within me: the recollection of that river night in Glory at the camp-ground when I had taken Emma home for the first time in a borrowed phaeton and she was young then and I could smell the moist swell of her breasts and the unfound life between her thighs and the cinnamon sweetness of her coiled hair. And I had stopped the buggy by the water-works and reached over with an impulse so sudden that she was too startled to resist and kissed her mouth and neck and pressed my lips against the harsh taffeta into the young and deep valley of her breasts. And for the only time in all our lives together she seemed to welcome my caress and her hands rose and pressed my face deep, deep between those young, full bosoms. And so, that sickeningly humid night in that strange place so far away in space and years from Glory, I felt again that same bold and irresistible yearning. I should have known. I should have remembered that even on that one night when she had admitted me to her flesh, the night our child was conceived, she had kept herself hidden in the starched harshness of her flannel night dress. No, never once in thirty years had I ever been permitted a glimpse of Emma's body naked. And even on that one night in Glory she had lain there, clutching her night-clothes close so that I might not see, permitting me the barest entrance, and all the while knotted in a fist of such loathing and disgust that, long afterwards, I felt a pang of pity for her shame, and wished that God might have provided some wholly unintimate means for women like Emma to conceive when their minds desired the child that their flesh entirely detested.

I remember that night in Calcutta: a woman was singing somewhere off in the night: a long and endless wailing tune, that seemed only to quicken my desire. Emma in her night-dress was fixing the netting over the child's bed when I came up behind her, reached beneath her upraised arms and clasped both hands around her breasts. For a moment she seemed frozen; the thought flashed through my mind that she had died suddenly, upright in inflexible rigor like an emaciated Untouchable we had seen the month before in the market place at Madras. And then she began to make a sound. It was a noise so thin and filled with dread, so strangulated in its horror, so implicit in its denial of life that I drew quickly away. And then after a moment she turned toward my shamed and motionless figure and slowly picked up a brightly woven leather riding crop she had bought in the bazaar.

Christ bade us forgive our enemies, Emma said. But for Satan we must show no mercy.

And the crop rose in her hands and struck me across the cheek, again and again: she literally whipped me from the room and down the reeking stairs and into the starlight of the street. I stood a moment, feeling the blood like tears down my face and then I began to walk. And despite my pain and self-reproach and sorrow seemed to know where my feet were leading me. The voice of the woman still cried like a lost soul in the trembling beauty of the Asian night. And it was toward that that I walked; toward this woman, who, it seemed to me that night, would kiss the hurt from my face and touch my hand in humanness. And that was all. Nothing in my mind survived of the lustful impulse which had seized me in Emma's room. The voice seemed the beckoning statement of all womanhood. And for some strange reason the face of my mother seemed to rise before my eyes and I remembered a night so long ago in Hannibal when I was five and had run to Granny Marshall's house to fetch a poultice to bring and hold against the brush-burn on my mother's forehead where my father had struck her with the back of his gloved hand.

I found the Asian woman. And she soothed all my confused emotions and she touched my hand. And more. It seemed somehow when she beckoned me toward her shabby pallet that I was going there to expiate something, to punish myself in some strange way with pleasure, to defile my flesh that had so offended poor Emma.

But it wasn't till a year later till we were back in Glory for a brief visit that I found out the price of that night's encounter. I thought of that immaculate Oriental face with the strange, bright spot—like a birthmark—on its forehead and I remembered what seemed the lithe and slender cleanness of those small breasts and somehow lonely and long limbs. And yet I could not think of what had happened as the punishment of God. It seemed more the punishment of Emma; or perhaps even more profoundly the punishment I had done myself for shaming Emma in that way. At any rate, it was Marcy Cresap—that quaint and curious woman against whom all Glory has risen—who diagnosed and treated me for the social disease which had been my stigma from that night of heartsick expiation. And I could not imagine that a woman would not judge me and condemn me—me, a man of the church of God—and yet that Cresap girl looked at me with kindliness and pity each day I came for my mercury.

I have heard what they have said about her. I have listened to my fellow-pastor Tombes in his almost diseased frenzy against this woman. I cannot judge her, I cannot even understand her. And I must admit that I think her strange because she did not draw back in disgust or rise up in judgment when she discovered that the minister of Glory's First Methodist Church had caught syphilis from a woman in a far country and of another race. Do you blame me? Can you understand? I forgive Emma for all she is and I try to understand and yet I know that she has warped and changed the shape of my mind and spirit. I know what I have missed in life. But I know that I have earned and gained things, too—things perhaps more precious, understanding more profound, than God would have granted me as the husband of a lustful, healthy woman. I don't miss what I have lost. Because I never knew enough of it to know what to miss.

Emma spends her days and evenings at prayer meetings or at the penitentiary. And here's the strangest thing of all, and I have prayed to God for years of nights to let me understand it. There is a man in the penitentiary who is serving a life sentence. In a way, he is Emma's favorite convict. Maybe he has given himself more fully to her kind of religion—I don't know. She visits his cell twice weekly and she treasures a leather book cover which he made in the prison shop and gave her. She keeps her Bible in that leather cover and I have watched her in the lamplight of many evenings touching that cover, often seeming to fondle it, as if it were live flesh. It is as if the cover was more precious to her than the scriptures it shields. She has even brought influence to bear on the prison warden to see that this convict has special privileges. And here's the thing that tortures and bewilders my mind about Emma. This convict is serving a life term for rape. Rape! Do you grasp the frightful irony of it?—the enigma of this woman who for thirty years has denied herself, me, our son and countless others the indulgence of their bodies. And yet among the fourteen hundred men up yonder in that prison she chooses as her protégé—a rapist!

Sometimes a madness seizes my mind and I envision Emma as a woman of clandestine and tortuous deception. Perhaps she has loved sex all her life! Perhaps she has had lovers by the dozens! Maybe it is I she finds repulsive and untouchable—a creature as impotent and immaculate as I always seemed to be in the eyes of my tortured mother. Or is it God Himself who teases us with jokes like Emma? I am not fit to preach—that much I know. The thoughts, desires and questions that enter my mind sometimes on quiet Glory nights when Emma's at the prison and I am alone and prone to such blasphemies—these clearly disqualify me from my post. If my congregation ever knew! And do you know something?—sometimes I wish with all my heart that they did know and knowing drive me out, out of the church, out of Glory even. Then maybe I could go somewhere and be a human being!

Three years ago my son Hubert died. It was a blessing, I realize. For the three years before his death he had stayed locked in the east room at the top of our old house on Purdy Street. He had cut a little opening in the bottom panel of the door and hinged another little door within it. Neither Emma nor I ever saw him in those three years. Emma used to carry his meals to the top of the house, rap twice, and pass them through the little door. An hour later she would come and fetch the dirty dish and cup. And yet once in those three years I did manage to speak to him. It was very late one Sunday, Emma had long retired, and I had been alone downstairs reading my Bible and the *Sonnets from the Portuguese*. I went upstairs very softly and stood outside Hubert's room for a moment. I spoke his name quietly through the panel. Perhaps he thought my voice was some religious visitation; he'd grown so queer in his thinking since the days in the missionary service. Perhaps he would not have spoken if he had known it was his father. In a moment I heard his footsteps shambling to the door, there was a pause and I was about to walk back downstairs again. And then I heard him speak.

I have seen the light, he said. I am converted.

And that was all. And never more in either of our lives was I to hear the voice of my son again. I said nothing to Emma about the incident. For some reason I wanted to keep it to myself. I liked to think that Hubert was converted to the way of life in which I believed—such as it was. I could not bear to believe that Emma had won his spirit and his conviction. It seemed dreadful enough that she had reached into the breast of the rapist and lifted out his love of woman. It seemed to me that prison had done him harm enough and then, on top of that, Emma to come to his cell and teach him the hate of life.

Talk about Hubert in Glory was constant. People said he was queer. Reverend Tombes and Doctor Follansbee started the gossip around that Hubert had gone insane and that Emma and I kept him locked in his room so that he would not get out and be committed to the Weston Asylum. People are not really unkind. They are lonely; they are bored. In the barrenness of their lives there sometimes comes the chance to create a fiction. It is something they can talk about; something to fill the lonely gaps of silence between couples who have lived together for years and found nothing to say. It is a joke that young people can banter about over sodas and tutti-fruities at Spoon's. Still it was a heartache to me and a matter of anger for Emma. I saw pity in the faces before me in the congregations on Sunday and I hated that. I don't want pity! I accept my life and I want nothing changed! Because it is too late to change!

It is a fact that Hubert became unbalanced in the months of that winter in which he died. My only consolation in those months was that in the eyes of God he was a child. I found comfort in the belief that he had found Christ and when his time came to be taken he would be received into the arms of the Almighty. It seemed to make up a little for the failures of my own life as a minister. It made it easier to face the fact that I had failed as a husband—as a man. In those last months the house would be filled with the sound of Hubert's voice. It was the voice of an unbalanced mind: a chatter and a gibberish that no sane person could understand; the singing of hymns that had neither reverence nor melody. Emma's lips pursed in curious satisfaction. I could not believe that she was so cruel as to be happy at the insanity of her son. I had known cruelness, coldness in Emma but I could not believe that her misanthropy went that far. And then I discovered why Hubert's state gave her pleasure.

Are you happy? she said to me one night during supper. Have you at last found satisfaction, Scott, in having made your wife's life one of misery and disgust? And is your pleasure now complete that your Godlessness has brought down His holy wrath against poor Hubert? You know that, don't you? Hubert's sickness is God's punishment against you for your life of lustful hypocrisy.

And so I knew. Emma was glad that Hubert was insane because it gave proof of her God. Her God and not mine, I assure you. It fulfilled something in her to know that all she had ever believed in seemed now manifest. My life of shameless carnality was at last rewarded. My son had been stricken mad. I think my wife Emma will be received in Paradise. But I think God is going to have to do a lot of work on her. I cannot envision Hell for Emma, despite the hell which, in some ways, her thoughts have given me. Emma will get to Heaven. But she won't like it.

At last all sounds from Hubert's room ceased. My impulse at once, of course, was to call Doctor Follansbee. Emma said she would not hear of it. She said if Follansbee came he would force us to have Hubert committed to the Weston Asylum. I said that Hubert might well be desperately sick up there and with no one to tend to him he might even die. Emma replied that God would look after our boy and that nothing could happen to him while he was in the arms of Christ. I said nothing for a week or two. The room kept its silence. The house which had echoed and rung to the incoherent cries and chants of the insane boy was now still. In the evenings after supper I would sit in the parlor listening, hoping, and hear nothing but the blowing of steamboat whistles in the evening mists of the river, or the games of the little foreign children beyond our fence in the barren flats by the smelter. At last I suggested again to Emma that we call Doctor Follansbee or Doctor Blick.

I am adamant, Scott, she said. We will have no doctor come into this house and send poor Hubert off to Weston. His sickness is your sin—his isolation is his way of staying away from a father he detests—his madness, if it is that, is God's punishment of you for all your shameless indulgence in the urges of your flesh!

Then we will send for someone who will not bother Hubert, I said. Someone who will not come here and go away with a mouthful of gossip that will hurt us all. Someone, too, who can look after Hubert if he is sick. And that person is Marcy Cresap.

Emma said nothing, wandered off into the parlor and, in a few minutes, came back.

I don't like that woman, she said. But I'll grant she's no gossip. And as far as her position in Glory goes, she doesn't have the power to send Hubert away.

So Emma agreed. And that night late—it was long after supper—Marcy Cresap's touring car pulled up out front under the chestnut trees. I told her about Hubert. I said he had made no sound for weeks. And I said that it had been two weeks since Emma had taken a plate of food up to him.

Let me go up alone, she said.

And to my surprise Emma agreed to that, as well. It's my opinion that she was a little frightened of what she might see when Marcy opened the door. It seemed Marcy was gone for an hour. Emma sat in the lamp-light staring at me with a judging and vindicative smile on her pursed lips. At last Marcy appeared in the parlor door. She stood a moment looking first at one and then the other of us. Her eyes were soft with mercy and with pity.

Your son is dead, she said. You'd best let me call Marple's right away. He seems to have been dead for many days.

Dear God! cried Emma, though her eyes were dry. My boy is in the arms of Jesus.

I'm sorry, said Marcy Cresap and put her arm around Emma's shoulder. I left them alone and slowly climbed the stairs to Hubert's room. I wanted to be alone with him for a while before they took him away. I was crying. It seemed somehow in that moment that he had suffered in his life far more than I. More, indeed, than his pathetic mother. I could hear Emma and Marcy Cresap talking downstairs in the parlor. Outside the open window of the upstairs hall a rain crow cried in the branches of the sycamore. I opened the door that Marcy had closed behind her. And I knew then why she was keeping Emma downstairs.

I have seen the light, I seemed to hear my son's voice say. I am converted.

And looking at him there I guessed that he had meant what he said; that it was, indeed, the sanest thing he had said since we left the mission. He was squatting on the floor, his emaciated legs folded beneath him, his arms resting on his knees. For a moment, I would have sworn that he was alive. Before him, against the wall, stood the ancient sandstone Buddha which was, with the exception of the leather thong that she had lashed me with that night, the only souvenir Emma had brought back from India. Hubert's eyes were glazed and open; they were fixed, even in that week-old death, with zealous intensity upon the smiling face of the stone and heathen god.

Emma never knew. Marple's hearse came very shortly and took Hubert away. Some time later Emma contributed the sandstone Buddha to a raffle sale the church was giving for the relief of famine-sufferers in West Bengal.

Shortly after Marple's hearse had left, Emma collapsed and Marcy had to put her to bed. Later we stood together—that strange woman and I—alone in the parlor of the silent house. The rain crow was still blowing softly in the branches of the old tree. We could hear the voices of the foreign children laughing and crying out yonder in the flats beyond the fence.

Hubert was converted, I said simply and smiled and was still.

Reverend, I have seen God in strange places and I have seen Him in strange faces, said Marcy Cresap. And a lot of them were stranger than that smiling face of stone.

And she was right. By Heaven, she was right! I've thought of that night so much since then. And my life doesn't hurt like it used to hurt. We're a queer family and each of us, even Emma, has sought God in his way. I'm just glad that one of us found Him.

Luke Strider

Grass has always been my business. Green things have always been my pride. It was that way with me when I was living and I haven't changed a bit on Glory Hill. Still it took me a spell to get the hang of watching things grow from the other side. I mean down here watching the roots of things go spreading out in a miracle of searching. Back in my life in Glory I was the best grass-cutter in the whole Ohio Valley. And when it come to trimming hedges there wasn't a hand in seven counties that could shape the tops as even as I could. Once in a while I miss the feel of shearers in my hands, the snip of clippers, the clean whir of lawn-mower blades. My nose yearns for the spritely, slightly sour smell of fresh-cut grass. There's a good greenness to that smell like the sap of earth itself. Nobody cuts grass good in Glory since I went; there's not a one can trim a hedge right either. I miss it all sometimes. Folks needed me. Plain and simple as my job was, I was a person who counted for something in Apple County. And flowers, too: I could tell you a thing or two about flowers. I mean the growing kind, ones planted and happy living in the soil. Once they were cut and tied up in bouquets they were nothing but bunches of death to me. I hated them that way. Green things: they belong to the earth and I always said if you weren't going to eat them, leave them be.

Back in Glory I was someone people counted on. The best families in town wouldn't let a soul touch their hedges or their lawns but Luke Strider. That may not seem like much to you but you think about it a while and you'll see how important my job was. Why, if it hadn't been for me the green things in Glory might have took over and the whole town run to nothing but a tangled forest. Maybe I wasn't important as Doc Follansbee or old Mill Rogerson but just the same I did something important in the town that nobody could do one-tenth as well.

Yes, I'll not deny I miss it all back there. Winter was pure misery for me, with nothing green to trim. When spring come spurting up out of the old, cold land I was like a man reborn. On the first day of spring I used to treat myself to a double-dip ice cream soda at Spoon's. I used to ride my bicycle up Jefferson avenue whistling like a boy and not even holding on the bars. It was just like my veins was filled with new, green blood like all those budding things. It was like the whole world tore up the past and made a brand new start.

I never even minded the way folks in Glory used to laugh at me behind my back. They didn't think I knew. But I knew. They said I was queer and strange. There was a few people in Glory that never made fun of me. For example, Captain Davis Cresap and his daughter Marcy. They was always kind to me and treated me like what I was: a man who could do something better than anyone else in town. When folks used to mock me for riding my bicycle down Lafayette Avenue no-hands and eating an ice-cream cone I'd shut my ears to them. I had my work to love. I knew what a grand, important thing my job was. Sometimes in those dazzling summer days back then I'd stop shoving my lawn mower and smell the grass and look up at the sky. I felt a splendor in my hands. It was like I was cutting the hair of the earth; it was as if I was personal barber to the Lord. Those times, those thoughts made up for the laughs and snickers I would hear. I knew I counted for something.

Besides, us Striders has always been different. My mother's brother's boy Bill's a famous evangelist. They say when he gets really going in a tent or church the folks rest in the palm of his hand; they tell me he can change the world's worst drunkards and call the blackest sinners to the side of Christ. Mama and Papa—they're different, too. The day Papa proposed to Mama she was sitting alone on the porch swing reading the *Century Magazine.* Suddenly Papa sprang up from nowhere out of the spice shrub by the steps. He stood there a minute and recited three poems by Robert Browning. That's how romantic Papa was! And then, without another word, he vaulted over the porch railing, kneeled by Mama's knees and clasped her hand. Now, how many girls could resist romance like that?

The only thing about Mama was she couldn't stand the notion of me marrying. I met a mature woman one summer across the river in Sandusky. It was the only time a lady got me by the heart and wouldn't leave go. In a month we was married. But nothing I could say could convince Mama that this lady hadn't married me for the family name. In another month we gave it up and got divorced. Mama said to Papa afterwards: *She enticed him with Jello!* But that wasn't so. I was drawn to that lady because of her mature beauty and respectable ways. Still, I'm just as glad it turned out as it did. I'm not one of those that's cut out for a life of marriage.

That Sandusky lady and me never even had a honeymoon; I never so much as laid a finger on her in all our month of marriage. For what we had between us was a pure and spiritual thing. There was never the taint of the flesh. And so I came back to Glory and my hedges and grass again. She was just as happy that we separated as I was, though there was never hard feelings between us afterwards. She wrote me a post card now and then and I always answered, mostly poetry, and life was just about the way it was before. I had my work and my little soda treats at Spoon's and a moving picture now and then. And over here on Glory Hill it's best, I reckon, not having someone back there to break your heart with missing them.

I had my pleasures in the life back there. Pleasures besides my hedges and my grass. There was my trap-drums and my correspondence course in boxing. Lord knows I had muscles enough: when I'd flex my arms for folks the biceps stood up as big as oranges. Still the course in the manly arts meant something special to me. The funny thing is I never had a fight in all my life. There wasn't a man in Glory knew as much of fists and fights than me but still I never used them. Sometimes in the evenings in the bedroom I'd shadow-box and one spring night I went out into the moonlit brightness of Purdy Street and shadow-boxed the shadows of the trees. Lem Carmichael's wife Clara must have seen me from her bedroom window because she told it all over Glory next day. And the folks all laughed and said again how queer I was. Nobody seemed to understand a thing like what I felt that night. I don't care how much a man loves life there comes times when he wants to hit out at something. I don't mean really hurt something. I mean just hit out at something, even the shadow of trees. It's like a dose of salts, it clears out something foggy in the soul.

Sometimes up at Spoon's or in the Court House Yard or up at Seat's Drugstore Soda Fountain I put on little pugilistic shows. I like to show the kids how to defend themselves. Even if they never lift a fist to mortal man, it's good to know. It gives a man the sense no one can hurt him. I tell the children to take the Charles Atlas course. Dynamic tension. A good body's something a fellow prides himself upon: except out here, except on Glory Hill. Muscles out here are only food for grass and lunchtime for the trees. And that's a thing that makes me happy, too. I like to know the body that I built is something that will come up in the spring and all the toughness in my once-proud arms be heartwood and sap for Glory's apple trees, and the color of eyes that Mama said I got from her side of the family will turn up in the work-shirt blue of wild geraniums. For skeptics and such who think there's no beyond, there's this, at least. Death has its chemistry, for sure, and that's a poem. And even men who don't believe in God should take pride that their flesh will feed some things, and come up through the earth and make grass green, and even in their rot make something live: even if it's only the lunchtime apple of a child.

Well, let's stop all this gloom!—I'm happy here. Up in that other world I had my grass, my hedges, boxing lessons and my drums. I played in Glory's Town Band years ago. And there was some said I should be working for Keith, or playing with the minstrel orchestras they have, on the show boat that comes to Glory every spring. But I'm content. I never wanted that wild, sinful life: playing my drums to make folks want to drink and carry on and, God knows, all the rest. I played a solo concert on my drums up at the prison many years ago. And all the boys just loved it—so they said. And once I played on Sunday up at church—me and Miss Emma Whittaker was all. Just her a-playing old hymns on the organ. And me and my trap-drums serenading God.

But there was some in Glory misunderstood, and said the Methodist Church was not a place for drums, and said I had profaned the house of God. And mind you, this was spring, at Easter Time. Right at the start of everything that's green. And before long they took revenge: there wasn't one would hire me to cut grass, or trim their shrubs or even prune their trees. Marcy was on my side and so was Tadd—you know: the editor of Glory's *Argus*. And Marcy wrote a letter to the paper and said some things that made me pretty proud. She said my drums in church meant no disrespect nor blasphemy to God. And then went on to say that everyone has his way of praising the Lord and none was fit to judge if some of those ways seem unusual. She said I was a good man and someone who worked to make the town a prettier place. I reckon by that she meant my grass and shrubs. And then she said the folks of Glory should be ashamed to keep me from my work. And said no one in all of Glory County knew how to trim a hedge or cut grass better than Luke Strider.

By ginger, I felt proud. But all her letter did was make things worse. And the few folks who still kept hiring me—they let me go. And even Miss Emma, who played the organ that day, smirked and said she'd only let me play to let me have my way, because she knew how queer I was and said she'd be half-scared if she had turned me down. That summer was a little death for me—no, worse than death for I've found death is kind. And there was nothing kind in Glory then: in the hot months of that long summer time. And Glory folks all cut their grass themselves, and trimmed their hedges too, and, Lord, they looked like some poor country boy's hair cut by his Ma. We barely got along that summer— Papa was sick. And all the little money Mama had was spent for doctors who charged us like we was Glory's richest family. And that, I guess, was part of their revenge. Gee, how I missed the lawns I'd used to tend; the good feel of the clippers in my hands, the pride I took in the long, level tops of hedges glowing dark green in the suns of noons.

And then the license came due on my dog. He wasn't much of a dog as far as fanciness or pedigree goes. But he was mine. And maybe it was because I had no wife nor child to love that I put such a store in that old hound who used to follow me slowly along the hedges while I'd cut, and share my ice-cream cone at Seat's Drug Store, in the gold heat of humming summer days. And watch me while I shadow-boxed at night, alone there in my room or played the drums. He loved my drums, that dog, and knew a trick—his only trick—of dancing while I played, waving his paws and standing on his legs, and waved a little flag I'd tied to one paw. He was a caution, that old dog of mine. And when the time to pay the license came, there wasn't a single penny in the house. I knew that Marcy'd pay it if she knew, but I was too proud I guess to ask for that. Pride's my worst weakness, I know, but you must realize: There's no one else like me in all of Glory, or Apple County either, for that matter. No one who knows how grass should look, nor shrubs, nor hedges either one. And that may not be much but it is something. Yes, it is something. And so they came one evening around five and took my dog away and tied him up to the big sycamore by Whittakers. And they shot him and burned him on the dump, beyond the very end of Angel Swamp. I never cried or nothing; I'm no child. But I'll tell you it took time forgetting. Yes, it took time. And all that night until I fell asleep, I sat upstairs alone beside my drums, and played with that last thing I had of him, that funny little flag he used to wave. So much for that. It doesn't hurt me now, those griefs grow cold. And over here I've seen him once or twice, playing among the trees on Glory Hill, chasing the ghosts of rabbits and of mice. And once he came up here and licked my hand.

The first day of the week I died I'd gone up to Seat's Drug Store for and ice-cream cone. Doc Follansbee's older brother Harp was there and Charley Seat and Doctor Alfred Blick. The minute I come in old Charley winked and Harp and Doctor Blick both smiled and give each other nudges and settled back, I guess, to have a little fun with me. It didn't bother me, for I was used to Glory people baiting me that way. And I don't care a whit because I'm proud. I know my worth, I know what I can do. My grass is all the honor that I need. And fame through Apple County for my shrubs—that's all the boost my self-respect requires.

Luke, said the Doctor, show us all that trick. The way you hit that fellow and knocked him cold. You know—that time in Cameron at the fair.

Doc Blick, I said, I think you've got it wrong. I never hit nobody in my life.

They say you did, said Charley. Come on, Luke. Show us that fancy uppercut of yours.

I stood a minute staring at those three and wondering what weakness in them made them need the teasing of someone as plain as me. If teasing was what they wanted why not pick on someone teasing really hurt: somebody big in Glory, someone stiff and vain, somebody with his chin stuck up with bluff. For all they thought of me I didn't care. They called me queer. They said that I was strange. But they'd forgot one thing: I have my grass. I am the barber of the Lord's green earth. Charley was rich, his drugstore made a mint. Doc Blick was richer even yet than him. And Harper had his wealthy real estate. There was but one thing that I wanted there. And that thing was a chocolate ice-cream cone. I looked at those three men and I felt proud. For all the pain that ever I had caused was maybe that hurt that leaves feel when they're cut. And someday I'd be just like grass myself—and fall beneath a bigger blade than mine: the scythe that heaps the sheaves on Glory Hill.

Come on, Luke, Harper whined again. Roll up your sleeves and teach us how to box. Give us a lesson—show us your uppercut. I've heard folks talk about it for a year. Until I've started in to doubt you some. Maybe it's all a fake, I tell myself. The tales I've heard of Luke Strider and his mighty arm.

I didn't care, it wasn't vanity. All I wanted was to be left alone. I stood and stared a while more at those three. And finally decided it was easiest if I rolled up my sleeves and shadow-boxed, there in the noon-time amber light of Charley Seat's Drug Store, and be a fool if that would shut their mouths, and let me eat my ice-cream cone in peace.

And so I did. I stripped my shirt sleeves high as they would go and flexed my biceps big as oranges under the skin and danced around a little, like it told me in the book, and struck a phantom in the air and struck again at sunbeams through the tinted bottles in Charley's window and lashed out at the anger at something that was suddenly up there before me in the air. And then I did my uppercut. And somehow I lost footing and misjudged and slammed my tight clenched fist into the marble edge of Charley's soda fountain. And stood there a moment staring up at my hand and watching the blood run down in little ribbons over my arm. While Charley laughed, then stopped, and looked ashamed. And Harp Follansbee covered his mouth like he had to cough and turned away.

Here, Luke, said Doctor Blick. Better let me have a look at that.

No, I said. No, indeed. Thank you. But, no, indeed.

And I walked out of Charley's Drug Store, half sick to my stomach with the pain which was starting and dizzy from the bleeding, I reckon.

And got a dirty bandanna out of my hip pocket and wrapped my hurt hand tight so the people on Jefferson Avenue wouldn't see and laugh or go tell it all over Glory. I didn't even let Mama know and I stayed up in my room, sitting on the edge of bed till the bleeding stopped, just sitting there staring at my drums and the little American flag that my old dog used to wave and thought about Harper Follansbee and Charley Seat and Doctor Sam Blick. What had they wanted from me? What did they need from me—these big, successful men? What was the point and what hurt thing was there in each of these mighty men that made him need to make a fool of somebody as unmighty as Luke Strider? I guess if I'd ever come up with the answer to those things I'd have known a lot. I guess if anybody knew that they'd know what makes hate work.

It wasn't for nearly a week that the hand really started getting bad: all proud and hurting and by noon that day my whole arm was streaked like agate—it was almost pretty. I was a fool. Because I wouldn't let Mama call Doctor Blick. I wouldn't let her call any of the other Glory doctors either because I knew well and good that Doc Blick had already laughed and told them what a jackass I'd been up in Charley Seat's Drug Store that day. I never had used to care what people thought of me: whether they thought I was queer or not, but this time I did. Maybe it was the pain and feeling so hot with fever that changed my mind. Mama said we had to get somebody or I'd die.

Then call Marcy, I said. She'll come. She'll know what to do.

But she's no doctor, Mama said. She's only the County TB nurse.

She's my friend, I said.

And then I added something I hadn't meant to say and I swear I could have cut my tongue out after I'd said it.

And she never laughs at me, I said.

Mama went and called her and directly she pulled up in front of the house and came upstairs and looked at my arm. Or so I found out later. Because I'd lapsed off unconscious for a minute and my whole body felt as sick as my hand was. I think Marcy knew it was too late to call anybody or send me anywhere and I think she knew I wasn't afraid because she said: Luke, I'm proud of you.

I must have been half-simple with fever because all I could say was: But what about my grass, Marcy? What about my grass?

And then my mind seemed to clear up something marvelous and everything in the room: Marcy, Mama, my drums, my manual from the boxing school, the little flag—everything was clear with a kind of glittery brilliance. Mama was crying and the tears on her cheeks were bright as diamonds. Everything in the room seemed to have a red halo around it and everything I looked at so vivid that it almost hurt my eyes. Marcy was holding my hand—the one that wasn't hurt—and I kept thinking: Gee, what if they cut my other one off? How will I ever hold the shearers or push the mower then? But I think I knew, not long after that, what was happening. I was sorry in a way. Mama would be so lost with me gone and Papa so sick. And I liked my life. I'll even say I loved it. It wasn't much in the way of excitement or adventure but somehow it mattered. When it came to grass, there wasn't a man in Glory that could fill my shoes.

The last thing I saw was Marcy. And the last thing I said was so crazy and queer I bet they still talk about it in Glory, except that neither Mama nor Marcy would ever tell. I looked at Marcy and then I seemed to see clear through her and what I saw was so wonderful I felt like I wanted to jump up out of bed and run straight into it. It was a land and it was green but with a greenness of which I never dreamed: flowers and trees and grass and hedges and shrubs more beautiful than I could ever tell. That's why I said this crazy thing and it was the last thing I ever said. I looked at all that green and lovely land and I said: Gee whiz!

And then it was over. And now I'm here. And no one else on Glory Hill is quite like me. And yet for so long out here it was all glumness for me; listening to the rain way up yonder in the trees so far above upon the earth I lie beneath. And then the marvel of it began. The wonder. All the chemistry of me seemed to go striving and wandering out into the land: the flesh of foot and face, the strong muscles that I loved, the hands that used to drum so wonderfully, the eyes that loved once looking at Mama and that old dog they killed: everything finding its place and its way into the earthy scheme of things. I have dissolved. I have broke loose. And all of me that grieved the losing of my precious trade—it has found its riddle answered. For I am what I always loved in life the most. I am grass! I am grass! And every inch and atom of me rises up and rises higher still—and wakes to find itself in every green thing!

Doctor Ira Grant Stribbler

It will take a lot more than Allie's nagging to convince me that I was to blame for Dollie Hazlitt's death in Wheeling that night ten years ago. It would seem to any reasonable person that ten years should be long enough to forget about a thing like that. Dollie was a fine woman and I know that she was Allie's closest friend but even so, ten years is a long time to hold a grudge. And yet I never expect Allie to forgive me; if our married life together lasts for another fifty years I know she'll still be throwing it up to me. The truth of the matter is that Allie's never gotten over the fact that her own father was a harness-maker in Glory while my family was among the wealthiest and most distinguished in Echo Point.

My father William Grant was the finest surgeon Wheeling ever had and his father was one of the city's first mayors and one of the finest corporation lawyers in the history of the state. My people had a sixteen room house and five hundred acres of land in Ohio County fifty years before the War of Independence when Allie's forefathers were poor dirt farmers scratching for a living twenty miles south of where Glory now stands. And that's the heart of Allie's hatred if you want to know the truth. Thank God I have my practice and the strength of character that comes from good breeding or she would have driven me insane long before now. I give no thanks to Fate for the life I've had. It seems that it would be enough that we lost our only child—that and the grief I suffered when I lost the Wheeling girl I really loved long before I ever knew Allie Clemens even existed. Sometimes I think how different my life might have been if Louise had lived and I'd married her instead of Allie. Louise and I had everything in common; we moved in the same Wheeling circles, she had class and breeding, she'd had the finest education money could buy at Mount de Chantell and Amherst, she'd studied music at the finest Paris conservatory, spent a year in Switzerland and Menthone and she was the prettiest and liveliest debutante of the 1915 season. She had everything a man of my background and stature could ask for. We were made for each other—Louise Liszt and me. Breeding, culture and money. How many nights I've dreamed of what our life could have been together. But it was not to be.

Not six months after our engagement in the fall of 1916 my father examined Louise and found she was hopelessly consumptive. Even with the best of care it was plain she could not live till Christmas. I was so distraught I postponed returning to medical school for a month so that I could be by Louise's side. She was marvelously brave and didn't seem to look forward to death with any fear at all. I was beside myself. All my plans, the life I had looked forward to as the husband of Wheeling's loveliest girl—everything had collapsed. A wife with the social background of Louise would have helped my Wheeling practice enormously. But now, in my grief, that was not what I cared about. I thought only of my darling girl so soon to be snatched from my arms. It would have been the gayest, most elaborate wedding of the year and now all those plans had to be canceled. The engagement ring I had given Louise was a five carat blue-white diamond from Jacob Grubb's Jewelry Store and now that extravagantly expensive ring was worn on a finger that daily grew more wasted until at last her hand had grown so thin that she could hardly keep it on.

There are as many cruel gossips in Wheeling as any town, I suppose, and don't think their tongues didn't wag when word went round that I had gone to Louise's bedside one September afternoon and asked for the ring's return. And they still talk about me, some of them, as if I had been the most heartless wretch in the world for asking Louise to give me the diamond back. What good was it to her then? And what sense would there have been if a piece of jewelry like that had gone with her to the grave? And even if that had not happened, there would have certainly been relatives who would have kept it. Well, I cared very little for what they said about me and I care less even now. Louise understood. She smiled at me in the most loving way in the world when I asked her. She knew as well as I did that she had no more than a month to live—six weeks at most. She slipped the ring off her finger and pressed it into my hand.

At least I thank you, Grant, she said, for the love I've had. And don't even listen to what they're saying at your wanting your ring back. I understand, Grant. I think I know you better than anyone has ever known you. And I only pray this ring will find its place on the finger of someone who cares for you as much as I have. Thanks, Grant, for everything.

Still I knew then I wasn't likely to waste a five carat ring like that on anybody else. I had bought that ring for Louise and for no one else. Our love meant that much to me, at least. And Jake Grubb was very understanding when I returned it and he paid me every cent it cost me. And still the gossips chattered. And they weren't content to slander my good name with the affair of the diamond ring. A few weeks before Louise died I began keeping company with another prominent Wheeling girl, Catherine Speidel. By an unfortunate chance the Speidel home in Echo Point was directly behind the Liszt property. Almost every Sunday in the last weeks of that September, Catherine and I played two or three games of croquet on the lawn of her father's huge property. By an unfortunate mischance over which, surely, I had no control, Louise had a clear view of the lawn from her sick-room. And so the slandering tongues of Wheeling society said that I had insulted my dying fiancee. They said that I could have waited, at least, till Louise was dead before I strolled about before her eyes with my arm around the waist of another girl.

Lord, what unfairness! Louise had said she wanted me to be happy, hadn't she? It only goes to show how narrow minds can distort the best of motives. I knew Louise could see Cathie and me from the window of

her room. And I knew, too, that she wanted with all her heart for me
to find someone to fill the aching emptiness in my heart. How many
times she had told me that she wanted me, after her death, to find a
girl who would love me and be an asset to my career. Well, what had
I done but that: Catherine Speidel was the daughter of a family every
bit as old and prominent in Wheeling as the Liszts were. In a way,
indeed, marriage to Catherine Speidel would have helped my practice
even more than marrying Louise would have, since Catherine's father
was on the Board of Directors of the Ohio Valley Hospital. And when
Louise died, at last, no one grieved more than I. Catherine said I was
inconsolable. And at her funeral I sent the biggest wreath of flowers of
any there. On top of everything, Catherine's friends told her I was only
after her for her father's social importance. Apparently they did a
pretty good job because before a week had passed Catherine broke a
date we had to attend the new Rudolf Friml musical comedy at the
Virginia. And I'd bought the two most expensive seats in all the house!

Is it any wonder I started drinking that winter? I was drunk when
I met Allie and drunk when I proposed and I was half-tanked when I
married her. And if I hadn't drunk pretty steadily during the years of
our marriage we'd have been divorced long before now. Somehow now
it doesn't matter. I'm past the age when romance means anything—I
mean the pure, honest love like I had for Louise and even Catherine
Speidel. Besides I know people here in Glory. And I know what the
nasty talk a divorce always causes would do to my practice. It doesn't
matter now. We live together in the same house, that's all. But it's like
we were prisoners—shackled together in hate.

I've seen a lot of marriages in my life. And I think the couples that
are bound together in hate are wedded tighter than the ones in love.
Take the case of couples like Mart and Lorry Sneed. I've never seen two
people living under the same roof who loathed each other more. And
yet when Lorry died of cancer last winter Mart went around Glory like
a lost soul. It was like taking a back-brace off a man who's worn one
all his life and seeing him fall limp. It was awful to see! I've seen man
and wife in love and when one of them died the one that was left just
seemed to go smiling through; it was like something he had had with
her or she with him was something that fulfilled them. But Mart just
seemed to dwindle. It was the hate he missed. It was the silence of that
big house which for thirty years had echoed to the venom of that

woman's vicious tongue. Mart's life without that hate was empty now. Finished. It's a pity he wasn't a drinker. That might have saved him. God knows, it's saved me. Not that I ever let it hurt my practice any. I keep a pack of cloves or sen-sen in my vest and no one ever knows. Except Allie. She seems to take a particular pleasure in pouring out the hundred-proof alcohol I get from the hospital. Or else she finds my extract of juniper and dumps that down the commode. She blames Dollie Hazlitt's death on my drinking. And if I hadn't slapped her face one night and told her there was more where that came from she'd have gossiped that lie all over Glory and ruined me.

Dollie was a Wheeling girl and nobody thought more of her than I. As a matter of fact, I used to take her to dances at the Stratford Springs long before I met Allie. That was even before I started courting Louise Liszt. As a young girl Dollie was never much of a beauty and she was a mighty poor sport. I got a little lovey with her one night and pinched her leg and she slapped my face. And I always suspicioned after that that she told Allie I'd been fresh with her. Still she was a good enough sort in later years, she liked a drink now and then and she was a whiz of a bridge player.

The night of the accident we'd all had dinner at the Fort Henry Club in Wheeling and gone out to Dollie's family's estate in Woodsdale and while Dollie and Allie were busy talking out front I sneaked a few extra drinks. That was in 1918 and Elsie Janis was supposed to sing at a big Liberty Bond Rally in Wheeling so we all decided to go back to town and see it. Allie kept saying I'd had too much to drink to drive and though there wasn't a word of truth in it she got me so nervous I guess I got a little careless. The road up Chickenneck Hill was wet from a spring rain and I was sore at Allie and going a little faster than usual when suddenly we began to skid. If Dollie hadn't panicked she would be alive today. But the minute we started skidding she opened the door and tried to jump out. And when the car slammed into the rock along the side of the road the door pushed shut and cut both Dollie's legs nearly off above the knee. She bled to death before we could get her into the Wheeling hospital and there was nothing I could do. Allie was in the nervous-disorder ward of a Pittsburgh clinic for a month after that and when she came home our life together was worse than it had been before. She still keeps a framed picture of Dollie Hazlitt on the mantel where I'll be sure to see it every night when I come

home. And she's always playing Dollie's favorite tune—"Poor Butterfly"—on the Victrola in the evening when the light through the parlor
curtains falls on Dollie's picture and lights it up. God, how I've lived
with that woman since then I will never know. If it wasn't for a little
nip now and then I could never have stood that life we've had together.
And when I was in the Ohio Valley Hospital last winter for cirrhosis
of the liver Allie only came to see me once in the whole month I was
there.

She's found a new best-friend since Dollie died however. And that's
that woman Marcy Cresap who's trying to drive every doctor in Glory
out of business with her communistic ideas about Public Health. If her
salary was paid by Apple County it would be easy: I could get her
fired like that. But she gets her money from a bunch of Jew officials
in the Public Health Service in Washington. Don't worry though. We'll
get her yet. She's fighting something that's a good deal bigger than she
realizes. They sent a doctor in from Washington to help her with her
schemes and plots but he was a Jew, too, and the doctors in Glory made
life so miserable for him he soon tucked his kike-tail under his legs and
ran.

Marcy was the one that started this socialist business of free toxin-
antitoxin against diphtheria in the Glory public schools. From the beginning there wasn't a soul in Glory on her side except old Doc Cecil
and Tadd Cockayne and if it hadn't been for Tadd and his damned
newspaper the plan never would have been got over. God knows, I know
a thing or two about diphtheria. Didn't my only boy George die of it?
And who do you think he caught it from but the children of those trash
at Angel Swamp that Marcy Cresap's always sticking up for! I'll say it
and I'll say it here in public. In my opinion Marcy Cresap was responsible for my child's death. That's right! She as good as killed him. And
it was one of her Jew assistant's hypodermic needles that did it—a
needle he'd stuck in the arm of one of those diseased Angel Swamp
cretins and then forgot to sterilize before he stuck my boy with it. God
damn that woman—the doctors of Glory will see her in Hell before they
let her put over her schemes for so-called public health!

Sure. I'm for toxin-antitoxin. Any doctor with a modern training is!
But I'm for respectable, decent families bringing their children in to
their family doctors and paying for it. It doesn't cost that much. But
when you consider all the children of all the well-to-do families of a

town the size of Glory it adds up to a pretty fair sum of money. And doctors aren't any different from you. They've got expenses and families to support just like you do. And with a plan like this Marcy Cresap has for free shots in the schools it means nothing more nor less than the first step toward socialized-medicine and socialized-everything-else. Communism. Well, what else does it add up to?

The first winter she tried it we defeated her. That was mainly because of public feeling in Glory against that Jew doctor that was with her. There were a few cases of diphtheria in Apple County that winter. Most of them were in Angel Swamp and down the river in some of the little towns where the population is mostly coal miners and shantyboat trash anyway. Well, the doctors stood up in a body and demanded that the children of Angel Swamp people be kept out of school. Marcy and that damned Tadd Cockayne started screaming that this was undemocratic and God knows what else and so the poor children kept coming to class. That spring a small epidemic of diphtheria broke out. Well, what else would you expect? Again the doctors yelled blue murder. Meanwhile the children of decent families were getting their shots from their own family doctors. My boy George was away for the Thanksgiving holidays visiting Allie's sister in Marietta and didn't need any. Meanwhile the Cresap woman kept up her fight. And between her and that miserable, socialistic *Glory Argus* they won. She and the Jew doctor started giving free shots in the schools. They even gave them to the Angel Swamp trash. Now it's the opinion of everyone who knows anything about the Malthusian theory and just plain common sense that nature has a way of taking care of people like that. They're a burden to the County and a burden to themselves. Besides that they're a disgrace to the human race. If you ever saw the way those Jukes and Kallikaks live, breeding among each other, spreading disease everywhere among respectable people, drinking their pay away and then expecting the State to keep them—well, you know what I'm talking about.

My boy George came home after Thanksgiving. I know I should have given him his toxin-antitoxin shots that night. But he was always such a lively, healthy little kid. He looked so good that night. And I was up in bed trying to throw off a cold with a pint of gin and I never thought of it. Someone spread the word—and I have no doubt it was Marcy Cresap—that I was on a big drunk that Thanksgiving. And I'll be damned if my own wife Allie didn't side in with her. She said I'd fallen down the stairs and hurt my back so bad I couldn't even make it out to my car to drive to my office and get the needle and the ampules. And that was a damned lie.

The next morning my little baby George went to school. And as Fate would have it, that was the morning Cresap and her Jew doctor were giving the toxin-antitoxin shots. George looked feverish when he came home for lunch that day. I took his temperature. It was a hundred and three. I put him to bed, called Alf Blick to examine him. I was still feeling rocky from my bout with that Thanksgiving cold I'd licked and didn't feel I was in any shape to look after him myself. I had another drink to calm my fears while Blick was on his way.

Blick came about three o'clock that afternoon, examined my boy and said it was diphtheria. A bad case. I stood there at the foot of my baby's bed and wept bitter tears while my wife Allie stood in the doorway with her fists clenched in her apron, whispering at me that it was my fault that George had diphtheria, that I should have given him the shots before he went away. I turned and cursed her. It was the first time in all our married life I'd done such a thing. I come from a respectable, genteel family which never used foul language. With the kind of folks Allie had I guess she wouldn't understand that. At any rate, I stood there by my boy's bed and cursed at my wife like a trooper. She covered her face with her apron and ran downstairs. After a while she came upstairs with a bowl of slop she called hot chicken broth and tried to get the boy to take it. That whimpering, back-country fool! She might have known he was doing well enough to swallow air, let alone her greasy broth. She stood there by the bedside and there was no sound in the room but his rattling breath.

Ira Stribbler, she said, you're a disgrace to your profession. You're an insult to the name of manhood. It was through your drunkenness that you killed poor, lovable Dollie Hazlitt. And now your drunkenness has sentenced to death your only child!

Hold your tongue, you common slut, I said.

I'll not, she cried. The night George took the river bus to Marietta I begged you to give him his shots! You were sitting in the sun-parlor too drunk to walk. You said he didn't need them.

He didn't need them, I told her, and that was true. It was a dirty hypo needle in the hands of that Jew doctor that infected him.

I walked to the door, shoved her aside and went downstairs. Alf Blick was in the sun parlor by the front door, looking out at the flakes of snow that had begun to fall. He didn't look at me. I judged that woman Cresap had turned him against me, too. But I was wrong. I asked him if he wanted a drink because I was going to have one to settle my nerves. Alf's not a teetotaler but he never drinks before sundown. Besides he didn't need the drink like I did.

It was her that's sentenced my boy to death! I said. That woman Cresap and that Jew doctor with his dirty needles. Needles filthy from the diseased blood of those Angel Swamp trash who ought to be dead anyway.

Alf laid his hand on my shoulder. His face was kind.

Grant, he said, what I'm saying is just between the two of us. I know how you feel. I can't blame you. I hate that woman as much as you do. And we've all got to stick together if we're going to beat her. But as a matter of medical fact that shot your boy had couldn't have given him diphtheria.

It did! I yelled. You know it did.

It couldn't have, Grant, he said. It's only been an hour and a half since they gave George his shot. From the looks of him he's had diphtheria for better than twenty-four hours.

You're a liar! I shouted.

Grant, I told you I was on your side, Alf said, and I'll have to admit he was mighty kind after the tone I'd taken to him. Personally, I'll be just as happy if the people in Glory *do* think it was that school shot that infected your boy. But it wasn't. Grant, I'm pointing no finger of blame at you. But that boy of yours should have had his toxin-anti-toxin a week ago when the epidemic broke out. But you're a doctor and a goddam good one. And you know as well as I do that no boy's going to get diphtheria from a dirty needle in this little length of time.

Will he pull through, Alf? I whispered.

Alf was still for a moment.

You better have another drink, Grant, he said. That's all I can say.

Will he pull through! I yelled.

No, Alf said. No, Grant. There's no power on earth can save him. It's gone too far.

Oh, Christ Jesus, I whispered. What's the answer to it all? Why in God's name did you put us here if all it means is this?

When I got upstairs again Allie was lying on the bed across the boy and I knew he was dead. I finished my drink and hid the glass behind the bureau where she wouldn't see it. I stared at her with loathing and disgust. I thought about my life and what it could have been if I hadn't married her. I looked at the small feet of my dead son sticking up under the bedspread. I stood there thinking that I would give up my practice, my money, my home, everything if only I could talk to him for one single minute. It seemed to me suddenly that I had something desperately important to tell him. There was a thing between us that needed explaining. But I didn't know then, I haven't known since, what that thing was. I knew in my innermost mind that Marcy's shot hadn't given him the diphtheria. I'm still man enough and doctor enough to admit the truth when it stares me in the face. But I knew she was to blame for my boy being dead. I knew I wouldn't have been drunk that night if I hadn't been so furiously, insanely mad at her. And I determined then that I was going to lead the doctors' fight in Glory against that woman and defeat her if it was the last act of my life.

Allie never moved. She stayed there stretched across my child George's dead body all that afternoon and long past sundown. It was snowing hard by then, the big flakes falling past like the ragged pieces of the life I could have had. And it wasn't my fault! That was what maddened me. It was none of it, any of it, my doing really. I felt like a checker that had been moved across a board by some big hand. And the game was a cheat. A cheat!

I thought of the Angel Swamp children that were healthy and alive that night. And my boy dead. Why? Why? I thought. Why couldn't it have been one of them instead of this child of beauty and breeding and good family? I wanted to get down on my knees and pray but I couldn't. Because I hated God. I hated His hand that had moved me like a checker across a board. I wanted to pray. But the words wouldn't come out. I couldn't pray to Jesus. Because I hated God for Him as well. I hated God because he had let Him be a Jew. Why did God make Him be a Jew? Can you tell me? A Jew like that kike-doctor giving shots up there!

I got down on my knees anyway. I was a man empty of everything. I wanted to pray. I had to pray. Something in me felt if it didn't pray I would choke to death on something fighting in my throat. And finally I prayed. With the snowflakes falling past the parlor window like the pieces of the torn-up love letters of all lost hope I prayed. And because I was crying, too, the prayer came out in thick and ugly words. I think I was a little crazy that night. I wasn't drunk any more. I swear to you it wasn't that. I was crazy with praying, that's all! And the craziest thing of all was who I finally found inside my heart that seemed decent enough to hear my prayer. Yet, even the prayer was crazy. If you'd seen me there and heard me you'd have sworn I was out of my head! I couldn't pray to God for He was heartless. I couldn't pray to Jesus who's a Jew. Who's left? Well, when I tell you you'll think I'm a fool. I know it makes no sense: the one I prayed to nor the prayer I prayed. There was my child fresh dead upstairs, and all I could think of were those frivolous things that happened back so very long ago I hadn't thought of them in all these years. But it was praying. And do you know to whom I prayed? Louise Liszt. I know it's beyond reason but there it is! Something old and wild and sweet came rushing back to fill me with repentance like a knife, and a half-forgotten grief more deep than hell. I prayed to her down there upon my knees: Louise.

I asked her to forgive my taking back her ring—for pulling it off her trembling, thin hand on that sunshiney day the week before she died. And then I asked her to forgive the croquet games, those Sundays long ago, out on the Speidel lawn where she could see. And me with my arm around young Catherine's waist, with only a week until Louise would die. Weren't those the craziest things to pray about?—a gold engagement ring, some croquet games? While upstairs lay my little boy fresh dead! And yet that ring, Louise, those games, the shame—came tumbling, rushing back to fill my mind, until, to save my very life, the fact that just upstairs my boy was lying dead was something I couldn't realize just then. I squatted there, like any faith-deluded fool, and prayed to a girl now dead these ten, long years! And in the awful moment after that, I felt I couldn't bear it if no answer came: I felt I'd go stark mad if after all I'd prayed—and praying's a thing that's hard for men like me—if after I'd prayed some something in the parlor silence there, failed to give me some sign that I'd been heard: a whisper, a fall, maybe a rustling sound. Or just a snowflake's strike against the pane, in one, still feathery answer from somewhere. It must! It must! I'd die unless it did. Some something speaking to me down there on my knees. Something that was a gesture from Louise—telling me God to Whom I could not pray, nor his Jew son whom Life had made me hate!

—Louise to tell me God or His Jew Christ, that one of Them had somehow made it right—the ring I'd ripped off of her hand that day, the
croquet games in those queer, Sunday dusks—a sign from her that one
of these Gods she loved had made the wounds I gave her hurt no more!

Timothy Holt Baird

At last I knew it was hopeless to fight it any longer: I couldn't keep my hands off him. There is something about boys that age that's as tender as any girl. I've read a lot—Plato and Catullus and Oscar Wilde. The world thought different once of men like me. I've read books and I know. That surprises you, I suppose—a man like me, a guard at the prison taking time for books. I couldn't have lived without them. With all that hate and suffering and human cruelty around me every day— I'd have died long before I did, without the solace of beauty. I guess I've always been the way I was back then—I never could remember when it began. Maybe my first girl did it, I don't know. Yet there are doctors and educated men who have the theory that men like me are born the way we are. A something in the chemistry of glands. And yet I look and act like other men. I couldn't have been a guard unless I had. They had an old psychologist years ago up at the prison who studied the men to see what made them tick, to probe and peer and guess what made them kill, what made them rape and rob and all the rest. I thought once that I'd ask him about me, what made me like I am. I gave that up though, fairly quick. I had to laugh. He hadn't been there more than thirty days till I found out that he was one like me. Don't that beat all? It wasn't any time at all until the word got round among the prison guards and he was fired before two months was up. The others have all told you, I expect, how much time there is to think on Glory Hill. I have regrets; that much I can't deny. And yet I think that the thing I dream of most—the one thing I'd have changed about my life, and it's the thing, alas, no man can change! And that would be that if I had my wish, I'd have chose being born in ancient times: back in the days of Greece or Ancient Rome, when men like me weren't looked upon as bad.

My father was a man who beat me black and blue. Yet he was never drunk: it wasn't that. He wasn't religious, nor even very strict. I don't know what it was he got from beating me. There never seemed any reason; he'd come home, tired from his job—he was a puddler in the Weirton mills—and sit around and brood and get so blue and mad at everything, the way things are, until he'd work himself into a rage. And fetch his belt off and come after me. Yet, still I don't blame him for how I am. And God knows my blessed mother wasn't to blame, she loved and prayed for me until she died. She died from some disease that no one knew; none of the Weirton doctors could tell what to name the thing wasting her away. And yet, not one of them knowing what it was, they wrote her out prescriptions by the ton and kept my father broke getting them filled. And not a one of them that ever helped. The night she died she started turning blue from head to foot with funny mottled spots. I was sixteen and didn't know what to do, or who to send for. And besides we were so broke the doctors wouldn't've come anyway.

Something inside me seemed to break and change that night. My father watched her dying in a rage, the dry-eyed fury that's far worse than tears, and sat beside the stove, watching her flesh grow blotched with blue and listening to her breath which thickened and bubbled like the sound that the last water makes when it goes down the drain. And then at last it stopped and she was gone. And Father went to the table by the bed and snatching up the Bible that was there, ripped it in half and then walked to the door and stood a while defying with his eyes the winter sky all lit up from the mills. And then he threw the halves of the ripped Bible at the sky, where the blast furnace flames belched out their hell, and stood a moment more, cursing as I had never heard him do, spitting out words I didn't think he knew, and shaking his hard, big fist against a thing, or maybe a someone far up in the stars: those infinite specks of heaven the mill smoke hid. And then for the first time in all my life he came toward me gently across the room, and took my head in his big hands, pressing it close against him there. I couldn't understand. And somehow this was worse than all the times he'd beat me with the belt whose buckle now I felt so cold and cutting in my cheek. I ran out of the house and left him there.

And nothing I was feeling seemed like grief. All I could feel was turmoil in my breast, shortness of breath, and fear of something huge, something that swelled above the tall blast-flames, and something that twitched and worried in my pants. I ran down Pulaski Street to a bad house: a place I knew where girls sat on the porch in chairs and swings, waiting behind the vines of honeysuckle that smelled to me like sin. And the old Polish woman asked me in and gave me a young Ukrainian girl named Sofie. Can you beat that? My mother hardly cold and here I was in bed with my first girl. And my last. I never wanted women after that. When I got through and stood there in the room, buttoning my clothes and breathing the Lysol smell and looking at that poor Ukrainian girl—she didn't even look as old as me—lying there on her dirty little cot, smiling the saddest smile I ever saw. I ran out of that place as fast as I could run. And threw up all my dinner in the street. That was the last. There's never been a woman since that night for whom I didn't feel pity or disgust. Or else I'd just feel nothing for them at all. And very soon I got the way I am. My first time was a cop in Steubenville who saw me on the street and bought me dinner and took me to a show. And afterwards we found a rooming house down by the railroad yards and that was it. That was when my life like this began. The cop said he would buy me all new clothes, and get me a radio and take me to shows. But afterwards he seemed to change his mind. Because he took me in and locked me up in jail.

It's all so good over on Glory Hill. Now nothing burns and stirs or rises up to shame me with how different I am. Here flesh dissolves and with it those desires that were as much a torment for the ones that men call normal as they were for me. There's torment here for some but not like that. There's sorrow and regret but not for things that men's flesh made them do, it's different here. And back in life there were two kinds of love, while over here there's only love itself. And it's as much for woman as for man. Or child or beast. It's simply love, that's all. Sometimes I think that's all it was back there.

When mother died I ran away from home. I rode the freights and wandered around the land. I've slept at night in forty different states, and shared my grub with men in jungle camps. I picked fruit in the South with Negro men, and women too, and sheathed the wheat in the big golden harvests out in Kansas. I dug for iron ore in the Messabe Range, and heard the speeches of Debs and Mother Jones in Homestead and joined the Wobblies and learned how to fight. And then I came to Glory and got a job as guard up at the penitentiary. That's where I met the best friend of my life: a boy named Harley Walters. Harley was from a farm in Tucker County and big and lean like Lincoln in his youth, with a slow smile and poems in his head, and much too kind to have the job he had. He wasn't strange in the same way that I'm strange. But still he understood and knew the way I was and never snubbed me for it, nor ever said a word, nor talked of it. It seemed that Harley for all his manliness and love had no desires of any kind at all. He spoke to me of a girl he'd married once. And three months from the day that they were wed, she died in 1919 of the flu. Sometimes I thought that all desires like that, fleshly desires of any kind, had gone from him with her. Harley was someways sadder yet then me: a man who's born to love once and that's all.

All the other guards had girls in town: young, loose and single girls in Glory or else they went to Benwood now and then and spent some week's pay at Parez's house. And funny as it sounds I'm not ashamed to say I loved Harley more than any single soul in my whole life. And not the way you think—let's get that straight. Where men and boys are concerned I'm strange. I'll tell you that and I'll not be ashamed. Because it doesn't matter any more; over on Glory Hill all these desires blend into one, and whatever love you cherished back in life, out here on Glory Hill it's all the same: man, woman, child it's just plain love, that's all. And that's the way it was between us two: Harley and me— we seemed to understand. We were both men and proud of being men, each in his way, and yet it always seemed that when it came to sex we each had none, or maybe both—who knows? Wise men don't know.

Sorrell was the warden in those days. And never a finer man has held that job. But Harry Marlin was captain of the guards and somehow

Sorrell never knew what kind of captain Harry Marlin was. Some men are just too good ever to see evil—Sorrell was that way. He never knew. If he'd have ever known he'd fired Harry on the spot. Harry had grown up out in Angel Swamp. He ran away from home when he was young and somehow washed off all the stain and shame of his poor childhood, went to school, went off to Pittsburgh where he worked a while and then came back to Glory good as new. Good as new and better than other men. Or so he thought: Lord, how he loathed the poor. And most of the cons in prison once were poor, children of white-trash families or from the stink of mine and mill towns up and down the state. Harry was just a guard when he began. But something gentle and blind in Sorrell made him think that Harry would make a good captain of the guards. So Harry made it—he had reached the top. And promptly set out kicking those below. Lord God, I never saw a man who hated men whose families were poor or worked the mines or sweated in the mills. It seemed that Harry Marlin's life was spent in climbing to a place where he could kick and shame and beat all that he once had been. Each time he had a man strung up by the wrists, or beaten with a whip or starved for a week on water and stale bread, it was like Harry was whipping Angel Swamp itself, or beating it, or dangling it by its wrists. It was a place he hated and not men. It was his past and not the cons he tortured.

And Harley for all his sweetness hated Harry. No gentler soul I've ever know than Harley, but when it came to Harry Marlin's ways, his methods there as captain of the guards, Harley was a raging cup of hate. And Harry Marlin knew how Harley felt and every single chance that he could find he'd order Harley to the cellblocks with a cat, and make him drag out prisoners to the room where things I hate remembering took place, and order him to lay the whip on hard, standing by Harley watching with a smile, making sure Harley made each whiplash count. Harley began to change within a month. When I first knew him he was full of peace; we'd sit up in the towers by the gun in the long morning hours while Glory slept, and Harley'd read out poems from a book. Walt Whitman, Tennyson, and William Blake. I never found out where he'd learned these things, or when and how he'd started loving them. Maybe some teacher or librarian in some small country town took him in hand when he was very young and put a taste for poetry in his head. Or maybe it was the wife who died while she was so young: maybe she was the one who made him read, and left him that gentle legacy when she was gone. In those days Harley even tried to write. He had a little ledger from somewhere: a book made for the keeping of accounts, and Harley used to fill that book with poems all the time. I've wondered since what happened to that book. The poems weren't too good, so no one cares. No one but me. Because I'd like to have that thing to keep of Harley and his life; those poems to remind me of those nights.

You probably read it in the *Glory Argus* about how Captain Harry Marlin died. Harley killed him—shot him through the head. Harry had ordered Harley to whip a con, half dead from TB, and Harley had refused. Harry gave the order once again. And the second time Harley said he wouldn't. And Harry Marlin took the whip himself and commenced to beat the man with all his strength. Harley said nothing, calmly took a rifle down from the racks of guns along the wall, aimed it carefully at Harry and calmly shot him through the heart.

A woman here in Glory heard the story: the way it really happened, I mean. Her name is Marcy Cresap and though I never met her I know she must be good as gold. Because she was close to Warden Sorrell and she went to him and told him what she'd heard and asked him to give the case an exposé. And Sorrell spent a week investigating, and gave the story to the *Glory Argus*, and even went and testified at Harley Walters' trial in his behalf. But feeling in the town was running high. And Sorrell's kindness did more harm than good. For somehow it seemed that some mighty big men hated Sorrell and wanted to smear his name. Some said that Sorrell had his eye on the Governor's chair. They said the most important men in Glory would fight to ruin Sorrell to the end. And so they did. And finished Harley, too. Ruined his case and sent him to the chair. And, Lord, how shrewd they were in what they did. One man and one alone turned the trick. And that was the little, fat prison doctor, Alfred Blick.

In all the years I'd worked there as a guard I'd never once suspicioned anyone knew. I mean about the fact that I was strange. How could they know? I never talked nor acted like they do—the ones you see dressing in women's clothes. And never in all my prison years did I have anything to do with any con. Nor any of the guards I worked with either. The only one on earth I loved was him!—Harley, my friend, the farmer with the poems in his head! And yet Blick knew about me—how I was. How he found out is something I'll never know. But just the same he found out and he knew and played it smart and used it to frame Harley. Not once in all that trial was my name said—not even by Blick in all the lies he said. But slick as any lawyer he fixed Harley—fixed him forever so there was no chance. Finished his hope of even getting life.

That Doctor Blick: how can he sleep at nights? How can a man keep living after that? How can he stand his own face while he shaves, or bear his body's smell when he's in bed? He stood up in that court-room on that day—and swore that Harley Walters was a fairy. That was the word he used: a fairy. And he said Harley was in love with Harry—Harry, he said, a decent, normal man who'd served and fought in France for country and for flag—while Harley was kept home be-cause of what the draft board doctors knew he was. I stood up and shouted it was a lie. And got thrown out of the courtroom into the street. I came back and shouted it again. And got fined a month's pay for contempt of court. But it didn't matter. I was half out of my mind with outrage and grief. I knew that Harley was going to his death for a murder. But I knew just as well that he'd have gotten off with life or twenty years if it hadn't been for me. I saw then how the rottenness of my life had caught up with me. I saw how a good and decent man was going to his death for something that was queer and twisted in me. And yet I wondered how things could have been any different. I asked myself and God in the deeps of my soul how I could have changed any-thing. And it seemed to me that everything my life had ever meant had led to this—the death of the only real friend I'd ever had. I swear, for a while there I began to wonder what kind of God it was that could sit there so high and let such cruel things be. I even wondered if there was any God at all: or just an empty chair where He had been.

Because nobody in that courtroom even so much as listened to me, let alone believed me. Some of my fellow guards even tried to shake my hand and said what a brave, fine man I was to lie and try to deny my manhood in public that way all for the sake of a friend.

Harley Walters went to the electric chair in December of 1924. I was home in my room in the boardinghouse on Water Street that night. I lay there on the bed and watched my alarm clock inch around toward nine o'clock: the hour. I remembered a lot of things that night. My mother's death, for one. And the picture came clear as being in my mind: my father standing there in the doorway in Weirton shaking his fist at God somewhere beyond the steel-mill glow. I thought about the little Ukrainian girl on the cot that night, too: I remembered the sad smile on her face and the strangeness in her eyes. Had she put a curse on my life with those eyes that night? Was there some damnation of my soul hidden behind the stillness of those lips. Or was God punishing me for being different from other men?

Oh, I tell you how wonderful it is to be over here on Glory Hill at last! That torment in my flesh—it is all gone. The shame of my desires is all forgiven like something ugly in the streets of a mill town covered over and blessed at last by a fresh fall of snow. God has said: don't worry any more. And Harley said it, too. He came here one night and stood above my grave and spoke his blessing plain. And then he said some verses from the poems he used to read beside the guns in those dark nights high in the prison tower. It's all healed over now, like an old, deep wound that's gone away and not even left a scar. But it was hell back there in Glory. And there was more hell to come, I was to find.

In the spring last year a Glory jury sentenced a boy to twenty years for murder. The boy was fourteen years old. His name was Jerry Thomas. Marcy Cresap got into the case and fought like a mother for that child. She went all the way down river to Captina to find out what had really happened. The boy had asked his father for a bicycle and the old man refused him. That night the boy hid behind the chicken-house with a .22 target rifle and shot his father through the left temple, killing him instantly. That was all the facts the jury had in the case. Marcy pried and poked around Captina for a few days and found out that the boy's mother was dead. Marcy wanted to know how she had died. Three years before the man knocked his wife down a flight of steps in her eighth month of pregnancy and she died of a miscarriage that night. The boy saw it. Maybe he loved his mother. Maybe he never forgot. I loved my mother. And there are some things I'll never forget and I was born all of thirty-two years ago.

The boy was given a special cell in the State Prison at Glory. Sorrell wasn't warden there any more so there weren't many special privileges for the young convict. Still there were some. The new captain of the guards had heard it said what a fine, Christian, selfless, masculine man I was. He assigned me to look after the boy. Every day he was permitted an hour's exercise in the prison yard. They built a special pen

of steel bars to keep the older convicts away from him. That was to
keep the bull homosexuals from getting him. Can you imagine? And
they give me the job of guarding the boy! Every morning the boy used
to play basketball by himself in the pen while I stood by with a high-
powered rifle. He would bounce the ball against the bars and catch it
when it bounced back. Sometimes he would look around, forgetfully, as
if he thought there might be other boys there to play the game with him.
But there was no one. No one but me. Me and Marcy Cresap. She used
to come regularly once a week and bring the boy magazines or some
candy or a toy. One day after I had taken the boy back to his cell she
laid her hand on my arm and looked into my eyes.

Tim, she said. I know your problem. I want you to know I have never
condemned you for it. God makes us all in strange shapes, I guess. I'm
a little queer in many ways myself. And I just want to say that I remember you that morning at Harley Walters' trial. And that's all I
needed to show me that you are more of a man than most of the men
guarding the men in this hell-hole. That's all, Tim. Take good care of
Jerry. There's no one in West Virginia I'd trust to look after him
more than I trust you.

Then she went away. I was glad she left. Because I started to cry and
I wouldn't have wanted her to see me doing that. I stood there thinking
about my life. I thought about Mama and my poor father—him maybe
the most pathetic and wounded of us all—I thought about the years of
my friendship with Harley and I wished, as I had wished so many times
before, that I could have gone down to that green room in his place. I
thought about the little boy, too—Jerry Thomas. And I knew I loved
him with a sweetness that made me ache whenever I saw him. And it
was strange. Sometimes when I was guarding him there in his steel
cage, listening to the thump of that lonely basketball, I would close my
eyes and remember things. I saw myself when I was a boy. I looked at
Jerry and it seemed that he summed up everything that I could have
been if something in the making of things had been different. Let the
doctors and philosophers figure it out. It's bigger than me. It's too
much for my poor mind. Let them decide whether Harley was wrong
when he killed Harry Marlin. Or let them judge me for the way I am
different from other men and the kind of life I've had. Maybe they'll
have something to say about Plato and his child-lovers, too, when they
get done. I only could think that Marcy's faith in me was all wrong—

that it was a real, male man that fourteen-year-old boy needed to watch over him. I could feel it all building up inside me—wantings I hadn't felt for fifteen years; things I hadn't even felt for Harley Walters.

Every morning when I knew it was nearly time to go to the boy's cell and fetch him it was an agony to me. Even before I could see him through the bars I had his image in my mind and heart. I saw the softness of his face and the dark curls that framed it, the wistful, lonesome sorrow that shone in his dark eyes. I could see the thick lashes of those eyes, shadowing the pupils until they seemed darker than they were. And the slender, rounded shape of his young body, hardly touched yet with the hardness of maturity. A boy that age is little different from a girl. His flesh is soft and scarcely shadowed with hair and his fingers are slender and delicate as the stems of blossoms. At night in my boardinghouse room I used to lie there half-mad with my dreams of that child. I cursed my life that I and he had not been born into a different age—an epoch of poets and of love which knows no sex. One night I thought insanely of helping the boy to escape and running off with him to Chicago or New York. I knew somehow that I was nearing the end of things. Because, with all my sensuous thoughts of that tortured and lonely child, who had been so criminally imprisoned by the State of West Virginia, I could not help remembering, as well, the face and the words of Marcy Cresap that day in the prison yard.

There's no one in West Virginia I'd trust to look after him more than I trust you, Tim, she had said.

The words ran over and over in my mind. I thought of them until gradually, at last, the vision of the boy's face began to grow dim in my fancy. And yet I knew that in the morning it would come back. I knew that I was nearing the end of things. I determined to quit my job as guard at the prison in the morning. And yet in the hours before dayrise I knew I couldn't; that I must see my boy again. And I knew that I was powerless, in this life, ever to leave him. I went to the prison that morning, waited while the wheel-gate slowly turned to let me in. In the prison yard I kept my face averted so that I would not have to see his. I listened to the monotonous, tragic drum of the basketball against the steel of the bars. I heard the caged pace of the child's big prison shoes. I reached in my pocket. I had brought the boy a gift when I had come to work that morning. I prayed that he would treasure it forever.

I stared at him through the bars—so beautiful and trapped and doomed in that hideous penal place. I reached my gift through to him.

I want you to have this, Jerry, I said. It is very precious. It belonged to a very great man. Even when you are grown up I think you will always be able to look at it with pride. And I hope it will always offer you fresh experiences of beauty.

He dropped the basketball, came over, took it from my fingers. For a moment he looked up at me with such an expression of appreciation as I had not seen him even give Marcy Cresap when she brought him candy and toys. His face shone with radiant pleasure. It was as though something had bent the bars a little. I knew now what I had to do—I knew that, at last, I was powerless to fight it any longer. I went into the guardroom of the prison and stared for a second at the gilded memorial photo of Captain Harry Marlin on the wall. I lifted a high-powered rifle from the gunrack, put the muzzle in my mouth. I pulled the trigger.

Over here on Glory Hill there is calm now. My love for that child, the little convict, has not vanished: only the flesh and anguish of that love is gone. I think of his soft eyes. I see them as they shone that morning. I remember that day and that moment. And I yearn forward to the day when he is a man and can read those Dialogues of Plato: the little book that Harley Walters gave me by the gun on the tower one April night a thousand years ago.

Billy Barger

They came for me with the warrant right into my president's office in the bank. I know the Apple County Sheriff had to do his duty, still, it would have been easier if he'd served the warrant on me at my house. No bigger scandal has hit Glory in thirty years than my arrest. Tadd Cockayne wrote it up short and decent in the evening *Argus*. Afterward I thanked him for doing that. The minute I looked through the plate-glass window and saw Sheriff Jessie Fronapfel walking across the street I knew the jig was up. And I knew my career was finished. I guess I even knew my life was drawing to a close as well. I knew that when they were all through with me, my strength would be all spent and all desire to go on living would be gone as well. Still I blamed no one; even after indictment I said that I was wrong, I pleaded guilty, and asked for no mercy from the jurymen.

Yet it was hard, I'd always been so proud. I'd worked so hard to get up where I was. I'd lived in Glory's streets since I was born, and all my kin were Glory folks as well. I went to Glory's schools and after that, got my degree at Harvard Business School and spent two years after in Philadelphia, studying at Pennsylvania's Wharton School. My father'd been a banker thirty years, and when the Farmer's Valley Savings Bank was formed in 1890, I was one of those most prominent Glory men who founded it. Oil was booming down at Sistersville and towns in river counties south of here and though our capital when we began was less than seventy thousand dollars soon we grew like Topsy and by 1901 our assets totaled more than half a million. Schwab and Carnegie were the Valley powers then and it was me that talked tough Charley Schwab into investing money here in Glory—the zinc smelter east of Angel Swamp.

Business is queer—it's like men drawing straws to see who pulls the shortest one which means that he's the sheep who must pay for the rest. In speculation honor's not what counts. It's luck that says who loses and who's won. I'm not complaining, mind you, for I know the way things are and knew it from the first. With eyes wide open I walked into this, knowing the chances, knowing the awful price which might be mine: and if the time should come when one must pay it might as well be me as anyone. And so it was, and so the dice were thrown. And it was me they chose or maybe Fate did all the choosing of the goat that day. I blame no one: surely none of the rest of them who were as deep in all of this as me. I went to trial making no complaint, knowing my guilt and knowing I would pay.

But still it is a bitter thing to know that men esteemed in Glory walk the streets and have men bow to them and shake their hands, while Glory people think of them as gods or paragons of clean commercial ethics, stainless as saints, these whited sepulchres. And when they die and go to Glory Hill high polished marble monuments shall rise, graven with all the honors of their lives. And many years from then these Glory folk shall revere them as founders of the town, great citizens of spotless consciences, whose names are cast in bronze on Glory churches, and spoken with reverence each Memorial Day. These are my cronies, these my closest friends, business associates, fellow Masons, brothers in Apple County's patriotic societies; these men I prayed beside each week in church. And even now I'll not condemn a one; at least no more than I condemn myself. All that I say is this: If I am black, then all my blackness will not make them whiter. I could name Glory names to make you stagger, and turn away and sicken at the wheels of commerce turning in this land. You'd pale and say that such things couldn't be. You'd name me men who gave cash in the thousands to build the finest churches in this town. But you'd be wrong in thinking that is all. For they were in this; as deep as ever me. We were all one and what we stole we stole, together, with full knowledge of our theft. Yet it was I who paid for all the rest. And sometimes now when I sit on my porch, trying to get a little morning's sun to darken up the bleached skin prison gives, I watch the folk of Glory going past, and see my old friends snub me with a smirk, hating my sight as if I were just scum, and thinking that it was I, and I alone, who stole the savings they had spent their lives in poor and thankless labor scraping up—there in my rocker weak from those three years, my stomach ruined from the food I ate, I sit there fingering thoughts like they were coins: Pennies in a beggar's dirty purse. Some of the things I feel is bitterness, but that somehow's the least of what I feel. And what's more, bitterness is less terrible by far than all the other thoughts I sit there counting one by one like some sick blindman's hoard. I think of friendship—not that it's a joke, or nonexistent, or an outright lie that men think is the truth. I think instead how little of it there is. Rarer than radium, friendship is in life. And loyalty, the same. And then I think how small a store of warmth there is in man. I'm one who's an authority on this. Three years in prison in my own home town. And two years after that, here on the porch, watching the folks of Glory passing by and throwing me looks of hate more dark than death.

The day that Skippy Wofford sentenced me he sat up there behind the judge's bench and cried until the jury was in tears. He wrung his hands and covered up his face and sobbed and flung his arms to either side, knocking the holy Bible on the floor. The bailiff picked it up and brushed it off. It wasn't hurt. That Bible in that room on Skippy's bench has seen and heard enough to make it tough or deaf; its words gone meaningless. And Skippy cried some more and said that never in all his years as Apple County judge had he been faced with the heartbreaking task, the painful duty to send his dearest friend to spend three years in West Virginia prison. And still he wept and many in the room were weeping, too, though all those pitying tears were not for me but for poor Skippy Wofford, faced with a job that needed braveness so. And while I stood there waiting for the sentence I thought back to just sixteen months before, when Skippy and some others I won't name had gathered on a rainy night in spring in a locked, smoke-filled room in the Mound Hotel. And there I watched while Glory's biggest lawyer gave Skippy a check for ten thousand dollars. And Skippy's services for this generous gift were to manipulate the court at the trial of a prison guard for murder so as to sway the jury's mind to think that Warden Thomas Jackson Sorrell was a liar, and so ruin his chances for the governor's chair.

I thought of a morning in Wheeling, too, when Skippy and those I will not name agreed to take some money from my bank—and I was with them, that I'll not deny—and it was more money than most of you will ever see, and gamble it on some western oil shares. It's Apple County history that we lost. But nine of Glory's leaders were involved. On Saturday we knew that all was over; and only hours till Monday morning came and soon the embezzlement would show up in the books. Well, it was clear to anyone with sense and the smallest grain of civic responsibility, that nine of Glory's biggest businessmen couldn't go off to prison. What would happen to the town? And what of the Glory people's faith in business? The future of the bank and more than that was hanging in the balance that was clear. One of us had to go though —that was clear, too. And who seemed more fitting than the president of the bank himself?

Skippy stopped crying after a little while. And the proper judicial sternness of his face presently returned; he got hold of himself, leaned forth painfully, for he was a hunchback. And thrust all sentiment aside as was his duty. And sentenced me to three years in the pen.

I'd never married and I thanked my Lord for that. At least, I had no wife and children who would suffer, cringing beneath the shame I'd brought upon them. I went home to the big house father built. I walked the halls and rooms the livelong night. I touched things, leafed through books, fingered the cups and plates of Havilland china, picked up the silver from my mother's table. And stared at my black diplomas on my walls, my father's picture hanging in the hall. It seemed that night I paced there with a hunger, a need not far from madness to be there, to touch, to look, to feel, to smell. And so that last night all I did was walk; upstairs and down, through every room and hall, with every light in all the house turned off. I knew each thing, each room, even by dark. I didn't need the light to read each book, to see my father's firm face smiling down as terrible as all those jury eyes. I felt around that house as, in his dark, a blind man's hands feel round and know his body. My last night there—I knew it would be that. For even when I came back in three years after, I would walk in the door a stranger there, the enemy of everything that waited, too sick to read, tired of my trinkets' touch, and disinherited by my father's eyes.

In prison they were kind and that was worse somehow than cruelty would have been. They favored me and let me in the yard to walk alone at night beneath the moon. And all that I could think as I looked up was that this same moon shone its cold, sweet light outside, lighting the town of Glory beyond the walls, falling in that bright square that I remembered across my mother's rag rug by my bed. They treated me as someone special there: and that, peculiarly, seemed somehow wrong. I watched the walking dead down in the yard, the pump-guns of the guards fixed in the slits, cut there like windows in an evil castle. I had an easy chair up on the porch where sometimes in those endless afternoons the warden's children played. It was a timeless life, slow with the tedium of a senseless patience.

And in the second year that I was there—I guess I'd thought too much, yes, that was it—the concept wrapped itself around my mind tight as a python: nothing could shake it loose. It was a thought so simple that it seemed the smallest effort should have shook it loose. And yet it clung and gripped and would not leave. And all the madness of my boredom there seemed now, in retrospect, a happy vacuum. It was pure treason that had seized my mind. And thinking it seemed to me ten times worse, and laid upon me twenty times the guilt, of anything that I had done before. No act in all my life seemed quite like this: a pure obsession that closed up like a fist and crushed in me the last spark I had left of conscience, honor, pride in America. And this is what it was, what it still is—It seemed to me that what crime I had done was wider, bigger than the ring of only nine men. It seemed to spread until it filled the land. Until it seemed to me that wealth—all the Republic's rich and high-heaped treasure—was money just as black as what I stole.

I tell you it was something in my mind that prayer or reason simply couldn't shake. I spent hours in the prison library, reading the trash they have there for the men, novels of the wild west or the sea, and the poems of Ella Wheeler Wilcox. I tried to keep my mind immersed in these, so that I wouldn't think my awful Thought. And yet it would come stealing through the bars, into my cell, each night when all the prison lights blinked out. I thought of myself as someone's soul possessed by the hanged and wandering spirit of a Bolshevik. Sometimes I would give up and let it come and take my mind, run shrieking through my brain. Most of the wealth of this great land of ours—this was my thought, in essence—has been stolen. I thought of the speculation I had made—the oil stocks that failed—embezzlement. And then I thought of the men of America who'd played the same wild game as I had played. And won! I'd sit in the rocker on the prison porch and watch the gray men wandering through the yard, like pale and wasted phantoms grazing on pastures of an utter emptiness. And I wondered why *they* were there—mind you, not why *I* was there! I wondered at the thousand Angel Swamps and all the mine and mill slums in the land. And with a vision almost too dreadful to bear I saw these lost men plain—why they were here! And I saw other men like Skippy and me and the rest. And then I saw the bigger ones like Schwab and Carnegie and Mellon. And with a sense of deep and shameless treason, a question against all that this country means: its progress, industry and enterprise—I looked down in that sea of aimless men and wondered why Carnegie was not there. Or Schwab or Mellon or the rest of them. I tell you I thought that nothing I had done, the funds I had embezzled through the years, the thing that Skippy had sent me to prison for—nothing I'd done, I say, seemed half so awful as thinking this thought of mine.

I'm out now and I sit on the porch all day. I try to be here when the sun falls strong; I moved my rocker so I'll feel its heat. It seems somehow important that I get a little color back so men won't look and see my skin like things which live their lives in subterranean streams and never have known the light. I can't bear strangers seeing in my skin the dying paleness which a prison gives.

There's few that ever come to see me here. I sometimes sit for days on end without a neighbor or a passer-by who even nods his head. Not that I blame them—these are honest folks. People who work and work till they can work no more and put away the little that they can. I've seen mill-workers labor thirty years and when they die their savings in the bank, five or six hundred dollars usually, goes to their family. And what happens then? Every dollar of it goes for funeral expenses: Marple's costs a lot, and so do flowers and granite and the hearse. All that some poor Slav worked for thirty years, and skimped and saved, follows him to the earth. And leaves a house of children needing shoes.

Maybe I think too much of Death these days. Here on my porch, watching the town go by. Yet those three years up there in prison, you must not forget, sped up my life and aged me thirty years. Even here in the sun I feel the slight, small chill of something in my bones. Like some sad music which is tuning up deep in the shamed and empty chamber of my flesh, and soon a hand shall lift its baton high and strike it sharply and something will begin. And something end—end and beginning both: I think Death's that, don't you? Oh, I hope it's that.

I had a little money which I saved up in the prison workshop making pants. As for the food I eat, my taxes, and the dollar a month my chewing tobacco costs, thank God I had a little money saved in Davis Cresap's bank—the Mercantile. The money I saved in prison wasn't much —two hundred dollars from those three long years of work. But I'll not touch a single cent of that—not for myself: that money's got to count. It's got to go for something particular. When I came out I offered it everywhere. I tried to give it to the Red Cross Drive. But Elsie Challoner said she'd not defile the Red Cross name with money from a thief. I offered it to Glory's Methodist Church, the church my father helped to found back in the year of 1872. They said my gift would stain the house of God, and they, too, turned me down. And I protested that all the churches here in Glory give together every year to make up baskets of food and toys for those in Angel Swamp. These children freeze each day, walking to school. They go home every night to corn-meal mush and bacon-fat and cold blackstrap molasses. I asked the Methodist pastor if he thought God would object too much were I to give a little money for some Christmas gifts, things that would make the winter months to come a little easier in Angel Swamp. I told him my two hundred dollars was money I had earned, at sewing machines up in the prison shop. I might have pointed out to this humble servant of the Lord that he was not ashamed to take the check for eighteen hundred dollars every year from John Wickerman who made his fortune out of that very same prison clothing shop. I didn't though. It wouldn't have mattered any.

The money that I live on these last years—the little sum in Davis Cresap's bank—is just enough to see me to the end. Last week I had a stroke, and I know well, almost to the moment, how long I have to live.

The money in the Mercantile will buy my simple meals, tobacco and the rest—the little that I live on every week. But as for money left to bury me there will not be a single, solitary cent. Thank God for that. Because I'll be content to lie in any spot of earth they choose. So long as it's somewhere in Apple County soil. That two hundred dollars would do marvelously, to give me the biggest funeral I could want and something simple written on a stone. But not a cent of it will go for that! For that two hundred is particular. It's something very special in my plans.

Isn't it queer? That a man like me who in his time has handled millions now thinks just of this—two hundred dollars. I've spent two hundred dollars in a night in giving Wheeling bankers fancy meals! But this two hundred's special. In some ways I feel as though it is peculiarly marked, and maybe even blessed in some strange way. There was a child I saw up in the prison. I used to watch him almost every day, standing inside a cage, bouncing a ball. They told me he was only fourteen years old. I used to sit there on the prison porch and think of what I'd done and feel ashamed. But nothing ever made me so ashamed as when I watched that child playing his pointless game. For what I stole I feel ashamed for me. But for that child I am ashamed for Man. And he's the one my money's going to. God knows what it will mean to him or if he'll ever find a place to spend it in that place. Still maybe sometime twenty years from now, when he has paid society its bill, he'll find some money in the prison bank and wonder where it came from and from whom. Maybe I'll be there watching on that day, though he won't see me smiling by his side. Perhaps in twenty years my soul will be free of its greed and cleaned by sorrow at last so I can follow that boy out of there, and stay with him a little while and speak, from time to time, in heaven knows what way the dead can speak to those alive and young. Maybe he'll need me then, who knows? Because I know that when a man walks from there, anger walks with him, vengeance has his hand, and retribution whispers in his ear. And who knows?—maybe by then I'll have the power to speak to him inside and make him think. And when he takes that money of his, and walks into a country hardware store and lays the bills down one by one, and pauses. And then speaks up and says: Give me that gun. I've got a score to settle with the world.

Perhaps some voice of me can whisper through and tell him that I lived once in the world. I'll tell him, if I can, one thing I learned. One

thing that's made this life's hell worth the game. One thing I learned
and maybe nothing else. And that one fact is this: The only human
vengeance that succeeds, is the revenge men take upon themselves. In the
long run of things the robber robs himself, and no one else in all this
queer, wide world. And every murderer's fallen foe is he!

Yesterday morning someone spoke to me. For a moment, sitting
there half asleep, I thought it was the breeze among the trumpet vines
playing jokes on my ears. But then I opened my dozing eyes and looked
down toward the pavement. It was Davis Cresap's daughter standing on
the steps, waiting to be invited up. I motioned to her with my cane and
stammered some foolish thing, half-silly with pleasure hearing someone
speak my name.

Colonel Barger, I've a bone to pick with you, she said, her eyes
twinkling with friendly mischief.

Come sit by me, daughter, I said, gesturing toward the empty canebottom rocker where no one had sat in more years than I can think.
She sat, watching me with those eyes of hers, a smile teasing the corners
of her mouth.

Someone, she said, deposited two hundred dollars in the prison bank.
They put it in the name of Jerry Thomas. Colonel, I have suspicions
about you!

Marcy, I said, solemnly, speaking as convincingly as I could. I don't
know what on earth you're talking about. Now where in the world
would I lay hands on such a sum as that!

She reached across and smacked me cross the hand. She rocked and
smiled and pursed her lips in pleasure.

All right, we'll let it lie at that, she said.

When I reached in my inside pocket then and fetched my pencil out
and with it the small black book and opened it and pressed it steady on
my knee so that I could write—my hand is not as firm as once it was—
Marcy watched me as I wrote another name, beneath the three names
already written there. And by the name I wrote the number four.

What's that? she said. And what have you written down there, Billy
Barger?

I wrote your name, young woman, I replied. I keep a tally here. This
small black book's a sort of human ledger. I wrote your name after the
other three. And then I wrote your number.

What number? Marcy said, tilting her head.

The number four, I said. Because you're the fourth.

I'm the fourth what? she smiled and tried to look.

The fourth friend Billy Barger has in Glory, I said. The fourth mortal who in these past two years has reached his hand in friendship to me here. I've four friends now and they're all here to read in this black book I carry night and day.

Marcy smiled and softness crossed her eyes. She reached across and touched my palsied hand and squeezed it and got up and said good day. When she had gone off Lafayette I sat and thought about this small black book I keep: all of the treasures chronicled on that page. Four friends I have! Four friends in all of Glory! Lord, that's a lot! Four friends who've passed the test, who've come through fire to touch in kindliness this thieving hand. Four friends I have in this great, wide earth. Think honestly a minute and tell the truth! How many of you out there can tell himself that he's as rich as Billy Barger is?

Anton Jacob Heller

Search for my bones in Potter's field among the hanged, the disinherited, and those so poor their name is but a number; I am not there. Look for my name among those graven on the stones on Glory Hill; you will not find it. Yet my eternal home is in the earth; deep, deep within the earth. I am too deep to even feed the grass. I am so deep I listen in the nights to the eternal rustle and the creak of rippling rock seams old as earth itself. Sometimes I think I even feel the heat of the molten stone at the world's center, in its fiery core. There's purity down here; nothing decays. I lie beside the four who died with me four hundred feet beneath the Benwood tipple.

We share a little room, carved out of coal. The other nineteen miners died in the blast; we five were cut off in a little room at the end of a corridor. No fire touched us, we didn't even hear the explosion. We knew when it happened though: a silent blast of air raced swiftly past us, then came sucking back, and instantly our safety lamps went out. The rats screamed in the blackness, some men cried. A mine mule bucked and whinnied in the dark. I was afraid for a while like every other living thing within that breathless, stygian corridor. But after a while I sat down against a wagon, opened my lunch-pail and began to eat the food my wife had fixed the night before. Four hundred feet above me sirens wailed and ambulances came clanging from every town all the way from Glory up to Wheeling. I didn't hear them though, I didn't care. I didn't scream and fight and break my fingernails against the 6 million tons of coal and slate and earth that lay between me and the Benwood sun. I felt ashamed for some of the men who did. I thought: What's the sense of all that? Death must come for all someday, someway, and this way seemed so clean: here in this dry, black room that we had carved out of the boweled, bituminous darkness of the earth.

I ate my lunch, I finished every crumb. The company officials argued among themselves four hundred feet above. Some among them said there was a chance that one or two men had survived down there. But the mine was burning. And mine is property. And the only way to quench a burning mine is to seal it airtight. If they left the mine to burn while they sent down brave men searching for survivors, the fire would get a grip. And even if they saved someone the mine would burn for maybe thirty years. And mine is property. At last, the company men agreed—the chance of any of us living was quite slim. And so at last they sealed it at the mouth. The fire was over soon and so were we. We simply fell asleep—simple as that. And up above us four hundred feet the company officials breathed relief. For mine is property. And you can always hire new men.

There's seldom a sound down here. Of course, there's always the rippling earth; the great seams hunch and whisper like the surf of some vast sea of stone. The old earth nudges and shudders in her sleep; restless with a billion years of dreams. And sometimes when there's stillness I can hear, far above me, steamboat paddles a quarter mile away, churning the waterways of the Ohio.

Still, being here is strange. I've come so far. When I was young I never thought of this place, never in wildest dreams imagining that here would be my end. I've traveled far. And I can hardly think how many years it's been since I started out.

In Austria our family was neither poor nor rich. My father ran a little store in Linz. Yet we were a family full of honors. Haydn played at my great-grandfather's wedding. And for generations one of the family heirlooms was a precious letter from Mozart repaying a debt and thanking my great-grandmother for a cake she'd baked and brought him once when he was sick. That letter and a lock of Haydn's hair went up in smoke the night they burned my father's store. It was the day after Luccheni, the assassin, killed the Empress Elizabeth. My father was always talking politics in the coffeehouse; some boys came that night and burned his store. The cruelty and disgrace of what they'd done drove him mad; he ran away that week and none of the family ever saw him again. Years later after I'd come to America, a Slovak agitator in the Pittsburgh steel mills told me he thought he'd known my father, and that he had died in Russia in the 1907 revolution. It is queer but somehow the horror of the fire that night stayed in my memory as something more terrible than my father's disappearance. My fear of fire was something that never left me. Perhaps that's why I was grateful and uncomplaining at dying in the dark coolness of that chamber in the mine.

I settled in Glory in nineteen hundred four. It was Davis Cresap's Mercantile Bank that loaned me the money to build my little notions store on Jefferson Avenue. I'd come to town that year with nothing but a peddler's pack of combs and pewter thimbles and papers of pins. I slept those nights that winter in the B. & O. boxcars down along the river. Davis Cresap took one look at me and loaned me a thousand dollars without collateral. Some of my store I built with my own hands, some of it was the help of kindly neighbors; most of the thousand dollars went for stock to fill the shelves. By the fall of nineteen hundred five I'd paid the thousand back with interest and had enough to send to Europe for my wife Louise and my four sons: Moishe Walter, William Clarke, Luther, and Chaim Mathias. For a while in Apple County it seemed as if I had come at last to the Promised Land, the long ago surrendered earth of my progenitors. For all the country folk had Hebrew names: Jacob and Sarah, Solomon and Rebecca, Abijah and Rachel, Ruth and Nehemiah. It was as if Apple County was the Israel of ancient times. Sometimes I'd forget when waiting on one of them, and speak in the old tongue.

All of my sons came to America with their mother save one: my oldest, Moishe. He stayed and joined the army of Franz Joseph and later transferred to the troops of Germany. And so by 1918 when the Great War was nearly over, I had two sons fighting against each other.

My son Chaim Mathias fought in the AEF and came home decorated personally by President Wilson for wiping out a whole platoon of Germans. I've wondered often, but I've never known. The thought is as terrible to me now as it was then. I remember the opera singer Madame Schumann-Heinck—she had a son on each side fighting, too. And when word came, long months after the armistice, that Moishe had been killed at St. Mihiel, fighting for kaiser and for fatherland, the thought grew more deep and dreadful in my mind. For it was in that battle that my Chaim had won his bloody honors. And Louise never understood it that I kept a gold-framed picture of the singer Schumann-Heinck over the big Victrola in the parlor. And sometimes in the quiet Glory nights I'd come downstairs alone in my night-shirt and play her records in the darkness there. And when I played her "Stille Nacht" that Christmas, Louise was shocked that I should wish to hear a Christian hymn. How could I tell her? That voice, that song was something which I shared with Madame Schumann-Heinck, whose grief, surely, was every bit as big as mine. It was a Christian hymn but it was more. It was the anthem of everyone who since the dawn of time has grieved a war and thought to kill was wrong.

When my boy Chaim came home from the service, his medal's dull shine brightening up his khaki, I could not speak to him. Up in his room he had a canvas suitcase full of souvenirs. A thousand times I thought about those things: imagining them inside that dreadful case. I never asked to see. Chaim never offered to show me. I had a horror lest he should. I knew the things soldiers brought home from wars: fragments of lacy things from Paris sweethearts, maps, reports and commendations. And other things, unspeakable things: snapshots and cigar lighters, cigarettes and volumes of poems, blood-stained diaries and packets of mouldering letters. Nothing that I could do would change my mind from the wild, despairing thought that in that case lay something that Chaim had taken from the body of the brother Moishe he had slain. The chances were improbable, I knew. And yet it was fear as sharp as instinct, and even now in this black, peaceful place I think of it and wonder. I'll never know. And maybe it's best I never do. For God knows in the chance and gamble of a war things stranger than this have happened. Chaim left Glory soon. We could not talk; I simply could not speak. And furthermore I didn't want him to speak. Because I dreaded I would hear him tell me what he had said to me in awful tones in the nightmares of countless anguished nights.

I never heard from him again. He went out West. He disappeared as thoroughly as had my father so many years before. I prayed for him often in the Methodist Church. There is no synagogue in Glory for we were Apple County's only Jews. And prayer is prayer, God is God. For me it doesn't matter where I pray. Churches to me are little different than warring armies, above which something Mighty watches them in mercy and listening pity, pausing from time to time to turn His sacred face away in grief. Louise protests. But I'm the master of this house and master of my spirit as well.

Luther and William Clarke have done well. Luther's in Pittsburgh with Carnegie Institute. He has become an archaeologist. Sometimes down here beneath these tons of earth it seems I hear his spade and bare hands picking, digging and sifting through the bright Muskingum soil of Apple County; young Luther picking and searching through the earth with strange professional desperation. I hear he searches through the Indian mounds of people who lived here three thousand years ago. There's something of furious hunger in his picking; a lone and savage sorrow to his search. I hear he seeks the bones of ancient men and arrowheads and cherts and old campfires. Yet sometimes in my stillness here I smile, and wonder whether Luther's search is simpler than ever he has guessed: that with his mattocks, brushes, spades he is not searching, searching, searching—hoping to find something quite different deep within the earth: the peaceful skull of one old Austrian Jew.

We had so many happy years in Glory: my sons, my wife, and I. And yet I think I always knew that it would end. We were not a people made for peace. Something in the blood and destiny of our family seemed always doomed to downfall. And nothing we wished or did or prayed for different could ever make it change. Our neighbors were so kind through all those years. I remember the long cool mornings by the counter in my little notions store, chatting with Tadd Cockayne about Bryan and the Bull Moose Party and the earthquake in San Francisco, giving little things to neighbors' children, sharing a glass of dandelion wine out back under the coolness of the crabapple tree. Those were sweet times. And then in 1917 all was changed.

It was not something that changed overnight. I'd felt it, sensed it, smelled it coming on. A mutter in the streets, murmurs at nights, the gathering snub of friends, old customers who came one day and never came again. And suddenly I dreamed back in my mind and saw my father's store burning against the sky of that so distant country, long ago. Does the world change? One night Jefferson Avenue was filled with laughing girls, their faces bright and flushed with the desire for love which, strangely, comes with war. Boys in uniform were everywhere. And up by Davis Cresap's Bank on the corner, Elsie Challoner was on a bunting-draped platform and the little Glory band was playing "K-K-K-Katie" and all the war tunes of the day and she was selling Liberty Bonds. That night, after the street grew quiet, and all the town of Glory seemed asleep, I put a record on my big Victrola. It seemed a silly thing to do, I suppose. "Stille Nacht" in the midst of summer. Yet that song was far more than Christmas, don't you see? In the dark parlor I could see the square of the gold frame that hung upon the wall: the shadow of that woman looking at me, and her voice singing with power; a power made more great because the sound came thin and tinny out of the tuliphorn. And there was something between that woman Schumann-Heinck and me that night; something stronger even than anything I'd had with my Louise. "Stille Nacht" in the middle of July! Anyone passing along the sidewalk hearing would have thought me mad. And, in a sense, I was. Mad with the wonder and the awfulness of a question I knew even God could not answer! Why men must hate. Why brother must fight brother. Well, someone, indeed, was in the street that night— a someone who, passing by, heard that thin voice and stopped and listening knew the words were German.

Have you the slightest concept what that one word meant in those grim days? German? For all those listeners cared I might have played "Deutschland Uber Alles" on my Victrola. Meanwhile I had fetched my fiddle from the piano. Many's the night back in the old, good times when Louise and our sons would play together, while I was leader with my father's violin. The record voice sang on and I began to play, softly so as not to wake Louise, perhaps, too, somewhat shameful lest the town should hear me playing Christmas tunes that sweltering Glory night. I didn't see the men gather outside, under the sycamores along the sidewalk. My shop was just next door to our little house. I heard a rock go smashing through the window and someone shouted something in the night, out there beyond the trees. I ran outside, still clutching my bow and fiddle in my hand. There was no moon that night and there was not enough light from the stars for me to see if any of the men wore khaki uniforms. I think they were all quite young. Does it matter? Another

rock went smashing through the window of my store and when upstairs
I heard Louise rising from bed, frightened and bewildered out of sleep,
I called back sternly for her to stay there. I leaned forward a little,
thrusting my head toward the dark cluster of figures on the pavement.

What do you want? I cried. What are you doing?

Hun! shouted one. Baby-killer!

Your own son's over there, ain't he, Jake? another voice cried and it
sounded like young Roy Huggins, one of my best customers of happy
days gone by. Your own boy's in Kaiser Bill's army—raping women in
Belgium, ain't he, Jake!

Hun! another shouted. Dirty German!

I staggered back as if one of their rocks had struck me. My eyes filled
with the hot tears of rage. My mind filled instantly with that terrible
vision of my childhood: my father's burning shop that night in Linz,
the flames billowing up like rags of hate, the sparks indistinguishable
from stars. And then I leaned against the oak tree by my porch and
laughed and smelled the drifting sweetness of the honeysuckle on my
little porch. I laughed and sometimes since I've wondered if they heard
me. I was not even German, I was Austrian. And, in plain matter of fact,
I was neither, being a Jew. So all I had to do, said common sense, was
to reach in my shirt and fetch out the little star of David which hung by
a chain round my neck, and step out there and show it to them. And
say. I am no German. I am a Jew, you fools! I am a Jew!

Is it hard for you to fancy why I laughed? Knowing within my heart
what gathered there, what smouldered and glowed about to burst to
flame, the hatred bunched up out there in the street. And knowing that
in a year or five or six the hatred of these boys against the German
would be a thing they barely could recall. The war with Germany might
last six years. But war with Jews, I knew well in my heart, would live
and last as long as man and his need to hate. I tell you I laughed, leaning against my tree, smelling the summer sweetness of my vines! A rock
came rushing through the air and struck me on the leg. Instantly, the
pain and something else: some stubborn need within me flamed up hot.
I'll let them know what I am, these poor fools! I'll let them know and
they'll not even know.

Come on out, you dirty Hun! bawled a voice in the night, a voice like
every voice of hate I'd ever heard, voice of a different language to be
sure, but just the same the same voice I had heard in twenty different

lands with different tongues. A voice, indeed, like those my father heard the night they threw a torch inside his store. And everything within me bade me fight, but something in me that hasn't perished yet, that even the suffocation here can't quench, something bade me fight their hate with beauty. For a moment I think they actually fell back, hearing my violin there in the shadowed yard; I'd lifted it furiously, tucked it beneath my chin, lifted my bow and threw my heart proudly into their nameless, hating faces by playing Beethoven—one of theirs, one of mine, one of yours, one of God's, one of us the world's!

Someone among them giggled, someone cursed; they thought I had gone mad. It was easier for them, with what they meant to do—thinking that I was mad. I might as well played "Turkey in the Straw" and then gone out and told them Lincoln was Chinese for all it meant to them. But I didn't care! I played on. Beethoven! Beethoven! I have never played so well!

They burned my store that night. My father's stunned and tongueless dread which had sent him fleeing mad across eastern Europe, his shame, the nightmare of my livelong life, was re-enacted now before my eyes.

There are good people in Glory. Louise and I stayed for a while in a room at the Glory Hotel and were not charged one cent. Thank God, my youngest, William Clarke was away at summer school in Cornell studying medicine. Davis Cresap offered to personally lead a drive to raise funds in Glory to rebuild my house and little store which burned that night. But I refused. And thanked him. And said good-by to something; adieu to life, I guess it was. I was forty-eight by then—too old to learn a trade. I found work in the Benwood Mines and Louise and I shared a single room in a boardinghouse in Mingo Junction. There is courage in us all—I have seen it. I have witnessed braveness beyond measure in others and myself. And yet I know that when the cord is broken—the golden cord that binds our spirits whole—there's nothing, not even God, can mend it back. And so it was in me—the broken cord.

It's queer—I went back in the ruins that morning. I found the photograph of Schumann-Heinck. The gold was gone, the varnished frame was blistered, the glass was scorched and blackened but not cracked. The picture was still hot as though with something in it angered for my sake. I wiped the black from off the glass and saw the face beneath it almost plain as ever. Again that woman's eyes and my eyes met and touched and spoke, saying some sacred things. In the panic and madness of running in the yard that night, I'd dropped my violin and smashed it under my feet. So that all I had left in the world of all we'd saved and treasured and built in Glory was that picture, which even yet reeks of holocaust. And yet that picture and that woman's face were somehow the finest treasure that I owned. Louise and I got by, I learned the mines. Things went on for a little while all right.

My youngest boy William finished medical school. He went to Washington, studied Public Health. He's back in Glory now working with that woman—Davis Cresap's daughter—somehow her name always escapes me. Marcy! Yes, that's it. Young Marcy Cresap and my boy William. The town has risen up to fight them now. The strong men in the Court House every day call the young Cresap girl most everything. They've hurled a thousand insults in her face—they've called her by a thousand scurrilous names. But there's just one name that they call my boy. They call him Jew and, for them, that's enough.

Even when he was young I loved him best. I'm proudest of him now— my William Clarke. Luther digs up the bones of dead men, studies them a while, frowns in puzzlement because they do not answer. Luther, my dear boy, leave the dead their sleep! Moishe by now's been plowed up by some farmer, and feeds the young French corn with flesh I fathered. God only knows where Chaim is—out West. He's got his medal and his trunk of things. Things that I never wish to know or see or touch. But William Clarke works with Marcy Cresap. They fight together for free health in the schools. My boy William Clarke fights disease! His is the war that's fought to keep men living. Isn't that wonderful, somehow— when you think of it? My youngest and beloved William Clarke. You know, I think this fight is good for him. I think it's good for him to hear them shouting: Jew! Jew! Jew! Because he's young and has so much to learn. And yet as I lie here beside my comrades, four hundred feet below the new and prospering Benwood Mine, I sometimes think that when my boy is older and wiser in the genius of his science, maybe he'll go alone into some room, and suffer there and ponder there for years, experimenting time and time again as men have always done—Pasteur and Schick. And after a while he'll come out weary-faced, but shining-eyed with wisdom in his hands, and maybe some new vaccination in his head and tell the world how he has fought to make our little time on earth less hard. Typhoid and Scarlet Fever—my boy knows these cures, or at least how to keep men from getting them. And yet—and yet—someday—and this hope and this prayer, this tough conviction, makes these bones to come alive and wake, to shine and sing a psalm here in my dark!—Someday my boy shall peer into his glass and see the germ that makes men call him Jew!—and hate and hate and hate him all for that. And he shall turn to them with caring eyes. And he will heal them with those two Jew hands.

Other Johnson

I've done some bad things in my day but murder is not amongst them.
My life's packed full of enough sins to keep a preacher busy for a year
and never talk about the same sin twice. But not even a preacher could
say I pulled the trigger that killed Fletcher Bledsoe down at Captina
that winter night. And nothing anyone can ever say or do can make me
say I did, no matter what they do to me.

My father Macabee Johnson was a proud man and a Christian. His
skin was that kind of deep and lusterless black you don't see much
among Negro folks these days. On the other hand, my mother Lulu
Annie was almost white—lighter than a yellow girl; she could almost
have passed. Between the two of them they had thirteen children. I was
the twelfth. My cousin Hagar says the May morning I was born my
father came in from work, took one look at me nursing there at mother's
breast, and he said, What!—another Johnson. I guess maybe they'd
just about run out of names for babies by then because that's what they

started calling me from that day on—Other Johnson—and that's what I was christened. My mother bore one more child after me and my father decided that was enough. That's the reason he had my youngest brother baptised Macabee Quits. My folks were poor and they were ignorant but I've never been ashamed of them. My grandfather Jeremiah fought for three years in the Confederate army and died down in Tennessee at Chickamauga. I'm proud of my people even if they were only impoverished and superstitious field Negroes. Yet even though I've struggled all my life to improve myself, I've never once thought of myself as better than them. For all the misery of their lives they left me with a strong body, a brave spirit, and a faith in God.

When I was seventeen I used to do odd jobs for the wife of Mister Armph Smithers who's now the Glory Chief of Police. He was a brakeman back then for the Ohio River Division of the B. & O. and his job kept him away from home a good bit of the time. Mrs. Smithers was a slight, brown-eyed woman with rich chestnut hair that she always kept in a neat little bun at the back of her neck. She was one of the stillest persons I ever met; her face was so calm and quiet that you'd never guess she'd ever had a thought or trouble in her mind. I used to keep the yard clean, carry ashes up from the cellar, cut wood for the smoke-house and to help Mrs. Smithers carry jars up from the basement and scald them during the canning season. In the spring and summer I used to take care of their garden: hoeing the corn, picking bugs and cut-worms, and put new stakes up for the tomato plants as they grew. I got a dollar a week and my lunch every day, promptly as the schoolhouse bell struck noon.

In the beginning Mrs. Smithers never said much; telling me what she wanted done in as few words as possible. Her voice was so soft and meek you could hardly understand what she said and her face always seemed to hold that same expression of peace as tranquil as the waters of a pool. But soon I noticed, when I'd be sitting there eating my lunch out on the canning table on the back porch, she would stop her work at the stove and look up to stare at me through the kitchen door. I am black as my father Macabee and I thought for a while she was looking at me as a novelty, with all the brown and light-skinned Negroes around Glory. On my eighteenth birthday Mrs. Smithers brought me out my lunch as usual and then she went back in and commenced fooling around the stove and presently she came back out and put a little birthday cake on the table before me. I was so embarrassed and confused I just stared at the green beans and ham on my plate.

Happy birthday, Other, said Mrs. Smithers, and still nothing had changed in her expression and her tone.

I thank you kindly, ma'am, I said.

And she folded her arms and stared at me a while more.

I bet you wonder how I knew it was today, she said. Well, I went up to the courthouse last month and looked it up in the birth records. And that's how I knew.

Yes'm, I said, sitting there like a fool, staring at my beans, afraid somehow to look at the little white cake she'd baked.

You're a fine young man, Other, she said. And I wanted to do something nice for you on your eighteenth birthday.

Thank you, Mrs. Smithers, I said, and stole a look at the cake; it was beautiful, all right. But I knew somehow I couldn't touch it. There was something about the whole business that scared me. All of a sudden Mrs. Smithers turned and went back indoors. Directly I could hear her sewing machine rattling away upstairs. I never touched a crumb of that cake. There was something about it dangerous; a thing that almost seemed to warn me. She gave me a fruit-cake box to take it home in. On the way home I dropped the box off the Grave Creek trestle into the water. I know it was an ungrateful thing to do but I couldn't help it. There's no way I could have explained that cake away to my father or mother when I got home. There was no way I could explain it to myself either.

It was nearly a week before Mrs. Smithers spoke to me again. I mean about anything personal like the cake had been. I was down in the basement putting a fresh coat of whitewash on the stones of the little cool room where she kept her mason jars of canned things in shelves along the walls. Suddenly I realized that Mrs. Smithers had come halfway down the cellar steps and was standing there watching me. I felt that cold foreboding sense again. But this time there was a warm feeling with it. And the warm feeling scared me worse than the cold one did.

Come up to the living room, Other, she said. I want you to help me move some furniture.

I washed the whitewash off as best I could at the old pump by the coalbin. I went upstairs. But my legs were trembling every step, like all the strength was going out of them. When I went in the parlor Mrs.

Smithers had taken the muslin cover off one of the chairs and was sitting their staring at me. It didn't look to me like she needed any furniture moved, especially at that time of year when it was spring and all the chairs and davenport were still covered with white sheets. The blinds were drawn and the white shapes of those things in that room were like ladies in white Easter dresses standing around watching.

Lordy, it's warm for the month of May, Mrs. Smithers said. I think I'll rest a minute before we start moving that furniture.

Yes'm, I said. I'll go back on down to the cellar and get the white-washing done. You can call me when you're ready, Mrs. Smithers.

She didn't say anything right away, not till I was halfway toward the door.

Other, she said, wait. There's no hurry about that whitewashing. Sit down and rest a spell. Pull that cover off the little chair yonder and sit down, Other.

Now, there's one thing I wish to get straight. I am a man and a human being and I know my worth in the sight of God. Right now you're probably thinking about some of my race who are ashamed of being Negroes and scared to death of doing something wrong around white folks. I mean the kind that's always yes'n this and yes'n that and afraid to act even human for fear white folks will think they're what they mean when they use that word: uppity. My father's poor and he's ignorant but he's a man I have always loved and respected. I know my value. It wasn't that I felt I wasn't as good as Mrs. Smithers that made me feel funny about sitting in that chair across from her. I have never crawled nor truckled to any man because of my race. Still it seemed to me that day that some things are fitting and some are not. I was a dollar-a-week handyman and Mrs. Smithers was my employer. It seemed I had no business loafing around that parlor with her that day. And besides, I had that feeling again—there was something queer about it all, parts of it didn't dove-tail somehow; I felt a danger to it like you feel a thunderstorm in the summer air long hours before it comes. Like when you lay your ear to a rail and hear the rushing of the train come thundering miles and miles away.

Besides, Mrs. Smithers went on. I like talking to you, Other. You're always so respectful and you work so hard—I never get a chance to know what's in your mind. You're intelligent and I can tell you're sensitive.

What you mean is I'm intelligent and sensitive for a Negro, I said.

I knew before I said it that it was impudent but I couldn't keep it back. I had felt somehow as if Mrs. Smithers was trying to make a fool out of me.

No, she said. That's not what I meant. I mean you're a fine young man with a good mind and keen instincts. And that has nothing to do with being white or black either one.

She sighed and looked away toward the drawn blinds.

I'm sorry you misunderstood me, Other, she said. I was only trying to be kind. And I wanted to be your friend.

I looked at her there: that expressionless, pretty face of hers almost showing sadness and something in her voice that sounded as gentle as Mother's. I felt ashamed of my impudence. I felt as if I'd been ungrateful to someone who really liked me.

I'm sorry I said what I did, Mrs. Smithers, I said.

Then please sit down a minute, she said. I won't bite you. It's such a lonely place, this world, and life's so short—and there's not many times that people can ever really talk.

I felt worse than ever. It's an awful streak in me: that stubbornness and suspicion. This wasn't the first time it had made a fool of me. I sat down in the little chair and pressed my hands flat upon my close pressed knees. I stared miserably at the pattern in the oriental rug.

Will you be my friend, Other? asked Mrs. Smithers. Or are you afraid to let yourself be kind and human?

No, ma'am, I said. I am not afraid of anything.

Then do me a favor, said Mrs. Smithers. Share with me a little glass of dandelion wine and show me you're not afraid to be my friend.

All right, I said. Thank you, Mrs. Smithers.

I never told her how my father and mother and my cousin Hagar feel about strong spirits. Big as I am, my father would have beaten me half to death if ever he'd caught me with a tincup of liquor in my hands. I didn't want that dandelion wine. But still it seemed I had to make it up somehow to Mrs. Smithers for acting the way I had. So I drank it.

And now it's years later and I know enough about hooch to know that wasn't any dandelion wine in that glass. My head began to whirl and my legs felt like jelly. Still I felt a queer, new freedom stirring inside me and a kind of warmth that spread up from my legs like some sort of a good-feeling fever. I'd never had a drink before. That's why I drank it down so fast, I guess. I looked at Mrs. Smithers. Her face was a little pink and there was a cluster of tiny beads of perspiration on her upper lip. But her face was still calm and expressionless. Except for the smallest smile in the world as she looked at me. I wanted to get up and see if I could walk around. But I was afraid to try. It seemed certain I would fall flat down on that oriental rug and make a worse fool of myself than ever. The liquor was like a stoked fire in my breast; I felt strong and proud and confident. It seemed to me that I had been a child for eighteen years and now in a twinkling I was a man. I wanted to kiss Mrs. Smither's hands and thank her. The gratitude I felt seemed like a hot, swelling warmth in my loins. Mrs. Smithers stood up. She looked at me with something fresh in her dark eyes and walked out of the room. I listened to her footsteps climbing the stairs. I sat there, waiting, wondering if I had said something without realizing it and made her mad. For a second some of the old, childish fear leaped back. But it was gone a moment later. Mrs. Smithers seemed gone an hour. But it was the drink that made it seem like that, I guess. Because I heard her voice directly speaking to me from the top of the stairs.

Other, she said. Would you come up here?

Something in me wanted to run; something else didn't. I wondered if I could walk or not. But when I stood up, my legs seemed to work better than they had in all my life. It was as if I floated on that oriental rug, and all the tiredness from lifting that whitewash brush all morning was gone. Still something deep inside me whispered, Danger. But I refused to hear it. I went upstairs.

I'm in here, Mrs. Smithers said from the bedroom.

I opened the door and went inside. She had changed her clothes and it seemed to me she was wearing less. She had on some kind of shiny, silk Japanese coat and it was so long I could hardly see that her feet were bare. There was something sad now in her face, and something else: a kind of glazed and lazy warmness in her eyes. Her mouth was different, too. It was open a little and it looked as though her breath was coming hard. Suddenly that face which had always seemed unchanging as a mask swiftly altered. She shut her eyes and her white teeth came out and bit her lower lip and big tears began streaming down her cheeks.

Oh, I'm sorry, Other! she moaned. I'm sorry. But I'm lonely. I'm nearly crazy with loneliness! I'm sorry, Other! Forgive me, please!

And without opening her eyes or taking her teeth from her lip she reached up suddenly, opened the Japanese coat and let it fall around her

feet. I had never seen a naked woman before. As close as we all lived
in that old ramshackle house below the tannery down on Water Street,
I'd never ever seen my mother naked. I'd never even seen any of my
sisters bare except when they were babies and that doesn't count. Macabee Johnson would have skinned any of his women if he'd ever caught
them running naked where one of us boys could see. I'd seen the pictures the children drew with chalk on the sidewalks back of the school.
But they were nothing like this. Those pictures were like sticks. Mrs.
Smithers naked was like a slender young apple tree full of fruit. The
bun at the back of her neck was undone and the long tresses of her
chestnut hair fell on either side of her small, round breasts. All the
scaredness vanished and the warmness took command of everything. I
thought I had never seen anything beautiful before in all my life till
then. But still she was crying, her head bowed, the tears dropping to
the small pink nipples of her breasts.

I'm sorry, Other, she sobbed. Oh God, forgive me if you can, Other.
But I'm so lonely. Armph's away so much my loneliness almost has me
mad! Are you frightened of me, poor boy? Forgive me! I've watched
you so long—a thousand lunchtimes I have watched you, Other! And I
know you've never been with a woman! Forgive me, Other. I've scared
you! And I wanted only to give you something warm and kind—the
only part of me that I can give. Forgive me! Oh, forgive me. Am I ugly
to you? Is it repulsive to you—seeing me like this? Will it help any if
I stop my crying? Wait! I'll be all right! Oh, no. You *are* scared of
me! I can see it. I'm ugly to you. Then go away. And forgive me if
you can!

It went on all that summer. At first it was only once a week and then
it got like a hunger out of hand. I dreamed of her white beauty every
night. At night I slept with a wash-rag in my mouth for fear my father
would hear me talking in my sleep: saying her name, or maybe saying
those words she taught me to say to her when we did it. They were the
words the boys used to write, down on board fences by the tannery. But
now she had made me say them shamelessly, she'd made me think of
them as words of beauty. In years to come I used to think about her
face: that mask of quietude and cool respectability. Who could have
guessed what passion and savage affection lay behind it? I've had my
share of women since that summer. But nothing to compare with what
she was: those fingernails that ripped and raked my back, her small

white teeth biting my black shoulder till it bled. And that voice of hers: always so soft and calm, yet when we did it her voice would gasp and choke, whispering those words furiously in my ear and then, toward the end, spitting the love words out in a grating scream.

The war with Germany broke out that year and I joined up. I saw a world I never knew there was. Even with her I'd never known there was any other place but Glory. It seemed till then that all the world there was was a land bounded by river in the west and by the quick rising hills against the east. I learned another world while I was away. I learned to drink and slept with women in the French farms: more women than I can count, I'm ashamed to say. I thought I'd become a man that day in Mrs. Smithers' parlor with the drink burning in my stomach. But I wasn't really a man until that War. I came home to Glory in the spring of 1919. It seemed a dull old town after all that. I lazed around the house and rolled cigarettes and my father never said a word: He was so proud of me. I didn't do a fool thing that whole spring. And never once in all that time did I ever think of Mrs. Smithers. But that didn't mean she wasn't thinking about me. I was walking past her house on Purdy Avenue that afternoon. Funny, I'd even forgotten where she lived. Suddenly I heard a woman's voice say my name. I turned and saw her sitting in the rocker on the front porch.

Other, she said. It's good to see you home.

Evenin', Mrs. Smithers, was all I said, and something in me wanted to get away from there.

Come around to the back, Other, she said.

I understood her not wanting me to walk right up to her there on the front porch. There'd be talk in Glory or maybe worse and I didn't want any trouble right then for either of us. I was feeling pretty important and good those days; I didn't want anything to upset the applecart. I had on my work clothes so it looked all right. I went around back and saw her coming out the kitchen door.

Come inside, Other, she said, and I did.

She looked at me with that old calm, unruffled stare of hers a minute.

You've been home nearly six weeks, Other, she said. Why couldn't you take the trouble to come around?

I've been mighty busy, Mrs. Smithers, I lied. Busy what with one thing or the other.

Aren't you going to give me a kiss? she said, so I did, but it wasn't any good; there wasn't any more feeling to it than when I come home and kiss my sister Alberta on the cheek.

So it's that way now, is it? said Mrs. Smithers.

Which way? I said. I don't know what you mean?

Have you got a girl? she said. I guess all the Heroes of the Argonne have girls, don't they?

I wasn't any Hero of the Argonne, Mrs. Smithers, I said. I wasn't in anything like a war, really. I was in one of the sanitation units they had to take care of company latrines.

But just the same, she said. Nothing is the same, is it? I mean, you've found out there was a bigger world than Glory and plenty of women in it, isn't that right?

No, ma'am, I said. I mean—well, I still want us to be good friends.

You do, do you? she said, her face never changing. And that's all. None of the way things were before. Give me another kiss.

I started to, I reached out to her, but I just couldn't go through with it. Something was gone. Maybe she was right. The world out there: the one beyond Glory, the bigger world. It had changed me inside.

Yes, she said. I was right. That's the way things are now.

She looked at me with her dark eyes gone cold and hard a minute more.

We'll see about that, Other, she said. We'll just see about that.

I looked at her; I couldn't believe she had been as hard as that before, it had to be something that had happened inside her since. But I knew it wasn't. I'd learned the world out there. I'd come back knowing she had always been that way. She kept on looking at me and suddenly her big eyes narrowed to slits of hate.

Well, maybe we'll see about that, she said. My husband quit his job on the B. & O. last winter. He's got a new one. He's something pretty important now—he's Glory's new chief of police.

I haven't done anything wrong, I said. Mrs. Smithers, what's the police got on me?

Not the police, she said. The chief of police. I'm his wife—remember? Other, I think you'd better give all this a second thought. I mean, before you decide to stop what we had together.

But, Mrs. Smithers, I've changed, I said. I've grown up this year. I wasn't a man back then—I was still a boy. And a man changes his mind about a lot of things when he leaves off being a boy.

Does he? she said. Well, I haven't changed my mind. Not about a thing. Is it my husband you're afraid of now? He's still away from the house most of the time. I hardly see him from breakfast till midnight. Is that it? Are you afraid?

No, ma'am, I lied.

Quit calling me ma'am, she said. If I remember rightly you used to use a lot more fancy names to me than that. Don't let me hear you call me ma'am again. It sounds like a yardboy.

I was a yardboy once, Mrs. Smithers, I said. And content at being that.

Is that so? she said. Well, you weren't any yardboy up there in my husband's bed.

Mrs. Smithers, don't be mad, I said. Let's keep on being friends. I'll even come and do the work I used to do. And I won't charge you a cent.

You don't mean the work you used to do for me up in the bedroom, she said. I don't remember you ever charged me for that, either.

I think I better be going, Mrs. Smithers, I said.

I don't think so, she said. No, I don't think so at all, Other.

She looked hard at me a minute and then an idea seemed to hit her; her face softened and she came up against me and put her tongue in my ear. I couldn't help it. I pushed her away, holding her back at arm's length. That's when her face began to go to pieces. And it was a queer thing. I remembered her face being like that before: the times when we were up there in her bed and I was doing it to her. And suddenly it was plain that what she was feeling now wasn't much different, actually, from that. I've had enough women out in the world since then to know. Those times up there she had been fighting me, hating me, using me; maybe I was like some kind of weapon she could use to hurt someone. Or maybe hurt herself. I wanted to get away from her so bad it was awful. I was scared. Even when I sailed off to War and not knowing what was coming or what War would be like I hadn't been so scared.

Think about it, Other, she said.

Think about what, Mrs. Smithers? I said.

You know, she said. Think what might happen here in Glory if a lot of prominent and well-to-do white folks found out Armph Smithers' wife had been raped by a nigger.

In a week I was trapped. I'd worried myself half sick thinking what Mrs. Smithers could do to me and probably would and I commenced to drink. That was my big mistake. Or maybe it wouldn't have mattered; maybe they'd have gotten me anyway in the end. One night I was upstairs in a combination poolroom and saloon down at Captina. I saw the argument start. I know the name of the man who started it. And I know he was on the payroll of the Glory Police Department. I hardly knew Fletcher Bledsoe, the man who got shot that cold, winter night. He was a crapshooter and a gambler and a waterfront brawler: I knew that. He hadn't hardly hit the floor till the Chief of Police Armph Smithers came through the door. He beat me with his billy till his arm got tired, I guess. I never raised a hand to him for I knew that's what he wanted. I knew if I lifted a finger to that man he'd shoot me on the spot. I might have been a Negro all my life; that night I was a nigger.

They took me in to Apple County Courthouse and booked me for Fletcher Bledsoe's murder. Two days later Mr. Ansel Carruthers, the prosecuting attorney and Mr. Charles Wofford, the County Judge, came to the jail to see me.

Skippy, said Mr. Carruthers. I think I know a way we can save this nigger from the gallows.

How's that, Anse, said the Judge, and I could tell by the way they were saying the words that they'd figured them all out before.

The only way I know, said Mr. Carruthers, is for him to plead guilty of first-degree murder.

How's that gonna work, Anse? said the Judge, as knowing as could be.

If he pleads guilty, said Mr. Carruthers, the case won't go to a jury. The case will go to you, Skippy. Now, you don't want to see this poor nigger hang, do you? After all, it was only another nigger that he killed. And a worthless, shiftless, trouble-making nigger at that. If it was a white man it'd be different. But it was only a nigger, Skippy!

Well, what will happen if he pleads not guilty, Anse? said the Judge, and I felt like throwing up my jail-breakfast I was so disgusted with this game they were playing with me.

Well, said Mr. Carruthers, shaking his head. If his case goes before a jury there's about one chance in ten he'll get off with anything less than the death penalty. Still, there's a chance of maybe Life—and if that's the odds he wants to play, then there's nothing you and me can do about it.

Then Mr. Carruthers looked at me and bit off the tip of a Wheeling stogie and spit it out.

Well, what about it, boy? he said. Do you want to play along with us? Plead Guilty and we'll guarantee you here and now that you won't go to the gallows. Plead Not Guilty and the probabilities are you will. Well, what do you say?

But I didn't do it, I said.

That doesn't matter, said Mr. Carruthers. Maybe you did and maybe you didn't. What matters is how you're going to plead.

I'll not plead guilty, I said, to something I didn't do.

Even if it means your life? said Mister Wofford, the Judge.

I thought about it a minute.

Even if it means my life, I said.

Mr. Carruthers waved his head toward the door: he wanted Judge Wofford to leave him alone with me so he could do some more persuading, lawyer-style. When we were alone together Mr. Carruthers stuck his head real close to mine.

Listen, you damned fool coon, he said. Your trouble is you don't know anything about the Law. Now, what this county wants is a conviction. Nobody wants your neck—not even the Chief of Police. All anybody wants is a conviction.

Is that what the Law means? I said. A conviction?

Law, said Mr. Carruthers. Or politics. It's the goods you deliver. That's all people want. And if you repeat that in court I'll deny it.

But I didn't do it, I said.

Well, suppose you didn't, said Mr. Carruthers, and I knew all of a sudden that he knew I hadn't done it. What's that got to do with it? We want a conviction. Can't you get that clear? Plead guilty and your case will be heard before Judge Wofford. And Judge Wofford and I both give you our word of honor that when Skippy tries your case he won't give you the death penalty. Isn't that enough? Our word of honor?

Your word of honor is shit, I said.

The next morning the jailer came and said there was a lady to see me. Come to think of it, he said it was a woman—not a lady. And you could tell by his tone what kind of woman he meant. Directly she came into my cell. She said her name was Cresap. She said she'd known my father and mother for thirty years in Apple County and once when I was little she got an old doctor named Cecil to come paint my throat when I had the tonsillitis. She said she didn't think I was guilty but she wanted to know from me.

Did you kill him, Other? Miss Cresap said.

I didn't, Miss Cresap, I said. On God's name I swear it.

I wanted to tell her all about Mrs. Smithers and the things that we did before I went to France but I didn't. Bad off as I was, it didn't seem like a gentleman should betray a woman in things like love. The funny thing was Miss Cresap knew all about it.

Has the woman's husband threatened you? she said.

Which woman? I said.

Has Chief of Police Smithers been in your cell and abused you in any way, Other? she said.

No, Miss Cresap, I said.

Then why is your cheek and your left eye swelled up that way? she said. Where did you get those cuts on your forehead?

I looked at the floor. Maybe I was paying for it. Maybe it all was something due me. My father and mother had raised me better. Still I wouldn't have done it that first time if it hadn't been for that drink she gave me. And then upstairs—it was the first time I'd ever seen a woman that way. It seemed like the first beautiful thing I'd ever seen. It was something I remembered like Adam might look back to Eden on that first dawn when the Lord woke him up with that rib gone.

I tripped and fell, I said. When they was taking me up the Courthouse steps, Miss Cresap.

She looked at me and shook her head; her eyes were kind, though.

You didn't kill that rascal Bledsoe, did you, Other? she said.

No, ma'am, I said.

Then how are you going to plead? Miss Cresap asked. Guilty or Not Guilty?

I didn't do it, I said. I'm a man. I'm the child of proud people. And maybe I'm stubborn—maybe that's it. I've done some bad things in my life, Miss Cresap, but I have never done murder. And I won't tell any court anywhere that I'm guilty of something I never did.

Not even if it means your life? Miss Cresap said.

Not even if it means my life, I said, and I knew I meant it.

Miss Cresap looked at me a minute. Then she sat down on the bench they give me to sleep on. She covered her face in her hands and I could see her shoulders gently shaking. I wished I hadn't said anything to make her cry. All I had said was God's truth. I laid my hand on her shoulder and patted it and then I left it there. But she brushed it off and softly cursed into her fingers.

Why does it always have to be money? she murmured. God damn it, why does life and death in Apple County always hang on a cross of gold? If I had money I could get you the best lawyer in Wheeling and have you out of this in three weeks. It's always money! God damn it, why? Is gold Glory's curse?—is money the price of life in Apple County? Babies dying of diphtheria, young mothers choking to death with TB! Typhoid!—Scarlet Fever—Syphilis! And this—yes maybe this the dirtiest sickness of them all!

She came to my trial. She sat there every minute of the four days. And when I got the sentence to life imprisonment she covered her face with her hands the way she had that day and cried again. Long after that, on the prison farm at Camp Fairchance, I told an old bank robber about those two times. He said I was a liar. He said nobody in Glory had ever seen Marcy Cresap cry. But he's wrong. I saw her twice. And since I caught TB inside the walls she began to fight to get me paroled so I could go to the sanatorium at Terre Alta. But that wouldn't work. So she swung it with the prison board for me to get transferred out to the prison farm where I'd get a little sun and fresh air and the fresh vegetables we grow. She comes to see me nearly every week. And brings me a few old books or a little money for the library I've got started here. It's something I thought up to keep busy; to keep from getting a little crazy from the life here, and something to give the other men a chance to read a story now and then.

I've had a lot of time to think out here at Camp Fairchance. I've thought about Father—my mother died last year and I know it was from grieving over me. I've thought about those queer days working for Mrs. Smithers and growing up and how calm and quiet her face always was, despite the crazy want and rage behind it. I've thought about that first time, too, and the terrible anguished loneliness in her face up there in her room that day. That was real. Even if she called me nigger afterward, that day she clutched me as a man our first time there. She's lonely again now—I know it. I can feel it. And I feel sorry for her loneliness. I always think of her with some strange thanks in mind. Because that day in her bedroom I was something she loved in some sad, crippled way. I was a man that morning. It wasn't till after that that I was nigger. And what she woke in me is a splendor yet! Just in remembering it!— I'll never forget! I was so young, I didn't know a thing. And by some blind and twisted way she taught me life. I'll never forget myself as I was then: like Adam blinking his eyes in stunned astonishment and ecstasy among the world's first dawn. So now I am out here and she's back there. We're both locked up for life—each in our way. Both of us serving sentences till we die: Me in my prison here among the corn.— her in her bare feet pacing a loveless room.

Private Lloyd Eldreth Weaver

When I was alive in Glory the only time anyone ever noticed that my right chest was gone was when I stood against the wind. That's when it would blow against my shirt and press it against the big hollow where my ribs and chest used to be. That's most likely the reason none of the fellows up at the Legion Hall liked me coming around there for a drink or a game of stud. I served for two years with the infantry in the Great War and when I came home from Walter Reed Hospital in 1920 they made me a member of the David Rogerson Memorial Chapter American Legion Glory Post Number Twelve. Still there never was a time until my death in 1927 that the boys didn't edge away from me when I came to the bar for a drink. I guess I can't much blame them. Everybody up there was always swapping stories about how thrilling and wonderful those years in France were. For a lot of those fellows it was the only important three years in their lives. Most of them were nothing before and they were nothing after. So those three years were something to

181

hang on to and remember and talk about. All the patriotism and bravery and glory of that time! It was only natural for them not to want someone hanging around who was a walking testament to the other side of war. There wasn't much glory about the gas attack that caught me two miles behind the French lines in the fall of 1918. The boys up at the Legion Hall wouldn't have minded somebody with a nice clean wound like a piece of shrapnel in his shoulder. But whenever they'd see me walking toward the bar or a card table they'd move away or look in the other direction. It was as if they had seen something in me that made them ashamed of something.

Mom always knew how they snubbed me up there. But she claimed it wasn't because of my caved-in chest at all. It is true that I always wore my old army jacket to keep it from showing. Though everybody knew that under the right side of that jacket there was nothing at all. But Mom claimed they snubbed me because I was born a woods colt. That's a name that means a bastard. Mom was a lonesome country girl from Silver Hill back in 1896 and she lost her head in Zack Lindsay's buggy one night and nine months later I first saw the light of Apple County. It's a queer fact but it's true that back in the country and amongst the really little towns of only eight or ten houses nobody treats a woods colt different from any other child. They may giggle and poke fun at the mother but a baby is a baby and there's always room somehow for one more at the table.

In bigger towns like Glory folks feel different about such things. I know for a fact that they always felt different about me and when I was a boy and a mother looked out and saw her boy playing with me she'd always come to the window and yell for him to come indoors. I never blamed them for it. But still it did make me feel different. I used to loaf a lot alone down around the river bank gigging for frogs or fishing for cats or maybe just staring at the water, the way it was at sunset when it looked like the old Ohio had a billion diamonds floating on top. Or maybe I'd stand for an hour or two waiting to see the *Queen City* or the *Wheeling-Sunfish* packet go by. I was a lonesome boy, I guess. I know I never felt as if I amounted to much. Maybe that's why when the Great War broke out it seemed a chance for me to go somewhere and amount to something. I thought of some of the old Apple County men who used to loaf around the Court House porch talking about Bull Run, Kerntown and Lookout Mountain. And sometimes I'd hang around Ike Mobley's clothing store listening to Cap Evans telling about when he rode up San Juan Hill with Teddy Roosevelt. In those days war to me was flags and drums and danger and a chance to amount to something. Nobody ever bothered to tell me about gas. It's a funny thing about wars and the way men like to remember them. I was only ten years old but I remember the Panic of 1907. Now panics and wars is both terrible things to hit a country. But they're different as night and day. In a war men dress up in uniforms and march and amount to something; in a panic they're lucky if they've got shoes and they slouch and loaf instead of marching: in the eyes of friends and family they don't amount to a thing. In some ways a panic hits a country worse than a war. Still it's always wars they put up statues to. I've seen a lot of courthouse yards around West Virginia but I've yet to see one where they put up a statue to the memory of a depression.

Mom always swore Zack Lindsay was my father. She said he was the only one it could be because he was the only man she ever let come near her. But Zack Lindsay spent thirty years denying that I was his son. Zack owns seventy acres of land on Roberts' Ridge and he has a hundred head of registered Jersey cows and the biggest dairy business in Apple County. In the Great War he was a Colonel of the Infantry and before that he was in the Cavalry fighting Pancho Villa down in Mexico under General Pershing. He's a man who amounts to something here in Glory. I reckon some men would be proud to have Zack Lindsay for a father. I'm not one of them. I hate like sin to doubt Mom's word but I hope to the Lord she's wrong. It's something I don't want to believe. Because every time I've ever come in the Legion Hall when Zack Lindsay's there he snubs me the worst of all the rest. But I guess that's because he was a colonel and I wasn't nothing but a dumb old buck private. I hope that's it. It's the queerest feeling in the world, going around never knowing who your own father was. It's like having a head full of respect and just dying for someone to give it to.

Not that I didn't respect Mom. And love her, too. We used to live down on Water Street near the wharf-boat in a little house with a big willow tree in the yard. Mom took in washings for a living all her life. I can see her yet, stooped over her washtub on the little bench in the willow tree's shade, with Octagon soapsuds up to her armpits, scrubbing out somebody's long underwear on her little washboard. I don't think there ever was a woman in Apple County worked so hard for so many years as Mom did. And never once complained. And she was too proud ever to go to anyone for charity, even when things was hard and rations short. I remember how everyone was complaining about the hard times back during the panic in 1907. But for Mom and me there never was much special about a panic: there just seemed like there was more of us in it. Still we got by pretty good. There always seemed there was plenty on the table at suppertime. It may not have been eats as fancy as they serve up in the Mound Hotel dining room but I never walked away from Mom's table empty.

There's a woman here in Apple County by the name of Marcy Cresap. A lot of folks love her. But a lot of folks hate her, too. And I doubt if there's a man in Glory hates her more than Zack Lindsay. And there is two big reasons why; two things she done to make him so sore he like to had a stroke. The first one was about me. When I come out of Walter Reed and they give me my train fare back to Glory I wasn't much better than I was when I went in. I hadn't been home two days before Marcy come to see me. I can see Mama yet, coming up from the yard, rubbing her nose with her sudsy hand and trying to fix her hair so's she'd look nice. Marcy had her husband Lou with her and he was a doctor. Marcy's husband took me up town to his little office and ran some X rays on me and thumped and listened around and made me spit in a cup. A week later Marcy come back to the house with the news that I was going to have to have my lung and five ribs took out of the right side.

I went down to the wharf-boat that night and me and Jellico Newby, the wharfmaster got drunk on some Wheeling bootleg whisky. I went a little crazy and Jellico claims I jumped in the river to drown myself and if he hadn't fetched me back to wharfside with a gaff hook and hauled me out I would have made it. The next week Marcy Cresap fetched me off to the Glendale Hospital and they done the operation. And when I was strong enough to get around the ward she shipped me off to Terre Alta to spend a year trying to get built back up. Zack Lindsay got mad as hell at that. He jumped on Marcy first and then he come down to the house and bawled poor Mom out. He said he was one of the biggest contributors in Apple County to the Christmas Seal drive. And he said they had no business spending all that money on me because what I had wasn't TB, it was gas.

I come home in a year, still sick as a cat and looking like I'd been flogged out of hell with a pine thong. I had circles under my eyes as dark as dusk and so hollow you could have stuck two grapes in them and they wouldn't have fallen out. I dreaded to shave in the morning for having to look at my face. It was a face like Death eating a cracker and the smallpox scars I'd had since I was twelve looked deeper than ever. That face of mine made me think of the wall of a white stone barn in Picardy where they used to line men up and shoot them: it looked like a thousand men had been shot against my face and nobody'd bothered to patch the bullet holes.

Well, Zack Lindsay raved on and on for nearly a year and when Christmas come he went around Glory telling everyone not to give to the TB drive because that woman Marcy Cresap was misappropriating the funds. I felt just terrible. I wished to God Marcy had left me as I was rather than get the whole town up against her. I thought of all the good people who wouldn't get help for the TB all because of me and that damned gassed lung of mine. But if it wasn't that it was something else. Because in two years Zack Lindsay started out after Marcy Cresap worse than ever. Marcy's husband and her little boy were both dead by then and she was going it alone except for a doctor name of Heller who had come in from Washington to help her out. This time Zack Lindsay was mad because Marcy had gotten after him about his cow-sheds and dairy barns. Marcy had gone round Apple County picking up milk bottles off of folks porches and looking to see what was inside. She got Tadd Cockayne to print her story in the *Argus*. She said she'd found as many as two and three big dead flies inside of a lot of those bottles of milk. She claimed she'd found pieces of cow droppings, too, and cow hair to boot. She said the butter Zack Lindsay was selling all over Apple County was full of flies and pieces of manure, too, and she said even the cream was filthy. She told everybody in Glory that Zack Lindsay was so cheap and stingy that he had refused to put screens in the windows of his cow barn and his milking sheds.

A lot of the people laughed at that. A lot of them couldn't afford screens for their own houses and it made them sore at Marcy for saying that cows deserved better houses than they did. And then to top everything off Marcy come out in the *Argus* with the claim that out of Zack Lindsay's herd of one hundred Jersey cows, twenty-six of them had the TB. That got a big laugh, too. Nobody ever heard of a cow having a human disease like TB and someone come up to Marcy in front of Mister Ganz's Store one morning and told her eight of the work horses down in Dick McFadden's Livery Stable had the fallen arches and what was Marcy going to do about that. Marcy paid their jokes no mind. She came out in that night's *Argus* demanding that those twenty-six sick cows in Zack's herd be destroyed. She got some kind of a court order from the U.S. Public Health Service in Washington, D.C. and had them shot, too. Zack Lindsay never forgot those cows. He never forgave Marcy Cresap. And he has not forgiven her to this day.

The year after I come back to Glory my chest hurt me something unbearable. I commenced to drinking. I knew how Mom felt about liquor and God knows how I fought the temptation. I went to Reverend Tombes one Wednesday night after his prayer meeting let out. I stood there on the church steps before him under the stars and young green leaves of that sweet spring night and asked him if he would pray for me and help whip the demon of drink that had seized me. He asked me if I was baptized in the church. I told him Mom always told me I couldn't be because I was a woods colt. He asked me if I was a member of his church. Well, he knew perfectly well and good that I wasn't. I never owned a good suit in my life and the clothes I wore before the war and the old army duds I wore afterwards—they weren't the kind of thing a man dresses in to enter the house of God. I told him I wasn't a member of his church but I quickly added that Billy Sunday had saved me once during a revival at the camp ground. I'll never know to this day what he would have said next. Because just then Elsie Challoner and Harper Follansbee's wife and some other ladies come over and started talking to him about that year's Church Drive for the Relief of Hindu Lepers.

Excuse me, boy, Reverend Tombes said. Come up to the parish some day and talk to me when I'm not busy.

That spring my drinking got like a fever. I couldn't get enough. And when I got enough I'd forget it was enough and drink still more. Yet I never asked Mom for a cent of money for my drinking. God knows, my drinking cost her enough in grief and unheard prayers. I used to drink so much I'd lay all day down on the river bank under the willows, that same river bank where I had stood and found peace as a child, drowning my eyes in the diamonds of sundown. I'd lay there all day and wake up at four or five in the morning and open my eyes and see the bobbing lights of the lanterns of the men in skiffs, laying their trotlines in the summer fog. And then I'd wander the streets of Glory half-mad with thirst for a drink; it was like a crazy, chilly fire inside me and nothing but a drink could put it out. Sometimes I'd open one eye down there among the polkweeds and goldenrod and see Mom up there under the big yard willow, bent over her tub, scrubbing her wash in the suds. Sick as I was, half-blind as I was, I could see the glitter of something on her cheeks. And I knew it was tears, not sweat. And I'd chew the grass and dig my fingers into the good bottom-land earth the way I used to hang on to the world and hug my body close out there in no-man's-land beyond the barbed wire of our lines. And I'd swear and vow and promise never to touch another drop of drink again.

And by afternoon of that very day, as soon as my shakes had stopped enough for me to walk, I'd be on the Glory-Wheeling streetcar, walking back and forth up and down the aisle, trying to raise a nickel or two bits. I used to keep a spare dollar always. That was so I could go up to Murphy's Five and Ten on Jefferson Avenue and buy up things to peddle on the streetcar: shoestrings, gum and Jew's-harps; packs of safety pins and lead soldiers and maybe two or three of those black-rubber, strap-on bow ties. I wore my medal, too, the one they gave me in France because I'd been damned fool enough to give my gas mask to a boy from New River whose own gas mask was ruined with bullet holes. And I wore my old A.E.F. cap and my puttees, though half the time I had the shakes so bad I hadn't wrapped them on proper. I sure must have been a spectacle to them people on the streetcar. Half of them bought my junk just to get me out of their sight. And then when I had three or four dollars I'd get off the streetcar two blocks from the Russian Church and run as hard as I could to the Polack's speakeasy next door and get myself a quart of moonshine strong enough to eat the threads out of a pair of furnace gloves.

I must have got hold of a bottle from a bad batch once. Or maybe it was just the fact of how much and how long I'd been drinking. I'd been going steady for a week or ten days, I guess. I'd gotten my little disability check from the government and instead of giving it to Mom as I usually did I blew the whole thing on booze that week. The day I ran out of money I had drunk two quarts of moonshine between sunup and noon that day. And since I was still thirsty for more I went hunting and sniffing along the sidewalk up Pulaski Street in Benwood. Out in a vacant lot behind the Kroger Store I found an old legless miner from Mingo Junction and he was drinking something he gave the name of "Open Switch." It tasted the worst of anything I'd ever drank and I found out later it was buttermilk and white gasoline. I had a few nickels in my pocket and my chest was almost killing me—it hadn't hurt as bad since the night of the gas attack—so I caught the streetcar back to Glory. I knew that something terrible was about to happen and I knew I had just about enough time to make it. I ran all the way down Seventh Street to the river and across Water Street and hid myself down in brush-filth and iron-weed where Mom couldn't see me. I found a half pint I'd lost the night before—it was half hid under a rock along the shore—and I sat there trying to focus my eyes, trying to remember when I'd put it there.

All of a sudden I seemed to grow cold sober. My chest still hurt like flames burning their way up to my shoulder, but my head was clear. It seemed to me I had grown deadly sober. It was the little bottle in my hand that was drunk! I laughed and fell over backwards, staring up at the little half-pint bottle in my hand. I wasn't thirsty for it—it was thirsty for me! All of a sudden, in the flash of a miracle, I had become that bottle's habit. I knew that because the bottle was talking to me, it was telling me so! I declare I never had something hit me that amused me so much in all my life! I roared with laughter. Then I drank the bottle dry in about four long drinks. Everything was very quiet. It seemed like I could hear things clear up on Jefferson Avenue in the middle of Glory. It was dusk by then but there were no diamonds in the river that night. There was only mist that crawled and wisped across the still green water. I tried not to look at it. I forced my face away from it. But in the end it was no use. Because even without looking at it again I knew well and good what it was. And I knew it was going to finish me. I'd seen that wisping cloud before. It was chlorine. I looked round me at the bushes up the bank beneath the willows. But they were not bushes now, they were moving men, comrades I knew had died that night in Picardy. I listened to one of them screaming for nearly five minutes before I knew the voice was mine. The cloud of chlorine nibbled at my sleeve.

In Apple County jail that night I raved. Police Chief Smithers hand-cuffed me to the bars of the cell and tied my feet up with a length of towline. I raved there all that night till my voice gave out and all I could do was stare, choking in silence, at the mobs of long dead soldiers shouldering toward me down the corridor. Twice I knocked myself out, banging my head against the bars. When Police Chief Smithers came in

and threw a bucket of stale, warm water in my face and told me if I
didn't shut up he'd hit me with his billy, I swore at him and told him
he didn't fool me in the least. I knew well and good who he was. He
was Ludendorf. My chest felt like somebody had shoveled red-hot coals
under my coat and buttoned it up again. Around noon that day I got
hold of myself. But when the sun went down again the voices began,
speaking to me from every wall, whispering through the bars, singing
"Avalon" somewhere down the end of the twenty-mile-long corridor.

I thought it was Mom I saw coming toward me in the cell that night.
And round her head there hung the dirty halo of a washtub. And the
harp she played so dreadfully in her hands: it was no harp at all but
her old washboard. Mama came in the cell after the dead soldier had
unlocked it. And she pulled up my torn sleeve and stuck me hard with
something sharp and I shut my eyes and leaned against the bars and
Mom said something and presently the dead soldier came back, looked
at me a minute with his rotting eyes, and then undid the handcuffs on
my wrists, the towline round my feet. I looked at Mom again. But her
sticking my arm that way had made me quiet now; quiet and wise, crafty
and all-seeing. I felt like I was drunk all over again but in a quiet way.
And I saw it wasn't Mom at all. It was Marcy Cresap.

They fooled me, Marcy! I sobbed suddenly. They fooled me! They
never said the glory of it was gas! Oh, Christ, Marcy, I'm so sick. My
chest's like I'd been shot there with a Maxim! Marcy? Don't leave me.
This place!—it's filled with them—the Jerries and our boys, too. But
it's not right, Marcy. It's just not fair of them! Because they're dead.
They're every single soldier of them dead! And that bastard up front—
the one in mufti. I bet he's a slacker, Marcy! Because he lied to me—he
fooled me, Marcy Cresap! He fooled me! He never told me a word about
the gas! Oh, by the way!—Marcy, *you'd* know—Did Pearson come
through? You know his mask was shot to hell!—and before I could
get my own around his face, he was half-gone already! Did he live?

She led me to the wood bench which is supposed to be a bunk in
Glory's jail. She pushed me back as easy as a child. Then she lay down
beside me and reached both hands down to put them round my wrists,
to keep me from clawing at my eyes again. I slept a while. Then woke.
And slept a spell more. Woke again. And it was like that the whole night
through. But Marcy was still there, lying beside my stinking body in
my filthy clothes, with both her arms around me, and trying to tell me

every time I woke up that it would be all right. I began to fight sometime near the hour of sunrise. But Marcy Cresap's strong, she held me down. And what with everything and all the pain that kept on piling up in my chest, I guess I wasn't much to fight, my arms were weak. I cried a spell. And then the voices all began again: Chester and Larry, Bill and the boy whose name I never could remember: the freckled one from Fargo, South Dakota. They were all talking at me from those walls: angry at me and cursing me and wishing I would die, because I'd given my mask to Pearson instead of one of them. Marcy hung on. She cradled me there all night. And sometime early in the morning, when I could see sun and fog beyond the bars, she jabbed my arm again and I fell back and slept the best long sleep that I remember since I was a boy up in my old bed in Mom's house.

For her sake I am proud and thankful that I beat the drink habit that last year. Maybe I was just too wore out; maybe that's all it was. Maybe my body was so wasted by then that liquor wouldn't even have made me drunk. I like to think it was will and prayer that did it, though. That and Mom. And Marcy Cresap. I never touched a drop that whole last year. I remember the last time I was up and around was the day I cleaned my good tie with gasoline, brushed my coat, and went down to the little airport along the river between Glory and Glendale. That was the morning Lindbergh landed and Judge Wofford and the Mayor and Harper Follansbee drove him all around Glory, showing him the town and ending up on the Apple County Court House steps. And I was sure glad I'd cleaned my tie and spruced up a little that day because seeing Lindbergh and that army man with him, Captain Keyhoe—that was the last important thing in all my life. I watched Lindbergh and the captain take off in the Spirit of Saint Louis and I cried and waved my old khaki cap like the derndest fool in the world.

Good-by! I yelled to the little speck of the plane. Good-by, Lindy!

Yet when I walked up Lafayette Avenue under the cool trees that hot day I thought to myself: You're saying good-by to a lot more than Lindy, Lloyd Weaver! You're waving your cap so-long to more than that.

And so it was. But it was pretty easy. It happened in my sleep one August night. I woke up choking like it is when you swallow smoke. But I could feel the hot gush spurting through my fingers foolishly trying to hold it back; my whole flesh was angry and resisting the red fountain that was finishing it all for me this side of things. But after a while I chuckled and let go.

We never had a plot on Glory Hill. It never seemed we ever needed one: nobody died. John Wickerman's wife Cora talked him into letting me have a place on the Wickerman plot. There's no stone marker there but that don't matter. Every Armistice and Memorial Day the David Rogerson Memorial Chapter American Legion Glory Post Number Twelve puts a little American flag up there in the grass. Funny, but that means a lot. It makes me think maybe it wasn't all of it something they lied about and fooled me with. It's nice to think that some of it means flag. And not just gas—gas, the thing the mayor and the preachers and the rest never once mentioned that recruiting day. For a while I had a lot to worry about though and I still do. Maybe it doesn't matter but still I worry. I mean that business about Mom. She knew her own time was coming not long after I was laid here on Glory Hill. I guess those Octagon suds had just clean run out and all the bluing gone. She was like a frantic thing that winter. She went and pleaded with John Wickerman for the last little space beside me in the Wickerman plot. And yet he couldn't—I can't blame him I guess. The Glory Cemetery Association has something they call Perpetual Care. That means they tend your plot: the graves and grass and shrubs and all forever. For eternity. I have to smile. I wonder if even the Glory Cemetery Association knows the size of that word: Eternity. Anyways the price of that last remaining space on the Wickerman plot was enough to pay for Perpetual Care for the whole forty square feet. And John didn't want to give that space to Mom and give up all that Perpetual Care. Eternity's a pretty good deal in a thing like that. I don't blame him exactly.

But still Mom was desperate. She ran around Glory all that early winter like a cat looking for a place to have its babies. When John Wickerman said she couldn't have the space to lie by me, Mom took it hard. But then she figured any place on Glory Hill would be close enough. We can hear each other's voices pretty good over here. So she ran from family to family in Glory—folks whose washes she'd done for forty years. But it wasn't any good. It was like a minstrel show with all the seats sold out. So when Mom passed on last December she never knew when the light went out that she would have a place on Glory Hill after all. She's over at the far north corner. By the shadow of the stone angel on the Blick plot. Mom's buried beside Marcy Cresap's father Davis. I wonder sometimes what they have to talk about down there. Or what Mom does to while the hours away: there's nothing to wash out here on Glory Hill. The rains of April—they take care of that.

I think a lot of Mom here in my place. My chest—it never hurts me any more—and almost all the bitterness I felt once has gone, too. The little flag up in the grass six feet above—it's washed-out and faded some since last Armistice Day. But I'm glad it's there. Maybe it doesn't mean anything, but I'm glad. It's not a joke Life played on you, like gas.

I think about my father too, out here. I'm sure of one thing now—it's not Zack Lindsay. It couldn't be. I will not let it be. Because after that night when Marcy came to jail and laid beside me all those hours of horrors, holding me and giving me medicine and fighting against the blow-torch madness of delirium tremens, fighting it with nothing but a touch, a smidgen of kindness and a whispered prayer; after that night, Zack Lindsay spread it round, gossiped the stinking lie of it everywhere, polluting Glory's telephones like a sewer, telling the Glory folks that Marcy that night had come there and laid with me for something else. He's told it everywhere in Apple County. That man, if anyone can favor him with the name, he's told the folks that Marcy lifted her clothes and did with me the thing I never done. I never had a girl, naturally. Before the war I always was too shy. And when I came back I was ashamed lest any girl should ever see my chest scooped out until my backbone showed and I was always too sick to want anything to do with a girl anyways. But that Zack Lindsay—he has spread the lie.

He's not my father! He couldn't be. I wouldn't let Life play this last bad joke on me! It's anyone on earth but that dead-souled Zack Lindsay. Any one! And yet—I have never once doubted Mom's word—there never was another man for her. So all I know is this: It's not Zack Lindsay—and it's not someone else; I've got Mom's word. And so, I guess, I have no Pap at all! Now isn't that a riddle fit for a man to puzzle out and untangle for eternity? Brother, that beats them all! I've got no Pap.

And so I play a little game; I tell myself a little story here. I never was the sort to go to church. How could I be?—I never had a suit to wear! And so I kid myself, I play this game. Maybe it's sacrilegious but I don't much care! I'm really not religious worth a dern. So I can play this game and kid myself along. I tell myself the Pap I have is God! Well?—what else would you do in my place?—choose Zack Lindsay?

Not me! Never! I'll always kid myself along somehow. And when the Pap-subject comes into my mind, I'll say: Lloyd Eldreth Weaver, your Pap is God!

Now wouldn't poor Mom scold me if she heard that?—me saying that her lover was the Lord?

Arthur Malcolm Keynes

Tolerance is not one of my strong points. There are three human weaknesses which I can neither countenance nor forgive. And these are Stupidity, Pretension, and Greed. Most of the other false colors in the human spectrum I can overlook. But as for those three I am harsh, accusing and implacable. That's the chief reason my family and I don't live in Glory any more. They'll tell you a lot of different reasons why I was fired from my position as chief chemist at the Rowan Glass Factory. If you believe them then I will know that you are either Stupid, Pretentious, or Greedy. And I'm afraid I shall be unable to forgive you. But then I am sure that if you are one of these three, you will not care what I think of you.

For the most part, the people of Glory despised us. The reason they despised us was because they considered us dangerous. Or rather they considered our ideas dangerous. My wife Betty, my two sons Jack and Donnie and my daughter Liz—we were what Glory labeled as Free

Thinkers. I have no idea what that phrase means to you but I can assure you that to Glory it spelled out peril. The danger of ideas. Any idea, of course, is dangerous. If it is not dangerous it is not even an idea. It is only Habit, which is safe. And the reason for this is that Habit is an Idea which is dead and fossilized. Once, centuries ago, that idea was quite dangerous. But through the years it hardened into a safe and meaningless belief. A hundred and fifty years ago the ideas which fused together this Republic were treason. Today they are habit. And any idea which questions them now—that's treason.

We settled in Glory the winter after the Armistice. My job with the glass factory was a good one. I was competent and well trained for it. In 1909 I got my Master's Degree in chemistry at Cornell University. Then I spent two years' post-graduate study in the chemistry of glass and ceramic glazes. My wife Elizabeth learned Social Work at Lillian Wald's Henry Street Settlement. I met her while I was in the army in western Pennsylvania where she was doing work among the miners in the Pittsburgh area. That region was not new to her. She was born in the Squirrel Hill Section of Pittsburgh where her father was a powerful and wealthy steel magnate. During a strike in 1910 he walked out of his office and saw his wife and daughter on the picket line carrying signs. Without a pause or a word he walked back into his office, sat at his desk, wrote out his resignation as president of the mills and sold his stock before noon of that day.

At the beginning things were reasonably pleasant for us here in Glory. The Rowan Glass Factory had been established and financed in 1894 by Davis Cresap and several other honest and forward-looking Glory businessmen. In those days the glassware was all blown and handshaped by skilled craftsmen. The lovely tumblers, dishes and goblets were etched by hand. By the time of the 1907 Panic the factory commenced to lose money and Walter Rowan and G. Vernon Tompkins fired all the glass-blowers and installed machinery to do the work. The designs in the glassware were now etched by hydroflouric acid. The old artisans wandered off and found work in the mines or sat at home on the back porch drinking away their little pensions. By the time I came to the Rowan Glass plant all the methods had been completely modernized. The glass-ware produced was strong and useful but it lacked all the charm and beauty of the old, vanished days of craftsmanship. I tried to give it back a new beauty.

Since the lovely shapes and patterns of the old times were gone it seemed to me that I could bring to Rowan Glassware something almost as beautiful. Color. I began to experiment with small batches using cobalts and copper oxides. When Walter Rowan found out what I was doing he had the company manager Albert Biddle Beam send me a memo of the most mild reproach. The evening of that same day Calvin, the son of Karcher McCombs, the company president, drove home drunk with a carful of youngsters from his high-school class and crashed headlong into a tree on Jefferson Avenue. Both of Calvin's legs were broken, but he got off the easiest of all. Two boys and a girl died instantly, and Darleen Yost, the only daughter of a Glory mail carrier, went through the windshield headlong and was blinded for life. Karcher and his wife had invited us all to a dinner party at their home that night and he did not feel, apparently, that the accident was any reason to call the party off. Doctor Ed Follansbee had assured him that Calvin's fractures were simple ones and that he would be up walking again in less than a month.

If young Calvin had been the child of anyone in Glory but Karcher McCombs, a charge of manslaughter while drunk would have been filed against him and he would have served time in the Pruntytown Boys' Reformatory or even at the state penitentiary. As it was, Rowan's lawyer Robert Kemple got together with Ansel Carruthers, the prosecuting attorney, and certain simple arrangements were agreed upon. An expensive private nurse from Wheeling and Doctor Ed Follansbee were the only persons permitted in Calvin's hospital room until the last trace of any liquor smell was gone. My wife Betty said she absolutely refused to attend the dinner party that night. I talked her into changing her mind. I said that a first-hand study of Karcher McCombs that night was a psychological phenomenon I wouldn't miss for the world. I had to see how a man could play the pleasant host on the same day his son had been responsible for the bodies of three young friends lying up in Marple's Funeral Home and the permanent disfigurement and blinding of a fourth. Karcher solved that problem as I had known he would: he got tight. Not drunk, mind you, but just high enough to keep his mind off sordid thoughts and spend an enjoyable evening. Everything might have gone off smoothly if Chester Yost hadn't come hammering on the front door a few minutes after dinner. Karcher went to the door. We could all hear Chester Yost cursing him out slowly and eloquently, from where we were sitting in the study.

Chester, nobody could feel sadder about all this than I, Karcher was saying. Try to think of it all somehow as the will of God, Chester. You're a church man. Go home and pray. And remember that God moves in a mysterious way, His wonders to perform.

Chester cursed him out again and his voice had broken a little; he was crying.

My girl will never see again, you son of a bitch, said Chester Yost.

Chester, I don't blame you for feeling bitter, said Karcher McCombs. But try to turn your thoughts tonight to that great soul, Helen Keller. There was a woman who was blind from birth. And deaf and dumb as well. And think what beauty and faith her life has brought to us all. Try to think of her tonight, Chester. Maybe your girl has felt the great hand of destiny on her shoulder today. Can't you look at it in that light?

And not only blind either! Chester went on, as if he had not even been listening to Karcher's inspirational words. She'll be disfigured, too. And only this morning my girl was the most beautiful child in Apple County. They told me at the hospital that no number of operations could ever bring that beauty back! Don't use the word destiny to me, you bastard. It was liquor; that's the word you don't dare say! Your boy was drunk!

That's not so, Chester, said Karcher McCombs. My boy has never touched a drop of drink in his life. His mother will swear to that and so will I. Chester, get hold of yourself. I understand your feelings. And I want to do the little I can to make it right. I want your girl to have the best hospital care that money can buy. I want to have the finest Pittsburgh eye specialists and plastic surgeons examine her. Money is no object. I want to pay for all of it. And knowing you're probably under a little financial pinch at the hospital right now I want to give you this as a starter. Chester, take this five hundred dollar check as a token of good faith in my intentions.

I remember how nobody in the study that night was able to look into anybody else's eyes. We heard something rip and the scuffle of feet out on the front porch. Chester Yost had dragged Karcher to the edge of the porch and knocked him down the flight of steps to the flagstone walk. When Karcher appeared there was a blue mark under his left eye and his collar and tie were torn open. He brushed himself off and stared at all of us with apology on his face but not the slightest trace of guilt or sheepishness.

I'm sorry about all this, he said to us. Men of that class always tend to get a little over-emotional.

He poured himself a stiff drink of bootleg Scotch and turned his back on us. He seemed waiting for the liquor to gather up the loose ends of his frayed feelings and tie them neatly together. Presently he turned around. His face was mottled and a little drunk now and his eyes were furious. He looked at his wife Helen with such savage intensity that he did not seem aware of anyone else in the room.

You're to blame, he said. You know that, don't you, Helen? You were the one who gave Cal his first drink, not me. And before that it was you who made him so rotten-spoiled that it sometimes makes me ashamed to know he bears my family name. You're the one who should have faced that man out there tonight, not me.

And with that he threw the remainder of the liquor in her face.

Somehow I have always felt that Karcher never forgave me for having seen that. Walter and Vernon and Albert were there too, but they were his superiors so it didn't matter. I was merely the factory's chief chemist and, besides that, both Betty and I were, relatively speaking, strangers in Glory. Within a week I knew that Karcher McCombs' attitude toward me had altered sharply—that he, in fact, hated me. I knew it from the boisterous and somehow needlessly elaborate courtesy with which he suddenly began to treat me.

Not that I blame Karcher McCombs for our having to leave so fairly soon after that. Karcher was part of it, all right, but he was not the only one in town who hated us. We never belonged in Glory from the beginning. There was scarcely a single one of our family habits that did not come under the frowning scrutiny of most of the town. The way we lived and thought, the books we read, and how we raised our children: all these things seemed to most of Glory folk evidence of the most heretical and outrageous Bohemianism. Even the fact that Betty was my second wife was a subject for delicious gossip. My first wife Ellen Marie Connell and I were married in high school. In 1903 Ellen gave birth to my daughter Liz and died a few days later of puerperal fever. Betty and I have had two sons—Jack and Donnie. The gossip in Glory had it that I had divorced Ellen to marry Betty.

From time to time hints and fragments of Glory's other objections to us came back to me. Since Ellen's tragic death because of a doctor's dirty fingernails I had had a rather strong interest in public health;

Betty's work in the slums of Pittsburgh gave her a background and en-
thusiasm for health reforms even stronger than mine. That was what
attracted us originally to the only young couple who seemed to be doing
anything about it locally: Lou Delaplaine and his wife Marcy. It was
common knowledge around Glory at the time that Lou was hopelessly
tubercular. What neither Betty nor I knew, when we first made friends
with this charming and dedicated couple, was the passion and unreasoning outrage with which they were hated by most of the really powerful
people of the town. When word got round that the four of us were
friends it was as if I had given the announcement to the *Glory Argus*
of my daughter Liz's engagement to a Negro. The spring before Lou
Delaplaine's death he, Marcy and their child had found a dilapidated
and deserted log cabin on the highest point in Apple County—a little
piece of untilled property at the top of Roberts' Ridge. The place needed
tar roofing and a new chimney but it seemed to them a place where Lou
would be up out of the damp river mists of the Glory nights: a place
where sunlight and fresh country air might give him if not a last, desperate chance of beating his TB, at least a reprieve. At that time, neither of
them knew that the child was infected as well. Betty and I used to go up
there two or three times a week that spring. The girls would cook a simple
outdoor dinner while I took an extra hod and trowel and helped Lou
patch up the crumbling mortar of the old chimney. I'll never forget the
stars up there those cool spring nights: they seemed almost to drift down
in our midst, they seemed so close that hands could reach out and touch
them. I loved those nights. Betty and Liz and Marcy getting dinner, the
boys climbing among the apple trees, and Lou and I singing at the top of
our voices. Oh, yes—that caused talk, too. We were both Gilbert and
Sullivan fanatics and after we'd stop exchanging choruses from *Iolanthe*
or *Ruddigore* I used to climb to the chimney top and pose there like a
Roman orator, waving my trowel at the stars which seemed to hang
below me in the night, and recite long verses from the *Book of Job*,
which I know almost entirely by heart.

Either we were followed up there one night or a young couple overheard us from a parked car down the dirt road a ways. At any rate, word
quickly spread round Glory that Lou and I alternated dirty limericks
with sacrilegious recitations from the Bible. I wonder if the *Book of Job*
has anywhere on earth ever sounded as fitting and lovely as it did on
those spring nights on that unsoiled hill, among the stars and young

spring winds of that brave year. Yes, brave. Because I don't think either
Marcy or Lou were kidding themselves any longer about the outcome
of his infection. When two people in love know they have a limited time
left together they either grow dour-faced and self-pitying, hating the
sight of one another, or they try to pack into those last few months a
sort of ferocious adoration of life. And in the months of that summer I
will swear that Doctor Lou Delaplaine and his wife Marcy shared together more love and fun, more passion and devoted work, more sheer,
bared zest at being alive than most couples are lucky enough to experience in fifty years of life together. To be sure, the lengthening shadow
of Death was always there before them. But it seemed to trouble them
no more than would the shadow of a tree, knowing together somehow
that both shadows owe their being to the fact behind them of some everlasting sun; or of some unquenchable lunar eternity. I am not a sentimental man; in most ways I am a hard one, but somehow the sheer, uncoun-
terfeited courage of those two moved me to feelings which often, in the
light of our supper fire, caused me to knuckle moisture from my eyes
and grate my teeth and complain that the smoke from our campfire
made my eyes tear. And then Lou and I would do some more mortaring
of the chimney of that, as yet, uninhabitable house. And I'd clamber
to the topmost stone and throw my head back and see a shooting star
and shout in a voice which those two had given fresh pride in being
human:

Man that is born of a woman is of few days, and full of trouble.

He cometh forth like a flower, and is cut down: he fleeth also as a
shadow, and continueth not.

And once I paused, remembering, and thought I had chosen a verse
that might depress them. And then I would look down and see the face
of Marcy Cresap smiling up with purest joy in her eyes at the splendor of
Job and know that what I had said had made them think nothing
of the kind; that nothing I, nor anyone, might say could shake the grip of
these two loose from life. Nothing but Death himself could do that
thing, and not even he—Lord Death—perhaps. While up there in the
hovering, close mystery of the stars, and the green wind of that spring
tousling our hair, and the country smells of comeback and fresh-starts
sweet as the waking earth in all our noses—up there it seemed that life
and death were equally and splendidly implied, and measured out between the night and earth in quantities of such twinned, undifferent

importance that neither could ever be more terrible, immeasurable, and dazzling than the other. And I would fling my trowel toward the Great Bear or the Pleiades and cry:

Because thou shalt forget thy misery, and remember it as waters that pass away!

And thine age shall be clearer than the noonday; thou shalt shine forth, thou shalt be as the morning!

And thou shalt be secure, because there is hope; yea, thou shalt dig about thee, and thou shalt rest in safety!

Also thou shalt die down, and none shall make thee afraid . . .

It was strange but Lou's impending death did leave me affected with a curious sorrow. Curious, I say, because it was nothing really to do with Lou that came to mind. Short as it had been, the life he and Marcy had had together was patently and shiningly so splendid, even so complete, that it did not seem to me that if both of them were to live another forty years that they could possibly discover any joy more absolute than that which they had had. Strangely, the thought of Lou's dying made me feel acutely something I had not felt especially strongly when it happened: the death of Ellen, my child-wife. We were both so young. No, that's not it. We were both so desperate—that's it. Both of us nearly penniless, both our parents dead-set against us; it's as if when Ellen died back then I didn't dare feel grief. It's as if had I let myself grieve her then I would have instantly gone to rack and pieces.

But that summer it suddenly came alive and hurting in me. And it was the thought of Lou's impending death that triggered it. I don't know how. Maybe I thought that had he come to tend her and deliver her of child that night that his hands would have been clean. His oncoming death reminded me of the mindlessness, the needlessness of hers. I think Betty understood; perhaps she even sensed it in me. Whatever she thought, she was marvelously understanding. Particularly since almost every atom of parental devotion within me seemed to turn suddenly to my daughter Liz. It was unfair, I guess: the boys—Jack who was nine and Donnie eight—they probably needed me more that summer. Because they were at that age of infallible instinct: they seemed to know something was going to happen to their playmate Bill and their friend Lou. Still Liz and I have never been closer than we were that summer. She was just turned eighteen with blue-black hair like Ellen's had been and violet eyes like my mother's and the kind of total, stunning beauty which, in a town the size of Glory, is a fact of instant and outspoken suspicion.

For the first seven years of her life I had raised Liz alone, and yet when Betty married me nothing about that upbringing changed: we were both in complete agreement that the only way to teach a child cleanness and candor of spirit was to teach it honestly. To most of Glory, of course, this philosophy of child-rearing was pure obscenity. Betty and I never made a point of going around the upstairs naked simply because it seemed a good way to teach unashamedness of nakedness. Most of the time nobody could ever find a bathrobe—that's all it was. And in the summer, at least, we'd all take baths when we came in from work or school and not bother to dress again simply because it was so comfortable the way we were. When someone would think of it he'd pull down the window-blinds upstairs but most of the time nobody ever bothered. It didn't seem to matter much to us. Because nobody had ever learned to feel that anything on, in, or about their bodies could conceivably be shameful. So what was there to hide? That did little to improve our local prestige either. The Methodist minister lived next door to us and on the other side dwelt two maiden ladies by the name of Peabody. So that if we had staged Roman orgies on the front lawn at noon the gossip could have been no more brutal.

Nor was that the worst of it. I told you earlier that I am not a very tolerant man. In fact, I am a snob. Which is only another way of saying that I should prefer the very best thoughts and actions in people as opposed to their meanest, shoddiest sides. In addition to my intolerance and snobbery there are other qualities which afflict me; tendencies which did more than anything, probably, to finish me at the glass plant.

I have a keen, sarcastic wit, a loathing for self-pity, and an occasionally ungovernable temper which, I regret to say, I have sometimes vented upon my own family. Walter Rowan's first assistant, Kimper Darling, is a particularly uxorious and truckling sort, the repulsively ideal type for the role as underling to a managerial mentality. Kimper is the kind who corners you by the water cooler after staff meetings and, with nudges and in a whispering voice, tells dirty jokes whose point invariably hinges on deformities or indignities about women's bodies; the kind of man who unfailingly causes me to suspect sexual impotence. His wife, a massive Wagnerian amazon is Glory's most pathetic and notorious hypochondriac. As some women's power over their mates rests in strength, Hilda Darling's lies in weakness; she is always on the point of becoming an invalid. And so one night, during a bridge game, when I referred to this couple as Kimper and Whimper, the thoughtless witticism was being circulated all over the Rowan Glass works by ten o'clock next morning. That did me even more damage than the news that we were subscribers to the *Nation* and *New Republic*, and when Liz chose for her last reading in Senior English a scene from Ibsen's *Enemy of the People* we might just as well have packed up and left that day. It occurs to me since that perhaps the theme of that great play may have brought home a little too sharply the very things that Marcy and Lou Delaplaine were fighting for in Glory. The polluted waters of the spring of Life itself!

Neither Betty nor I has ever told a child beneath that roof what is Wrong in life and what is Right. We have told them only what we believe to be beautiful and what we believe to be ugly. We have taught them that life is full of decisions and that every decision has its consequence. We have told them they can never enjoy the Rights and Privileges of this world if they stamp upon the Rights and Privileges of other people. We have tried to help them understand that Poverty is a disgrace to their home even more than it is to those of the poor. We have hoped that they may see that sickness anywhere on earth is an insult to the health of their own bodies if the sickness of those others leaves their hearts and hands unmoved. Neither Betty nor I have ever sent any of our children to Sunday school or church. That is so that they may have a chance to become religious. And there has never been an evening in all our years together when each of us has not been expected to recite after dinner some delightful or thrilling new passage he has learned that day from the Holy Bible.

When the word came back to my ears that my daughter Liz was a degenerate young slut I went to my dresser drawer and fetched out the 25 caliber Mauser automatic my brother Jeff brought home from France. It was a warm summer night. I stood for a moment with the pistol in my hand glaring out at the dark. What was I going to shoot— the town of Glory? I laughed in a chill of relief and took the clip of bullets out, hurling them out in the shrubbery where I prayed they would lie forever, rusting. I took a ball-peen hammer from the kitchen cabinet, hammered the gun barrel out of shape and dropped it in the garbage can. I stood a while, leaning against the frame of the screen door in the kitchen, looking at the stars among our yard of poplar trees. I listened to the river frogs far off among the cattails below Water Street, choiring in shameless reverence of eggs and birth and all the raw and lovely ways Life chooses to begin. Betty was working with Marcy that night. Liz had a date somewhere with someone. The boys had gone to the Orpheum to see Douglas Fairbanks.

I had known for some time about Liz's friendship with Glory's only artist—a man named Harold Post Robinson. It was Marcy and Doctor Delaplaine who had brought him up to the hill that spring where we were trying to fix the cabin to save Lou's life. Harold did the whole roof himself—every sheet of tarpaper, every roofing nail. That cabin roof may be famous years from now. A Robinson original! And while Lou and I took turns reciting verses from Isaiah, Harold in his good baritone hummed an aria from Bach none of us knew. We sat up there that night long after the fire we'd built had gone out with the stars. Below us the mists of morning lay on Glory. We heard the rooster crows from twenty farms, scattered around the quilted humps of those eternal hills. The boys, wrapped in robes, had long ago crawled in the car to sleep. Liz sat with her legs tucked under, her head against my shoulder, watching us all with wise and drowsy eyes. The string of smoke from our old and burned-out supper fire stood gray and still in the pure air like the ghost of someone slender. Harold had been reciting Blake for an hour. But, after a while, he had fallen still. Nobody said anything for a long while; all of us, it seemed, like creatures in genesis witnessing earth's first sunup, heard sheep bells far off tinkling like some forest carillon summoning beasts to praise. Suddenly Marcy Cresap Delaplaine began to speak, almost absently, and yet with sleepy conviction, her mouth smiling, her voice saying something so oddly beautiful I will never forget it.

You, Arthur. And you, Betty, she said. And you, Hal and Liz and the boys sleeping yonder in the car. And me. We're all doomed for a little while. I mean Glory's got it in for each of us. And in the end Glory will win. They'll drive us away. And it will take us a little while to find a new place, a new beginning, a grand comeback.

Then she laid her hand on her husband's hand and squeezed it hard and looked at him.

You, too, old darling, she said softly. You, too. It will take you a while to find your lovely comeback. But I bet you make it sooner and easier than any of us.

The fact of the scandal about Liz was that she and Harold Post Robinson got to be friends. Wasn't that a dreadful thing now? And wasn't that a riddle to the ones in Glory who said Hal hated women!

In September of that year Hal finished a small bronze statue of Liz. I was the first one he showed it to. He came into the living room that night and unwrapped it and stood back from it where it stood upon the table. I called Betty and the boys downstairs to see. And later Marcy and Lou came up to see it, too. Liz had kept it a secret. But not for the reason Glory women thought. She had wanted it as a gift for me. And I am a hard man, an intolerant man; I am sarcastic and acid-tongued and awful-tempered. But I stood there that night with the tears in my eyes, blurring that lovely image of my girl, my first-born child, my Liz. I knew two things suddenly that night, things I guess I'd known for longer than I supposed, things that small bronze figure said to me. I knew that Harold Robinson was a great artist; I knew my daughter Elizabeth was a splendid woman.

Who spied into my house that night, who stole across my lawn and peered through my window? I'll never know. It doesn't matter. Maybe no single person spied at all. Maybe just something evil in the night out there looked in. By midnight all the party-lines in town were tied up and fighting for each other. By morning the word was everywhere in Apple County: my daughter Liz was an immoral woman; she had posed without clothes for that artist, Harold Robinson. How disappointing it must have been to all of them: they couldn't add the finishing touch to the tale—that Liz had had immoral relations with Harold Post Robinson. For everyone in Glory knew that he liked only boys.

Maybe I would have resigned anyway. I like to think I would have. Yet, in the final summing up of things—what does it matter: Glory's everywhere. All the good of it; all the evil, too. We live now in a town that's just the same. And it's a thousand miles from Apple County.

It wasn't just the statue of Liz that made them decide. It was everything about me and my family. It was everything we stood for there in Glory. It was Liz reciting that Ibsen speech in Senior English. It was Betty choosing a nasty book like *Main Street* to review before the Tuesday Arts. It was me and my Kimper and Whimper. It was the boys playing football with the Negro children on Water Street, or looking for arrowheads with the waifs of Angel Swamp. It was all of us running around the upstairs with no clothes on, just like that favorite family of

Reverend Tombes: Adam and Eve and their two loving sons Cain and Abel. It was all of these, summed up and totaled neatly like a row of deficits on a ribbon of paper in the adding machine up in the office of the Rowan Glass Works. We had to go. You can see why, of course? When we were gone, the town would once again be safe. Safe, at least, from Arthur Malcolm Keynes, and all his shameless and immoral family.

I'm a good chemist. I don't make mistakes. That much I know, and I can look back on my work in Glory with pride and a feeling of distinction. Walter Rowan, G. Vernon Tompkins, Albert Biddle Beam, Kimper Darling, Karcher McCombs and some richly bribed workman in the plant one night fixed me once and forever. They spoiled a batch of expensive ruby glass and blamed it on some lab mistake of mine. It wasn't hard to do. A handful or two of extra chemical tossed in the vat while still the glass was hot. Enough to throw the color off just a shade—a shade of difference from the specifications. The glass hadn't even been poured when Walter Rowan called me in his office and regretfully told me the news. He said it wasn't the first time; he said I'd spoiled a dozen other batches.

Arthur, I like you, Walter Rowan said. I'm sorry things have got to end this way. Good luck. And here's a check for three months' pay. I know you'll have no trouble finding something new.

I took that last stroll along the high catwalk above the glowing, molten vat of scarlet glass. I leaned over the rail, I dropped what I had carried there from home, right after they'd called and told me the news. I watched it fall and disappear into the batch of ruby red they said I'd ruined. Then I went home and told Betty to start to pack.

A thousand years from 1921—or maybe two or three—the men with spades will come where Glory was; the archaeologists who scrape and wonder at what the world we live in now was like back then. They'll sift through Apple County's dark rich earth, and ponder, and put our coke bottles and tin cans and the crankcases from our Fords into their museums. But one day they will come upon the loveliest and strangest riddle of them all: a giant blob of glass once dumped out there in the town trash heap beyond the place men then called Angel Swamp. A huge red lump of glass, scarlet as the blood of life itself, catching the light and glowing like some crimson, fallen star. Lord, how they'll rack their brains at this—these men! And stare and scowl and try to plumb its meaning. Maybe that day they'll change their minds about our gods.

Maybe those men will scrap their old, snide notions that what we worshiped were the cold, hard gods: Stupidity, Pretension and blind Greed! They'll stare inside that one great lump of glass and see in its center, fixed in its glow forever, deathless in bronze and safe from earth's corrosion, in grave, wise charm, with tilted, listening head, the shy, fresh nakedness of a pretty girl.

Chester Yost

A man can love his child too much. Especially when it's an only child. And especially when it comes to a man like me with a child as pretty as Darleen was and a wife as crazy as Matty. I never come as close to murder in my life as I did the night Mister McComb's boy Calvin smashed that car up drunk and made my daughter blind. After I went up to his house that night and knocked him down the porch steps I stood there looking at him cringing on the sidewalk. I thought a minute whether it might not be worth while to stomp him to death right then and there. But I didn't. And the reason I didn't was because it came over me suddenly that Darleen's being in that car that night was more my fault than his.

Nobody can ever tell me any different: my wife Matty married me for one reason. And that was to get away from home and her uncle Gaily Rosebud. The first time ever I laid eyes on Matty she was thirteen years old. Me and five other boys was working the hay-harvest on her daddy's farm up near Jacktown. Matty used to come up the pasture two or three times a day with a bucket of ice-cold spring water with a dipper in it. And when we'd go down the fields to the house when Matty's mama blew on the conch-shell to tell us lunch was ready it was always Matty who set the food before us. We ate out on a long table in the yard under the shade of a big sugar maple. The other five boys never paid Matty any mind. They all had girl friends up at Jacktown: housemaids and waitresses who worked at the Big Diamond Lunch. Besides I reckon they felt thirteen was too young to go fooling around with. As for me, I could hardly keep my eyes off that girl.

She was one of them that gets ripe early—too soon, in fact. Ever been around one of them eight- or nine-year-old girls that makes you squirm in your chair and want to get away from there? That's the way Matty was back then. There was certain things about her that seemed indecent on a thirteen-year-old girl. Maybe it was something around the eyes, the way she smiled, a certain way she moved sometimes, slow as a cat. And there was a smell about her, too—like she was a thirty-year-old woman. It didn't belong. It somehow seemed indecent. Many's the time I was glad to be back up in the fields again working off steam with a scythe or a pitchfork. But you know that girl wouldn't let me alone? It was like she could read my mind. Or maybe sense the lust in me like an animal can smell fear. Many's the time, when she'd come up the high grass with that bucket of cold water, she'd dipper out a drink especially for me. And she'd hold it up there, dripping, and tease me with her eyes. I just used to thank God none of the other boys noticed. It'd be just like one of them to go tell that fierce-tempered daddy of hers to keep an eye on me. And God knows he might have fetched down that Winchester of his and chased me clean into Cameron.

Matty's mother was a plain, fat woman in a blue cotton dress and a face as common as bread dough. Her black eyes didn't show any more sense than a pair of raisins stuck in a pie. A woman like that always puts me ill at ease; you never can tell what they're thinking. Her brother who was a horse-breeder by trade was a shifty sort who always had a grin on his face like the corners of his mouth was held up with glue. I never trust a man who smiles all the time. It always tells me his face is holding something back, hiding some thoughts that's in his mind. It's not natural to smile all the time: there's just not enough things in the world to keep a normal man amused that much.

Matty's uncle's name was Gaily Rosebud. He lived with his sister and her husband to help around the farm. He hadn't bred horses in years. They say he used to win first-prize all the time up at the Jacktown Fair. The way I found out about him and Matty was pure accident. It was September. Down in the woods it sounded like the locusts was sawing down the world. Me and them other five boys was cutting hay up on the ridge. The blade of my scythe needed honing so I went down to the barn to fetch the stone. I just barely stuck my head around a corner of the little room where Matty's daddy kept the tools when I seen Gaily Rosebud and Matty in there by themselves. Gaily was sitting on a nail keg and Matty was standing up real close to him with her eyes shut. Her face was all flushed but I could see tear marks on her cheeks. Gaily had his hand up under her little short dress and he was moving it back and forth and breathing hard. I forgot all about the whetstone and went on back up the hill to the place we'd been working. I was so mad at that dirty old devil that it didn't matter if my blade did need honing; I cut more hay than all five of them other boys that afternoon. Every blade of timothy felt like that Gaily Rosebud's scrawny neck. That night I saw Matty in the hencoop with a pan of cracked corn in her hands feeding the chickens. When she got done and headed back up toward the house I called to her. She smiled when she saw me. When she come over she smelled like cracked-corn; and I could smell the sweat of her, too, like a grown-up thirty-five-year-old woman. By God, for a minute there I got madder at her than I was at that ornery uncle Gaily of hers.

Let's go for a walk, I said, looking the other way.

Where to, Chester? she said.

Anywheres, I said. Up the road to Jacktown will do. Missy, I've got a word or two to say to you.

About halfway we turned off the road and went down and sat with our backs against one of the haystacks in her daddy's fields. I could smell the fresh-cut clover and the timothy and I could still smell that cracked-corn smell on Matty's hands. I could smell her skin-smell, too: that grown-up smell that made me just want to tear out and bite something.

It's about you and that uncle of your'n, I said, cool as a judge. You might as well know it—I seen him and you down in the barn this afternoon, Matty. The cat's out of the bag, young lady. And if you want my opinion that ornery, dirty devil needs a thrashing he'll not soon forget.

Matty looked at me a minute. She was still. Then she cleared her throat and stared off down the pasture. The field hands in another farm was still working, burning brush-filth and the smoke of it lay like blue dreams in the thick stand of locust trees down in the holler.

There's nary a thing I can do to stop him, she said.

Can't you go tell your daddy? I said.

By the time daddy'd stopped throwing a fit Uncle Gaily would have lit out and be gone, she said. And it would be me that would bear the punishment of it all.

How long's it been a-going on? I said.

She figured a minute, counting on her fingers.

Since I was nine, she said. That's four years ain't it?

By God now! said I, clenching my fists till they creaked. By God!

I never knowed what he was doing the first time, she said. It went on one whole summer. And one night I tried to run away and he grabbed me back and I told him I'd tell daddy. And he said if I told daddy he'd lie and say I made him do it. And then he said, if ever I told anyone, he'd show up on the day of my wedding and tell my husband everything and spoil my life.

I blew my nose in my hanky and looked at the smoke down in the holler.

Do you like it when he does it? I said.

No, she said. I hate it. I hate him! Chester, I just can't stand it much more. I've just about made my mind up to run away to Cameron and stay with my aunt!

A man like that, I said. By God, a man like that!—he should be horsewhipped clean out of Marshall County.

Well, she said. He's mama's only brother and the sun just rises and sets on him. And daddy—he dotes on him, too. Daddy says he just couldn't run the farm without him. Chester, it's me that's got to go.

A child like you, I said. You're too young to run away alone. By God, I've half a mind to go down to the house and have a talk with your daddy myself.

She turned her big black eyes on me, wide with terror. She laid a hand of cold fingers on my wrist.

Chester, you dasn't! she whispered. Oh, Chester, you dasn't! Daddy'd kill me if he knowed!

Her big eyes filled with tears but her mouth was steady. She lifted her knuckles and rubbed the tears away, made her mouth smile at me and laid over against me, shutting her eyes, and putting her arms around my neck.

Listen, Chester, she whispered, her lips moving on my neck. Promise you won't tell daddy and I'll give you something.

What? I gasped. What'll you give me?

You know what, she murmured.

Well I was just naturally beyond words.

I do it good, too, she said. You just ask some of them boys that hangs around the Big Diamond Lunch up at Jacktown, Chester. They'll tell you how good I do it.

Godalmighty, I said, trying to get her arms loose from round my neck. You mean to say your Uncle Gaily ain't the only one?

I hate him, she said. I just naturally despise men that smells like horses. She scowled.

Besides, she said, he's so old he can't even do it no more. All he can do is just diddle around. That old Uncle Gaily! I just naturally despise him. He's got a pecker like a turkey's wattle.

The morning after the hay-harvest was done, her and me run off to Cameron and got married. I look back on all the misery of it now and yet, I swear, if I had it to do over it would be the same. That thirteen-year-old girl had me crazy. And when I married her it seemed like I was marrying something every man in Marshall County was going to miss so bad it hurt, now that I had that little Matty all to myself. It was like I was winning the biggest raffle in life; like I was stealing a girl away from every man on earth. I swear I felt like no man anywhere was ever going to get any more ever, now that Matty was out of circulation. And the idea of all the men and boys that ever had done it to her: that never crossed my mind. She had chose me. And I knew how different things was going to be now that we had tied the knot. But they wasn't.

I got a job working at the Purina Feed Mill in Cameron and Matty just kept on going the way she always had. Even a year later, while she was carrying Darleen, she never stopped; at least not till she got so big no man nor boy would look at her. After the baby come she took a couple of days rest and drank up about six dollars worth of ice cream sodas and then she was off again. I swear, even before poor little Darleen was weaned the child would be sucking at one tit while some worthless farmhand would be playing with the other. Cameron isn't a town big enough for a man to stand it with his wife carrying on that way. So I put in for Civil Service and two months later I got a mail route in Glory. Glory's about six times the size of Cameron and there's a movie-show there and five or six churches and there isn't a summer goes by that a Chautauqua show or Gentry Brothers Circus don't open on the big lot down by the smelter. They've got a camp-ground, too, and a big revival-auditorium and there's hardly a year that Sam Jones or Billy Sunday don't show up and save a few thousand souls. I figured maybe things like that might slow Matty down. But they never.

Not in all my life had I had a woman until our honeymoon. But from what I heard the boys say, it didn't take much loving to keep a woman bright-eyed and happy. Not a wife like Matty, though. Trying to content that girl was like trying to dipper out the whole Ohio River with a tea-spoon. After the Great War I used to look at her sometimes and, I de-clare, besides all the grief I felt, she made me purely marvel. There she'd sit—a girl hardly into her twenties—and I'd think: Matty, if you was to take on the whole AEF, Coxey's Army, the Moose and the Woodmen of America it wouldn't be no more to you than eating a cracker before dinner. I used to feel so helpless I'd want to cry. I'd look at her pretty little back when she'd be washing dishes at the sink and I'd say to my-self: Chester, she's like trying to put out a brush-fire with spit.

Meanwhile, Darleen was growing up to be the prettiest little thing you'd want to see. I used to take strange comfort in thinking that she was surely going to be prettier even than her mother. And she was. She had a pert little black-haired beauty about her like Colleen Moore and a figure to beat a follies queen.

The year Darleen turned seventeen Matty was thirty-two. You'd think the years would have slowed her down a little but they hadn't. There wasn't a wrinkle on her face nor a gray hair in her head and her figure was as curvy and slim as ever. It wasn't till you looked in Darleen's face that you could see the difference. There was something about that child—was it in her eyes? Yes, I reckon it was there. A quietness that was almost sad. Not that she was a gloomy girl to slouch and sulk around the house. Four or five boys in her class in Glory High was chasing her like she was a star from the movies and yet I could see how different she was from Matty. A little good-night kiss on the swing out front, it never went no further than that. I used to look at her and think: I wished

I had met a girl like that back in 1903 when first I laid eyes on Matty. I reckon my life would tell a different tale.

The summer of the accident Darleen was bringing boy friends home to sit on the porch with her almost every Friday and Saturday nights. First thing I knew Matty would ask them in the kitchen for lemonade and ginger snaps and the next thing she'd be making googoo eyes at Darleen's beau. I was worried the first two or three times but I could tell that poor Matty didn't stand a chance. She must have known it, too, because suddenly her whole life began to change. She joined the Church of Christ and after a while she decided that wasn't toney enough and transferred to the Methodists and the next thing I knew Matty was singing in the church choir. It must have sure hit her hard to know her daughter could get men that she couldn't have. And it must have made her blink when little Darleen kept those boys interested without ever giving them nothing more than a little hand-squeeze and a good-night peck on the cheek. It was like Matty had been smitten by the Hand of God and made to kneel in humble thoughtfulness. I looked back on all those years and tears would come to my eyes. Little Darleen had done a miracle somehow. My one, my only—my little girl! But sometimes a man can love his child too much. Matty was going to church choir practice twice a week, prayer meetings on Wednesday, and church twice on Sunday. She'd walk up Jefferson Avenue and never give so much as a sidelong glance at any boy nor man that she passed by. The funny thing was she kept me out of her bed, too, and bought an old four-poster from the secondhand lady on Lafayette Avenue and put it up in the attic and made me sleep there. Well, I didn't much mind. I was close to fifty-four now and the years with Matty had just damned near played me out. To be truthful that woman's constant heat had pretty well finished me by forty.

The early months of that summer were, in some ways, the happiest of our marriage. For so many years I had troubled my soul that Darleen might somehow find out about her mother. My living nightmare was that my little girl would turn out just like Matty. I got so I didn't even trust the high school boys who'd sit out under the honeysuckle vines on the porch holding Darleen's hand. I don't trust honeysuckle. It is strong wine to the nose and a mocker to the senses. It got so I used to tiptoe around the side yard and peep through the vines at Darleen to make sure she was behaving. One night I tripped and fell on the garden rake and Darleen looked out and saw me in the moonlight laying there and commenced to giggling. That made me so mad I was awake all night. Sometimes when she'd be out there with a boy I'd feel a kind of panic like a spooky horse; sometimes I just couldn't bear the thought of some boy with dirty nails holding my little girl's hand.

Matty's church work took up more and more of her time and I used to go half crazy in the evenings with no one around, no one to talk to or even look at. Just the sound of that porch swing slowly squeaking out there in the dark.

Matty was one of the most popular members of the choir; for that matter everybody in the Methodist Church liked her. I reckon none of them knew about her years on the farm of her father, or at Cameron, nor even the years in Glory. Matty had a way of slipping around from bedroom to back seat to hayloft without anybody noticing. If any of those ladies ever guessed, poor Matty's church work would have ended there. I know those Methodists!

The night of the accident Matty was late getting home from choir practice. I had a funny feeling that night. It seemed to me that a blessing had come into my home—a change in the life of Matty, thanks to God. And yet I had not thanked Him. I had never so much as showed my face inside His church. It come over me like a cloud of gloom: that guilty thought. So I fetched my straw hat, brushed my shoes and walked up Jefferson Avenue toward the church. I decided I was going to talk to Reverend Tombes that night even if I had to rouse him out of bed. I had made up my mind to join the church. I wanted to find some little way to give my thanks to God for Matty's change. I was scared not to. I was scared if I didn't He'd take it all away and Matty'd go rampaging off again. The big front doors of the church were bolted tight. I went around to the side door, found it was unlocked and walked into the little room where the Missionary Society meets. I could see the rows of the little, yellow folding chairs, like the ones at Marple's Funeral Home. There wasn't a sound anywhere. I didn't know what the other rooms were; I'd picked up Matty one night after Missionary Meeting or I wouldn't have known that one. I tried another door and walked through the darkness, suddenly hearing voices somewhere. I found another door and opened it. I'll say this much for Matty: this time she looked surprised and even a little bit ashamed. In all the years I'd chanced to walk in on her before, she'd never bothered any more than to look at the fellow and say, Well, sport, shake hands with my husband! This time she just gasped.

She had all her clothes off except for her rolled stockings and high-heel shoes and the preacher was standing there with his BVD's on looking like a suck-egg mule. It's funny. I felt real sorry for him. He didn't look like he had anything more to do with anything that was going on than a bone does in a hound's jaws. I turned around and started away, going through the same old motions I'd been practicing for all those nineteen years of marriage. I was used to it by now. I felt a funny disappointment about something in the back of my head, though. There had been something I had wanted to tell the preacher. And now I couldn't think of it to save my life. I opened the door.

Wait! said Reverend Tombes, grabbing for his pants. Listen here now.

Yes, preacher, I said.

Listen here now, he said, shaking his finger at me. You can go tell this all over Glory and it won't matter. You know that, don't you! You can tell anyone in Glory and nobody will believe you.

I know, I said. I wasn't figuring to tell anybody, preacher.

Well, it'll not do you any good if you do, he went on, his voice rising. Because your wife's reputation in this church is above reproach. And as for me—I am the minister of the biggest church in Glory. Tell it where you will! It'll not matter, my man. Because everybody knows me. I bring them inspiration!

All right, I said. Everybody knows me, too, for that matter. I just bring them their letters twice a day. But, don't worry about me saying anything. I don't care. Preacher, nineteen years of caring has left me clean played out of caring.

Just remember, said the preacher, that we are all prone to the temptations of the flesh. None of us is perfect in this world. Forgiveness is love—you must learn that!

Preacher, I said, I learned that under a haystack up near Jacktown on a night in the hay-harvest twenty years ago. Matty, I'll leave the door unlocked for you as usual. Good night.

Try not to judge harshly, said the preacher, and I could tell it was all bothering him something fierce. Think of this woman who is your wedded wife as a poor, weak temple of flesh like each of us which now and then must falter in its steps. And try to think of me as a man of God.

A man of God, I said, but I was talking to myself now. All right. And all of them—the men, the boys—the thousands of them all the way from Jacktown to Cameron to Glory—all of them, too, then—men of God. For didn't I hear it said once somewhere that God is love. Now let me leave. And, you two, get on with your loving. Man of God—woman of God. Then go on loving!

I almost ran home. Some of the way I think I did run. I can't remember all of it. It wasn't them I was running away from. If seeing that could make me run then I'd have been running all those twenty years. I was running toward someone. I thought about the preacher; I felt for him. I felt sorry I couldn't make him understand that I didn't hate him, nor her, nor it: there'd been too many times before for that. But he couldn't understand that. He was sure I hated him. He couldn't understand a man not hating him for that. Sometimes since I've thought about that poor soul, and, deed to God, I think that's all he understands is hate. To tell you the truth, when it comes to love I don't think he understands it as good as Matty.

I could see Darleen's boy friend standing stiffly in the light of the screen door, tipping his hat and saying good night. I stood waiting till he was gone; I was trembling and shaking with some terrible emotion, but still it didn't seem that it was anything new. Darleen had hardly banged the screen door shut till I ran up the steps and on the porch. She turned, frowning through the dark to see who it was. Then she smiled and ran out on the porch into my arms. I clenched my jaws till my teeth creaked. I shut my eyes and held her in my arms, feeling my legs like jelly and something else. All her youngness was there inside the ring of my holding, all her warm youth pressed against me. For a minute I could smell the burning of that autumn night below Jacktown, the way the dusk lit up the tops of the locusts in the holler, the boughs with the blue smoke like dreams among their leaves. I could feel Matty again. Wild and young and somehow deathly, wonderfully dangerous. I couldn't help it. I had always been this way. Is it a curse?—is it a sickness of the soul, the thing I felt? Darleen's face, shadowed by the dark curl of her short bobbed hair, moved back and her black eyes searched my face, a little scared.

Daddy, what's wrong? she said. Daddy, you're hurting my back.

Well, it seemed the most natural thing in the world; it seemed like the first time me and Matty touched each other's faces. I kissed Darleen

on the mouth and pressed hard on her lips and I swear I could almost
hear the bright bells on the harnesses of the big Belgian mares up the
road in the dark where the lights gleamed at the Jacktown fair. I kissed
her hard as I had always wanted to kiss Matty when she'd come home
all mauled and mussed and loved-out, ready for sleep. I put my tongue
hard against Darleen's teeth and my hands went fumbling down among
her dress. That was when she screamed and tore away like a wild
thing and ran off the porch and I could hear her high heels clacking
off up the bricks and I stood there thinking: It's always been this way.
That's what you wanted in Matty that soft night, that tired night in the
dusk after the heave and sweat of that day in the hay harvest. Youth.
Youth, I thought.

Youth! I cried once aloud.

And then I stood there in the firefly dark, smelling the honeysuckle
and the smell of youth Darleen had left on me, like spicy dust that
moths leave on your fingers. And I suddenly understood that filthy
dirty ornery old man Gaily Rosebud—dirty old Uncle Gaily. And I knew
I wasn't any better than him; I knew I never had been, even back then.

Darleen ran crazy into uptown Glory that night. She found a crowd
of boys and girls she had always snubbed in school. Not snubbed—
that's not what I mean. Boys and girls she never had a thought or
pleasure she would want to share with, that's it. Cal McComb—Mister
McComb's boy—him and the others—and she went with them. And Cal
was drunk and run into a tree and Cal broke both his legs and three of
the children died. And my Darleen—blinded for life; her beautiful face
scarred forever.

It was Miss Cresap, from uptown with one of them Glory health officers
—she come in her car and asked me to come sit beside her in the front
seat while she told me. I didn't say nothing for the longest while. I
didn't cry. I didn't feel sick or sad nor nothing. I didn't feel nothing.
Miss Cresap asked me if I wanted some ammonium to smell or a drink
of water or anything and I said, No. Then I said No two or three more
times. I can't remember what I was saying No to. Maybe to just everything. Or maybe to nothing at all. It's funny—I never thought a thought
about Matty. I reckon she was still up there fooling around with
Reverend Tombes.

That was sure a damned fool thing I done later—going up there and
punching Mister McCombs. He never had nothing to do with it, except

maybe for giving his boy the booze. I felt like such a fool when I walked away from there afterward, remembering how bad I'd wanted to stomp Mister McCombs to death. What for? Would that bring back my baby's eyes? Would it take the scars off my Darleen's face? I didn't blame Mister McCombs when he called the Glory Courthouse and had Chief Smithers lock me up. I sat there for a long while in that cell, the first time in my life, too. And all I could think about was the way Matty had felt beside me up in the shadow of that haystack near Jacktown that autumn night so long ago. The cracked-corn smell on her fingers; the woman smell on her child's body. It had been the same with me and Darleen that night—the very same. And I knowed suddenly that it had always been that way in me. And I knowed, too, how long I'd looked at little Darleen that way, and keeping it all stoppered up like sour home-brew about to bust its cork. And then I thought about that business in the church room. Them there. Him and Matty. That was what busted the cork.

Miss Cresap come after about two hours and paid my fine out of her own purse. Then she slipped Chief Smithers an extra twenty to keep it all quiet so's I wouldn't get in bad with the Civil Service and lose my mail route. She drove me home and parked a good long while out there in front, under the trees. I was glad not to have to go in right away and face up to Matty. After what I had done. I told Miss Cresap what I done, too. And, because I sensed somehow she was the kind you could tell things and know they'd never breathe a word, I told her about Matty. I told her about Matty all the way back to Uncle Gaily Rosebud and the days in Cameron and all of it up to that night in the church. I told her about that, too, and she just sat there listening and biting on her lip. I told her about all the thousands of men and the way Matty was and how I couldn't hate her for it. And I told her how hard I tried to make the preacher understand I didn't hate him. He couldn't understand. He couldn't. He was mad like I had stole something from him. I sat there awhile more without saying a word, I was pretty well talked-out, fought-out, jailed-out and played-out that night. But all of a sudden the riddle of it all just come back and choked me like fingers round my throat. Miss Cresap sure must have thought I was cracked. Because all of a sudden I just taken and drawed back my fist and let go and it's a pure wonder I didn't bust that little round piece of glass in her speedometer. I turned and looked at her before I got out of the car. My knuckles was bleeding and scuffed but they never hurt. And I gestured with that bruised hand in the air like I was trying to grab ahold of something: atrying to take hold of a thing invisible up there and never let go of it.

Miss Cresap! I shouted like a crazy man. What does it all—? I mean, God damn it, what does it all—?

What does it all what? I thought directly. Well, I don't know to this day what I was trying to say. I haven't the foggiest notion what I was trying so hard to ask Miss Cresap. But, you know it was queer! She seemed to know plain as day what I was trying to ask.

I wish I knew, Chester, said Miss Cresap, laying her fingers across my bruised fist. I wish I knew. Maybe someday we'll all know. And won't it be funny if we find out, at last, that all of us—you Chester, Darleen, Matty, that old uncle of hers, the preacher up there tonight, me—that all of us, always, have been hunting through heaven and earth: the dirt and the stars, searching ourselves and each other, looking, forever looking for the same one simple thing?

Judge Alexander Campbell Peabody

Last August when I left the Weston State Hospital for the Insane it was in the usual way: they shipped me home in a B. & O. baggage car on the morning train to Glory. Not many people have ever left that asylum in any other way. And perhaps that's just as well; the world of the living on the outside might frighten them with its absurdity. My oldest daughter Mabel saw to it that I had a nice burial on Glory Hill with the slightest possible publicity. Marple dressed me in the same old gray alpaca coat in which I had so often addressed the State Legislature. And also Mabel respected the two requests in my will. One was that, instead of the usual Christian funeral service, a passage from Thoreau's *Essay on Civil Disobedience* and a chapter from the *Book of Job* be read over my grave by my old friend Thomas Jackson Sorrell. The other was that I be laid to rest with my right hand holding my worn university copy of Holmes' *Autocrat of the Breakfast Table*. Having held a lifelong suspicion that either of the other worlds beyond life might turn out to

221

be rather dull places, I felt it pardonable to equip myself with a book which surely would keep me amused till Doomsday's horn shall sound. Both of these wishes merely confirmed in my daughter's mind that she had been right in 1924 in signing the papers for my commitment to the asylum.

Oratory was a gift a few scattered people still remember me for in West Virginia. But as for dirges and lamentations, I was always a little above that sort of thing. So if you're listening now to my voice in the expectation of a jeremiad of self-pity I'm afraid you'll be disappointed. I loved my life—every moment of it: the sorrows and disappointments just as much as the joys. I respected my life, too. And because of that, I suppose, it was natural that I respected the lives of others.

I loved both my daughters Mabel and Rina. And I loved my wife Sade, too. But I am afraid I loved my son Wesley Rush Peabody more than any of them. It was wrong of me, I suppose. And yet he seemed a continuation of myself, a perpetuity of all my beliefs, and something immortal of my flesh as well. Even more than that it seemed to me that Wesley was destined to achieve things in the State, perhaps in the entire nation, which I had never seemed to have the power or luck to do. In 1907 when Wesley Rush graduated from Law School at the University he was the youngest as well as the most brilliant member of his class. When I offered to take him into my own law office in Glory he told me he felt his life had a mission which could never find fulfillment in Apple County. I shall never forget the light in his eyes that morning, the joyous look on his face, the ring of the true crusader in his voice. He sat awhile in my small office and talked, the words tumbling in torrents from his heart, his fist rising to pound my desk from time to time as he spoke indignantly of the rampant and rising power of the Trusts in America. He said he believed that if the barons of coal and steel succeeded in crushing the Knights of Labor that the rights of the working-man would vanish and with it would die the very lifeblood of the Republic itself. His voice fairly sang as he spoke of his heroes: Mother Jones; Altgeld, the sublime and self-martyred governor of Illinois; John Mitchell, the head of the miner's union. His voice grew deep and raging as he talked of the Homestead Massacre in 1892 and the great Anthracite Strike of five years back. His eyes were moist as he rose suddenly from the chair, walked across the room and stood looking a long while, silent, at the framed picture of my friend Clarence Darrow.

I've got to learn politics, Father, he said. I know I could spend a life-time here in Glory fighting for the good things you've always stood for. I could save a few men from the gallows up in that reeking dungeon, the state penitentiary. But somehow I want to strike at the roots of all this. I want to dig right to the source of this evil and destroy it at its origin. And I know the only way I can achieve this end is to find a place in politics.

I was still a moment: half of my silence was an inexpressible joy and pride, the other half was my concern that Wesley Rush didn't know how shabby and sometimes shameful the road could be to reach these glori-ous ends. I prayed to God to inspire me to some speech that would fore-warn Wesley of these things and yet which would not, at the same time, discourage that splendid ardor.

You dream someday of being elected to the state senate, I said.

Father, I think of that as only a little pause along the way, said Wesley Rush. What I really dream of is the senate of the United States. In a position like that I could fight—I could do something!

I closed my eyes, touching the lids with a thumb and forefinger, and prayed he would not misunderstand me.

Of course, I said, you know that getting there's sometimes a hard and dirty road. Even the greatest statesmen of the Republic have some-times had to lie a little, retreat a little, make friends with evil men, speak often to the people as if they were confused and blinded children, pretend to stand for the very things they hated, and shake hands with the same powers their souls had sworn someday they'd defeat. You know these things, don't you, Wesley?

Oh, sure, he said. I know these things, Father. Even the greatest crusaders have had to shut their eyes sometimes to what expediency made them do. In the beginning even Lincoln himself had to speak out from time to time against the blacks. But I know that in the end it's worth it, Father. Because, in the end, I know that I and the things I believe in will win.

Remember Altgeld, I said, as casually as I could. In the end he lost. He pardoned the Haymarket anarchists. And in that gesture finished his career forever.

But, Father, don't you see? cried Wesley Rush. In the end he lost. But all that he stood for won—and it will live forever.

I rose, went over, put my arms around my son and held him against my heart. We had never been this close in spirit.

I think you understand, Wesley, I said. I think you'll get there, my boy. God keep and bless you.

But in my heart I felt the chill of coldest fears for Wesley Rush. And in my mind, although I couldn't admit it then, I saw him bravely riding off to crucifixion, death at the hands of shrewd and ruthless old-guard politicians who would hand him a rope, and swear they were with him, give him a handclasp and a friendly cigar, and send him away to watch him hang himself. How often I'd seen it happen in my time: a man who starts out pledging to save the world, he finds that getting up there calls for toughness, and so he gets tough and finally wins his goal: the high place from which he once dreamed he'd rescue suffering, starving men he once had loved. But now that he's there, something inside him's dead. The getting tough—that was what calloused his spirit. That tender heart is now cold as stone: too cold to give a damn for people he once worshiped, too busy now to remember all his vows, too rich sometimes to remember even the faces of his people, too rotten at last to care for anything on earth but his fat stomach, convention whores, and the huge checks of managerial gratitude.

Wesley Rush was away from home most of the time those years. I'd sometimes read the labor papers: the singing, glowing praises of my son. He seemed to have a genius for keeping a rare and wondrous kind of balance. His popularity was growing among the people of the state, his name was getting bigger every day in the state capitol. He was popular with politicians, popular with labor leaders, popular even in most powerful business circles. My pride increased. I knew that all my fears had been wrong. I thought to myself: You fool, you're growing old that's all. You've got no faith in youth. Maybe you were even a little envious that day! Jealous of what you knew your son would be! The things he stands for—they're the same things you've fought for all your life: fought for and lost and haven't even been blessed with the curious dignity of honest defeat. People in Glory don't see you as a fallen hero. People in Glory point at you and laugh: crank, eccentric radical, author of some silly and privately printed books. And all your idealism impotent and flabby, as if faith were some kind of prostate gland which got so swelled, at last, Ed Follansbee's scalpel had to cut it out. But somehow I didn't mind. Even the misery and nagging of my home couldn't drag my spirits down. I knew my boy Wesley Rush Peabody was going to win; that he was going to be all the greatness I had failed to be.

Sometimes in those years I dreamed back to my own boyhood. Born on a rocky, wretched patch of hillside farm in Pocahontas County, child of a mad and visionary Scotch-Irish father who fought to farm that land as if his hoe were a sword and he was engaged with the very earth of those steep, flinty hills in some queer kind of battle to the death. But nothing would ever grow. And he would hurl his hoe, cursing, into the scrub pines and laurel and ride off for a month or two to preach hell and salvation in the light of camp-meeting torches and praise God and curse the earth God made: that earth which every summer for forty years had tricked and beaten my father to his knees. And yet each spring he'd always start again. Spending the little money that we had for onion sets and seed corn and a new hoe to replace the one he'd always thrown away and somehow never was able to find again.

My mother was silent and patient; barren after I was born. She was a sweet-faced Christian who never complained. I used to hide in the polk-weeds and watch my father down there on the hill fighting the land as if it were another man. And I'd cry and beat my little fists bloody against a spruce tree and pray that someday we'd quit the farm forever and move to a town like Clarksburg and live in a decent house and see my father quit his senseless feud. My father and those hills!—he couldn't win. I used to lay abed at night and think of us living in a town, where every summer I'd go with my father to see Buffalo Bill's Wild West Show, and ride to church on Sundays in a decent buggy. But still my father bowed his beaten head each spring and hurled himself into the battle with the hillside. And nothing ever grew. Nothing but weeds and me.

All of that happened nearly seventy years ago. And yet, in those years when Wesley was running every term for State Senate, those far-off times seemed close as hours ago. Each voting-time for Wesley seemed like the sowing-time had been for my old father. I prayed it wouldn't be like that for Wesley. I prayed the seeds he scattered would come up; that something, at least, would grow. Then a few years before the Great War Wesley's fortunes changed. He was taken under the great, gray wing of United States Senator Goff Rogerson, the father of Glory's richest man Millard. Goff seemed bent on finding his protégé a place of power. Wesley Rush was on his way. I had my hopes, I had my prayers. But both of them were haunted by misgivings. Goff Rogerson was one of the most popular politicians in the history of West Virginia. He was a millionaire many times over and yet everybody knew he was just as common as dirt. Nobody hated nor envied Goff for his wealth and power. Instead it seemed that common men wished to keep him always before their eyes as reminders of what they themselves could become.

Whenever Goff came to Glory he sat around the evenings in the Mound Hotel and told the boys a few off-color stories and set up liquor and passed out good cigars and made grand promises, most of which he kept. Nobody cared about the bigger promises Goff made to other and more influential men. He kept those promises, too. Nobody would have believed the stories about those promises, not even if they'd been shown the proof of them on a sworn and notarized paper. Everybody loved Goff Rogerson. He was like a kind of mirror for every man; a magic mirror that showed them the reflection of what they could be and not what they were. He was common as dirt. Goff was almost seventy-five in 1910: a grand old man, a pride to the state, and one of the big powers in national politics. Everybody had forgotten—or hadn't bothered remembering—how Goff Rogerson had made his fortune back in the Sixties. During the War Between the States Goff's family owned a huge stand of timber over in the eastern counties. The beginnings of Goff's family fortune were simple. He sold railroad ties to the Union Army and hired Rebel guerrillas to tear them up, providing a constant supply and demand. After the war he invested this small fortune in coal and started making his big one. By 1900 the state had named a town after him and a College for Negroes. Goff Rogerson was for everybody. By 1905 they dedicated a twelve-foot steel statue to Goff by Gutzon Borglum; it stands today in a small square near the state capitol building. Goff was for everyone: even foreign artists. And by that time he had a keen interest in steel which gave the statue a rather material appropriateness. And he had an even more heartwarming interest in Wesley Rush Peabody. All I could do was sit by and watch. And pray. It's a queer thing. But, in the many times that I sat around talking to Davis Cresap or Tom Sorrell, the subject of my son and Senator Rogerson was a topic which neither of them ever mentioned. I was thankful for that. Because I was worried. I knew the beauty of Wesley Rush's ideals. But I knew, as well, how fragile such ideals can often be. And so I waited.

My wife Sade and I were never close. In most things I worshiped the ground she walked on and yet it never seemed that we ever got truly close to one another. There was rarely, in all our years of marriage, a time when we sat down together for more than three minutes and talked about anything. She never seemed interested in what I ever had to say. As for the things which interested her—crocheting, the Women's Christian Temperance Union, her flower garden, recipes scissored out of the *Delineator,* and the Methodist Missionary Fund—I used to lie awake at night trying to think up thoughtful and interested things to say to her about these subjects. Deep in her heart—though she would have died before she'd have said so—I knew she felt a deep humiliation at the way most people in Glory felt about me.

Years and years before I had been one of the state's outstanding criminal lawyers. After fifteen years of successful practice I was elected Judge in Apple County. One spring morning a company policeman was shot to death at the foot of Misery Hollow on the Parr's Run Mine Property. I knew the man. He had been in my court twice on a charge of public drunkenness and once for wife-beating. I had set him free on probation. I knew, too, something which few people in Glory know to this day. I knew he was not one of the regular company policemen on Millard Rogerson's payroll. I knew he was a Baldwin-Felts strike-breaker brought in from the southern part of the state and I took the trouble to find out that he had served time for robbery in the state penitentiary right here in Glory. For a time no one was arrested for this man's murder. Then one evening Chief Smithers, Sheriff Dunn and two special deputies—one of them a Parr's Run Mine guard—brought to Apple County jail an illiterate Russian-born steelworker from Benwood. They said they had found proof in a trunk in the man's roominghouse that he had killed the guard. At the next term of court the man appeared before me charged with first-degree murder. It was then that Ansel Carruthers, the prosecuting attorney, produced the single exhibit which was to prove the man's guilt. It was an old forty-four caliber revolver. I asked to examine it carefully. All my years as a criminal lawyer had not failed me. I had handled a lot of murder weapons in my time, and I knew that this was not one of them. I recognized that revolver. There could be no mistaking it. It was an old gun that Police Chief Smithers had kept for at least ten years in the bottom drawer of his desk. I knew that gun could never have found its way into the hands of this wretched man. He sat at a table in the courtroom, with a cheap lawyer at his side:

a man nearly as illiterate as himself. The court had appointed the lawyer in his behalf: an appointment which had been made without my knowledge.

Mister Carruthers, I said, I know this gun. And so do you. And so does the Glory Chief of Police. It has laid in the bottom of his desk for the past ten years. Mister Carruthers, do you offer this as exhibit A for the State?

Ansel's face was plum-colored. He struggled with himself for a moment before he could answer.

I do, your honor, he said, presently.

In that case, Mister Carruthers, I said, rising from my seat behind the bench, I do not now find it compatible with either my personal conscience or my civic responsibility as a judge of this court and a member of this bar to sit any longer as a public officer of this county administration.

I was calm, I was beyond the point in which men shake with rage: my hands were still as steel. I was disgusted and sick at heart. I thought swiftly of men I had sentenced in the past. I scarcely dared wonder whether I had examined the evidence against them as scrupulously as I had this. It seemed to me that every human being I had ever sentenced, however lightly, was suddenly innocent. It seemed to me that every conviction in every court on earth since time's beginning was morally wrong. I turned and went into my chambers. I tore off my black robe and threw it in a pile in the corner. I walked through the courtroom in my street clothes without looking at anyone on either side of me. And I never came back.

That night Tom Sorrell called on me at my home and took my hand and sat awhile with me in the parlor. He did not speak. I could not look him in the eye. We had been close friends for more than twenty-five years. And yet on one thing we had always disagreed: the justice of the death penalty. Tonight in that silence we seemed to speak a thousand words. And yet there was nothing that either of us could say aloud. And so as we sat there with the cool spring wind blowing the curtains and filling the room with the scents of new-rising life, there came a ring at my doorbell. It was young Marcy Cresap.

Father's pretty sick again, she said. It's his heart, you know. Otherwise *he* would have come tonight, Judge Peabody.

She smiled and brought something round that she had been holding behind her back. It was a bouquet of violets from the Cresap yard.

He asked me to bring you some small remembrance of him, she said. So I picked these. They're his favorite flower.

Thank you, Marcy, I said, taking the little flowers from her hand. And thank Davis for me. They're a beautiful gift. And a plain one. And, I reckon, that's right. Because after today I'm a very plain man.

She quickly shook her head No and suddenly stepped forward boldly, put her arms on my tired shoulders and kissed me on the cheek. I'll never forget that. Young Marcy Cresap kissed me on the cheek that strange spring night. I'll bet my daughter Mabel talks about that still.

I tried to start up my law practice again in Glory but it was no use. The town wasn't the same. And neither was I. Somehow something had been picking at my brain like a bird's beak since that awful day in court: the bird's beak of conscience, it was; the ceaseless pecking, pecking of a thought. I closed up my little office and moved my desk and all my law books into the little room just off our parlor. For the first two weeks I just sat there, staring at the books, my old Oliver typing machine, the picture of Darrow on my wall. And then I began to work.

Every year for five years I wrote a little book and sent the manuscript off to a publisher in Chicago along with a check to pay for the printing and binding. And every book was about the same thing: the obsession, the madness, the hole the bird's beak of that thought had picked at last clear through my head: my little books were arguments, pleas and essays—sometimes even rhymes—against the taking of men's lives by the law. In the beginning, I suppose, I thought someone would buy the books from me. But even if I hadn't thought that—it wouldn't have stopped me. Dead men hung in the gallows of my dreams. Their dead hands struggled slowly free from the leather thongs that bound them. Those hands reached up and tugged the black bag from their faces. And mercifully, forgivingly, almost tenderly, those eyes looked into mine. Yet in their deep regard I could read something else behind their faces: a plea for mercy. No, not mercy for themselves. The judgments I had passed on them had made it too late for that. Mercy for those to come.

No one bought my books against legal vengeance. Even now—a year after my death—they lie piled high in moldy boxes in the cellar. No—I am wrong. Each year I found three customers for each new book. One was Tom Sorrell, one was Doctor Will Cecil and one was Davis Cresap. I ran ads for the rest in the newspapers of distant cities. Few answers came. At last I went up Jefferson Avenue with a market basket full of my little books and passed them out free to any who'd take one. Some time later I would see them lying in the gutter where they had been tossed away after a moment's glance. It was not an easy time for Mabel and Rina, my two girls.

Mother would be so ashamed! Mabel sobbed one day running indoors and upstairs to her room. She had been out in the front watering the lawn and shrubbery with a garden hose. She had seen the crude picture of a gallows and a dangling man which some of the neighbor children had drawn with chalk on the bricks of our sidewalk. I fetched a scrub brush and a pail of hot water and went out front to erase it. I looked down at it a moment. Then I went back indoors.

No, I thought. Let it stay. Let it be seen there on my walk—the image of the savagery and cruelty I stand against. Let people going by see it. And let them think of this frightful picture—drawn by the hand of a child: a hand which may someday hang a man—or, just as probably, a hand which may be bound to its twin hand with a leather thong: the thong they bind men with before they let them drop. Let the picture stay there on my walk. And let it stand for me and the great evil thing I once upheld but which I shall now fight, in whatever years of life are left to me.

Sade died in 1910. I missed her dreadfully. Sometimes at night I would wake up thinking of things I might have said to her about her canning, about the Women's Christian Temperance Union, or her garden full of flowers. And yet I knew that, even if her head lay that very moment across the bolster from me, in the morning I would not be able to remember what it was I meant to say. Mabel was back from New York. Rina's tragedy had driven her deep into the doll house of her childhood. But I still had my dreams of Wesley Rush. A lot had happened in the years since that morning we had talked in my law office. Now Wesley was the junior United States Senator from West Virginia under the aegis of the mighty Goff Rogerson. My son seemed more impassioned than ever; he voted and spoke for civil rights, for help for the aged, for mine-safety reforms, for aid to neglected children, for investigation into conditions in the state mental and penal institutions. I decided, in the innocence of later life, that I had been mistaken about Senator Goff Rogerson. I walked along Jefferson Avenue with a new spring in my walk, giving my little books away. Perhaps it was my fancy but it seemed to me that fewer people laughed behind my back; the children no longer drew ugly pictures on my walk out front. I thought to myself: They respect me. They know I am the father of Senator Wesley Rush Peabody. And they know that a son's ideals do not come from nowhere. They must know that Wesley Rush is everything his father meant to be. And they must see in my face how happy I am that it is he instead of me.

It was in the winter of that year that my son reached the end of the rope which Goff Rogerson had so carefully played out inch by inch. And when Wesley Rush reached the end of that rope he found a noose. I understood so clearly the working of Goff Rogerson's mind. He had spied my son early in his career. He had seen him as a young man of idealism, courage, ambition, and a passion for social reform. He had seen my son's great potential for popularity among the masses of people. And I believe that Goff Rogerson knew that, with or without his powerful sponsorship, the boy would rise to a position of power, in any event. Still—better to have him close where he could be watched, better have him handy where he could be controlled when the moment came, good to have him nigh where the bright light of his young beliefs could illuminate the myth of Goff Rogerson's own great liberalism. And, most essential of all, convenient to have young Wesley Rush so near for what must be done; near enough for his hands to take the rope, and then to let him have his way awhile, and play the strong hemp outward inch by inch, until the noose at last would tighten round his neck.

It was in 1919. The land was in a state of madness amid the clamor and hysterical purges of Wilson's Attorney-General Mitchell Palmer. Wesley Rush made a speech in the senate in defense of Eugene V. Debs, a protest against Debs' imprisonment in the penitentiary in Glory and later in Atlanta. Goff Rogerson's speech that followed was a masterpiece; I will say that for it: it was the sheer genius of Machiavellian treachery. Goff spoke in sad, apologetic tones as if he were trying to explain away the thoughtless rashness of his young, impetuous protégé. He said the boy had spoken thoughtlessly. Goff Rogerson's eyes filled with tears from time to time but his strong, devout and dangerous voice did not falter. He said he could not have concerned himself more with Wesley Rush Peabody if he had been his own son.

Nay, think of him not as treacherous, murdering Brutus! cried Goff Rogerson on the floor of the Senate that afternoon. See him with mercy if you can find mercy in your hearts! See him as sad and innocent Anthony, lured and beguiled by the seductive Cleopatra of disguised Bolshevism!

Then he had a drink of water. He tasted it wistfully, classically, as Socrates might have taken his first sip of sad hemlock. But the water in that glass that day was heady and victorious wine for Goff Rogerson. His young challenger had finished himself and Goff knew it. Still he went on for another half hour. He quoted Shakespeare, he quoted Will Rogers, he quoted Jefferson, Paine, and the Holy Bible. And even in a stroke of masterful daring at the end, he quoted Lenin himself.

This boy, he cried, at last, is guiltless. He did not think!

In times of national panic the people do not want boys in their Senate. Especially, do they not want boys who do not think. Wesley Rush Peabody was ruined. And none knew better than I that his ruin had begun the day Goff Rogerson took him under his gray and smothering wing. His term finished that year. Everybody knew he would not run again. I heard from him once—a card from Detroit telling me that he had taken up Christian Science. A year later a story was published in the *New York Tribune* that Wesley Rush Peabody, former junior United States Senator from West Virginia had become the legal counsel for the New York State Communist Party. I lost track of my boy for months after that. I was getting over the first of a series of strokes which finally freed me from Weston and brought me home to Glory Hill. Early in the spring of 1923 I read that Wesley Rush was in Europe studying the collapsed economy of Germany. Weeks later in a Paris interview which appeared in the *New York Sun* my boy was quoted as saying that the single threat to the prosperity of Europe and the peace of the world was the Jewish domination of European banking. Three months after that someone cut out and saved for me a news clipping telling of Wesley Rush Peabody's trip to the Vatican and his imminent conversion to the Catholic Church.

One cold day in January 1924 my boy came home to Glory. He took a room at the Mound Hotel and did not come to see me or his sisters for a week. The morning he called that he was coming, Mabel made Rina bundle up and go with her up to their Aunt Stella's. Mabel said that as far as she was concerned her brother was dead and she swore an oath before me that never again in her life would she speak his name. Wesley Rush looked older. Older than a boy of thirty-three should look. I wanted somehow to put my arms around him. But all that I had ever put my arms around before was gone. He seemed very quiet and self-possessed.

It's good to see you, son, I said.

He picked up one of my little books from my desk, turned it over in his hands a minute and then threw it back.

You're still writing those things, he said.

Yes, I smiled. Still at it, I reckon. What about you? Sit down, boy. It's been a long while, you know. They tell me you've been all over the world. Tell me a little about things over there.

I've only got a minute, he said quietly. I haven't got time to sit.

I read about you now and then, I said. Where you were. What you were doing.

I looked at him steadily a moment, wondering whether I should mention it.

They tell me you've joined the Catholic Church, I said.

Where did you ever hear a wild tale like that, for goodness sakes? he laughed, and began to pull his collar up around his neck and moved toward the door.

Well, I said, uncomfortably, I suppose you'll be starting up a little law practice here in Glory now. With all your experience you should be a whiz by now, son.

No, he said. Nothing at all like that. I'm through with all that. When I came back to New York I worked for a while with the American Legion. I've got enough money saved up to get along for quite a while. I'll probably be working with the Legion here in Glory.

He stared at me a moment more and my heart ached a little to see so much hate in his face.

Well, good-by, he said, went out the door, closed it and walked off through the snow.

I never saw him again. I couldn't sleep that night. I couldn't sleep for nights after that. It's bad enough when a man thinks he's wasted his own life. But, when he thinks he's spoiled his son's as well, it's hard to sleep at nights. But still I'd wonder what was the wrong I'd done. And sometimes I'd think it wasn't even Goff Rogerson that was to blame. I used to lie awake there thinking and smelling the old glycerine-and-rose water smell of Sade still in the pillow and I'd wonder if maybe the men who deeply believe—who fight for one thing all their lives alone—for truth, freedom, maybe even the men who fight for wrong—if maybe they aren't slowly dying out. I'd lie there wondering if there wasn't something queer about our new century that makes of boys the man my son became: scuttling in terror back and forth between the barricades, never sure, after that first big awful wound which comes to everyone, which side they're on. Maybe it wasn't me nor Goff nor politics nor any of the other things to blame: The way my boy once was—how he is now. What makes it happen that way, I'd like to know? It seems as if it's some queer virus in the air of this bewildering century we've begun.

Don't blame Mabel for having me sent away. I got on her nerves real badly toward the end. I'd walk the house at night—I couldn't sleep. I'd slip downstairs in my bathrobe and carpet slippers and feel around my old desk in the dark: those piles and piles of books nobody wanted. I got to going up to Charley Seat's with prescriptions Follansbee had written and pretty soon I'd need them more often. Because I knew I had to sleep: my walking the house all night wasn't fair to Mabel. And I slept. Because Follansbee was prescribing laudanum. And before spring came I got so I was using three or four bottles every week. Then one day Follansbee said he wouldn't give me any more. And I felt so sick and weak by sundown of that night that I went up to Charley Seat's drugstore and begged him to let me have some without a prescription. Charley chuckled and shook his head. So I went on home. And around four in the morning Mabel came downstairs and found me with the light on in my office. I was sitting in front of the old Oliver. Mabel said my typewriting had wakened her. And she asked me what I was doing.

Starting another book, I said. Sorry I woke you up.

Starting another book, she said. Another of those books on *that!* When will you give up, for heaven's sake?

I'll never give up, I said, my hands trembling, my eyes full of tears.

We'll just see about that, she said.

Never, I said. I'll never give up. Daughter, that's the way I'm made!

Father, I don't mind telling you I've reached the end of my endurance, she said. I might as well tell you I know what was in those two bushel baskets of empty medicine bottles out back. *Dope!* And don't think everyone in Glory doesn't know about it, too!

Well, now, I said softly. I wonder who told them.

Father, I've got to have a talk with Doctor Follansbee, she said. I think it's only fair to tell you. I'm going to call him in the morning. Something has got to be done!

And so they did it. Yes, something was done. Between Mabel and Follansbee and Skippy Wofford I was in Weston before the dogwood even bloomed. And after those three asylum years: the only real hell my life has ever known, I came home once again—this time to Glory Hill.

I don't rest well these nights. It's quiet here. It's peaceful here on Glory Hill and everyone here is kind. It's Wesley Rush that keeps me up these nights. I hear him sometimes running through the dark, the footsteps of a man in mortal terror. And here's the awful part—his terror is the kind that will not be appeased until he's made some other person feel a terror worse than his. He organized the Ku Klux Klan in Apple County. And what a shady, skulking lot they are. They run and shout and thunder through the dark, like children playing ghosts in pillowcases, children who play with matches in the closets and set the house on fire. The ones they're after now are Davis Cresap's daughter and the young Jewish doctor who's her aide. They burn their crosses up in Misery Hollow and high on the clean, good rim of Roberts' Ridge, dirtying the night with yellow, flickering hate; dimming the moon with scared and sneaking flames.

God pity my poor son's friends, God pity him. He doesn't know what I know on Glory Hill. He can't see things eternal as I see them here; his eyes can't grasp, as mine can, old times gone and time unborn, up in the risky womb of years to come. He doesn't know how swift the flames from burning crosses spread; he doesn't grasp the thermal point of hate; nor know that little fires like his in time may streak out like blood-poisoning through the land and set the whole earth belching like a torch, and leave this lovely star God gave us once, a little cinder blackening in the sky.

That little fire, that burning cross can do that. So listen to me, you out there. Can you still hear my voice in Glory? Then promise me if you see Wesley Rush Peabody tonight you'll make him put his burning crosses out. It matters!—do you hear? It's your world, too!—it's every bit of world you'll ever have!

Now, let me sleep.

Professor Kenneth Henshaw Founds

My life proves one thing, at least: a man can't shut sex out of his life for ten years without its catching up with him in the end. Time without love has a way of piling up like unpaid bills until, at last, there comes the day when they are too-long overdue, when postponement is impossible any more; and when the awful sum of them, plus interest, must be paid. On that day some men go gently mad and sit behind the drawn blinds of a furnished room, answering the thousand whispering lips of women in the air about them. Some men fetch rifles and calmly stalk the town shooting down those God told them just last night were bound in thick conspiracy against them. Others dash suddenly to desks and snatch up pen and ink and scribble symphonies or write, from the store in them of love-remembered, the simple lyrics that live a thousand years. And other men, like me, merely begin to move like sleepwalkers under the spell of some sightless and sense-drugged indiscretion and end up with nothing worse for punishment than being fired and hounded out

236

of town. Sometimes I reckon that sinners, criminals and poets are only men trying savagely to remember something. I mean men like me who strive for reason with unreasonable gestures, seek for beauty and sometimes do unbeautiful things; creatures groping their guilty backward way to innocence itself: a face, a tune, a memory, a toy, a something once misplaced in the misted mythology of us each—a green child playing in a green, lost garden.

It's been a long time since I've been to Glory. I see the *Glory Argus* every morning though; I have them send it to me in the mail. And these days when I read of Marcy Cresap and what those men in Glory are trying to do to her, it's almost all that I can do to keep from going back. They're nailing her like Christ against that courthouse wall! My Marcy—my darling! My first, my only love! I want to go back there and stand by her side and fight for her. It takes all the strength of will that I have left to keep me from doing that. And that's the bitterest knowledge I have to bear—the knowing that my being on her side would do her more injury than her enemies could; they'd jeer and point and slander her all the more. They'd say: Just see what kind of man she has for a friend! Ken Henshaw—degenerate betrayer of schoolgirls. Wouldn't you know his sort of man would be on her side?

And all the women on Mabel Peabody's party line would suddenly remember Marcy and me in school together and how I was her steady beau in Glory High. And they'd whisper about the beautiful spring night in 1912—the graduation dance—and Marcy's card was marked so she'd have every dance with me. And out of all that innocent loveliness they'd fashion some ingenious ugliness and give it to the men to use against her there. Because my name is mud in Glory now—No, worse than mud: there's something clean in mud. And so I have to helplessly stand by and watch what they're doing to Marcy down in Glory and never raise my voice or lift a finger in her defense. Exile is my penitentiary cell, and silence is the lash Time flogs me with.

I can remember hardly a moment of my childhood when our house wasn't echoing with music. My beautiful young mother played the piano and my father sang in a gay, brave baritone. We had a Pianola, too, and the biggest collection of piano rolls in Apple County. And the fine Edison phonograph my father bought was one of the first in Glory. Even when I was four years old I was certain that I was going to grow up to be a band-master like John Philip Sousa. There was something else I was sure about, too, and that was who I was going to marry. I think the first time I decided to marry Marcy Cresap was when she showed me her little tea set. A tiny pot, three saucers, three cups and all of them rimmed with bands of genuine golf leaf. The first time I had tea with Marcy was one summer day out in the shade of her father's favorite apple tree. Her mother had made us little cucumber sandwiches. We sat round Marcy's small playhouse table, drinking tea from the little cups and eating our cucumber sandwiches. From time to time I would pour a little more tea for the enormous doll who shared our lunch; its wax face had melted and run a little, giving it an expression of lumpish and sagging fortitude. That made it look exactly and unfortunately like poor Mrs. Genevieve Brast whose husband drank. For this reason Marcy never called the doll anything else and whenever Mrs. Brast came to visit, Marcy's mother had to hide the doll upstairs in the clothes-press.

Poor Mrs. Brast, Marcy would whisper to me behind her hand so that the doll would not hear. Her husband *drinks.*

And sometimes on wintry afternoons when all the day was a gray dusk except for the falling snow, Marcy would bring her tea set over to my house and we would sit up in my playroom beside the snowbound window, while downstairs my mother would be playing Debussy or MacDowell or Chaminade on the piano and Marcy would be pouring tea and chattering away to a whole roomful of the strange and distressed creatures of her fancy: Mr. and Mrs. Cobbloy and their retinue of children, neighbors and indigent relatives—paupers every last one of them and dreadfully dependent on Marcy for aid and advice. I know I had as much imagination as most children and yet it seemed to me sometimes that Marcy really saw these people: their frozen, red noses, their ragged, tatter-demalion, scarecrow clothes, the chilled toes poking out of broken shoes. She was constantly worrying about them, ceaselessly advising them, offering them food, fetching doctors for their sick babies, sighing gravely to herself over the haplessness of their lives. It was a strange fantasy for a child of four and yet it never left her. She would scold me sometimes because I had not reached into the empty pockets of my small britches and fetched out a handful of imaginary money to give them. An odd dream for a child of four. But then Marcy was no ordinary little girl.

When her father's coach-dog Brutus died one summer they buried him in the back yard beneath the apple tree. And it was there that I once found Marcy in the hum and fragrance of an autumn day sitting before the small grave in her little rocking chair and singing. And because she knew it was an occasion for sadness and respect she had thought it best to be singing a hymn. And since she could think of no hymn in particular just then, I suppose, she was singing the old Temperance song "Father, Dear Father! Come Home With Me Now!" The words didn't seem to make much sense but Marcy's voice seemed to hit squarely at the sad, sweet melancholy of the old coach-dog's death. I stood there hidden by the puzzletree and wept shameless tears for poor Brutus in the cold earth there beneath the shiny tips of Marcy's little shoes.

But it was the wretched and needy family of Cobbloys that took up most of Marcy's thoughts in those years. There seemed never a day went by when one of the Cobbloy children didn't need shoes, when Mister Cobbloy wasn't in the County Jail for beating poor Mrs. Cobbloy; there was never a respite for Marcy from the unremmiting round of the injuries, shortages, slights and sicknesses of that Cobbloy family which, to her alone, was visible and real. And she would worry over them, love them, tend them, fetch help for them when help was to be had. To this day I can see her solemn, little moon-face lift from the tiny teacup and stare out our window at the ragged, pristine majesty of slowly falling snow.

Poor Mrs. Cobbloy, Marcy Cresap would sigh, taking a sip of tea and rocking a little faster, her big eyes watching the snowflakes with a little frown as if she considered each of them a mean little joke which Winter had come to play upon the poor. It's her sister Lettie now. She's sick abed again with the quinsy! The worstest she's ever had it, Kenneth! And would you believe it?—that old Doctor Scallywag wants ten cents to come see her and she hasn't got it. She simply hasn't got it!

Marcy, Marcy, did you guess back long ago in those old winter dusks that the Cobbloys would forever be with you and always with broken shoes and croupy coughs and snuffling noses to be wiped on ragged sleeves? And did you ever guess, above your little teacup there behind that winter's window, Marcy, that Doctor Scallywag would never change?

I grew up accepting Marcy Cresap. I mean the way you accept breathing or Christmas or opening your eyes in the morning. I do not mean to say that I ever grew used to her. For, like breathing, she brought to my nose unendingly the smell of new and different flowers;

like Christmas she was the mystery, the surprise which sometimes catches at your throat, of packages secret, clasped and sacred in their whispering gilded papers and their cradles of bright ribbons; like opening your eyes in the morning she was never knowing for sure what things your eyes would see that day: you knew only, as your gaze wandered round, blessing the sweet, dull commonness of your bedroom, that those eyes soon would be looking at Marcy Cresap, fresh-faced and scrubbed, waiting on her steps to walk with you to Glory school. I know now what Marcy Cresap was to me in those years. She was All to me. She was love, she was comfort, she was beauty and wisdom, she was mad romance. And because she was so subtly all of these things to me at once, she was never any one of them to me separately. It was growing up together that way, I guess, that made it be like that.

If I had met her when I was fifteen or maybe eighteen she would have been each one of those things separately, I think. I would have told her I loved her in a different way, meaning, perhaps, a different, better thing. We would have gone off, like other couples did from Glory High, and stopped the mare somewhere and spooned in Papa's buggy till the moonlight got too bright for a girl to hide her blushes any more. I just always knew that someday Marcy Cresap was going to be my wife. And because that knowledge was always with me, safe and shiny as a buckeye in a schoolboy's pocket, I never gave a thought to what being married would really mean. I guess I never really thought of married people ever doing anything while they were married except loving each other. I don't mean I didn't begin to have strong feelings of sex when the time came, and I can't really say when that time came. I know I used to think that if Marcy hadn't come along when I was four I would have been left in a really bad situation. Because when I was three I had decided that I was going to marry my beautiful young mother, Teresa Founds. The obstacle of my father's probable objection was a distinct problem to me. I've heard a lot of talk about some of the theories of these alienists and Viennese psychologists about boys and their mothers. I don't think I quite understand them. Because I don't mind telling anybody that I was in love with my mother when I was three and I was determined I was going to marry her. Heaven knows what we'd have had to do with my poor, wonderful father if Marcy Cresap hadn't come along when I was four. And from then on nothing changed. Marcy was born to be my wife.

Can any of you out there remember the first time you looked at your hands and were amazed at their remarkable ingenuity? Does anyone listening to my voice remember the first time he looked at the moon and how it was a shock and a wonder and, only after a little while, a joy, an ecstacy. Custom blinds us, and habit slays, at last, that first sweetness of our inborn wonder. Lord, after we grow up we're like old drunks who've grown so jaded they can't taste that vintage of amazement on their tongues any more; nor feel that wine's first, wild nudge of wonder at their hearts. Like discovering hands and never forgetting; like firstsight of the moon that never grows common; like breathing that is always breathtaking; like the tongue's first taste of this world's wild and warming wine: the mind's eye that sees always the soul of earth's most old and common things forever fresh. That's what Marcy Cresap was to me. And not just *to* me but *around* me, *outside* me, and *within* me, as well.

I know about the other couples around us in Glory High School: some of them had romance, some had love, some had sex. Where Marcy was concerned I never could separate those three somehow. When I'd finish playing a Debussy prelude in the parlor I'd feel full of romance and I'd run next door and get Marcy and make her come listen while I played it for her. When I'd see somebody on Jefferson Avenue who was poor or crippled or drunk or maybe just lonely I felt love for that person and I'd go run tell Marcy about it and we'd sit up half the night talking about a world where such things couldn't be. And sometimes when I'd feel the hot swell and surge of wild, young sex within my body I'd close my eyes and I'd see a face. But it wasn't a face of someone I wanted to do anything to—I mean, to stop that state I was in. Sometimes the face was that three-year-old's image of my beautiful mother; sometimes it was Marcy. But whenever I got that feeling and that condition, I'd run next door to Marcy and by the time I got there and saw her lovely shadow in the screen door all of the hot and feverish and nameless want, all of the localized excitement, so to speak, would have spread around through me like a glowing fire. And all of me all over was what had just been down there before. I guess you think that sounds pretty crazy. But can't you understand?—it had to be that way! The pictures the boys drew sometimes along the Glory sidewalks, the little books some of them used to pass around in school, the words they used to talk about the parts of women and the parts of men and what they did to each other with those parts, the stories some of the fellows used to tell of things they'd done to girls on moonlight joy-rides down the river road—what, in God's name, could any of these things have to do with Marcy? I hope you will forgive my saying it but it's just like I had shut my eyes back then and tried to imagine a picture of the Almighty God sitting on a commode.

The only single time in all those years when I felt anything for Marcy that was near what the others meant when they said Sex was the date we had in the early September of that year she went off to school in Little Washington, Pennsylvania. It's funny but that was also the night I realized for the first time that Marcy and I weren't going to get married. Not ever. It was our last date. She was all excited about going away to boarding school next morning on the train. Her mother had spent half the summer buying clothes for her at Good's and Stone & Thomas' and Steifel's and all the best stores in Wheeling. You'd have thought she was buying Marcy a trousseau. I look back on it now and wish it had been that. I wish so much it had been Marcy going off with me on her honeymoon next morning instead of to Washington Seminary. As I say, she was gay and excited that night about going away. She had never been away from Glory in her life except for a couple of trips to Pittsburgh with her mother to see a musical comedy and do some shopping. But underneath Marcy's excitement that night I could sense something very solemn and really sad in her. Well, I think we both knew it was our last date. And we both knew that my life was going to go streaking off in one direction and hers in another. I'm sure I knew that night that Marcy would meet somebody else and marry him.

Call it premonition. Or maybe just call it knowing how somebody thinks and what they're feeling and what they'll do because you grew up so close to them that you don't know yourself any better. It sure was a beautiful night. It was really past the end of summer. But summer seemed to fight dying hard that year; it seemed to hang on clear into the fall with a sort of wistful, longing tenacity. It was September; autumn was really here. But that night, summer seemed to tarry and pause an instant more before it sped forever away. Ever notice sometimes how the seasons seem to sense and share your moods? That was how it was that night: Summer seemed sad about the end of Marcy and me.

Marcy took my cheeks between her hands and kissed me softly, quickly on the mouth.

Aren't you excited, Ken? she said.

About your leaving tomorrow? I said. I guess I'm not much.

Not about me, silly, she said. About you! In two weeks you'll be clear away up Boston at the New England Conservatory of Music! Glory's most wonderful and shining musical talent!—the only genius Apple County ever had! Next to Daddy, of course! And Doctor Will Cecil!

Sure, I said. I'm excited. Sure.

She took my face in her hands again and pulled it down close to hers. Her dark, big eyes with their lashes thick as water-color brushes— they searched my face with love and with sorrow, too.

Ken, she said, in a small voice, I won't change if you won't. Ken? No, don't pull your face away. Ken? Did you hear me? I won't change if you won't. Ken?

Listen, Marcy, I said and there were tears on my cheeks. I won't ever change. I won't ever, Marcy.

She didn't say anything, she just put her arms around me and laid her cheek against my neck. I knew she wouldn't change. Marcy couldn't change. She had always been the same. And I knew that she would marry another man. But that wouldn't mean she had changed.

That's when I kissed her so hard that night, and pulled her so close against me I guess I scared her a little. For a little moment there I was desperate. And everything in me of what I guessed the fellows meant by Sex—that woke in me right then. It was like part of each of Marcy and me was going to die that night and we had to pack everything into Now while there was time. Don't misunderstand. I didn't touch her the way I used to think sometimes I wanted to touch her. I didn't get fresh or anything. I just kissed her very hard and held her very close against me. It's a queer thing to say, I know, but that next winter in Boston I picked up a young burlesque dancer in Scollay Square and we went to her place and we went the whole way. I mean, the thing that's queer about it is this: what I did to that little Irish girl up in her hall-room bed wasn't as everlasting and choking and wild and crazy beautiful as just holding Marcy there and kissing her for the last time that night. Nothing before had ever been like that, nothing ever was afterward. I used to wonder after I heard that Marcy'd gotten married if her husband ever got jealous thinking of me. Wouldn't you feel jealous if you knew someone else had had your girl during the fourteen years when she was discovering everything: God, the universe, herself, and Apple County?

When the World War broke out, the army turned me down because of the rheumatic heart I've had since I was small. I told them the army needed bands to march to but they still wouldn't take me. It's cowardly of me, I guess, but I've wished so often since then that I'd been taken and gone over there and died. Not that I wanted anybody grieving for me. It's not even that I wanted to escape the pain of living. I just felt somehow I'd had a pretty full and perfect life up to that night when I kissed Marcy for the last time. It's not that I was jealous of the man she was engaged to, it isn't that I didn't want to go on living without her. It just seemed like my life was somehow rounded-out and perfect up to then. A completeness so splendid that anything after would be somehow excessive and tasteless. But Life's not like stories that always end where they should.

In 1917 I got the job as music teacher at Glory High School. The school didn't have a band in those days and so most of my work was with the Glory High School Glee Club. I never worked so hard at anything in all my life. Whatever else they tell about me back in Glory, I'll bet they still remember the Handel's *Messiah* we did that first Christmas after the war was over. I rehearsed those girls and boys until the other teachers complained I was keeping them from their other studies, but I rehearsed them still harder. And on Christmas Eve, 1918, I led them in the final and near-perfect performance in the choir loft of the Glory Methodist Church. I felt a pretty deep sense of satisfaction that Christmas. Even with mother and dad both gone I felt as if this were the best Christmas I'd had in years. There wasn't a glee club in the state that could match the one I'd built with patience and love and hard work there in Glory High.

When mother and dad died within a year of each other while I was away at school I told my Aunt Blossom in Louisville to sell the old house. Now I lived in a little furnished room on Jefferson Avenue just over Brother's Restaurant. I lived and ate, I breathed and thought nothing but the intention of doing a good job as Glory High School music teacher. It had been nearly seven years since I had held Marcy in my arms that autumn night. The sound of locusts that night was the sound of summer hating to let loose. I used to lie in the dark on winter nights and hear the soft break of beating snowflakes on the window of my room and, in my heart, I could hear those locusts cry. I tried to forget the other time I'd touched a woman: that night in the room of the dancer from Scollay Square. I made myself forget it and I succeeded, too. And I was to keep all such feelings and emotions and memories shut out of my mind for three years more before they broke loose again. No, I know it now: a man can't shut sex out of his life for ten years without its catching up with him terribly in the end. It's like the bursting of a boiler.

The trouble began in 1922. What made it happen? Was it all my fault? What made that high school full of girls turn on me like amazons that spring? For months that winter it had been going on behind my back, without my ever knowing. I tell you I wasn't looking for that sort of thing. I thought once afterward that it was some climate of the times: those first years of the stumbling nineteen twenties, years of reactions to a fearful war. Children reflecting the pellmell, jazz-crazy recklessness of fathers and mothers more like children than even they themselves. Maybe that was part of it. A sixteen-year-old Glory High School junior named Carmel Stribbler was part of it, too. Carmel had the kind of flexible, pure soprano I'd been looking for ever since I came to Glory High. I worked with her a little harder than the rest, trying to build the chorus of the glee club around that strong, young solo voice. I suppose she was pretty. You know, even now I find it hard remembering. Even now the only face I ever see behind my closed lids in the instant before sleep is the face of Marcy. Yes, I think Carmel was probably quite pretty. As I remember her, she had that loose-mouthed and almost drowsy precocity which strangely puts an older man on his guard. It is like the waking of a forest creature, ravenous with hunger after dreams, yet shy in its first quest after food.

It was hours after school let out that mild April evening when Carmel came up behind me on the back steps of the Glory High. I had been sitting there in the twilight, straining my eyes, working out some choral parts for the graduation recital. Carmel stood so close behind me that the edge of her short spring coat brushed against my shoulder. I was startled and nearly dropped the staved sheets of music paper on my knees.

Well! I said, feeling like a fool. Well! Carmel.

She laughed lightly and popped her gum, then took it carefully out of her pink mouth and stuck it on the back of her geography book.

I didn't mean to scare you, Professor Founds, she said.

Oh, you didn't, I said, feeling more stupid and off-balance than ever.

I just wanted to talk to you, she said as carefully as if she were reciting by rote. About something, she went on. Maybe it could be very important.

If it's about the graduation day recital, I began, but she stopped me.

No, she said. No, it's nothing like that. This is something very personal.

I sat still, silent, studying her as best I could, her oval face showing palely against her dark hair in the twilight of that dying April day; I felt a vague sense of terror.

I might as well get right to the point, she said sitting on the step beside me.

She threw me a quick sidelong glance, her gleaming eyes veiled by her lashes; she smiled.

You don't mind it, she said, my sitting here next to you?

No, I said. No, surely not. Now what's this personal problem of yours, Carmel?

She frowned into the sunset as if fixing a condemning eye upon all abstract evil.

It's about Betty Lou Carmichael and Sally Wolff and Jackie Smeed, she said. The three worst liars in the whole glee club. Professor Founds, words just completely fail me when I try to tell you what tale-bearing, lying hypocrites those three girls are!

I tried to search the pretty features of her face for some clue to what she was trying to say. But that face was like a pure, white sheet of paper upon which nothing has ever been written.

What have they been lying about? I said.

You, she said, and put her gum back in her mouth.

What about me? I asked, trying foolishly to smile.

Oh, everything! she gasped, popping her gum again.

Everything, I said What do you mean—'everything'?

She sighed, a long exhalation with which she seemed trying to express the confounding hopelessness of her mission to save me.

You'll just get sore if I tell you, she said. You'll probably think it's all just some orneriness I made up.

Listen to me, Carmel, I said, wanting to seize her by the shoulders and shake it from her. Sometimes students say things about their teachers that are trivial and harmless. But sometimes it can be something important. Sometimes gossip can hurt people—even ruin them. Carmel, you and I have come to be good friends this year.

Professor Founds, she said, with a distant and forlorn despair in her voice, I've come to look up to you as much more than just a good friend.

I stood up, straightening my sheets of music, feeling a vague dizziness; I laughed lightly.

It's probably all nothing, I said. It's probably just some little joke that's going around about me. But thank you, Carmel, for worrying about it.

She stored the wad of gum far back in her teeth, clenched her eyes shut and began blurting it all out in a breathless monotone.

It's no little joke. It's a big and terrible lie, she said. It was after practice last Wednesday afternoon. Jackie Smeed started it. She said you were the handsomest teacher in the whole school. She said she went for you in the biggest way. And Sally Wolff said you didn't have a wife and you never dated any of the other teachers or any girls at all. And Betty Lou Carmichael said her boy friend said he knew why. He said you were a pansy. And Jackie Smeed said that was a lie. She said she had good reason to know because she said you kept her after rehearsal one night and locked all the doors in the auditorium and she said you took her back of the curtain and made her take her jumper off and petted with her till she got so hot she didn't care what happened next. And she told us what happened next. And it was—well, you know what—she said you went all the way with her. And then Sally Wolff said she never meant to tell a living soul but the same thing happened to her, only this time it was up in your room over the restaurant. And then Betty Lou Carmichael said she'd bet us her weekly allowance for the next two months that she could make you, too, and that once you'd had her you wouldn't want it with any other girl in the whole school. Oh, Professor Founds, I could just die. I feel so awful sitting here having to say these awful things to a person as fine and clean as you.

She began suddenly to cry, the gum clenched between her molars, her face masklike in its immobility, the big tears simply tumbling out of her wide eyes and dropping off her face onto the backs of her boyish schoolgirl hands which clutched the geography on her bare knees. I sat stunned and voiceless, blushing like a child, and feeling again a chill of weak-kneed terror. I reached out and patted the girl's shoulder consolingly, as if it had been she who had been wronged and needed comfort. The shudder of her weeping stopped suddenly, she dabbed the tears angrily off her cheeks with the heels of both hands and thoughtfully commenced chewing her gum again.

If you just knew those girls, she said. That Jackie and Betty Lou and that horrible Sally Wolff—the things they do! There's this man Clarence Dudley—he's the shoe clerk up at Mobley's—and there's this sheriff's deputy named Dallas Barger who runs the tire repair shop back of the Hupmobile Agency on Jefferson Avenue—and they're always taking girls back in Dallas' repair shop. There's hardly a night during the summer vacations when Sally or Betty Lou or Jackie Smeed aren't up there drinking homebrew and smoking cigarettes and everything else with Clarence Dudley and Dallas Barger and some other men. And they're not the only girls from Glory High either. I could name you a dozen more, at least, and almost every one of them in the glee club, too. Joanne Harris—she's another. And Geraldine McCann.

I don't want to know, I whispered. Don't tell me any more, please. I don't want to know.

But, listen, she said. You ought to hear who all goes up there! Girls from the very nicest homes in Glory! Jobell Bosworth and Doris Ann Shrieves! Girls from nice families like that!

Please, I said. Carmel, please, if you don't mind. I don't want to hear.

I covered my face with my hands strangely as if to hide something shameful that might show there for Carmel or someone else to see and comprehend.

Oh, but, Professor Founds, she cried, you've just got to hear. Because those other girls I named—they've been bragging about you, too. Doris Ann was passing a note all over study hall yesterday. I won't soil my mind by repeating the words she used. But the note said you did it better than Clarence Dudley or Dallas Barger or any of those other men.

Some of the sheet music fell out of my hands, I watched the white pages of the spring oratorio drift like white moths off across the gusty April twilight. I was trembling; my whole body helpless with unreasoning and savage rage at the child sitting so erect and ruinous on the stone steps by my feet.

Just—just shut up! I shouted. Just shut up about the whole thing. Can't you see you're part of it when you repeat it? Can't you understand that, you little fool?

She stood up and looked at me with all the hopeless pathos of youth in her wide, sorrowing eyes.

Go home! I said, backing down the steps, feeling the sheets of music beneath my shoes. Just go home and stop repeating all this insanity.

Stop repeating it, do you hear! You're making it worse. You're part of it.

I never breathed a word of it, she said softly, to any living soul on earth but you.

I don't believe you, I said, furious and needing somehow to reach out and give her as great a hurt as I knew how.

Her big eyes filled with tears again and she pressed the geography tight under her breasts, and looked at me with a soul full of anguished reproach.

I would never say anything to hurt you, she said. Because I've come to look up to you as much more than just a good friend. I don't care if you hate me, Professor Founds. It won't change anything about the way I feel. You'll always be the most special wonderful human friend I ever had!

She turned then and ran up the steps under the dark trees toward home. I stood a minute with my eyes closed, fighting to get hold of myself. I had forgotten about the sheets of lost music: the pages of the spring oratorio which blew now across the football field and hovered in the air, small as snowflakes against the dusk. When I started slowly up the stone steps I felt something soft and clinging beneath my shoe. I sat down and stared stupidly at my shoe sole and then began blindly, furiously plucking away at the stuck wad of gum, cursing softly in the darkness while my fingers, sticky with it, gave up the faint and sweetish smell of mint, and something more which, drifting up, increased my outrage in one fragile gust; a fragrance which seemed to linger in the mint: the scent on my fingers of a girl's young mouth.

I walked the streets of Glory for hours that night. I remember when I opened the door to my little room the clock in the Apple County Court House was tolling the hour of ten. In the darkness I could smell her faint fragrance the minute the door had closed behind me. Face powder, chewing gum, the flowery soap that young girls use. Yet more than any of these the smell of youth! I could see the pale shape of her face presently: silent and unmoving against the darkness, and then she moved toward the window where the light cast up by the street signs showed her spent and spiritless silhouette against its dusty amber. I felt as calm as if we had been old lovers. I felt as used to her as I was used to breathing, or Christmas, or opening my eyes to the light of each new morning. I watched her bend slowly to the movements of undressing as if I had watched her do this a thousand nights before. And when she came padding softly barefoot across the carpet and stood against me my hands reached up and cupped the upcurved, nippled sweetness of her breasts with no more sense of strangeness than once those hands had felt when, dimpled with infancy, they had groped hungering upward to the still clearly remembered bosom of my beautiful young mother. And what I did with her then was what it seemed to me I had always meant to do with someone faceless, yet lovely and familiar, beneath me now in the pillow. It seemed to me there, cradled in the mad, rocking-chair wildness of her young body's soft ferocity and need, that I had gone for ten years, inflicted with some monstrous and comic absentness of mind. You see how the years caught up with me that night; how all the old and unpaid bills of love and all their years of gathering interest suddenly came due! It was aching, it was wonder, it was Eden; and something in my breast sang with hurt like the missing rib that God had taken to make her from that night. And then, at the end, she breathed a quickening storm and wailed and arched her back like a pale, white bow and sank her young teeth in my shoulder to the bone. And the white bow of her body sprang and straightened and sped the arrow that slew me into sleep.

I lay long there, listening to her breath and the sounds of Glory out in the April night. I thought how harsh I'd been to her that evening on the steps. I was about to ask forgiveness when she yawned and struggled free and sprang like a nymph toward the open window, peering into the little lights of Jefferson Avenue a single story down, hiding her nakedness behind the curtains, the outline of her hair and neck and shoulder black against the yellow April mists beyond the window, and her hip touched by light in one fiery line. I sat up in my narrow cot and watched her, considering how I should phrase my asking forgiveness, for how I'd struck out in such a senseless anger at her down there on the steps behind the Glory High. And suddenly her hand moved and her fingers flew up and waved three times at someone she had seen, someone down there in the Glory streets who'd watched and waited for that little signaling wave. Her hand flew to her lips then and I heard a girl's low giggle in her throat.

Carmel? I whispered, and she turned and laughed again, softly with mischief and with a triumph, too: a victory old as man and maid on earth. And in that instant her whole, round pretty face was lit plain from the street. She laughed again, and strangely I laughed, too. It wasn't

Carmel Stribbler, at all. It was one of the other girls, Jackie Smeed, that Carmel had told me the awful tale about: the one who'd started the shameful lie about me. I closed my eyes in heedless, uncaring madness and laughed again. I opened them and looked at Jackie Smeed and thought: Well, it sure isn't any lie now. I put on my old bathrobe and went to the window and stood behind her. Down on the sidewalk across Jefferson Avenue, Carmel and four other Glory High School girls leaned against the wood fence in front of the big chestnut tree by the vacant lot behind the Hupmobile Agency. Carmel Stribbler saw my face in the window and smiled, she lifted her fingers and blew me a kiss. Then she and the other girls turned and walked back toward Dallas Berger's tire repair shop.

But you must understand this: it didn't matter to me. I mean that it wasn't Carmel who had been in my room that night. It was someone faceless I made love to in the darkness there: someone faceless and yet familiar to me as breathing, as Christmas, as opening your eyes to every morning's light. It was always that way in the darkness: even when the other girls started coming: Betty Lou and Sally and Joanne Harris and Geraldine. And, at last, Carmel herself. I made love to them all. And yet always I was making love to only one. Because the darkness enchanted them, it cast its spell upon them, taking their names away and letting them be known to me only as youth. Youth, the green thing I had lost back in my life's green time. Youth which never really comes again!

I always knew how it would end. But it didn't matter to me. It is not every man who can step into a darkness and be seventeen again. It went on all that summer. And it went on clear into the second semester of my last year at Glory High. In the end the insatiable trek of them to my little room; the savage and unappeasable hunger of youth began, at last, to show its wear on me. Sometimes alone there on my narrow bed, thinking about the wild flesh of those girl-children—it frightened me. I read somewhere once that high-school girls are cold and passionless infants. But when I thought of Carmel and the others—I tell you, it frightened me. Sometimes it scares me thinking of it yet. Because I know there will always be men like me who cannot keep themselves away from youth, or youth away from them. And because I know that, in the end, such men must always suffer and be destroyed.

Back in Glory these nights deputy-sheriff Dallas Barger rides loathing through the town, his big gun strapped to his buttock, with one eye hating the children of the poor, and with the other seeking out the children of the well-to-do. Up in Brother's Restaurant he still brags of the night he arrested me in my room. Yet at my trial the girls refused to testify. And so the charge was dropped. But I was through. I never taught again. The news of my infamy was bulletined to every school board round the land. I wandered north of Glory, up the valley. I found work in a little music store in Steubenville. There I sell sheet music, ukelele picks, strings, hillbilly guitars, ocarinas, secondhand pianos and records by Paul Whiteman, George Olsen and the Two Black Crows.

I am not bitter at my lot. I found my youth when youth came seeking me. Seducer of children—Spoiler of the innocent: that's what my name will always stand for back in Glory. And yet, what mortal creature on this earth does not forever yearn to merge itself in youth, to wed its yearning flesh to youth's gay willingness, to find, in other youth, the youth it lost? As for the horde of girls who came like tender amazons and sniffed me out, hot on my spoor, and then seduced me savagely as if I'd been their bride—the thing they sought in me I'll never know. Sometimes I think I know—I can't be sure. I think they came like constables, at last, and made me pay up every cent with interest— creditors of their sex who seemed to know, as surely as if they'd summed it in a ledger, that I had ten years' bills unpaid to Woman: the piled-up debt of love no one escapes; the love I pledged once to a little girl, above toy teacups with real gold-leaf rims.

A Houseful of Twenty-Seven

There's not a bit of use in twenty-seven people all trying to talk at once. And that's how it will be if one of the rest starts in. Directly, six or eight others will think of things they want to tell. And pretty soon all twenty-seven will be chiming in till it won't make any more sense than a treeful of catbirds. And I think it matters—your knowing the true facts about us all there that winter: twenty-seven people living together in a one-room house not much bigger than a B. & O. boxcar. Better let me do all the talking for everybody.

God knows who built that house. God knows when. Sometimes I think it was never built at all. Sometimes I think the wind just come up one day and blew it together. It had that look: like a pair of pants that's been patched so much you can't tell which is patches and which is pants. Still, it stood; whatever it was stuck together with, it held. I reckon it would be standing yet if Miss Cresap she hadn't come along last year and burned it down. At any rate, there was living there under

253

that roof: me, my woman Josie, her old pap, them nine kids of ours, and fifteen total strangers. God knows where they're all at now—scattered to the four winds, I judge. God knows where I am, too. I reckon I ought to say God *knew*. He should. Because till two weeks ago, when they taken Him away, God was in the cell next to mine right here in the West Virginia State Penitentiary. Does that surprise you? I guess now you'll start looking at me funny and saying I'm crazy like them guards and that prison doctor Blick that's always cracking jokes about me all the time. Well, you just go ahead and think what you please. I tell you Almighty God was locked up tight in the cell next to mine. When it comes to Justice, the State of West Virginia don't spare nobody.

I hold no grudge against Miss Cresap for coming out there with matches and coal oil and burning that place down. I'll have to admit that a houseful of twenty-seven is packing people pretty tight. Still there was winter nights when we all sort of kept each other warm. When you're poor sometimes the only stove you've got is someone else. And bitter nights sometimes when that stove gets cold you've got to give it a poke with a joke or a tune or shake its ashes loose with a little loving-up. I bet back in 1911 when it was just me and Josie alone in that place we would have froze to death if it wasn't for each other. We used to keep each other warm tickling and hugging and laughing at some derned-fool story we'd heard somewhere once. The trouble is we run out of stories. That's when Josie started having kids.

For sixteen years babies come out of that girl like popcorn jumping from a hot skillet. And there was hardly a one of them that wasn't brought on by a cold snap. I'm not talking now about our first-born Honey Darling. When I got Josie with her, it was a warm June morning out behind her pap's stables. The old man had sent for me and a boy named Stalnaker to come clean out the well. Stalnaker knowed a moonshiner about three mile up the dirt road toward Lynn Camp. We hadn't hardly got there at sun-up when Stalnaker taken off across the field. He said he was going to get a drink if that moonshiner still lived there and he said he'd be back in half an hour. Here it was nearly eight-thirty and I could see I'd have to clean that well out all alone. I'd have walked off the place myself but jobs wasn't easy for a man like me to come by. Two years before I'd lost my right hand above the wrist in a sawmill down on Middle Island Creek. I knowed the days when I could be picky about a job was gone forever, so I went to work alone. Early that morning I hadn't paid Josie no mind when first I seen her. She was moving around in the mist, feeding the chickens, slopping the hogs, and gathering eggs. By the time the sun was over the ridge and the mist was gone she was up in the shed milking.

Working with one good hand and a stump tires me easy, so by ten o'clock I taken a little rest. I walked up the yard toward the place where I'd hung my jacket on the rail fence; I kept my chewing tobacco in the pocket where it wouldn't get all wet from the muck and mud from the well. Josie had finished her milking and churning and she nearly bumped into me coming out of the shed as I passed. She'd just had a big drink of foaming warm milk and her upper lip was still white with it. She looked so pretty I just wanted to bend over and lick that milk right off her mouth. I thought she'd push me aside and go on up to the house but instead of that she smiled at me as sweet as a child. So we commenced to talking about one thing and another till I forgot all about that plug of tobacco. She chattered away about her pap and his horses and she just couldn't keep her eyes off that stump sticking out of my shirt sleeve. I told her one of them Filipinos cut it off in the Spanish American War and I could tell that really got to her. There was the derndest racket in the world going on up in the stables and I hadn't been around real farms enough in my life to know better than to ask what it was. She got red and laughed and then she looked up bold-faced and told me. Her pap was breeding a mare to his stallion that morning. Him and the man that owned the mare was walking her up and down outside the stallion's stall to get him ready. The stallion could smell the mare out there and he was trying to kick down the stall-gate to get at her.

Josie wasn't the prettiest girl I ever saw; in most ways she wasn't pretty at all. But the way she stopped talking after she told me about the racket up in the stable, the way she just seemed to stand there waiting for me to do something, the way her eyes seemed to get bigger and scareder by the minute: my throat got so tight I felt like I was choking. I taken her hand like we was going for a walk down through the pasture where the dewdrops still glittered on the cobwebs like the diamonds of a queen. We went down behind the stable and stood there a minute with that hot mist of sweat and horse manure all around us and breathed the clean, wild smells of it and listened to the stallion's hooves still smashing, trying to kick the whole damned stable down. And then the racket stopped, a gate creaked and a man cursed somewhere and sprang

aside. And there was a racket of hooves on the stable floor and then a
whole thunder of thudding, striking hooves up in the yard and then the
wildest shrieking whinny I ever heard. Josie heard that sound and gave
a shiver and shut her eyes; she taken my hand and pulled me down on
top of her in the Queen Anne's lace. The smell of her was like butter
and warm, fresh milk and her breath came groaning in my ear and her
little, wild hands didn't know how to do anything right. But everything
got done right. And when Josie sat up directly, straightening her hair
and rubbing the mud and grass stains off her bare legs, there was a little
spot of blood on her clean, white petticoat. And there was our first-born
girl beginning inside her. There was something inside me, too, right
then: a sweetness sunk deep as a fish hook, and the harder I pulled the
deeper it went and the sweeter it hurt.

That autumn when Josie started getting big her pap beat her with a
buggy whip and chased her off his land. I was coming to see her that
night when I seen her walking up the dusk. I had about fifty dollars
saved up from the summer's work so we come into Glory. I guess I
wasn't thinking too straight. Because it seemed to me we could get along
pretty good in town on that much till spring anyways. We stayed that
night in a little boardinghouse down on Water Street and sat up a while
in the rockers on the porch with the other boarders, watching the fireflies
down in the weeds and a big show-boat come past all lit up with a brass
band on board heading for Raven Rock or Cresap's or Captina or some
place off down river. I squeezed her hand with my good left one and she
knew that was as much as to say that I promised her someday to take her
on a show-boat ride like that. But, you know, I never did. That night in
the room Josie carried on something awful and made me go stand out in
the hall because she didn't want me to see her get undressed with her
stomach that way. I stood there scratching my back, trying to figure out
a woman. I'm surely not a man to think of such a sight as ugly. In sixteen years to come I was to watch her belly's rise and fall as regular as
the rise and fall of seasons. Directly she whispered real loud that it was
all right to come in. She was in bed in her petticoats, with her back to
me and her legs all scrouched up so I couldn't see her. I give her a little
kiss on the side of the neck and I remember how her hair smelled that
night: like fresh bread baking somewhere.

I got something to get off my chest, Josie, I said directly, in a shameful whisper. It's an ornery lie I told you.

What is it? she whispered, thrilled, for there's few things a woman enjoys more than a man getting an ornery lie off his chest.

I lost my hand in a rip-saw in a mill down on Middle Island Creek, I said. I wasn't in no war.

I laid still a spell, listening to her breathe, figuring I shouldn't have told her, scared.

Does it make any difference? I whispered.

She turned around real quick and put her arms around me. She wasn't ashamed of her belly any more, she pressed it against me and kissed me real hard and we lay there, falling asleep, listening to the show-boat blowing its whistle down river for the Devil's Elbow.

There's no two ways about it: I got off on the wrong foot in Glory. Stretch it as we might, that fifty dollars didn't last us much more than six weeks. I walked the streets of that town asking for any kind of a job. Josie and me was boarding with an old woman named Honesty Noller and the five dollars a week we was paying included two meals a day for the both of us. I hope someday I'll see that kind old woman's face over on the Other Side. She said she'd take care of us both till Josie's baby come, but I had my pride. At least, back then I had it. Later, I give it up. When you're poor, Pride's another mouth to feed. And no matter how much it eats, you never see nothing grow fat. So me and Josie taken off together again. And, far gone as she was, she tried to get housework. If ever you want to witness something hopeless you just go watch a pregnant girl and a fellow with one hand asking around for work. Lord, it was so pathetic we both sat down on the curb in front of Koontz's Candy Store on Jefferson Avenue and laughed till I bet everybody that seen us took us for drunkards. So that afternoon we went back to old Mrs. Noller and asked her if we could stay one more night. She cried and kissed us and said for all she cared we could stay forever.

Next morning Josie was feeling sick as a cat so I went out alone. It's a good thing she didn't come along. Because that was the morning I throwed a fit on the sidewalk in front of the Episcopal church. I've had fits for as long as I can remember but this was the first time I'd had one in better than a year. I thought for a while there I was over them. But this was one of the worst: it was like a whole yearful of fits all saved up for this morning. As bad luck would have it, just as I hit the sidewalk here come a whole bunch of ladies of the Good Samaritan Bible Class down the steps of the church. It's just pure fate I didn't trip one of them;

somehow they managed to step around me without me hitting or kicking one of them. Folks that has seen lots of fits in their time tell me I throw one of the most energetic they've ever seen. Once in the mill down on Middle Island Creek I twitched loose from the strong arms of two husky mill-hands and throwed myself across a board and into the saw. That's how I lost my hand. God knows how I'd have come out of this one, if someone hadn't helped me, for I had already swallowed my tongue. When I opened my eyes I thought I'd gone to heaven and was looking at an angel. It was a girl—almost a child—she couldn't have been more than fifteen and she was all dressed up in her best coat and bonnet and she was bending over me with spit and slobber all over her hand and teeth marks in two of her fingers where she'd been getting my tongue out.

Are you all right now? she asked calmlike.

Yes'm, I said. Deed to God, I'm sorry and ashamed. Right here in front of the church. Deed to God, I feel the worst fool in the world. I come out this morning feeling spry as could be and on my way to look for a job when—

But this is Sunday, she smiled, and took her clean little lawn handkerchief out of her purse and wiped the sweat from my forehead. Nobody ever gets work on Sunday. You should rest and look tomorrow!

Sunday! I gasped. Deed to God, I never even remembered. Here lately one day's just about like the next.

I sat up and brushed myself off and felt like crawling between the bricks in the sidewalk. Because here come another platoon of those ladies down the church steps and the preacher in their midst. Suddenly the little girl stood up and turned her back on me and clenched her fists and stamped her feet.

Yes! Yes! she cried, like she was still talking to me. Can't you tell it's Sunday, mister? With all these good Christians of the Good Samaritan Bible Class stepping daintily over you!

I thought for a minute she was mad at me; I couldn't tell for a minute if she was yelling at them or yelling at me for them to hear. But then she turned and put her skinny young arm under my arm and helped me up. I was too embarrassed even to thank her. I didn't see her again till years after that. Miss Cresap still looked beautiful, she still looked young; but there were sunset shadows of grief under her eyes, she wasn't that little girl any more. She was still mad at something. But I knew for sure, at last, it wasn't me. And she hadn't forgot that Sunday she helped me get up and watched me run off so full of shame and disgrace I forgot to even thank her. But she wasn't mad at that.

Josie and me come at last to Angel Swamp that winter. Nobody ever moves to Angel Swamp. I don't reckon, in the whole history of Apple County, it could truthfully be said that anybody ever moved to Angel Swamp. Still a lot of families end up there; a lot of them start out there, too. There's a road from Glory to Angel Swamp; for that matter, there is two or three. And yet a man could say that Angel Swamp don't really lay at the end of roads; it lays at the end of the way things are.

It was just starting to snow the day Josie and me moved into that old one-room house we was to live in for sixteen years; the place Honey Darling was going to get born in, and then Rachel, and after her, thirteen more kids—and seven of them was going to live. I picked up an Indian arrowhead out of the naked earth in front of the door. I held it up to Josie and she smiled.

Well, Josie, I says, it looks like somebody else lived here before us.

She kept fussing around the place, talking about what she could do to make it nice and how lucky we was to get it and what she could do to fix it up pretty. I kept moving around, too. I don't know about Josie, but I was moving around to keep from freezing my hide off. That old wind come in from the Ohio River like a razor and stropped itself against your skin. But, just the same, Josie and me was feeling pretty good. At last we was moving into a place of our own; a place of our own, at least, till somebody come along and said it wasn't.

Around nightfall it was snowing pretty hard. Still away off yonder on the rise we seen someone coming, carrying something; directly here come two or three more. They was Angel Swamp families bringing us housekeeping presents just like they used to do for young married folks down in the country, when I was a boy in Wetzel County. Mostly they was things from their own houses: things they'd found on the dump: an old army cot and a mattress, a piece of carpet to nail up until we could fix a door to keep the wind out, a bushel basket of stove wood, a suit-box full of old baby clothes and some jars of food the women had put up that fall, and one little boy with a lame leg come hobbling up on his stick and give me a hound pup stuffed in a gray wool sock. Everybody stood around staring at us whilst I got a fire going in the cracked old iron stove and wrapped a rag around the stovepipe joint so she would draw right. One young girl come over to Josie and folded her skinny arms in her skimpy coat and stared down at the fire behind the little iron door. I mind the way the light lit her face; she smiled queerly, and there was a mean, pinched contrariness around her squinty eyes.

You folks sure is nervy, she says. Nobody else'd come near this place for the past year. I reckon you wondered why it was empty.

Why, yes, I said. How come it's empty?

The typhoid fever, she says, smiling a little more. It wiped out three people summer a year ago. Right in this very house.

She searched and studied my face, with the fire dancing mad and mean in her eyes.

Ain't you scared? she says.

No, I says, standing real close with my face grinning all crazy and my nose almost touching hers. We ain't scared. Because me and my woman, we both got the smallpox this morning. That's why we come here. Everybody knows the typhoid and the smallpox can't abide each other. And when they gets inside of you they rassles themselves to death. Say, ma'am!—what's that breaking-out there on the tip of your nose?

She lit out the door like death was trying to run up her leg and all the other people hollered and laughed and some fellow passed around a mason jar of moonshine liquor.

God knows who built that house. God knows when. Still it was roof and walls, it was stove and home, it was sheltered bed of birth and death for Josie and me and ours and all the rest, for the bitter and the sweet of sixteen years. Some heartwood of the cheap planks of that shack are part of the give and toughness of my body's sinews still, up here in prison; some of my sweat and spunk and blood and some of the careful spit a man must, now and again, aim thoughtfully at walls to keep from caring too much when something's gone past where caring can help: those juices of me went into that poorly carpentered wood, and went up with the smoke when that wood burned. Whatever else has got to be said about that house, that much good, at least, I just had to get spoken out.

The trouble with—No, I'll not call it trouble; I'll just say—the way it was with Josie was she never could say no. Whether it was the love in summer which would hit us both sometimes because of how good the wind smelled blowing down from the orchards on the ridge, or the moon, or the way one of us looked, or the frogs' hot, croaking voices in the dark down in the misty cattails by the creek; or the love in winter which was, often as not, the afterthought of two bodies warming themselves by one another's heat till the stoked coals blazed and bubbled out of hand. Summer love, winter love, she never could say no to me. And I couldn't never say no to myself. And whatever the thing was we added up to, the total of us two like scribbled numbers summed up on a grocery bill—that thing couldn't never say no to some loud, big Yes that clasped us all around: bigger than us, the house, or Angel Swamp; bigger than the black garden of the stars that bloomed round Glory and its ring of hills, like roses growing wild in some dark wood. And it wasn't just to love neither that Josie could never say that one word: No. It was to them that come a-begging and if she didn't have it to give she'd run off somewhere and borrow it to give. And if there wasn't none to borrow, she'd ask that beggar in and together we'd all set and spit and talk and grin to keep our thoughts from thinking what a bad joke not-having was. And sometimes when the beggar'd steal something from the house he'd never even thought of till he seen it there, Josie'd laugh and poke my ribs and say: See? That's what he come to ask for in the first place. So it's all right! We never had to send him away empty-handed after all.

I swear, our oldest girl Honey Darling growed up in her mother's image. She's just like that. Her tongue just never learned how to wrap itself right to spit out that word No. You might just as well have tried to teach a dog to say "apple butter." I don't mean that she was ever easy with the boys; no more than Josie was, sixteen years before. For when a man come and taken Honey Darling, at last, it wasn't easiness that made her give: she thrust herself strong into his hands like a kid giving a Christmas present to someone who has waited his turn; waited for the one present with his name wrote on it with the big red crayon of stubborn girls who save themselves for the goodtime Christmas morning of giving it away.

Most of the gals of Angel Swamp was easy little rips who gave what they had away before they hardly even knowed what else their things was for; not Honey Darling, though. Though, as I say, she wasn't a gal to say No. But whenever a boy got her down in the dark, down on the creek bank in the firefly dark where the lilac smell blowed cheap and sweet as a busted bottle of dime-store per-fume, whenever some fellow'd come pawing around her sweater or his hand try to go spidering up her bare leg she'd just laugh and squirm away and tease his hot thoughts round to thinking something quiet. Tomorrow, she'd promise, maybe. But it was always maybe, and tomorrow was never now; and now was a Christmas present with somebody else's name wrote on it and that name was never his. And the funny thing was: none of them ever got sore and they'd always come asking for her again, scratching their heads and blushing and thinking maybe tomorrow was tonight. And cussing themselves for the derndest fools in the world; but grinning just the same and feeling their boy-hearts quicken at Honey Darling's sight there in the door.

How we all got by those sixteen years in Angel Swamp I'll never know. But we got by. The kids picked berries in the thickets and went up Misery Holler to gather greens or little bunches of wild flowers. I'd find a little sassafras sometimes and we'd go selling those from door to door. Sometimes I'd find a little work: one-handed jobs. One time I felt a fit coming on and told the kids to mind the pails of berries and I went up in the alley back of the movie house and Rachel—she was Josie's second-born—she come with me to keep me from swallering my tongue. Fellows who've seen some fit-throwing in their time, tell me I throw one of the liveliest, most comical kind of fit a man would wish to see. And so that day them kids of mine they made a line there at the alley mouth and wouldn't let nobody through to watch my fit until they'd paid two pennies to see the show. I must have throwed a humdinger that afternoon —I've still got the scar on my forehead where I laid it open when I hit the wall. The kids taken in close to thirty-five cents that day. So we had a piece of bacon with our greens that night.

That was the week Josie's old pap come to live with us. He'd lost his farm to the bank and had nowhere to go on earth; he was old, with a cough and spitting blood. And he didn't seem to remember the time he'd flogged poor Josie off the place, with no more where to go than he had now. And Josie, if she remembered, bit her tongue and smiled and kissed his cheek and taken him in: that woman couldn't say No, not even to him. It didn't matter much: there was always something to go round, or nothing at all, and one more mouth to feed couldn't much change that. But after him it just seemed like they started coming from everywhere: strangers we'd never seen—men with that homeless smell of slept-in clothes, and the unwashed and gray faces and hands that water couldn't change now, not even if it was hot and there was soap. Some women come, too: a man and his wife sometimes, and Josie kept having babies every year—except that one year we missed: the year she'd been to hear Sam Jones, the evangelist, and wouldn't let me a lay a finger on her all that winter after. I put up with it, too, and never said a word and never looked to get it somewheres else. Josie just smiled.

I don't think it was the fear of hell, at all, or shame of the flesh that made her turn her back to me that year. I reckon all she wanted was a little rest; a time to let her poor, worn body just be her own for a spell. But if it wasn't new babies coming, it was strangers: wanderers coming roofless and hungry to the door of that old, funny shack in Angel Swamp. And I was as bad as Josie, after a while: I couldn't say No to them any more than her. A houseful of twenty-seven—that's what it was toward the end. And there was times when it was even more than that: strangers who'd come and maybe just pass the night or stay a week or two and presently begin to fret and itch with the knowing that something golden surely waited for them somewheres up the line. And off they'd go some morning, riding the freights into the river mists.

There was convicts, too. And that's the reason the State gives me why I'm here, locked up in a cell next to the empty one where God used to be. Across the creek from Angel Swamp's the prison farm. And sometimes in the late of afternoon, before the guards come with their pump-guns to herd the boys into the trucks to drive them to the barracks up the hill, sometimes the guards they take their time in coming, or look the other way. And that's to give some of the cons a chance to take his favorite Angel Swamp gal down in the bushes. I'd give a lot to know how many of the neighbors' knocked-up gals is carrying convict's babies. And that was one of the things that brought Miss Cresap raging out here a year or two back. She raised pure hell with Harry Marlin, captain of the prison guards, and he just grinned and spit and looked the other way, like he wanted to show her the way it was done, and he said: Hell, lady, we can't watch them boys every minute. And besides— what if they do get a little of that Angel Swamp stuff. If it wasn't them it'd be some of their paps or brothers or the neighbor's boys.

Miss Cresap she tried to get Harry Marlin fired. But he pulls too much power in the county and with the warden and the Glory law. And all she got was more folks mad at her. And then on top of that she started in that week about that houseful of us twenty-seven there. It was Josie's old pap she was worried most about. Him coughing and spitting blood all round the place: and Josie nursing the last kid we was to have. Miss Cresap she come with that old, white-haired Doc Cecil she works with and they could tell with just one look at Matty's pap that he was too far gone even to be worth inspecting. And then they made Josie spit in a cup and Miss Cresap fetched her and the baby into Glory in that big old touring car of hers and taken pictures of Josie's chest and scratched her arm and scared her half to death. Miss Cresap she come back out and said that Josie's pap was dying from the consumption and he was giving it to everyone else in the place and something had to be done.

How many of these people here are yours, Harvey? she asked me.

Well, I said. They's ever' one of them my friends, Miss Cresap.

I know, she said in that soft, queer voice of hers. But I mean how many of them are your own family?

There's me and Josie, says I. And there's Josie's pap and there's them nine kinds. Miss Cresap, I never did learn to do sums right. How many does that make?

Twelve of you, she said. And fifteen total strangers.

It's the dead of winter, Miss Cresap, I said. I can't just shove them folks out in the road. People come here and me and Josie never asks them in till we see plain in their faces there just ain't nowheres else.

We'll find somewhere else, Miss Cresap said. I don't know where nor how. We'll find jobs. We'll find homes. I don't know how, Harvey, but we'll do it.

Miss Cresap, why not just let things be? I said.

Harvey, said Miss Cresap laying her hand on my arm, you know I've tried to help you through the years. I wouldn't ask you now to do anything I didn't know was best.

But that old pap of Josie's, I said, shaking my head. We can't just throw him out in the road, Miss Cresap.

I'll get him in the sanatorium, she said. I'll get both of them in the sanatorium. I'll find beds for them if I have to go out and steal them. I can tell you, Harvey, there's no hope for the old man. But there *is* hope for her.

Hope for who, Miss Cresap? I said.

For Josie, she said, her fingers squeezing my arm. You know she has it too, don't you?

She ain't got nothing, I whispered, so scared I could hardly stand on my two legs. Not Josie. No. There ain't nothing wrong with Josie.

She's got tuberculosis, Harvey, Miss Cresap said. Doctor Cecil and I both examined her. He says if she doesn't get rest and sunshine and good food she can't live a year.

By God, she gets rest! I shouted, trying to stand between Miss Cresap and that houseful of twenty-seven. She gets sunshine and good food. Just as good as the rest of us.

She'll die, Harvey, Miss Cresap said. Harvey, did I ever do anything deceitful to you? Did I ever lie to you or try to hurt you?

Not till now, you never! I hollered, like the God damndest fool on earth. Not till you come around here talking about taking my Josie away from me.

Not for more than maybe two years, said Miss Cresap.

That's too long! I blathered, so mad I had started in to cry. That's too damned long!

Harvey, it's long, Miss Cresap said. But it's not as long as TB will take her away.

That's when my head seemed to snap inside. I know now I was crazy. Everything I did from then on was crazy. The thing I said to Miss Cresap then, that was the meanest, craziest thing of all.

What do *you* know? I hollered, stamping around on the frozen ground. You derned old máid! What do you know about loving someone and then somebody wanting to take them away for two years! Josie and me—we ain't *never* been apart! What would you know about being apart from someone you been so close to so long you can't sleep of nights unless their back is warm up agin yours? What do you know about that, Miss Cresap?

She stared quick at the backs of her chapped hands and then looked up quick at the sky: the clouds was gathering for a big snow that day. She looked back down at me, her eyes was kind of tired. She opened her mouth to answer but I wouldn't let her.

Josie ain't got TB! I yelled. She's strong as you! You reckon she'd have milk for the baby if she was sick? I say she ain't got TB!

Miss Cresap got in her old car and drove off back to Glory. It started in to snow. I raged around down on the creek bank till past sundown. I just sat there with the snow piling up on my bare head and not giving a dern for nothing. I tell you I went crazy that day. And that night it just got worse. I was so crazy I couldn't even feel the cold nor the snow on my shoulders and on top of my bare head. It was late when I got back up to the place. I stood there in the dark, listening to all the snores of them all piled and heaped around me like stove wood in the blackness. I heard Josie's pap somewheres yonder starting up that bubbly, hacking cough of his. I stood there, a crazy man, in the midst of that houseful of twenty-seven. Except there was twenty-eight that night.

I thought about that extra one and it just seemed to make me crazier than ever. It was the convict that run off the prison farm two days before. It wasn't the first runaway we had hid in that house. Every two year or so some trusty would wait till the trucks was loading and the guards was busy taking the count and then swim across the creek in the dusk and run up and hide somewheres in Angel Swamp. And they always seemed to come to me and Josie; they always seemed to pick out our crowded and crazy house to hide away in. It was just like always. Except this time it was different. I had seen the look in Honey Darling's eyes when she saw who it was had run away this time. And I remembered the summer before when her and him had hollered back and forth across the creek to each other when he'd be hoeing beets up in the fields and Honey Darling would be sitting on the bank, fishing for cats. Amongst the snores of all the sleepers I imagined I could hear the whispers of Honey Darling as she lay, at last, in the arms of the one she'd held back for through all them nights of summer boys. I knowed I was going to lose her; a man don't have to look twice in his daughter's eyes to know when she's ready to go. I knowed when the young trusty found a moonless night and swung up on a slow freight that he'd be holding Honey Darling in his other arm. And that made me crazier than ever that night. I wasn't just going to lose Honey Darling; they was trying to make me lose my Josie, too. In the midst of that houseful of twenty-eight I stood there quiet and calm with craziness. Josie couldn't have the TB. I wouldn't let her. Honey Darling had the right to whatever love life told her to choose. But losing Josie was another thing.

I went out and stood in the door a spell staring across Angel Swamp glistening under the new, big moon: the snow was piled everywhere. For a while, at least, everything in sight seemed to look brand new; all the mean oldness of the pinched and bare earth that smelter-smoke had killed, even the tumbledown shapes of shacks and busted fences, it all looked like the snow had come to cover dark wishes and forgive them. I wouldn't let Josie have the TB, I figured in my crazy head. It had to be something else. It had to be something that wouldn't make them take her away from me.

And then it come over me. It was Josie's new baby, Jessie. My mind filled suddenly with the picture of Josie as I had seen her that morning before Miss Cresap come, her face old and tired, bending over the baby, her dress open, trying to press her breast into the blue, wrinkled mouth of that sixteenth baby. For a minute I remembered Josie that June morning behind her pap's stables; even in the stillness of fresh snowfall in that cold night I could hear the thunder of the stallion on the stones and I could hear the mare's high, whinnying cry. I thought about that first night in the boardinghouse on Water Street and the lights of the showboat and the brass band pounding and the broken promise to Josie that someday I'd take her on a boat ride like that. And I remembered Josie turning to me suddenly in the bed and pressing her belly against me in its first fullness and the way we fell asleep that way. And her hair that smelled like fresh bread baking somewheres. And it come over me with a crazy sureness that it was this last, this sixteenth, this one baby too much that was draining all the strength out of Josie's breast. Yes, it was that. It wasn't the TB at all! And when that baby was taken away, then Josie would be well and strong again.

I was like the cold-bloodiest murderer in the world as I went tiptoeing back among the snoring, stacked sleepers and felt my way toward Josie in the dark. I taken the little bundled up thing carefully out of Josie's tired arms. Josie moved once in her sleep, but she was too wore out for even the baby missing from her arms to wake her up. I went back out to the doorway, stood a second, and then set my feet crunching out through the snow. I knew what I had to do. I knew what it was that was taking my Josie's strength all out of her chest. It was this poor, sorry, helpless little thing. I knelt there in the snow by the busted fence and closed my eyes, holding the little thing against my own chest. God, I thought if only I had breasts to feed you with! Lord, how I loved the poor little thing. But I hated it, too. I hated what it was doing to my Josie. I felt like poor Abraham in the Scriptures when he stood with the knife raised over his Isaac, and my poor arm waited for the Angel of the Lord to stay my hand. I lifted the corner of the ragged, dirty blanket that had sheltered the faces of so many before. I wanted one last look at my lastborn. Its face didn't look much bigger than a dried apple; and it was wrinkled that way, too, with the queer, tight look I seen once on the face of a midget in a circus I went to once with my Pa. The little baby's face was plainly lit by the cold light of the moon. Its small eyes stared at me like the glass eyes of a toy. I knew then why Josie hadn't been able to get it to take her breast; I knew the baby had been like that since early that day, before Miss Cresap came. I tore the blanket away, feeling wildly of its little body: the arms and legs like little sticks of wood, the cold and swollen belly. I choked and wept a spell, holding the little thing against me, rocking to and fro on one knee in the snow. I looked up at the sky. Clouds like old clothes was blowing across the moon and over the hills that rimmed round Glory on every side. I lifted my fist and shook it against the air; I raised my hand in fury against the stars.

It was You up there! I roared. You done it!

I was crazy for real now; crazy with grief and shame and rage.

You! You! I screamed at the sky. You done it all! You done it to this little thing! You done it to her in there! You done it to me! God forgive you, God!

Then I just knelt there a while more, rocking in the snow on that one knee, clutching the cold, little thing against my chest. After a spell I looked around me, wild-eyed and crazy and lost out there in the queer light of that moon and all those watching stars. I saw the clean whiteness of the snow. I knew that's where I would bury the little thing. It seemed to me that it would stay buried forever there, under that whiteness, that great forgiving whiteness. And I did that. Then I went back inside that crazy place, that household, that snoring houseful and I lay down and felt some stranger's foot against my shoulder, and another's hand against my shoe, and I listened for Honey Darling's whisper but I couldn't hear it now. And I knew somehow that her and the boy had got up in the night and gone.

It's for that—for hiding out the boy—that the State claims they put me here in prison. But I know it's not for that. It happened too many times before and they never done anything to me. The State says they give me twenty years for harboring criminals. But I know they put me here because they think I murdered Josie's least-one, the last born, the one I buried that night there in the snow. And I never done it. You heard me say how it all was. It wasn't me. The baby was dead before I taken her from her mother's arms. There's only One who could have done it. And I know who that was. Up until a month ago they had Him in the cell just next to me. I used to press my mouth up against the bars so's He could hear me and I would whisper.

Confess it, I would say. You might as well. Confess that you taken that little one's life, God.

But all the sound I ever heard from Him was tears. And I used to beat on the bars with my pail and the guard would come and I'd try to explain it to him but it wasn't any good. And Josie she come to see me once before they got her that bed in the sanatorium and I tried to tell her. And she just cried and tried to kiss me through the screen. And I even told Miss Cresap.

It was God! I whispered to her. I know it, Miss Cresap. It was Him who killed my baby! If he'll just own up to it! But he won't!

She just looked at me with sad, kind eyes and never answered. And directly she told me that she burned down that old house with kerosene and she said she'd got new homes for most of the people and all my kids was being taken care of somewheres round and about the country-side. But I wasn't paying her much mind. I wanted to make her under-stand it wasn't me that killed that little thing.

Well, Harvey, she said, if you were God and if you had done a thing like that, wouldn't you feel sorry after a while and wish for someone to forgive you?

I thought about that a good deal. I laid there awake and then I shut my eyes and decided I would forgive Him. I thought about it all next day, too, and I even went and whispered through the bars to Him.

It's all right, I said softly. I ain't mad no more. I forgive you, God.

But he never even heard me. He wasn't even there. Because they'd taken him away and put him up in the part of the pen they call Death Row. And I never laid eyes on so much as a shadow of him again. Though I did try to pray. I wanted to pray to someone to forgive him. But that don't make no sense—for who's there left? Who do you pray to when the one you're praying for is the one you're praying to? And both of them is dead! Can you tell me that.

Oh, he's dead, I tell you. Because last Friday night the lights got dim and the stars they hummed and the moon let out a scream; and the curses of lost men, like me, howled in the weeping dark. He's dead I tell you: the forgiver and the unforgiven both. Last Friday at nine they burned him in the chair, and I could hear it singing like a throne.

Craven Quick

The Cresap woman won't ever tell it. That's because she doesn't want to
drag out the name of the Other Party involved. What she saw that night
in South Wheeling in that room in the Diamond Hotel is a secret as safe
as if it was locked up in a strong box in the Apple County Bank and the
key thrown in the Ohio River. She'll never tell it. I know her. She might
like to blab it to try and ruin me but she'll not. No matter how hard
and dirty I and the other decent folks here in Glory fight her she
wouldn't dare ever use that against me. Because she knows it would only
ruin the life of the Other Party. While it wouldn't hurt me a bit. Because
no one would believe it was me. I know what kind of friends I've got
here in Apple County. Staunch and true. A man's friends and neighbors
get to know him pretty good after forty-five years in a town this size.
They know me. And they know I'm a man. A man's man. They know
the way I've raised my boy Bud up to be. A man's man, too. And I'll
have to say I did that single-handed and without any help from Beuna.

270

If I'd have let Beuna have her way she'd have raised Bud to be a namby-pamby that the whole town could kick around without his so much as raising a hand to them. But I fought Beuna all the way. I made up my mind to teach Bud to stand up to life. I did it with my will and I did it with a buggy whip and willow switches when he was little. And when I figured he was big enough I taught him with my fists. It took me a while but he finally got the idea. It took a lot of beatings—a lot of bloody noses and black eyes—but I taught him. In the end I won. I made a man's man out of my boy.

And I'll tell you straight that it was a good thing the day Bud finally realized he'd have to stand up and fight back when his old man knocked him down. A mighty good thing. Because if he hadn't I'd have killed him. I'd a damned sight rather seen my son lying in his grave on Glory Hill than have him grow up into the kind of whimpering piss-willie his mother tried to make out of him. God knows she'd made a pretty good start of it before I noticed anything was wrong. Beuna was a Wheeling girl with a lot more education, soft-living and free-thinking than a woman should have. Plus that she's a snob. You get a combination like that in a woman and it can mean sheer ruination for a son. Bud was eight years old before I realized just how much damage she'd done him. Harper Follansbee and I are partners in the real-estate firm up on Jefferson Avenue. We closed up early one fall Friday afternoon so I stopped by the Legion for a drink and went on home. School was just out. Beuna had gone up to Pickett's to do some marketing for the week-end so I was alone when I heard Bud screaming his head off out in the backyard. I went back to the kitchen and peered out through the curtains to see what had happened. Well, I just naturally couldn't believe my eyes. There was Bud with three dirty little Polack miner's kids on top of him. They had chased my boy over the picket fence into the yard and now they were piled up on him and they were whaling the tar out of him. Bud broke loose and got up and for a minute I was sure he was going to turn around and make me proud of him. Instead of that he starts wailing again for his mother and comes tearing up the back steps and through the kitchen door. I caught him by the arm and swung him around.

You got your direction a little mixed up, didn't you, Bud? I said.

He threw his arms around me and pressed his face against my belt; he was wailing and blubbering words I couldn't understand. I unfastened his fingers from behind me and thrust him back and held him in a grip of steel, forcing him to face me.

Stop that bawling, I said. Stop it. Bud, I said stop it!

But he just began to shake and yell all the louder so I slapped his face and when that didn't shut him up I did it again and he just stared up at me with his eyes full of cowardice and his breath coming in thick hiccuping sobs. What I saw in my boy's face that afternoon made me feel like going over to the sink and puking.

You're not running into this house, I said, controlling myself. Not from a fight you're not. You better get that straight right now, Bud. You got your direction all mixed up if you think you can come running in here from a fight. Now, mister, you turn around and go back out there and stand up to those boys.

But, Pa, I can't! he wailed. I can't, I can't, I can't!

He started to blubber and bawl again but when he saw my right hand draw back he flinched his face and shut up again. By God, I must say I really controlled myself that day. I wanted to grip my fingers around his throat and throttle those shameless, thick sobs.

There's three of them, Pa, he gasped. And they're bigger than me.

What's that got to do with it? I said. What did that ever have to do with it?

They're them real tough kids from up Misery Holler, Pa, he yelled.

I glanced swiftly over his head through the screen door at the three grinning faces watching and listening to it all through the pickets of the fence. I wanted to tell Bud that those faces belonged to Polack trash; I wanted to tell him that when the day came when an American couldn't stand up to any number of their kind then we might as well rip down Old Glory and turn the country over to the Bolsheviks. But Bud wasn't ready for that lesson yet. I know boys. I hadn't taught Boy's Bible Class at the Glory Methodist Church for twenty years without learning a thing or two about that. I knew how to handle Bud at this stage of the game.

Pa, don't make me fight them boys, Bud whimpered, trying to lay his head against me again. Pa, please.

I shoved him away from me and held open the screen door.

Get out there, I said.

Pa, I can't I can't I can't, he wailed.

This is your last chance, Bud, I said. Either you go out there in the alley and fight those boys or you'll wish to God you were dead.

With a last sob of despairing cowardice my boy threw himself against me; his hands clutching my back seemed to burn through my shirt with disgusting contamination. I threw him back and turned around and went up the backstairs. When I had found what I had gone after I came back down to the kitchen. Bud was sitting on the chair by the stove holding his head in his hands.

Put this on, I said, holding it out to him.

Bud stared up at my face and then looked back down at the thing I had fetched from Beuna's bedroom.

What for, Pa? he whispered.

Put it on! I said, and when he began to back away from me I sprang forward and forced the skirts of the dress over his head and shoulders. He stood limp and staring while I slipped his arms into the flouncy silk sleeves. When he stood before me with the hem of his mother's dress in heaps around his feet I stood back. I undid my belt and took it off, folding it.

Now, mister, I said. I think you better pick up your skirts and start out that door pretty quick.

Pa, what for? what for?

Because if you stay in here I'm going to use this belt, I said. And if I use this belt your mother's going to need a new dress. And, mister, you're probably going to need some new skin.

Pa, you crazy? he whispered, with a gasp of impudence.

I didn't hit him hard. Still it was hard enough. The strap didn't leave more than a red mark on his face but it was good enough to tell him I meant business. He went slowly across the yard to the back gate, holding up Beuna's flower-print dress so he wouldn't trip on it. I stood on the top step of the back porch holding up my pants with one hand and pointing to Bud with the belt.

Boys, I hollered to the little Polack trash behind the fence. My little boy's decided he wants to be a little girl. Maybe you can find some little girls for him to play with. Or maybe he hasn't made up his mind yet. Maybe you can help him. And I don't give a damn how you do it.

I heard them titter and watched the three heads rise above the pickets, giggling and pointing at Bud.

Then I closed the screen door and the kitchen door and bolted it and went out to the front of the house to see if the evening paper had come yet. It was there all right but when I sat down in the porch swing to read it in the golden light of that late October afternoon I couldn't keep my mind on a word I read. All I could think of was my horror and disgust at what I'd seen in my son that day. And I knew what I'd done was right. If those boys beat Bud up so bad that I'd have to send for Doctor Ed Follansbee it was still worth it. If they put him in the Glendale Hospital it was worth it. Even if they killed him it was better than to have him grow up a weakling and a coward. I knew what I had done was right. It was good Psychology. And you ask anybody around Mound County about Craven Quick and they'll tell you I've got a natural-born sense of Psychology and it's always sure-fire whether it's women or real-estate or boys.

Well, I sat there on the porch swing that afternoon with the evening *Argus* on my lap but I was thinking about too many things, too many memories, to read it. Beuna, I guess. That's what I was thinking about. Remembering Beuna and the carefree years before I met her: the good old days of youth and freedom, nights with the boys when we'd drive to Benwood and leave our boater-straws in the buggy seats before we piled in and broke up a meeting at the Slovak Union Hall and then went off to get drunk at the Sanchez woman's whorehouse while her pretty little ladies-of-the-evening ran around in their teddy-bears and poured us drinks and nursed our split knuckles before they took us to the rooms. Still Beuna and me were happy there for the first year or two. Nobody in Wheeling ever thought Beuna would marry me. She was thick as thieves with that snotty, social Echo Point set of pansies and their rich, spoiled sisters and I was a boy from down river at Glory and the ones that didn't hold that against me said a tall, handsome girl like Beuna Windsor would never marry a tough little tank-town saloon fighter who was only five-foot-two. Well, a lot of men have been fooled about that: my stature, I refer to. A few dozen wop steel-workers are wearing their noses a little different because they figured they could whip a little sissy in a striped blazer and a straw hat.

Yes, I sat there on the swing that afternoon thinking about the good old days and what a swell gang we were and how those wedding bells—they sure did break it up. I remembered the Elk's Gaiety Follies of 1908 when we had a benefit-show with all the fellows dressed up like chorus cuties: every one of us—the most regular guys you'd want to meet—we were wearing panties and brassieres and little lace skirts like the Ziegfield girls, with rouge and lipstick and face powder. It sure was a panic

and the climax of the show was a mock beauty contest—A. K. Pyle won
first prize for the daintiest arms and shoulders. Al Blick sang "Kiss Me
Again" like Fritzi Scheff, and yours truly took first prize for the prettiest
figure in the whole show. Tie that one, if you can—the meanest, toughest little one-hundred-and-fifty-two pounds of scrapping dynamite in the
Ohio Valley hearing himself called "petite and roguishly demure" by
the judge that night. Well, after the show we all drove down to Benwood
with our costumes and wigs still on and went into a Pulaski Street
saloon looking for fun. The place was full of Hunkie millhands and it
was payday and a lot of them were drunk and before they caught on a
couple of them come over and start flirting with A. K. Pyle and some
big Polack had his arm around my waist and asked me if he could buy
me a drink and I nodded yes and made googoo eyes at him and soon as
I got the drink down he stuck his big garlic-stinking face down to kiss
me and that's when I let him have it. With my knee. I mean I really
gave it to him right in the family-jewels and laid him out gagging and
retching in the sawdust. Then we all lit into them and what I mean to
say it was the kind of knock-down-drag-out the boys still tell about. We
sure took that place apart. I thought about it there in the swing that
afternoon and I thought about Beuna and me getting maried the next
year and the morning Ed Follansbee came out of Beuna's bedroom and
told me I had a ten-pound son. Well, I was just as proud of him then as
I was ashamed of him now. And that was the moment I swore a solemn
oath that as far as Bud was concerned I was going to make him or break
him.

He got a pretty bad beating out back that night. And it was just the
first of a lot more beatings to come. The word about the dress got
around among the kids pretty fast and from the time Bud was eight
until he was well into his teens there was hardly a week went by that he
didn't come home with a split lip or a black eye. I used to look at his
knuckles to see if they were scuffed up any and if they weren't I knew
he'd turned yellow again. And when he saw that look in my eyes he
never had to be told what to do. He'd march ahead of me down the
cellar steps to the coalbin and take his pants down and I'd lay onto that
boy's butt with my belt till it bled.

One of these days, I would tell him, you'll figure it out, Bud. One of
these days you'll get smart and realize that no whipping you're ever
going to run away from in the schoolyard is half as bad as the one I'll
give you when you get home.

But there was six of 'em, Pa! he'd whisper, nursing his butt with one hand and trying to pull his knickers up as easy as possible with the other.

I don't give a hoot if there was sixty, I said quietly. Number has got nothing to do with guts, boy. What have I always told you? It's not the winning that counts, my lad, it's how you play the game.

I caught him once trying to trick me the winter he was just turned thirteen. He was on his way home—running as usual—from a bunch of niggers who'd decided to help out with his education in life and jumped him on the railroad tracks down by the zinc smelter. He lost a front tooth that time and his lumber jacket was half-ripped off. The niggers decided not to chase him into our neighborhood so he was alone when I saw him through the parlor window. He knew I'd look at his hands when he got in the house so he was down on his knees ripping the skin off his knuckles against the street curb. That was the first time I ever struck him with my fist.

Beuna was sick most of the time in those days so her wailing and protests didn't count for much. She only succeeded in making what decent home life I had left to me a living hell. So the responsibility of raising Bud up into respectable manliness lay on my shoulders and mine alone. Whatever credit goes to anyone for the man Bud turned out to be I don't mind claiming for my own. I saw to it that he spent an hour and a half each and every night up in his old attic playroom exercising with the dumbbells and building his body up.

I'm going to leave you, Craven, Beuna said to me one night. I'm going to take Bud and go to my mother's in Wheeling. You can't touch either of us there.

Can't I? I said. You haven't got a very good memory, have you, Beuna?

She stopped packing and stood in the closet doorway with an armful of dresses, staring at me with scared, weak eyes.

What's that supposed to mean? she said, shaky-voiced.

Parkersburgh, I said. That night at the Legion Convention in 1920. That's what I mean. By the time I get through with my divorce charges against you I don't think even your fancy father or your fine Episcopalian mother will be able to stand the shame of having you under their roof. Think that over for a while, my fine wife, and then decide if you want to finish packing.

You can't—you couldn't—prove it, she whispered, sitting down suddenly on the rug against the closet door.

Four respected and influential Legionnaires would be glad to testify, I said. Would you call that proof, Beuna?

Well, Beuna's memory seemed to make a sudden recovery. Because she swallowed once or twice and shut her mouth and then she began to cry. And I left her in disgust and went downstairs to see how Bud was coming along with his homework. I felt drained and weary. It's not easy for a man to have to be a father to his son and a mother as well. That's how I thought of myself sometimes—father and mother both to that child. Maybe that's the main reason I hadn't been able to touch Beuna's body in more than eleven years. I had to be so much of the mother to our son that when I got done being father, as well, there was no desire in me to be a husband. Not that I'm not as passionate as any normal, red-blooded American male. I need a woman as often as the next man—more, in fact—but it got so I couldn't look at a sickly, complaining wretch like Beuna and see a woman any more. And so when I got the urge I did what any normal man in my position in Glory did. I got in the old Buick and drove to Benwood to the Sanchez woman's house, got good and drunk and picked out a girl. There's no man alive who knows me better than Doctor Ed Follansbee—by God, the good old times we used to share—and Ed would be the first to tell you that there's no man in Mound County, young or old, who can show a girl a better time than Craven Quick.

In fact I got so wild and rammy one night that the Sanchez woman threw me out. I guess one of her girls must have complained she just couldn't take care of that much man. Ed and I got drunk Thanksgiving weekend three years ago and drove to Benwood. We were pretty tanked up by the time we got to Sanchez's and we must have had the better part of a quart of bootleg Scotch before the girls took us up to the rooms. I don't remember what all happened. I remember making some kind of a little joke to the Sanchez woman after I'd fooled around in bed with the little Hunkie girl for a while. I remember telling her I didn't like any of the damned big-assed peasant bitches she kept in her house and I remember asking her to send out to one of the South Wheeling hotels and getting me something else. I gave her a fifty-dollar bill, too. The next thing I knew I was standing out on that windy back porch of the whorehouse trying to get my coat on and listening to Ed arguing with the Sanchez woman through the open doorway to the kitchen. Ed came out directly. He staggered against me in that freezing wind that blows up across the freight yards from the Ohio. The Sanchez woman stood hollering in the kitchen doorway. I turned and saw her in a blur of angry, drunk tears.

Listen, you son of a bitch, she said. And you mind to remember when you get sober. Don't you never come back to my place again. Because I don't put up with that kind of stuff around here. I pay the law and I run a decent house. Just mind you remember now. Don't come back no more.

I could hardly see. I just remember the bleary big hunkie shape of her standing there against the oblong of kitchen light and the shape of the big nigger that works for her—I seen him coming up behind her in the yellow glare. I thought to myself: Why, between me and Ed we can whip that big yellow bastard easy. But I knew we were both too drunk and Ed was already tugging at my sleeve, his shoes slipping and crunching in the cinders. And then the Sanchez woman slammed the door and left us alone in the cold, cold wind. I put my arms around good old Ed and hugged him. I could hear my voice like it was someone else talking.

Old friend, I kept saying. Good old friend, old friend old friend. Where's all the old good friends gone, Ed? The wedding bell rang the life out of them. It rang the hell out of them, old friend Ed. It's the goddam bell of hell. And you know what? It's not a wedding bell, it's a funeral bell.

Ed will tell you. I was too much man even for that old Spik madam to put up with. I probably asked her to send out and get me fifteen or twenty extra girls from the South Wheeling hotels, line them up in the kitchen, and watch me take them one by one. Ed's been with me all the way. He knows about Beuna. He never condemned me the night a year later when I told him I couldn't bear the sight of Beuna any more, with that white scar since her hysterectomy. It wasn't that I couldn't forgive Beuna for not being a woman any more. It was everything else that had come between us. She was still young and I guess she still had her looks. But every time I'd catch sight of her nakedness—that white scar like a crooked blue string across her belly—I'd feel like something was turning my stomach inside out. I'd look at her and for a minute sometimes I couldn't think what she was—man or woman—she was only a creature with something slashed away. And yet the marriage had to hold together

—I had to keep it together. I had to raise Bud. I had to make sure he turned out good—a man's man. Let God judge me as He will upon His throne of wrath and mercy—at least He can never say I didn't fight to make a man's man from my boy.

Beuna and I got separate bedrooms after that. Sometimes I'd hear her crying through the wall. In the dark. But there again is a case of where that psychology-sense of mine saved me. I knew she couldn't be crying because she wanted me as a woman wants a husband. Because there wasn't anything left in her to want that with. And so I reckoned she was either crying that way to keep me from sleeping or else crying out of sheer, stubborn fury that I had taken Bud out of her arms and was trying to raise him the way she didn't have the guts to do. Lord, I know women's minds so well sometimes it just plain scares me.

So back in 1913 when I quit having anything to do with Beuna, I commenced going to the Sanchez woman's house in Benwood. And I kept on going there till that cold night in the Thanksgiving Day weekend of 1925. After that I never went back—mainly because of Ed Follansbee. I wasn't a bit afraid of that damned Spik madam myself, you understand. But I couldn't see the good of getting Ed messed up in a lot of nasty gossip. Ed's got a fine, clean name and a good practice here in Glory. And his brother Harper's my partner here in the Real Estate office. So after that when I got hard up I'd drive the old Buick up to South Wheeling and check in at the Monongah Hotel. Hallie Hubbs runs the place. He's Republican Committeeman for the District and swings a lot of weight with the Hunkie labor vote up there. So it's a nice, safe, little old place to go. Hallie keeps about ten girls in the rooms and he changes them every couple of months or so. Beuna knew about the whores all those years. She knew it when I come back after the Armistice and commenced to going to the Sanchez house again. The first night I got home to Glory I went there. I never much cared whether she knew or not. That kind of thing couldn't concern her much any more one way or the other. Still I felt a little pity for her; a little of my psychology-sense told me she still had some need for attention. So when the American Legion held their State Convention in Parkersburgh in 1920 I took Beuna along and sent Bud over to stay at Ed Follansbee's. Beuna was thirty that year and still had her figure and her looks but I knew what a sterile joke her beauty really was.

We got a nice room at the Chancellor and I made up my mind to try and show Beuna a good time. I took her to a couple of movies and we ate at a good restaurant the first night we got there and I had the nigger bellboy bring up a good quart of Scotch. I hadn't forgotten what she accused me of forgetting either. She said I'd forgotten the time we spent a week in the same hotel the first year of our marriage but I hadn't. I don't forget things. I just hadn't mentioned it out of tact. Things sure were a lot different between Beuna and I that week we'd spent together in the Chancellor Hotel eleven years before. Beuna was a woman back then. That week was like part of our honeymoon. So this time I just hadn't talked about our being there before because it seemed like I would just be reminding Beuna that she wasn't one any more.

I came back to the room early one evening. I'd spent most of the day with some of the old gang—boys I hadn't met since the Armistice —and I was in a darned good mood. The street out in front of the hotel was milling with boys in uniform having themselves a good time and somebody was trying to get the band together to put on a little impromptu concert. The minute I got in the room I could smell it in the air that Beuna had been up there for a good while drinking alone. I heard her in the bathroom and I went over and opened the windows to air the room out. I leaned on the window sill and looked down at the boys in the street, the flags, the cute little river rips hanging on to the sleeves of old buddies of mine from France, the brass of the band instruments flashing against the crowd. I felt good. Then I heard Beuna say something behind me and her voice sounded low and queer. I turned around and I couldn't believe my eyes.

She had on a pair of whorish fur mules and black cotton stockings rolled below her knees. She had on the damndest, silliest pair of black step-ins I ever saw and I've seen a lot of them in my day. She must have had a hard time finding them because they came up high enough to cover her navel, to cover that ragged white scar on her belly. And she had on a brassiere I swear she must have borrowed from one of those hustlers down in the street. And she had an expression on her face she must have copied from studying pictures in Photoplay Magazine—a silly smile on her mouth and her eyelids done up like Theda Bara. I couldn't help it to save my life. I busted out laughing.

Don't laugh, she whispered, covering her mouth with her painted fingers. Oh my God, Crave, please don't laugh.

Well, what the hell am I supposed to do? I said.

Crave, please, she mumbled. Just while we're here. Crave, please.

Please what? I said, certain almost that she'd lost her mind.

Want me, she said. Please want me, Crave.

Want you? I said. Want you for what?

Crave? she said. They've almost all gone away. Where did they go, Crave? They went while we weren't even looking.

Where did what go, Beuna? I said.

The years, she said. Crave, for God's sake want me before all the years go running out. Crave, please.

I got up with a sigh and started toward the house-phone. I wanted to phone down to the dining room and have them send up some hot black coffee so I could get her sobered up. But I wasn't halfway across the room till she had thrown herself against me, her fingernails clawing at my back, her hips pushing senselessly against me. Her breath disgusted me. That mixed with the smell of some strong, expensive perfume she must have been saving for years because there had never been any reason for Beuna to buy perfume in the years between. She kept trying to kiss me and all I could do for a minute was stand there, half-retching, trying to get it into my head that this was really Beuna. She was crazy. I swear to God she was. And the worst was yet to come.

Listen, Crave, she whispered wildly with her wet, loose lips against my neck. Listen, I'll be anything you want. I'll do anything. Listen, Crave. I know what those girls do. I know, Crave. Turn out the lights if you don't want to see me, Crave. Turn them out and make believe I'm one of those girls. I'll be good at it, Crave. Listen, Crave, I'll surprise you.

Get away from me, I choked, trying to get her hands loose without her tearing my shirt. But her hands were suddenly everywhere; I couldn't keep up with them. And then something did tear and I knew she had ripped open the fly of my uniform and I just stood there stunned, trying to get it into my head who this was. And when she got down on her knees I thought she was looking for my trouser buttons that had scattered across the hotel rug. But she wasn't. She was still on her knees, against me, her fingers tearing at me, and I knew she wasn't on her hands and knees looking for any goddam buttons. I stood there looking down at her, letting her have her way for a minute, letting my old psychology-sense take over again.

So that's what you always were, I said quietly, watching her have her way with me. That's what you've always wanted. And I reckon Ed Follansbee would have to cut something out of your mouth before you'd stop wanting that.

I knocked her sideways and left her crying on the fancy oriental rug, taking the door key with me, locking the door behind me. I swear to God I walked like a man in a trance. I walked down six flights of stairs and out through the crowds in the lobby into the crowds in the street. I knew how to handle her. God, I know women. I knew I had to be as tough with Beuna as I'd be with Bud. I had to drive my lesson home hard. I bumped into a boy named Whitey Masters I'd known in France. Whitey was an Albino; a queer, gawky-looking sort of fellow with a skinny throat and an Adam's apple with some little tufts of that queer Albino hair sticking out of it. There were three other fellows with him: all good clean country boys like Whitey. I trusted them. I can tell when a man's clean.

Listen, Whitey, I said. You and those other three go on up to 613.

I handed him the door key; I remember how his palms felt against my fingers: calluses as thick as lizard skin.

Thanks, lieutenant, Whitey said. What's going on up there.

There's a good-looker waiting up there, that's what, I said. A real good-looker. And she's raring to go. She could take on the whole A.E.F. tonight. Go on up and show her a good time. And have a good time, too, yourself. And say, boys—

They all leaned forward and round me to hear because a crowd of screaming girls burst out of the hotel on the arms of their boys. I winked at Whitey and the others.

She's French, I said.

And I winked again. Whitey didn't get it but the other three did and they moved off toward the steps of the hotel. I felt bad. I felt sad the way I'd felt the day I'd had to make Bud put that dress on and go out there and take his medicine. But I knew I was letting Beuna off easier than I had Bud. I knew those four boys wouldn't do anything to Beuna as bad as what I'd probably have done if I'd stayed in that hotel room with her another second. I almost beat a little Slovak girl to death one night in the Diamond Hotel for trying to do what Beuna wanted to do to me. I knew I'd handled things right. The old psychology-sense was back in business again. I looked up at the windows on the sixth floor and listened to the hustlers and town-girls screaming back in the lobby. A bunch of good old buddies of mine were trying to sing "Keep the Home Fires Burning" while the band was tuning up over on the steps of the Chancellor. I looked up at the windows of the room again. But there wasn't anyone there yet. I decided to go somewhere and find some old buddy of mine who had a bottle. There was plenty of good liquor around that night. Not rotgut bootleg stuff either but real Canadian Scotch. I looked up at the window again just as the band began to play. Beuna was leaning out over the window sill with her mouth open and Whitey Masters was leaning over her shoulder, pulling at her arm. Beuna was screaming her head off; I could tell by her eyes and the way the tendons showed on her neck. But the band was playing and everybody was yelling and singing and nobody could hear her and nobody would pay any attention if they could. Whitey must have gotten her back in the room with the other boys all right. Because when I looked up again the window was empty and the curtains were blowing in.

By God, I need a drink, I said out loud and went off through the shoulders. I need a drink real bad.

And I did. A man like me doesn't take it any too well to find out he's been married to a woman for eleven years, the mother of his son, and never known in all that time that she is queer for men. I didn't even stay out the rest of the week the Convention was set to run. I got Beuna on the morning train and took her back to Glory that day.

Well, it worked. She let me alone after that. I mean she let me alone about everything. For a month she stayed in her room with the door locked and then for another six months she never said a word to me, nor looked me once in the eye. She was a changed woman. She had learned her lesson. She didn't even bother me about Bud any more. And I must say Bud was coming along pretty good before long. I don't mean he'd learned to stand up and fight yet but at least he had learned to take his medicine without whimpering when he came home later and had to face me in the coalbin. And I never once lost my faith and courage. There was something beginning to glitter in that boy's blue eyes. It was just a little spark at first but when I saw it I knew Bud was going to win through. And in the end I was right. On Bud's fifteenth birthday I got him a pair of boxing gloves for a present. But that was only half the present. I got a pair for myself, too—that was the other half.

You're too old to whip with this, I said to him that winter night in the cellar, and while he watched I opened the furnace door and threw the ragged buggy whip into the roaring flames. From now on, Bud, you and me are going to settle our differences with these.

When I knocked him down he got up again, though he still had that bewildered look on his face like he didn't know what to do, like he couldn't believe I wanted him to dare do such a thing as hit me back. And it went on like that for nearly a year with me punching him around the cellar and only occasionally him swinging a kind of halfhearted punch at me like he didn't mean it and was only doing it because he thought I wanted it. I knew he wasn't anywhere near the right way of thinking. I knew there had to be something to start him off, something to trigger him, so to speak. And one summer night a year later the old psychology-sense came to my rescue and told me what it was. We were sparring and I was knocking him down out in the back yard beside the chicken coop and when we were in a clinch I put my mouth right down close to his ear and let him have it.

Son of a bitch, I whispered and jumped back, punching him along the chest and shoulders. You're a son of a bitch, Bud Quick.

What? he gasped. What'd you say, pa?

I said your mother was a bitch, I muttered, still laughing, still dancing around him.

It was the first time he ever hit me and, by God, if he didn't land one that set me down hard on the grass. It seemed like from then on he seemed to wise up. He lost that silly, sheepish, schoolboy smile he'd always had and the glitter in his eyes: it was clear and set now. By God, I'd won. By the time he was eighteen he was damned near as good as I was and there wasn't a boy in Glory High, no matter how big they was, who'd care to tangle with my Bud. It got so there wasn't much fun in our bouts in the cellar any more. They were just about even every time. I felt twenty years younger. Once Bud had become a man we were closer than brothers. Many's the summer night when I couldn't stand Beuna's complaining any longer that Bud and me would roam off together into the town looking for fun. It got so the two of us was a familiar sight around Glory in those dusky evenings. And there wasn't a man around who didn't watch his step around us either. I felt like the old lost years had come back to me again: the long-gone times I'd thought of that afternoon on the porch swing when Bud was out back, in Beuna's dress, getting his first taste of life as it really is. We prowled the streets together till the clock in the Central School tower struck nine and then we'd head for home. And many's the night we'd nurse our bloody fists in the same washbowl and maybe, for fun, I'd toss up a handful of hot water in Bud's eyes and catch him off guard with a short snapping punch up alongside the cheek.

It was a good year. In some ways I think it's the only happy year I can ever remember having. It's like I'd gotten hold of an old piece of myself that had gotten lost somewhere back there in the trash of the years, behind all the ugliness of Beuna. Back in the trash of all those years I'd dug it out with my hands and made it live again. And looking at it there in my hands I was proud because I knew it was something I'd beaten and whipped and thrashed into truth again. Looking at it there in my hands sometimes it seemed like the victory I had won wasn't Bud at all. It seemed like it was me. And then, suddenly, the good part of it was over. Bud changed. Oh, I don't mean to say he turned soft or cowardly. But he changed though. After supper I'd fetch my hat and clench a Marsh Wheeling stogie between my teeth and be all set for our evening raid; flexing my fingers and cracking my knuckles and feeling my fists. And I'd stroll through the house calling for Bud. But it got so half the time he wasn't around. And when he was around he'd make up some excuse: say he felt like going to a movie or up to Spoon's for a claret phosphate or maybe just lying on his bed reading some fool book. The good part of it was over. I'd be all set for our evening ramble, my muscles aching for a good work-out with a couple of pool-room bums.

Bud, let's go see how the wise-guys are, I'd say.

I'm reading, Pa, he'd mutter, and never take his eyes up from the page.

But what about the wise-guys, Bud? I'd say. There's bound to be a few out tonight looking for a knuckle-sandwich. Was there ever a night we went out looking that we didn't come across a couple of the wise-guys, Bud?

But it was over. The good part of the year was done. And it got so Bud went out nearly every evening as soon as the dishes were off the table. I played a little coy for a while; I acted like I didn't even notice. And then Bud was gone every evening for two whole weeks. So one night I followed him. I thought maybe he might be going out looking for fights on his own; I wanted to think it was that. But it wasn't that at all. When I caught sight of Bud up under the big elms by the courthouse statue he was with another boy and two girls. The four of them were standing around laughing and eating ice-cream cones. For a minute there the first fool thought that hit my mind was that they were laughing at me. I couldn't hear what they were saying; just the low murmur of Bud's voice and then the other boy or one of the girls would laugh. And for a minute the thought stabbed me like a knife that what Bud had said was something ornery or disrespectful about me. Isn't it a panic the damned fool thoughts that will cross a man's mind when he's scared? I don't mean to say I was scared. What I mean is that all of a sudden I had the wild thought that somehow I'd lost Bud. I went home down Seventh Street with the first cool wind of autumn blowing up from the river. My shirt was soaked with sweat; I felt cold. I sat out in the dark on the front porch for a long while listening to dry leaves blowing along the pavement out under the big maple. Pretty soon I heard Bud whistling; I heard him kicking through the leaves on his way home. When he got up on the porch I cracked a match on my thumbnail and lit up the stump of a cold stogie.

Evening, Pa, he said and pulled the screen door open.

Hi, fella, I said. It's almost ten o'clock. I got to thinking maybe you'd run into a couple of the wise guys.

No, Pa, he said. Me and some kids from school. We's just fooling around up on the courthouse corner.

Yeah? I said. Are they scrappers like you and me, Bud? Did you bump into any of the wise-guys?

No, Pa, he said, still holding the screen door open. We's just fooling around. This real good friend of mine Dallas Gorby we run into these two girls we know in school.

Well, it got worse. Bud and this boy Dallas Gorby spent just about every evening together that fall: sitting around Spoon's eating ice cream with those two girls or some of the others from school, or loafing around the courthouse statue, and once or twice I heard them together out on the back porch talking about the girls. One afternoon I saw them out in the back yard sparring around with the boxing gloves. It gave me a queer feeling: seeing those gloves I used to wear on somebody else's hands. I strolled out on the back porch and stood watching.

Hey, there, I said. Either one of you tough guys care to take on Jack Dempsey?

Bud looked up, grinning, and shook the sweat off his face; he commenced stripping off the gloves.

No, thanks, Pa, he said. Me and Dallas are late already. We got to get up to the library before nine to get some books for a history test tomorrow.

I went back in the kitchen and sat down on the wood chair by the stove.

Goddam, I thought to myself. Wouldn't it be something if Beuna has been putting poison in my food lately.

Because my stomach had been nearly killing me all that week. And that night it seemed worse than ever. I saw Ed Follansbee for a check-up the week before Thanksgiving but he said I was sound as a dollar and to quit smoking so many stogies. But I didn't. Because my common sense told me it wasn't stogies or poison food or any such damned rot as that. Those stomach-aches of mine were just that old psychology-sense of mine giving me the red light, so to speak. The human mind sure is a complicated thing and mine was trying to tell me that things weren't going right with my boy Bud. I'd already checked around town about this Gorby boy. His father got killed in the Benwood mine in 1924 and the boy's mother had brought him to Glory to live with her sister down on Purdy Avenue. Hardly the kind of boy I'd pick out for a friend of any son of mine. And I knew the kind of girls they were hanging around with, too—girls whose folks couldn't afford to outfit them in anything better than Sears and Roebuck dresses and half of them looked like they'd made their own in the high school sewing class. Well, I guess I don't have to spell it out: what girls of that class are looking for in the way of a good time. And if you've never lived in a town the size of Glory you don't know how the folks of that class of girl can make trouble when one of them gets in a family way. I didn't blame Bud for the company he was keeping. He just hadn't learned any better yet. I was fair about it, as I always try to be. But I knew—just like I knew the day those Hunkies chased him home—I knew the time had come for another strong lesson in Bud Quick's life.

And that's what led up to that night in the Monongah Hotel in South Wheeling—that night of all the slander and misunderstanding and the downright filth which that Cresap woman created in her own mind: the shameless lie she doesn't ever dare to tell about me in Glory because nobody would believe her if she did. And because of what she knows it would do to the Other Party.

It was two nights before Thanksgiving of this winter and I made sure ahead of time that Bud wouldn't have any plans made. I'll admit to one mistake—I shouldn't have been drinking as much as I did that night. Bud and the Gorby boy were sitting out on the back porch eating black walnuts and throwing the shells into a little bonfire they'd made. I had half a mind to order the Gorby boy off my place but then an idea hit me. I'd had a feeling from the first that this boy wasn't quite all a boy should be: something a little too full about his mouth, something a little too round and trim about the upper part of his legs. So I decided I'd test him out and maybe I would succeed in showing him up in front of Bud. I had it in my mind that night to find out for certain just what kind of stuff that Gorby boy was made of. I was going to strip him down to the truth. And I had me another good tumblerful of Ed Follansbee's hospital gin before I went out on the back porch.

Come on, you guys, let's take a ride, I said.

Where to, Pa? Bud said.

Never you mind, where to, I said. I figure you boys are men enough to get your ashes hauled. I figure it's time you learned what a real woman feels like. You've been fooling around long enough with these little high-school vamps. I'm going to take you up to the good old Monongah Hotel in South Wheeling. I'm going to pay a couple of Allie Hubbs' little girls to fix you boys up.

I studied the Gorby boy's face real good as I said it and saw how he flushed up red in the firelight. He looked at Bud and kind of grinned and then stared off quick into the bonfire with his head turned away from me. I laughed to myself and went back to the kitchen. I fetched that quart of Ed's gin and three glasses.

It is also, by God, time you started learning to handle your liquor, I said, and poured out a round.

I had myself another glassful of the gin myself. Yes, I'll be the first one to admit that I shouldn't have had any more. Not, at least, for a few minutes. Because that night was the first time in my life that things sort of got ahead of each other—mixed in their natural order, so to speak. I remember Bud telling me he didn't think he wanted to go and then I got him or the Gorby boy to have a drink or two of Ed's gin—I forget just which it was—and I can remember the long, slow, careful drive up the Narrows and through Benwood and McMechen and the big orange flames from the blast furnaces and I kept on driving easy, because the dirty streets of the South Wheeling slums were slick with a fall of fresh snow. As I say, I wasn't really drunk and yet things sort of were getting ahead of each other, so to speak, and a lot of it now is hard to remember. Hard but not impossible because I've got a perfect memory, drunk or sober. I can remember Hallie and the two little Hunkie girls but then somewhere later it just seemed like all the strain and weariness—yes, the God damned loneliness—of that autumn seemed to catch up with me and I—yes, by God, I'm not ashamed to admit I'd been lonely that year and here it was Thanksgiving nearly and I could think of damned little to be thankful for with a wife like Beuna and my boy slipping through my fingers like one of those greased girls at the Elks' Smoker that year. So I fell asleep and when I opened my eyes I was lying on that hard, little bed in one of Allie Hubb's hotel rooms and I heard somebody throwing up in the washbasin over on the table by the window and I turned my head and looked.

Bud, get your clothes on, I said. You and me's going home.

But it wasn't Bud. It wasn't Bud, at all, it was that damned Gorby boy and he was standing there naked as he was born and still slobbering sick and the muscles of his stomach were jumping under the smooth skin of his belly and tears were running down his face.

Where the hell is Bud? I said.

Bud ain't here, he half-screamed, choking and hiccuping, his fists clenched at his sides. Bud ain't here. You know goddam well Bud wouldn't come! You damned—you dirty-damned—

But he started getting sick again and flung his head around to the table and stood there heaving with his silly, little girl's buttocks twinkling at me in the light from the gas flame by the door. I tried to get up but the fatigue and strain of that autumn were still in me. I was too dizzy to sit up with all that loneliness and strain in me. I laid there looking at the stained ceiling and for some damned reason it made me think of that hotel room back in 1920 at the Chancellor.

What do you mean—Bud wouldn't come, I said, speaking carefully so the boy wouldn't get the idea I was drunk.

I didn't give a damn about him but still and all I didn't want him getting the idea I was drunk. I didn't want him thinking I had done anything I couldn't remember because I was drunk or for some such reason; I remembered everything about what I'd done: Bud being there and the girls and all of it. Things just had changed around a little in their natural order that's all. I don't mean I hadn't had a little too much to drink but still I remembered everything I'd done in the Monongah Hotel, in that room, that night. I don't forget things.

What do you mean Bud wouldn't come? I said. And where'd the girls go? Where'd Bud go? Where's my boy?

I turned my sick head on the bed and saw the Gorby boy again. He was sitting on the edge of the busted old Grand Rapids easy-chair, still naked, holding his head in his hands and gasping and swallowing softly.

Where's Bud? I said. And where's the girls?

He shook his head slowly, still not lifting it, still holding it in his hands.

Did you get fixed up? I said. Did you and Bud get your ashes hauled?

He shook his head again slowly and groaned. I stared at him a minute and laughed.

And that's when Allie knocked at the door and I didn't pay any attention for a while and he knocked harder and when I asked him what he wanted he said that Nell Gorby and that damned Marcy Cresap were outside in the hall and he said if I didn't let them take the boy home— he said if I didn't open the door and let them in to get the boy that the Cresap woman was going to call the Wheeling police.

When the boy heard that he hopped around, getting into his long underwear and looking for his pants and directly he opened the door and Allie stayed back in the hallway whining and explaining something I couldn't make out and presently the Gorby woman came blubbering and blathering into the room and took her precious darling out. And that damned Cresap woman stood at the brass foot of the bed looking down at me, shaking her head like a preacher, and when she spoke I thought at first she was talking to herself.

God's pity on the poor little thing, she said.

God pity him hell, I said, turning over on my face, showing my backside to her. He got his ashes hauled. Don't let him tell you he didn't. For I was here and paid for it. He don't need your righteous pity.

I didn't mean him, Craven, she said. I meant you.

I laid there for a long while feeling the helpless outrage gather inside me at this piece of impudence but I felt too sick to turn around just yet and set her back on her heels. I just felt like sleeping. That's all I wanted right then. I felt somehow like I'd lived a hundred years more than God ever meant for a man to live and still He wouldn't let me die. But, at least, I could die in a little sleep. And when I woke up and knew somebody was standing at the foot of the bed I thought the damned bitch was still there, still standing there and looking down at me with her phony righteousness and her mind full of all the dirty accusations and slanders she's never still dared utter to this day. I let out a groan of rage and turned over on my back again. But it wasn't Marcy Cresap. It was Bud.

Where the hell were you? I said.

I got here as fast as I could, he said. I missed one streetcar and the other one came slow because of the storm.

You're a damned liar, I said. You came here with me. You and that Other Party you've picked for a friend.

He shook his head slowly and watched me.

By God, are you telling me? I shouted, trying to get up. You been here all along. You and him. And the girls. I told Allie clean girls. Young ones, I said. Nice neat Polacks and Ukrainians with twinkling little butts. Don't tell me, mister.

He opened his mouth, closed it, and then he opened it and spoke again, so cool it made me proud.

No, he said. I didn't come with you. Don't you remember? You took Dallas. I didn't come. But it's all right, Pa. It's all right.

He smiled at me.

Want me to help you get cleaned up, Pa? He said. Want me to help you get dressed? The last streetcar's at midnight and I can take you home.

I frowned at him and turned my head.

You mean you didn't have no girl? I said. Allie didn't fix you up?

He shook his head and smiled again.

Why? I shouted. Why? Why!

He shrugged the way he had on the porch and then he got red and looked away to one side.

I got a girl, Pa, he said. A nice girl in Glory. In school.

He looked back at me, square in my eyes, and cleared his throat.

I'm not saying these girls—the ones you like—Pa, I'm not saying they're not nice girls, too, he said. It's just that I got my girl. A real nice girl, Pa.

He sighed and came over to the side of the bed and laid his hand on my bare shoulder, waiting.

Want me to help you up? he said.

Get your hand off me, mister, I said.

I felt his hand go way and was sorry for a minute I'd been so harsh. He meant well. By God, that boy Bud is good. He'll do anything for you. But just don't ever try pushing him around. Because he's just like me. That boy Bud is a man's man.

I just thought you might want some help, he said. I wasn't meaning to be fresh, Pa. I thought you might need some help getting that stuff all off and getting dressed. It's half an hour till the last streetcar, Pa.

What stuff? What are you talking about? I said.

Pa, he said. Pa, I'm not saying bad things against you—I'm not laughing at you or anything.

Why the hell should you laugh? I said, and fought my way up out of the dirty sheets and staggered over to that big long, dirty mirror on the back side of the door in that old hotel room in Allie Hubb's Monongah.

God, I been lonesome, I said, but I wasn't talking to Bud so I didn't care. Godalmighty, I been a lonesome man.

I saw myself in that dirty mirror.

I'm sorry, Pa, said Bud. Maybe we can go to a movie or something this week. I'm sorry I been out every night. I reckon you were lonesome.

But I was still talking to myself.

Lonesome, I said. Sure as hell. I've been lonesome for more years than you been living. I got a lonesomeness inside me older than death.

And I couldn't take my eyes off that damned, ridiculous, lonesome spectacle of myself there in that brown and bleary mirror. I looked up at a loose piece of wallpaper on the ceiling and shut my eyes.

Wanna fight? I shouted, but I was still drunk and I forget just who I was shouting to. I chuckled a hiccup and turned weaving round to Bud. I waved my hand to the mirror.

Just like the good old days, I said. The good old gang. Just like those grand old pals beyond recall. Didja know?—I won first prize, mister. Well, I did. "Demure and petite." That's what the man said that judged the contest. Ain't that a panic? Me!—Craven Quick! "Demure and petite"!

I turned around. I just couldn't keep my eyes off that image in the mirror. Dressed up there in black lace step-ins and black silk stockings rolled under my knees and French high heels and that fancy blue brassiere with the cups stuffed full of paper from the bathroom down the hall and my mouth done up with purple lipstick like Clara Bow's and my eyelids dark like Bebe Daniels'. That's what was there. And that's how I was and it's what the Cresap woman saw. That's what she'd tell on me if she dared. But she won't. Because she knows it would hurt the tender, young reputation of the Other Party. Yes, that's what she saw: me all dressed up like a girl in the Ziegfeld Follies and never had enough sense nor heart inside her to understand it was all because I was lonesome unto death, lonesome and looking back to that gay and free night twenty years gone by when the most regular bunch of guys you'll ever want to meet held the Elk's Gaiety Follies of nineteen and eight. That's how lonesome I was, you see? I was thinking back all those lonesome twenty years.

For God's sake, Bud! I yelled. Let's go find somebody to fight! Let's go tear up that Mick's saloon again!

I don't want to fight, Pa, he said. Thanks.

He laid his hand on my shoulder again.

Thanks anyways, Bud said. Come on home, Pa.

Damn home! I said. Go home. There's no home. You don't want to fight anybody. Then *you* go home!

I stood there looking at myself in the mirror and when Bud opened the door to go the mirror went away and when he closed it after him the mirror came back. And so did I. I stood a spell more looking at old first-prize, demeure, petite me and then I remembered where the gin bottle was and I went over and poured myself a good drink. And I sat there on the edge of the sagging mattress and drank it slow and you could sure smell the lonesomeness in that room. After a long while I looked up quick and there I was in the mirror again, only this time sitting down. I remembered the way somebody sang "Kiss Me Again" —sure it was young Doc Blick in a high, sweet falsetto—and the prize he took because everybody swore it was just like Fritzi Scheff.

"Sweet summer breeze—" I started to sing. But I couldn't finish it. I finished the drink though. And I poured another one. Because I was crying. I thought maybe some more of Ed's hospital gin would stop my crying. But it just made it worse. Lord, I must have looked a fool— tears and rouge and mascara running down my face and the lipstick smeared all over the back of my hand when I tried to stop crying. I only thank God that Bud had gone. Can't you see I'd rather be struck down dead than ever have my own son see me cry!

Jenny Purdy

My, it's such a fine spring evening! If you happen to be in Glory tonight
while they're still out on the porches would you tell them please that
Jenny Purdy is just fine? Especially Bud Quick and Miss Pet Weightman and Mister Paxton and Marcy Cresap. Papa won't be there—that's
the only trouble. After last Thanksgiving Day Papa stayed around
Glory the rest of the winter, but last week he gave up his greenhouse
and went wandering away with everything he owns in Mama's old straw
suitcase. Tonight he's staying at the General Polk Hotel in Old Washington, Ohio. So if you get to Old Washington, Ohio, this summer before Papa goes away again, would it be too much trouble to tell him
his Jenny's doing fine and loves him very much? Even if it doesn't do
any good—even if he doesn't believe you, I sure wish you'd try. I know
how hard it is out there to understand why we have to be here on Glory
Hill. It's even hard for us to figure out. Over on the Gassaway family
lot there's a man who used to be Governor of West Virginia and a big

294

coal and steel operator and heaven knows what all and he never stops complaining. The other night he was carrying on worse than usual.

I could have been the greatest of them all! he groaned. Morgan, Mellon, Carnegie—the pack of them. I could have had this country in my pocket. And just when I was really on my way I got cut off in my seventy-third year. And by cancer! The same common, disgusting complaint that killed Joe Callahan, the town drunkard. By God, the impudence of some afflictions! Why, I could have been—

But just then the wind began blowing loud in the high old spruce above his monument and he had to stop a spell. Mad, I'll bet, at the impudence of wind.

I could have been the Caesar of American industry, he grumbled, when the starry dark grew still again. And here my genius rots on Glory Hill!

Judge Peabody—he's the old man in the lot near ours who was so kind to me when I first came here—he couldn't lie there in silence listening to any more.

Even worms, my dear Jim, he said. Is free enterprise.

Well I must say that's a mighty crude way of pointing out the coarse chemical predicament we're all in out here. Yes, even you, you old fool! said Mister Slade.

Yes, even me, said the Judge with a chuckle. Even me. But decay isn't the only industry on Glory Hill, Jim. Have you ever considered the chemistry of dandelions? Did you ever talk to Luke Strider over there about his grass? One of these days, Jim, I bet you sell all your stock in the worm business and buy shares in a tree. And, oh, what lovely dividends are leaves!

Well, things like that never bother me a bit out here. What bothers me is getting lonesome for Papa and Bud Quick, Miss Pet and Mister Paxton, and Marcy Cresap. I just never get upset about all those serious, big thoughts about life and death like the older ones do out here. I just know I was part of something once and I'm part of something still and I know I always will be. But then I was luckier than most of them around me. Because I was only sixteen when I died. So I hadn't really lived long enough to forget anything important. I came to Glory Hill still remembering what we're all born knowing and then spend the rest of a lifetime forgetting. I guess little children never worry about death and where they'll go because they can still remember birth and where they were.

The first week I was here last winter was really bad though. It was just after Thanksgiving and way off in Glory I could hear the sound of things being wrapped and hidden away and all the children were whispering, so I knew it wasn't any time at all till Christmas. I just thought about poor Bud Quick and Papa and the rest of the people I loved and what a fool thing I'd done to die like this and spoil their Christmas. I could hardly stand myself those nights. And besides there was Mama lying only four feet away from me and she hadn't said a word since I'd been there. I was sure she was mad at me or maybe her feelings were still hurt.

Mama died when I was ten and she was always laughing and telling jokes to Papa and me and I remember how Papa used to play the piano and Mama would sing. Miss Pet and Mister Paxton always said she had the sweetest voice in Mound County and she did. Yet for days after I came to Glory Hill she never even said hello to me. And I lay there remembering the night before she came down with the typhoid fever—the last and only time Mama was ever sick—and I hadn't cleared the supper table and dried the dishes for her the way I always did. Instead I forgot somehow and ran out to see if Bud Quick was in our yard. And he was, so we ran off together up Lafayette Avenue into the green, bright summer town and Mama did those dishes all herself. And came down sick next day. And so one winter night I thought about Mama lying, quiet and thinking, so near by me and yet with the farness-away of all those eight years between us and that old, lost summer.

Can you ever, ever forgive me, Mama, I thought, mournfully, and just yearned to reach out the fingers of my thought and touch hers and ask her if it was the dishes that night. And pray she'd say it wasn't. But I didn't. I just kept still and listened to the wind. It sang in the elm tree and the cold grass way above me. And round me I heard all alive and sound-asleep things, wrapped safe inside the worn, old cloak of earth: curled moles that dreamed blind dreams and burrowed mice and chrysalids of paint-box butterflies—creatures just like me, maybe. I knew they were there, I could hear their sleep and feel them everywhere as far as my mind imagined earth could go: not just on Glory Hill but back in our yard among the roots of Papa's perennials and the cellar-bins full of irises and canna bulbs and winter onions and in the whole earth of Mound County where primrose promises lay sleeping, full of the come-back and promises of tomorrow. And I thought of each of them, like me maybe, just scarcely daring the most timid hope for that first, warm morning—like Genesis Papa used to read me—when the foot of April would fall walking on the land. That season when the old men's first horseshoes would start chinking against the spike in the evenings down in the vacant lot behind McFadden's Livery Stable. And the wild Pittsburgh calliope of spring's first showboat would come singing through the green leaves toward our town: a beautiful circus come walking across the waters like our Lord.

But still that night I knew it was winter. And I was lonesome for Bud Quick and Papa and everybody. And I was miserable knowing I was going to spoil their Christmas. There was nobody to talk to about all of it, either. Because I was still a stranger there on Glory Hill; even Mama hadn't said a word to me yet and Judge Peabody had noticed my being there, all right, but even he hadn't said anything yet; I guess he knew I needed a while to think. It had started in to snow that night. I could hear the hissing whisper of the little flakes; they struck in swirls of crystals against the dried-out bouquet of frozen daisies Papa had left there three weeks before. I could hear bells ringing out somewhere in Glory's streets. Then directly I heard Captain Calvin Lake's old Spanish-American War cornet playing "Silent Night" just the same off-key, awful, grand way it used to sound. And then I could hear May Anderson's bass drum thudding time and Sophie Sochek whanging on the tambourine and Junior Gumm just standing there looking humiliated and not making any sound at all. I could see how they would look, too: Maisie, Captain Lake and Junior Gumm, the deaf-mute boy, who always brought along the old yellow wood clarinet and seldom remembered to bring along his music book and hardly ever got to play. I knew where they'd be standing, too: on the bright, windy corner of Third Street and Jefferson Avenue near Mister Ganz's Store window where all the nicest presents were, unless, of course, you went to shop in Wheeling where presents cost too much.

It got awful quiet there on Glory Hill that night. Everybody was remembering things, I guess. It was the quietest I ever heard anything: all those thoughts remembering back to the thousands of Christmas Eves. Lord knows how far back Christmas Eves were being remembered there that night—a hundred years, I'll bet. There were more bells blowing on the wind now and I could pick out each one from the other and know which church it was coming from. Captain Lake's old cornet was having a terrible time with "It Came Upon a Midnight Clear" but it seemed to be saying if it got through the Spanish-American War all right it could surely pull through something beautiful like this. I kept on feeling everybody on Glory Hill hushed, remembering. Then I suddenly wondered to myself what they were remembering out on the rain-washed, grassless flats behind the Penitentiary in Potter's Field where people who can't afford burying get thrown away. I sure hoped the wind was blowing the sounds out their way, too, that night. But I hoped they all had something nice to remember: something they got once that wasn't all used up and spoiled before they got a chance to love it a while and wear it out. Or maybe a present they gave somebody once that they didn't really need but really wanted: something that cost too dear for common sense or maybe even useless and yet hoped-for more than anything. And therefore more necessary than church, more holy than bread. Then I heard Mama. She just cleared her throat a little the way she used to do when she was getting ready to sing and Papa started the wrong chord on the piano. Before I knew it the band back in Glory was playing "Noel Noel" and Mama was singing along with it in the same grand, clear voice she had back in those lost summer nights in the parlor. And for a minute it seemed to me like the stillness of everybody on Glory Hill got deeper than ever. But the band and the bells blew clear on the wind and Mama sang sweeter than ever and directly Judge Peabody joined in with a deep voice like a soft trombone, and then Luke Strider commenced singing in a sweet tenor and so was Lloyd Weaver, the boy who lost his lung in the Great War in France and I couldn't get over how good he sounded; back when he used to sing in the aisle behind us in the Presbyterian Church it didn't seem like he'd have enough breath to get through Old Hundred. Before long just about everybody on Glory Hill was singing: So many voices presently that I couldn't hear the snow any more. The only one not singing was me—I just couldn't yet. First I had to get something off my mind; I couldn't think of anything else till I found out. Mama stopped singing when I reached across and said her name.

Jenny? Oh, it is! It's Jenny, she whispered in the voice I'd always known.

Jenny, she said shyly. I'm so ashamed. Nearly a month gone by since you came here. More than three weeks passed and I haven't once had the gumption to raise my voice in comfort to my own child here beside me on Glory Hill! Jenny, Jenny, I was scared—ashamed. You always used to tell me I had the nicest speaking voice in all of Mound County.

And so—she went on, angry with herself, it seemed like—so I was afraid, at first, even to whisper. Think of it! My own child. Gracious, the pride and vanity of old fools! Afraid even to reach over and whisper my own child's name. Jenny, Jenny, I was scared you'd hear my voice over here, after all these years, and you wouldn't think it was a nice voice any more!

Oh, but it was nice. It was Mama's voice just like it used to be. The wind still blew now and the snow hissed in the grass but the band back there was gone, the singing hushed, the bells stilled. Back in muffled, snowy Glory everyone hurried home to light the trees.

Mama and I talked the whole night long. We talked till late into that Christmas forenoon; told old family gossips, jokes and tales; remembered queer things, sad things, funny ones, too; things that ended once, things that haven't ended yet, things that never will. The ones we talked of most were Papa and Marcy, Bud Quick and Miss Pet and Mister Paxton. Odd isn't it, when you think of it a spell?—the way the living haunt the dead. Even now, on this perfect spring evening, I think about poor Bud back in Glory. And about Papa stumbling off into the land like a lost soul and sleeping this very night in a big oak four-poster in the General Polk Hotel in Old Washington, Ohio, with two things under his pillow: an old picture of Mama and me and a road map of the whole U.S.A. Well, maybe they'll get by and be all right—come through it all some way. I sure wish I knew. They sure wish they knew, too.

Maybe we were always too close together. No, I don't mean that—it's a fool thing to say. When people care for each other they can't ever get too close to each other—there's too little time for them for that to ever happen. I didn't mean that. Please pretend I didn't say it. And whoever you care for a lot—or even just have to put up with—get close to them as you can. Right now. This very minute. Because the years—why, they're over in a twinkling.

We *were* a close family. And it didn't stop where the fence did either. There was always room for somebody strange, someone new. We lived in the little green bungalow at the bottom of Lafayette Avenue. Papa was the man that raised flowers in Glory in those days. In the wintertime he grew them in his small greenhouse and in the summer our whole three acres of back yard was flowers clear down to the banks of

Grave Creek where the cattails grew and the green frogs sang all spring. Whenever anybody in Glory wanted flowers in those days they came to Grover Purdy's bungalow. Flowers for weddings, birthday parties and funerals; flowers for gardens and sometimes just a little begonia in a brown pot for a rooming-house window sill. Bouquets of flowers, ropes of flowers, and sometimes just one flower. Just for smelling. Or looking.

Mama baked bread and rolls all year round, cakes and cookies for occasions and hot-cross buns at Easter. I never could make up my mind which smelled better—Mama's kitchen or Papa's greenhouse. Sometimes the smells got mixed up together—cakes, manure and Papa's sweet wild violets; hot-cross buns, bone meal and ginger bread. One big smell and, Lord, it was like perfume for a Queen. As for me, I kept busy, too. When I was nine—the year before Mama died—I sent away for a magazine route and if you care to take the trouble to look up the records sometime you'll discover that for three years in a row Jenny Purdy sold more *Saturday Evening Posts* than any other child in the whole fifteen-town territory.

That was when I first met Bud Quick. Bud was only eleven then and two grades ahead of me in school and, sad to relate, about the only time I ever saw Bud he was having awful fights out in the schoolyard. I never stopped and watched Bud's fights but just the same I knew from the other children that he always got the worst of it. And Bud knew I knew. And for some queer reason he despised the sight of me for knowing. Every other child in Central knew Bud always got the worst of it. And, if he hated them for knowing, he didn't show it. But knowing I knew was a thing he could hardly stand. Not that he ever hurt me or said a mean word to me to show his resentment. But I knew from his glowering glances—the burning hurt look from one puffed-up, blue-black eye whenever we'd march past each other during fire-drill—Oh, I knew. And did it puzzle me? Well, not so much. His hateful glances made the girl in me grow warm as Mama's fresh-baked bread. I knew his hate wasn't hate at all but something perfectly delicious he hadn't found out yet. In the winter during school, of course, I only sold my *Saturday Evening Posts* in the evening. But when spring came I could start early in the foggy dawn, if I wanted to, and sell my magazines till there were fireflies in the evening meadows.

That summer when I was going on ten—that summer when Bud Quick and I fell for each other forever—I always used to watch him with a sort of tender curiosity. I mean, I couldn't figure out the reason he was always chasing cars. I'd see him sometimes—a lonesome-looking little boy with bushy hair and the yellow memory of winter's last black eye—spring from the steps of his front porch and go chasing some perfectly ordinary-looking old Buick touring car clear up Seventh Street to the courthouse. His eyes would be wild and his bushy head strained forward to see something. Sometimes a smile would light his face or else again he'd go stumping back home, glum with disappointment, his hands jammed into the pockets of his knickers. Then he'd sit on the porch and watch the cars go by—there weren't too many in those sleepy summer afternoons of 1921. Sometimes three or four would go by in a couple of hours before one would happen along that looked interesting. Then off he'd tear again and once he chased one clear up Seventh as far as Jefferson Avenue; I know because I followed him, watching him with that funny, warm curiosity he made me feel, a something almost scary with excitement at wanting to find out what Bud Quick was chasing so I could chase it, too. It was funny, I used to notice, that I'd stand there under a big maple tree on Lafayette Avenue and watch Bud go pounding up the sidewalk after a muddy old Reo and I'd get all short of breath. Funny, I mean, because Bud was doing the running and I was standing still. It was halfway to August before I guessed. And one afternoon I got my chance. And with my heart in my mouth I told Bud Quick I knew and fell in love. He came slouching down past the Grand Theater, his face miserable after a Pierce-Arrow had outdistanced him around the Soldier's Statue on the Court House Corner. I stepped out bravely from behind the popcorn machine with my magazine sack under my right arm and looked up at the light bulbs—I didn't dare look him in the face when I spoke.

I saw it, I said. It was a South Dakota. And the one you missed this morning up by Peabody's—it was just a plain West Virginia. Only the reason it looked different was because of the yellow mud. For a minute there I was just like you—I thought it was a Rhode Island, because they're almost that kind of yellow—

I thought he was going to hit me for a second but then he got so interested in finding out for sure it wasn't a Rhode Island that he frowned seriously and forgot to be nonchalant.

Jenny, are you sure? he said gravely. I was just positive it was. Are you *sure?*

Positive, I said. Absolutely, positively positive.

And my heart was like a melting caramel.

That was our first summer—Bud and me: the summer of the license plates. He'd already started the first day school let out so it wouldn't have been fair, he said, to make me start a list all my own so late in the summer. So he let me share his. And even though that was late in August we saw ten more new states before the leaves began to turn. With me it was sharing something with him but it was something more than that for Bud—when Labor Day was past and the school satchels and crayons and pencil boxes appeared in the show-windows of Mister Seat's Drugstore Bud seemed almost in a panic.

Summer's nearly over, Jenny, he said sadly one day. The cars from other places are going home.

We got thirty-two states, I said cheerfully. And that one we almost saw by the *Argus* office *could* have been an Alabama.

But Bud Quick firmly shook his head; not standing for any female maybe's.

Thirty-two states, he said. Definite. You got to be definite or it's just ridiculous. Thirty-two, Jenny. And that means sixteen we didn't get.

And he slammed his palm with his knuckles.

Dern, he said. And summer's gone. It didn't seem like longer than it takes to blink—and here comes fall. And summer's gone.

Still it wasn't as bad as Bud Quick said that day. I got Michigan and Vermont and my first kiss the day before the first day of school. And that made thirty-four and Bud Quick's first kiss, too. And even though we laughed about it in the summers up ahead, we neither of us ever collected license plates again. Bud always seemed to have some trouble getting out of the house—I didn't understand why then. Still once or twice a week in the last days of that Indian Summer Bud used to come down Lafayette Avenue and sit on the porch with me, and Mama'd be in the kitchen making sea-foam candy and Papa would be talking to Miss Pet Weightman while Mister Chalmer Paxton puffed on one of those chokey, long, awful-smelling stogies and ate one of Mama's fresh cinnamon rolls and adored Miss Pet through his twinkling little pinch-nose glasses.

After a while I'd take Bud Quick's hand and we'd go out on the back porch to sit on the broken step and look at the sad, beautiful three acres of the last of Papa's summer flowers: it was like the death of a forest fire

—all embers in the dusk. And the willows beyond, on the banks of the creek, filling up with mist and the gray-blue of dusk-fog and the bowed green hair of the willows was sadder than the very saddest of Miss Pet's favorite Victrola records. If it wasn't for the smells of Mama's candy blowing out through the screen door I'll bet I'd have cried in Bud Quick's handkerchief. When the sea-foam was cool Mama'd call us all and Bud and I'd run with our pieces down through Papa's hollyhocks and last, late roses to the creek and sit in the mist under the willows like gray dreamers in a green dream. And I always waited and didn't eat any of my candy till Bud Quick ate a piece of his and then I'd grab his bushy, shy head and kiss him quick on the mouth. That kind of kiss had a burnt sugar taste that used to make me shiver all over. And then we'd sit and talk till the fireflies came out and Mama called us from the kitchen door.

Oh, but still I was a perfect little fool about one thing in those days. I used to think Bud Quick was ashamed of me. Because he told me never to come to his house, never even to stand out in front under the sugar maple and call to him. He said it was because of his mother who was sick and his father who studied a lot. He used to talk for hours about his father, his face peaceful like somebody sleeping: his father was the kindest, smartest man in the world. But he studied a lot because he was a philosopher and a very poetic soul and he just couldn't stand company or persons shouting out under the maple tree. I was real impressed, I guess. Bud's father sounded like the kind of kindred soul that would get along just grand with Papa and Mister Paxton. So I waited a spell and then I told Bud that the first spring night his mother was feeling better it might be nice for his father to bring her down to our house to meet Miss Pet and Mama. Poor Bud's face turned the color of buckwheat batter. But he thought of an answer.

Oh, no, he said. Mom's nerves is too bad for that. And Pa's busy every night studying and reading and thinking.

That's when my feelings were hurt. Can't you always tell when somebody you love is fibbing? But after a while I told myself it wasn't that Bud's mother and father would think Mama and Papa were common. I thought it was because of Miss Pet and Mister Paxton. And that was almost as bad. Because I loved them almost as much as I did Mama and Papa. But to hear most people in Glory talk you'd think Miss Pet and Mister Paxton's romance was the worst scandal the town ever had.

Heaven knows why. Miss Pet lived alone in her dead father's big, gray house up on Tomlinson Avenue and Mister Paxton lived by himself in a room at the Mound Hotel. Even the worst gossip in Glory could never say that Mister Paxton ever so much as set foot inside Miss Pet's stained-glass front doorway and the only time anybody ever saw her and Mister Paxton at the hotel was when they ate their turkey dinners every Thanksgiving and Christmas Day in the hotel dining room or once a week when they'd spend a summer evening in the front lobby playing whist or euchre. And when the first stroke of nine o'clock sang down through the courthouse trees Miss Pet would get up, fetch the little parasol she always carried in those summers and even if they were right in the middle of their game Mister Paxton would bow and take her hand and kiss it and Miss Pet would walk homeward past the whispering porches all alone. Still those two just seemed to shock and mortify the town. Maybe it was something one of them did a long time ago, too long ago for me to hear about, too long maybe even for anybody to exactly remember.

Mister Paxton came from a real quality family in Wheeling and Miss Pet was the very soul of genteel manners. Still I heard Mrs. Stribbler tell about a time she'd decided to be hospitable and ask Miss Pet and Mister Paxton to a lawn party she and some other Glory ladies interested in missionary work were giving to raise money for the Friends of Fiji. Mrs. Stribbler said Miss Pet and Mister Paxton each used her privy twice during the space of an hour and Mrs. Stribbler and everybody must have felt that was terribly common. I guess we were the only friends those two had in Glory. For as long as I can remember they came and sat on our front porch in the summer evenings. As soon as it got mild enough for Papa to hang up the porch swing and bring out the wicker chairs we'd see them coming down Lafayette Avenue under the locust trees. And when the nights past Indian summer got too cool they'd kiss our cheeks and say good-by till spring. I guess with all the talk about them already they'd never let a front door close behind them to set folks' fancies thinking the worst of what they couldn't see. So there was never a winter that we saw them, though never a Christmas that their presents didn't come: from dear Mister Paxton gloves for all of us that didn't fit, from darling Miss Pet another year of *National Geographic*. Between the two of them I think it was Mister Paxton I fell in love with first. Because the absolute purple passion of his life was amateur magic tricks.

And they never worked—that was the part I loved. Because when you're only four or five and somebody does a trick that fools everyone but you, it makes you feel extremely wise. Except that when I got to be seven I found out Mister Paxton's tricks really didn't fool anybody; they only pretended so. To make him feel good. So I pretended, too. He used to send away for his tricks to a joke-and-magic store in Toledo, Ohio, and one of them was a little thing you stuck in the roof of your mouth to throw your voice. Mister Paxton was always making Papa laugh by pretending to make ghosts call somebody's name back in the darkened summer parlor. That was the only trick that fooled and scared me in those days. Because in the summertime Mama always kept the blinds drawn in the parlor and covered the furniture with white muslin sheets so the sun wouldn't fade the plush.

No wonder Mister Paxton loved Miss Pet. She was so elegant; the soul of gentility and so kind. In the summer she carried her little parasol. When she opened it it wasn't much bigger than one of Mama's pie plates. Miss Pet said that was because the skin of her face was always so delicate; her cheeks always smelled like rosewater-and-glycerine. Her hands were sensitive, too: they smelled like lemons and she always wore white string-mesh gloves. Miss Pet used to say things that made most Glory people think she was a secret drinker. Though I, of course, knew better. And the things always made the most perfect sense to me. One evening the spring after Mama died she looked up and saw the dirigible Shenendoah drifting huge and silver over our house and she smiled at it politely and softly said, Good evening. One Christmas Eve Doctor Hettie B. Johnson invited all the children of the Presbyterian Sunday School to her house for some refreshments, carols and a short talk on venereal disease. Doctor Hettie was past eighty years old and had done years of experience in welfare work and she invited Miss Pet to serve the cocoa and fig newtons and Doctor Stribbler's wife to play the piano. When we'd all finished with the carols and were waiting to eat Doctor Hettie introduced her Polish maid to the children and said she had rescued her from a Benwood house-of-fame.

And what did you do there, my dear? Miss Pet asked politely.

The young girl frowned and commenced picking her nose.

I was a hustler, she said.

Oh, I think that's grand, said Miss Pet happily. I do so firmly believe in everyone keeping busy!

Well, Mrs. Stribbler looked just awful and so did Doctor Hettie. But I was only nine and it made sense to me and there wasn't a snicker nor giggle from any of the boys so I guess it made sense to them, too. Poor Miss Pet, brave Miss Pet. She never let the meanest scold in Glory still the unself-conscious poetry of her heart. I think sometimes of the night during the discussion period after one of Reverend Toombes' Wednesday night prayer-meetings. When everybody else seemed to have run out of anything else to say Miss Pet asked for her turn with a little wave of her hand.

I always think of God, she said with a sweet and thoughtful little smile, as someone really ahead of His time.

Well, most of Glory thought its worst of them: Miss Pet and Mister Paxton. And even thought bad of us, I've heard, for being fond of them. Some Glory people even went to Wheeling for their flowers. Papa didn't care though; not a bit. When the first dogwood bloomed in Colonel Bruce's yard and the new moon of spring lay like a lock of child's hair on the sky, we'd start watching for them along the brick sidewalk down Lafayette. And when summer was long ended and the last locust hushed and the boys kicked through the leaves and looked for chestnuts on Roberts' Ridge and waited for first frost to come and turn the pawpaws black as mitten leather—we'd wave so long to them both and Mama'd tell Mister Paxton to watch his catarrh and hope Miss Pet wouldn't have quinsy again this winter. And wait for them to come again next spring.

Well, I haven't told you all that could be said of them. Maybe I haven't been really fair. So don't be too harsh in judging the ones in Glory who treated Miss Pet and Mister Paxton the way they did. There was something about them that somehow I've dreaded telling. They were homely. I mean if you saw them now—even on this fine spring night when you're in a kind, warmhearted frame of mind—you'd probably say they were the two homeliest human beings God ever made. I've got to be fair. Miss Pet, to most everyone, had a long, droll, hound-dog face like John Bunny's girl-friend Flora Finch in the movies. It was a face, poor dear, that looked like some undertaker had started to embalm it and been called away to the phone before he could finish. Mister Paxton's face was pear-shaped, beet-red from high blood pressure and he wore a hair-piece which was too small and with the part in it pointing in different directions each day since he never managed to stick it on the same way two mornings in a row. With his purple face and huge cheeks he looked, poor darling, when he smiled, like someone had kicked open a spoiled eggplant. Now I guess I've been fair—I've said the worst that anyone can say of them and still be telling the truth. And maybe that's what Glory held against them. It seems like when people, too homely or too pretty, fall in love there's just something naturally suspicious about it in some people's minds. Folks feel better about it when plain, common-looking people go together. I guess they figure the pretty people are sure to be drawn to do sin—and the homely ones have got nothing else to do. Now that I've been fair and told the worst of them I've got to tell you this strange fact. I saw Miss Pet and Mister Paxton for the first time when I was six months old in Papa's arms on the front porch. I grew up seeing them. And, next to Mama and Papa, I thought they were the most beautiful faces in the world. As a very little girl I knew their faces were strange—but so was my rag doll Charming Charley strange—and Papa's prize red rooster Admiral Dewey. And birds and stones and the mottled face of the moon and the tiny-bearded pansies down in Papa's garden and the big-toothed horses down in McFadden's Stable—they were strange. But they were beautiful. And what can beauty ever be but that?—a strangeness grown common and sweet as breath, with one thing added to make it special and high above the rest—that funny kind of moreso-ness that love gives things inside: lighting their darling faces like those human lamps we used to carve from pumpkins, Bud and me, each Halloween. Nothing on this whole, wild world ever gets beautiful till somebody starts to love it and it finds out. If you just want to see a kind of human miracle sometime, then you go love something homely and watch its lamps light up. Papa knew. So did Mama, though she never said.

My Lord Almighty! Papa used to cry, running back into the kitchen where Mama'd be whipping up a saucepan of black-walnut fudge. Katherine, I look at them two setting out there on the porch in the moonlight with the shadow of the honeysuckle on their faces and, God Almighty, Katherine, they're beauties. My God, Katherine, I never seen such homely faces on this earth but they're beauties.

Hush that swearing, Grove, Mama'd whisper, beating the fudge furiously. Bud and Jenny's yonder on the porch.

But, Katherine! Papa'd cry. Them plain, ornery, downright ugly faces—My God, they're beautiful! Beautiful!

Father, stop that! Mama'd whisper again. They'll *hear* you!

But they never heard. Mister Paxton would be busy amusing Miss Pet with his latest sleight-of-hand or maybe making her think it was old Captain Brast, dead for thirty years by then, whose voice was singing "Dixie" back in the haunted summer parlor.

Say what you will, Papa would observe, licking a fingertip of Mama's fudge. There is few prettier sights on earth, Katherine, than two homely people that's *found* each other.

There's a lid for every pot, Mama would say.

But ain't they beautiful? Papa's voice would cry.

Mmmmm, Mama'd answer. They're kind. They're good. That matters more. I haven't noticed their faces now for years.

Mister Paxton, we'd hear Miss Pet's high, sweet voice lilting through the house. Don't you find it wholly forgivable that poor, dear Woodrow Wilson got married again?

Or else she'd go walking off alone down into the back yard among Papa's roses, sniffing and fondling the blossoms, her thin figure pale in old white dotted-swiss, once elegant and dear and now fresh-lavendered but frayed with shabbiness: her shape would seem to me then like some moonlit ghost of a dead china doll wandering into the flowers of an old nursery carpet. Sometimes she'd hum a tatter of a little tune—something on one of the old phonograph records she used to bring down from her old house and give to Papa to play on our Victrola: she hadn't one of her own—it was sold for junk or groceries long ago. The saddest tunes in the world. Caruso and Nelly Melba—that sort of singer. Sadder than love itself, I used to think, sitting by Bud Quick there on the broken step. And wonder why he never let me come up to his house or even call to him out under the sugar-maple tree. I didn't understand back then. I wish I'd known. I wish I hadn't asked him what was wrong the day I caught him limping past the popcorn stand by the Grand Theater. He quit limping right away and bit his lip and wouldn't say a word to me for hours that day. I wish I hadn't teased him the day I asked him to go wading with me in the creek with two of Mama's old jelly-strainers to catch pollywogs. But I did. I kept it up till he went way up in the brush under the far willows and took off his shoes and stockings where I couldn't watch, and waded out into the water up to his knickers and then came over to where I was. And when he slipped and went off in the deep place and I helped him kicking and gasping up into the cattails

I saw the scars: old white ones and fresh red welts all up and down the back side of his legs. He knew I'd seen, too, because he looked at me real quick and then he lied.

I derned near took all the skin off my legs, he said. Shimmying down an old pine tree up near Lynn Camp last month. Me and Pa. He took me there. He takes me everywhere. Pa's writing a book, Jenny. It's all about the Natural History of Mound County. My Pa sure is a whiz when it comes to Nature. You just show him a wild flower or a bird's egg and see if he can't name it—in Latin, too. And Greek!

I waited till he went home before I cried. I went up and stuffed my head under the feather pillows on my bed so Mama wouldn't hear me. But she heard me and came upstairs and asked what was wrong. And I lied. I decided I wouldn't be rotten enough to try to make myself better than my poor, dear Bud.

My legs, I said. I hurt them! Skinning down a tree, Mama! But they're all right now!

Jenny, child, she said; I could smell vanilla and the sweetness of strawberry preserves in her apron when she pressed my head into her old blue dress. Jenny, child, let me see. I'll fetch some witch hazel and stop the smarting.

No! I screamed, pushing away from her. Let them be! Don't touch my legs, Mama! I *want* them to hurt! I *want* them to!

I'd never screamed like that at Mama before; I never screamed at her ever again. In a week she was dead. Well, I'd bust out crying, telling you that, if she wasn't beside me now on Glory Hill. Time sure is a good handkerchief, isn't it? Mama died in late August of 1922. There'd been such a to-do all that summer about our well and the cistern out behind the greenhouse where Papa used to fetch water for his plants. That was the first time any of us ever met Marcy Cresap. She came down to the house one morning in the spring of that year and she and Papa sat out among tulips and hyacinths in the greenhouse. She said there was an open privy up by the Thompson house below the little apple orchard on the hill above us. And she said it was poisoning our well just as sure and certain as if somebody was dosing the water every day with rat poison. Papa looked up at the old rattle-trap Thompson house; behind it the apple trees were milky with first blossoms like somebody had just sprinkled them with shatters of a broken china dish. He looked at Marcy Cresap and thanked her.

There's nothing I can make them do, said Marcy Cresap. Follansbee and Quick Real Estate owns the property. And when I went to them they said they couldn't do a thing. Mister Thompson got laid off at the Smelter last fall and since then they haven't paid a penny on the mortgage. So Harper Follansbee turned it over to the Mound County Bank to settle—they made the loan in the first place. When I went to the bank John Grimm laughed and said as far as they were concerned Follansbee and Quick still had the liability of keeping up the place. And when I went to Harper Follansbee he told me to get a shovel and a honeydipper's license and clean out the privy myself. I said the privy shouldn't be there in the first place—whether it was open and overflowing or not. I said it was polluting your well, Marcy went on. But Harper was due at Rotary Lunch and I never got an answer to that.

Papa thanked Marcy again.

Wiley Thompson's a good man, Miss Cresap, Papa said. He's got enough troubles on his shoulders now without my going up there and telling him to move his privy. He's been a good neighbor to us, Miss Cresap. And besides that—

His privy is poisoning you, Mister Purdy, Marcy Cresap said. It's poisoning your wife and children.

Papa looked kindly at Marcy.

Begging your pardon, Miss Cresap, he said. But I've only had the pleasure of knowing you for about fifteen minutes. I've been a neighbor to Wiley Thompson for twenty-two years. Harper Follansbee is a nice man and so is Mister Quick. And John Grimm bought flowers from that very garden yonder for his daughter Twila's wedding. Now I don't figure men like that are likely to sit around on their hands and let me and my family drink from a poison well.

But they did. And the week after Mama died of typhoid that August Harper Follansbee stopped Papa in front of the Mound County Bank and told him how sorry he was to have heard the news.

So summer went and took Mama with it. Marcy came to see us every couple of weeks and we got to be friends that winter. Though it was weeks and weeks before Papa could ever talk to Marcy without turning his face away to keep from meeting her gaze. And in the spring Miss Pet and Mister Paxton came back. But it wasn't the same. Papa tried making candy one night but it burnt in the saucepan and when I smelled it I ran out to the kitchen. Papa was standing there crying with the hot pan still in his hand and the tears hissing on the gas-spider and when I took the saucepan away from him there were big thick blisters on his hand where it had burned him and he hadn't even felt it.

Bud didn't come down to see me till the night after Mama's funeral. He didn't knock at the door or twist the bell like he always did. I didn't even know he was there till I saw his shaggy, stooped outline sitting on the back porch. He just seemed to be dreaming to himself and watching the old fog gathering in the willows by the creek the way it always had and always would: fog wisping among the drooping willow leaves—like memories and secrets and promises haunting the ghostly hair of sad, green queens. He didn't say a word for a while. But I think I made him feel better when I went down and sat on our broken step. Because that's when he came and sat down beside me and gave me the book. By the light of the new risen moon I could read the gold letters on the worn cover. It was The Poems of Rudyard Kipling. I reached over and gave his arm a thanking squeeze and opened it to the blank page in the front and read the writing there:

For Miss Jenny Purdy—a small token of sympathy and condolence following her sad, tragic and heartbreaking loss—one of the favorite books from my own large library and which I pray she will find comfort in reading. From her good friend—Craven Alfred Quick.

I looked at that handwriting I'd seen a thousand times over Bud's shoulder in Central School and then I started crying. It was the first time I'd really cried since Mama died. But I was crying for Bud, too, so now it was twice as hard. I threw my arms around him and cried all over his little jacket and I felt him sort of choke a couple of times like he was crying, too, but when I looked at him after a spell his eyes were dry, though his face was grave and grieving.

Well, I said directly. I'd like to thank your Pa myself for his kindness but—

And I felt him stiffen.

—but I know how busy he is, I said. Studying and writing, I mean. So I'll get you to thank him for me.

You sure do understand things good, Jenny, he said. You sure do. My father's a real busy man.

I felt the creek fog against my cheek and pressed it quick to warm it against his.

I never said so before but I just have to tonight, I said. I love you, Bud Quick. Oh, I love you, Bud Quick!

Papa never mentioned Mama's name that fall, nor once that winter, nor the springtime after. He was always either staying alone by himself out in the greenhouse or else bustling around in the parlor with a chilly, terrible cheeriness I couldn't bear. One night that summer we were all out on the porch and Papa and Miss Pet were talking about the best way to dry rose petals for sachet bags and the first thing you know he seemed to cheer up a little like the old times and for a while it almost seemed like Mama was back in the kitchen about to call us in for candy-time. Mister Paxton reached in the pocket of his alpaca coat and fetched out a little wooden egg and made it disappear. Only for a second, that is, because the little blue egg was hardly gone before it fell out of Mister Paxton's sleeve into the shrubbery.

By God, now! Papa roared, laughing. By God, Chal, I know now where them eggs had been going all these years. By God, Chal, right up your sleeve!

Hush that swearing, Grove! came Mama's sweet voice plain as could be from the parlor. They'll *hear* you!

Nobody said anything for a long time. We sat there a while listening to the locusts up in the trees in Colonel Bruce's yard and presently the *Queen City's* whistle came blowing faintly up the river dark. Then way off in the queen-anne's-lace in the meadow beyond the creek a fox barked twice and set hounds baying from hilltop farms asleep for miles around. We had all heard it: that voice of her from the darkened, summer parlor. Everybody was thinking the same thing for a minute and then, I guess, everybody was thinking, No, it wouldn't be that at all. And then gave up. And just sat there dumb and stumped with wonder on the brink of the enormous night.

Before God, Grover, I swear to you—, Mister Paxton started in a broken voice.

I know that, Chal, Papa said, reaching over and laying his hand on poor Mister Paxton's knee. I know it wasn't you.

But Mister Paxton just seemed to sit there stunned. His violet face in the ragged shine of gaslight through the curtains of Papa's bedroom had turned the color of ashes. When suddenly Miss Pet, darling Miss Pet, inspired as always to whatever occasion, folded her thin fingers in her dotted-swiss lap and, with a voice surprising and sweet as any school-girl, sang four whole verses of "Blessed Be the Tie That Binds."

Do you wonder now at why I miss them so out here tonight on Glory Hill?—and why I worry and think about them every night? My dear, defenseless ones. Bud Quick, I guess, the most of all. And that's selfish of me, I know, because Papa is the lost one tonight—lying wide awake and staring at the light-crack under the hotel door out there in Old Washington, Ohio. But it's Bud I think of most. We sure had a fine time growing up together. We saw each other every day at school and we saw each other three nights a week for all those six years. I didn't know for a long time that Bud had to wait till his folks were asleep and then climb out the bedroom window, crawl over the back-porch roof and shinny down the apple tree to come to see me. When I found out, he said he didn't want to go downstairs and out the front door because it would disturb his Pa who always sat up till nearly daylight studying and improving his mind. Though I knew there wasn't a light in all that house past ten o'clock. But I never told Bud. And I never asked why. I was just happy and proud he loved me enough to lie.

It's funny, it's a kind of miracle, really, that Bud's folks never found out about him and me. Especially the way news gets around in Glory. But they didn't. I guess it made us closer: having to squeeze and portion out the time we had together. I guess it kept growing up from seeming so startling—physically, I mean. I know some of the boys and girls in school found it humiliating. Bud and I were always together so much, I guess we just never noticed what was happening till after it happened. In all those six years Bud Quick and me only had three misunderstandings: one big and two little ones. The first little one was the time Margaret Kump won first prize in the Sophomore English Class Poetry Contest. Bud said he knew all along my poem was best and he said he'd found out the reason mine didn't win was because Margaret's aunt was treasurer of the Mound County School Board and the teachers who had to pick the best poem were afraid to make her mad. Well, when I simply refused to make a fuss about it Bud got so mad he wouldn't speak to me for three whole days.

The other time was about Bud needing eyeglasses. He was always getting awful bruises on his face and I couldn't imagine why because he'd long since stopped having fights with the other boys at school. Bud said he got the bruises because he was nearsighted and always bumping into things at home. Such as doors. And he simply wouldn't ask his Pa to buy him glasses.

The big one we had was all my fault and I never denied it wasn't, not even to Bud. It all started over a silly poem I wrote. It wasn't really silly —it was actually very serious and poetic; I just mean it would probably sound silly if somebody read it and took it literally. I always gave Bud all my poems to read, so naturally I gave him this one. Well, the main idea of this poem was about my being a wood nymph coming out of an apple tree and going down by the creek bank and standing naked in the fog, waiting for the night mists to hide me from the Moon, my Mother, before I called to my lover who was a centaur out in the Elysian meadows. Bud didn't say a word when he finished reading that poem. And even a week later he wouldn't tell me whether he liked it or not. And then one summer night last August we were down by the creek looking at the funny old bullfrogs with Papa's flashlight and Bud suddenly started acting strange.

Jenny, I want to see you, he said softly.

Well? I laughed, shining the flashlight in my face. You're seeing me. You see me all the time.

No, he said in a chokey, scared kind of voice. I mean I want to see you like you were in the poem.

I began to feel all soft and wise and wanted; I felt grown-up and quite old: thirty, at least. But I felt scared, too.

Naked? I said in a squeaky voice.

Bud nodded fast in the dusky light of the full summer moon.

Why? I breathed, chewing a piece of bitter grass and pushing a cattail back and forth with the tip of my shoe.

That poem, Jenny, he said, wildly, softly. I think about it all the time. Jenny, it's great. My God, it's greater than Longfellow! I learned it by heart. Every night this week I dreamed it: seeing you come out of that little apple tree up in Mister Thompson's yard.

Well, it was a *mythical* apple tree, I said. It so happens, Bud.

That doesn't matter, he cried. I saw you in my dream when you came out of that apple tree naked and ran down here. Jenny? You're not even listening to me.

I shivered and smiled inside and turned my face away quick and stared at the far-off lights on the tipple of Panama Mine.

Mmmm-hmm, I said. I'm listening.

"Naked in the night-blessing fog," Bud declaimed, quoting from my poem in hoarse, wild monotone. "Fog wisping among the drooping willow leaves. Oh, night mists, hide my nakedness from my Mother Moon, until my lover gallops nigh—"

Bud, let's don't do everything too quick? I pleaded, suddenly sensible. That's how the sweetest, sacredest things get spoiled. It's like opening each other's presents before Christmas morning—

Jenny, I won't touch you, he pleaded. I won't do a thing but look. I know how we promised each other we'd wait till we got married for that. Jenny, I feel as strong about that as you do. We'll never let it get like it is with those others up at school. Cheap and common, I mean. Jenny, I just want to look at you. I want to see you the way you were seeing yourself when you wrote that poem. "Stripped of the fraud of flimsy, mortal robes," he cried, quoting again.

As a matter of fact, I said, I wasn't really seeing myself naked at all. Not really *naked*. Not the way you mean. I meant making my *soul* naked. If you really understood my poem at all, Bud, you must have known what I was *really* feeling.

Jenny, I understand all your poems, Bud said, very intensely. And I always know what you're feeling.

Well, I said. If you really understood me at all you'd know I surely wasn't speaking about actually being undressed.

What *were* you thinking about then, Jenny? he said, poor dear, all bewildered now.

I was thinking about goddesses and romance, I said, lifting my face poetically to the moon. And . . . eternity.

Jenny, won't you please? he begged, presently.

Well, I'd never heard Bud Quick beg for anything before in his whole life and for a minute I just couldn't stand him. And I felt for the first time in myself a fierce, glad sting of cruelty and power. And that was when I said that harsh and foolish thing.

Bud Quick, you seem to think I'll just do anything daring, I said. Since I foolishly consented to smoke one of your awful Spud cigarettes in the greenhouse last Sunday night!

In the faint moonshine I could see Bud's wild, sad face through the corner of my eye. He slowly lowered his head and sat down suddenly on the grassy bank, cradling his mouth in his hands.

Jenny, forgive me, forgive me, he said through his fingers. Inside I'm nothing but the lowest, orneriest poolroom rake in Glory!

I stood there looking down at him. I felt heartsick with love for him and hate for myself. Helpless, I watched him get up and go running off up through Papa's garden toward Lafayette Avenue, toward the lights on the corner of Seventh Street, toward the door of his dark home. I stood there crying for a while and calling myself perfectly awful names and wished Mama was up yonder in the kitchen to go tell how terrible a girl I was and then have her tell me I really wasn't. I prayed for a while for Bud to come back. But he didn't. And I got mad at him all over again because he didn't and that made me start crying again. I stared down through my tears at the stupid white pile of my clothes scattered beside me on the grass. And stood there crying and shivering and naked in the fog and promising God that if only Bud came back he could look at me as much as he wanted. And touch me, too, if he wanted. And if it was a touching I didn't want I'd just want it because it was something Bud wanted. Because his wanting it would be the thing that would make it be beautiful and make me want it, too. But he didn't come back. I decided the prayer I prayed was just against God's principles. With the big, warm tears splashing on my breasts I stood there still. And nothing but the moon and those big, ugly bullfrogs to see how pretty my naked-ness was.

Well, I forgave Bud and I forgave God but I just couldn't forgive my own fool self. I swore by the moon that I'd never write another poem in my whole life. Leaving my clothes in the grass and still sobbing bit-terly, I walked up the path through Papa's garden, kicking the flowers as I passed. I stumbled into the greenhouse, blubbering and hurting my bare toes knocking over watering cans and flowerpots in the dark. Thank heavens Papa didn't hear me, poor darling! The dear soul would have run up to the bedroom for a blanket or his winter overcoat and sat up worrying over me all night long. I felt around till I found the almost empty pack Bud had hidden behind a potted geranium. And the little box of matches. Then I sat down there, bare and cross-legged, nursing my bruised shins, and smoked all seven of those dreadful Spud cigarettes and loved Bud more than ever and caught the worst summer cold I ever had.

We didn't see each other for an eternity after that. Though once in a while I'd catch a glimpse of Bud and his Pa out walking the streets of Glory late at night. It gave me the queerest feeling. Every time I'd see them hurrying along the misty streets, side by side like boys playing soldiers, I had the strangest thought that someone was after them, chasing them: they always walked so quickly, their faces when they passed beneath a street lamp looked strained and pale. I used to get the idea someone was really behind them in the fog, trying to catch them, wanting to hurt them. And I worried about that. For all the good it did me: worrying. Because it went on that way for months later. Bud wouldn't come near me; he wouldn't even meet my eyes when we'd pass in the halls at school. And every day I thought I'd rather die or be blind than have to see another morning with no Bud in it.

And then one night, long after, Bud came back. He said he was awful sorry about everything, that it was all his fault and it had been like a bad dream: the months since then. He told me he loved me more than ever now, really desperately, he said, but he didn't have to tell me that; I already knew, though my heart fairly split apart with joy when he did. He kissed me: a shy, careful kiss at first—like we were relatives. And he seemed older, graver somehow. He had this sort of thoughtful sorrow all around him like a pale, sad glow. His best friend was Dallas Gorby, a nice boy who was a Junior up at school, and Dallas had a girl named Clary Jeanne Pleasants from down the river at Hannibal and the four of us used to go on dates together. We'd buy ice-cream cones at Seat's Drugstore and on hot nights we'd go eat them under the big, cool trees by the courthouse statue. Sometimes we went to the movies at the Grand Theater or sat in Spoon's Ice Cream Parlor drinking claret phosphates. Bud laughed and kidded a lot. But there was this new feeling about him: older, serious, almost like he was thinking himself into a fever about something. I remembered the old times when he'd never take me anywhere at nights. And now that's all he ever did with me. I remembered how hurt my feelings used to get because I thought Bud never wanted to be any place with me where his folks could see. Now I thought what a little fool I'd been back then: not to be thankful for the beautifulness that being alone with him was. Now it seemed like all that mattered to Bud was being with me where people could see; and making sure we'd never be alone. Till finally I couldn't stand it any more and made up my mind to ask him the reason why.

It was a cold, beautiful, clear night last November. Bud twisted the door bell just as Mama's old blue china clock was striking seven in Papa's bedroom. I had my coat and hat on, sitting on the carpet-stool behind the curtains of the bay window in the parlor. I waited till Papa let Bud in. I ran out in the little hallway and threw my arms around Bud and kissed him. His cheek was like a cold red apple; I just wanted to bite it. Bud seemed to have made up his mind about something that night, too. I stood back a little, cocked my head and smiled at him there in the yellow, bubbly light of the little gas flame by the mirror. Bud's face was quiet. It was like one of those pictures of a battlefield when the war's over and somebody won. I searched his grave, gray eyes, wondering which side had lost. And suddenly I had the warm, fine feeling that it wasn't ours. We walked up Lafayette Avenue past Colonel Bruce's, squeezing each other's fingers through our mittens. The wind in the big trees' high bows blew; the dark was winter-black and crackling cold and all its billion stars, like flames, came close as flashing candles down around us. I knew now that Bud was bursting with something to say as much as me: I could feel it quivering—even through the mittens—clear to the tips of his fingers. Bud wiped his forehead with his other hand.

Whew! he said. It's sure a caution how overheated a person can get on a night as cold as this.

Please don't perspire, I said. You'll catch your death!

Bud cleared his throat like he finally made up his mind to blurt something out. But after a minute he gave a sad sigh and I knew he'd given the idea up. I decided it was my turn to try being brave.

What would be really nice right now, I said, is cocoa.

We can go have some at Seat's Soda Fountain, Bud said gloomily.

Of course, Mister Seat always makes his cocoa with water, I said.

But I paused before I said the next thing; not wanting to rush Bud's thoughts.

Naturally, I make mine with milk, I said mildly. With a drop of Mama's Golden Rule Vanilla Extract. And a tablespoonful of marshmallow cream on top.

And so, in a little while, there we were back in Mama's old kitchen, drinking cocoa and listening to the winter wind's cold sighing in the shutters. Well, my good hot cocoa certainly thawed out Bud Quick's tongue. After about twenty minutes he finished telling me how he felt about himself that night by the creek. He said that was when he discovered how rotten he was inside, how unworthy he was ever to be in love with me. He said he knew then that he couldn't ever trust himself alone with me again. I knew better than to try to argue. I smiled down sadly at my cup and watched the funny little membrane of milk twitch and shiver on top of the cocoa.

And so until we have the right to be, he said, we can't ever be alone together, Jenny.

You're alone with me now, Bud Quick, I said quietly.

But he waved his hand scornfully and gave a worldly smile.

Things never happen to people, he said, in kitchens.

Then he commenced talking again about how rotten he was inside: the worst old reprobate in Mound County. And he said how, when he quit seeing me that long, awful time, he just didn't want to do anything but go out and smash things and hit people—anything to keep himself from thinking about love because if he thought about love he would think about me. And he said if he thought about me he'd always see me naked like I wrote in that poem and then he'd want to touch me. So the only thing he could think of doing instead was to run Glory's streets at night looking for things to smash or punch. He said it was a good thing his Pa was such a strong, philosophical soul, because if his Pa hadn't gone along with him—trying to hold him back—Lord knows what he'd have done.

I sat there listening to Bud's passionate recital; half-dreaming, half-hearing what he was saying, half-saying to myself a lot of girl-thoughts all my own—thoughts I had the good sense, surely, never to tell Bud, because they'd have scared him out of my life forever. That night in the greenhouse I must have done some pretty important deciding. The first thing I got settled in my mind that night was that I really belonged to Bud Quick. Clothes on, no clothes, touching me, doing whatever it is people do when they're in love—no matter what Bud wanted, I decided that night, it would be just fine. I told myself when you belong to people and won't let them do what they want, to their own personal belonging—why, it's worse than stealing! And even if what they want to do is something you simply couldn't dream of ever liking, your letting them do what they want so much must make you happy, too. Still that wasn't the end of my thoughts there in the greenhouse that night; I knew it wasn't all that simple. Yes, I realized I belonged to Bud all right. Still, I knew I simply had to keep my head. Yes, everything I was, in heaven or earth, belonged to Bud Quick. But in a manner of speaking it was in a trust fund. Yes, whatever Bud wanted—it would have been just fine with me. The trouble was it wouldn't have been just fine with Bud—afterward, I mean. So I knew I mustn't let him do things to me till we were together in a way he wouldn't consider common or bad. Married, I mean. Anything else would ruin our being together and make him hate me and feel ashamed of himself. And if that ever happened, I knew I'd just rather be dead.

Oh, I thought all this out very carefully and seriously in the greenhouse that night. Does that sound scheming and deceitful to you? But I wasn't scheming—I swear it! And it isn't really deceit. It's Pretending. And Pretending—for a girl—is merely being considerate, polite and tolerant with some special boy's morals. Even when his notions about morals seem so odd and unearthly she can't begin to understand them. It just baffles me why boys make simple, beautiful things so complicated —like nakedness and love and babies. But they just do. I guess it's their consciences. So, naturally, when a girl's in love she's got to protect that love from getting ruined by the kind of consciences boys have. And, I guess, even when a girl's not in love and just going with somebody, she's got to protect the boy and herself from the kind of opinions Glory has. Well, you know it as well as I do—girls aren't really Moral. Heaven knows we've got enough on our minds managing to be such two difficult things as Practical and Romantic. I'm just absolutely certain there never was a real girl ever lived who ever had a real consience. Boys have morals; girls have standards. I think that's just about the only big deep-down difference there really is. Maybe that's why all the big religions get invented by boys. While girls never seem to have to invent anything more beautiful than love letters and grocery lists!

Well, the more Bud talked that night the more I knew my greenhouse hunches had been right. But the more he talked the more I loved him, too. I had to almost bite my tongue to keep my head. Because I couldn't stop thinking about Bud wanting to see me naked. And just thinking about that made me feel pretty all over, from my hair ribbon to my toes. Under my clothes it just felt like all my skin was pink and glowing with happy prettiness to think Bud wanted to see me naked. My head got all dreamy and sleepy and my knees felt loose and useless like the time when I was five and Doc Busby gave me laughing gas to cap my tooth. Bud's voice kept on talking till I *did* have to bite my lip. I bit so hard my tongue tasted coppery and I gripped the wood chair seat till the pink ovals of my fingernails ached. Oh, how those fingers yearned to go flying up to the high neck buttons of my pretty, green watered-silk blouse. I just hoped and prayed Bud Quick's morals held out. Because all my common sense and every bit of all my wise pretending would simply turn to water if Bud so much as touched my shoulder with his hand. It's odd, I thought, that life must be this way. But so it is, I seemed to hear Mama say. Yes, so it is, my dear. And so we must abide.

—to marry me! Bud gasped out suddenly at the end of a rushing, pellmell sentence that had begun back Lord knows where.

I sat foolish, dumb as a pudding-stone, still biting my lip, scared to open my mouth to say Yes because I knew if I so much as breathed or moved an eyelash I was going to cry. So I just nodded fast and swallowed very hard twice. Though I might as well have said Yes because I cried anyway.

And so we sat there till, like bells beneath the ocean, Mama's china clock chimed midnight in the ticking deeps of the winter house and we talked about how we would run away to Maryland and marry the day after Christmas. And then when it was past one o'clock we both stopped talking, smiled for no special reason and just looked at each other's faces. And when Mama's clock chimed the half-past we had sat there all that time, hushed, across the kitchen table from one another, nothing of us touching but our eyes and thoughts. I thought what a marvel it was that the cold, bony moan of winter wind could make me feel so rosy-warm. I smiled and blushed suddenly, thinking, pleased. Bud asked me what it was that made me smile so and blush and softly stroke my left hand with the fingertips of my right. But I knew I dasn't tell him.

Yes, till the very end I never could tell Papa we were running away. And Bud Quick never told his folks either. Though he did tell Dallas Gorby and made him swear on the memory of his dead mother he wouldn't breathe a word of it—not even to Clary Jeanne Pleasants. And, of course, I told Clary Jeanne after school next day and she swore on the Bible on Miss Duckwell's desk in Home Room she'd never betray it to a living soul—not even Dallas Gorby.

Though, of course, it wouldn't have really changed anything. Because our running away, our getting married—it wasn't going to happen. In the afternoon, two days before Thanksgiving, I got this awful pain in my chest. By sundown it had gone away but then—just when I was clearing the supper table and taking Papa's plate out to the kitchen—it came back. Hard this time; it hurt so bad I fainted and broke four pieces of Mama's beautiful Haviland china. I can just barely remember

Papa carrying me into Mama's bedroom. Then it got dark again for a while.

Well, sure—once in a while out here on Glory Hill I get to thinking and dreaming back and then I half-wish I'd been brazen and lost my head to Bud Quick that night in the kitchen. Sometimes I wish I'd been just totally shameless and jumped up and run round the kitchen table and made Bud Quick ravish me. But that's only curiosity, I suppose: wondering what it was we missed, wondering what they make all the fuss about—that big, wild wanting that struggled inside Bud; the curious, little wanting that wandered inside me, unawakened, hushed as sap-rise in a spring tree, there within the folded, red petals of my flesh. And I'm glad we never did. I guess it would have made Bud's sadness all the worse: another thing we did for him to miss, some part of him buried out here with me. Yet, maybe we lost something because of what we never did. I don't know. Maybe I'll never know.

But I do know something Mama always used to say: *Child, the things we lose are the only things we keep.*

I don't know. Maybe that's how it is. I didn't have it all with Bud, I know—all of living, I mean. But still I swear I had the best. Bud Quick and Jenny Purdy loved longer than some people ever live. We never had a baby, never lived in the same room together, never got tired, never grew old, never got gray hairs. But I know we shared a time on earth that's longer than the sum of centuries some married folks are spending back in Glory tonight. And we never had but those two little and that one big misunderstanding. If ever Jenny Purdy was the riddle to anything in the universe Bud Quick was its answer. That makes me remember something Miss Pet said once. It was a spring night like this and we were all out there together on the front porch and Papa was playing "Ah, Sweet Mystery of Life" on his mandolin and Mister Paxton had just finished a new trick that left a broken egg for poor Mama to clean up off the porch rug. And Bud Quick was a solemn, bushy-haired little boy sitting over on the step near the fragrance of the sweet-shrub bush, eating his share of Mama's sea-foam candy.

I awakened this morning, Miss Pet sighed blissfully. Thinking of the most beautiful solution in the world.

Indeed, dear lady, said Mister Paxton politely. And what problem was troubling you?

Prob-lem? said Miss Pet, frowning thoughtfully. Why, really, I don't recollect there was any! I just woke up and there it was plain before my eyes—this simply delightful solution. Dear, dear, dear. I suppose they *do* go together, Mister Paxton. Though I should fancy solutions are much more pleasant when one isn't fretting about some *problem!* Mister Purdy, do you know I don't think I've ever *had* a problem in my whole life! Though, I must say, I'm forever thinking up these perfectly lovely solutions.

Yes. Bud Quick and me. Together we were that: some kind of perfectly lovely solution. I don't know if it ever had a problem; somehow it never needed one.

That night when I opened my eyes again I was under Mama's bright, old apostle quilt, in her big spool bed, and Papa and Doctor Ed Follansbee were bending over me. I just looked at Papa, so lorn and frightened there. I decided I mustn't wait another night to tell him about Bud and me running away to Maryland to get married in only five weeks. I hated myself for not telling him before—I knew I simply had to tell him now. Still I thought I better wait a minute till the pain got better; by then it was clear down in my arm. It was like a stoked fire throbbing in the flesh clear to my fingertips; it hurt even to breathe.

Jenny, Jenny love, Papa said. Now that you're awake I'll run phone right away for Bud Quick. That's who you need! Why, it'll do you more good than all the pills and tonics in Doctor Ed's bag yonder, won't it now? Just seeing good old Bud!—won't it now, Jenny love?

Lord knows how bad I wanted Bud right then. I never needed anybody as bad in my whole life. But I simply couldn't bear the notion of him seeing me without my hair brushed and a perfectly shameful shiny nose. I took a breath to ask Papa for my powder box and the sterling-silver-handle comb-and-brush set Mama gave me for my ninth birthday and my genuine tortoise-shell mirror. But then the pain seemed to flame out from my fingertips and flow into things in the room till I could feel *them* hurting, too; even the faded purple flowers in the old wallpaper flinched and flamed in agony. And I fainted like the worst old sissy in the world.

And it was dark, but it was a queer dark—I could almost see Bud Quick inside it. I could *feel* him, at least, as plain as you feel me here now. And he was in trouble, it seemed. Yes, it was Bud and he was in trouble and I couldn't lift a finger to help. I heard my voice whimper impatiently back there among the dusty roses of the wallpaper. And it got empty again for a while, darker, and then it cleared up the way when the summer moon comes sweeping through sometimes on stormy

nights and lights up someone's face. And that's when I knew it wasn't
Bud in trouble at all: it was somebody Bud loved who was in trouble.
And that someone wasn't me, but that didn't matter. What mattered was
somebody Bud loved in trouble and he must go and be there and help.
Then I heard Bud's voice. I heard it in the room as clearly as if he had
been standing there with Papa and Doctor Ed, behind the darkness. And
do you know?—he was saying the strangest, loveliest thing I think I
ever heard anyone say.

Thanks anyways, Bud said. It's just that I got myself a girl—a real
nice girl, Pa.

Oh, I loved him so much for that it was bigger than the pain.

You just wait, Bud Quick, till I see you, I thought to myself. You're
going to get the nicest, biggest kiss you ever got in your life!

But then I was flying away in the dark, off through the snow, away
from Papa and Doctor Ed, though I knew I was only going for a
minute. And presently I could see a queer room, somewhere north,
nearly to Wheeling, it seemed, and the someone Bud loved, the somebody in trouble was there, needing him just terribly. Yet my eyes
couldn't see. They couldn't see! And I couldn't tell who was there in that
queer, awful room but I knew it was the somebody Bud loved and he
had to go be there now—now! And all I could think was: Bud, somebody really needs you! You mustn't come to see me tonight! Because
I'm going to be just fine but somebody needs you who isn't going to be
just fine—ever. Bud, please listen! In a queer little room up some
place south of Wheeling someone needs you ten times more than me!

I wasn't being noble or anything, I was just being practical and
honest, knowing Bud the way I do; knowing Bud had to go be there by
someone who was small and scared, needing him terribly. Needing him
even—how strange to me it seemed!—needing him even before I ever
was born.

No, Bud. Not here! I thought. Not here. Not me. Him. Him!

And I willed it and willed it with nearly all the strength left in me; I
willed it with almost the last, stammering pulse of my ruined rheumatic
heart.

And then I half-saw him there: the little one in that room, beyond
the flying snow, in a somewhere south of Wheeling in that sleeting,
ragged night; yet only saw him blurred, as if through tears somehow
not mine but his: him, slumped in a half-moon's shabby dusk of gas-

light's blue-gold flame. And I could make out the small shape, the huge sorrow of him now. And someone stood beside him, bending down, being kind.

Bud's there! I cried, and almost cheered in thankfulness. Bud's there!

I felt a pure peace clasp me round, to see Bud there: strong and quiet with simple-mercied gentleness beside the sobbing child; Bud bending like a father to the little lonesome thing who whimpered and crouched, sick and desolate, the child's face of him hidden in its headlong, nightmare terror behind his pathetic little mask of tears and streaming circus paint.

I opened my eyes suddenly; I saw Papa and Doctor Ed Follansbee.

Jenny love? Papa said. Is everything going to be all right now?

Grand, I said, speaking perfectly clearly, and smiled at him. Everything's just grand now, Papa. Bud's going to be all right. He's where he had to be. He went there the way he had to and he's going to be all right. He's really there, Papa.

Where, Jenny? said Doctor Ed. Where did you imagine you saw Bud just now?

Why, with his crippled boy, I said.

And then I grabbed Papa's hand and squeezed it real hard.

Bud's just grand, Papa. He's going to come through just grand. You just wait and see. Bud's on his way!

And—with a little shiver—I was, too.

Tally Vengeance

Her real name wasn't Vengeance. It was Natalia Lazarevitch when she and her man came down here from Mingo Junction in the spring of 1919. But ever after that night last September when she left Glory on the west-bound evening train she was Tally Vengeance. As I recollect it was old Colonel Bruce who started them calling her that. Though— even without the name—it was vengeance the people would remember her for. Still, it was more than just vengeance: I saw it as a brand of indestructible pride; something straight-backed and high-chinned without being stiff-necked. That, too, and a stealthy, peasant patience, as well. And, of course, that breed of wild, stoked slag-pile burning femaleness you don't often run into in the preacher-scared and custom-shackled life we've fashioned for ourselves here in the Republic. Maybe back in the old-world Serbia where Milosh Lazarevitch brought her from, Natty wouldn't have stood out as anything wonderful or dangerous. Or even peculiar. For all I know, the women in those Balkan states are all like Natty. If they are, God help the kings: it's no wonder they're always getting into wars. Because when that woman got done working out her notion of justice here in Glory you'd have thought Halley's Comet had gone through the roof of the First M.E. Church and thrown off enough cinders to set fire to the business district, the Elks Club, and half the respectable homes in town.

Let me be the one to tell you about Natty Vengeance. Because you'll never hear it from her. The Lord only knows where she went when she caught the ten o'clock west-bound that cool September night—or where she's at now. And even if she was still here, her own voice couldn't— even if it would—tell you what Natalia Lazarevitch was and how she got that way or did what she did and why justice seemed to her something more precious than religion, respectability and personal pleasure. Or, for that matter, even personal safety. Natalia Lazarevitch couldn't tell you these things: she was a Serbian and couldn't talk more than a half-dozen words in English. And maybe, being the kind of woman she was, she never knew what made her do things anyway. Women like Natty do most of their thinking in their hips; they are moved about upon this earth by the silent—and sometimes dangerous—logic of the womb. I've only come across two or three like that in my day: females without enough brains in their heads to know how to pluck feathers off a chicken, but with all the mother-wit and knowledge of a genius down in the hunches and instincts of their glands. And there's never any sense asking that kind of woman why she did something. Because her reason for it has to travel all the way up from her hips and by the time it gets to her vocal cords there's not a bit of truth nor a grain of sense left in a word of it, not even to her. But there's still another reason you'd never get the facts about Natty from her own voice. She'd never tell you. Not in Serbian, English or Choctaw Indian. Natalia Lazarevitch would consider the reasons she did what she did to Glory as something that was simply not a damned bit of your business.

Well, that was something else I admired about her. Spiritually, I mean. Because I'm like that, too. My life—past, present and future— my sins, my business, ambitions, failures, good luck and bad, my pleasures, wounds and disappointments; the good side of me and the ornery side—I look on them as all mine and strictly private. I feel beholden to no man to tell him why or how or when I ever did anything. So if you're inclined to want to know everything there is to know about

Henry Winemiller, you just better go ask some of these other big-talkers here in town. The only trouble is you'll soon find out they don't know much more about me than you do. I don't mean to say I'm hiding any great, dark secrets. On the other hand, every secret I do have is personal and private and I'm not about to spend a great long while blathering about myself like quite a few of these voices of Glory I've been hearing.

My old Mom, God bless her memory and keep it ever green—she died of consumption when I was a boy down in Braxton County more than fifty years ago—she was like that. So I started life not saying much. And a man doesn't run a barber shop in a town like Glory for thirty-seven years without improving the swiftly vanishing art of keeping his mouth shut. Lord knows, if I ever started talking about the things men tell me whilst they're cranked back in the chair I wouldn't be safe from my own razors. It puts me in mind of a stogie-roller in Wheeling once who ran in and told a priest he'd got a little sixteen-year-old dime-store clerk in the family way. He said he figured it wasn't too black a sin since the girl was illegitimate herself and so that kind of finagling around couldn't make much difference to her anyway. Well, directly here come the priest tearing out of the confession box. And he like to thrashed the clothes off that poor dude. I guess I won't have to draw any pictures for you to tell who that little girl's secret father was. I'm not telling that to knock anybody's religion. I'm just talking about big mouths.

Naturally, I'll tell you as much about myself as you need to know; enough so what I tell you about Natty Vengeance makes some sense. As a matter of fact, there's not much to tell about me that's very interesting. I'm fifty-seven, sober and single, have all my teeth, live in a nice little room over my barber shop in the two-story building which I own, and I hire one extra barber, Densel Yoho. I shave, cut hair, renovate toupees, sweep the shop myself and chew a little plug tobacco. Since I keep my mouth shut, except to spit, I keep my ears open, in order to hear. On the mug shelf on the wall by the deer-antler hat rack you can read—in letters of rainbow hues and gold-leaf script—the names of Apple County's most substantial men. They are Glory's bankers, investors, farmers, fruit growers and mine operators, lawyers and doctors, real-estate leaders, mill owners, stock speculators, preachers, small children, two bootleggers, five or six steamboat captains and a heavy-set lady girl-scout leader from a certain town down the river whose face hair I shave—with the blinds drawn, after sundown—twice a month. The bootleggers come all the way down to Glory from a certain city for their shaves because, it's my guess, it makes them upset having their faces covered with towels where they can't watch the passing cars in their home town. The bankers and business leaders give me two bits and a dime extra when Densel Yoho gets through with the whiskbroom, and the bootleggers get the same shave and the same haircut and leave me with a twenty-dollar bill in my hand. But I'd sooner have real-estate men or mine owners in my chairs. Because many's the time while I'm shaving a lawyer and Densel's cutting a banker's hair and maybe there's a state-senator over by the window, waiting his turn and reading *Grit* or *Pathfinder* or *Iron Age* and they'll get to chatting a little about good, healthy stocks on the Wheeling or Pittsburgh exchange and directly the senator'll drop a word about some stock that's going to get a lot healthier after the next session of the legislature.

So—every now and then—Densel Yoho and his brother Layhew take over both chairs for a few days whilst I take a little business trip up the Ohio. My big mouth never earned me a plugged nickel in my life but being a barber has taught me that my ears are worth more than my shearers, though you'd surely not guess it to look at me. Most folks in Glory think I'm worth about as much as the clothes on my back. Well, I guess a lot of them will be in for a good surprise when I kick off one of these days and a few of them gather up in Case Resseger's law office and hear him read off the will of Henry Winemiller, Glory barber. I expect it will make some folks sore. And I'll reasonably guarantee it'll make a lot more a good deal sorer when Case gets to the part where I leave half of it to young Marcy Cresap's TB Sanatorium and the Apple County Health Association. Whilst the other half I plan to leave—Well, now never you mind about that. I've talked a good deal more about myself than I ever should have.

Natalia Lazarevitch—Tally Vengeance—that's the one I want to tell you about. But where do you start in to tell about a woman like that? You could study that woman eight hours a day for years—you could watch her hang out a Monday wash or kissing her children with their towheads and red-scrubbed faces out on the door stoop when the first bell rang at Central—you could stare at Natty Vengeance till your eyes fell out and never know a bit more about what it was she had than you did before. It was looks, all right: she had them. But it was more. Sometimes you might see her kiss her man good-by before he went whistling up to Lafayette Avenue with his lunch pail full of good things she'd fixed him, on his way to work in the Benwood mill. You'd see him get that kiss and think about the things in that lunch pail that her hands had fixed and put there and you'd feel a little like not opening the shop that day and going up to the Elks and spend the day getting drunk. Sometimes I'd look out the window and see her pass on her way up Seventh Street and the comb and scissors would start to shake a little in my hands for a second or so. You'd look at her and feel it. Yes, that's what I'm trying to say. It wasn't a thing you could see or hear—it was a feeling. Any man raised in the country, around animals, knows what it is. The way they feel things; well, there was a little animal in all of us feeling the big animal in Natty Vengeance. Like a spoor, maybe. Or the thing creatures scent when they're in heat. Yes, heat's what it was. It was like that Natalia Lazarevitch was always in heat: a proud, fine bitch who wouldn't ever give so much as a look at the whole, wild, sniffing, whimpering pack of feisty mongrels she led behind her through the streets of Glory all that year, and the whole pack tumbling pellmell on top of each other, sometimes snapping at each other and getting kicked or run over by cars or maybe just dropping on the sidewalk out of plain exhaustion: it never mattered.

By God, I still don't know what she had. I've been with a lot of women here and there, now and then. When I go up the river to Wheeling or Pittsburgh it's not all business. Once in a while—But never you mind about me. It's Natalia Lazarevitch I'm talking about. This thing she had. By God, I don't know. I'll bet if any of those scientists ever figure out what it was that woman had it's a cinch, within a year, they'll be passing laws against it. Because it was a community problem, a real public disturbance in Glory when Tally Vengeance came up Lafayette Avenue to Kroger's every payday. Because there wasn't a man within looking distance—even the oldest—who didn't catch his breath a little and feel the old springtime of his poor, dead youth stir inside him and then rise up like Lazarus from the tomb. Every man wanted her. And every woman in Glory hated every man for that. Though they might all just as well have stopped the wanting or the hating either one. Because there was only one man in Natalia Lazarevitch's life—that whole time she never looked at any man but her husband.

Milosh Lazarevitch made good money at the Benwood steel mill. Natty always used to cut his hair for him, I guess—it sure looked it—and I reckon he shaved himself. But once a year he used to come up to my barber shop—June twenty-eight, rain or shine—and have a shave and a haircut and a slicking-down with a tonic nobody but him ever asked for—I'd bought it from a Parkersburgh drummer fifteen years before and been stuck with three bottles of it. It had stood back in the corner on the marble shelf so long it was so dusty and fly-specked and greasy you could hardly make out the fancy label: Ellwell's Authentic Louisiana Jasmine. And when he'd had the works Milosh would go marching proudly off home to his Natalia and the two kids, smelling like the parlor of a Polack whorehouse on payday night. Then later on that evening you'd see the four of them up at Spoon's or Charley Seat's soda fountain whispering and giggling together—in Serbian, I reckon, because some of the Glory ladies said they weren't ever able to pick out so much as a word Natty ever said. And they'd be sucking orangeades through straws and directly they'd all troop out licking double-scoop ice cream cones and go down to the Grand Theater and have a big time whistling for Tom Mix or crying for the Gish girls or hissing Monte Blue, though the Lord knows what they thought the shows were about: even the kids couldn't read the titles yet. Milosh would be dressed up in a big stiff black suit that looked like cardboard, like one of those suits they put on convicts after they get through hanging them and put them out for public viewing up at Peace's Funeral Parlor. Natty would have on a big-brimmed leghorn straw hat with a bunch of celluloid cherries and a shiny rayon dress with a big flower pattern of six or eight different colors—and this was something else the women of Glory couldn't forgive—the loudest, commonest dress off the nigger racks at Ganz's Store and yet when Natty put it on it didn't hide a thing, it made everything she had, in fact, look a little better; you'd have thought it was the fanciest, good-taste, twenty-five-dollar New York City dress from Steifel's up in Wheeling.

I think the Glory women hated Natalia for her hair a little bit, too. Because it was thick and the deep-brown glossy color of a polished buckeye and she braided it in a sort of chestnut crown around her head; it must have fallen clear to the backs of her calves when it was undone: a whole lifetime of hair, you might say, and there was hardly a woman in Glory that year who hadn't had her hair cut to what they called a "boyish bob" or else had it cut page-boy style with bangs in front like Coleen Moore. No, indeed, Natalia Lazarevitch's hair didn't help her popularity much among the Glory wives. When Natty was alone on the street I used to look out the window, and, I swear, she always gave me the idea she was tall. Though she wasn't as tall as Milosh; she came just about an inch or two above his shoulder. Then I figured out one day it was because of the way she walked, straight-backed as one of Remington's Indians and with her white, round chin held back and a little smile sort of teasing around the corners of her pink, full mouth. Since then I've seen that smile in my recollections— yes, I'll be honest, I see it some nights in dreams—and I try to figure out what she always seemed to be smiling about. But I'm never sure. Sometimes I guess she was thinking it was only two hours or five hours till the Wheeling streetcar dropped Milosh off at Twelfth and Lafayette and she was smiling to think how he'd look when he ran down the yard under the big willow beside their litle house on Water Street. But I never knew for certain.

Sometimes I'd think she was laughing at the other women but I know it wasn't that—not, at least, in the beginning: she never noticed them. Or else she just felt good and was smiling at the goodness of being alive and being the kind of wild, full woman she was in whatever sort of a day it was, beneath whatever sort of sun or cloud. More often I thought it wasn't any good kind of smile at all; that maybe it was the little cruel grin of a woman who is waiting for an injustice to happen to her—and who knows it's got to happen because that's how the world's made—and who knows how she'll get even because that's how she's made. Maybe. By God, I don't know yet. And when I'd get done with every damned fool answer a man could think up for the thoughts behind that smile I'd start getting all sore and American and hot under the collar and tell myself: Well, by God, she ought to be smiling. Because she's a citizen of the greatest Republic on earth. And she's living in the finest state in it and has a nice little home for her family in the valley of the prettiest county in the state. And her kids are going to school and growing up in the swellest, nicest town in the county. Though I'll grant you I couldn't imagine any part of the U.S.A. not looking pretty good after Serbia.

Hell, I'd never even heard of the place till Natalia Lazarevitch and her man Milosh came to town. Some nights when I couldn't sleep and

I'd lay there awhile listening to the electric fan and the kids roller-skating down Seventh Street and I'd start thinking about Serbia. Serbia, I'd say it over to myself a couple of times in my mind and sometimes I'd say it out loud in the dark, Serbia. And I'd try making up pictures of it in my mind, the way I imagined it looked over there where Natalia was born. And sometimes it was so real in my mind it was like looking at a colored photograph on a new calendar or sometimes I'd start adding a little to it: a palm tree here, maybe a quaint little jungle-type cottage there till it seemed as elegant to me as an expensive hand-painted oil picture. I used to get really artistic up there in the room, in the dark, in my thoughts about Serbia. Serbia, I'd say to myself till I fell asleep, Serbia. But after I was asleep I wouldn't say Serbia any more. I'd say, Natalia. And twice that summer I got disgusted with myself and the barber shop and had Densel Yoho call in his brother Layhew and take over both chairs while I went to Pittsburgh for a weekend. And it wasn't on business either; it wasn't any hot market tip I was chasing. And both times I came back to Glory worse off than when I left it.

I'd stand in the dark awhile by the lonesome depot and smell the warm river night and hear the rattle of Hook Madden's telegraph key back in the station and listen to the lonesome cry of the evening west-bound way off now, down among the river hills. And I'd walk up Seventh Street under the big trees and know I'd have to go up to the room directly and lie there with the worst old hangover in the world and wanting to burn my BVD's because they smelled like disinfectant and some poor, cheap, Soho, Polack girl's perfume. Through the open window I'd hear old Mrs. Tigglebeck's Victrola whining and squawking away across the street and the fan would whine on in the dark and I'd stare at the little square of light the window made on the ceiling over the big framed picture of Mom and try not to think about it. I mean Serbia. Mrs. Tigglebeck's Victrola keeps going till sometimes ten o'clock of a night and the sort of records she plays are just what you expect. She must not own but four or five and being the sort she is—an old, morbid-minded whistle-tit who never misses a single funeral on Glory Hill plus every time they hang a man with no family to claim him and have to bury him down back of the smelter in Potter's Field—as I say, it's no surprise that her two favorite records are "The Wreck of the Shenandoah" and "The Death of Floyd Collins." Half the nights I had to listen to those damned things I felt like heaving a shoe across Seventh Street.

But the second Sunday night when I got back from Pittsburgh I was glad to hear that old Victrola: that's how blue I was; glad for anything to listen to, something with words to keep my mind off Serbia, anything to keep my thoughts away from the woman in the house down on Water Street, smiling in her sleep, clasped in big Milosh's arms, and all her grand hair, thicker than ropes of carved mahogany laying dark all round her on the white pillowcase. So I laid there thinking about all those gallant Navy lads and their brave commander out in Ohio that night, plunging to their doom in that awful line-storm. And I thought about the time we'd all hear a sound from the air like a hundred motor-cycles and run out in the middle of Seventh Street and see the big silver Shenandoah floating right over Glory, so close you'd wonder how it could clear the hills across the river. And when the other record com-menced I killed a little time thinking about Floyd Collins, poor boy, dying that way, trapped in his Kentucky cave. But I still couldn't get sleepy somehow and I still had you-know-who in the back of my thoughts and directly the old woman put on a Two Black Crows and I listened to that for a spell, though I knew all the jokes by heart, and directly that got me to thinking about the darkies up Misery Hollow by Parr's Mine. And, naturally, darkies got me to thinking about Hunkies and they set me thinking about Slovaks and Spiks and the next thing you know I was right back to Serbians again.

Well, next morning I felt just terrible and everybody else in Glory must have been feeling the same way, too, because nobobdy came in for so much as a mustache-trim before ten o'clock. I just sat there on the chair by the window, bluer than ever, and stared at the hair-tonic ad on the wall over the cash register that said: *It's Too Late for Herpicide*, and listened to Densel stropping his razors. Densel Yoho and his brother are two of the best damned barbers in the Ohio Valley but Densel's mind goes off on a strange, disordered tangent every six months or so. He gets these seizures, so to speak, and comes to work in a baseball uni-form, cap, cleated shoes, catcher's mitt and all, and just stands around chewing gum and grinning till I send him home and call his brother Layhew. Later in the day you'll see Densel up in the middle of Seventh Street by the courthouse, squatting and punching his glove, his eyes bright and his jaw working faster, waiting for the ball. I can always tell when his spells start coming on: he's moody and nervous for a few days and then he buys four or five packs of Fan Tan Chewing Gum up at Charley Seat's candy counter. A normal, intelligent person can make a sensible remark to Densel when he's like that and he'll come back with a fool answer that'll make them wonder if he's got all his buttons. Layhew takes over Densel's chair for a few days then and directly Densel seems to get it all worked out of his system because he'll show up for work in a couple of mornings, bright as a pin and starts fetching his towels and stropping his razors like he hadn't been anywhere but home overnight; I don't think he remembers what's been going on because he's never been back more than two hours till he asks me how my trip was. Well, that morning I was sitting there staring at the bald head of the man who was too late in the Herpicide ad and still thinking about what I'd been trying to keep from thinking about all night.

Densel, I asked, though I should have had better sense; he had that moody scowl on his face and I could smell the Fan Tan a good ten feet away. Densel, where is Serbia at? In the Balkans—that's where Serbia's at, isn't it?

I have my fears about that, Henry, I have my fears, said Densel, chewing faster and not even bothering to turn around. Gehrig, Lazzeri and Koenig never looked better, I'll grant you. But them aching legs of Jumping Joe Duggin could ruin Huggins' whole infield combination this summer!

I just sat there, disgusted, and stared at the twisted suspenders on Densel Yoho's big fat back.

Call Layhew! I shouted before I stormed out and slammed the door behind me. You hear me, Densel? You get Central on that phone right this very minute and have her ring up Layhew and you tell him to get right over here. You hear me, Densel? I'm going up to the Elks Club for a drink.

I've always made it a hard rule never to take a drink till the sun sets. But a man can just stand so much. And yet sometimes when he's stood all he can stand, he finds out he can still stand a little more. Because when I came back to the barber shop I found out Densel not only hadn't called Layhew but had left the place empty with three men waiting for shaves and gone home to put on that damned baseball suit of his. So that I only had but the one chair working till long after lunch; Layhew had to come up river all the way from Captina.

I didn't eat my supper at the hotel that night. I went down to Joe Lowrey's Resturant on Lafayette Avenue. When I thought about what I planned to do that evening I felt like I didn't want a lot of people I knew sitting across the dining room from me, watching me, and maybe guessing what was really in the back of my mind. It was a fine June evening with a little breeze from the river. As soon as the sun went down I hurried up past the courthouse toward Tomlinson Avenue. The little hairs on the back of my neck still had that tingly feeling like a lot of folks were staring at me. There weren't any people in the Glory Public Library except Miss Aurora Twigg, the librarian, and a couple of little girls looking at magazines in the back. I felt uneasy, though, when Miss Twigg looked over her eyeglasses and smiled at me. Books, a whole room full of them; I guess it was books that made the place smell queer like that: musty and close and queer, like somebody's old trunk. I'd never been in the Glory Public Library until that spring night; not once in my whole life.

I don't mean to say I'm not a reader. And I'm not just talking about newspaper and magazine reading either. Up in my room I've got a whole shelf full of those little blue books from Haldeman-Julius out in Kansas. I've been sending away for them for years—just little blue paper books and most of them only cost a nickel and I've read every one of them from the one on bee culture to Judge Lindsay on Free Love. Just the same I felt nervous in the library that night with Miss Twigg looking at me and smiling. What's she grinning at? I wondered. Does she know what's really there in the back of my mind? I told her I wanted to see some sort of a geography, one with maps in it and not just U.S.A. maps or state road maps. Finally, I just come out straight and said I wanted a map that showed the Balkans. And having gone that far I said real quick: Serbia. So she smiled again and said it was an atlas I needed, not a geography and she went and fetched this big flat dusty book and found the place for me and went away and left me there at the table. Well, a map's a pretty dull thing to look at, usually, except for the colors or if you're planning a motoring trip somewhere. But I'm not ashamed to say that when I saw that map that showed Serbia it was like a love letter. Through the dead, musky air of that breathless room, quiet except for the little girls whispering over their *Literary Digest* pictures in the back, I could almost smell the lilacs that grow in the back yard of a certain house on Water Street. I could fairly see the color of a spray of them against dark hair roped in thick coils and almost too thick to take the tooth of a comb. Serbia was there right at the tips of my fingers and I moved them all around its different counties like some torn-up patchwork quilt: Croatia was blue and Slavonia was river-green and there was pink Montenegro and bright-orange Bosnia and one called Herzegovina that was faded violet.

It just shows you how little you know, I thought silently. For I always thought the Balkans must be islands. Warm islands somewhere off near the coast of India, maybe. Palm trees and warm days and cool nights with the winds blowing lilac through the window screens. But it's not islands at all. It's up near Hungary so it must be cold. It's not islands like I thought, at all.

Gracious, Miss Twigg whispered, hurrying toward me with another book and laying it flat on the table she commenced leafing through the pages. Gracious, she said. I gave you the old one without thinking, Mister Winemiller.

The old what, ma'am? I said.

The old atlas, Miss Twigg said. The 1910. The one before the War.

What War? I asked, like the worst ignoramus in the world; because I really didn't know what she was saying.

Why, the Great War, she said, smiling, her eyes bright with natural surprise. Here you are, Mister Winemiller. The Balkans. 1920. Yes, *here* we are.

Her finger pointed; I looked at her hands, how thin they were with a little, old-timey engagement ring—her mother's, I reckon, because Miss Twigg wasn't married. Her hands looked clean but dusty, like your fingers get from handling moths, only it seemed like it was all over her hands, on the backs of them, among the pale-blue veins. Dust of books, I thought. I followed her fingers as she pointed. It said Jugoslavia.

But where's Serbia, please? I said, and felt like a lot of things were going wrong somehow.

Oh, I'm afraid it's gone, Mister Winemiller, she said. Just simply gone. Just swallowed up in the treaties. Clemenceau and poor, dear, late President Wilson and those other fine, earnest, weary souls. Mister Winemiller, did you ever notice what a startling resemblance Lloyd George bears to our own dear Deacon Ambers?

But I wasn't listening to her somehow; she's a good-hearted soul and mighty well educated but I always get a little nervous around people that whisper all the time.

But where did it go? I asked, still like a dunce, not getting wise to any of it.

Pardon? whispered Miss Twigg. Where did who go, Mister Winemiller?

Serbia, I said. I'm afraid I don't understand maps very good, Miss Twigg.

Swallowed up! she whispered, with a little flutter of her fingers over the table, flinging them over the outline of the vanished states like a flurry of dusty pigeons. Gone! she whispered again. Absorbed. Digested. Ah, the Great War changed so many things! Only today I saw poor Mister Rogerson down at Kroger's—his boy, you know; his only son. But then why should I be telling you about the War, Mister Winemiller? You, who served in France with the AEF—you, who saw Europe first hand! Still, you might like to read up—to recollect a little. Wait now. I have just the right books for you.

And she tiptoed off among the big shelves of musk and gloom, still whispering to herself, and left me alone there, staring at the place where Serbia was but wasn't any more; staring dumb and thick-headed. And getting sorer by the minute. I felt like running out and catching the next Wheeling streetcar and jumping off right in the middle of Benwood or McMechen and giving some people a piece of my mind. I felt like going up there and collaring all those Hunkies and Polacks and Slovaks and Slavs and Montenegroes and Serbians. I just want to get hold of them all and holler: What the hell's wrong with you people? Haven't you got any pride? Haven't you got any patriotism? I just looked at a map and listen, you dumb bohunks, you know what? Your countries— they aren't there any more. You hear that, you dumb Serbians? There ain't no Serbia? How come you let a damned fool thing like that happen? Hell, we've had better than a hundred years of wars in the U.S.A. but, by God, you can still find it on the map. No wonder you people have to scratch a living out in the mines or sweat the marrow out of your bones in the steel mills. You don't deserve any better!

I just felt like taking both those map books and throwing them out in the middle of Tomlinson Avenue. But directly I commenced to cool off; I sat down and leaned my elbows on those maps and thought about it. I knew I didn't give a damn about the rest of them: the poor fools up yonder in the steel slums south of Wheeling. It was Natalia I was thinking about. If I was mad it was because of her; if I felt sad it was from thinking how a woman like her must feel. I mean how it must be to be proud of a place you come from and then suddenly it's not there any more.

Directly here come Miss Aurora Twigg back with a great, huge stack of books in her arms. She put them down in little heaps and I looked at her hands again. Covered with dust, like moths leave behind. Dust of books, I thought. Dust of kingdoms.

There now, cried Miss Twigg softly in a chokey, pleased little whisper. There, Mister Winemiller. The whole history of the Balkans.

I sat there a spell looking at the three piles of dusty, musky books that covered now the quilt squares of the maps. I felt real grateful to Miss Twigg for her time and trouble but I didn't want to read any of those books. I don't think I could have even made my hands touch them. They disgusted me. There was something unclean about them. They were dusty like Miss Twigg's hands and the dust seemed like it was in my throat, choking me. I thanked her and ran out of there.

Lordy, it was hot on the bed in my room that night; the fan didn't seem to move the air at all. But I was so busy thinking I hardly noticed; thinking and looking out at a few stars I could see through the screen in the corner of my window. I thought about a lot of stuff, trying to grasp it all, trying to read some kind of map of things that I was on, before something got signed by beaten kings or winning presidents or neutral God; hurrying to find the shape and meaning of me before they all signed something and brought a new map out, and me not on it anywhere any more. There wasn't many sounds outside in the street that night; I guess it was the heat. Miss Tigglebeck's Victrola was still; she must have gone to bed early, or was back in her little kitchen drinking death-black coffee and reviewing all the obituaries, axe murders and fatal auto wrecks in the *Glory Argus* and the Wheeling and Pittsburgh papers.

Around midnight I heard Densel Yoho. He wasn't bothering anybody; he never does when he gets these simple spells. He was somewhere out yonder in the dark; I judged him to be up near the courthouse corner, squatting right out in the middle of the trolley tracks, spitting in his mitt and punching the leather with his fist every now and then. Play ball! he'd holler out from time to time and then he'd squint and focus hard down the deserted street, or else scan an eye along the star-paths of the big June velvet night for a long, high one out in left field. But, hell, who's got the right to say what's real or empty fact, I'd like to know? Densel's desperate ball game out in the empty street—the old woman fighting each night, with flirting flattery, to charm away the black drummer whose overdue visit has got her hypnotized with dread—some poor, dumb Serbian's pride in a country canceled out by ministers and kings: a homeland long since scissored off the map—and me up there in my room with my fool fingers dreaming they feel the thick weight of dark and wondrous hair. Well, who's the crazy one, I'd like to know!

I laid there sweating on the bed in my BVD's, my hands behind my head, and thought about the rest of the sane and sensible folks in Glory. Well, I couldn't keep from chuckling out loud. I swear, there in the close, hot dark I could feel all of it out there in the night: the wanting, the hating that was going on. I could feel it like a thickness in the air: all the men out yonder in Glory asleep in their beds and just scheming and dreaming for the means to get at that woman in ways real nice and cozy. And all the wives beside them, dreaming and scheming of ways to get at her themselves—but in ways not quite so nice and cozy. Which ones of us all were the fools, I'd like to know. Who were the crazy ones that night in Glory? I heard Densel Yoho cuss and throw his glove down with a loud smack against the bricks; directly he commenced hollering at the umpire. When I dozed off he stopped hollering, but he was still arguing in a low, choked, hopeless voice. I could half-hear him in my sleep, in my dreams of Natalia's hair: those bright braids thick as carved wood; poor Densel was saying it was the Black Sox Scandal all over again. He was saying the game was crooked—fixed from the start.

Well, maybe it was. Because the very next morning Marcy Cresap came in my barber shop asking for money. She waved at me with a smile and went over to Holly Withers, who was waiting his turn, and asked for a donation. She had an old blue coffeepot in her hand; it sounded like there was about six or eight dimes and nickels in the bottom. Marcy knows I like her. And she knows my barber shop is a good place for soliciting donations, especially when both chairs are busy and there's two or three fellows waiting their turn. A barber shop is a place where few men like to look cheap.

Who's it for this time, Marcy? I hollered across to her.

I remember I was shaving A. K. Pyle's neck and I knicked him a little when she told me.

It's for Mrs. Lazarevitch and her two children, Marcy said. Her man was killed at the Benwood steel mill this morning.

Just then a young blond-haired boy named Filipovitch went hurrying up Seventh Street; when he saw Marcy through the window he came tearing inside. He undid a big safety pin from the pocket of his blue work-pants and tugged out a wrinkled wad of greenbacks and stuffed it in Marcy's coffeepot. Then he whipped off his cap and gasped when he saw John Grimm and A.K. and the police chief Holly Smithers and all those important Glory men there. He swallowed fast, his pale-blue eyes bugging out, and clutched his cap against his shirt, striking a kind of pose like a fellow about to make a speech he's already done six or eight times that day.

That there money's from the men in Mike's crew, Miss Cresap! he cried in a tight kind of singsong voice. I was there and seen it happen! —when Mike Lazarevitch got killed! We'us all jist so nervous—Oh, it was somethin' jist ter'ble. The superintendent—he sent the whole shift home for the day! Holy Jesus, and please excuse me for cussin' thisa-way! But it was jist somethin' ter'ble, folks! Mike—he was up there on the walk above the crucible and he leaned accidental and the wood-rail on the scaffolding—it busted! And down came Mike a'fallin'! Holy Jesus, and he never even reached that hot metal! And, for God's sake, please excuse my cussin'. Down come Mike a-fallin' and when he come about fifteen foot from the blazin' top of that molten steel—Mike he just disappeared. There'us jist this little blue flame and a puff of smoke! —Whissshht!—Mike he jist disappeared in the middle of the air! Never even had time to give out a yell. Jist—whisshht!—and Mike was gone! Holy Jesus, and please excuse my bad talk but it was jist somethin' ter'ble to see! And that there money, Miss Cresap, that there's from the boys that worked with Mike! For Miz Lazarevitch and them two kids. A hundert seventy-six dollars and eighty-three cents! Holy Jesus, Miss Cresap, I thank you and excuse my bad talk, one and all, God amighty!

And he tucked his cap on inside-out and backed off, stumbling and blushing through the door, and run off hard up Seventh Street. Directly John Grimm opened his alligator wallet and gave Marcy a twenty-dollar bill and so did Holly Smithers and Claude Wayman, and A. K. Pyle coughed and fetched around in his snap-purse and come out directly with a five, folded up small so nobody'd think he was tight. When Marcy come round to me with the coffeepot I rang open the cash register and turned my back on them all so's they couldn't see what I was giving. I wasn't about to have them know. And I'm not about to tell you either.

Well, Milosh sure had a queer funeral. Way up on the side of the hill above Benwood, far up beyond the last, dirty slum-house privy where something green, at least, grew—though nothing much more than goldenrod and polkweed and a few skinny sumacs. A queer sort of funeral with all those Serbians and Polacks and Hunkies standing around plus a few valley-Americans: me and Marcy and Tadd Cockayne and his boy Albert and old Doctor Cecil. And they had this preacher from the South Wheeling Orthodox Church: an old man with a beard like the picture of Walt Whitman in Judge Peabody's library. A strange sort of feeling you got, standing there with him praying and sprinkling and making signs in the air, like it was all happening on some foreign hillside and not in Mound County, at all. He did his preaching in Serbian and then some in English for the ones who had forgot or never knew and talked in a high, proud voice about Milosh Lazarevitch who had fought bravely with his brothers and sisters against the Turks and the Austrians and then come to America and become a good American without forgetting his brave heritage.

Right in the middle of it Mabel Peabody come up the dirt road in her 1922 Pierce Arrow with old Miss Tigglebeck in the front seat beside her and they parked a good distance off, watching and listening while the preacher, his white beard blowing in the hill winds of that fair June morning, said Milosh Lazarevitch was now and for everlasting in the high company of his people's undying heroes: Saint Sava and King Marko and the holy Prince Lazar and somebody named Stephen Dushan —a mill-worker friend of Milosh's I reckon. No, I'll not soon forget it: the queerest sort of funeral, without even a hearse or county coroner's ambulance to bring poor Milosh up there, but instead of that a big, muddy, six-ton Garford truck with WHEELING STEEL CORPORA-TION stenciled on the cab, and a cheap, black wreath on the windshield. While, looming up in the truck-bed, was this gigantic mass of cold steel with Milosh in it—six or eight tons, I reckon, if it weighed a pound: a great, enormous cone: ragged and ugly as the meteor they got up in the museum at Pittsburgh. And somewhere in it—I guess that's how they figured—was whatever ashes of Milosh Lazarevitch that didn't go up in that little blue flame when he fell.

Natalia's dark eyes had watched, proud and brave in her bloodless face, above the smooth cheeks that looked soft as blossoms above her chin and then seemed to tighten and gleam where the scrubbed skin stretched over the flat, high bones; and her broad bow mouth with its full underlip was not shaking, it didn't seem even tight like women's mouths when they don't dare cry, though the little smile didn't play in the corners that day. And all she ever did that even seemed close to grieving was to shut her big eyes gently when the twelve millworkers, struggling the huge mass out of the truck and down the makeshift ramp of girders, let it go, at last, with a single-voiced shout and let it plunge with a ponderous rumble into the enormous company grave.

My! *That* lady sure is a cool cucumber! I overheard Mabel Peabody exclaim to Miss Tigglebeck when the services were over; Marcy and me were just walking past her car.

Were you watching her face, Nevada? Mabel went on. She never shed a single, solitary tear. Not that I'm really surprised: a woman of that sort—and a foreigner besides. I declare, Nevada, I don't know how I ever let you wheedle me into driving you up here to witness this common spectacle!

Ah, now, Mabel, said Miss Tigglebeck. There is some grief that's past all tears. And it's true, dear—the poor thing is a foreigner, and foreign ways are strange, sometimes beyond our understanding. Still—just look yonder, Mabel: her two fatherless little waifs!—see how the one tries to hide her eyes with her bonnet brim! Look how the other tugs at the black fringe of the mother's shawl, trying to stuff it in her little mouth to staunch the sobs! Ah, the poor soul—widowed with those two little girls! And so far far from the land of her forebearers! Mabel, whatever shall she do?

Well, that's sure not a hard one to answer, sniffed Mabel Peabody, glaring out the window at Marcy and me. She can always go back where she came from!

Marcy was pulling at my sleeve, but by that time I didn't care; I shook loose and walked through the tall grass right over to that Pierce Arrow running board, and stuck my head in the window.

'Be a little hard to go back to Serbia, wouldn't it, Miss Peabody? I said, with an educated smile.

And *why* would it, Mister Winemiller? she shouted, backing away from me a little.

Because—it's—not—there—any—more—is why! I said.

Then, tipping my hat politely to Miss Tigglebeck, I turned on my heel and went off with Marcy Cresap who drove me back to Glory.

And so it commenced. A week passed—then two—and by the last week in June it didn't need a mastermind to guess what most of Glory was up to. I lathered and shaved men daily while they smirked and hinted at the mention of Natalia's name; I trimmed some mighty important heads and watched their faces through the snip-snapping scissor blades and saw their winks and gloating leers and knowing, wiseacre nods. And after I'd whiskbroomed them off they'd tarry awhile by the door, whispering and chuckling Natalia's name behind their hands and the big, gold lodge rings would twinkle as their fingers twitched in ornery anticipation. Nights when I'd have my supper in the hotel dining room I'd see the women's smiles and hear their whispers, too: the Glory ladies had their plans for Natalia, as well. Though, what with the little wife sitting right across the tablecloth from them, the men kept their mouths shut now, though—from time to time—one of them would get a dreamy look and stare out the plate-glass window into the mists that rose from the river in late June's moonlit dusk, and smile a little smile, and pick their teeth behind a hotel napkin, and ponder what the next move should be now.

Because the first move had already been made for them. I mean Milosh's death. Natalia didn't have a penny to her name. When Marcy Cresap told me that I couldn't hardly believe it. I asked her about the hundred seventy-six dollars and eighty-three cents the men in the mill chipped in. I asked her about the coffeepot money, too, and Marcy said Peace's Funeral Home had taken all of that for Milosh's sandstone marker and she still owed money to the steel company.

What for? I said.

Well, said Marcy, her eyes flashing a little behind her spectacles. It seems that hill above Benwood where they buried Mike is company-owned. Maybe some day they plan to expand—they'll build a plant there or dig a mine—Lord knows. Meanwhile, they use it for that. For burying. There's half a century of men up there who died in the mill. Some just got old and wore out; some had accidents. When a man dies like Mike died they always bury the whole thing that he fell into. Henry, I guess there must be better than a dozen eight-ton chunks of steel stuck into that smoky hillside. The company's sentimental that way. It's just lucky she doesn't have to pay for all that steel Mike spoiled. As it is, they're only charging her for the worth of the land where he's buried.

She chuckled and turned her head away real quick; I could see an angry mist in the corners of her eyes.

Up at the funeral home last week, Marcy said, Tom Peace's boy made up a real good joke. It was the day they ordered Mike's marker from the stonemason down at Marietta. Folks all over town are still chuckling over it—the cute motto Tom Peace's boy said they ought to use on Mike's tombstone.

What was it? I said.

Rust in Eternity, Marcy said.

But I guess that wouldn't have been worth Glory's trouble. Natalia couldn't read English; she'd have missed a good joke like that. And so Glory went about getting at her with jokes she could understand—even if they weren't quite as funny as the one Tom Peace's boy made up. A woman doesn't need to understand English for her and her kids to get along, but she's got to eat, she has to pay the rent, there's a gas bill every month and doctors send bills, too; there's the week's groceries to buy at Kroger's every Friday and children's clothes don't last forever. One night toward the end of June I was awake as usual, thinking about Natalia, and I couldn't figure it out to save my life. It just seemed too queer to have an answer: all these businessmen in Glory making it so hard on her—all these men who were itching so bad to get on her good side. Well, I know I'm a fool but I didn't have to strain my brain much figuring that one out. It was plain as daylight that somebody was putting the screws on every one of those men: the doctor, the grocer, the real-estate fellow, the clothing-store keeper, the nabob up at the gas company, the shoestore owner, the dentist, the steel company secretary, the tombstone contractor and all the rest—though I'm not mentioning a one of them by name. Yes, somebody was putting the screws on them to put the screws on Natalia. A whole little chattering bunch of somebodies, to be exact—and every single somebody among them wearing a skirt!

However tender—or however ornery—a businessman in Glory might have felt toward Natalia Lazarevitch that spring, can you just imagine now him giving her credit or, worse still, money and coming home that night to anything less than a household full of nagging, married hell? So—by the end of that month—Natalia's back, at last, was flat against the wall. To my knowledge there was but one Glory merchant who went down to the little house on Water Street with any sort of suggestion. Natalia sent the children out of doors and fetched in an old one-eyed Croation miner's widow—a bone-setter by trade—to stand by the stove and tell her in Serbian what the man had come to tell her in English. Well, it sure was a nice little plan, all right: Natalia was to get a whole year's supply of groceries and all she had to give him was a whole year's supply of something else. I remember that night well—I rented a bottle of leeches from Seat's Drug Store and fixed up both this certain party's eyes pretty good, but his nose was bad for months; even though, I declare, it did look sort of scenic and grand the way it went from deep violet and baby blue through all kinds of green and orange and tan and finally ended up in a finale of pale yellow ochre, like the sunset in the Maxfield Parrish picture that hangs over my washstand.

Though she hadn't really hit back yet. She wasn't Natty Vengeance yet. Natalia Lazarevitch could have fetched a black iron skillet up side the head of every big man in Glory and not even touched them the way Natty Vengeance would touch them in due time. Was fated to. Yes, something in me will always believe it was fate: every bit of it. There was something fixed and irresistible the way people went through their movements from first to last: beginning with Milosh, the day he fell, clean till the night Natty Vengeance left Glory behind her forever.

Marcy Cresap saw what was happening: the men in Glory sick with the fever of wanting Natalia, the women of Glory hating Natalia, not because the men were sick, but because it wasn't them that got them that way; knowing they couldn't anymore get a fellow fevered-up that way than they could raise a thermometer stuck up a corpse on Peace's cooling table—hating Natalia Lazarevitch as only women can hate woman, whilst hounding their men, day and night, to drive her off the brink of Glory. Marcy saw all this happening; she fought it the way she fought everything like it in Apple County—not ever hating the haters, just hating the hate. But even Marcy couldn't change it now. Because, by this time, Natalia was mad.

She couldn't get work and she wouldn't take charity. And one sweltering June morning a delegation of ladies of the Glory Associated Charities came smiling down Water Street to Natalia's kitchen door with three apple crates full of old winter clothes, several cans of lard and two big bags of flour. Well, charity from that quarter didn't surprise me a bit; if there's one thing women can never resist, it's a good, close sympathetic look at someone they're destroying. And what is even the best of charity but the bared backside of contempt, cheaply perfumed and offered for a kiss?—the last insult scared winners ever seem able to cook up against spunky losers.

And it was work Natalia wanted, to keep herself and the two little girls together. She'd asked at the glass plant, the back doors of Glory's restaurants and cafes, the aeroplane factory, the two hotels, the enamel works; she'd gone from house to house offering herself as housemaid, cook, washer woman, grass cutter. Nothing. Meanwhile, though she had enough to eat for a while from the little cellarful of things she'd put up the fall before, the rent was due. And the gas bill. And the rest of the bills. So she tried selling a few things from her cellar shelves: mason jars of apples and spiced pears and green beans and queer, strange Balkan eggs—sleek and velvety things—boiled for two days in olive oil, Serbian-style. But, of course, no one ever bought so much as a single jar of fruit, or an asafoetida bag, or a sheep's-milk cheese, or a posey of wild flowers from the stuff she hauled rattling behind her, in the old child's wagon, through Glory's leafy streets. And, before long, men who'd worked with Milosh in the steel mill—Serbians from Natalia's own outlandish abolished hills—came courting and asked honorably for her widowed hand in marriage. But she drove them away with shouts as wild and final as if they'd been Glory Rotarians with something less permanent in mind. And folks started wondering why she didn't just pick up and go somewheres else—a place like Steubenville or Weirton or even back to Benwood, to the old battleship-gray frame house where she and Milosh had lived and had their kids before they came to Glory. But it was too late for that now; something had got hold of that woman's mind that was fiercer than pride or getting-by or even just plain survival. Natalia Lazarevitch was mad. And here's a funny thing: that wisp of a smile was back in the corners of her mouth again: the smile-ghost nobody'd seen since they buried those six tons of Milosh up on Benwood hill.

I'm not ashamed to say I laid awake those nights—sweating with scared notions that one of those big, laughing mill-hands would finally win her. Or that maybe she'd just give up, at last, and run off with the kids somewhere new. But she didn't. Though, before long, I was to wish to God she had; before many weeks I was to curse myself for ever being thankful she was still there. But, you see, by now she had to stay. They could have tractored her house down and set fire to the ruins and rubble and she'd have stayed; she'd just have taken her kids and her three laying-hens and her two sheep and gone out to sit under the big willow, while that ghost-smile kept on teasing the corners of her mouth, like little, licking flames. Because Natalia Lazarevitch still had something she planned to do with Glory before Glory was done with her. And I guess I was the last man in town to know she'd already commenced doing it.

There's one big trouble to living a life like mine: I mean, following a trade where you have to keep your mouth shut for thirty-seven years. And that is, once you ever do start talking about things, there's no shutting up. Lord, when I think of some of the things I've told you, it makes me wonder if my senses haven't left me—I've owned up to stuff I wouldn't have even whispered to Mama's picture up there in the dark of my room. So I might as well tell how I laid awake every night of those last weeks in June scheming for some way to get round Natalia. Well, I know—every other male in Glory was awake scheming that himself. Only, God help me, I wanted the crazy, wild she-devil for my wife.

Falling in love, like mumps, is better off having while you're a boy; it's mighty disorganizing when it hits you in the fifties. Like a butcher's sledge, it slams you between the eyes and before you know it you haven't got the judgment of a reasonably dumb fourteen-year-old.

One night in the hotel dining room I caught myself mumbling out loud during my peach pie and saw a few people staring at me, curious naturally, and realized suddenly what I'd been saying. I'd been working out the sort of speech I'd say if I went down to Water Street some June evening and proposed. And had half a mind to go do it right then and there. Not knowing yet that the time had come when it was way too late for that; never guessing that Natalia's queer, dark vengeance had already begun.

I snuck into the library; I just had to go there that night. Because it was the only place in Glory that had Natalia's picture: the only likeness I could think of that I could look at whenever I wanted and touch with my hands. For me the beautiful colors of the map in that old dog-eared, out-of-date atlas was a picture of Natalia Lazarevitch; the only one I had—a face that crazy kings and crook-ministers couldn't ever treaty-out of being. Let them repeal the maps; let them scrape and ink out, paint over and reprint the shapes of all those queer Hunkie home-lands—they still couldn't embezzle away the tough pride of some people. And with all their monkeying around, they couldn't ever change the smiles in the corners of some women's mouths.

The library was just the same as the first night I came there: Miss Twigg was fussing around with her little cards behind the desk, the two little girls in the back were whispering together still; it was like nobody'd even gone home since then. Then Miss Twigg spied me.

Ah, Mister Winemiller! she cried with a hushed gasp. So you *did* come back for some more books, after all!

No'm, I said. Just to look something up. In the atlas—the *old* one, that is.

Oh, dear, now! Miss Twigg whispered. Dear dear now! What shall we do! It's busy I'm afraid.

Busy, ma'am?

Those two little ladies in the back, she said, *they're* looking at it! But I suppose they'd be just as happy looking at magazines.

Miss Twigg held a dusty hand up to one side of her mouth and leaned closer, whispering softer still.

Poor little things, she said. Before their father died they used to come here often of an evening. But now they're here every night. Till closing. Then I see them from my bedroom window—wandering the streets long after I've gone home—sometimes they sit yonder on the courthouse porch till past midnight. I don't think the mother wants them home evenings. Heaven only knows why not—they're such little dears. That *strange* woman—

What woman? I said, though something in me knew already.

Why, Mrs. Lazarevitch, Miss Twigg gasped softly through her fingers, and seemed to breathe out little puffs of book dust when she spoke. The foreign woman down on Water Street. The *widow*, she added, then bit her lip and glanced away quickly as if she'd just said a word that ladies shouldn't use.

Children! she chirped brightly, and fluttered off before I could stop her. Mary—Sophie! Come let me give you the new *Delineator* to look at! It's simply full of pretty pictures. And there's a splendid new Butterick dress pattern! Has your mama taught you to sew yet, my dears? No—I suppose she hasn't. Still, there's lots of colored pictures, so come now, my lambs. Mister Winemiller wants to use the atlas and I'm sure two well-mannered little ladies won't mind giving it up!

I looked behind me at the door but it was too late to run. I just seriously felt like hiding somewhere amongst those dusty bookshelves before I'd let those two children of hers see me there and maybe recognize my face and know what I'd come there to look at. Sophie pouted but little Mary just smiled bashfully and stuck a finger in her mouth when Miss Twigg spread the new magazine on the table before them and shoved the atlas to one side. Then she turned, smiling, and beckoned to me with her fountain pen. So there was no way out of it for me; I had to go sit in the chair right next to those two and make some kind of show out of it. So I went back there and sat down somehow and just stared at the tops of my clammy hands on the open page before me without even knowing what it was. And to make matters worse, the oldest girl, Sophie —Mary was the shy one—the bold one, Sophie, she spoke to me.

My, I jist love maps, she whispered, looking around at me with big, frank, friendly eyes. Don't you? I reckon—next to movie shows—there's nothing I'd rather look at than maps. Don't you? When I git old enough to git a job at the glass factory that's the very first thing I'm gonna buy me!—a map book just like that there one.

I cleared my throat and I must have been purple with shyness; I've given a lot of Glory children their first haircuts and spent thirty-seven years learning how to talk to them, but these were *her* children and that was her map under my hands. I just felt like my tongue was an old shoe.

Of course, she went on in that bold, hoarse whisper, I don't plan on working at the glass factory more than a month. After that I'm going to be a movie actor like Norma Talmadge. Next to Mama, Norma Talmadge is the gorgeousest lady I ever did see. I think she's gorgeouser than Clara Bow. Don't you. I just know I'll get to be a real famous movie actor. Because I'm always pretending I'm somebody else. I reckon that's why I just love map books. Because I'm jist always pretending I'm somewheres else than where I'm at. I can jist sit and look at maps for hours and hours—can't you? I jist sit there looking at maps and dream I'm far far away.

I sat there staring at the backs of my big hands. But I had to smile and something tight inside me seemed to burst and spill and run all through me till it warmed my clammy fingers.

Don't you? the bold child Sophie was saying suddenly, her fingers laid with lonesome friendliness upon my sleeve.

Sure, I said. You just bet your life I do.

Me, too! whispered Sophie loudly. Oh, me, too! I'm jist dyin to go there!

I sat quiet a spell; I wondered how a man could break the news about something like that to a child without breaking her heart as well.

Suppose it's not there any more, I said.

You're jist kiddin now, she laughed, and even shy Mary had to giggle at my foolishness.

No, just suppose, I said. A body can't be too sure of things in such a world as this. Things change. Sometimes they go away.

You're jist kiddin, she laughed, more tickled than ever and Mary had to stick her little fist in her mouth, rocking with sneezy, muffled chuckles.

Places don't go away, she said scornfully. My, you sure are an awful kidder.

Sometimes they do, I said. I'm a good deal older than you and I know about these things.

Where to? she whispered, with great, huge, solemn eyes, a little scared-looking now. Where could places go?

Nowhere, I said. Things like wars come. And when the war's over the place isn't there. It's just gone. So there's nothing left for the men to do but make the maps over. And old maps—like this one—they don't mean no more than pictures in a fairy-story book. D'you see?

She looked so puzzled and sad I wished I hadn't tried to explain; her big eyes shone with lonesome sadness, half sore at me, and the little smiles that played in the corners of her child-mouth, they were gone. But I kept on anyway; I had to let her know the way things are.

So if you got dreams of going back, I said firmly, either you or your sister—or your Ma—if you're fixing to go back to Serbia—

That ain't Serbia, she said, cocking her head with puzzlement at me. I never said a word about Serbia. That there's a map of Texas! That's the place I always pretend I'm at!

I looked down suddenly, feeling strange, foolish feelings, and looked at the map of the U.S.A. under the heels of my big, dumb hands.

When they got the war done, she begged, in a half-scared whisper and tugged at my sleeve, was Texas gone?

I shook my head and queer thoughts made me tremble; I shook my head No real hard again and slapped my hand on the map.

No, by golly! I said out loud. The war never changed nothing on *this* map! And no war never will!

With a little sigh of glad relief the child clambered across the arm of my chair and leaned on her elbows, turning the thumb-marked pages of the atlas till she found what I wanted.

There! she said, with a stab of her finger on the page. That there's Serbia.

And she leaned closer—frowning, searching— her breath so close that it stirred the little hairs on the back of my hand.

And that there, she said, with another finger-jab, that's where my Mama was born and there's where Papa was born and that's where Uncle Danilo got killed fighting the Turks and that's where—

And she kept on pointing and talking and I looked at the queer names on that queer map of No-Place-Any-More and thought about the people she was talking about who had vanished just as totally and the towns that hadn't even mattered much when they were there, queer-named towns where nobody of any importance ever did anything important enough for anybody to take notice of and how they'd all so soon been forgotten; a beautiful land it had been, but I kept thinking: Whatever had such lost, outlandish flyspecks on a canceled map ever done that touched a single human life in Glory or changed a soul in the whole great U.S.A., for that matter—except to send a woman out of its ragged obscurity to change the life of me? I looked at all the meaningless, lost, queer names of them as they passed under the little girl's finger; the sad small towns where nothing, but Natalia, ever happened: Travnik and Topola, Pruska Gora and Dubrovnik and Zagreb. And Sarajevo.

Suddenly on the first stroke of the courthouse striking nine, Miss Twigg tapped her little iron bell and tiptoed back, still whispering, to tell us it was time to go. The two children ran off ahead of me into the pearly river mists.

Wait now! I hollered boldly. You kids leave me walk you safely home. It's too late at night you going down there to Water Street in such a fog as this.

But I could barely make out their small shapes in the corner lamp post's smothered bloom of light.

Good night! cried brave Sophie. Good night, mister!

You go home now! I hollered, stern as if I was already their father. You hear? Go straight home now!

We dasn't! sang out shy Mary, with a sudden, sorrowful boldness of her own. Mama don't let us never come home till after the clock's struck twelve! Mama don't—

Hush! I heard brave Sophie whisper in the mists.

—Mama don't finish entertaining her gentlemen till twelve! shy Mary finished, heedless.

Hush, I said, you little fool! cried Sophie in a rage, and I heard the smart smack of a slap and off they scampered somewhere, small Mary wailing and Sophie scolding, deep in that white woolly wilderness of night.

And so it was that I first came to know—what most of Glory had known already: how, in that desperate, queer last week in June, Natalia Lazarevitch had started selling her favors for a price. I tell you I took it hard. I thank the Lord I'm not a drinking man or, I tell you, I'd have been a goner. As it was, I had Densel and Layhew take over both chairs whilst I took off a week out-of-town to pull myself together. I couldn't have stood the sight of Pittsburgh just then, so I took a trip over to Uniontown where the Methodists were throwing a big spring Tri-state Revival. I went religiously four nights in a row and watched while the world-famed evangelist made kindling wood out of four perfectly good kitchen chairs. But the night he hollered out in front of three thousand people: "Women, cross your legs and close the Gates of Hell!" I got up and walked right back up the Sawdust Trail and went out of that tent disgusted with everything—chairs, Methodists, women, hell and myself—and went back to the tourist home and laid on the bed listening to the delighted ladies who'd commenced singing "Beulah Land"—with crossed legs, I reckon. I thought out things pretty thoroughly those last few days there, away from Glory. I knew that nothing had happened back there that could ever change my mind about Natalia. I knew she could put-out for money in every town between Aliquippa, Pennsylvania, and East Liverpool and I'd still want to marry her. What had me really stumped was why she was putting-out to the very men in town she hated worst. Until I remembered something else; Natalia was mad. And when a woman like that gets mad she's not about to give up nor give in either; she's more likely working on some female scheme to make a man wish, before she's done with him, that he'd been born a gelding.

So June came to its end. And then commenced one of the strangest summers Glory'll ever have to remember. For me it seemed the saddest since the one when Mama passed over. But just about everybody else in Glory seemed to be having a pretty good time. The men had Natalia when they wanted her. The women had her where they wanted her.

Their tight-lipped mouths showed the Christian victory of seeing her beauty forced to be what they'd all suspicioned it was meant for from the first. They'd seen her upstart Hunkie pride forced into public prostitution. And no woman ever minds immorality in a town when immorality is the price of justice.

I guess I could have gone crazy without much trouble that summer if it hadn't been for Marcy Cresap dropping in for a chat now and then. And when nightfall came there were two folks in all of Glory who befriended me, listened to my yowls, talked back, kidded me a little, prayed some and scolded a lot. One was old Miss Tigglebeck and the other was Densel Yoho. Nights of laying up there in the old room, evenings with nothing to do but think, and the dark ceiling like a moving picture screen with pictures of Natalia and all those men— sometimes I'd get scared I'd turn dog-mad and go running down to the house on Water Street. So I'd go sit in Miss Tigglebeck's front parlor and drink Postum and listen to her Victrola. And for a while I'd forget my own miseries thinking about that poor boy trapped in that Kentucky cave and about gallant Captain Lansdowne and all the young lives doomed on the Shenandoah's last trip that night. I got so I even worked up a little interest in Miss Tigglebeck's scrapbooks of obituaries and the murder of the little Parker girl by the fiend in California and whether Harding's death was natural or not. Miss Tigglebeck would come up now and then with some first-rate little nature note she'd gleaned from Headstone Footnotes, the curiosity column in *Evergreen Memories,* the American Mortician's Monthly, or maybe a comic remark from Cript Quips, their joke department. I'd drink Postum till I was half sick and sleepy and listen to Vernon Dalhart whining away on the machine: "One dark, September mor-ning—the ear-th was fa-a-ar be-low; the migh-ty Shen-en-doah. . . ." And I'd shut my eyes and I could just see her, the way she used to come gliding low over Glory—just clearing the courthouse trees, it seemed, and the way you'd feel cool for a minute in that long, gigantic shadow that flitted over the streets and up the building fronts and across the back lots. It doesn't sound like much to you, maybe, but it kept my thoughts away from Natalia for a while. And when I didn't have Miss Tigglebeck I had Densel.

That Densel Yoho is a tough one to figure out. He's as kindly a soul as you'd ever went to meet and forty weeks out of the year he's as bright as a new dollar. He only has these baseball seizures once or twice a year; I guess all that fuss over Babe Ruth's world record last season was the reason he had three. When he's got that uniform on, Densel hasn't got the sense of an epileptic ape. But once he's got it all worked out of his system he comes back sharper than ever. His brother Layhew is a boob by comparison. When Densel gets over one of his fits he hides his glove and suit and baseball shoes somewhere in the boardinghouse he lives at and comes back to work. He never remembers a thing he did. But he looks as refreshed as if he'd spent a week's vacation out in Kansas at Doc Brinkley's clinic. I don't know where he learned it at, but Densel's got a strong philosophy about women. That's how I first got round to confiding in him my feelings about Natalia. Pretty soon we got to eating supper together every night at the hotel. Afterwards we'd pick our teeth a while and have an extra cup of coffee and then go down on Lafayette Avenue for a few games of balkline or three-cushion at Leaky Waldorf's Crystal Billiard Lunch.

Aw, stop your sweating, Hen, said Densel one cool August evening. That woman'll straighten out directly. She's busy working on something, that's all.

It'll wreck her, I said. Her constitution won't take it. It'll kill her, Densel.

Constitution! said Densel. *Kill* her. Why, Hen, putting-out six or eight times a night don't tire a woman like that as much as you'n me sweat over a game of rotation pool. You listen to me, Hen. That woman'll straighten out directly. And she'll quit putting-out. Because she'll never be worth a damn as a hustler. It's just not her speed—she's too hot-blooded for it. Hustlers is like nuns, Hen—scared to death of a real good loving. So they both have to get as far away from it as they can—some place where, most of the time, there's nothing around but a bunch of other women. That woman's not like that—she's a hot-blooded devil, a real one-man-er. He sure had himself a female—that poor bohunk that married her. I'll bet it wasn't hot steel that killed him at all. He likely went up in smoke just thinking about what he had waiting home for him. The poor, dumb Polack. They should have buried the bed and not that hunk of pig iron—

He wasn't a Polack, I said sternly. He was a Serbian.

Polack, Serbian, Lesbian, whatever, said Densel. That's not what I'm talking about. I'm talking about that woman. She's just hustling now because it's part of her scheme. Lord, when I think of those damned fool men, he sighed, and chalked his cue. Those poor, damned fool men.

Well, in your judgment, what *is* her scheme, I said.

I don't know, said Densel. You don't know. These fool men in Glory don't know. Their wives don't know. And I'd lay even money she herself don't know. The only thing in that woman's thoughts is getting even. One day she got the word Revenge in her head and, from then on, her head didn't have no more to do with it—the rest was all juices and glands and instincts. She's not thinking, Hen. She's *feeling*. When that kind of woman starts thinking she ends up doing something stupid.

I leaned on my cue and sipped a little of Leaky Waldorf's near-beer; I gazed out the gloomy, dusty poolroom window at the yellow light from Tadd Cockayne's gooseneck lamp still burning in the *Argus* office. All I could feel was that awful doom of ruin I felt so sure was waiting for Natalia somewhere up there in the weeks and months ahead. I heard a steamboat blow her lorn lament; like some cry of a nightbird's fatal omen.

They'll get her, though, I murmured. Can't you see that, Densel? In the end, *they'll* get her.

Who? said Densel. Who'll get her.

Them, I said. You know these married women in Glory—all those wives. Don't tell me they don't know. Don't tell me they don't give a hoot: their husbands slipping down to Water Street. Every night—the minute the sun's down and the fog's up. Oh, don't think they don't know, Densel.

Densel stuck his cue back in the rack, chuckled and tossed a quarter on the felt.

Sure they know, he said. They know that woman's putting-out. They know she's gone to hustling. And what do you reckon that makes them do, Hen?—shed a charitable tear for one of their fallen sisterhood? And a bohunk sister at that.

Serbian, I said. I sure wish you'd try remembering that fact, Densel. Natalia is a Serbian. A mighty proud people. And without any map any more, I added, in a slightly superior tone. Except the maps of our own Apple County.

Serbian, said Densel. Whatever. I'm talking about women now and they don't make any maps of that. Whatever. Because it don't matter a bit: whatever breed or denomination she is or they are—that's not what I'm getting at. I'm talking about that woman on Water Street putting-out and every other woman in Glory knowing she's putting-out. And glad she's putting-out because putting-out's what they've always wanted her to have to do since she and the poor, dead bohunk first come here from Benwood with the kids. Don't you see it, Hen?—the way they're all settling back now to enjoy it for a spell: the sight of her crawling in the ditch of harlotry and disgrace. Just wanting what they always wanted: to see her stuck-up, godawful, terrifying beauty have to crawl. And have to put-out for a living. Even if it's their own men that are getting what she's putting out. They'll watch her for a spell, see her get what they reckon is coming to a working-stiff's wife who dares walk with her chin stuck-back that way and her eyes crackling with pride the way hers always done. You know. Like the queen of something. Maybe that's what she was back there. Queen. Of Serbia. Or Timbuctoo or China. Whatever. Because it don't matter where. What matters is here. In Glory. What matters is the way she held her head up on Friday nights when she come into Kroger's on the dead bohunk's arm: the way she always looked like she was getting ready to smile but hadn't quite started yet. All that, Hen, plus that godawful femaleness that didn't leave nothing safe around it after it walked past.

Just coming here to Glory in the first place—wasn't that enough to get them sore, Hen? Instead of staying up in Benwood or McMechen or Mingo Junction with the rest of the Polack steelworker trash? Wasn't it enough? And then behaving like she was some sort of a six-generation, English, valley-born, Legion Ladies' Auxiliary, dame of the DAR, Methodist preacher's wife and Beauty-contest Winner at the Panhandle Peach Festival, to boot? It was too much, Hen. By God, it just wouldn't do. So they had to work it round and wait till life whored her down to humbleness. And now they'll enjoy that for a spell. And when they get tired of playing with the mouse they'll eat it. Except that I'm betting on the mouse, for some queer reason. I'm betting that by the time the cat figures it's time to get ready to move, the mouse'll be having herself a regular cat church-barbecue! In a way it's almost sad, Hen—all them women tonight up there in Glory—they're just sort of mesmerized in the spell of their own reflections. Now, there's nary one them doesn't know that woman's finagling around right this very minute with somebody's husband. But do you reckon there's one of them whose pride would let her own up that it's hers? The party lines are all humming tonight, Hen, but they're all talking about somebody else!

We had long since left Leaky Waldorf's; we'd talked all the way down Lafayette and up Seventh. The way Densel's voice carried through the fog when he got worked up, I was half-scared some woman would overhear. Miss Tigglebeck's light was out, I noticed with disappointment. But I talked Densel into staying out a while longer and we went and sat in the dark in the barber shop and Densel had him a sip from the hair-tonic bottle we kept disguised between the bay rum and the Herpicide.

Densel, how'd you come to know so much about women? I asked, though maybe I shouldn't have done it.

By staying shut of them, he said.

Never had a gal? I said, and shouldn't have asked that either.

Got one now, he said. She taught me all I know about 'em, Hen.

How'd she teach you? I said.

By being dead for fifteen years, he said.

And then he sat studying the lights in the river mists beyond the glass and cleared his throat and took another big swig from the hair-tonic bottle.

I loved her, he said. But I never understood her. Not when she was around. She loved me, she teased me, let me have my way with her, then run off with a laugh and married a harvest hand from Braxton County, died in child-bed, and left me fifteen years to figure it all out. No, not all, by God. Not all. I still get stumped by women when I'm around them. When I'm alone it's all as plain as daylight. But when you're around them it's no good ever trying to figure them out and it's purely fatal to try outguessing one. Don't ever try it, Hen. Not even with the dumbest woman ever born. You'll lose if you do—just like those poor dudes are going to lose. When the bohunk woman gets done, it'll be them that suffer. Even the wives—they'll be winners in a way. Because they belong to the same team, the same breed; the bohunk woman will get her revenge in a few months and the wives will be enjoying theirs for years to come. Yes, it'll be the men that'll pay the piper. Because the game was rigged against them before they ever started. They're out there tonight—taking their turns at the house on Water Street—thinking they've got their wives and the bohunk woman both out-guessed. That's a mistake, Hen. Don't ever make it. When it comes to the love-game every woman born is a genius. That's because they invented it. Every bit of it: the rules, the prizes, the penalties. They invented everything from doing it to the words that's used to do it with to the dunce stool you get sent to if you don't do it their way. Don't ever try to outguess a woman at *that* game, Hen. You might as well go try to tell Edison how to change a light bulb!

He glared around him suddenly in the twilight from the street lamp; for a minute I thought he was going to fetch the bottle for another swig but he merely cracked his knuckles one by one and glared at his faint reflections in the mirrors.

By God, Hen, said Densel Yoho. Sometimes I think I've got them all figured wrong, though. Sometimes I ain't sure of any of it! Not them— not males—none of it: not even Life. Sometimes I think it's all something—something bigger! Fate! We're all just shuffled thither and yon—men and maids alike—moved round by something none of us can do a God damned thing about. Like a game, Hen—that's what it is. Some sort of a dirty game that somebody's fixed! It's—! It's—!

For a minute I thought Densel was almost remembering something; I wanted to seem obliging.

I know, I said. Like the Black Sox.

The which? said Densel.

You know, Densel, I said. The Black Sox. That big baseball scandal here a while back—

Why, now I never did hear tell of that one, said Densel, and sat studying his hundred reflections a while longer.

And please don't never mention that damned game to me, Hen, he said directly. I never seen a baseball game in my life and I don't care if I never do. I couldn't tell you the difference between a touch-down and a punt. And a few weeks from now, Alec Pyle and John Grimm and the rest of them fanatics will be setting up there at the Elks with their ears glued to that damned Atwater Kent and coming down here afterwards to get shaved and I'll have to listen to nothing but baseball talk for the rest of the summer. So just kindly don't never mention the name baseball around me, Hen.

He stared off, kind of grumpy and baffled for a bit, but then his face brightened; I guess he thought he was changing the subject, though I could fairly smell the Fan Tan gum and neat's-foot ointment in the air.

Say, Hen! You never did say! he cried with a genial grin. How was your trip?

Well, that was the longest summer I can remember in Apple County since the year of Mama's last sick spell. Those two summers were a lot alike; they both ended on the same sort of September evenings: nights with that same first feel of fall; twilight all dusty with sundown and goldenrod, and green smells of the hay harvest blowing in the wind from every ridge and river meadow. It was on that same kind of autumn night when Mama passed over that Natalia Lazarevitch caught the west-bound out of Glory. I'll long remember those nights; they both left me waiting, heartbroke, puzzled, maybe hoping, maybe just watching, for a long whiles after, for someone who might be coming back. Or maybe only waiting for another such September night to come, when I could ride west-bound out of Glory, too, and someone nice up-the-line, in some sweet, grassy, little hick-town depot, hunting for my face along the dusty day-coach windows. That kind of fall evening.

Though it all commenced in the morning—a Monday, it was: Labor Day. All the men in town were home having their day of rest: taking down porch swings, mowing lawns, or changing furniture around in the parlors. A few events had been announced for the holiday. Major Tinkum was going to stunt his Curtis Jenny over the Ohio River and his wife Cayce was going to walk the wing. Murph "Mile-a-Minute" Mooney, former Glory High track star and popular free-lance Christmas card salesman, was going to race a seven-foot Lithuanian all the way down river to McKeefrey. And that night there was to be a concert by the Prison Band.

Around noon I was all alone in the barber shop, dressed up like a fop—and a fool, too, because I didn't even plan on taking in the band concert. Still, maybe it was a hunch made me spruce up a little that morning. For I had just finished combing my hair down flat and neat when I spied the three of them coming up the deserted sidewalk on the other side of Seventh Street: Natalia and the two little girls. They marched right across the street, too—making a big racket, talking and joking about things, and pulling that half-busted, old, child's wagon behind them—till directly they stood right out front, staring through the window, waiting for me to come unlock the door.

You close, said Natalia, with a flirty shrug. Aw, sure! I bet you close! Everybody close today. Sure!

And she chuckled deep inside.

Even Natalia! she laughed. *I* close today.

Well, yes, I *am* closed, I said. Yes. And No. In a way No. And in another way Yes.

I cleared my throat, scratched my neck, commenced over.

Yes, I said. I just this minute opened.

She smiled like the sun; it brought back summer, a-hurrying.

Yes? she cried. You hair-cut Sophie?—Mariya? You hair-cut them kids pretty like you hair-cut my Milosh on Saint Vitus Day?

Well, I couldn't say a word for a minute. Because somehow I couldn't get it through my head: Natalia there, what she was saying, me there looking at her—none of it seemed real. She didn't understand my stillness either. Because she looked worried a minute, then gave a rich laugh and fetched a dollar bill out of her patent-leather purse and waved it under my nose.

Pay cash hair-cut; she cried, smiling. No credit. No pay-later haircut Sophie—Mariya. Pay cash. Credit bad thing this here town!

And she swung her slant-eyed, savage stare off up the empty morning, while a smile turned in the edges of her mouth like flame curls burning paper, and the look those eyes gave Glory, it was a whip that bit but made no sound.

No credit! she shouted softly in that milky voice and laughed and I saw the painted fingers on her flowered hip digging the round flesh, warm beneath the flimsy of her frock. Natalia Lazarevitch!—only one in this here town say: Okay, credit! Okay—sure! Pay later!

Then she turned her high chin round and set that stare on me, looking hard and deep for a spell, and then the look came kindlier; she had that kind of eyes: hard like agate now, cold as river-ice, and then—in a twinkle—soft as big, wet marigolds. She smiled, seized Mary's fingers in one hand, Sophie's in the other, and herded them through the open doorway. Now as she bent, first from one to the other, laughing and whispering low, fast words in Serbian, I couldn't keep my eyes off her hair: those braided coils, that thickness like the good grain of clean-turned wood, but the color—well, how can I tell you?—I've seen it somewheres in country kitchens long ago: that smoked-gold gleam like copper kettles get—a sooty glitter; and something like the color of the twined and toasted loaves of that queer, shiny bread they sell in Hunkie mill-town bakeries. It was all I could do: keeping my hand back; my fingers ached with wanting to touch that hair.

But it was the hair of little Sophie I found presently beneath my hands, while shy Mary waited her turn, sucking a pink thumb now and then and, each time, Natalia, murmuring some low, strange word, would gently strike the plump fist from her lips, then settle back to watch my handiwork, while—once now and then—shouting some teasing, foreign words at Sophie and Sophie'd answer back and then all three would laugh. My hand shook some; I'll not deny that those were the two slowest, carefullest haircuts I ever gave. Can you wonder?—with *her* right there, not eight feet away; so close I could hear her breathe and the rustle of her clothes when she moved and, each time she'd laugh, I'd look in the mirror and see her bright lips leap like redbird wings and fly back from the white flash of her teeth; I'd see those fine, small bosoms spring and jump in her common, gaudy dress at every gasp of almost-weeping laughter—Lord, you could feel that woman's heat like standing against a round stove in a store!

And I've cut children's hair by the hundreds in my thirty-seven years —it wasn't that. It was her watching me work, watching the scissors and comb in my fingers and looking out to make sure I did it pretty, the way she said I hair-cut her Milosh: special, de-luxe, nothing but perfect would do. You'd have thought they were young princesses that came and clambered up to sit straight-backed on the child-board in my barber chair that day: the little, laughing, whispering daughters of a queen; some empress from a land too wild and beautiful and queer to put on maps, and not ever in the coarse and common colors of this poor schoolbook earth. Yes, I had to work slow, careful—my hands shook so, with her watching, but even if she hadn't had eyes to watch me, even if she'd been blind as old Ransome, the piano tuner, just her there—being—that would have made me tremble. And under my finger-tips the fair, clean hair—fine as milkweed floss—of bold Sophie and the shy Mary and me knowing that each of them was a smaller piece of her, until at last they got to seem all one, all Natalia, and me the man to head that footloose home. Every time I breathed the whole damned barber shop seemed filled with them; it reeked of the scrubbed, wash-tub immaculateness of them all: that smell of cleanness, starched cloth, girl-smell—a crazy kind of musk and yeasty sweetness, like a walking bake-shop smell that went with them where they went. Till, as I say, they seemed mixed up in one: soap and clean hair and the fresh-ironed gingham of cheap dresses that had been washed too often because she would sooner have them shabby rags than not be just as clean as the pink-scrubbed skin beneath the darned and threadbare sleeves and rickrack hems and the little girl necks like bobbing flower stems in collars raggedy as wornout valentines.

And I was hopping mad on top of that—just perfectly furious thinking what I'd say if somebody like A.K. or John or Holly Smithers or maybe some of their wives was to show up right then and make some smart remark; I kept on having these imaginary conversations between them and me—they'd say something cute about me having that common harlot in my place and cutting her children's hair and then I'd think up a comeback to that and end up throwing them all to hell out in the middle of Seventh Street anyways. In a way, I was half-disappointed nobody like that did show up; I sure had some snappy quips, real sarcasm, if ary one of such as them dared open his yap. But nobody came. And it's just as well they never, I reckon. It took me long enough to get done as it was and I drew it out a little extra anyways, wanting to please her, wanting to keep her there a spell more. And I never gave two better child haircuts, if I do say so. And when I was done, Natalia clopped over, like somebody who'd never got the hang of walking in those high spike-heels; she scrambled her fingers in her shiny, violet purse and fetched out some money.

How much cost? she said.

I waved my hand and got red-faced; I stared down at the little wisps of pale curls round my shoes. I couldn't bear stepping on them.

Nothing, I said softly, and shook my head and still couldn't look up at her.

She was quiet a minute and I didn't have to see her dark eyes to know they were blazing.

How much? she whispered, sore as hell. One dollar? Two maybe? How much cost hair-cut my Sophie—my Mariya!

I just shook my head and stared at her high-heel blue shoes and the slim ankles in the white cotton ankle socks.

Free, I muttered. I done it free, that's all.

She jammed two wrinkled dollar bills in my hand and stood back with a little snort of scorn.

Free? she laughed, and said some more words in her own queer tongue and the little girls both laughed. *Free!* she mocked. No such thing as free in this here town! No free, mister! And no credit! Natalia Lazarevitch—she only credit in this here town! Here! Take!

And she waved another green dollar bill an inch or two from the tip of my nose.

More? she sneered. Four dollar maybe?

And that's right when I got mad and snatched the dollar out of her fingers and crumpled all three of them up and threw the ball of green money in the cuspidor.

Not four! I shouted. Not three neither! Not a goddamned one. Haircuts for grown-up adults is a quarter in this shop and kids is twenty. But I meant them two as a gift. And it wasn't meant as barter neither. I reckon there's nothing now you've got I'd want much to swap for, lady. Why, they really got it smeared all over you, didn't they?—A.K. and John and the rest of them!—they really made you stink a little with their greed, lady! Why, you don't even know the face of common kindness any more. I guess you must have sold them bastards a little more of yourself than you reckoned to!

Bold Sophie stared and shy Mary sucked her thumb. And Natalia's eyes narrowed, searched, got wider then, and darker, deeper somehow: older than some queen's eyes remembering her dead king's ways or the real ways of any man—she'd been so long away from that, I guess, she'd clean forgotten how to judge a gesture's honesty or filth. But suddenly the old softness swept back in her eyes: wet marigolds lit up again by sun. And she shrugged and gave a queer, sad laugh and clattered off, beautiful and foolish in those high heels and dime-store anklets, and went to the marble shelf behind the chairs and commenced lifting the tonic bottles, one by one, and raising each one to her nose with gingerly and childlike carefulness, sniffing the tops before she put them back. I smiled and went right to the back where I kept them: the three bottles of the tonic that nobody but him ever wanted. When I handed it to her she took it, sniffed, sniffed once more, than a third time, harder, and her dark eyes burned like altar candles.

Hah! she cried. This one! Sophie—Mariya!—come! Hey!

And she doused their bowed, obedient heads—Lord, it made me think of some wild, foreign baptism!—and fetched a comb and doused their bright hair some more with the stuff and shy Mary took a deep breath, smelling, smiling, while bold Sophie only smiled a little—in her mouth's corners—her mother's smile, and stood still and straight and awful proud while Natalia's strong hands worked the comb and patted and laughed, straightening a lock here or a stray strand there, and cried a little and stroked hard with the brush, sniffing and laughing some more and crying some more and then murmuring things in Serbian which somehow sounds like both. With the brush in the right hand, the comb in her left she stood back then, cocking her head, judging her work and presently gave a grunt that it was right. Then Natalia shut her eyes and drew her head back, breathing in deep—smelling, I reckon, the unearthly, godawful sweetness of that Elwell's Authentic Louisiana Jasmine—and her long nostrils flared like a mare's does, and I watched a little pulse beating in the tall, milky column of her throat while she kept on smiling a spell more—smiling harder, it seemed, at some thought that went roaming back—and then two wild tears sprang swimming out and hung in the brush-thick lashes of her clenched lids. But right away she flung her eyes open wide, shook her head fast and laughed a shout and went running at the two little girls, waving the hairbrush, threatening and hollering, jolly and teasing.

Outside! Go! Go! Outside now! she shouted, whacking their bottoms and hurrying them shrieking and laughing out the door and down the steps. And you *wait* now! You hear, Sophie!—Mariya! You wait now! I come. You hear!—*wait* now!

And she came back and stooped and picked up the green wad of money where I'd thrown it like an old quid, stared at it in her fingers, shrugged, chuckled and stuck it back inside her purse. Then she turned and came over and stood in front of me, close to me, and studied my face real careful all over; her eyes were still wet; dark—the way it looks inside a great pine forest after a rain—and I knew it was a dark of kindness, and I have prayed since that it was, maybe, something more.

Now, I give *you* something, she said and touched my cheek with a finger.

Sure! I give *you* present now, she cried in a low soft voice. I give you thing I never give one man since my Milosh—

Natalia gave a thoughtful sigh while her queer, dark eyes searched my old, silly, American face and I could feel her slow breath against my chin.

—Not even man I do bad thing with, she whispered, savage, and lifted her fingers to touch my other cheek. Never! Not one man in this here goddam town! I never give *this* thing! Oho, never! I give this thing only my Milosh. Now—I give you.

And Natalia Lazarevitch held my head in all her fingers while she lifted her face and gave me one soft, slow kiss across the mouth.

Some days go and you never know what happened to them. The summer Mama passed over—it was ten o'clock in the evening—and I couldn't tell you what I did till sunrise of the next morning; it was the look of the daylight told me Mama was gone. A thing happens to you— a death, a wonder—and you look round directly and it seems like two minutes has ticked-off but it's really hours, months, maybe years that's gone. That day—that's how it was.

Around sundown Densel Yoho came tearing up to my room, two steps at a time, all out of breath, and sat down, panting, with both hands on his knees, in the canebottom chair by my bed. He didn't even look at me lying there on my back; he just stared wild at the worn place in the dusty Oriental rug.

Well, it's happened, he said. She waited all this while—the whole summer. Didn't I tell you, Hen? She bided her time and then, by God, she struck like lightning. Didn't I tell you she was feeling it all out, waiting, biding her time, Hen?

What's happened, Densel? I asked quietly.

Her. That one. The Hunkie widow, he said. Serbian. Whatever. Her and them two little girls—Hen, they've rung every doorbell in Glory this afternoon. By God, they really made the rounds, hauling that kiddy wagon behind them like a chariot of fire!

What the hell are you talking about? I said, sitting up on the bed.

Her. That Serbian. Or Whatever, he said, smiling. Woman amongst women. A justice amongst men. Lord God, Hen! Nigh every doorbell in Glory—there's hardly a one she's missed. Her and the littlest one, Mary—up on the porches, ringing the bells—or knocking on the screen doors. Polite knocks, too. Get that, Hen—easy, genteel knocks. Polite; but businesslike. It was a spectacle long to remember: her and the littlest one up there on all them porches, knocking, ringing, one house after the other. Whilst the oldest gal—what's her name?—the one they call Soapy —her standing out front on the sidewalk, by the kiddy wagon, reading from that big cloth-backed ledger book—calling out the Party's name, how many services rendered, the total bill due. Three dollars at one place—nine or maybe twelve dollars owed next door. A few lucky ones like A.K. and Doc Stribbler headed her off and paid her before she got as far as the porch steps. Cash, too. And when they give her a big bill the gal Soapy made change from a stogie box full of greenbacks in the kiddy wagon. Then her and the little one would go on to the next one. And whatever amount the gal Soapy found in the ledger column she'd holler out that number. And that was it. She could have asked three times that much and got it, too—they'd have paid just to get her out of sight before the little woman saw. But she's honest. Not a penny more nor a penny less—she only asked for what she'd earned—hard earned. One of the wives would answer the door now and then. Quite a few ladies screamed, fainted, went into hot flashes and sinking spells. And whenever that happened, why, her and the little girl Mary went and sat politely on the porch steps to ride out the storm. Sooner or later the man of the house come running with the cash. Anything to get her out of the little woman's sight.

I laid back down on my pillow, sick-hearted, picturing it: those proud, strong hands held out like a common bill collector, that brave face shamed.

John Grimm had a light stroke a little before three o'clock, Densel went on. His missus phoned Holly Smithers and demanded he rush right over and put the woman under arrest. Holly knew better. He was next page in the ledger. He came simpering and soft-soaping out the front door before she got near his porch. He figured to wheedle and bluff her off his lawn. She turned and said something in Hunkie—or whatever talk to the big girl. And she—what's her name?—she, Soapy, she reached in that old wood wagon and fooled around amongst a big pile of souvenirs and directly she come waving something over her head like it was Flag Day. A pair of initialed BVD's. I reckon Holly'd left them down in her bedroom once—probably one of them nights when Tacky Bledsoe used to go down Water Street on the city motorcycle to fetch Holly home drunk in the sidecar.

This town has crucified that poor woman, I groaned, staring at Mama's picture in the pale light of early fall evening.

Crucified her! Densel said. Why, Hen, how so? I'd say Glory has shared with that ignorant immigrant the homely business creed on which the Republic is founded. It has opened to her the golden pages of the thrifty Christian principles on which the Home is built. And don't never fancy she's such an ingrate as to let those lofty lessons go by unlearned—unprofited—unappreciated! It was Credit, don't you see? They taught her that one word from the beginning. They shoved that word in her face like an empty dinner plate—they nailed it to her wall like a sheriff's eviction paper—and then they whipped the rags off her babes' backs with it. Well, that's one word in English she learned good enough to savvy its meaning and worth and, I guess, learn how good it makes you feel to accommodate somebody and tell them there's no hurry about paying. Even when they held out cash-in-hand, I bet she told them to fold it again and stick it back in their vests and pay later. Credit. The one word they taught her good. Good enough to give credit to them who didn't even need it nor ask for it—credit, what's more, to them very same ones who'd not given her credit for a soup bone nor a loaf of stale store bread for her kids' supper. So that's how she's been putting-out to them all summer long—on credit. Well, what's being more American than how she done? Or Christian either? I mean, to give them sanctimonious tightwads the kindly terms they wouldn't give her. How's that for turning the other cheek? Oh, Hen, the beauty—the naked, lovely justice of this day! Lord, I don't see how this town can afford to lose a woman like that. She's a living symbol for our children. If Glory has a bit of sense they'll make her stay—they'll draft her if they have to! She could give speeches every few weeks to the Lions Club and get up and talk at a few Rotary Luncheons. And then, maybe, every Sunday or so, she could give a little chat to the Christian Endeavor or the Methodist Women's Bible Class or maybe even take over old man Toombes' pulpit and preach the regular sermon—off-hand, I'd suggest something on the Golden Rule. Then maybe they could pay her off with a few good hot chicken-pie church suppers. I reckon she'd enjoy a good meal or two after the lean summer she's spent. Not that she appeared exactly puny nor run-down up there in town this afternoon. When it comes to nourishment, a woman like that—

Whatever kept her from starvation—God knows, I muttered, staring at the cracked, old wallpaper on my ceiling.

As I was commencing to say—Never you mind about a woman like that starving, said Densel. A woman like her—just never you mind. I reckon the old Hunkie miner's widow give the little girls their meals. And you can bet she wasn't in much danger this summer of getting throwed out of her house for any back rent. If Harp Follansbee had so much as whispered "Eviction" in that woman's ear he'd have been black-balled by the Moose, castrated at Kiwanis, and shot by a Legion firing squad.

God knows, I went on, heedless. God alone knows what kept her strength up all these weeks.

Outrage, I reckon, Densel said. The body heat of hate. God knows—you're right, Hen: God *does* know. And sometimes it must just scare Him a little—looking at that wild rib he took out of Adam. God looking and seeing a woman like that, with a wildness like that—burning inside her like a coke oven. Well, Hen, you remember all them talks we had this summer—down at the Crystal, under the billiard lights—nights I told you about that wild, crazy female ferment I could watch working inside that woman like too much yeast in a bottle of warm homebrew. Don't you understand it yet, Hen?—how a woman like her can hibernate inside herself like a bear in a cave and live off the burning fat of her own wrath, and sleep, curled up, throughout whatever. And live on little else but that. Just holed-up there inside herself like a winter bear, sucking on that big, bitter paw of her instincts' own sweet vengeance and the long, little justices of time. And not minding all the slow while it takes neither, knowing when spring comes she'll uncurl, thaw out and go eat. And square up for a few things while she's at it. It's something they've got and we don't, Hen. I mean natural patience. We don't have it and we never will. I mean the kind of patience—like body fat—that nature gives women because they're the only humans that ever really have to learn how to *wait* for things.

Densel sat a spell, staring. Then he gave a queer, bitter little chuckle, pulled his folded, sweaty handkerchief out from under his collar and commenced cooling his red face with a cardboard fan from Tom Peace's Funeral Parlor.

Yes, it's been quite a day, Hen. Quite a day, said Densel Yoho. They canceled the foot race to McKeefrey, called off the band concert at the prison, and that damned fool aviator's wife has been up there walking that aeroplane wing for the past three hours and not a living soul but small boys has come out to wave at her. Quite a day. It looks like quite a night, too. A lot of the boys tonight will have to sleep in their cars. Some others has packed up and taken the streetcar to Wheeling to spend a few days. And I understand the Mound Hotel and Tomlinson's both is sold out and quite a few army cots has been loaned to the Elks and the Legion by the Red Cross. For a Labor Day spectacle I'd say it has even beat the one thirty years ago when they brought Bryan to the camp ground to do the "Cross of Gold."

Densel cracked his knuckles nervously, one by one, and glared at the Maxfield Parrish picture over my washstand.

Makes a fellow glad he's single tonight, eh, Hen? he said directly.

No, I said. It don't particularly.

Densel was still a while more, brooding worse, and we listened to the westbound blowing for Glory somewhere up the harvest-smelling dark.

Hen, I know what you're feeling, Densel said. You got a bad case on that woman. I've always known that, Hen. I thought maybe if it was me that broke the news about what she done today and how she done it—how she come through it all just looking elegant—the only one amongst them all not looking common nor whipped. Hen, I didn't want you hearing it from some of them boys in the shop tomorrow morning. The way they'll tell it—now and for years to come. Ugly and ornery and mean. Some wise guy even made up a new name for her already—Tally Vengeance—but it'll never stick, Hen.

No, I know. It won't stick, I said. She's Natalia Lazarevitch. Serbian. Lady.

Whatever, said Densel. Anyways, I guess you ought to know now that her and them two little girls is down at the depot waiting to go. That's her train blowing now, Hen. I thought maybe you might want to go say good-by or some such thing.

I done that already, I said.

Anyways, he went on, in a soft, furious voice, like he was working himself up to a quiet rage again at the way everything is. Anyways, Hen, I just thought my coming up here and telling you and talking all this fool talk for a while—Hen, I figured it might help ease the hurt. But it don't—does it?

Nope, I said; my breath was all played-out somehow, I couldn't say another word to Densel—not even thanks.

Densel picked up the cardboard fan again and sat glaring at the funeral parlor ad printed across it in thin, black letters.

Still, by God, it was *that*, he said, with a soft, bitter chuckle and his voice was like he was talking to himself now. Something kind of glorious —something kind of beautiful and fierce moving amongst us here for a while. By God, it was *that!* Like somebody for once had beat the crooked wheel! Like they'd finally won the game in spite of the fix—the eternal, goddam fix!

Densel got up and swung his arms a little, flexing his muscles, loosening his joints; he cursed under his breath and went off toward the door.

I'm going down to Charley Seat's before he closes, Hen, Densel said, without turning around. I'm all out of gum. Charley's got the only gum-rack in Glory that stocks my brand.

I listened to his footsteps down the stairs; I sort of envied him.

So now I've blabbed it all and it'll get back to Glory sure as hell. Still, I don't care. When a man's in my trade and has to spend thirty-seven years of his life keeping still I reckon he's entitled, just once, to out-talk everybody else in Glory. So, I don't care how many people know what I said or how sore they get or how many customers I lose. I've got me a nice nest-egg laid away. I'll get by just fine. And when my will is read, half goes to Marcy Cresap's TB Sanatorium—that's for Mama. And the other half—well, never you mind who that's for! Though, I reckon by now that's no secret to you either.

Natty Vengeance is still around Glory—in name, in whispered memory, sometimes in laughter, sometimes in awe. It was Natalia Lazarevitch went away that soft, fall night. And who knows?—well, the B. & O. runs eastbound through Glory, too. And if, one of these nights, Natalia Lazarevitch should come back and I'm not around any more to wave hello or cut her children's hair or ask her what I always wanted to but never could figure out how, I just want her to be all right. I mean, I don't want her ever again having to take those two children and go dragging a busted kiddy wagon up cool, rich streets just to get whatever her flesh and spirit tells her it happens to cost to stay alive on this earth a little while and still not stop being beautiful and mean and Serbian and unbeaten and proud and female. Just because a queen has her country stolen off the maps is no reason to have to go wandering away like that with two sleepy-eyed princesses, three one-way tickets, a paste-board suitcase full of rags and only one or two hundred dollars just to get her somewhere, anywhere, up the line. Somewhere, someday I want Natalia Lazarevitch to be a real winner in the little while of her life.

Play ball! yells Densel way off up the summer darkness of the Glory streets; there's a wind in the leaves and his voice is almost faint.

I get real mad about something all of a sudden. I run to the window, move the electric fan off the sill, pull in the window screen, and poke my head and shoulders out into the dark. Over my head I see the fixed, still stars in the windy autumn night; but they don't faze me one bit.

PL—AY BA—LL! I yell in a voice so loud you'd think I was holler-ing it at the world.

Doctor Janus Dalzell

Don't look at me that way. Do you think God or anyone on earth gives you the right to sit in judgment on me for going over with the others that day? I did what I did because of something I read in a woman's eyes, that's all. No, it was more than that. I did it because I believed it was right. The doctors of Mound County were in the right from the very first. The Cresap woman was wrong, that's all. Don't turn your head and walk away. Listen to my side of it, for God's sake.

The Cresap woman was practising medicine without a license—can you deny that? You surely know the years and years of poverty and sacrifice it takes to become a doctor. Is that something a man should see stolen away from him by some meddling do-gooder, passing out prescriptions like a candy-butcher and keeping Apple County peopled with the scum of Angel Swamp? All right, I admit it. Those weren't the reasons that made me go over with the others. They're good reasons but they weren't mine. It was something I saw in Miss Margaret's eyes that day, back there in her wheel-chair where she sat watching me, hardly ever blinking, looking at me over the heads of the packed court-room, her lips moving silently to herself, her eyes sometimes brimming with tears, her eyes talking to me, pleading with me. I did what I had to do. What I thought was right. I went over with the others. I did it for Miss Margaret. And I would do it again. Miss Margaret had a stroke five years ago and is paralyzed. I feed her her meals, bathe her, tend to her, carry her to and fro from bed to chair, though that's not hard for me for she has dwindled to the lightness of a child. And none of it has been hard: I love my wife. Surely she knows that, whatever else she judges me for. Don't you think she knows that? Never mind, you wouldn't know. I've seen it often enough in her eyes. I know. Even though, since the stroke, she hasn't been able to speak a single word, nor even a whisper. Not a single spoken word to me until that winter's day. After the trial. After the Cresap woman was beaten and finished forever in Apple County. There in that courtroom when everybody was filing out, heading home. That's when Miss Margaret spoke to me for the first time in five years.

But never mind about that now. It was as much a miracle as anything I've seen in a quarter century of medicine. A bitter miracle. But never mind about that. I think I've got the right to try and set you straight about me, what sort of galoot I really am, and whether I'm what you think or maybe a skunk of a wholly different stripe or maybe even not so bad at all.

Have you got any notion in your mind what it means to grow up in the eighteen eighties in a town like Twelve Dozen, West Virginia? They're some beautiful little towns in this state but Twelve Dozen wasn't one of them: it was jammed down between four or five bare hills like a grey rock clutched in a man's dirty fist. Martha's Creek was nearby but it was never deep enough to swim in in the summer and when it froze in the winter it was too rock-studded to skate on. My three brothers Willy, Jake and Morgan and me had about one amusement in those days and that was going up to the big frame Hippodrome Hotel in the evenings to watch Bixby Lemons, the proprietor, bait the drummers. Bixby was a man built like a cement sack that had got wet and hardened; short and stocky with a bullneck, bald-head and close-set, ball-bearing eyes. For a dollar Bixby would let any man in the lobby knot up his fist and swing however hard he wanted right square at Bixby's nose. And to make the dollar's worth more interesting Bixby'd have the cross-eyed night-clerk tie both his hands tight behind his back. Once in a while I'd bet my brother Morgan a nickle that Bixby Lemons would get a black-eye or a broken nose but I always lost. Because there never was the drummer came to the Hippodrome Hotel that could swing faster than Bixby Lemons could dip his head, swift as a snake, and take the blow square in the middle of his cast-iron forehead. Then afterwards we'd all go up to old Doc Turner's house and watch while he liquored up the sweating, anguished drummer and set three or four broken bones in his puffed-up fist.

Morgan and I had a laugh about old Bixby Lemon's head the night before Morgan sailed overseas with his outfit in the winter of 1917. Then we had a drink and drank a toast to all those thousand broken-fisted drummers and Jake came up to the hotel room with his arms around two rosy-cheeked Red Cross nurses and Willy was playing "Tiperrary" on the jews-harp—it sure must have sounded strange in that swanky old New York Ritz-Carlton hotel—and after a while I quit singing and laughing both and just went over and stared down at the cold, windswept corner of Madison and 46th Street, feeling ashamed to be there in civies with the war all around me and my baby brothers all set to sail for France next day. Willy was playing "Dixie" on the jews-harp and Morgan was dancing with both of the Red Cross girls at once and, bad lung or not, I felt like the worst slacker in America. There was a party going on in the next room and somebody came to the door and asked us over and Willy and Jake and the two girls went but Morgan stayed. Morgan had seen me there by the window and just knew, I guess, what was going through my mind; Morgan was always closer to me somehow than Willy or Jake. He still had his bottle of Hunter Baltimore Rye in his hand but he didn't offer me any more; I guess he knew it wouldn't help much.

You done your best, old Bud, you done your damndest and we all know that, Morgan said. There's not a one back in the whole state of West Virginia could say you didn't do your best. But you know as well as me, old Bud, that the trenches aren't the healthiest place in the world for a man with one lung gone.

And a man fifty years old, to boot, I said bitterly. You might as well say that, too, Morg.

That was the last night I ever spent with Morgan. He and Willy were both killed in action that spring in the Battle of the Somme and Jake died of gas gangrene in a base-hospital two weeks after the Meuse-Argonne fighting that long, cold winter of 1918. It didn't hit me for a pretty good while. I had my practice back in Glory, I had Miss Margaret and though we'd never had any children we were close. Some grief's a kind of time-bomb. One sunny April morning I walked out of an office with a waiting-room full of patients, climbed into my Packard and drove all the way over the hills and through a dozen dirt-road valleys back to Twelve Dozen. Mother and Pa were both gone, not a soul there was kin to me, not a face on the street knew me as I wandered aimlessly around that ugly, lonesome town; it was 1923 and Jake and Willy and Morgan were dead and duly buried, honored, preached over, praised and made silly by holiday orators. It's a wonder I wasn't picked up by the town constable, if Twelve Dozen had one by then.

I walked those streets crying quietly to myself and not even bothering to cover my face or to wipe away the tears and snot and slobber of a grief that seemed so fresh I could hardly tell what it was grief about. And rage. Hate, I mean. A thin, hot line of hate that seemed to run through me from head to toe, like a skewer. Around nightfall I was played out; plenty of people had stared at me that day, nobody knew me, not a soul remembered. Before I went back to the car I went in the Hippodrome Hotel and asked for old Bixby Lemons. A man past fifty, mind you, yet I had it in my mind I might give Bixby a dollar just for that one classic, sucker swing. Even if it broke my fist. I had to smash something, you see. I can't explain. Somewhere down the one Main Street of Twelve Dozen a boy was twanging on a jews-harp. No, the day clerk told me. No, he said, Bixby Lemons died of the flu in the 1919 epidemic. And I went back to my car not crying now, laughing now, something a little more hysterical than the crying had been, something making me want to go back to Glory and smash something there. But, of course, the long drive home through the cool night hills straightened me out and Miss Margaret was crying and waiting in the parlor for me. And, of course, by then all the meanness and hate and wanting to smash something worked out of me. The long drive home through the cool hills and seeing Miss Margaret again. I'd be all right. But Miss Margaret wanted to know where I'd been so I told her I'd gone back to the old hometown, such as it was.

It had to do with seeing Morgan and Jake and Willy, mother, I said.

Janus, they're dead, she whispered. Janus, you're all feverish.

No, I'm not, I said. And I know they're dead, I said, feeling the last of the hate draining out of me. I know that, mother. I was looking around town just the same though.

Janus, don't torment yourself, said Miss Margaret. They were killed, brave boys.

Sure, I know, mother, I said with a funny smile. I had a queer idea in my head somehow I'd find them—well, their ghosts maybe—and they'd tell me why in the hell I wasn't killed, too!

But I was all right. The grief stuck like a thorn, though, and hurt sometimes, but I kept busy, busier than ever. I was the first doctor in Apple County to have an office equipped with X-ray apparatus; my bout with TB in the three years after medical school had ended in a collapsed lung and I'd gone back to the University for another year's work in Roentgenology before I set up my practice in Glory. I've done well here; almost all the X-ray work has come to me and, up to the time the Cresap woman set up shop in Apple County, I was top man in the TB business. I've got two cars: a Studebaker 'President' Sedan for fun, funerals, and the fancier sort of house-calls and the old Packard touring-car for calls out in the country.

I've thought a lot about Morgan, Jake and Willy in the last few years but all that queer, feverish hate I felt that day like a hot wire running through me: it's gone. I knew I'd be all right. The ache—that's the only word I can use for it: an ache it was, like the cramp in your groin and belly when you're young and you've been out in the spring moonlight too long petting with a gal in a buggy and not getting anywhere: that ache I felt still when I'd think of Morgan, Willy and Jake lying scattered so far apart under the grass of Arlington and the poppy-covered fields of France—that ache was to last a while longer and ended in a strange way, as suddenly as it had begun. Here's how it happened: my hands were just commencing to go bad then; they're pretty much of a wreck now: I've lost three fingers off the right and the first joint of the first two fingers on the left. It's my own fault, sure, but a man can't work with X-ray as constantly as I have in the past twenty years and not get careless. But back in 1924 it had just begun—the first joint of the left index was badly involved and the second finger was already bothering me some.

Blick took notice of it at Rotary lunch one day and asked what I was doing to arrest it and then bawled hell out of me and then he asked me why I didn't take off for a few months, at least; maybe take Miss Margaret to Atlantic City for the summer. I laughed him off and said I was too damned busy taking pictures of his botched-up set fractures and those cases of catarrh and miner's asthma that turned out to be advanced tuberculosis. No, seriously, he said, he was planning on a three month sabbatical and needed someone to take over his practice and handle his work as prison doctor up at the penitentiary. I thought it over a couple of days: Blick's schedule was an easy-going eye-ear-nose-and-throat routine, mostly a practice taken up by the town's well-to-do neurotics, tonsils and adenoids now and then, not much to do up at the pen: really a pretty light schedule during the slow summer months between flu seasons. Miss Margaret had had her stroke a few months before and I was really waiting on her hand and foot. As for what had begun happening to my hands, I never gave it much thought and even now I didn't give much of a hoot whether I got away from the X-ray or not, whether it got worse or better; I guess I've always been pretty well resigned to that getting me sooner or later and didn't much care; I've never been much of what you could call a hypochondriac. It was Miss Margaret I was thinking about; that's what decided me to take up Blick's offer. And to tell the truth the work at the prison was a kind of novelty in my mind. So Alf and I worked things out and he sent his Mrs. off to Lilydale, New York for the season's big spiritualist convention there while he lit out for his summer home at Pillicock Hill in the little valley southeast of McBurney's Point.

It started off as a pretty quiet summer, tending to Blick's families, doing a few T and A operations in the office; taking care of Miss Margaret left me time for about two hours' sleep a night but I didn't seem to mind it: there was something about that prison that fascinated me in a funny kind of way. I guess I spent more time up there than Blick ever had, more than I should have, I suppose. That's when I really got to know the Cresap woman well and I'll be the first to admit that I liked and admired her. There were more than two hundred active TB cases up there then and Marcy Cresap had the notion they deserved treatment every bit as much as if they were decent, law-abiding citizens outside the walls in Glory and I pretty much agreed with her. She and I both had the suspicion there were a lot more than two hundred lungers

behind bars up there and since the prison infirmary didn't have any
x-ray facilities I donated the old unit from my own office when I got
my new outfit installed that July and she and I commenced weekly
Monday examinations on men that looked like possibles. We got along
swell and I'll be the first to admit she's an amazing woman and I expect
I was about the only M.D. in Apple County—with one exception—
who felt sincerely sorry to find out how bad she'd gotten out of line.
And I hated to join in with the rest of the County Medical Society to put
a stop to her meddling. I even helped raise funds at Rotary to help pay
for plates and developing costs for the pictures we took up there and it
ended up with me paying for most of it out of my own pocket. But I
didn't know everything back then about Marcy Cresap, that was the
trouble. It was the trouble with a lot of us in the County Society; it was
only providence that we woke up in time to how far she was carrying
things. What with looking after Miss Margaret and Blick's practice and
the extra work up at the pen I lost about twenty pounds that summer.
And I'll admit there was still that ache in me sometimes when I was
alone at night and the faces of Morgan and Jake and Willy would shape
themselves out of some fancy of dark and moonlight and the wallpaper
on the bedroom ceiling. And then one Friday night that August—a bare
week before Blick came back—the ache stopped and it's never come
back and it was the night they executed that Calhoun County boy who
killed his wife and her mother.

It was the year before they put in the chair so it was a hanging and
I'd never seen an execution before, let alone officiated as prison doctor
at one, and yet I wasn't the least bit nervous in the world. I even went
down that Friday afternoon and watched while they tested the rope and
gallows with a hundred and seventy pound sandbag which was the
Schneider boy's weight and I couldn't eat a bite of supper that night
and Miss Margaret kept lifting her eyes slowly and curiously to my
face while I spooned her her meal and about halfway through she
pulled away from me and motioned faintly with her fingers that she
didn't want any more. Maybe she sensed my excitement or something, I
don't know, though I didn't mention a word about the hanging that
night and I told her the paper-boy must have missed us that night.
Every evening at eight or so I carry Miss Margaret into the big chair by
the reading light in the parlor and hold up the *Glory Argus*, page by
page, so she can keep up with things, but that Friday I wrapped the

supper garbage in it and told her the boy had missed us. I didn't want to upset her; she was nervous in a queer, quiet way anyways, her hazel eyes turning to me every now and then and her lips moving a little bit like she wanted to say something. Except that there was no reason for it I would have said she looked afraid. I don't know why but I wasn't thinking much about Miss Margaret one way or the other that night; I undressed her and got her into her night dress and kissed her and turned the light out in the bedroom and it was long before eight o'clock; I wasn't thinking about Miss Margaret at all that night, I don't know why but I was thinking about Morgan and Jake and Willy.

I just couldn't seem to get them out of my feelings somehow and the ache was somehow stronger than ever and a whole lot of memories about things I hadn't remembered for years; I wasn't even thinking much about the boy Schneider. I could see Morgan's funny smile clearer in my mind than I could remember seeing Miss Margaret's face at bed-time that night, clearer even than I could recollect my own face that I glimpsed briefly in the hall mirror before I went out the front door on my way up to the prison. And I felt excited, too, in a strange sort of way: all kind of het-up with that feeling you sometimes get that you're just about to turn a corner and come face to face with something.

Well, Schneider or Shields or whatever his real name was—he didn't get any reprieve that night—and I'm not going to go into the details of what his hanging was like because it hasn't a damned thing to do with what I've got to tell you. I remember standing there on the lower level, below the seats where the two Wheeling reporters and the boy from the *Glory Argus* and the rest of them were, I remember listening to the Methodist preacher up there with Schneider and the warden and the two guards, he was reading something from the Scriptures and I was down there with the stethoscope around my neck remembering things about Morgan and Jake and Willy that I hadn't thought of in thirty years. And they were happy, kind memories, too: things that brought the sting of tears to my eyes and the old ache seemed stronger than ever. Now, I want to make one thing quite clear: Schneider's neck didn't break when they dropped him, he just hung there a while and when he had quieted down I went over with the stethescope. And the thing I want to make clear to you is that even though Schneider's neck didn't break he hung there a more than sufficient time to be dead. The heartbeat I thought I still heard when I pronounced him dead—that was purely my imagination. This isn't exactly the easiest thing in the world to tell about because in a way, I suppose, it reflects on my objectivity and self-control as a physician. And yet I won't lie about it: I pressed that stethescope against Schneider's bare chest and it did almost seem to me—in my imagination—that I could hear the hard, strong pounding of his heart, though I know perfectly well that it was the pounding of my own, the blood that seemed to come rushing to my head in that moment when my thoughts were so sharply, keenly full of Morgan and Willy and Jake.

Even after they'd cut him down and I was alone with him upstairs in the prison morgue—his stripped, big hillboy's body stretched out with his toes turned-up and the rope-burns fresh in the flesh of his neck—it still seemed to me that when I pressed that stethescope under the nipple that the sound of a faint heartbeat was there. I guess I panicked a little —something that hasn't happened to me ever before in my life. I stared and the more I looked at that purple, contorted face the more it seemed to me that Schneider was still alive, that I'd made a monstrous error in a mighty serious affair, that I was somehow ruined and that, strangely, I'd disgraced the memory of my three slain brothers. You can see how my imagination had gotten the better of me. I was overdramatizing a simple matter out of all proportion to common sense. Because Schneider was dead all right; my reason as a medical man tells me that: I know the look of death, the angles and postures of it, the feel of its cold flesh, the cyanosis—Schneider was quite dead. That's why what I did next doesn't really matter.

The fact of my thrusting my crippled hands around the dead man's throat and tightening with all my power and keeping his broken throat in that savage grip so long that it was difficult at last to loosen my numb, ringing fingers—keeping that strangling grip around the dead man's throat till I was sure that he was dead (though I *was* sure!), keeping that grip until my sobs had stopped and my breath came back, choking that hanged man with my trimmed and half-amputated fingers until the last—the very last—of the old strange ache went out of me and with it my last thoughts about the sad futility of my brothers' deaths in France. I think you have the right to know about all this: something I've never told another living soul. I choked the hanged man with my hands in the prison morgue that night: a strange, queer thing—perhaps even a momentarily mad thing—to do. But I want you to know that Schneider was dead.

I suppose a smart alienist could make out a pretty good case against my sanity but, as things turned out, I never felt better, worked better, nor prospered more than I did that fall and winter. Blick got up at Rotary Lunch one day and I could tell from the smiles of Ed Follansbee and Ira Stribbler that they and the rest of the County Medical Society were in on the surprise—Blick got up and gave a short speech about my unselfish and brilliant work in Apple County in the whole field of respiratory diseases and especially tuberculosis and even more especially what he called "the selfless and disinterested pioneer work" I'd initiated up at the penitentiary. I might take time right here to point out that the man Schneider was tubercular himself and would have died within a year, and that choking to death the way he did—on the end of a noose—well, I've watched enough TB patients go out when the trachea, throat and upper respiratory system gets involved to say with certainty that hanging spared that boy a much worse death. Anyhow the Rotary and the County Medical Society paid me a pretty warm tribute at the luncheon that day and presented me with a plaque which, till quite recently, hung on the wall in the parlor beside the window Miss Margaret likes to sit by in her wheel-chair and besides that they fixed a little brass plate on the back-rest of my chair in the dining-room at the Mound Hotel: my permanent and regular seat at all Rotary lunches and the twice-yearly dinners of the County Medical Society.

Quite an honor, so far as I'm concerned—not much, I know, as honors go in this wide world, nothing, surely, as splendid or significant as the names of William, Morgan and Jacob Dalzell back in the American Legion hall in the hometown and on the big painted wooden Honor Roll of Monongalia County War Dead that's staked out on the lawn, under the big elms in front of the county courthouse, between the muzzles of the big, bronze Federal cannons. The plaque hangs in my office now; Miss Margaret doesn't understand some things I guess and she never will. That day in court when the Cresap woman was up before the whole of Apple County for trying, like a thief in the night, to steal from the men of the medical profession the hard-earned honors of their qualified positions—Miss Margaret sat in the back of the packed court-room throughout those three January days, sat there in her gleaming wheelchair with her eyes never moving from my face. And I tell you I tried with all my soul to read in those eyes what they were trying to tell me. And so I did what I did because I believed it was right and because I misread what those eyes were asking me to do, I suppose. Because when every member of the Apple County Medical Association save myself and old, senile Will Cecil—when all of the doctors walked out of the courtroom in mute protest right in the middle of the Cresap woman's shabby speech in her own defense—Doctor Cecil and I stood alone, Miss Margaret's eyes pleaded from me something I could not read and something which I couldn't have done even if I had understood her.

I was just standing there listening to the lies and sob-sister stuff the Cresap woman was pulling about the men of my profession in Glory and I was still thinking, at the same time, about the fight against disease being something bigger than personal considerations and for a while there I was like a man holding a rope-end in each hand in the middle of a tug-of-war. And all the while Miss Margaret's deep hazel eyes were watching me, talking to me, asking the impossible. Because the fight against disease is a matter of doctors standing together like soldiers, shoulder to shoulder: the fight against disease wouldn't stand much of a chance if the men best equipped to wage it didn't hang together. Lord, that courtroom was hot that winter afternoon: steam-heat and the packed bodies of three or four hundred people. And they were watching me, too: a sea of faces all fixed on me and old Doctor Cecil, and I bet three-quarters of those faces or, at least, members of their family were patients of mine.

The Cresap woman was making her defense and you can bet she was pulling out all the stops on the organ, though she wasn't shouting, she was just standing there looking at everybody and the court and telling them what she had done and what her opinion of the County Medical Society was. For some fool reason I thought about that chair over in the dining-room of the hotel where the Rotary luncheons and the County Society meetings were held. I watched the last of the backs of the doctors walking out of the court-room while the Cresap woman was attacking them and I couldn't help thinking about that little brass plate screwed into the back of my chair and I knew that plate was solid gold. The men I was watching file out, the men I was turning against, they were the ones who made it gold, their trust and tribute and fellowship made it gold. And here I was standing there beside an old fool like Will Cecil and turning my back on the men who had given me that plaque and that brass plate, and with it their trust and faith.

But it wasn't all as easy as that. Because I knew the Cresap woman—
in the beginning, at least—had done a good deal to get the sanatorium
money raised and I knew that—until she'd taken it on herself to start
practicing medicine, at least—she'd done a lot of good in fighting com-
municable diseases in Apple County. To hear her talk now though you'd
have thought she was the most selfless and disinterested pioneer in the
whole field and all the study and work of the County Medical Society
men didn't matter a hill of beans. You can call me a fool if you want
to but praise counts for something with me; a doctor doesn't get much
of it in his life and I've had little enough in mine. I don't mean that
praise means more to me than the good, solid knowledge of doing a
good job quietly and unostentatiously; I'm not a glory-seeker. But I
know one thing: it just made me furious to hear certain people in
Glory give Marcy Cresap all the glory and honor for fighting TB in
Apple County. I stood there in that hot, packed court-room beside old
Will Cecil and looked at the eyes of all the people I knew, the ones I'd
treated, ones I'd cured, ones whose loved family members I'd had to pro-
nounce incurable. I didn't know what they were thinking. I looked at
the plea in Miss Margaret's eyes and I didn't know what she was thinking either. I glanced quickly around at old Doctor Cecil; he was standing there, senile and queer and radical: a big man with a shock of snow
white hair and straight as an arrow for all his oddness and his eighty-
five years. He was smiling a little and his eyes seemed to me to be looking over the heads of everyone there, stubborn and prejudiced and un-
yielding. I doubt if he was even listening to what the Cresap woman
was saying: God knows he never listened to what anyone else in Glory
ever said and he had long ago cut himself off from the friendship or
even speaking-terms with his fellow doctors: there had even been talk
during the past few years of trying to have him expelled from the
County Society.

I suddenly felt I had no business being left alone there with a man
like that; I felt like a fool being on his side of an issue as big as this:
he was dead-wood as far as all this was concerned. The Cresap woman
was still talking and even I wasn't listening now, I shifted sheepishly
from one foot to the other and tried not look at anybody, not even Miss
Margaret, because I knew this was something I had to search out in
the deeps of my own soul. I found myself thinking of queer, unrelated
things. I thought about how proud Morgan would be of that brass plate

and I imagined him standing in front of me, looking at me with that old, crooked smile of his and laying his hand on my shoulder and looking down at my hands half eaten away by x-ray exposure and saying: "Don't you worry now, Old Bud. You've done your bit and it was in a war every bit as big as the one I fought in and you've got the wounds to show for it. Be proud, old Bud, and stick with your buddies because an army wouldn't last very long if buddies didn't hang tight. You never killed a German, old Bud, but just the same—." Morgan was that kind. He'd think that brass plate was every bit as important as his medal and I know he'd tell me so if he was still alive. God knows I miss him sometimes. The ache may be gone but I miss him. Sometimes the riddle of death gets too big for me to ponder and I just feel like I'd have been better off if I'd gone to France and died with Morgan and Jake and Willy; sometimes I get a feeling that it's all some kind of God's own joke and then I throw those damned lead gauntlets clean across my examination-room and go under the x-ray with naked hands. It's only occasional times like the tribute at that luncheon, the plaque, the brass plate and times like that that I realize I'm worth something, that I'm fighting for something in Apple County.

Well, at some point during the course of Marcy Cresap's oration I remember old Doctor Cecil calling to the other doctors to wait and hear what she had to say in her defense. But by that time I'd made my way down through the packed court-room aisle toward Miss Margaret. I knew by that time where I belonged; I knew my loyalties belonged on the side of the men of my profession. I heard Doctor Cecil's voice booming behind me and then it ceased while some of the doctors strolled back into the court-room out of curiosity, I suppose, to hear what the Cresap woman's wind-up would be; they were smiling, amused and she was close to the end. I elbowed my way over to the little clear space the folks had made for Miss Margaret's wheel-chair and she looked up at me as I laid my hand on her shoulder.

Well, mother, I said. It looks like this fiasco's about done. I think the people finally realize who's best able to look after their health in Apple County. Mother, let's celebrate and have supper tonight at the hotel.

But she shook her head at me and the eyes behind her glasses filled with tears.

What's the matter with you? I said. Are you sick? Is it too hot in here? Here, let me wheel you out into the fresh air.

But she shook her head at me again and I guess I got a little irritated because she pulled herself away from me, wheeled the chair back away from me, and kept looking at me in that queer way and shaking her head. After what I'd been through up there I guess I was about at the end of my rope; my nerves were edgy and I guess I just wasn't up to any of Miss Margaret's sulks.

Listen, mother, I said, patiently. Have you any notion of what I've been through up there today? It wasn't an easy thing to decide. I know the good side of the Cresap woman's work. Do you have any idea of what all was going through my mind while I stood up there beside that old doddering Cecil—standing alone there against every other member of the County Society; my colleagues and buddies? Can you appreciate what conviction that took? And do you know what finally decided me? Do you, mother?

She nodded with effort and her lips opened and her mouth and throat strained and worked, groaning with the effort to speak, her face twisted and her eyelids squinted shut with the struggle of shaping the word. And she said it; it came out thick and labored but I understood it all right; the first time she'd spoken in five years and when it came it was like a blow in the face.

Pride, she said; yes, that's what she said, and that's when I lost my head. Pride she called it, squeezing the word out of her paralyzed face with all the clutched, straining effort of her frail body. And I knew how she meant it, too: Pride like that kind the Bible means, that pride before a fall, the pride of vainglorious fools, and it wasn't that, it wasn't that, I tell you; I did it because I thought it was the thing Miss Margaret's eyes were begging me to do: I went over with the rest of the doctors because they were my buddies and we were in something we couldn't fight alone, nobody wins a war alone. And yet Miss Margaret had had the cruelty to drag out that word Pride and rebuke me for it; I tell you it was like spit in my face.

Pride! I shouted, but nobody noticed because a lot of the doctors were shouting with laughter just outside in the courthouse lobby. Yes, I'm proud, I said to Miss Margaret. But it wasn't pride the way I think you mean. Pride! I shouted it again. Well, now since you've found your-self able to speak to me today, mother, perhaps you'll tell me what's been going through your mind these last two hours while I've been up there suffering and sweating before the people of Apple County. Shame

I suppose you'll say. Is that what you were feeling about me while I was up there wrestling with my soul? Don't you know that I chose the way my conscience told me it was right to choose? Come now, mother! Do you mean to tell me that you didn't feel a little *pride* yourself? Pride for me?

But again she shook her head and again she clenched her face like a fist, gaping and gasping with effort till a little slaver gathered in the corner of her working mouth and her whole body trembled and strained to speak again.

Pi-ty, she said, at last.

I had to get away from her then; I love Miss Margaret, God above knows I love her but I had to get away from her just then or else say something that would forever scar the rest of our lives together. I found Alf Blick outside in the smoke-filled lobby; he was laughing at something Ed Follansbee had been telling and four or five other members of the County Society were passing around a silver flask of moonshine, drinking toasts and I got Alf aside and asked him if he'd mind driving Miss Margaret home in his Buick and I'd come back and get her wheelchair later. I said I was feeling a little woozy from that damned courtroom heat and wanted air and that was true enough; I felt like something was choking me and my clothes were drenched with sweat. Ed offered me a swig of liquor but I turned him down and hurried off. It was cold outside, like there was snow in the air; the sky was slate-grey as cat-ice above the bare January trees but I felt like it was August inside my clothes and sweated like a fever had just broken. But the fever was in my mind and it was rising, not breaking, I guess, because right then I did a damned fool thing. I went over to the hotel; Jim Doobey, the day clerk, never even noticed me when I hurried through the lobby and into the dining-room. The kitchen doesn't start serving till five so the dining-room was deserted, not a soul there now, not even Clara McCluskey who comes there every afternoon to use the hotel pen to write a postcard to her married sister in Toledo. The chairs were all moved around and I had a little trouble hunting out mine, the one with the brass-plate, my chair of pride and honor. But I found it, way in the back by the door to the kitchen, under the gaslight where one of the kitchen help had been sitting, I guess, because there was a *True Confessions* left there on the seat. It was getting dark outside in the late winter afternoon and the light from the gas-jet by the swinging doors was wavery and poor. My brass-plate was still there and after I'd spit on my pocket handkerchief and rubbed it real hard a while it seemed brighter, clearer, almost like gold; bright as the medal on my dead brother's chest. But even as I stood there staring at it I knew something was broken, something spoiled and gone forever.

Pity! I whispered, spitting the word out, hurt and bitter, in the silence of the empty dining room. And then I commenced cursing softly to myself and my eyes filled with tears and I couldn't make out the words on the plate nor even the shape of it, just a blur of brass; something that had meant so much to me, something that was lost and spoiled forever for me now, it was just brass now—Miss Margaret had done that, she had taken away the gold of it with just two words—and I cursed softly to myself and fetched my overcoat open and fumbled around in my vest till I found the little mother-of-pearl pocket-knife Miss Margaret gave me the first Christmas we were married and I commenced digging at the screws that fixed the brass-plate into the wood of the chair-back; I broke the blade of the little gold knife twice but I got the thing unscrewed at last and stood looking at it a minute more there in my hand before I swore some more and bent it out of shape and dropped it in the cuspidor on my way out through the lobby.

I went out down the steps and crossed Seventh Street to the court-house, blowing my nose and hoping nobody'd see my face, what a fool I'd been, and I made up my mind I'd tell the boys, Alf and Ed and the rest, that some drunk or maybe a souvenir-hunter had taken the plate and it didn't matter anyway. It didn't matter anyway because a man doesn't really need that kind of honor if he knows he's right in this world, if he knows he's right with his conscience; I made up my mind I wouldn't let the boys replace that damned plate either and I swore right then that I'd find myself another chair to sit in at the luncheons and I've kept to my word; I can always spot that chair with the pocket-knife marks and the marks of the two little screws in the yellow oak and I've always made it a point to sit somewhere else.

It was colder, I felt a snowflake against my cheek and hurried back into the courthouse. I fetched Miss Margaret's wheel-chair and got it down the stone steps and headed home. It's a funny thing how an empty wheel-chair makes a man feel so awkward; I mean, you feel a little bit like a fool pushing an empty wheel-chair up the sidewalk, especially around dinner time when folks are usually looking out of their parlor windows watching for the newsboy or husbands coming home to supper. I pushed that wheel-chair up Seventh Street and watched the snow flakes gathering on the black leather of the empty seat. And the old rage, the old hurt, the ache, it came back for a minute and shook me like a chill. I lifted my face to the grey darkening sky and glared, filled with the most helpless fury, while the snow flakes brushed my face like little cold, jokes.

Who the hell you think you been kidding? I said out loud.

But I swear to God I don't know if I was asking Him or Morgan or someone else; I guess I never will know who.

Martha Ann Turk

As you came through the big white front door just now I'll bet you couldn't help noticing how bright and shiny all the brass things are: the knocker and the handles and the brass-plate round the keyhole and the name-plate with his name still there: the old-fashioned letters scrolled into it like wild, winged things in flight in a burning brass sky: William Quincy Turley Cecil, Doctor of Medicine, and even the key on the inside of the door and the latch and the hinges that don't even show: they came in for their share. They ought to be bright enough to notice for I've been out on the front porch the livelong morning with my good rags and a can of Golden Rule polish, rubbing that brass till it fairly smoked and a good thing, too, for I'd have been in for it today for sure without something to polish and so much to tell you about him and Marcy Cresap and the way things were and all the rest of it; when I'm mad or feel a bad cry coming on I'd be sunk if I didn't run quick and polish something for dear life, shine something till it sings with light and whether it needs it or not and there's always metal somewhere in this old, big house that needs it, though sometimes when I'm mad enough or too full of tears the brass won't serve: it's there's not enough of it, so I fetch out the old Cecil silver and light into that like it was three days till Christmas and shine and rub and polish all the old, grand things his grandmother fetched across the Alleghenies in an English chest in the time before there ever was a Glory, biting my lip and talking to myself and rubbing those soft old silver things till the light within them shines like the light in the eye of love and it does me a world of good for after a while all the grief and rage and elbow grease are clean played out of me and I can stare, at last, at my fool's round face like a silly blob of cream in the silver bowl of a spoon.

Such a morning was this one and such a mood was I in that there was nothing for me but the brass out front because I knew you'd be coming and I wanted the big white door to look its prettiest besides, so I've been out here since I sent the children up the river road to the school in Glory, rubbing away with my rags and polish long before the river fog rolled off and biting my tongue till it nearly bled to keep from saying things, even to myself, about the disgraceful Doctor Dalzell and the shameful way he told it to you: about Doctor Will and the things Doctor Dalzell called him and the lying, false-hearted things he'd have had you believe about Marcy Cresap and the way it all turned out in the court that day; my blood fairly boiled and the brass shone brighter and brighter in the green and shimmery light that rises from the river when the sun brushes it from its first waking rise in the cold autumn treetops of the eastern ridges.

Lying, false-hearted things he'd have had you believe about the day before the very last day of the whole, disgraceful court business last winter: the afternoon the doctors, every last man of them save William Quincy Turley Cecil, walked out first in the very middle of the little piece that Marcy Cresap stood there speaking in her own defense: attacking nothing but sickness and filth and greed; saying no word against a single one of those men of medicine who would not give her the courtesy of hearing her out, speaking no name of any one of them who had refused to visit the sick that she, on many's the bitter blizzard of a river night in March when the very snowbound hills of the roadless county districts seemed seized with the sickness of a stunning chill themselves, the sick that she had gone, at last, by sled, on some half-frozen horse, or sometimes waist-deep snowy miles on foot, to see and tend or sit by, at the very least, until they'd got their dying done. And never once in all those years administered spoonful, needle or a pill of medicine that one of those lazy-marys hadn't sent her out to give on his prescription while those fine Hippocratic gentlemen stayed snug and tucked in quilts beside their hot-water bottle wives and Marcy paid the druggist for the medicine from her own poor, shabby purse.

Oh, the brass sure must shine like God's own golden gates this sweet October morning, for I rubbed it till my fingers blistered at the wrath of my remembering those mean, ungenteel afternoons in last year's January court! For I was there and saw it all and heard it all and smelled it all, I might just as well add, for the courtroom was close and steamy and the air reeked with the stench of ungentlemanliness and worse and I mind well the sight, throughout those shameful afternoons: Judge Wofford, draped like a gaunt, black raven of bashless partiality, covering his thin mouth with his hands to hide the smiles that quivered in its corners and eyeing poor Marcy with an oysterish, wintry satisfaction and croaking a silent Nevermore to her good works into the grey soup meat knuckles of his clasped and disguising fingers. Yes, the brass sure must have caught the river's lights and winked and glittered good at you when you knocked today! Yet I was rubbing and polishing for pride as much as anger; remembering the way Doctor Will had stood up there, his blue eyes flickering in the bridled fury I so seldom saw in all the good, dear years I watched those eyes face every kind and sort of mortal creature and sickness and the aftermaths of all the kinds of human neglect and orneriness that you could fancy, saw him stand there and call to the men to stay and hear a lady speak her defense, asking them to stay if not as doctors then, at least, as gentlemen and Christians. While all the buttery little dairymen and You-Know-Who and Thingamujig, the real-estate partners, and Master Mighty from the mills and the coal lawyers with their truckling, dusty clerks all lolled about the court, paring their fingernails one minute and then peeling an apple the next and with the same blade, and the rich doctors' nurses propped up along the ringside seats like rows of cold-storage chickens stuffed with stale, sageless bread and with little sprigs of green giggling meanness, like sprigs of parsley sticking out of their You-Guess-Whats.

Yes, it was William Quincy Turley Cecil, him alone of all the doctors who stood by Marcy that day and presently five other people came and stood beside him, though none of them doctors, except Charley Williams who was a dentist, and Orville Birdsong from Cameron who is a Republican Committeeman but a gentleman and Christian nonetheless, and Tadd Cockayne, the fine and fearless *Glory Argus* editor, Mary Ellen Weaver who was a public health nurse like Marcy and young like Marcy once was, too: her face wild with the same hoping wildness Marcy's had when first it began to catch fire with her dreams. And it fairly makes my blood boil when I think of how Doctor Dalzell told it to you: not so much as breathing the name of a one of these and making you fancy, what's worse, that Marcy's cause was lost and sunk and done for, because it so happens that it was the very next day's session that she won and won despite the trifling and conspiring of the whole pack of them, won thumpingly because there wasn't a smidgen nor whiff or proof that ever she had taken it on herself to practice medicine nor done one deed amiss nor ever once acted outside her lawful authority under the US Public Health Service, nor ever given so much as a needle or spoonful of cure or comfort without its being within her legal duties and many's the time by prescription and with some lazy, greedy doctor's bidding, blessing, right of proxy, right of way and hurry-up wave and a "Please, for God's sake, go instead of me this bitter winter's night and leave me kindly to my quilts and steamy, warm wife."

She won, I say; there simply wasn't a legal tree to hang her from; though you'd never hear Doctor Dalzell say such a thing and you may thank his lying silence for the brightness of the door-brass this gold October morning with nearly a year gone by since that Then and this Now and so much that's happened in between, so much I can scarcely bring myself to the telling of it and never would dare hope an explaining of it, so senseless and sorrowful are those events since then, since that victory. And I can only helplessly tell of it: the thing that happened after the victory, that defeat that was to come with the end of that winter and come so senselessly that only a God more wise and just than we may judge or justify or even, I sometimes fancy, in a seizure of holy sadness more terrible than ours, that He Himself cannot somehow believe it and must strike the match of his lightnings and stare in the moment's glare in bafflement and gasp, sorrowed and confounded, and then go grieve it in the wind or wander off to weep it in His rains. Though it is true that Marcy Cresap won her fight last January and Apple County won, as well, and I know Doctor Will was right last spring when he said that Kindness and Loving everywhere on earth had won their little day that day though he added shortly afterwards that such victories are like the seasons and pass away and every field must yearly yield to the cold share of the plow and planting be begun again and all the struggle be begun again as if, each spring, no green new thing ever has split the earth before and sent up tender starts before to startle the eyes with each new summer's genesis.

Marcy won and Apple County won and we all forgot that that was only the winning of that then, for Marcy was soon to lose another fight, another thing, and Doctor Will—but don't let me tell about that yet for if ever I commence that part of the telling I'll be running away from you before you can sneeze twice, seeking my good polishing rags and the old Cecil silver and never get to tell you anything. And there's so much that needs telling: I've listened throughout the whole babble of what's gone before me, the sweet and the sour alike, heard all of the voices of Glory speak their mind and heart and maybe speak it truthfully and maybe not but speaking, I judge, the best they could, God pardon us all. I've listened, I say, and listened hard and fair and yet never once heard mention of the full and Christian name of William Quincy Turley Cecil, Doctor of Medicine, and it just makes me bite my tongue till my blood boils to have heard snap-purse sneaks like Doctor Follansbee and fat Blick and Wofford and old Stribbler and the lickspittle rest of them and not one man enough to ever say his name. And it shames me, what's more, that it should fall to me to tell you of him for I am worth so little to undertake so grand a duty, with no knack for words except my poor Welsh father's gift of using them too much and wantonly and none of my English mother's sweet gift of keeping still and making stillness speak as lovelily as rests in the music of a shouted song, nor having any education of my own past country-school fifth-grade, except the learning I've scissored out and pressed flat and stuck in here and there, like pastings in a fool's scrapbook, from hearing Doctor Will and reading the books he made me read from his great rich library and prowling myself among its high shelves since he went away that stormy April night, trying to pick and choose like a nincompoop child with its Saturday penny wandering amongst counters of candy all in boxes whose labels it can't tell one from the other. And whatever I say of Doctor Will I may be sure that Glory's scolds and gossips will twist it round their mischievous fingers into the shape of some indecency and for that I care not a whipstitch, praying only for the fairness of you who hear the telling of my voice that you will not think ugly things of his memory, forgetting me and my good name entirely, if you please: a foolish woman of thirty-six years who was his housekeeper and loved him like a kinsman for ten of those.

It was a summer night nine years ago that Vergil Turk grabbed his trombone and his painted cardboard hat and ran away with the circus, leaving me here with three helpless children and nowhere to go but down the river road to Lord knows where and it was on that very morning that Doctor Will said I was free to do as I pleased but that, indeed, he wished I would stay for he loved the sound of children in the great, cool silence of his mother's house and nobody since her had ever turned out a peach-cobbler to his taste save me and when I said that there'd be talk in Glory he said there'd always been talk in Glory and there always would be where he was concerned and it might be nice for them to have someone pretty to talk about for a change and he said that gossip was a tonic and a therapy for some poor souls and my staying on might keep them from the earth of Glory Hill a few years more. And there was talk, for I heard it myself and Lord knows I felt it often enough beneath the stares at church and it made my blood fairly boil to think of minds more gnarled and mean than lightning-cursed old apple trees who could fancy orneriness like that of a man like him, already in his eighties and with a memory of a youth more rich with women than could fill the lives of ten of them, a man whose mistress now was the fertility of his own intellect, a man kind as God's neighbor and educated in the finest schools of Europe and with a knowledge of medicine that would have shamed the best of them, and moreover it put me into a daily rage, until he taught me better, to have them think of me as a slut so forward and shameless as to carry on beneath the very roof and in the dwelling-place and very presence of my three half-orphaned darlings, Jewel and Sam and Joe.

But they'd have talked in spite of me, trust in that, and doubtless the talk began the very week of the night Doctor Will took in Vergil and my two babies and myself already big with Joe, welcomed us in from the rain of the river road the night the circus went broke up on the flats below the smelter and turned out Vergil with nothing but a wife, his hacking cough, ten cents, his cardboard hat, trombone, a straw suit-case full of clown silks and a piece of tent-canvas to keep the downpour off his babies' heads: Lord, the very sluice-gates of heaven seemed bursted that night and Vergil and me and the kids went off in the rain across the meadows till we spied the old, great frame house under the willows on the river bank, below Glory, at the dwindling cow-path end of Water Street. And that was the night my fingers first lifted the brass door-knocker which I was to keep polished brighter than burned gold from that night on. He took us in and when the summer morning shone all whites and blues and greens and yellows like a country salad in a bright delft dish, poor Vergil fussed and fidgeted above the plate of sausages and corn-meal mush and the babies laughed and flung their oats and cream in careless spoonfuls all round the great, huge kitchen floor while the old man watched and smiled till Vergil pursed his lips thoughtfully as if he had nothing but money in the old suit-case upstairs and asked the old man about trains and Doctor Will smiled some more and said he feared they didn't allow trombones in the fancy parlor-cars of the B&O and waited a spell then, that gracious wait of gentle folk who know that the difference between the offering of a kindness and the tossed coin of charity abides in the very spirit of that measured, genteel pause.

Why hurry away? he said presently and fetched Jewel off her straight-backed chair and commenced to feed her oatmeal from the blue bowl on his knee. Stay as long as you please, my dears. I love the sound of children in a house and the feel of good people in the old rooms around me. Besides that, sir, I have many patients and very long office hours and often I'm called off into some roadless, distant district of the county and don't get back till long past midnight and you'd have the whole house to yourselves while I'm at work or away down river or off all day in the hills. I know it must sound quite selfish of me, sir, but even in a house of so much space and plenty I find myself longing for the sound of someone moving in the other rooms.

I sat there fairly shrinking into my clothes for Jewel had oatmeal and cream all over one leg of the old man's clean alpaca trousers and was daubing a spoonful of it now all into his neat, long white moustache; poor child she meant to feed him.

Thank you, Doc, Vergil was saying. Couldn't think of such a thing but thank you kindly anyways. No No No, couldn't think of such a thing!

But I knew Vergil and I could read his poor wayfarer's trifling eyes and the very set of his thumbs in his suspenders that, indeed, he had already thought of such a thing and had made up his mind and was good as settled, for a spell at least, and his stomach growled like breakfast was moving over to make way for lunchtime and supper and so on through a whole almanack of meals and till the itch and whim to wander should seize him again. And Doctor Will he made it all so easy— and what is gentility but such easemaking?—saying again how he loved the racket and whisper of children and the feel of people in a huge, old house so full of rooms like an empty candy-box with nothing but a fragrance of old chocolates in the honeycomb of its quilted paper rooms, though in time I came to know that it was not true loneliness that made him want people round about: the very richness and provendor of a mind too full of thoughts ever to be lonely was something that he constantly must share: that great, wood house with all its ancient wrinkled mirrors and the oil-paintings in the halls and the waiting, thinking silence of his books and the striking of the clocks like the cough of old, gold birds and the silver spoons and spode and boneware that never touched a mouth and the huffing, steamy rebuke of a potful of kitchen coffee with no one to drink it with at night while he shared some simple, highborn country thought that had come to him in the winds of his daylong county drive.

And we were not the first to share his jokes and roof and books and vittles and thoughts: the house had nearly always had some wanderers in its rooms: gypsies and wayfaring families, the rootless of this cranky, footloose land, or sometimes quaint, queer, doddering delegations of old school friends: doctors who had studied with him sixty years before, and more than one thief, I suspect, and now and then a runaway from the prison-farm, or some child or grandfather or man-and-wife that he'd fetched in from Angel Swamp or Misery Hollow to lie in featherbeds as old as the Republic and get their strength back sipping hot barley-and-mutton broth from a recipe that had warmed Jefferson's old bones or die with some sweet, faint comforts, at least, and with kindness holding their hand to the very last wink of the candle: yes, these—the very ones the hospital wouldn't take—these were the ones the County

Medical Society named when they tried to get Doctor Will booted out
of the Association for running a hospital without a license as they called
it, though Doctor Will knew the law and never went over the number of
sick a doctor may take into his own home to treat, nurse and tend.
Sometimes when they were bad and far-gone and near-the-end Marcy
Cresap would come and lend a hand while Doctor Will was off somewhere in the county and her presence in that house all night sometimes,
that was only another splash of coal-oil on the dirty little campfires of
their gossip and false-witnessing.

They laughed at him in Glory and spun tales like spider's nests and
called him a dirty, ignorant old country doctor and he was none of
those things save old: spotless in summer in his white linen suits and
with degrees in doctoring from great schools in Lausanne, Switzerland
and Paris, France and who could have still taught medicine to the oldest
of them in Glory and he was no more "country" than the sky itself whose
blue he had seen through the spires and domes and belfries of Europe's
greatest capitals and he was not even old, except in years, and unless
thought and wisdom and mercy themselves are old. And in the years after
Vergil ran away I was his guest, though I fought through every day to be
his servant; I was his friend, though I would have proudly given myself
to be his lover—despite Vergil and the blood-hot longing he had left
behind him, burning like stoked coals in my bones—but he never wanted
that from me: his life had had its rich fill of that, I reckon, for there were
the two oil-painted pictures of Suzanne that hung in his plain, little office
and the tiny actress on the library mantlepiece with her little waist
pinched in with whale-bone stays and her great, dark eyes above the
painted Japanese fan smiling sadly out at someone from the little frame
of carved sterling with its little scattered rubies and the queer white
jewel of smokey, milky light, hung like a stage-play moon above her
head. He never mentioned her, though I guessed she was French for I
cleaned the glass with ammonia-water twice a week and polished the
silver bright as poplar leaves and rubbed the little moon till it shone like
a queen's pearl and, though I couldn't read them, I always saw the frail,
foreign words she'd written there with green ink in a child's big careful
hand and of course I knew the word Paris and the year 1889. Though
I always guessed that she was not Suzanne, the other one, the one in the
two hand-painted pictures—I could tell by the eyes and her build, for
she was naked as Eve and proud to show herself, as I was myself in my

own girlhood when I married Vergil that night in the hotel down the river in Kentucky, proud in her flowering girlhood with breasts like round, firm custards turned out onto a plate and fine, long round thighs and flesh so delicately veined with life and pink like cream poured over a bowl of crushed, fresh berries with the stain of the juice just ever so faintly mingling.

The two pictures of her hung on the wall above the old desk in his office and though he had spoken of her often I would never have known her name if I hadn't heard it from the men from Wheeling the summer morning they came and devilled him for hours to sell her to them and he sent them away with a laugh and armfuls of lilacs from the yard. And you can be sure that Suzanne's pictures came in for their share of Glory's talk of the queer, old, dirty country-doctor in the big house at the end of Water Street. And though the pictures never shocked me for they were the very image of a proud girl's innocence and glory and I have seen sluts and whorish hypocrites in throat-high blouses and ankle-length skirts and yards of petticoats while underneath the sneakiest, outhouse thoughts lay festering like a wound beneath its bandage of dirty gauze; though, as I say, Suzanne never made me blink an eye, still I was puzzled, when I first walked into it, at the bare, comfortable plainness of Doctor Will's little office for I had been in many a doctor's office when I was carrying Jewel and Sally and Joe, though seldom the same one twice, for the circus never stayed in one town long enough for that. And yet the ones I'd been in had big white glass cases full of fearful-looking pliers and scrapers and pullers and glistening bright steel knives and awful-looking tool-chests that looked more fit for changing tires than touching the poor, scared flesh of the sick and there was generally a book-case made of ugly yellow oak full of books with names of terrifying ailments and in the corner, hung up by the nape on a thin cruel rod of brass, a skeleton grinning like a landlord at a public auction and with his head askew like he'd meant to ask some last, important question about Life before the medical-students took out his tongue.

And so, most naturally, my first glimpse of Doctor Will's office made it seem to me a strange, undoctorish place: a great frothy bunch of lilacs in a stone jug on the deep white window-sill behind him and a shelf of poems on the wall and a nice bright oriental rug and comfortable chairs and a little cot with a bright apostle quilt thrown over it in case someone felt faint. And on the walls, to either side of the bright bow-window behind his chair and desk, the two oil-painted pictures of Suzanne, full length and glowing and joyous: one of her grand front like an orchard of fruit and gold-pink fields of everlasting harvest and the other of her shameless, glorious backside like a young girl spanking, steamy-hot from the tub and hurrying off to her clothes-press all quivering with the anticipation of her clean clothes' pretty kiss and the night of a grand ball somewhere with a dance-card full of love-mad boys. And many's the day when Doctor Will was away in the country districts and not due back till God knows when that I'd come there in the afternoon smelling of laundry soap or furniture polish or with shortening and flour to my elbows from the week's baking and my hair all a mess, I'd come at that hour when that grand north wall caught the river light from the windows and sit there for a long while, reverent as church, bathing myself in the light of the two Suzannes—that skin a-shining warm as summer lanterns, those breasts and the cupping lift and droop of the proud girl's firm, fine behind, gold-pink with healthy life: like cups of sun they seemed.

And one such day it come over me in a revelation and I knew that when some creaking, cracking, wheezing, aching, limping, ailing, feverish, maybe-dying creature dragged himself to that office to be treated that that's what Doctor Will intended his eyes and thoughts should be filled with: the naked flesh, flank and face of health and life; life, life, yes, forever life and not the piteous, clacking, fleshless, grinning, ruined scaffolding of our poor, sweet bodies' brief habitation but life, forever life and not the fleshless framework of beams and joist and shingles: the rain-ruined rack of some helpless morgue pauper the anatomy students had carved away and plucked like turkey-bones a week after Christmas, the mean poor minimum of what we all some day must come to: not that but life, life and all alive, glowing, sweet, naked, cidery health like her: the twin Suzannes: that's what he wanted them to see, not death. And what's more he didn't want the sight of a cold, glass case filled wih surgery's dreadful stainless-steel clamps and saws to horrify the fancy of some poor sick child who might soon enough need to feel their tug and probe or the smothering little death of chloroform, not that but flowers: lilac, sweet-shrub or hydrangea or honey-suckle from the old, cool back-porch vines or maybe a great bouquet of his mother's prize General Washington roses, red as the lips that kissed the first blooming of them ninety years before: it was all a plan—the plainness of that room; the way Doctor Will planned it: not a doctor's office, like most, whose air wisped and whispered with phenol and iodoform, ether and linament but the smell of life in the air, and hope, and not fumed-oak cases of crumbling leather doctor's books of awful, big-named ills and their maybe-cures but shelves of poems and stories in colored paper wrappers and beneath the window-sill a wood chest painted blue and full of bright toys to tease a child's mind away from the ogres of his fear.

Oh, I dearly loved that room, that queer, wise doctor's office, and I'd sit there many's the afternoon for a little while when the river-light rippled sunlight and green water on the wall and I'd feel the light from the flesh of the two Suzanne's upon me like the golden gaze of Genesis on the Lord's seventh day and—well, I'd remember the nights when Vergil would look at me in the oil-lamp light of the circus wagon when the show was over and we'd be readying for bed and I'd be bare as her and yawning and scratching and taking a needless while about finding my night-gown in the clothesbox at the bunk-head, pretending I'd forgotten where I'd put it that morning so Vergil would be getting a good look at my beauties and come to me and I'd let on he took me by surprise and even there and then, alone in Doctor Will's office, by the light of afternoon and the glowing twin Suzannes, I'd feel my breasts hurt like they were full of milk again and wanting a child's tugging mouth and digging little hands to take them and I'd hear Jewel and Sally and little Joe laughing and chasing dragonflies down on the little steamboat landing by the cattails, under the big old willows, and feel the stirring nudge of memory in my womb of Vergil's getting me with them and remember how a woman's hands never feel so somehow right and fitted together as when she folds them across the rising proudness of her belly in the waiting time and once it came to me that surely that's how the ancient races of humankind first learned to clasp their fingers at prayers and that surely it must have been a woman who first taught her men and babies to do the same for how could anyone but a woman first find out the true praising joy of such a gesture?

And so I was one afternoon, sitting there and feeling heedful and guilty about three pans of cinnamon-rolls in the oven and a big wash soaking out in the tubs under the apple-trees but enjoying myself and indulging myself a little spell longer, letting my flesh chat back and forth with the flesh of the two Suzannes like a chat with neighbor-women over a backyard hedge, when suddenly Doctor Will came through the office door and I stood up quick with my heart in my throat, blushing and stammering as if he'd come upon me naked as her and so I was, I reckon, with not a stitch of clothes upon my feelings and he smiled and went to the little cupboard by the door and fetched out a bottle of elderberry wine and two glasses. I knew at first glance that he was off in one of his tempers again though I knew, as well, that it wasn't at me for being there; his eyes were sparkling like steel on flint and he was chewing his white moustaches and rubbing impatiently at the great freckling of liver-spots on the backs of his long, old, clever hands.

I almost smiled when he came round the desk, bowed and handed me my little glass of his own home-made wine for though he was always the soul of courtesy to me I knew when he grew particularly polite, stiff and courtly like the host at a dance, that he was about to go off again about the worthlessness of humanity and the hopelessness of ever lifting a hand to help it: it was a struggle sometimes for me to keep from giggling to hear him rant on about the ornery no-accountness of us all, himself included: what he called the "pride-drunk, pitiless sons of Senator Adam, the first of the Lord's cursed earthful of sneaking politicians with his blue serge fig-leaf and his Elk's minstrel wink: the inventor of pockets, my dear Martha—these being more easily picked than his neighbor's poor, bare hide." Every month or so he'd carry on that way, damning the whole of humankind since Eden, the words rolling quietly out of him with the fury and comic imagination of a circus roustabout though never once did he ever swear in my presence or even within my hearing: he made up great rolling oaths of his own, like pieces of poems or wild old river brags and it was seldom he ever had his spells like this in front of me, choosing to lock himself in the little linen-room beneath the second-floor staircase where there was nothing but an old carpet-stool to sit on and a candle in a pewter dish on an old wicker clothes-hamper and a cracked little walnut looking-glass on the wall—he called it his "contrariness room" and I'd hear him up there bawling himself out in the broken mirror, as delegate of all mortality, and after a half hour of that he'd come down stairs to the kitchen starved for his supper and pale and shaken-looking but relieved-looking, too, and directly he'd always ask me if he could play a game of jacks or hearts with Jewel and Sally and Joe after I got them washed and ready for bed. He took a sip of wine, sucked his moustache furiously and glared over his shoulder at Back-View Suzanne.

Senator Adam has been at me and Marcy again! he shouted presently.
He and his miserable, miserly, grabbing, gold-scraping, shite-poke off-
spring, Doctor Cain, M.D.! Martha Ann, I fear there's no hope left for
the whole hippocratic, whoring horde of us. I'm eighty-one now, I've
been practicing medicine for fifty years, and this morning at breakfast
I made up my mind that another ten years of medicine is every bit I
intend to put in! Half a century of trying to soothe and mend and stitch
and heal and suddenly it comes over me that I'm doing it all alone and
being called a fool for my troubles. And I *am* a fool! What in Time's
name is the sense to any of it! For Life is always fatal bye and bye—
and don't we every one of us have a pill for every ill but Death? And
yet there remain some few little things we have it in our power to do,
if only we would—to make the miseries bearable, to see that the patches
hold as long as we can make them hold before the seat of the britches
goes out and the whole suit falls to rags. There's that puny little we can
do, like hopeless, crazy tailors—if only we would. But them back there
in town—doctors of Glory who've forgotten the glory: the lovely, mad
glory! Why, they've forgotten even that they're doctors. There's not
a shameless one of them who won't demand that long look into a sick
man's pocket before he peeks down his throat. They've forgotten that
they're doctors, Martha Ann, that's what's wrong. Why, the meanest
insult they can think of to throw at poor, gallant Marcy Cresap is to call
her that—a doctor; accusingly, like it was a kind of disgrace, a degen-
eracy they wanted to forget they ever were themselves. I want to
seize and shake them by the shoulders and shout them awake, shout
them into remembering how a doctor is a doctor first and doctor always
and doctor till the last doctor comes hopelessly to doctor his own poor,
last, undoctorable gasp. Doctor first and last and always and even if he
goes broke and ends up in pauper's field being that.

Lord, I'm used to it myself—after fifty years I've got skin tough as a
catfish—but sometimes when I listen to them cussing out the Cresap
girl I feel like giving up my practice and turning to drink or laudanum
or stamp-collecting or pressing wild-flowers. I listen to their impudent,
ungentlemanly, covetous ravings and I don't hear the voices of doctors
at all—I hear the quacking gabble of big businessmen. They look at the
flushed and feverish face of some sick creature and suddenly they're
like poor Ed Follansbee's brother Harper estimating a piece of real-
estate. Well, I guess I'm a kind of real-estate man myself, Martha, but

the trouble with me is somehow I never much got interested in rents and property-values or those foreclosures on the flesh of poor, stupid mankind which spring from nothing more nor less than the sickness of his simple greed. I don't know the good real-estate from the worthless, I guess; sometimes I'm blinded by the cheapest Angel Swamp tarpaper and think it's fancy Morton Avenue stucco or maybe marble. When I see a piece of human real-estate I just lose my head and go wild wanting to fix its leaky roof, chink up its drafty cracks, seal up its poisoned wells, patch up its liver and lights, mortar up the cellar leaks, drive the bats out of its attics and shine up the windows of its eyes. And that's just because of my cracked and cranky nature; I can't help it. It's surely not that I love my fellow mortals. For if there's anything stronger than my everlasting disgust with the human race it's my appalled and staggering pity for it. I'm not one of those starry-eyed do-gooders of the Uplift Persuasion. As a doctor I give mankind the worst imaginable prognosis. It's a hopeless case, I fear. I take one good long sensible look at it and phone quick for the undertaker!

Now you know perfectly well that's not the way you feel toward folks, Doctor Will, I said suddenly, pleased and comforted somehow that he was having all this out on me instead of by himself up there quarreling alone in the candle-light of that close, camphory little linen-room beneath the stairs with nothing but his own face to argue back at him from the little walnut mirror. It's not how you feel at all, I said.

It is. It is, he cried, his eyes frowning into the sun and leaf shadows tossing their broken, calico light across his big, clean, stained hands folded on the desk before him and then he was still a spell, his head turned a little, listening to the sound the children made far away somewhere chasing milkweed fairies down the October meadow and then he smiled a little slowly to himself and lifted his old eyes to the river flames of the afternoon sun all quivering, watery fire in the quartered panes of the high, west window.

It's perfectly true that I deplore humanity, he said. It's just that I could never resist *people.*

And he sighed a deep sigh and shook his head sadly at himself and then it was as if he had forgotten I was there and remembered it suddenly: he turned his eyes quickly to mine, gasped, staring at me horror-stricken over his glasses, his cheeks reddening and his mouth open as if he'd discovered himself in some inexcusable impoliteness.

Good heavens, Martha, you must forgive me, he said, getting up all awkward with embarrassment. What ever in the world is the matter with me!—Am I getting senile so soon?—What unpardonable rudeness of me to have thrown all this on you!—Martha, will you please forgive me?—Upon my soul!

And he came hurrying round the desk, sheepish and fumbling, and lifted my hand and kissed it, still muttering mad at himself and then turned and hurried out the doorway.

Unpardonable, unpardonable, he was roaring softly under his breath and halfway up the stairs by now. To the room—to the room—the place where such purgative discourses belong! To the contrariness room!

But I called out on impulse in a clear, loud voice: *Don't go, please, sir!*—bold as brass as I was and a little giddy from the warming, grand elderberry wine and all the passion of his elegant outrage—Doctor Will, come back and don't give a thought to me. Please come back and say your words at me. Doctor Will, I'd be so proud—I'd be so beholden!

And I heard his footfalls pause on the old stair carpeting at the top and after a bit I could hear him coming back down again, quickly but soft-stepping as if he had his carpet-slippers on, but he didn't come back to face me and presently I heard him out on the back-porch calling to the children to come indoors to the shade of the vines and play a game of croquignole or parcheesi with him: he always wanted the children to play with after he'd been at the human race that way. And I stood a minute more in the doorway of that sweet, plain little room with the bright berries of the sprigs of autumn bittersweet burning in the corner of my eye from the stone-jar on the window ledge but seeing mostly the pictures on the wall again! me and the two Suzannes chatting back and forth between our skins, each pleased with the other for we were plainly both creatures who understood the unprotected, hideless innocence of men, feeling gold-pink and rosy with the wine of understanding and the untaught, knowing motherwit of femaleness till suddenly I smelled the scorch of my cinnamon rolls staining the air and I hurried away to the kitchen, praying they hadn't burned for there was nearly a pound of good country butter in each pan of them and knew I'd have to wait now till after dark and dry the wash piece by piece in the warmth of the oven door when the children were prayed and bedded down. Yet somehow I felt I'd served a plain duty to Doctor Will that day that mattered more than three pans of rolls and the little Monday wash.

It's queer how plainly I dreamed that night of my fine Welsh father, preaching like the psalmist from the great oak pulpit of his church long years before in the golden river Sabbaths down at Paden City and sometimes preaching on and on to us like a love-mad singer during Sunday dinner with my mother tending to the filling of the plates and her quiet smiles and slow, proud glances were all commas and periods and apostrophes and dashes and semicolons to the rolling, marvelous, chanting boom of my father's voice as he kept on with the sermon that wouldn't stop when church let out: praising the wonder of God and the beauty of His children and the savage orneriness of His children, the loving kindness and the scalding greed, the power of them and the glory and the shame all living side-by-side in the same soul, and most of all the pitifulness of His children whose travail and spiritual war was forever with the cruelty and tyrranous envy which marred the may-fly briefness of their little whiles on earth.

Yes, my father's sweet voice preached and sang the livelong length of my sleep that night and I could see plain as yesterday the big crack that ran down the dark, oiled woodwork of the big church lectern he stood behind each Sunday and I minded how some said it was the wild, big grip of his huge hands that made the split and how some said it was made by the lashing lightning of the parables and examples and the moral tales that came thundering from his fantasy; sometimes more pagan than Christian they seemed to some but none could dispute they were sprung from the rich, red womb of human truth. And I suppose if you've read some of the teachings of the new German doctors that Doctor Will used to talk about now and then that you will think that I dreamed such dreams that night because Doctor Will seemed to me like my father and maybe that's so and maybe it's not; a girl may dream with pride and fear and love of the first, grand man she ever adored without German doctors needing to make such a mystery and uproar over that.

And what if it's true?—I see no great cleverness in such a piece of self-evident guesswork: I'm often reminded of people I loved by some-one in a different time and place and not even resembling them so's that I could see; I mind one day when I was coming out of Kroger's on Lafayette Avenue in Glory with a great, huge bag of the week's shopping in my arms and I spied a ragged, blind man with a green guitar and a little tow-head child leading him along by the broken button of his coat and his ruined, pearly eyes thrown back to the sunlight and wind of the spring morning like he was seeing even more of it than I was seeing with all my senses safe and alive, and there was a sweetness in his face that favored the features of poor Vergil, so much so that I nearly dropped my bag and my heart hurt with love till I gasped and tears sprang to my eyes and I set the bag down on the curb and ran over and kissed him as hard as I could square on the mouth and took the change I'd saved out for my weekly soda and picture-show treat and dropped it in the little girl's cup.

And I suppose the German doctors would think up some shrewd and hidden meaning to that and say that what I really wanted was to take the poor soul off to a hotel bed and make the child run across the street to the picture-show while I let the blind man love me in the soft, wild way Vergil used to and feel no shame because he was sightless and wouldn't remember my face afterwards to tell it on me. Though it wasn't that, no nothing so simple: I had to kiss him out of queer thankfulness for something and I had to let him know that gratitude, for it was like I had seen some pure, unearthly knowing in his sightless, pie-shaped, smiling face as it weaved back and forth smiling and singing in the green, spring light. I am not telling you that I have never wished for the weight and pleasure of a man in the ten years since Vergil ran away, even if something has somehow always held me back from seeking it, and some of you, at least, have heard talk in Glory about my being more to Doctor Will than housekeeper which has always pleased me that they should acknowledge the passion and energy of that good man despite his more than eighty years. Though he was never my lover in that way. The plain fact of the matter is I never wanted any man but Vergil and perhaps you'll think that's an odd, unnatural nature for a woman of twenty-three—I was that age the night he ran away and left me—and surely it was unlike either my oldest sister Glynis or the middle one Gwen who lost their maidenhoods every hay-harvest and came back to father's forgiving house with innocence renewed and virgins restored or so it seemed for father never seemed to think too badly of such transgressions and smiled and knew their hot wilful natures were things unchangeable as Glynis' freckled face like a meadow of snow and buttercups and her short, snub nose or Gwen's long legs and quiet, slow speech and her eyes: one blue as a wild hyacinth and the other a deep and river green.

No, it was not chastity or the lack of it that mattered much to father though indeed it mattered much to my poor English mother, Yorkshire born and high-church to her death in stiff and suffering silence, yet it was not the joyous, brief frailties of the flesh but greed and cruelty and poverty on earth that father's preacher mind was set against and it was life and beauty and all the sad, gallant strengths by which men struggle to bind these two together that his sermons sang about and so Glynis and Gwen would weep and repent and find themselves maidens renewed each change of the moon, it seemed, and yet presently run to lay with handsome field-hands and travelling men in barn-lofts and pawpaw thickets and roll in the wet summer grass out back of the torch-lit tents of revival shows although before either of them was twenty they were married at last and nursing grand fat babies and turned into the finest, faithfulest wives a decent man could wish for. And yet, as I say, I followed my nature, too and perhaps that nature was unnatural for I never wanted any man once I laid eyes on Vergil—I stole him right out of my sister Glynis' arms that week the circus came to Paden City but she didn't care a bit: she had already repented and run back to mother to weep and swear, against her nature, oaths she surely must have known she could never keep—yes, it was only Vergil Turk for me from that time on; I never really could have stood another man's hands upon me once Vergil touched me: I was like some strange, contrary lamp and only he had the magic match to light its wick and once lit it burned on and it burns yet and when I think sometimes how cold and dark a world it would be without that soft, familiar light I dasn't complain that he ran away from me or call it ill fortune that my children and I— and maybe Doctor Will—were glad to live for a while within that lamp's warm glow of common, household sweetness. It's surely my fantasy, I know, for I am full of my father's nature, but often when I see the glow from the flesh of the two Suzanne's I fancy that she was just such a curious, queer lamp of a girl as I. Though I came to know it for a fact that the girl of the twin Suzannes never was a mother— Doctor Will told me that one day—he had known her well in the old-time days in Paris, France in the eighteen-eighties when he was there studying for medicine: she never had so much as a single child and yet my instincts had told me right about one thing for, though she had had many men, she had only had one lover and it was his flame, as my flesh and senses told me, that had lit her wick and left her glowing in the world alone, like a wild, contrary lantern, thank the Lord for that, for there was little enough light in her life, poor thing, for that one man, the bringer of the flame, was a drunken beast who abused and cursed and beat her from one end of her girlhood to the other and when she could not fetch home enough money hiring herself out as a model for the artists he would drive her into the streets and into the French saloons and threaten to kill her if she did not sell herself as a whore and bring in enough money to keep him in his drink.

The artist who painted the two Suzannes was a Frenchman who came to the medical school to study anatomy all over again and Doctor Will said he was a true genius, he had known it even then, because he was already in his forties and famous and accomplished and knew as much about anatomy as most young doctors and yet he felt he had not learned enough, back in his art school days, about the wondrous workings and cunning of the flesh and bones and muscles and joints and gizzard and all the rest: the miracles of the parts that live and move and flow inside us all beneath the secret mask of skin that is its holy home and he came to class all one winter and watched the young doctor students dissecting the poor dead bodies of paupers and dead prisoners and dead street-girls and whores and starved children and old men and women who'd died of loneliness or old age in asylums and charity-wards: a sorry, soul-sickening schoolroom that would have seemed to me, at least, though doctors get so they see these things impartially and to learn the goings-on inside the living and with no more disgust or sick-feeling than mechanics tinkering around the parts of an old Model-T. Still, after a while, Doctor Will said he got to feel the coldness of the dead about that school-room and know the need to warm his spirit with the sight of something alive and rosy and moving and by then he had learned all the veins and gristles and muscles and organs by name, inside and out, for he was a quick student and first in all his classes and since he and the Frenchman had got to be friends by then he took to going to the Frenchman's art studio and studying the naked men and women, alive and well and moving, and he said it was like the coming of spring after a hard winter to be able to look at a man's chest rising and falling as he breathed or a woman's arm as she raised it to fix her hair and not seeing that chest or that arm all flayed open and laid out, part by part, and none of the parts working any more: it was like a revelation and he got the feeling of living bodies back in his mind again. It was what he felt again from being there in the Frenchman's art studio and away from the reek of that bleak, cold schoolroom where all the lessons were death, there in the Frenchman's studio watching aliveness skin and knowing what was happening under its hide and the Frenchman knowing what was happening, too—knowing it even better than he did, Doctor Will said once, for he was a genius and a poet and Doctor Will was only a doctor and a student and I scolded and took issue with him at that—and watching another kind of life come alive on the canvas the Frenchman was painting on: skin there, too, with things happening underneath it as they were arranged and made to happen by the fashioning and shaping hands of the Lord.

Before Doctor Will left school in Paris, France, that spring he took those two pictures of the twin Suzannes; he had told the Frenchman that whenever he came back to his little town in far-off West Virginia he wanted pictures of Life to hang in his office, not skeletons or skulls or such poor tumble-down shells of the dead nor any of those dreadful, scarifying anatomy charts like the *Famous Debowelled Man of the Signs* on the zodiac page of the almanac: mankind with his poor, private insides all exposed like a plucked Sunday chicken on the kitchen sink with all its blue and purple and yellow innards spread out like glistening, soft jewels; No, it was Life, he insisted. And Doctor Will had set his heart on having the front and rear pictures of the two naked Suzannes for she was surely alive as any mortal being who ever lived, poor child, though alive half the time with pure outrage and fury and resentment at her lot: the very week the Frenchman was halfway done painting the front-view of her he had to stop and begin the backside-view because her whole right eye was puffed up in vivid violets and yellows where the wretch she shared her bed with had struck her with a whiskey bottle, yet she was surely a creature alive if only with fury and love, Doctor Will said, for she shuddered every now and then and shouted curses gloriously all the while she posed for her beautiful behind-view and hollered out that she swore to God to get shed of her man forever and go home where she was loved and wanted—she was a small-town river girl, like me—though she never did, poor love, and Doctor Will never knew what happened to her in the end though he had his sorriest suspicions that she was one who'd end up old and ugly and sick and poor, finding her way, at last, to a cold table in that stone school-room of the dead and all the sweet ruin of her youth's loveliness come beneath the student's knives at last.

And because Doctor Will honored life and swore that it was the luminous, naked image of it that he meant for sick people to see on the walls of any doctor's office he ever opened back in Glory, because of that the Frenchman kissed his face and gave him both the twin Suzannes and wouldn't take a penny's pay for them, and all the rest of that chilled, snowy French afternoon so long ago he and Doctor Will and the naked, wild Suzanne with nothing but a tattered kimona over her glorious shoulders and pink-cheeked from life and fury and love and the plain, country wine the Frenchman opened for the occasion, they sat and drank and ate bread and cheese, drinking toasts to Life every few minutes or so and praising it even when it was nothing but black-eyes and grand outrage and love for contemptible wretches, though they drank toasts at last to him who was alive if only in his contemptibleness and boozing misery and then, just at the moment when night fell on the great city and the old men went round lighting lamps in the grand French streets they drank damnation to corruption and old-age and sickness, lifting glasses to the Lord in prayer that some day Death himself would trip in his mean rounds and crack his boney head and die, though they all three wept a little afterwards, tipsy as fools by now, and laughed and all admitting that Death was immortal as Life himself so the Frenchman opened another bottle and they sat drinking it and half another one till the midnight churchbells rang, drinking countless toasts to the livingness of one another and roaring solemn, tipsy defiance to old Death whenever and wherever he would come to each of them.

How often I've thought I'd like to have met that fine, grand French gentleman—even though foreigners still make me nervous with their dark gypsy eyes and their queer gabble-gabble and ways of conjuring a girl's petticoats up and mesmerizing her underpants off before she has the breath or sense to really know what he's doing nor time to make up her own mind, as a decent girl should, whether she wants him or not, though by that time it's a moment or so too late and the silly thing can't even remember that she even unfastened something here and another thing there and actually helped him get the elastic of her drawers down over the swell of her thighs and accommodated him in getting the tight cuffs past the roses on her garters; no, not even my circus life with Vergil and all the Italian acrobats and German equestrians I ate and worked with nightly in those grand years ever changed my touchiness when I was close to one of them, for it was always in my mind how my poor sister Glynis got caught in the family-way by a Portuguese gandy-dancer on the B&O and Glynis, who was everything on earth before you could call her a liar, swore all she ever remembered him doing that night in his furnished-room was tattooing a little blue butterfly on her right breast. Still, I would admire to have called that dear French gentleman my friend, if only because of his genteel kindness to Doctor Will and because he was a genius like Doctor Will and, too, because he worshipped life to the last, stubborn rebellion of his days and I know that's true for Doctor Will told me he had heard how years later in the time just before the Great War when the Frenchman was in his seventies how he still painted his grand pictures of life even with his poor hands so crippled and knotted with rheumatism that he had to have his paintbrushes strapped to his dead, stiff wrists with bits of string.

And yet, for all his pride and love of those two oil paintings in his office, Doctor Will possessed a queer and wilful shyness about anyone who came there's ever knowing anything about them except to see them for what they were and take from them the tonic of their glowing glory and heat; he never mentioned once to me the Frenchman's name though that never mattered to me in the least since all the names of foreigners are alike, and I'd never have even known the name of the girl Suzanne if the men who came that day to try and buy the pictures hadn't let it slip. It was a bright May morning with the air cold and warm at the same time like wintergreen in your mouth and the sunlight flashing like an equestrienne's spangles on the wind-whipped waves of the river and when I let the men in the front door Doctor Will was out in the garden with Jewel and Joe, planting his first onion-sets, and before I could hardly shut the front-door behind them they made straight for the office: men in black serge suits like bankers or pallbearers idle between bereavements and they fairly reeked of Wheeling money and their stogies killed the sweetness of the wild-flowers I'd picked and put out fresh that morning. And they stood there admiring the pictures and talking back and forth about the two fine Suzannes and this was how I came to know her name for my two ears were pricked up sharp to catch the men at any mischief or thievery before Doctor Will could come indoors and take charge.

Suzanne, I said in a good, strong voice from the doorway behind them, for I wanted them to know I was there keeping an eye on them. So that's her name now, I said. Well, I've wondered so many, many times. Such a pretty thing she is. Suzanne. Well, I must say it's a name that somehow suits her.

What name? said the oiliest of the pack with a face wrinkled as the fancy leather of a chauffeur's glove.

The girl in the picture, I said. Suzanne. The name you just said. How well it suits her. The two Suzannes!

Well, now, said another, after they'd all looked at each other in odd amazement and smothered queer, snide chuckles. Yes, they are both Suzannes, madam—.

And being called 'madam' made me mad as it always does for I think of 'madam' in its usual household meaning.

—Suzannes they are, he went on and I knew they were all having fun with me for he said it different from the way I did.

What a pretty, pretty name for a girl, I said, heedless. Well, I always guessed somehow she had just such a pretty name—the two Suzannes!

And it was then that I got my first suspicion that something was not quite right with them for they snickered and smirked some more and puffed their stogie smoke in such foul clouds that I knew I'd have to air out the whole downstairs the moment they were gone.

Not her, my dear, said the first. Him. *He* was Suzanne—the painter of these masterpieces. Who knows what the girl's name was?—some poor nameless strumpet he picked up off the boulevards.

And that's when I grew certain they'd been drinking (as first I suspicioned) what with all their cheeky boldness and between their sneaky, simpering winks and their hucksters' greasy smiles at one another till I'd just about had all I could countenance and when one of them fetched a reading-glass from his coat pocket, polished it and, walking impudently over to the wall, held it up before one eye like a picture-show detective and commenced studying the darling flesh of poor Suzanne: that gallant girl now vanquished and brought down and so long ago laid at peace in her last, small claim of earth and, after him calling her a nameless strumpet off the streets, now staring brazen as brass at the magnified right buttock of her grand, defiant, life-loving behind till I thought to myself: Now, that's just a step too far, you sodden, dirty-minded old thing! (for I was sure now beyond doubt that the whole slick, trifling pack of them were all as drunk as the Lord) and I hurried off, my blood just boiling by now, and ran to the kitchen door to call Doctor Will in as quick as he could come. Yet, true to his gentle nature, he was polite and smiling and kind to them and he sent them packing back to Wheeling with long faces and squinty, baffled eyes already twinkling with new schemes and their arms full of lilacs from the yard and the backseat of their big Buick full of jonquils and dogwood and redbud and they piled in as best they could, sneezing among the blossoms and their minds full of pleasant hospitality and hopeless confoundment and yet I knew that, for all his calm sweetness, Doctor Will was furious and troubled that someone had found some secret about his paintings and what they really meant to odd, insensitive people, for it did appear that they were worth a great deal of money though that didn't matter a fig to Doctor Will: he'd wanted to keep all that money-value a secret in remembrance of old friendships and vanished, lost Paris afternoons, I know, and because he'd never wanted the two Suzannes to mean anything to anyone save what they meant to him and what he'd told the Frenchman he meant them to mean to certain, myriad others: the very face and flesh and impudent buttocks and rosy breasts and the glistening-eyed laughter of death-cheating life and whatever good comfort the sense and sight of such things might bring to poorly patients when they crept in to sit in his little office, downcast and scared and dog-sick, for all the world like great King Solomon when he grew cold and old, wanting the hot flesh of pink, young wives to warm his poor bones in the quilts of his winter bed.

Now in the apple heart of this fine October day I think back, after so much has happened and with those two dear ones dead and gone, and my mind sees a winter's morning when Marcy Cresap was in Doctor Will's office and they were packing up comforts and medicines to take to some sick family up near Lynn Camp, with snow so deep and the roads so lost that even the rural mailman's Ford was parked, frozen, in back of Glory's post-office, and I mind how Marcy was standing by the window right where you are now with the lemon-colored light of river morning caught just so in the curve of her cheek and forehead and I saw it then: the same glow that shone from the twin Suzannes on either side of her and I was to see it again when she stood up throughout those days in the county court, her face all wreathed in wrath and love and with that same Suzanne sadness, too, as if she knew there was something grander in her than the petty, mean thing she was fighting, for all the world like Suzanne's look seemed to say there was something older and lovelier in her cussing outrage than just mean fury at the male contrariness of the brute that used her and blacked her eyes; Marcy's face made me gasp in those days when I watched her in the county court for there was that same shining thing there; that said she knew she wasn't fighting the court or the Health Commissioner or the people of Glory nor even the doctors of Apple County but the old black drummer himself: Death and his hired-hands, greed and ignorance.

And it was even in her voice, ringing like a fine, gold bell, on that day she made her little speech of defense and all the doctors but Doctor Will walked out on her and I sat there among those packed, steaming throngs of Apple County folk, my eyes just feasting back and forth with pride between Marcy's face and the face of Doctor Will—his great shock of white hair mussed and tossed back and blowing in the light for all the world like the beard of God in the little green drawing of Him by some mad English poet that's hung on the wall by the head of Doctor Will's big, spool featherbed, and his lips quivering with anger and shame at them who call themselves men of healing and Christian gentlemen who would not stay in that court-room a moment or two to hear a lady's speech.

You say I practiced medicine. All right, then let me tell you how I practiced medicine, Marcy was saying, not shouting for the room was hushed, but in the clear, sweet voice that seemed to find its breath not in her poor, scarred lungs but in the deeps of her heart; I swear as I listened I thought it was as I had always fancied Suzanne's voice would have sounded if she had ever spoken out of the picture frame, out of the vanished years, though not in the strange gabble of French but in the plain words of Apple County speech.

Yes, she was saying. Let me tell you how I practiced medicine. Take for example a time back in January 1926—two years ago when we had that awful snow. I'd gone to Cameron to quarantine a case of diphtheria reported the night before. When I got to the house I found somebody else who'd gotten there a little ahead of me. It was the undertaker—tidying up the child and laying her out in her older sister's good Sunday dress. On my way to the train station an old man met me the minute I'd hurried inside the warm, little ticket-office. He wanted to know if I wasn't the county nurse because he said if I was he wanted to tell me about another child—his granddaughter—who'd died of diphtheria early that morning over on Laurel Run near Adaline. He was pretty upset because the house was full of the rest of the family who hadn't caught it yet and didn't know how to go about keeping from getting it. They'd already tried three or four different doctors and tried to get them to come and tell them what to do but none of them would bother. The

family was poor and besides the snow was pretty bad and not even a
road up that way—.

If the court will excuse me, cried out Doctor Stribbler, jumping to
his feet, copper-faced and huffing like a tea-kettle. I just want to say I
resent and deplore Miss Cresap's idea that poverty would keep a doctor
from his duties.

And I'd like to say, Doctor Stribbler, said Marcy, cool as an angel.
That I've had occasion to resent and deplore that idea a good deal
oftener than you have.

Or bad weather either! snorted the old fool. Though anybody with
common sense knows that sometimes snow does get too deep and roads
too bad for a doctor to get into certain districts of Apple County.

Yes, Doctor Stribbler, Marcy said, smiling a little. Weather's a good
deal like what you once told me you thought death was—a matter of
God's will. Though I surely hope you're wrong. I'd hate to think God's
will hangs on the thread of a five-dollar house-call fee.

Two or three doctors jumped up then and carried on and Judge Wofford, dozing and slumped up yonder in his black robes like a heap of
old umbrellas, roused up and told them to be still.

Well, I took the train back to Glory, Marcy went on. And quarantined
three other cases up Misery Hollow and a case out at Angel Swamp. And
then I called Doctor Blick and reported the family down on Laurel Run.
He said he sure did hate to send me all the way back out there in all this
awful snow but he just didn't see how he'd be able to make it out there
himself. Then he told me to load up my bag with anti-toxin and take the
train back to Cameron and see if I couldn't round up some doctor who'd
see to the job. And he said, if I couldn't get any of them to go, to give
the anti-toxin shots myself. When I got back to Cameron the doctors all
said they sure did hate to send me all the way up to Adaline in all this
awful snow but they just didn't see how they'd be able to make it up
there themselves. So I picked up my bag and headed out. I practiced
medicine.

It took a little while to get there because I rode by sled for twenty-
eight miles, walked through the waist-deep snow another five, and went
on horseback eight miles more. When I got to the house I found I was
late again; the child was dead and you may believe me when I say I
could see by her face how hard she died—choking to death with a
throat filled up with membrane that a culture-test later proved to be

pure diphtheria. Well, I rounded up everybody in the house and gave them twenty-thousand units of anti-toxin each. Yes. I practiced medicine. The old man and his son were pretty broken up over the little girl's dying so hard that way and their not knowing a single thing to do to make it easier for her—but then choking to death is hard to make easy for anyone anywhere. Neither the boy nor his father nor any of the rest of the family seemed to feel bitter or vindictive over what had happened though. The old man just gave a tired, sad smile and said a little bit of money around the house would have changed things a good deal because they'd gone round to every doctor in Cameron two days before and they all said they sure were sorry but they just didn't see how they could make it all the way up Laurel Run in all that awful snow. Yes, I practiced medicine.

She paused a spell and smiled a little to herself, remembering all of it, her head tilted back a little and the yellow light of the winter's day coming through the high court-room windows and catching in her cheeks till they seemed to be shining with a pink-gold light from within.

I wasn't the only person who came up there to help though, she said softly then, almost like she wasn't talking to the court at all. There was an old crazy preacher in the house and he was standing stiff as a tree by the little girl's bed shouting old gospel hymns—.

I don't believe this hearing is a fit place for any reflections on the cloth, Reverend Tombes orated from somewhere in the rear.

That's strange, Reverend, Marcy said. It was old Mister Lowdermilk. He was the same preacher you called a fanatical lunatic last summer when you and the rest of Glory's cloth made the sheriff close up his tent-revival meeting down on the smelter flats. But then I suppose cloth, like everything else, comes in different grades and prices. May I continue? Thank you, your honor; gentlemen of the county court.

There wasn't any undertaker there, naturally, so the old man and his son were doing what they could to straighten the little girl's body out and they'd pried her clenched hands loose from the bed clothes and straightened her fingers the best they could and since there weren't the customary two pennies to be found anywhere among them they'd closed her eyes and laid a bottle-cap on one eyelid and a lead plumber's washer on the other—none of them felt much like having her staring at all of us there. And her mother had considerately dusted her cheeks and forehead with a little flour from the pantry to cover up the blue discoloration of cyanosis. Well, anyway as soon as I'd given everybody their shots of anti-toxin I made the old man and his son promise that if I managed to get a doctor out of doors back in Cameron that they'd not fail to come up and meet him at a place on the dirt road six miles up Laurel Run and promise to pay him if he'd come and look after anybody else in the family who might happen to be down sick by then and I said, if necessary, I'd get the money somehow, somewhere myself. And then I left them. And when I got back to Cameron that afternoon I called Doctor Follansbee in Glory and begged him to come down and give me a hand. But he said he sure was sorry—he just didn't see how he could make it all the way down there because his new Buick just wasn't built for that kind of travel and besides he had a County Medical Society luncheon at the hotel that day.

Where was your good friend the eminent and aged Doctor Cecil, Miss Cresap? called out that sorry scoundrel Doctor Follansbee from somewhere in the room. Was he at the luncheon that day, too? Do you mean to tell us that the benevolent Will Cecil didn't want to face blizzards and snowdrifts and bad roads that day either?

Everybody gasped and then some of them tittered and I gave a quick glance at Doctor Will and just burned with pride because he never blinked an eye.

Oh, I neglected to mention Doctor Cecil, said Marcy. And for that I apologize to him and to the gentlemen of the county court as well. Doctor Cecil was out that day. He was tending to a family of twelve—three cases of diphtheria and one of double lobar pneumonia. The family lives near Bowman's Run just south of Nauvoo School in Seldom Seen Hollow and I doubt if many of you have ever noticed their home which is the body of an abandoned B & O caboose—not really one of the architectural landmarks of Apple County, I'm afraid, though the woods are lovely up there in the spring. Yes, it seems there were two of us tending the sick in Apple County that day. Doctor Cecil was practicing medicine. I was practicing medicine.

And I turned square around in my seat, searching amongst the crowd for the face of Doctor Follansbee which was a sight to behold just then for he was too angry at himself even to be mad at Marcy for a minute, having clean forgotten that Doctor Will hasn't been welcome at the County Medical Society luncheons for nearly fifteen years. Well, Lord, it was still in the court-room: you could really feel all the people thinking, weighing, judging, listening for what came next, though there was no noise amongst them but the whisper of children and a few croupy coughs and sniffling winter noses and the shuffle of the doctors' feet for those worthies were just about agreed to get up and stage their walk-out right in the middle of Marcy Cresap's speech.

At any rate, she went on presently. While I was on the telephone talking from Cameron to Doctor Follansbee, Central broke in on the line and said there was another family in a house up Speakeasy Hollow just north of Maggoty Run and that they'd been trying to get me for two days because the oldest boy was dying of tuberculosis. It was around five o'clock by then. I got a bite to eat in Cameron and then took off into the worst snow-storm within my memory and reached the family about ten o'clock that night. I'll not bother the doctors here with a foolish question but I would please like to ask a question of you gentlemen of the county-court. Did you ever see a person die of tuberculosis when the throat is involved? Do you have any notion of what they suffer—flaming with fever and unable to swallow a drink of water? Has any one of you seen them in those last, tormented, agonizing hours when they are beyond believing that any hell after death could ever be worse than this hell of Now?—or that there could be any heaven beyond life more splendid than the hushed, unknowing nothingness beyond that Now? That was what I found—that was what I watched. The boy had none of the simple medicines that make those last hours a very little bit easier. His mother told me that she had tried to get a doctor out there where they lived but that none would come through such a blizzard as that.

I sat with the boy during the whole night long, doing what little things were possible to make him comfortable. I took pieces of gauze and wiped blood and sputum from his throat because he was too weak to cough any more. I couldn't stay with him till the end. I had to get back to Glory because the health officer was in bed with a head-cold and there was much for me to do back here. But I didn't get back to Glory that morning. Because just after sunrise, while I was packing up my bag and ready to leave the dying boy's house, there came a knock at the door. It was an old timberjack with a hip crippled in a logging accident twenty years before. He had seen me the night before coming up through the blizzard on the ridge above Speakeasy Hollow and he'd started out after me around two o'clock that morning, leaving a sick wife and a dead grandchild of his own, dragging himself three miles through the drifts and laurel thickets to get there before I left. He was so breathless and played-out that it was a full hour before I could even understand what he was trying to tell me. Well, the dying boy's father helped me hoist him somehow or other onto the back of the horse I'd ridden up there and got on behind him with my bag and we rode down toward Maggoty Run and up Speakeasy Hollow a couple of miles more to the shack he lived in. It's a strange thing but I remember how beautiful the woods were in the snowfall of that morning—how they were so still except for the scolding chatter of squirrels and the soft hiss of the snow flakes on the leaves and the whisper of the wind. I think I'll always remember that morning somehow although—.

Are you a nature-lover, Miss Cresap? Judge Wofford murmured into the fist his face was resting on.

I am, indeed, your honor, Marcy said gently. Even the sometimes surprising nature of gentlemen. May I go on? The court has been so generous with its attention and I wouldn't want to be boring.

Not boring, Miss Cresap, said the Judge, rousing himself a little and shaking his shoulders loose in his black alpaca folds and thrusting his arms out over the bench before him as he shot his cuffs. Not *necessarily* boring. Depressing, perhaps. For, I must say, the people you concern yourself with—they don't seem to plan and manage very well for themselves.

The poor, sir, said Marcy Cresap. They have a poor way of doing things.

I should call that evident, grunted the judge. And don't you think, Miss Cresap, that many people of this hopeless class would be better off out of their misery?

Marcy smiled and looked toward the black lace of the cold, winter trees in the great, high, dusty window and then she smiled some more and shrugged a little.

In my work, sir, no one's hopeless till he's dead, she murmured. And as for misery—there's a share of that in every human existence. But there is joy, too. I hope your honor will grant me that even the simplest, shabbiest soul in Apple County is equal to a little joy now and then?

Indeed I will grant you that, Miss Cresap, said the judge. He is eternally equal to the joy of living off his betters—and when charity's not enough, of robbing them.

May I ask his honor if he believes poverty is a crime? said Marcy.

Poverty, Miss Cresap, is the wilful, indulgent father of crime, said the judge in his finest, fustian bombast. That is all.

And who is poverty's father, sir? asked Marcy then.

Miss Cresap, it is you—not I—who are here to answer to the county-court for misbehaviour! said his unhonorable honor. Nor am I here to answer the shifty questions of your well-known radical philosophy. I will tell you this much, however: I know far better than you the triflers you claim to champion. I have seen too many of their kind come to face me across this bar of justice! Lazy orneriness and wilful felony—that's what marks the faces of those that have stood before me here.

And some dirt, too, your honor, said Marcy pleasantly. Maybe one thing that separates some people from the judicial presence is not so much a bar of justice as a bar of soap.

They wouldn't wash if they could! cried out Willy Weir from the table of county-court gentlemen, before the judge could answer.

Probably not, Mister Weir, Marcy answered. Four or five generations of poverty and disease sometimes kills the taste for neatness. It's no treat to wash in cold, cistern water. And not much satisfaction in getting the blackness of dirt off a face just so you can see the pallor of its sickness. I am against dirt, Mister Weir, but sometimes I can't blame other people for not sharing my prejudice.

We know all about your prejudices, Miss Cresap, said Willy Weir who'd worked up a good grandstand head of steam by then. And we know what you're against. You're against the property and business and honest enterprise of the finest group of doctors and the best Medical Society in the whole state of West Virginia! Look yonder! They've had their fill of this and they're walking out! And I don't mind telling you that I and the other gentlemen at this table would like to get up and walk out, too, and we'd do it, too, if it wasn't for the respect we hold for His Honor, Judge Skippy Wofford and the august dignity of this court. Look at them go, Miss Cresap. They can't even stomach staying to hear you out and I don't wonder! Only two remain and only the Almighty knows what's in the conscience of those two. Will Cecil and Janus Dalzell just may not have the sense to know which side of their bread is buttered. Maybe nobody taken the trouble to tell them that Marcy Cresap is just as much against them as she is every other doctor in Apple County!

I am against no doctor in Apple County or anywhere on earth, Marcy said. I am against disease. That is my job. It should be theirs.

Don't bother telling us what you're against, Miss Cresap! Willy shouted. It's all pretty plain. You're against the respectable business of medicine!

I'm not against medicine, Mister Weir. Though sometimes I'm against its business.

Well maybe you'll go on and admit some more things, Miss Cresap! said Willy Weir, slapping his flat hand on the table-top. Your notions and ideas are pretty well known around Glory. Maybe you'll admit you're against business in general. Maybe your hatred of this fine group of doctors reaches out and embraces all of Apple County's businessmen —bankers and dairymen and real-estate men and all the rest! If the facts of your thinking were known—.

I protest against the turn of these proceedings! roared out Doctor Will from across the room while poor Doctor Dalzell stood there, white as whey, straining his neck to catch a glimpse of his poor, sick wife, somewhere lost in the crowd at the rear. I protest, I say, Judge Wofford! shouted Doctor Will. Miss Cresap is not facing an inquisition of her political beliefs. And I deplore the discourtesy of my colleagues in walking out in the midst of this lady's defense of herself. Gentlemen, come back—come back! This is unconscionable! Stay and hear this matter to its end if not as doctors then at least as Christian gentlemen.

But the judge, up in his fusty pulpit of earthly justice, only stared a little and muttered a little and then slapped his hand for silence on the worn, dead wood beside his Bible. And Willy Weir was far from done.

If the facts of your thinking were really known! he shouted. If we really knew the full extent of your attitude toward Glory businessmen—.

Unconscionable! Unspeakable! roared Doctor Will in his fine baritone. Gentlemen, come back! Come back! And you, sir—Judge Wofford —will you have the decency to let this lady finish speaking without the interruptions and the orations of this disreputable milkman whose herd of Jerseys was condemned by the county veterinarian himself and who has a clear, bright axe to grind in these proceedings!

Doctor Cecil, growled the judge. I'm not in need of you to remind me what is decency in this court. Another display of such contempt and I will fine you.

Then be good enough to fine me, Wofford! cried Doctor Will with a savage grin and both hands folded complacently behind him in the tails of his long alpaca coat: Lord, he was in his glory, for he was alone now; Doctor Dalzell had had all he could stand and was edging his way through the crowd to get his cold feet warmed in the company of the other doctors. Make it a good fine, Skippy! roared Doctor Will. For the

extent of my contempt of this whole star-chamber carnival is uncon-
cealable and vast!

And when the old devil fined poor Doctor Will fifty dollars he complained, calling him Skippy again, and said it wasn't near enough; that
his contempt was worth a hundred dollars if it was worth a cent and
went on jovially to add that he didn't dare say how big his contempt
really was for if he did he'd have to go to the bank for a loan to pay it
and Judge Wofford didn't dare threaten him with jail, knowing well
and good that there were enough poor patients of Doctor Will's in Apple
County that they'd have had to call out the State National Guard to keep
them from taking the jail down brick by brick and maybe the whole
court-house with it.

Let Mister Weir go on with me, Will, Marcy called out sweetly and
suddenly. He has a right to ask me anything he wants. Thank you, Will.
But you know I have nothing to hide.

No, Miss Cresap, and you couldn't if you wanted to! cried Willy Weir,
all overcome and trembly-voiced from the grand support he'd gotten
from the bench. You couldn't conceal from any decent citizen in Apple
County that you're against honest American democracy itself!

Well, I am against one kind of democracy, Mister Weir, smiled Marcy.

Hah! cried Willy, slamming both hands on the table. You admit it.

I do, said Marcy Cresap. I am against the democracy of microbes.

Says how? asked Willy Weir, cupping one hand round his brow and
squinting an eye shut as if somehow listening with the other.

I am against the fair, unprejudiced democraticness of bacteria,
Marcy said, lifting her own delicate eyebrow as if surprised he hadn't
understood the first time. I am in treasonable conspiracy against the
impartial free-enterprise of disease germs. My, Mister Weir, how un-
snobbish they are!—they'll infect your child in school with diphtheria or
scarlet-fever as generously as they will the Angel Swamp waif who sits
at the next desk.

All we seem to have heard from you during this hearing is about
Angel Swamp waifs and such, said Willy Weir. You don't seem to concern your duties much with anyone else but them—people living out of
charity-baskets up Maggoty Run or Seldom Seen Holler and such other
outlandish nooks and crannies of Apple County. What do you know
about the sicknesses of decent, respectable folks in Glory? Since when
did you commence concerning yourself so much about them?

Marcy smiled real quick but there was a sting of tears in her big, grave eyes and then she gave a little quick shrug over her shoulders like she was trying to shake loose a hurt, mad at herself for having let it touch her.

Well, Mister Weir, I helped Doctor Heller inoculate the children with toxin and anti-toxin in the third-grade room at Central School this winter, she said. Your little boy was one of the children, Mister Weir, and he seemed to me a most decent and respectable little boy.

And then she turned her face away, as if none of them were there, as if she herself was suddenly somewhere far from there; her eyes and thoughts all occupied in the sky and the filigree of tree that stood in the great, grey winter of the window.

And from other things—I know, she said presently. Some—other experience. My child. My husband. Both. Dead of tuberculosis. Yes, I do know. Really, I am qualified to speak, Mister Weir. My little boy was decent and respectable. My husband was decent and respectable, Mister Weir.

Willy grabbed a tumbler of water from the table and drank it slowly, gathering his thick wits' ends together, for the whole room's eyes were on him and directly he cleared his throat like a pipe-organ and spoke in the soft charitable tones of an undertaker.

With no wish to trade on your grief, Miss Cresap, he said. Nor to reflect on the memory of the deceased—Still and all, your husband was a doctor. It does seem strange that he couldn't heal himself or your child of the very disease which, I understand, was his specialty.

Yes, doesn't it, Mister Weir? said Marcy, smiling again, the old brave pink back in her cheeks again. I guess he failed, Mister Weir. I suppose you'll have to try to forgive him that. Just as I have learned to forgive the sickness which seems epidemic among the doctors who've just finished walking out of this court-room. My husband was a specialist in tuberculosis who died of tuberculosis. So it would appear that ambition and avarice aren't the only sicknesses that destroy good doctors, doesn't it, Mister Weir? And while you were reminding me of the death of my child and husband you might have added that—while we didn't have much money—we weren't really poor. So let me say this to you again—let me speak again my dark, sad, fearful tribute to disease. It dosen't care if you have a penny to your name. You speak to me of democracy, Mister Weir. Disease is the faithful comrade of rich or poor, ignorant or wise.

And Death, sir, is earth's great democrat. I only wish all doctors were as great.

But by now Judge Wofford plainly showed that Marcy Cresap had stolen enough of his show with that old fool Willy; he ruffled his robes like a blackbird's wings and stifled a yawn.

And have you done making your speech now, Miss Cresap? he said.

I don't think I have anything else to say, your honor, said Marcy. I've told you about my work the best way I know how. I'd appreciate the court's permission to leave before long. I've got to go down river to Captina sometime this afternoon to quarantine a diphtheria case and give the rest of the family their shots. Though there may be something more you'd like to know. I'm sure I've left much of it out. I know I could go on here for days telling this county-court of other people— miserable, struggling, sick beyond helping themselves any longer—.

Spare us that ordeal, if you please, said the judge, with a weary wave of his hand. Though I intend to say before I dismiss you that I could talk even longer than you about that kind. You call them miserable, struggling, beyond helping themselves. I do not intend for you to leave this court with such an impression unchallenged. I know that kind. They do not struggle except in the efforts of mischief, they do not help them-selves except to what does not belong to them. And as for what you call their misery—they choose it out of sheer perversity. If, indeed, they are still capable of moral choices at all.

Oh, they are quite capable of choices, your honor, Marcy said. And moral choices of great public importance.

Woman, I can't conceive of what you are talking about, groaned the judge.

Well, I was thinking particularly, said Marcy with a bright smile. Of the days when they come into Glory to vote.

Well, truthfully, I would surrender a year off my ordained span of life if you could have seen the tricked, pie-pale look on the old crow's face in that instant before he slouched down again into his heap of hearse-curtains and fetched up his big hand quick to cover his mouth, his face the color of cold plum butter, and his quartzy, black eyes popped out over the mask of his knobby knuckles, his looks flitting back and forth in stony panic among the staring, tittering, here-and-there shabby faces of the electorate ranked out there in judgment now of the judge. Well, it was a moon-faced, ornery little girl, wild as my Jewel, who saved the wretch's face from that sorry moment and turned the crowd's attention: a little bit of a thing, no more than five, with a dirty face and a runny nose and lost from her mother if, indeed, she had a mother in the room or anywhere in Glory, for that matter; she came clawing and ducking through and amongst the legs toward the front of the court-room, setting up a wail and darting hither and yonder, panicked, I suppose, from all that mobbed, sweating closeness or maybe just gone off, like a firework, the way children do (and often rather sensibly) after so much grown-up talk and tedium. Her shoulders were shaking in her ragged, little, hand-me-down coat and she was thrusting her round face back and forth before the foremost ranks of the crowd, blathering and blubbering and searching the tree-top forest of dumb, staring heads with her wild, big eyes and hollering every now and then for someone by the name of Jake.

Well, you never laid eyes on such a roomful of helpless men who'd have known well enough what to do if a prisoner'd run amok, and the women weren't a bit better; tittering and whispering amongst each other about the cute, devilish little creature, the ornery, heartless, bitches, and the judge, I suppose, was wondering if there wasn't some law in the statutes to fine a child a nickle and costs for court-contempt and then maybe stick her in a special little brownie-sized jail-cell if she couldn't pay, while all the table of fine county-court gentlemen were gawping and speechless at this bird-size outrage fluttering back and forth under their chairs and between their legs and then the bailiff made a grab for her and that's when I commenced fighting my way through the aisle of legs, stomachs, crutches, umbrellas and shopping-bags to get to the poor little thing before one of those beasts laid hands on her and only frightened her the more.

Whose child is this! bellowed Willy Weir at the top of his lungs.

She's Jake's, Willy! yelled out some joker from the crowd.

But who's Jake? hollered another smart alec and at that the whole court-room gave a roar of croupy laughs, the ornery, heartless wretches, for it was plain enough that no Jake was there and the poor little soul really beside herself by now, sobbing and hiccuping and her nose running down all over her hands. Well, my blood was just boiling by then and Judge Wofford was hammering the bench with his Bible and Doctor Will was trying to get to the child through the crowds that had bulged forward to watch the fun.

What's wrong with this child? screeched Willy Weir, ducking out of her way as she came scampering past him again, swift-footed as a cricket.

Lord knows, I was blood-boiling mad; she did put me so much in mind of my own wild, little Jewel and I was bound and determined to get to her for I know how to quiet scared children (it's all in the tone of the voice) and I was struggling to squeeze my legs and behind past the knees and stomach of a fat woman who was sitting there, wheezing with laughter, with a half-eaten Baby Ruth in one hand and mopping her streaming cheeks with the other and when Willy Weir yelled that out I just purely forgot where I was and all my outrage just swelled up in my breast and broke like a bubble: all my boiling wrathy impatience at the thick-headed dumbness of most men when it comes to the needs and natural history of little children.

What's wrong with her! I yelled in my fine high soprano. Why you old fool you, it just might so happen she has to pee!

Well, it was out of me before I could think; I could have bitten off my tongue for uttering such a thing to maybe humiliate the poor little thing's feelings even more, though I didn't give a tinker's dam for whoever else heard me, the judge included, still it just made matters worse; the whole room whistled, stamped and howled with laughter all the harder now, turning and stretching their ornery necks to get a glimpse of me, while there I stood still fighting to get over the mountain of that heaving, hooting, tear-streaming fat woman; Lord, it was like wallowing through a bathtub full of biscuit dough: I had one foot in her grocery bag and I was jammed between the back of the next row and her stomach and great, huge thirty pound breasts on the other, with her crutch-handle poked into my side till I didn't know whether to cry from pain or the fury of it all. And then I caught sight of Doctor Will's face as he smiled, his head turned; he was moving back to his seat again and for a second I got mad at him, thinking he was turning his back on that scared, frenzied little thing who was still wailing and yelling for the lost Jake, though I couldn't see her now, and the Lord knows I couldn't fancy anybody in the room doing anything for her but me, for she had so much put me in mind of my own Jewel when she flies off like that that I couldn't shake loose the feeling that she was one of my own.

And then I saw why Doctor Will had smiled and turned away: Marcy Cresap had run down there and scooped up the little kicking, wailing thing and carried her away, snatching Willy Weir's chair right out from

under his surprised behind as she passed, dragging it over into a corner
of the court-room, out of everyone's earshot, and sat the little soul down
in her lap with both their backs turned on the judge and the mob and
the whole solemn, disreputable assemblage and had commenced whispering to her, mopping back the sweaty, wild curls with one hand while she
fumbled for something in her pocket-book with the other and murmuring to her calmly all the while. Well, it takes a child a spell to run down
from such a sobbing, scampering whirl as that, like a bird flown indoors
that shrills and gasps struggling in the cup of your hand till its feathers
feel the trust in your gentling fingers, but Marcy had the child stilled in
no time with only the hiccup of a sob every now and then, her shaggy,
damp curls laid over against the squirrel collar of Marcy's old winter
coat and her nose running all over Marcy's shirt-waist till she fetched
out a handkerchief and made her blow and then held up what she'd
been hunting for in her pocket-book, smiling and holding the little white
thing up so the child's big eyes could see it before she popped it into her
mouth. Then she drew her head back against the squirrel and went to
whispering some more and presently the child brightened up and
directly the two of them were chatting together as if there wasn't another
soul in that whole hushed, sweaty room but the two of them, chatting
back and forth for all the world as though they were alone on a country
porch somewhere, gossiping like sisters before bedtime, in the summer
sweet of a firefly dusk.

Judge Wofford, I reckon, would have adjourned court for the day's
session about then, for the winter day was running out: a darkening,
smokey blue in the windows, and yet he seemed spellbound, watching
Marcy with the child with an expression I'd adore for you to have seen:
mixed, it was, and torn on the rack of twin emotions, as if he didn't
know whether to hate Marcy most or love the little girl more for popping
up when she had, to turn the people's staring, rib-poking judgment
from him after the mean little dirt Marcy had done him, when directly a
commotion set up in the back of the room and directly a skinny man in
a sweaty hat with no hatband came edging his way up the aisle through
the whispering, way-making crowd; it was the lost Jake, live as Lazarus,
who like as not had slipped out of the proceedings and hopped down to
a Lafayette Avenue bootleg-joint for a snort or two and left his child
alone, for he looked that sort: a sad-faced, shrugging loafer with saggy
jowls all boozy-veined like mausoleum marble and a long, snotty nose
like a rabbit-dog with distemper and a simpering, loose-memoried air

about him as though if the last trump of judgement sounded he'd forget
to take his soul along before he'd disremember to finish the nickle's
worth of moon in the shotglass by his hand; the sort that always has a
great, long greasy pocket-comb sticking up out of his hip-pocket, poor
wretch, though it was plain he hadn't set a comb to his shabby, bed-
mussed hair for a week: it stood up like dead cow-chewed pasture grass
when he snatched off his hat and tucked it up under the armpit of his
frayed, blue shirt and slunk up, bowing and smirking and begging all of
Glory's pardon, and taken the little girl out of Marcy's arms and made his
way out through the crowd again, mumbling something to her, though she
was sound asleep by now with her round face bouncing on his coatless
shoulder and one thumb stuck in her puckered, sweet lips. And he'd
hardly gone through the door before the crowd was treated to the next
act of the circus, for Willy Weir jumped up, as if he needed to make a
little greater fool of himself that day, stood a moment elegantly sipping
water and posing like the old magazine pictures of Mark Hanna, and
proceeded to stick another turkey-feather in his behind.

That little child was doped! he yelled out presently. And every one of
us in this court-room seen it!

Order, order, Mister Weir, old Wofford growled, slapping his raggedy,
dog-eared Bible on the worn judicial wood again with no more respect
than if it was an old telephone book used to swat flies. And then Doctor
Follansbee raised his voice from the back of the room for, by now, the
doctors had all come back in to see the fun.

Your honor, I think Mister Weir's interesting observation rates the
court's investigation, he called out, already beginning to work his way
up to the front of the court-room. Many of us present did see Miss
Cresap administer some sort of tablet to the child. And it is my judgment as a doctor that she was plainly under the influence of a sedative
when her father carried her out of here.

Miss Cresap, said Wofford, turning on Marcy with all his manliness
and self-assurance swiftly returning. Did you give that child something
to make her sleep?

I gave her something to stop her crying, Marcy said. And presently
she did fall asleep, your honor—.

Something perhaps to calm her nerves—perhaps to make her sleep,
Miss Cresap? called out Doctor Follansbee.

Yes, doctor, said Marcy. I always carry them with me. Apple County is full of crying children, it seems. So I always keep some in my purse—I never know when I'm going to need them.

Need what, Miss Cresap? said Doctor Follansbee, standing now with his elbow resting on the judge's bench. Them, Miss Cresap? What do you mean by 'them'?

Well, I call them my Stop-Crying Pills, Doctor Follansbee, Marcy said.

And what might a doctor call them, Miss Cresap? said the doctor. Or a druggist. What is their pharmaceutical name, Miss Cresap?

I don't believe I can answer that, doctor, Marcy said.

A woman of your vast claims to medical knowledge, Miss Cresap? said old Follansbee. Come now, Miss Cresap. A pill that stops a child crying that swiftly—that makes a child sleep like that child was sleeping! Come now, Miss Cresap, what is the medical name for your little pills?

I'm sure I haven't the slightest notion, said Marcy. Though you might ask Doctor Will Cecil over there. He's never without them. He comes across quite a few crying children, too. He might be able to tell you their chemical name. I never call them anything but that—my Stop-Crying Pills.

You mean Doctor Cecil gives them to you? said Follansbee.

No, said Marcy. I go into Charley Seat's Drug Store every few days and get them myself.

With a legal prescription for them, of course, whispered Follansbee, triumphantly.

Oh, Lord! called out Doctor Will before Marcy could answer, his white hair flowing wilder than ever and his face alight with the devil's own mischievous grin. Oh Lord, he cried. Let down Thy saddened, kindly laughter on us here. For a little child has mis-led them!

Order! Order, Will Cecil, or I'll find you in contempt again! grinned old Wofford, his own blood quickening to the chase. Now, Miss Cresap, the court orders you to empty your purse before it here and submit in evidence these—these so-called Stop-Crying Pills.

Gladly, your honor, Marcy said, her pretty face strained and drawn; beginning to show the ordeal of that day, and went over and dumped out everything in her purse under the judge's nose and went angrily fishing around among the spectacles and powder-compact and door-keys and loose pennies and the clean folds of a little flowered handkerchief and a green bottle of lavender smelling-salts and then reached into the spilled litter of her woman's things and held up a half-used roll of peppermint life-savers.

Yes, she said in a low voice, her eyes flooding suddenly and at last with all the damned-up tears of that day and, indeed, of the years. There, your honor. There, Doctor Follansbee. A powerful sedative for a small, scared child. Especially when mixed with the whispers of a few, soft foolish words. Yes. It was one of these you saw me give the child. So now, I guess, if you can't hang me for a health-nurse you can pillory me for a peppermint! If you can't keep me from fighting dirt and death then you must stop me from stopping children's tears. Here—do try one. Oh, you would do well to try one, your honor, if ever the tears of your own life's mercilessness should overtake you. And you, Doctor Follansbee—*do* have one of my Stop-Crying Pills! It might help quench the grief at your memory of wasted skills and squandered trusts and the sacred oath of the Greek physician which long ago you traded to the highest bidder—it might even help still in your ears the rattle of all the hard-breathing sick of all the ten thousand winter nights when the snow was too deep for you—the way was too far for you—the roads too bad for you—the pay too little for you—.

Order, Miss Cresap! roared Wofford, purple-faced as a thunderhead in dog-days and slamming again with the black, blasphemed leather of his Scriptures. Order, I say. I demand that you stop this outburst!

I will not stop! I will not be still! cried Marcy Cresap. For I am guilty and you can do your worst to me. That and no more. Yes. You are right! All of you! I practiced medicine! I practiced it when its own practitioners forgot its practice. I practiced it when they indifferently sent me out into the broken-hearted depths and reaches of Apple County to do their own jobs for them. Oh, please, *do* have one of my fearful, dangerous little pills, gentlemen! Learn at least one more of the awful ways in which I practice medicine. For it's true, you see, it's true! You've won! Your case against me is perfect and complete. For I go about spreading health among the undeserving—I propagate clear eyes, smiles and sound chests among the unbeautiful—I fight to keep alive the unprofitable. And I stop a child's crying with a peppermint in his mouth while I try to stop his dying with a needle in his behind! So it's your clear duty to get me discharged as health-nurse of Apple County and drive me forever out of Glory. For I am a trouble-maker—an enemy of doctoring's good business. *Because I practice medicine!* And I will eternally practice it so long as those men who have sworn to practice it can no longer distinguish between the green of one man's money and the red of another one's blood. And these—and these—! Oh, dear God, don't let me be such a weeping fool! These—.

For she was almost at the end of her breath by now and it was such a hurt in my heart to look at her so for I had never yet seen Marcy Cresap display such grief or her face ever break its strong, sweet quietude before; though still her cheeks shone savagely alive with the lovely, raging, pink-gold radiance of the wild Suzannes, and her great, dark eyes, flooding now with tears, flashed much as I fancy the eyes of the wild, wilful French girl's must have blazed in the white winters of those lost Paris afternoons when she, too, poor dear, railed and raved against still another sort of mulish male impudence. Then she turned suddenly from the doctor and the judge and faced the hushed, witnessing ranks of the gawping throng, staring with a child's bewilderment as if she had forgotten they were there and now faced them with surprised remembrance; and shame, too, as if somehow for a moment she had let them down by that very forgetting of them there, and some of them maybe sick and needing her. She stood so for a spell, gathering back her breath, and then shook her head roughly till her dark hair flung round like some flag of braveness; angry at herself, sorry for them, worried for them, ashamed of something dark and devilish in us all: something in her, in old Follansbee and the judge, something in Doctor Will, in me, in all of them out there: some dark, contrary devilishness in every human thing alive in Glory, Apple County and the wide, sad earth.

Yes, she murmured to them, nodding rapidly, her voice breaking a little more. You all know me, all of you. And you all know I'm guilty, don't you? You yonder—Bessie Sochek, Chester Yost. And you, Clackey Barker. You can come up and bear witness to it. You surely know it's true. I practiced medicine. But I guess—indeed, I guess I better stop now, hadn't I, and practice some on myself?

Then she laughed a little and cried a little at the same time and shook her head again, flinging the tears loose from her face the way a hurt and hounded beast flings blood free from its torn nose.

Well, I do have my Stop-Crying Pills, don't I? said Marcy Cresap with a soft chuckle and an even softer sob. And if these two gentlemen will forgive me I'm taking them back for I'm afraid I'm going to be needing one of them myself just now.

And so she turned and fumbled everything back into her purse and ran silently weeping out of the court-room, leaving such a stillness behind her that you could fairly hear the brush of winter sky lay dark dusk upon the panes of the great, high windows.

I didn't go back to court for the last day of the hearing for I didn't think I could endure another moment of it, especially if Marcy should lose, and my Sam and Sally were both sick in bed with croupy colds and Jewel's nose was already red and snuffly, and there was washing and cleaning and cooking to tend to—I'd already missed two days of my duties to Doctor Will and, Lord knows, he needed his hot suppers and clean sheets and bolster-slips when he came to his featherbed, dead for sleep. And somehow I didn't need to witness the end of it, for I sensed in my soul's deepest wits that the fools would outsmart themselves and that Marcy would win and so they did and so she did, as I have told you. Yet the last day must have been the worst of them all with the doctors and businessmen at her more savagely than ever for they were wild by now, seeing how the people of Apple County were all rallying to her side. And they fought her that last day with every foulness they could lay hands on, raging at her for the County Health Doctor she had brought to Glory for he was a Jew, though that was small matter now: he'd been fired from his job and scorned from the county long since, and they raved about her yearly two-thousand dollar salary and said she was biting the hand that fed her, though that was a bare-faced lie since Marcy had never taken a single penny from the county: everything she was paid came to her from Washington, D.C. and the Apple County Tuberculosis Association.

Tadd Cockayne's editorials in the *Glory Argus* had blazed like torches to show up the shame of the things being done against her: even how the doctors themselves had gone on strike against the County Sanatorium and wouldn't set foot in it and how they even threatened a strike against the Cora B. Fiasco Memorial Hospital and not to send a patient there if the Superintendent or the Board of Trustees ever helped Marcy or took in a single charity case she asked to have admitted. But since they weren't paying her salary, weren't even hiring her, for that matter, there was nothing the county-court and the men who owned them could do to discharge her and I fancy they sensed they'd pushed things far

enough anyway, with most of Glory and Apple County on her side by
now and elections less than a year away. And so the side-show shameful-
ness ended. And Marcy Cresap won. And the doctors and the dairy-men
and mine-owners and mill-presidents and the real-estate and all the
trifling, ornery rest of them crept back into the shadows again and
pondered how they might fight her through the years to come in quieter
and more crafty ways. Lord, the victory of that winter's afternoon on
the court's last day made Doctor Will seem half-a-life younger and he
plunged into work like a boy fresh back from Paris medical-school just
setting out in practice, and so the winter waned and the dogwood and
redbud gleamed like bits of stained glass in the grey woods above the
river and even the skunk-cabbage looked pretty in its dun, humble way
and the green frogs shrilled love shameless in the dusks and the big
spring moon shone like rubbed pewter over the river and the first show-
boat came to the Glory landing with its calliope chattering its pipey
racket back and forth between the hills like all the bawdy and outlandish
pipes of Pan.

It seemed for me as happy a time of life as I had ever known except
for those first circus years with Vergil and I would waken sometimes of
a spring night with the curtains blowing in the moonshine and the cold
air sweet with such a wildness of things aborning in the black earth of
the bottomlands and even in the very air itself that I should not have
been astonished to see wild flowers blooming round in the bedroom
shadows like the dark air had become as rich and thick as the fathering
soil of the valley; indeed, I was as happy as I was in those first years
with my new husband when the children to come lived as yet only in the
world of kisses and looks. And even sometimes wide-awake in the bright
spring mornings of my housework when the clean white curtains in the
windows kicked and filled billowing like the gay gowns of girls at a ball,
sometimes I would dream that Vergil had come back, as if he had never
run away, and possessed a new-made nature purged of its fool's poor
footloose waywardness; he was pipe-puffing comfort and solidness and
reliability itself, the kind who could walk into any bank in Glory and
borrow money in two minutes without collateral; though there's this
queer thing about some of us—and I knew it deep inside—that the very
madness in a man that drives him at last to leave his woman and children
and roof and bed is often the selfsame half of his nature she most
adores: the eagle-side of the silver coin of him that she can never hope

to hoard and dare not even too often take out of her apron-pocket for a peek and a little polish, for when the eagle hears its wild heart tell it fly, then fly it must and take the other side along with it: face and date and In God We Trust and all the whole lovely dollar itself. And a woman of my contrary, queer nature is given to keep but one such coin in the whole, little purse of her silly life.

And yet, as I say, sometimes that spring when I'd be widest waking and without the excuse of sleeping for my dreams—when I'd be dressing my wild Jewel or washing the face of grave, little Sam or combing out Sally's cornsilk glory of hair—in broadest waking I would hear Vergil's trombone on the morning wind; Lord, how sweetly he could play, and I'd imagine—no, I'd really *know*—he was down at the landing where he used to take the children sometimes in early summer mornings before breakfast and I'd be listening to "The Big Fat Man" and "Floating Down to Cotton Town" or " 'Lassus Trombone," tunes he played to make the children laugh—playing like he used to that summer before the night of the new moon when he heard the siren-song and ran away and his telling the children, in those mornings, that it was the blown beckoning of his songs from the gold bell of that battered, old band horn that would urge the sun itself up from the apple orchards on Roberts' Ridge and roll the fog off the dusky meadows and he would tell it with hushed prophet's zeal till they'd be moon-eyed with believing, certain beyond question that, if their magic father didn't play his tunes at just that hour of dawn, the sun wouldn't rise at all and the fog lay all day long in billows of pearly bunting to the rim of Glory's valley and daylight not come till heaven knew when.

For Vergil Turk was a wonder with little children and natural born to the show—Gentry Brother's World's Greatest Trained Animal Circus, it was—with a child-sized tent and child-sized rings and child-sized animals doing all their child-sized miracles and little bleachers with hardly enough room for grownups at all: no lions and tigers snoring and coughing with menace enough to people a thousand nursery nightmares, no chained mammoth elephant to whiff and puff hot steam against timorous, small fingers reaching to drop a peanut bravely into the two-holed terror of his trunk, and no sideshow of wrinkled, leering midgets like evil grown-ups shrunken down to come spy on children in their knee-high world nor vast, pathetic ladies in iron-pipe chairs, fanning themselves and smiling and drowning in their seas of sad blubber and grimy lace; nothing save small trained dogs and wise, amazing monkeys in gold and red suits and prancing ponies in their tiny spangled harnesses and a white lamb in scarlet boots who danced whenever the band played "Dardanella": all of them doing their turns and tricks as merry and wise as the enchanted creatures of bedtime tales and harmless as the wooden, painted beasts in toy arks.

I thought constantly of the circus days that spring: those years with Vergil in the matinees and glittering evening shows till I could almost swear the circus had come back to the smelter flats so clearly would my fancy hear the tunes of Vergil's trombone in those sharp, sweet April mornings and him playing all the old tunes except "Rocked in the Cradle of the Deep" which never failed to make me cry for it had been his solo in the evening show the night of our wedding before we went off to the country hotel for our one-night honeymoon. And most of my good-feeling was my pride for Marcy after that awful winter's trials and the way she had triumphed so elegantly and permanently—or so it seemed—and Doctor Will seemed to feel it, too, for he slaved at his practice harder than ever till I wouldn't catch sight of him from the dark of morning till the deep of night; he'd be off by himself sometimes and sometimes with Marcy in her old touring-car, tending some sick ones somewhere in another of Apple County's God-forgotten corners. And the summer came on and seemed even fairer than the gay, grand spring had been. And no one came to the house but tramps whom I always fed or else felt my own good meal that night like a cold hop-toad in my throat, and peddlers, salesmen and drummers by the score— there was hardly a week went by without its two or three of them and I never turned them away, poor things, save *him*: that one to whom I shall turn and tell you of presently. For I was always glad for a few minutes' sight of a stranger's face and a sample-case packed full of queer, strange useless things I could never fancy anyone buying and the half-hour's hopeful speech all of them had rattled off by rote so many times it was as sad as the songs of wound-up toy birds. And I'd offer them a cup of coffee and a piece of pound-cake and sit watching and listening by the window with the children round me as the poor souls prattled on about the wonders of their wares and, after unclasping their dented, ancient sample-cases, knelt to spread out their store of queer, unwanted things across the threadbare Chinese carpet in Doctor Will's office. And usually there was a free sample which the children saved up to play store with, though I always felt mean taking them when I so seldom ever bought anything; indeed, I used to thank my stars it was myself there to answer the door and humor the poor souls and not Doctor Will in my place, who'd have soon had the house heaped with encyclopedia sets, bottle brushes, hymnals, carpet-sweepers, home medical companions and patent-pending, three-in-one potato-peeler, cherry pitter, apple-slicers.

Yet I do confess to a weakness for the little brown bundles of the sassafras-man whose tea is still a comfort to something country in my spirit: kitchen, childhood ghosts, the cupboards of my mother—and I always placed a good order with old Mister Lovelady, the Golden Rule Man who came with his spices but twice a year: springtime and fall, and I declare I'd have paid him a price just to open up his suit-case and let loose into the room its smells for me to sniff in, swooning: crystal-ginger hot as love and cinnamon-bark and cloves and candy orange peel like a vagrant, out-of-season Christmas, and wintergreen, vanilla, nutmegs and tonka-bean all a-mingling to ravage the senses; in the moment after the lid of that brown sample-case fell open, all Asia filled the room. And before long I would fairly swear that through the blowing curtains, the common air of Apple County was all made whispery and wizarded with heathen, teasing tongues while the honest, plain river wind seemed breezing in off the geranium-blue latitudes of Africa's outlandish seas.

And yet among all that poorly, harmless, crackerjack caravan of drummers and peddlers that came and went with their cheapjack packs of this-and-that there was but one whose name I never knew, nor what he carried in his sample-case and vended for his living, for I could not abide the sight nor sense of the man's presence, though Doctor Will was civil enough to him when he chanced to be home when he called which was often, since he commonly came after sundown or even far late into the moonlit, cricket-speaking stillness of summer nights and I'll not forget to my dying day how always when he'd climb out of his rackety old Ford and come walking up the yard toward the back-porch, stepping cat-eyed and sure through the calico of moon-shadows under the leaves of the chinaberry tree—no, it was not my fancy that the frogs down in the shoals beneath the river mists grew still and the crickets out in the silver-hazy meadows seemed to hesitate and hark and house-dogs set up the sound of clamorous, faint barking in all the quilted, sleeping farms for miles around. And yet it was in the brightness of river sun-light that I first saw him: a cool, sweet June morning with a whipping

breeze and the tinkle of sheep-bells on the ridges and the air alive with
new green growth and the shouts of plough-boys blowing up from the
downriver bottomlands. The children were out in the meadow somewhere and I was in the kitchen baking: potsdam-cakes for them and a
spice-cake for Doctor Will when he got home that night for sometimes
he came in too tired for any supper but a slice of my cake and a cup
of cocoa. Till I die I'll not forget that morning he first came: that one
amongst all the drummers I could never bring myself to ask in and offer
a cup of coffee and listen to his chatter to humor him a spell and look
at all his unwanted wares and let him rest his feet and waste an hour or
so. And it did seem queer for me to feel such a shivery distaste for him
since he was a pleasant-looking sort and in some ways the most gentle-
manly of all and with his worn serge trousers neatly pressed and wearing a candy-stripe shirt with a celluloid collar and a shiny snap-on bow-
tie and a yellow boater straw which he was always quick to tip, as
courteous as a process-server, and neat, black patent-leather shoes that
were always bright as beetles and never seemed to show a speck of dust
from the road.

Yes, he was always the perfect picture of smiling, cozening gentility
and far more pleasant to sit with, one would think, than old Mister
Gumbolt, the vacuum-cleaner salesman, who wore no socks on his grey,
gouty ankles and simply reeked of snuff and who inevitably hauled out
his cracked, money-less wallet and showed me for the hundredth time
the awful hand-tinted picture of his poor, late wife laid out like a stiff,
stuffed doll in the satin and flowers of her coffin. And yet, for all that, I
found in poor Mister Gumbolt that comfort that I was somehow a comfort to him, if only for that little while, and he never frightened me like
this other one did. Indeed, till the day I die I'll not forget that first
morning I saw him standing there smiling with his sample-case in the
kitchen door and that's been nearly ten years ago, the year after Vergil
ran away, and I remember yet how the birds seemed to grow still in the
chinaberry tree in the yard behind him and the clamor of the green,
growing morning itself seem to halt for a moment, harking, waiting and
I couldn't hear the children hollering and hooting in the meadows and
the wind itself ceased in that instant of his tipped straw and his smiling
bow as if the spring day itself, remembering something of winter,
caught its breath and waited a moment, too. And for all that long ago
it's been I can't tell you even now what it was about this one of all those

wandering salesmen and peddlers which set my skin cold and made me want to gather the children close about my skirts in the dining-room and cover the old mirrors and latch the shutters and hum one of father's old Welsh hymns in a quavery, small voice the way mother used to when a lightning-storm broke booming over the roof above us and silvered all our faces in swift, frightening flashes through the slats of the bolted window-shutters.

Who is that man, Doctor Will? And what does he sell? I asked one August night after he'd chattered off down the river-road in his Model-T.

What difference does it make, Martha? It's nothing we want to buy, my dear, said Doctor Will, who'd been alone with him in his office for nearly two hours with the door closed and bolted and yet not so tightly as to keep from my ears the sounds of some savage, whispered contention between the two of them.

But what does he peddle, Doctor Will? I persisted, boldly. I think I should know. For sometimes he comes to the house when you're away— in the mornings—and I simply can't abide the sight nor presence of him.

But Doctor Will didn't answer; his face down-drawn and pale, like a man who has been bargaining long with a hard-driving huckster and just barely won by sheer love and will. And yet for all his weariness he was angry, too, with a full head of wrathy steam and off he went, without another word to me, to shut himself up for another hour in his con-trariness-room beneath the second-floor stairs and sat, I could imagine, glaring at his face in the little mirror and haranguing at the world for being as it is and it was then, overhearing his voice when it rose to organ-chords of noble anger, that I came to know the stranger as the Black Drummer and that was all I was ever to know him by and even to this day I know him by no other.

And sometimes in the nights of his visits with Doctor Will, I did a thing I'm still half ashamed to own to: a thing I'd never have dreamed of doing if I hadn't felt that Doctor Will might come to some harm in the course of that closed, strange interview and feeling, as I had felt since that first queer morning when I turned and saw the Black Drummer standing in the kitchen door with the whole day hushed behind him, that he was one who came to peddle nothing but a sample-case of dark and nameless ills, and feeling, too, that even if I felt nothing for Doctor Will's well-being or my own that I owed, at least, some caution for the children. And so, as I say, I did a shameless thing, though I don't regret it now: I stood by the bolted door and put my ear to the crack, eavesdropping as best I could at what Doctor Will was contesting with such grave, furious solemnity, though I could never catch more than a word here and a name there, for the Black Drummer never let his own voice rise above that somehow wearied, courteous murmur: it was Doctor Will whose voice rose furiously now and again and I would hear him slam his desk with a fist and gasp with the exertion of some strange savage bargaining; he'd seem to be beside himself and when his voice rose I'd hear the mention of a sick child I knew he'd been to see at Raven's Rock that morning or the mention of a miner caught the day before in a slate-fall up Parr's Run or a young woman with cancer of the breast who'd been to see him the week before and, when Doctor Will had grown still again, the drummer's spiel would go on evenly, quietly, as if he had all his wares spread out for show on the frayed Chinese rug and though, as I say, I could never distinguish a word of what he said I could hear the dark song of his voice and his way of speaking in a tired and sometimes even sad tone as if, as a salesman, he had long ago lost faith in the line and was tired of days of lugging his heavy, strange sample-case from the town-to-town of his eternal route and the nights in the gaslit rooms of the country hotels until, indeed, he had almost grown uncaring of the good-favor of the men in the home-office. I nearly pitied him. Indeed, until a certain morning five years ago I humored him for a few, uneasy moments at the kitchen door, though never asking him inside as I did the others for a cup of coffee and an hour of pleasantries and a glance at their wares, for somehow I never cared to see what lay packed within that strange, green cardboard sample-case of his.

It was a gold and green spring morning much like the first one in which I saw him and, just as before, it was baking-day and I was in the kitchen with an oven filled with rising bread and singing to myself and wondering which smelled better: the rich yeasty breath of the swelling, golden loaves or the green smell of growing things outside in the river morning. And without the usual warning bang and chatter of his old car coming up the yard I looked up suddenly and saw him standing in the kitchen door.

Nothing today. Nothing today, thank you, I said briskly, for I was taken unawares and angered at his startling me with such a brazen stealthiness that way. Doctor Will and Miss Marcy Cresap left for heaven-knows-where at sunup this morning and Doctor Will will not be back till past midnight if I'm any judge. And he'll be dead-tired when he does get home and I don't mind telling you I'd as soon you didn't come round to pester him with your huckstering at such outlandish hours as you've often come here before. Now if you're of a mind to report me to Doctor Will for impudence then by all means do so. I'll gladly bear the consequences of his taking me to task as the price well-spent of his getting a decent sleep for the Lord knows he gets little enough of that.

And I declare I'd have gone on till I'd worked my blood up to boiling and ordered him off the porch and out of the yard if I hadn't chanced to glance at him and see how desperately forlorn he looked: I'd never seen him so; all the shabby elegance seemed wilted out of him—there was a smudge of mud on the black toe of each patent-leather shoe, his peppermint shirt was grey and rumpled like he'd worn it and slept in it for three days and nights and the sample-case hung in his hand as if it were heavy with all the world's woes.

If I could just rest a spell, he said, with a ghost of the old, sad enterprise in his smile. If I could maybe have a cool glass of that good well-water yonder in the bucket.

I grumbled something and fetched him a tumbler of water, reaching it uneasily out to him, and it was then that I smelled his breath and knew he'd spent a night of drinking.

There, I said. Drink that for a change. It's water. It won't poison you. It may be a sight better than what you've already been drinking. Sit yonder and rest yourself on the porch step. I don't care for people stamping round my kitchen whilst I'm baking. If you want more water you can have it.

Thank you, he said, fanning his grey, weary face with his straw hat and drinking with the other hand. I'm tired, he said. So tired, dear lady. Thank you again.

And, Lord help me for a fool, I pitied him again and fetched him another glass of water and when he'd finished that he smiled a little and looked off toward the last misting wisps of fog on the river shore and spoke like he was speaking not for me but for himself or, perhaps, for the hard-headed men of the home-office.

Tired, he said. Tired. When can the drummer choose from his own wares? When can the peddler earn the comfort of the moneyback, guaranteed items he peddles to all others?

And then he sighed a sigh so soulful that I almost reached out to him the comfort of my hand; though, a moment later, I was glad enough I hadn't given in to any such rashness of womanish solicitude.

Believe me, he said sorrowfully. When I tell you how sincerely I sympathize with you, Martha Ann—May I call you by that name, dear soul? And will you believe me when I tell you I am sorry—deeply sorry—. I am at your feet, Martha Ann, over the death last week of your beloved husband Vergil.

I only thank the stars that I was standing with the kitchen-chair behind me to sit down in real quick (which I did) or I'd have fallen stretched-out backwards on the hard stone floor and likely knocked my poor head simpler than it is or broken dear-knows-what bones and had all that to add to poor Doctor Will's burdens. But a moment later I was on my legs again, my blood just boiling, and standing in the doorway with my feet planted square apart and both fists on my hips.

What do you mean! I shouted. You never set eyes on Vergil! You couldn't even know his name! Dead? Dead? Not likely! Not a wild, live boy like my Vergil! I'll never believe it, you black-hearted fabricator!

But it's so, Martha Ann, it's so, said the black drummer. And who more quickly able to know the truth of it than me? It's true, dear soul. Last week in Memphis, Tennessee. I *know*. For it happened in the territory—my territory. My route, you see, covers all the river counties on the Ohio south to Cairo and forty counties south of there—and below New Orleans clean to Poverty Point. The territory, dear heart. And so how could I help but know? Don't I know every death that happens in the territory? Isn't it my business to know? Though let me tell you this —and it should bring you heart's ease to hear it—that your beloved Vergil had an easy crossing. A little twinge, a quick gasp, a shiver and he was gone. Doesn't that comfort you somewhat, Martha Ann? An *easy* passing—perhaps the easiest in my entire line. Here. It's Item Twenty-seven in my lists. I can show it to you in the New Spring Catalog and set your doubts at rest. One moment and I'll fetch it out, dear heart.

And he squatted on the porch and already had one brass clasp unsnapped and was already fumbling wearily at the other and a moment more and he'd have had his dreadful old sample-case open and agape with the Lord knows what darkness and piteous horrors all packed tight inside it there and perhaps left me raving mad at the very glimpse of them, but sense and sanity seized me somehow when I spied my Jewel and Sam in the yard beneath the chinaberry tree and, because it was the only thing handy, I seized up the bucket of well water from the stool by the door and flung it full in his face. He stood presently, sneezing and drenched and wiping his face with his fingers and stood a spell, dripping and un-speaking, his face more forelorn than before and then shook the drops from his nose-tip and turned his melancholy face to me and stared while he squeezed the water from his frayed shirt-cuffs, gazing at me with a deep-eyed pity that only confused me and set my nerves on edge the more.

I wish you hadn't done that, dear heart, he said, softly. These are the only clothes I've got. Just look at me now.

And he sneezed again and shivered in the river-wind and, Lord save me for a fool, I felt a pang of pity for him again for he was only a poor drummer off the roads and clearly crazy as a loon and I didn't believe a word of what he'd said about Vergil's dying for how could he know such a thing even if it were so, which I knew it wasn't, for wild Vergil was stubborn and strong and ornery with life and I felt as mean as if I'd spit in a blind man's cup, remembering my good father's calling the queer and crazy-witted ones of this world as being God's laid-aside, un-finished sketches for the master canvas of man.

I'm sorry, I blurted, flushing and flustered. You're mean and mad and mischievous to come telling such outlandish lies about my Vergil. Still I had no right to soak you so. Take off your shirt and reach it in to me and then go sit yonder on the steps whilst I dry it against the stove. I'll even iron the cuffs and collar for you though you can't blame my dousing you for their needing that. What you want's an honest woman to mind after you, mister, if I may say so. And the decent companion-ship of a home and children instead of nights in shoddy drummer's rooms in queer country hotels. For some men haven't the nature that will endure the solitude of a wanderer's life, and it's loneliness that's muddled your mind if you want my opinion, mister. But all that's neither here nor there nor my affair. Take off your shirt, I say, and fetch it through the door to me and I'll do my best with it and then thank you to be on your way and not come here ever again in the mornings to trouble the usual good-humored tranquility of my nature and mix me all up when I've got a head full of important duties and an ovenful of bread to tend. Do as I say! Give me your shirt for you're shivering and you've sneezed three times already. There's always a chill in the river air these April mornings and I'll not have it on my conscience that I sent you away wet to maybe catch your death!

No fear of that, he murmured with another snuffling sigh and a yearning, sad stare at the sample-case by his muddy shoe-tips. Lord help me, no, dear heart—no fear of that.

And wild Jewel and solemn Sally and grave Sam stood ranked in a staring row in the yard beneath the chinaberry tree while the black drummer reached me his shirt through the doorway, his face shameful as a sheep-killing dog, and then slunk off to squat alone on the porch-steps whilst I went and did my best for his dirty, candy-stripe shirt and though I fetched out the iron and did all I could to tidy it up it was a sight when I was done and a shameful thing for any woman to give a man to wear, and if it had been anyone but him and my nerves in better shape I'd have asked him in to warm his rickety chest by the stove's warmth whilst I washed and ironed it properly. Still he thanked me and blessed me and carried on shamefully, poor thing, when I came back to the doorway holding his shirt, still warm from the iron, and went away down the yard, lugging that great burden of a sample-case as if it were all the weight of the world and, for him, no end of the world's long road or, at least, the road of that world he called his route, the territory. And though, Lord knows, he was to come again to the house it was the last of his morning calls, the last I ever saw of him, close-at-hand: head-bowed and slump-shouldered with that weariness whose meaning I could never quite define and climbed into his Model-T with the straw-hat jiggling on his head as he went down the yard-ruts toward the river road and banged and chattered off into the mists of that queer morning. And to this very day as I sit here telling you of it I will swear that he was mad and cracked and nothing more than that and I will never let myself believe for long that which in certain moments, alone and in weak-mindedness, I have let my poor mind fancy he may have been. I must surely own that I was indeed mad as a hare, for a spell that morning, for I wandered through that big house stunned and mumbling, letting my whole ovenful of elegant bread burn till the air of the whole downstairs reeked blue with the smoke of it, after I had stood in the back door and seen the dead robins and starlings lying about with upcurled feet in the seer, dead grass beneath the chinaberry tree and saw, as well, how its big, young leaves had lost their glowing greenness and turned dry and flannel-grey, some of them drifting down to earth in the mad black drummer's wake as if he had left behind him one evil and untimely moment of November in the cursed twinkling of a springtime morning. And the children were all crying except brave Jewel who was comforting Sam, and Sally, through her sobs, was trying to explain how he had only touched the drummer's hand with his fingers, begging a sample, and it was that, of course, that fairly turned my senses inside out and I sat for an hour in the kitchen hugging Sam hard against my breasts, my wits not comprehending till halfway through the afternoon that his small right hand was lame and withered blue and the fingers curled in like the little foot of one of the dead birds in the yard.

I soaked his hand for a spell in cracked ice and then packed it round with steaming hot towels and then took it out and rubbed it good to get the circulation back, trying to think what Doctor Will would do, and half-mad with wondering and fright and put him under all the winter quilts and comforters in the featherbed and trying everything I could imagine or remember and worked over him till late into the evening, forgetting all about Doctor Will's supper and prayed and sang hymns and talked to shapes in the lamplight shadows as if my dead Welsh father were there and scared poor Sally even worse when I thought I saw mother in the curtains and begged her to run and fetch some camphor-ice and put the kettle on for tea: poor meek Sally, she ran off wailing to the third-floor and hid in the clothes-press in the sewing-room, though Jewel was a strength of a rock to me that awful night: running to fetch more blankets from the cupboard in the hall and doing all the things I should have had the sense and strength to do for Sam was in the parched clutch of a fever, racked and chattering beneath the mountains of goosedown and flannel bedclothes. And Sally who wanted so terribly to be as useful as Jewel, overcame her fright from time to time and stole down from her hiding-place to creep into the midst of us and kneel by the featherbed and because she was too shaken with terror, poor child, to remember any prayer I'd ever taught her, could think of nothing to recite save her ABC's which she would say gravely, with tight squinched eyes and clasped, cold hands, in the high, brave voice of a boy and it seemed as grand a prayer as any said amongst us there that night.

That's queer, I was to hear Doctor Will say on a summer evening long weeks after then. It looks as if my chinaberry tree is dead. I guess I'll have to send for Wiley Kelts to saw the poor thing down. But it *is* queer. For it did put out such a fine growth of new leaves this spring.

I know it's an old tree but I did reckon it would last another five summers or so.

Still I never breathed a word of comment, for I'd never once told him of the black drummer's call that morning and when he had come home that night, at last, soon after midnight, he had taken a look at my Sam and sat up working with him till morning and brought him out of the ravings of his fever and said how lucky I was, sad as it was about Sam's curled, useless hand, because it might have been his legs and a lifelong lameness or, worse than that, no life at all. Though all that last summer, when he'd bring up the subject of Sam's illness, Doctor Will would look at me in that piercing, close, gentle way of his, smiling a little, scowling a little, his great white head tilted, suspecting something or other about it that I hadn't told him, and every week or so he'd put a toy in the child's good hand to keep him interested while he worked the lame hand out of the little pocket where Sam kept it hidden with a child's natural shame and he'd study it and work with it, purse-lipped and puzzled, and say it wasn't any sort of infectious paralysis at all since the tendons weren't wasted and slack and, besides, the symptoms were all wrong for that: turned round backwards and counter-clock-wise, as it were, with the paralysis coming first and the fever and sore-throat after, and then he'd study my face again with that curious, close inquiry of black eyes and it was all I could do to keep from blurting it all out to him: the whole wild tale of that black morning when the mad drummer called. And having kept that silence has anguished my conscience ever since. Now often in the nights of this lonely autumn, in the emptiness of this old house, with stillnesses seeming to stand listening in every room; October nights silent save for the dreaming breath and stir of the children in their quilts and the talking of the clocks and the old wind breathing its river myths against the glass of every pane, I lay awake till long past the hour when Doctor Will used to come home and ask myself again if I might not have warned him in time and saved the tragedy of those precious ones from ever being. If only I had been brave enough to tell him my half-mad guesses at the black drummer's nature. If only, I think, again and again in the dark, if only. And in the end I always tell myself that he knew. Nor will I soon forget the morning of a shopping-day in Glory five years ago this November when I was coming out of Kroger's with a bagful of groceries and spied that familiar, dilapidated Model-T parked up Lafayette Avenue under the trees and I stood a spell watching and presently saw Doctor Follansbee come out of the door of his office and walk the black drummer down the steps to the running-board: the two of them laughing and clubby as lodge-brothers, arm-in-arm, and the faces of each content with a deal well-made and pausing between puffs on their long, fresh Wheeling stogies to poke each other's ribs and kid a spell before the caller climbed into his Ford and even then the doctor leaned in, resting his elbow on the sample-case, talking shop a while longer and smiling and nodding, thick as thieves.

Well, Doctor Will never sent to Glory for the handyman and his saw because the chinaberry tree suddenly sent out small buds of second green that June, as if in a brave, vegetable utterance of life's impudent everlastingness, and though Sam's small hand got no better, at least, it showed no signs of wasting and, strange to say, it seemed to me a care-free, dreamy summer, with dry, warm days and soft, cool nights with great river fogs come up from the willows to stand round the land in blurred and woolly everywhereness, like mid-summer ghosts of Christmasses come back. And I've never seen nor sniffed such feasts of great white blossoms among the polished, dark leaves of Doctor Will's General Washington Roses: that ancient, vast bush that seemed to fill half the garden and with a trunk as thick round as a man's shoulders and which had grown there, it was said, from the first cutting planted by Doctor Will's grandmother in the fall of 1799. And strange, too, I suppose it may seem that, never since our first years, had my Vergil seemed closer to me than in those nights; it was as if, indeed, the mean and senseless lie the black drummer had made up to tell me out of the warped and fevered fancies of his mad mind had only implanted more freshly in my wits and senses the certainty that somewhere yonder in the land wild Vergil Turk, footloose and contrary notwithstanding, was more surely well and alive than ever.

And all the enchantment of those dream nights and days was sweetened even more by Marcy Cresap who now, working closer than ever with Doctor Will, came more often to the house. I cherished her visits and well do I remember the morning she called on the very Monday of that last week; she was looking for Doctor Will to take with her up Fish Creek to treat a boy with mumps and when I told her he had gone off long before dayrise with his breakfast in a paper poke and his hat on backwards she shook her head and laughed and stayed a spell anyway and we drank a whole pot of fresh coffee and she had two of my fresh cinnamon buns and we talked a good little while, as close as sisters, sitting on these very split-bottom chairs right here in Doctor Will's office, under the blushing light of the two Suzannes, and it was then that I told Marcy Cresap my feelings in the court-room in those winter afternoons and said how her own brave face had put me in mind of the angry, wild French girl up yonder in her twin, gold frames and she laughed at that and said, indeed, she'd felt as naked as that up there before the knotted ranks of her foes, though not nearly so pretty as that, she added; still she was pleased, I knew, that I had said such a thing.

And you beat them all so soundly, I said, warmly. And that's what matters, Miss Marcy. It was an hour of triumph.

No, she said, with a smile, the light of the river quivering in the dimpling curve of her cheek. I didn't beat them, my dear. I stood them off for an instant, that's all. You know this as well as I do, Martha Ann, for you are kind and wise and sensible-natured. That there is no beating anyone—no losing anything. Not in Apple County, not anywhere on earth, not in all the eternities of ticking time. There is only the ebb and wane of things—comeback and loss—leavetaking and return—nothing lasts, yet everything endures. And through the queer, imponderable riddle of that there run the threads of the simple things we seem to see: life and death; love and hate; goodness and wrong. For those are woven together so alike that it's an impudence of us, in our piteous little wisdom, to call one from the other. And do you know, Martha Ann, I believe that if all the voices of Glory—the quick and the dead alike—could speak of their lives they'd only be telling us that—they'd be admitting that—whether their voices wanted to or not?

Life is a misery, I said, stupid as a pudding, and not meaning that at all, yet tongueless to utter something wiser than that.

Oh, no! It's a glory!—a glory! cried Marcy Cresap. So long as we're bound to keep on doing what we have to do—what we were born to do!

A glory. Yes, I know. I know. I'm a fool sometimes, I said. For I know I'd live it all again—even the miseries of it—and live it a thousand times over, just for the pure, glad wonder of it; the queer blessing of being alive at all. And yet I swear that in those afternoons in the court while I sat witnessing you on the rack before those men—I never thought so poorly of this world as then. But then in the end I saw it wasn't so bad a place after all. Seeing you up there smiling in the faces of those shameless wretches in your hour of triumph.

But Marcy Cresap shook her head again and smiled softly.

In the work I've tried to do in Apple County, she said, I'm afraid there are no hours of triumph. There are only moments. There are those bright twinklings in time when even Death himself seems sickened at the thriving of his trade and turns his face away in disgust at the greed of his merchants. And, even for them, there are moments of lightning-flash vision—the flickering of an eye when man stops his savage, grinding getting and gives that one, close pitying look, that moment's mercy. Because in that twinkling he sees the face of his victim is his own—and himself no more than the shadow of his brother. A moment. One firefly wink in an immeasurable darkness. And then it goes out. But it always comes back. And always goes. And always comes again. It never ends.

But the sound of her soft, impassioned words brought back in a rush of remembering all my feelings in the court-room on those winter afternoons and I couldn't see anything just then but the faces of those doctors and I told her so.

It was all I could do to keep my seat amongst that mob, Miss Marcy! I cried out, my sight of her all swimming now in a blur of mad tears. For my blood fairly boiled at the sights and the sounds of those evil men!

But the doctors of Glory aren't evil, Martha Ann, smiled Marcy. They are sad and lonely men. For they have lost something they'll probably never recover. They're not evil. They're only poets who've forgotten how. If you feel anything for them feel pity. For they are just old and lonely bookkeepers now who've forgotten that once they meant to write poems in the smiling cheeks of children, put songs into the healthy lungs of men, bring kicking miracles out of women's wombs. And now all they care to do, poor dears, is scribble debts and credits in a ledger.

Well, not Doctor Will, at least. He's not forgot! Nor have you! I exclaimed in a pitch of wrath at the world of things that be. God pity Apple County on the day it should ever lose its Will Cecil or its Marcy Cresap!

Yes, but that's the very gist of all I'm trying to say this morning, Marcy said. For surely we'll not be here forever—.

And for an instant the little room seemed hushed until a solemn, curious smile stole round Marcy's mouth and she turned her stare to the gold and river-green and coppery sun lights in the white, dancing curtains and the tossing froth of lilacs in the blowing window and, beyond it, the fine country air of all that bright day shimmering with the sheens of watered-silk.

No, some day we will surely go, she went on. Doctor Will is very old. And as for me—well, I think I'm too ornery and stubborn to be going for a while yet. Still, if I should die tonight—would it all change?—would anything really end? Someone would come. It might be a while. But someone would come, Martha Ann. Before long somebody else would show up one morning in Glory at the health office door—contrarier and crazier with hopes and more troublesome than Doctor Will and me—and doing our jobs far better than ever we dared dream.

I'll never admit such a thing, I said. No one could ever take your place in Apple County, Marcy Cresap.

And yet if you really believed that, Martha Ann, said Marcy, glancing at me swiftly, with strange, dark reproach in her eyes. Then you couldn't believe in me. If you really thought that all I ever fought for will vanish when I go—then you couldn't believe in human life itself, which is all it ever was—all I've ever had the time to bother about.

I know that, dear, I know that! I shouted miserably, with an angry, foolish toss of my head. Oh, it's only that I haven't got the gift in my weak, poor wits to say what I mean to say! How else can I say words to tell you what I feel?—that you're you. That's all! Glory's never had but one and never another could be. What other words than to say you're what you are, that's all—that you're Marcy Cresap!

I am no one, Martha Ann, she said with a kind smile and leaned across to lay her fingers on my fidgeting, troubled hand. I am a moment. That's all I really am. I am a twinkling blaze of little anger—just like you, my dear, and like that girl up there in the paintings. We flicker for an instant in the gigantic preponderance of dark. And in that instant we fumble round to do what we must do in the time we've got to do it. We do what we have to do. And for me that's always been to try to patch up broken things. And the time of my light isn't long enough. Apply County is too full of broken things. And I guess that's true of all the world, as well—though Apple County's all the world I know. And even in this little world of Apple County—the time of the light just isn't long enough. Maybe that's why I'm always hurrying so. Because most of the time I'm so shamelessly vain as to think I can get them all fixed in my own little moment. I'm just like you, Martha Ann, and forget sometimes that some day someone will have to take my place —will have to finish fixing all the things I wasn't quick enough or wise enough or kind enough to do. And new things getting broken every day! So you see, my dear, someone just has to come. And because someone must, someone always does. That's what I mean when I look back on so many things through the years—that last day in the county-court—and swear to you that there's really no losing, no winning; no beginning nor any end. There's none of life so simple as that, thank the Lord, or the ones in Glory who've fought me so hard would have ended me long since. And to tell you the truth, I'd never have loved any of it with such a fury if it were all so dull and simple as that: the matter of a naked yes or no, good or bad, all love or hate, and life or death a hope-less certainty. I've adored the huge, staring puzzles of my mornings—the living, vast riddles of my every days, and each riddle with as many Apple County answers as there are Apple County noses—and behind each nose a thousand, contradicting Apple County answers more! For when have I ever once searched any face in Glory and seen all one truth and none of its opposite? And who in Apple County has ever despised me so much that he hasn't loved a little the very things that I've loved, too? Who is totally heartless here in Glory—who is hopeless? I'll never believe I've ever met one who was. I've never yet heard any voice in Glory that raged at me with a hate so loud that I couldn't hear behind it the nearly-stilled clamor of its lost, forgotten love. And I have yet to listen to a sick chest rattling so sharp with death that I couldn't hear the brave, contrary drumming of its heartbeat, wild with life! Who's all one thing and none of the other here in Apple County, Martha Ann? No one—and least of all me, for I have seen hate, vindictiveness, envy, bitterness and bad-minded outrage in my own face in the bedroom mirror at night that would shame the consciences of the doctors them-selves. The world's a babbling argument and everyone's a world. And every voice of Glory is a chorus—a wild, queer choir in the church of each one's flesh, and half the voices singing other tunes! Heartlessness? Hopelessness? Lord, how could I ever believe in such easy nonsensities? I'd never have stayed in health-work all this long while if I did. I've held my stethescope against too many hearts ever to believe in heartless-ness, and hoped through the vigil of too many sickbed nights ever to believe in hopelessness. I have faced diphtheria in a small child's throat and blind ambition in a doctor's mind and fought both of those ill-nesses the best I knew how. And for me, the glory through it all has always been the hope they'd both get well. The unpredictables, Martha Ann, the living, lovely riddles! How I've adored them!—even the many times they broke my heart. Creation never meant such tedious crudeness as a black and white to things—God is no bore!—there are all those vast, human gardens of innumerable, dazzling colors on every side of things and above and below them, too, and in their very midst! Birth, with all warm and glowing life behind it; Death, with all shining and strange life ahead!—and betwixt and between them both that wonderful, terrible, twinkling, rainbow moment that's a little like them each! Oh, come now, Martha Ann—whatever have I said to bring tears to your cheeks? Why,—next to Doctor Will—I'm the greatest optimist in Apple County! Just look out yonder into his garden! How glorious it is this year! I declare, never in my time can I remember a summer when it's seemed so wild with bloom. Why, it's all a great bonfire of flowers tossing the flames of their moment against the sky! Look at it, my dear—*listen* to it, my dear! The garden is saying everything I've said. For here it is August now—and not a green and flowering thing out there will live to see the snow, nor will it die and miss the spring. It will only hush and sleep a while and come again.

And I am quite good-humoredly resigned to it that you who listen now to my voice in this fair, keen October morning and who grew half-persuaded of my queer-wittedness after my tale of the black drummer's coming and all the black wildness in his wake—which was every word of it so true that I would swear to it before the two eyes of God Himself—I am certain, I say, that you will now be all the way persuaded of my madness when I say that Marcy Cresap's visit that morning filled my senses with the surest, saddest premonitions of everything which was, indeed, to come before that very week was out. Think what you must of me but bear in mind, if you please, that I am a country-woman with the mother-wit and wonder of the country-born—those other-senses, often city-stifled, or else bricked-up, condemned and smothered in the tomb of sophistication: the simple, witnessing wonder of all children in their unastonished cunning. And you who so fixedly deny belief in other worlds might well make certain first that other worlds do not believe in you. Still, I must own to it—that I do have more of my Welsh father's wild fantasy to my nature than any of the rock-solid Episcopalianism of my Yorkshire mother. And my father often used to say that though he was the preacher in our family, mother was the pure Christian beneath his roof and himself more pagan than he sometimes dared to think, and though mother would never listen to him when such a mood seized him, there was many's the night he'd gather Glynis and Gwen and me close round him in the lamplight and tell us of his boyhood tramping all over France and Ireland and all the shires of England—he'd run off from Wales when he was scarcely seven to keep from going with the other children to dig in the mines. And he'd speak of fairy-lights and speaking-trees and tiny men and girls who danced and fiddled in moonlit meadows while he watched them from the haystack which was his night's home, bed and shelter and he'd tell how, as a young man about to enter the ministry, he had nonetheless found small difference between the barbaric, rock temple at Stonehenge and the steeple spires of country Christian churches since they were both stone raised by man's hands in praise of God.

And if poor mother had not done with the dishes by then and fled next door to the kitchen of Jenny Stone, the plumber's wife, she'd cover both her ears with her soapy hands and run in the pantry and shut the door to keep from hearing father tell of Llew Llaw Gyffes, the Welshman who was born of a virgin exactly as our Lord was, or maybe even tell us again how he'd seen, in the meadows of Brittany, huge, long stones standing on end that were shaped like the privates of a man and a cross stuck on top and gospel pictures chiselled across them where the old, first Christian priests had come and made the best they could of what was already there and all of it one and the same till you couldn't tell where one man's worship left off and another's began and not much matter, really, since the praise of the flesh and the spirit were, in my father's notion, both holy sights in the eyes and thoughts of God's enormous mind. And always when he was done talking to us in those long ago evenings, he'd lay his hand upon the heads of Gwen and Glynis and me, each in our turn of age, and tell us that a pretty girl's healthy, happy body was a temple finer than any church or shrine or stone and he'd swear sometimes he thought, for all we knew, God might be a lovely woman and not the solemn, bearded patriarch the Bible pictures show and then he'd stand up in the lampshine and in his singing voice he'd shout the little song of Daffyd ap Gwylim: "My face towards the fine girl—My back to the pure God" and though he spoke it in Welsh we all knew its meaning by then, even poor mother who was always scandalized into a sick headache by it.

Please do try to understand why there's such a need in me now to speak of my father who, in his vagrant, beautiful strength was so strangely like my Vergil in his wayfaring, beautiful weakness. Please rest assured that in this moment of speaking to you my courage needs the comfort of such rallying remembrances. For the night of the drummer's return in that black August week was the night, as well, when Vergil came back to Glory. Doctor Will had come home a little after sundown that evening and Marcy Cresap was with him and behind them, stretched out on a make-do ironing-board stretcher in the backseat of Marcy's touring-car, was a little boy no more than five with his eyes closed and the flesh of his breathless face as pale as yeast, while his head all round was heaped with white bandages like a rajah in his turbans. Marcy said he'd fallen from a swing in the Glory playground and struck his head on the concrete and Doctor Will said it might be only concussion of the brain though it might just as easily be a fracture and because of that we carried him flat on Marcy's ironing-board up to the south room on the third-floor and put him in the great, high-backed walnut bed where Doctor Will was born.

I might just as well saved my breath for I knew without asking, since that lovely old bed was so seldom without one of them in it, but still I asked it anyway: Another one the hospital wouldn't take? And Doctor Will nodded; he was bending now over the child's face gravely, tenderly, to lift each eyelid with his long, wise thumb and shone his flashlight close to stare into each eye, one by one. And presently he straightened up and stood back from the bed, thrusting his shoulders back in that All-we-can-do-now-is-wait gesture I'd come to know so well; his eyes burning with troubled concern and his proud face full of a kind of guilty dumbfound and abeyance, while his big fingers gave forth a faint, swift whisper as they stroked his thumbtips in a movement of humble fury as much as to say that they had spent half their fifty years of doctoring in such impotent, desperate attendance. While behind us in the bedroom doorway, Jewel and Sally and Sam who had followed the whole, queer, creeping procession up from the yard stood clumped close together by the little, white, ancient washstand, staring at the small figure on the bed and sucked their thumbs gravely, their three white faces round as supper plates, wordless and wide-eyed as we before the still figure of the child whose littleness seemed so much littler beneath the great bandaged bunting of his out-sized head.

Little children like this, said Doctor Will suddenly, with a quick smile of angry cheerfulness. They're extraordinary, Marcy—isn't that so? You know how they lie like this sometimes for hours and you'd swear they're gone and if they were grown-ups and had such a crack on the head they probably *would* be gone and yet you turn your back on them for an instant and before you can blink your eyes they're up in the bed and calling for their supper. One minute you'd swear they were gone and in a twinkling they're ready for you to play some little game with them! Sometimes! You've seen it, Marcy. So many times!

And then he grew grave and, raging with his helplessness at not knowing the unfailing key to such infant miracles, he folded his hands behind him under his coattails as if to hide from himself their dreadful, mortal ineptness and stared down at the child's face again, waiting in wonder and hope, his great, straight frame alive and tense with them, and his face flushed and baffled before the maddening platitude that all his half-century's medical wisdom and all the medical books in all the vast, huge libraries of the great universities in France and Switzerland were suddenly diminished to a something simpler, littler than one small word that lay there before him, unfound, unknown, unreadable, behind a child's sleeping face. And all the while I stood back in the hallway's yellow gaslight, twisting my wedding ring and swallowing hard like a spineless ninny whilst I breathed in the courage of my breath to tell Doctor Will what there'd been no time to tell him in the shocked and scurrying urgency of the yard by Marcy's car, nor on the stairs up which the three of us so gentlingly had moved, scuffling and struggling on every step to keep the fragile burden of the hurt child level on the ironing-board between us. And when at last I found my senses to say it, I heard my voice as if it weren't my own, like words in dreams.

You have a visitor waiting out yonder beyond the garden, Doctor Will.

Thank you, Martha Ann. I'm quite sure I do, he said presently and went angrily to the window and drew back the little chintz curtain to glare down through the firefly dark, while Marcy and I stood behind him, so that we all saw plainly the flare of the kitchen match that blew and shone on the visitor's sallow face as he lit up a fresh stogie and leaned back against the sample-case in the seat beside him and settled down to puff and take his ease and sweet time waiting in the misty, deepening dusk.

Yes, of course he would be there, I heard Doctor Will's voice murmur somewhere as the night breeze from the river set the curtains fluttering over his shoulders. Why wouldn't he be there—waiting tonight? Hasn't he always been there in all the other nights—waiting for Marcy or me? Now stop your worrying, Martha Ann, and gather your wits together. All I ask of you is to stay here and keep watch by the bedside of this little child.

I can scarcely remember their leaving the room, the sound of their footfalls going down the stairs, nor Doctor Will's voice far down in the yard as he boldly beckoned the drummer in, for I was still numb with the fears of those hours since four that afternoon when the car first came rattling up the river road and parked out yonder beyond the western-most corner of the rose-garden, keeping back in the green cool of the willows and out of the mid-day's bee sweet blaze, while the drummer settled back to take his time and kill a few hours, waiting for Doctor Will. And now I sat by the bed and heard the distant slam of Doctor Will's office door and the faint brass cry of the key as he locked himself and Marcy in, alone there to face that scoundrel. The bed room was very still except for the sounds of three wet thumbs in the mouths of my own sleepy small ones and the slow, sharp breath of the child upon the quilt at my elbow, while through the open window, from far up yonder on the flats below the smelter, I could hear the thin, tinny brightness of the little brass-band tuning up for the evening show, for it had been on the morning of that very day that the circus came back to Glory. Lord, such a tangling of sounds un-akin, I thought to myself, though such is surely the common, odd clamor of life itself: the comic and fateful all wedded together to make the air preposterous.

The child's face on the quilt looked whiter than ever beneath the great bun of gauze and his breath seemed quickening and queer and I fancied to myself that he was not going to come round and the awful thought crossed my mind that if he died suddenly I should have no notion of what I should tell Jewel and Sally and Sam who would instantly and surely, with children's senses know, for they had never once taken their eyes from his face from the moment he was laid there. If it happened, I wanted them out of the sight of it and made up my mind it was safe to leave the poor child alone for the moment it would take to hustle them down to the second-floor bedroom, for Sally lately had taken over the nightly washing of Sam's face and helping him and Jewel into their night-clothes and tucking them and herself under the quilt before I came in to hear their prayers and kiss them and turn out the gas-light over the bed. And so I told them and got up and went toward them in the doorway to herd the cluster of them quickly before me down the stairs, when suddenly they broke apart from each other and stepping past me as if I weren't there and without a sound, walked to the bed and each laid something on the quilt. And I knew it was the moment they'd been waiting for through all this tedious while, holding

those things behind their backs with hushed, grave patience till the right
time came: Sally her long-awaited patent-leather ladies' purse with
Doctor Will's Christmas silver dollar still unspent inside it, Jewel, a
small green bottle of dreadful dime-store perfume which, though long
empty, she still treasured constantly on a string around her neck to be
lifted and sniffed at thoughtfully now and then, and Sam a coveted
moonstone he had found once in the gravel-pit by the river. I stood
a moment looking down at my children's heads and the things on the
quilt and bit my tongue hard for fear I'd say a word and be a worse
fool than I'd been that livelong day; I hurried them off downstairs to
their bed, scolding them before me the way I always do when I'm mad
at myself for some uanswerable thing I've watched them do; I stood for
a spell in the hallway's yellow light, hearing their hoarse, excited whispers behind the door which on that night, you may be sure, I locked
behind me, dropping the cold key between my breasts; hearing, too, the
sound of voices that blew up the stairway from downstairs through the
cracks of that other locked door to the little office just below: the
quaking rage of Doctor Will, the gentle, interposing murmur of Marcy's
eternal calmness, the jokey, pleasant cackle of the drummer's bargaining whine. Though I could make out no word of what they were saying,
thank the Lord, and presently went hurrying back up to my rocker by
the sick child's bed.

It seemed a long while that I sat there, though I remember once going
over to the window and drawing back the curtains to look out into the
winking, starry wonder of that lovely August night with the air rich with
the smell of fresh-mown meadows, sweet as the breath of cows, and the
whole darkness drenched with reeking wisps of the scent of Doctor
Will's jasmine like some wanton perfume in the scandalous, black hair
of a foolish girl and I could see just the palest beginnings of mist
on the bottomlands at the river's edge, though the night above was a
cloudless perfection with the cold, clean curl of a new moon and the
stars so thick you couldn't have guessed where stars left off and fireflies
began if the fireflies hadn't dipped and burned and seemed to breathe in
a breath of the dark before they burned again; and there was a breeze
that rose and fell and I could hear on the wind the circus-band striking
up "The Entrance of the Gladiators" up on the smelter flats as the
evening-show began and then, as it always had to me, it seemed a sad
thing to hear those horns a-mingling with the sounds of the locusts
crying the end of summer in the trees. And I thought to myself angrily

that it had no business to be a night so beautiful with its blowing fireflies and its stars and new moon and its smells of life and the good-time
tunes of the circus-band rising and falling on its wind and the dark of
it all alive with choiring locusts and twang of the green frogs under the
mists of the shore and all the valley's river sweetness wild with scents
and senses and sound of its living, green and flowering things out there;
no, it seemed a pure, shameful impudence that it be such a fair, fine
night whilst the black drummer sat on a chair in a room of this very
house, troubling Doctor Will and Marcy Cresap with the easy harangue
of his tirading, tireless enterprise, and all of it yonder in the night so
boisterously live and lovely whilst behind me on the quilt lay that hurt,
small creature with the whole of what Marcy would call his twinkling instant laid there in the measure, balanced between the huge
unfathomables.

It seemed, in that moment at the window, that I had never before felt
so hopelessly the queer, contrary, self-battling doubleness of things, and
when I turned again and looked again at the blanched and blushless
face of the child and heard his slow, hard breath, I felt so certain that
at any moment he would wink out like a dear, little broken lamp, that I
sank played-out in the rocking-chair, heartsick and blood-boiling mad
at life and death alike. As I have said, it seemed a long while that I sat
there, for I worked myself into as fine a state of fury and perplexment
as had come upon me in the court in those winter afternoons: I heard
the clocks in the house speak twice, so I suppose I sat so for an hour,
growing more troubled by the minute: I felt for the key in my dress-
front a dozen times, thinking after the safety of my Sally and Jewel
under the same roof with that rascal of a drummer and of my Sam with
his small hand already lame from the touch of him and I rocked and
rocked till at last I dozed off, I suppose from nothing other than plain,
spent outrage and dreamed I could hear all the voices of Glory out there
in the night, talking beyond the window, not speaking all at once in a
clamor, mind you, but each one in his turn coming forth to speak some
little thought about himself and a guess as good as yours at what on
earth his life could possibly have been about, and then it seemed that
Vergil was looking out at me from the bureau mirror, smiling at me
with his head tilted and his chin resting on the bent, gold bell of his
trombone; smiling at me with his old, endearing, crooked-mouth, bash-
ful way and not saying a word except with his eyes: that he was sorry he
hadn't done better but thankful just the same to have been here a while

at all, better or worse, and then my father stood in the blowing curtains in a fresh, white linen suit, looking at me for a spell with the fireflies and stars behind him, winking through his shirt-front and shining through his sleeves, and one hand reaching into the faded forest of the wallpaper for the hand of someone else who was dimly there: it was mother, I suppose, and directly his eyes gentled into a stern and dreamy strangeness and I clearly remember him saying: *Let mystery be mystery, Annie girl. For there's no either to things like these—nor any or. There's only being: before, between and beyond—and that's a splendor enough to blind the eyes of angels!* And I remember puzzling over that and thinking: What a queer thing—what a peculiar, queer thing my father just said and it was, indeed, a voice that woke me from my doze and no dream voice either for when I opened my blinking eyelids wide there was in the bedroom still the sense and echo of living speech. And I shook myself by the shoulders and scolded myself with a couple of angry pinches and gave the chair a couple of quick rocks with a thrust of my heels, simply furious and disgusted with myself for having let my head nod, even for that moment neglecting the simple vigil to which Doctor Will had entrusted me, and when I turned my glance anxiously to the bed beside me I might just as well have died right there in my clothes. For the quilt was empty and the child nowhere to be seen. I'll not tell you the fancies and unsensible horrors that crowded into my mind in that moment as I sat there, gathering back into myself the breath to run screaming downstairs for Marcy and Doctor Will.

I sure would admire to go to that circus-show tonight, a pipey voice said quite distinctly in the room.

And I saw him then, beyond the bed, sitting on the carpet-stool by the window, his huge white bandaged head balanced somehow absurdly on the face that rested in the cup of his hands, his eyes to the window in a great gaze of longing thoughtfulness, while between his bare toes in a little heap lay the gifts of Jewel and Sally and Sam.

Honey, honey, you shouldn't be out of the bed! I cried out and ran to him and then, in my joy, ran to the door to call downstairs the news and then back to the child again. Oh, my dear little dear, you're all right—you're all right! I cried out and ran back to the door and called for Doctor Will and Marcy though my voice was gone to such a whispery breathlessness they couldn't have heard me if they'd been just over the threshold so I ran back to the child and knelt on the rag-rug by his side.

But don't you think you should be back in the bed? I said gently.

Oh, no, he said with a grand, scorning wave of his hand. I had enough of that.

And then he looked at me and smiled politely and patted me on the arm with his fingers.

Thank you kindly, ma'am, he said solemnly. Don't worry a bit about me. I slept just grand.

And some pink was already back in his fat cheeks, though his face did still seem to be a little peaked and there were still small shadows under his huge, brown eyes, yet I thought better than to tell him how bad off he'd been and make a fuss with him about the bed; I only prayed he'd be none the worse for sitting up and that Doctor Will wouldn't be long in coming.

And you feel all right? I inquired in a voice as casual as I could make it.

Oh, yes. Just fine. I thank you, ma'am, he said. I feel just grand.

And then he returned the sad gaze of his round, wide eyes to the night beyond the curtains that blew around the great white bundle of his head.

Though I sure would admire to go to that circus-show tonight, he whispered wistfully to the tuneful wind and good-time sweetness yonder in the dark.

Oh, but it's far too late, I'm afraid, said I. For the show will be letting out in another ten minutes. Hear the band now?—that's "The Sheik of Araby". That's what they always play before the last act goes on. You see, I know all about circuses. For I used to work in the very one that's here in Glory tonight. "The Sheik of Araby"—that's the next to the very last tune the brass band plays. Oh, just listen, my dear, listen!

And though he'd turned away from the window now and was asking me if I had really worked in the circus and if I got in whenever I wanted without paying to see the show and all kinds of such natural questions I was scarcely able to answer him for listening. Because now it was "Rocked in the Cradle of the Deep." Vergil's solo. Don't you fancy I would know? Spend a thousand days and night with a trombone player and don't you know? The way he plays a tune that no trombone player ever to be born could ever play just that way again. Could the dullest ears and heart and memory God ever gave a woman make such a mistake? Not mine, at least. I knew; it was Vergil all right.

It was Vergil—alive and it was the child-alive and the beauty of the night beyond that window had been the world-alive if only my poor faith had not caught its foot and stumbled, unbelieving. And I squatted there listening to the horn of Vergil and the voice of the child while my eyes filled with angry tears at the lie the black drummer had brought to my kitchen-door that morning to tear open the living heart of me with grief, that black lie that my darling Vergil had died. And I bit my tongue with fury and my blood just boiling at the thought of him down there at that very moment with more of his black lies rolling off his black tongue right into the laps of poor Doctor Will and Marcy. For I thought of the child on the quilt: Death's living image not an hour gone by and now he squatted on the carpet stool by the window, alive, alive, good Lord, how alive! and tugging at my sleeve with his fingers and whispering questions, cherry-cheeked and shining-eyed, all awe and wonder, while I like a poor, dumb-tongued ninny answered him the best I knew how with all my thoughts such a tumult of gladness and outrage and joy and wrath and that other, utterly nameless human feeling which is the sweet marrow of our very souls' bold bones and bids abide in us that living, careless and cantankerous beauty which snaps its fingers under Death's own nose and then runs off to see the circus on the flats. Yes, it was all there in my thoughts, like a good stew bubbling in its pot at suppertime. And how I wanted to run out into the hall and stand at the top of the stairs with my feet apart and my fists on my hips and yell down in a voice that he would hear even behind the locked door of that little office: Liar! You old black, lying drummer you! You fake with a suit-case full of worthless this and that. You peddler with nought to peddle—drummer with no drum to wake the villages of Apple County with your bogus wares. My Vergil is alive!— hear his sweet horn yonder with the circus-band on the flats! The child's alive!—listen to his prattling voice in this room where only an hour gone by Death shared a quilt with him! Run yonder to your car, black drummer! Run off down the river road and hide in the mists, black drummer! And if you ever dare so much as show your dark face at my kitchen-door again I'll lay that sample-case upside your head!

And you may be sure there was another yearning in me, too—Lord, my heart was full of so many things that night! For I knew my Vergil wouldn't have come back to Glory that day if he hadn't wanted to see something of the children and me. Yet he had always been that way— that shy and strange! It was so like him to wait till night to tell me he was here—to know I'd hear his horn and let its sweetness speak for him and make me come. And even to this day it seems such a queer, unseemly tangling of times that the one night after all those long ten years that he'd come back to Glory and know I'd hear his trombone in the band and yearn till I ached with it to rouse and dress the children and run with them across the meadows and the railroad tracks, hurrying toward the twinkle of the circus on the flats—that this would be a night I couldn't leave. For Doctor Will and Marcy Cresap were still down in the locked office with that scoundrel. And Doctor Will had trusted me to stay with the child.

By twelve o'clock the evening-show was long out and I could hear the rousters shouting and their chinking sledges as they struck the tents and loaded the show in its wagons and sang till long past one, their voices and the barking of the little dogs and the rumble of their wagons fading into the distance on the river road. It was the end of summer. I fancy it was the last show of the season. But, as I told the sick child who'd wanted so badly to see the show that night—springtime is like sunrise. And summertime is only winter night's tomorrow. Summer will come back to Glory, I said. The circus will come back, I told the child. And Vergil will come back, I told myself. Though, strange to tell, since that night I've stopped waiting, looking, listening for that return. Maybe in the strangeness of my heart I don't even want it. In my queer way it's heart's ease sufficient to me to have heard him speak to me that August night—to have heard his trombone tell me he was alive and the black drummer had lied—that death could never lay its hushing hand upon his horn. And you must even believe me when I tell you now that I'm even glad I couldn't take the children and go to him that night. For ten years is a great while, really, and feelings dear to people sometimes change. Though I know that Vergil himself will never change: the good and the wayward of him either one. Yet often it's only heartbreak to go back to things—to search out those who left us once with love as the only legacy behind them. And so I abide content that I didn't go to him that night.

I have my Jewel and Sam and Sally and they are half of him, while I tell myself the other half of Vergil abides for-keeps in me—like a fourth child never born: singing in the play-room of my heart's gay days, weeping in the galleries of its now-and-then dark nights. Meanwhile, the far, muffled mutter of contention down in Doctor Will's office had long since ceased its drift up the breath of the staircase, and the child and I sat cross-legged on the rag-rug by the window, playing cat's-cradle with a length of darning-wool from my basket and listening to whip-poor-wills and owls dipping and whooping yonder in the misty meadows of the gold-dappled dark and the silvery scratch of crickets under the queen-anne's-lace; and giggling with scarey delight at the creaking sounds old houses make at such queer hours that are neither night nor morning, and telling each other little jokes and rhymes and chatting away in spells between the speaking of the clocks, though most of the chatting fell to me since the child couldn't seem to hear enough of my tales of the circus-days, and I'd hardly get one out till he'd be begging for another.

Ma'am, he said at last with a great grown-up sigh while his big eyes fixed upon me in a grave and worshiping stare. If I knowed as much as you do and had been to as many towns and seen as many things as you —deed to God, I'd go somewheres and start a store!

Poor little thing!—I knew from that how little of this world's good food and clothes and toys he'd known in his short five years that he'd always thought storekeepers nothing less than grand gods come to earth and I hugged him and we sat marvelling a spell at the little heap of gifts Jewel and Sally and Sam had brought to him and the way he guarded them so close between his small bare feet I swear I think he fancied they had come from fairies yonder in the twinkling meadow night and he sniffed at Jewel's little empty perfume bottle and presently, looking downwards as if not wanting to let on to me that it mattered so much to him, he asked where his mother was and if she was coming to fetch him home (asking "if", mind you, not "when" as though he'd long ago gained the good sense to expect to find more "ifs" than "whens" in the ragbag of hand-me-down fortune) and I told him then, as I'd heard Doctor Will say earlier, that his mother was across the river at Powhatan, where she worked as a house-maid, and that he and Marcy Cresap were going over at daybreak to bring her to him. And hardly had all the clocks in the house done with their scattered chimes at half-past two when I heard Doctor Will and Marcy laughing and chatting on their way up the stairs and the back-fire of the drummer's car as he rattled off down through the mists of the bottom-lands.

Just take a good look at our fine, little guest now, Doctor Will! I remember exclaiming when I saw their two faces smiling in from the bedroom doorway. Up and ornery and chirping like a fiddle! Lordy,

Doctor Will, when I first saw he was out of the bed and over yonder on the stool—gabbling away about circuses and the color creeping back to his cheeks and his eyes wide as big, bright pansies—it was all I could do to keep myself from running downstairs to hammer on the door and tell you!

But you wouldn't have had to, Martha Ann, said Doctor Will with a smile. I knew.

Yet how could you know? I thought to myself with a thrill of shivers. How ever down there—in the locked dreadfulness of those hours—how ever could you have known? something in me asked silently, and yet there had always been so many things that incalculable man knew that I kept to myself what seemed a foolish query. And Marcy came over smiling and gave my shoulders a hug, saying how half his getting better was due to me and my watching vigil by the bed, while Doctor Will, with much tickling and private jokes and whispering between them, got the child back under the quilt for there was a taste of chill in the air from the river breeze that billowed blustering in the curtains. Then both of them came in turn and kissed him goodnight and Doctor Will went and fetched the heap of little things that Jewel and Sally and Sam had brought and tucked them under the quilt-square by his neck and told him again how he and Marcy Cresap were driving down to Captina before sunrise to catch the first ferry to Powhatan and bring his mother across to fetch him home. And I remember how I stood by the door in the downstairs hall with Doctor Will after we'd waved goodnight to Marcy who'd gone home for her two hours' sleep and I looked through the door of the little office and saw to my relief that the twin Suzannes still shone rosy with defiant joy in the gold-leaf of their frames, for it had seemed to me, in my craziness that night, that the paint of her sculpted sweetness might be dark and tarnished after those pent-up hours in the black drummer's presence.

It's been a hard night for you, Martha Ann, Doctor Will said. Go to sleep now.

I'll sit up in the rocker, thank you, sir, I said.

There's no need to, he said, smiling again. He's all right now.

Well, I want to, I said. I really need to. I'd fret and lie awake from him. Indeed, I'd not sleep a wink listening for him to wake up crying in the fear of a strange bed, Doctor Will. I know the mind of a child in a darkness not his own. I'll sit up in the rocker.

And I bit my tongue to keep back the blithering tears I'd kept corked tight so long in the bottle of that night and wanted to blubber it all out into his poor, wearied ears, like any senseless fool of a female, that I chose to sit in the rocker till morning for a need of my own as much as the child's; I was bursting with words to tell Doctor Will of the splendor and wonders I'd heard and sensed and seen in that little room that night and how I was too great a coward to leave it for fear they'd all run away when the night ran out. I wanted to spend the rest of all the hushed, ticking hours till sunrise telling Doctor Will my happy, rioting thoughts about Vergil alive and the hurt child alive and, indeed, each of us alive and how my senses up there that night had all come suddenly to one swift, clear glimpse of that deathlessness of things as Marcy had told it to me that morning; and yet all I could find in the wit or tongue of me to blurt out in that moment was a silliness that shames me yet: This night has broken my heart with joy! I cried out with the mindlessness of emotion.

He smiled at that thoughtfully, courteously as if I'd said the wisest thing he'd ever heard.

And joy will come to break it again, he said. And so will grief. Taking their turns like sun and moon, my dear. For that's the way of the world —the way of hearts, at least.

And he kissed my hand goodnight and I remember before his going up the stairs his asking me if I'd bake a peach cobbler for him that day for he'd be coming in late that night and knew he'd be hungry for nothing but peach cobbler drenched in cold, thick Jersey cream for his midnight supper and I said I would and when he reached the top of the stairs he turned in the yellow light of the Welsbach flame by his bedroom door and leaned on the bannisters, looking down at me with that queer light caught in his great white mist of hair, his big face tilted thoughtful and smiling.

The human heart's a marvelous creation, Martha Ann, I'll always remember his saying. It's the only organ in the body of man that works better after it's been broken. Broken and patched and ticking away at the world again, better than ever it was before. But then you're a woman and I'm only a doctor, so I'm telling you something I judge you were born knowing and will always know, as woman has known it since that sunrise in Eden when she was shaped and rose, knowing and smiling, from that rib at the heart's very side!

And now as I sit here in the apple-bright, cold sunlight of this October morning and listen to the sound of my voice telling you how it was, that August night seems only a clock-tick moment gone. I remember how I sat awake all that night in the rocker by the child's bed, and though the lights were out, the moonshine in the window lay glowing in the curtains like a cold, blue-petalled flower. I couldn't sleep; it seemed I had no time to sleep, tired as I was. A great attentiveness seemed to grip my senses as I thought of Vergil alive and the child alive and the black drummer surely defeated forever in whatever towns of the territory he might wander and call. I stared in the dark, still seeing the look of triumph on Marcy's exhausted face in the hallway before she left and I felt the gentle, strong victory in Doctor Will's voice as he spoke to me from the top of the stairs. I sat awake all that night—as if it were too beautiful to miss, as if such a night as that would never come to Apple County again. I planned a morning in my kitchen fashioning the finest peach-cobbler ever baked, for Doctor Will when he came home late that night. And I witnessed again the wonder and witchery of the speaking, scented night beyond the window and it seemed that there was, indeed, as Marcy had said that day, no beginning to the stubborn everlastingness of things, nor any end. I dozed off in the rocker around the very hour when the last of the moon's cold shine paled into the first glow of milky dayrise in the sky on the eastern ridges.

I couldn't have slept but an hour but I was stiff in the chair with an old shawl of Doctor Will's wrapped round me and the light beyond the window was a thick, impenetrable world of morning mists. I shook myself angrily, shrugging the sleep and stiffness out of my joints and went downstairs, cross as a bear at myself, for Marcy had come by then and gone off with Doctor Will and I had wanted so to fix them both a good hot breakfast. It's a marvel to me yet that I remember anything of that morning: the river fog thicker and whiter than I had ever seen it, and I remember even less of the day that followed: that afternoon and evening through which I sat in Doctor Will's office as speechless and senseless as if I had died myself; that terrible while I sat alone after Tadd Cockayne drove down from Glory and told me about the accident. I wonder now if I thanked him for his kindness: I can't remember; I wonder now if he was crying, too, while he told me, though I would guess he was. At a little past seven that morning the two of them, in Marcy's car, went off the road in the fog two miles above Captina and were drowned in the deep place in the river bend called the Devil's Elbow.

Around ten that night I glanced madly at the two Suzannes, roused myself out of my stunned and shameful sloth, and hurried away to the kitchen to commence cooking, for the children hadn't had a bite to eat that day. I fried country ham and fixed a black iron potful of green beans and good, baked sweet potatoes and fixed Marcy's own recipe and my Sally's favorite: leaf lettuce wilted with hot ham gravy and vinegar over it. I even baked peach cobblers—one for each of the children, one even for myself and one more for something's sake. I cooked till past the strike of midnight and it was nearly one when I set before my four, starved dears the finest hot supper I'd fixed since Doctor Will's last birthday and sat and ate it with them, hungry as they, and all of us joking and carrying on the outrageous way we always did, as if nothing had happened at all, as if, indeed, nothing ever could. And the newcomer ate as if he'd not tasted a mouthful of honest home-cooking in weeks, his still big white-bundled head bent over his plate, some loops of its bandage come unwound and dangling under his nose and one tuft of corn-yellow hair poking out of the top after his hard day's play in the meadow and yet that head never once lifted for an hour while he stuffed his cheeks with my spiced-apples and buttermilk-cornbread and I kept filling his plate till I was afraid the famished little soul would eat himself sick. While from time to time I stole a glance to the starry night beyond the kitchen screen and wondered to myself about his mother for she had never come for him and, for that matter, she's not come yet and here it is eight weeks later. Though I've never once censured her for that, poor young thing, for heaven has fashioned the conscience of our natures all different as birds in a wood and I have often fancied the child's mother as a girl with three or four more like him to raise and with as many different fathers as there are faces to be washed each night and no man of them around to share the burden of providing nor ever so much as treat them all to a picture-show now and then: a pretty young thing, I fancy, with the selfsame free, forgetful nature as my own two sisters, Glynis and Gwen, and half that nature already crushed to earth and left to watch her youth's bloom launder away.

And so after supper that night I put them all in the same bed together and tucked them in and kissed them and went away quick to let them say their prayers alone, since I judged the newcomer would be embarrassed before me at not knowing any to say and I know my Sally well enough to be sure she'd teach him theirs. And when they were asleep I fetched my bottles and good cleaning rags and hurried round the hushed house in one of my incorrigible furies, polishing the brass of it till it glittered like a post-office at election time and when there were no more doorknobs, knockers and latches to do I fetched out all the old Cecil silver, as if it were two days till Christmas, and spent the livelong night in shining that. By daylight my eyes were smarting from ammonia-smell and the brassy blaze of everything in sight and my hands were bleeding blisters and so I went to Doctor Will's little office and sank into that split-bottom chair by the door yonder and sat a good long while, wordless except for my skin and senses speaking back and forth with the two Suzannes in our old way, for, indeed, she seemed the only creature in Apple County or the whole earth I could bear to share my feelings with that morning and we both laughed some and wept a little and raged in common helplessness at certain things and after a bit I went over to Doctor Will's little daybed by the door and fell asleep till seven when the children came down and woke me for their breakfast.

And I've kept you far too long; I've wearied you, I know, with my so many things to say. And yet there has been no single living soul in this house in all the weeks since August, save my four children, who's come to hear my voice tell how it all was. And I thank you for that: for listening with such kindly understanding, such patience and—I should fear—such ultimate bewilderment, now that I've finished. For what really have I told you?—where's the moral? Where's the beginning to any life's true tale told truly?—and where's its end? *There's only the ebb and wane of things—comeback and loss—leavetaking and return— nothing lasts, yet everything endures,* I often hear a woman's familiar voice speak clearly in this very room on these wild autumn mornings when the clear, cold air is filled with flying leaves and the river wind whips the empty lilac branches against the quartered glass. *And through the queer, imponderable riddle of that there run the threads of simple things we seem to see: life and death; love and hate; goodness and wrong. For those are woven together so alike that it's an impudence of us, in our piteous little wisdom, to call one from the other. And do you know, Martha Ann, I believe that if all the voices of Glory—the quick and the dead alike—could speak of their lives they'd only be telling us that—they'd be admitting that—whether their voices wanted to or not?*

I'll be leaving here soon, leaving Apple County behind me, taking the children somewhere else where I'll find house-work and a home where I can keep the five of us together. For one day early in September, Doctor Will's niece appeared suddenly in Glory from a town in east Virginia and sold the house and everything in it and gave me my notice in no uncertain terms. She was a great, bustling big-neck of a woman with grey, close-cut hair like steelwool and wore plain-tailored, expensive suits and flat-heeled, practical shoes: a lady strong in club-matters and church-work, I judged, from her manner and remarks during the three days she spent charging about the old house complaining about the poor house-cleaning I'd done and throwing this thing and the other into empty paper cartons in the hallways while constantly exclaiming that she couldn't conceive of an old man with a mind as fine as her uncle's allowing his house to become such a magpie's nest of trash nor of myself as a hired maid with a Christian conscience not taking things in hand and doing my duty by throwing out the junk when he was away. And one evening when I was coming down the river-road from Glory with the children helping me carry the week's groceries I spied her out beyond the chinaberry tree tending a great bon-fire of Doctor Will's books and papers and the toy-box from his office and other such things as she couldn't sell or couldn't understand. I stood in the kitchen door watching and wondering till she saw me and came up to the porch steps, smiling and livid with fury.

It's plain you'd planned on being in my uncle's will, she said. And so you were till this town's two best lawyers tended to that this morning.

I never wanted anything, I said, and it was the only time I ever answered her insults. Nothing of Doctor Will but what he left in my mind. And that, ma'am, is beyond the touch of lawyers and most likely even beyond their comprehension.

Oh, yes, I'm quite sure it was your mind and not your body my uncle found so interesting, she said. Don't think you're talking to one of those children out there in the meadow, my girl. It was plain what my uncle found in you—Oh, quite plain. Do you think I'm blind? Do you expect me to believe he'd have had those shameful, nude paintings of you hanging in his office if it was your mind he cared about? I'm not without eyes, my dear, nor certain respects to my dear Uncle Willy's memory—whatever his moral weaknesses may have been.

Where are the paintings? I breathed against the screen-door. Where is Suzanne?

But she said no more and smiled triumphantly and gave herself a crafty, righteous wink before she went back to her fire again and, snatching up Doctor Will's old garden rake once more, poked the ashes into flames of fresh gold-pink and stood back watching the smoke curl away on the Apple County wind; smoke blue as the dusk of some old Paris winter.

She went away that week, with the grudging concession that we could stay there in the house till the painters and carpenters came to start fixing it over. And it's perhaps queer that I can never think of her unpleasantly—she who had broken my heart a little more that afternoon and in the same awful act paid me the loveliest praise I've ever had. And the new owners have still not come with their workmen to take things over and nobody's bothered us yet about getting out, though we must be leaving soon, for the little money in the savings-account Doctor Will once set up for the children is almost all gone for food. I told Jewel and Sally and Sam and the child whose name is Luke Mark Matthew John Turk—I told them early this morning that we'd be going away somewhere, soon. And they stood there on the back porch brave and straight-legged as young fauns before they turned suddenly and fled into the heavy mists of the meadow and after a little while I could hear the sound of them far out in the white billows of the morning, somewhere by the landing, sobbing their young hearts out. They cried for almost an hour, till I was afraid they'd be sick, and yet I knew there was nothing I could do to stop them, nothing to help, nothing to say. And then around ten o'clock, just when the morning fog was rolling off, scarcely an hour before you came, they suddenly stopped. And when they all came sheepishly into the house the helpless child grief was gone from their faces as if cajoled away by some windy whim of the meadow. And when they trooped into the little office and stood before me yonder, all in a row, and I bent above each in his turn to tend to the wiping of cheeks, the blowing of noses, they were smiling a little bit; I'll vow to that. And I must swear to still another thing—knowing full well how often our fancy is capriciously persuaded to such senses. And yet it seemed to me so pungent and so real that I cannot truly bring myself to think it was illusion. It was a something so haunting and so sweet, a thing so everlastingly memorable and vivid that it gave full meaning to the valiant suddenness of those four, small banished griefs. It was on their breaths. Unmistakably. A scent of peppermint.

DATE DUE

8-10-77			